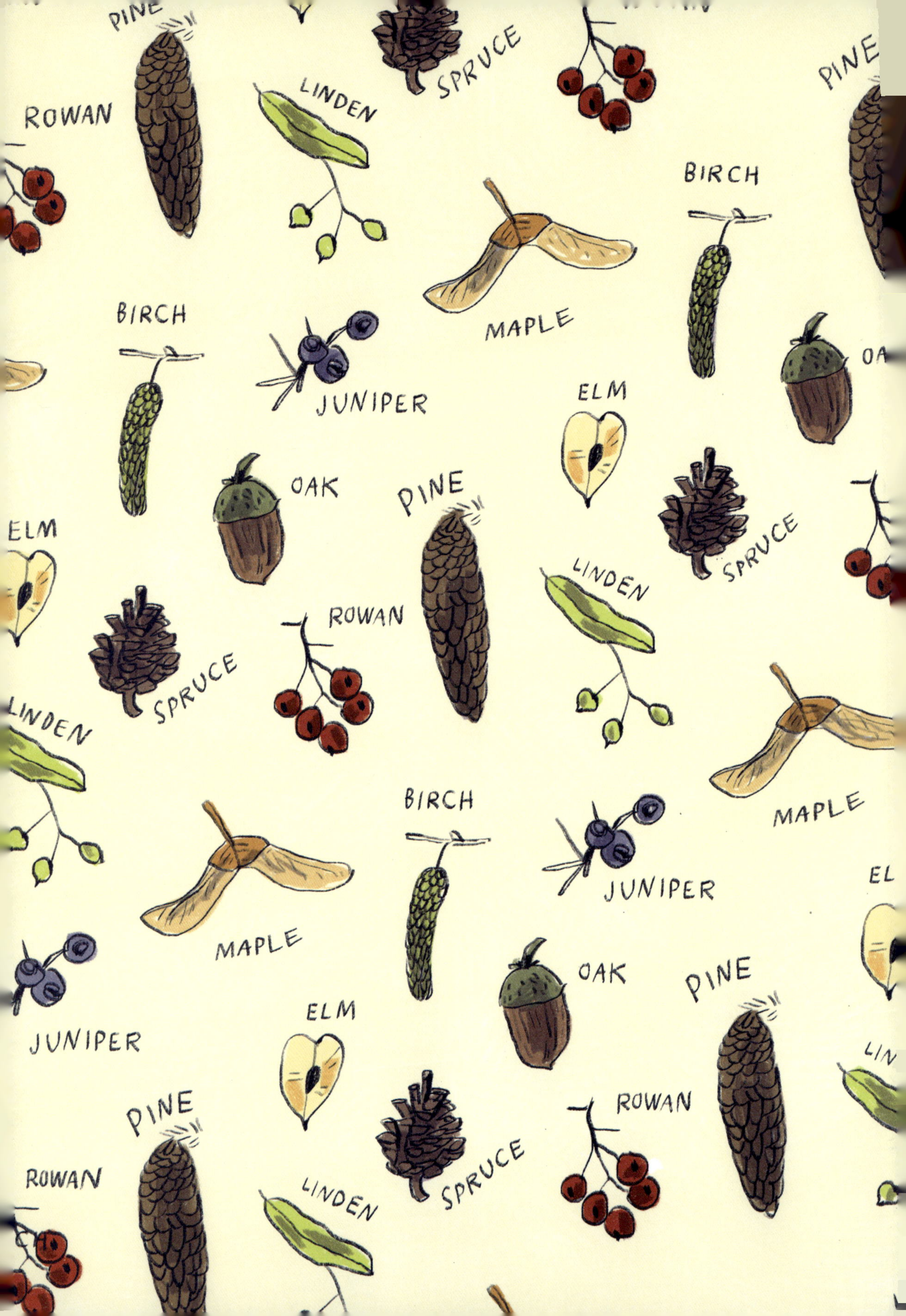

PINE
SPRUCE
PINE
LINDEN
ROWAN
BIRCH
MAPLE
BIRCH
JUNIPER
ELM
OAK
PINE
ELM
SPRUCE
LINDEN
ROWAN
SPRUCE
LINDEN
MAPLE
BIRCH
JUNIPER
MAPLE
OAK
PINE
JUNIPER
ELM
PINE
ROWAN
ROWAN
SPRUCE
LINDEN

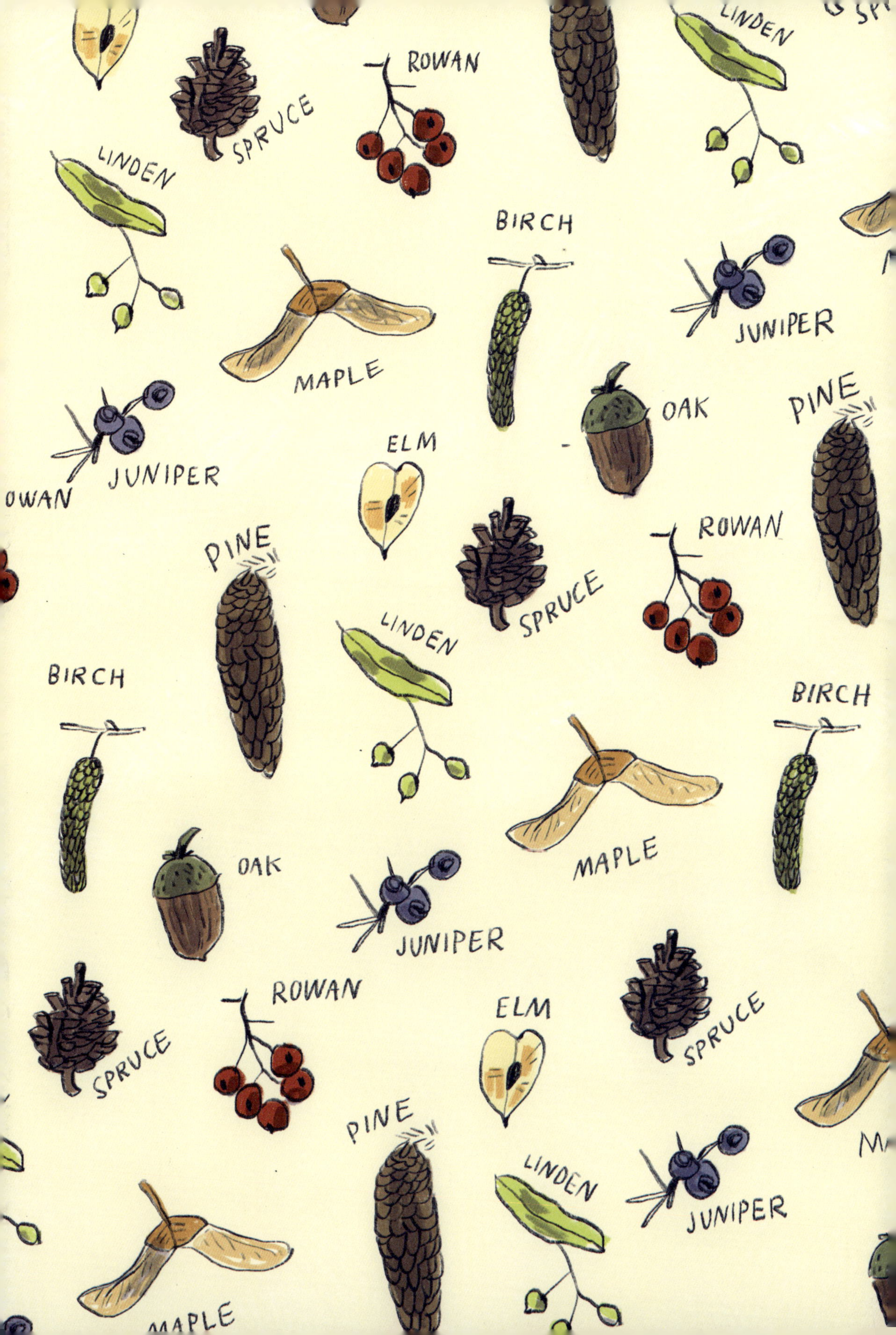

ROWAN
SPRUCE
LINDEN
LINDEN
BIRCH
MAPLE
JUNIPER
OAK
PINE
JUNIPER
ELM
ROWAN
PINE
SPRUCE
LINDEN
BIRCH
BIRCH
MAPLE
OAK
JUNIPER
ROWAN
ELM
SPRUCE
SPRUCE
PINE
LINDEN
JUNIPER

NORA DÅSNES is the author of three graphic novels, including *Cross My Heart and Never Lie*, which received a starred review from *Kirkus* and about which *Heartstopper* creator Alice Oseman said: "Reading this was like a warm hug." Both *Cross My Heart and Never Lie* and *Save Our Forest!* have been translated into sixteen languages from the original Norwegian. Nora studied illustration and animation at Kingston University outside London and speaks fluent English.

Visit noradasnes.com/english.

LISE LÆRDAL BRYN is a translator from the western fjords of Norway. She studied cross-cultural storytelling at the Johnston Center for Integrative Studies at the University of Redlands and literary translation at the University of East Anglia. She spends her winters writing in London and her summers working in a garden in Norway.

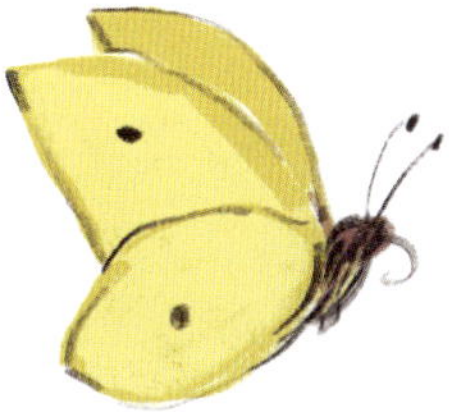

NORA DÅSNES

SAVE OUR FOREST!

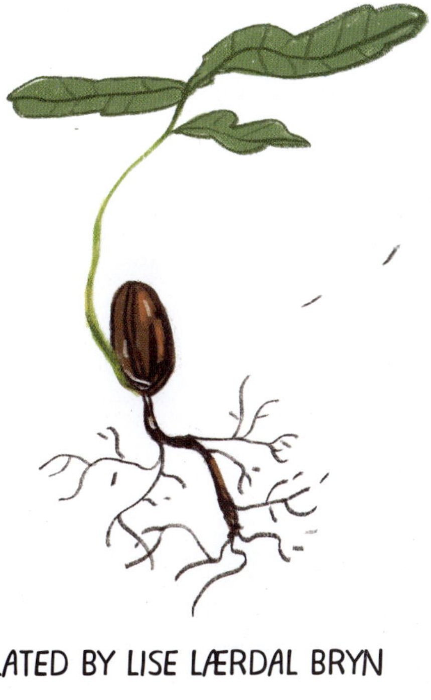

TRANSLATED BY LISE LÆRDAL BRYN

Hippo Park

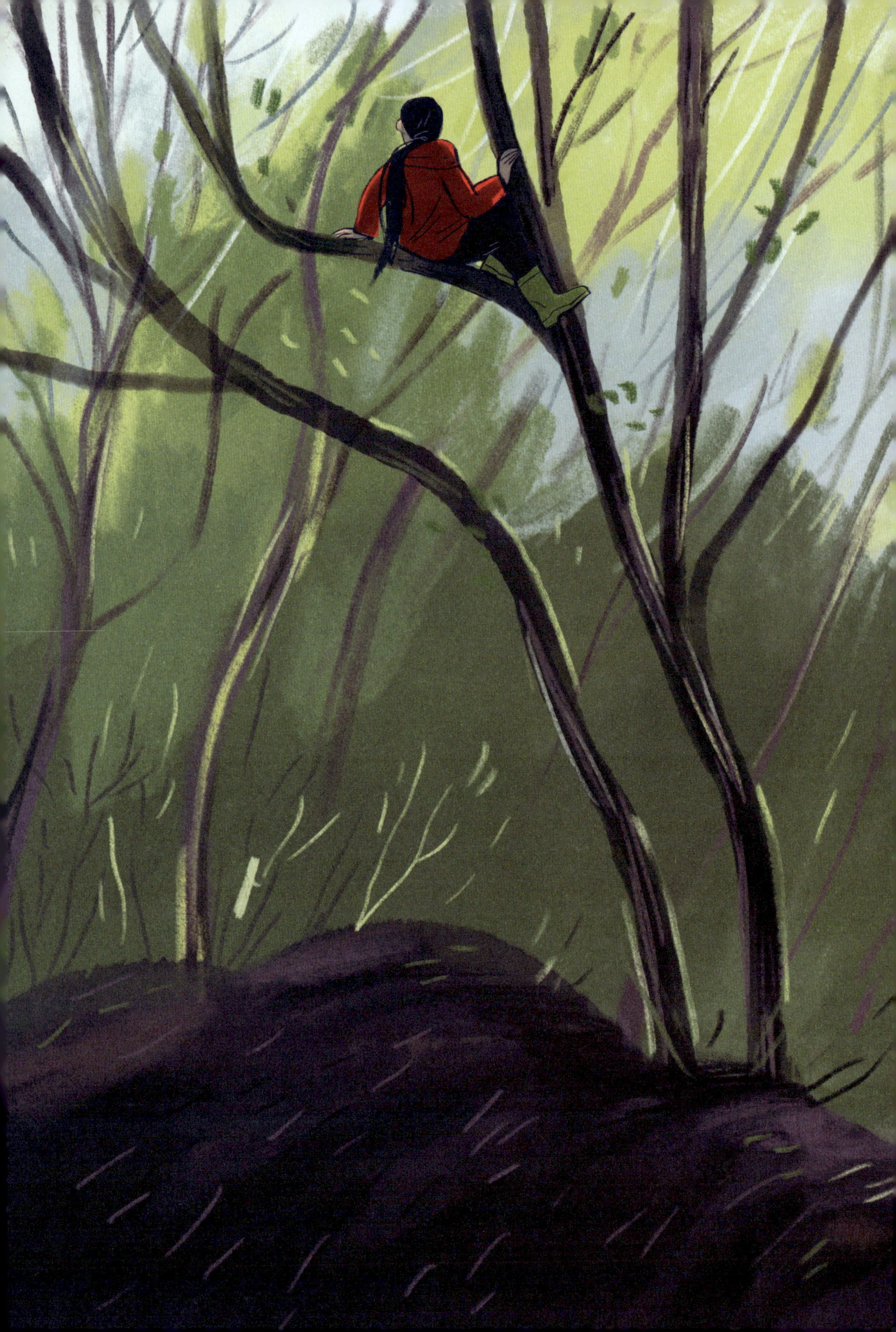

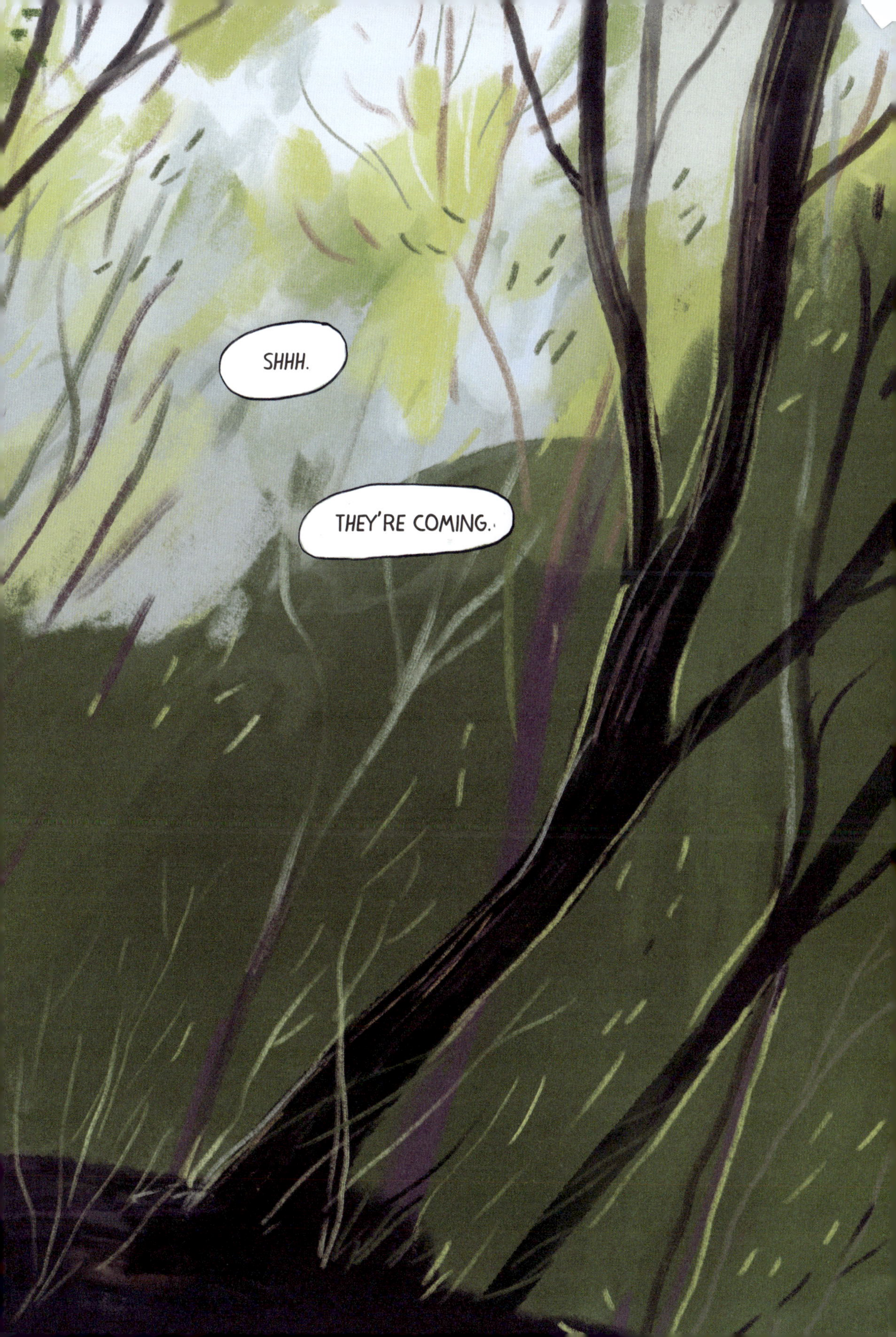
SHHH.
THEY'RE COMING.

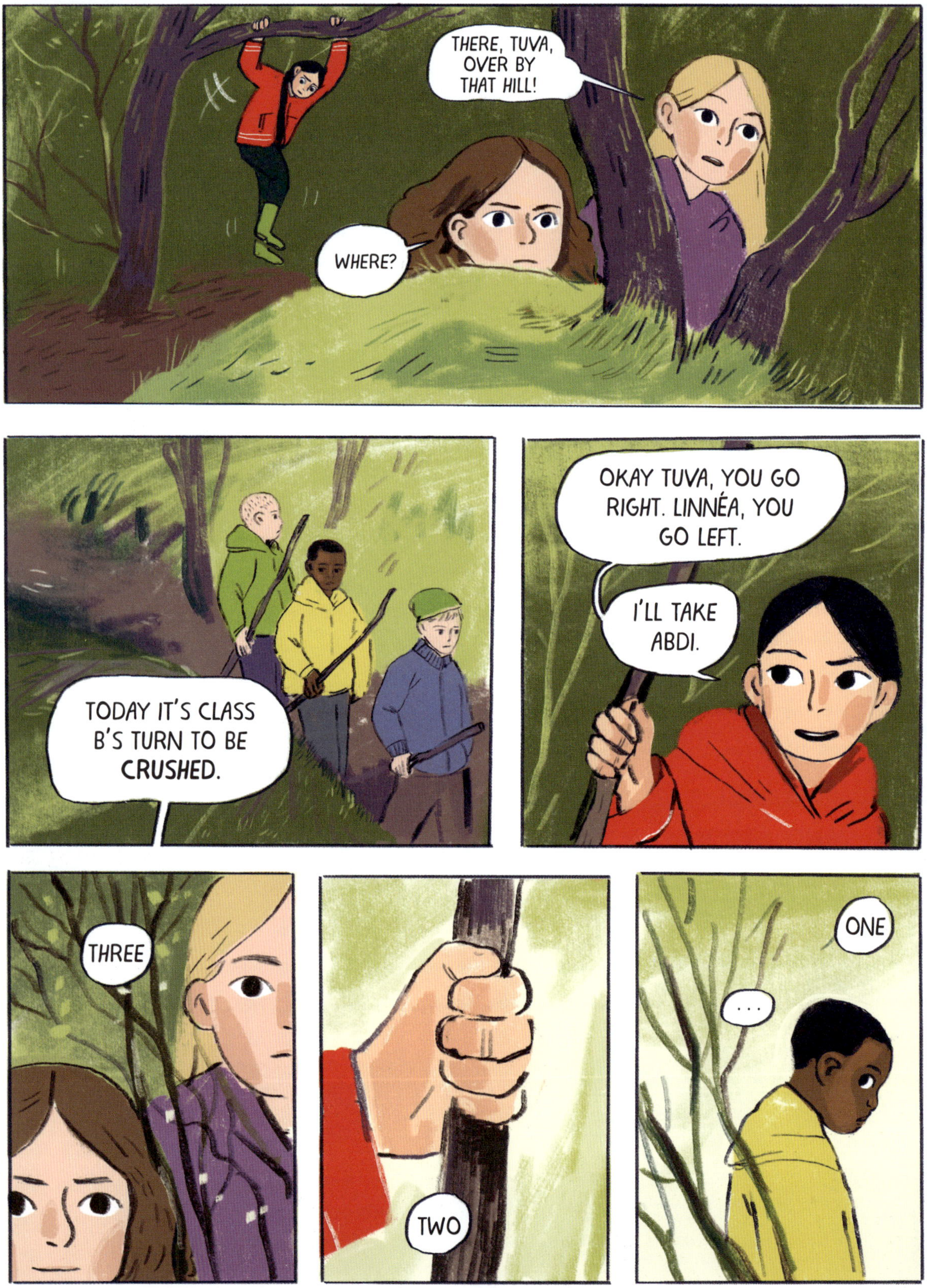
THERE, TUVA, OVER BY THAT HILL!
WHERE?
TODAY IT'S CLASS B'S TURN TO BE **CRUSHED**.
OKAY TUVA, YOU GO RIGHT. LINNÉA, YOU GO LEFT.
I'LL TAKE ABDI.
THREE
TWO
ONE
...

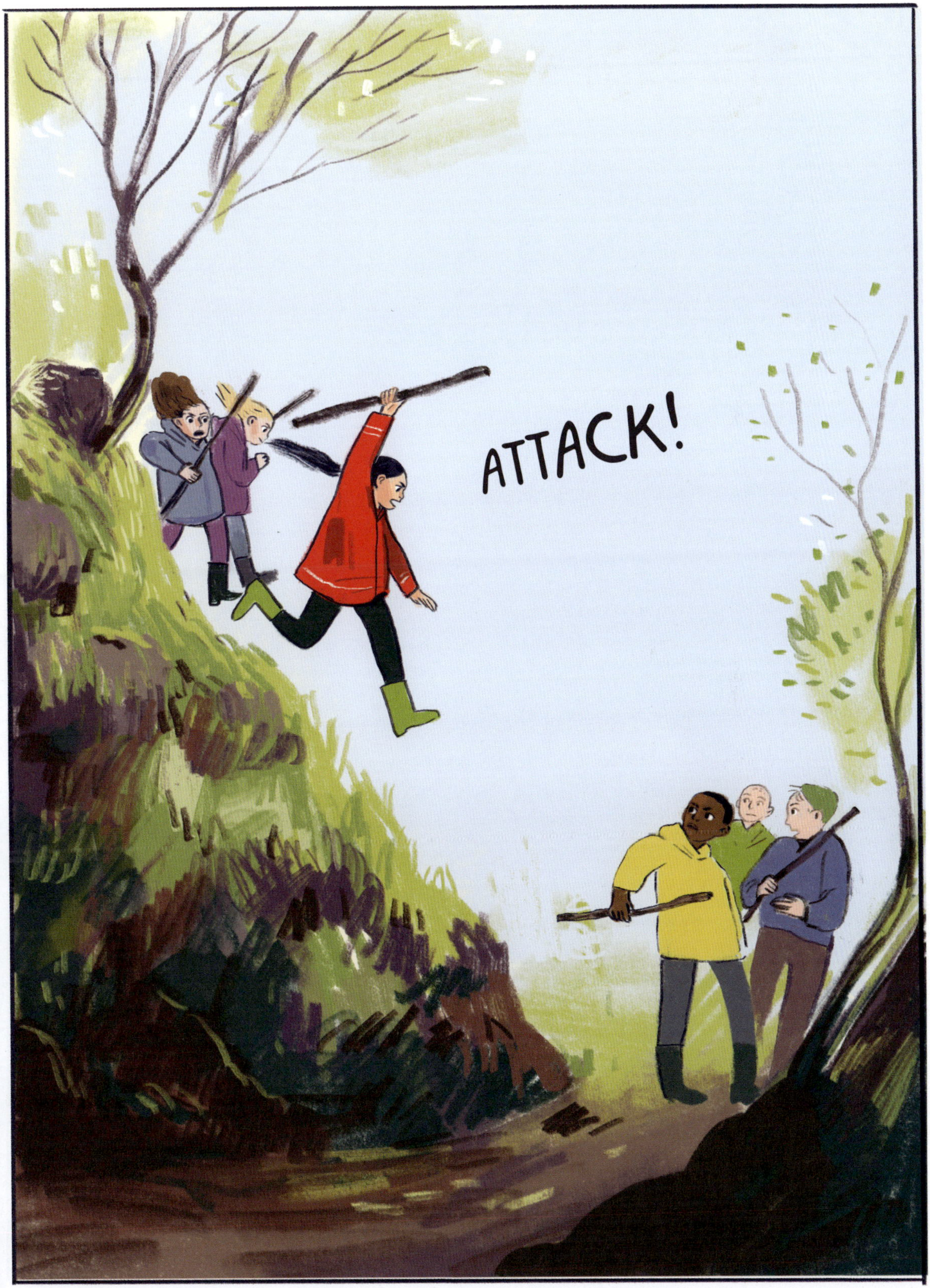
ATTACK!

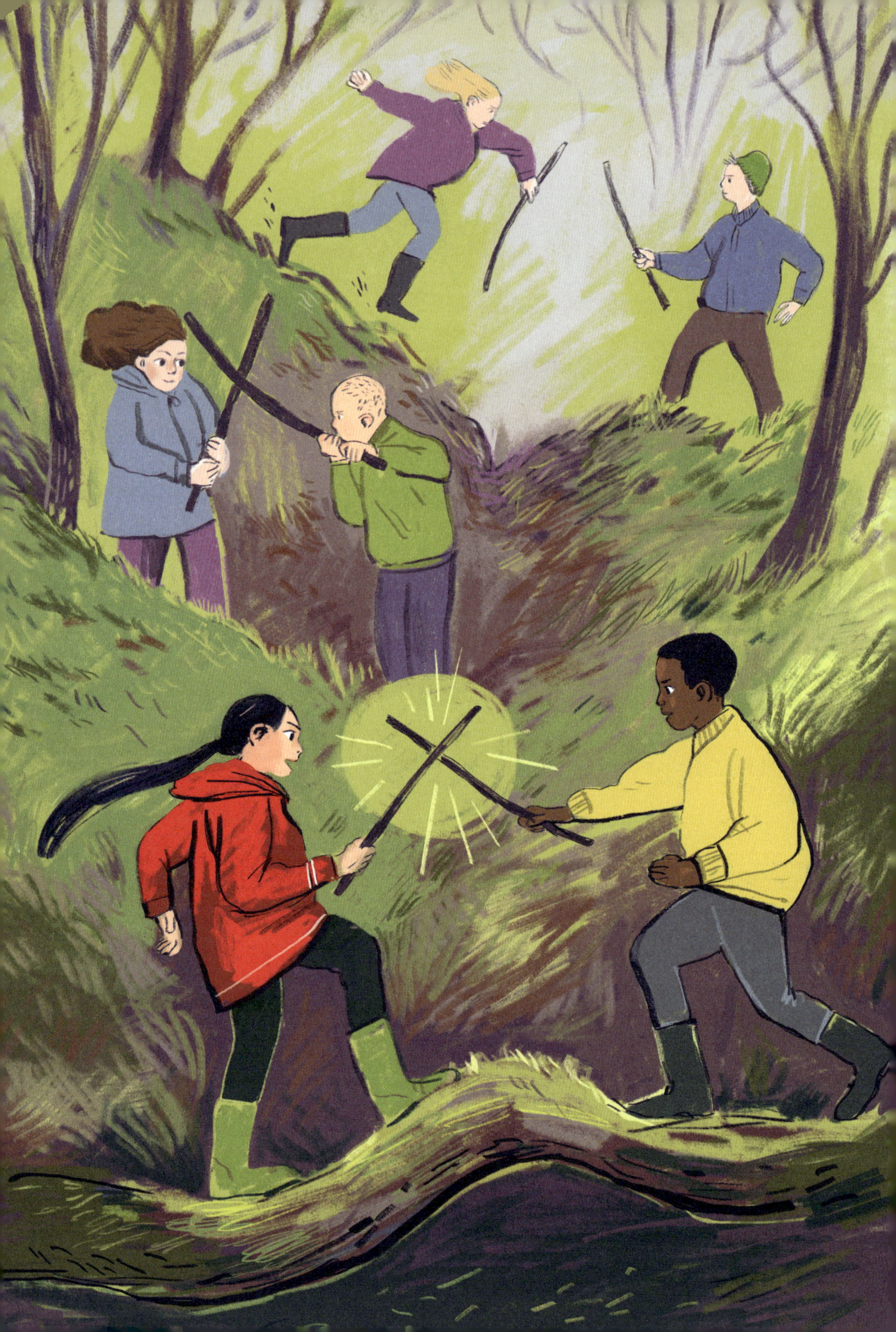

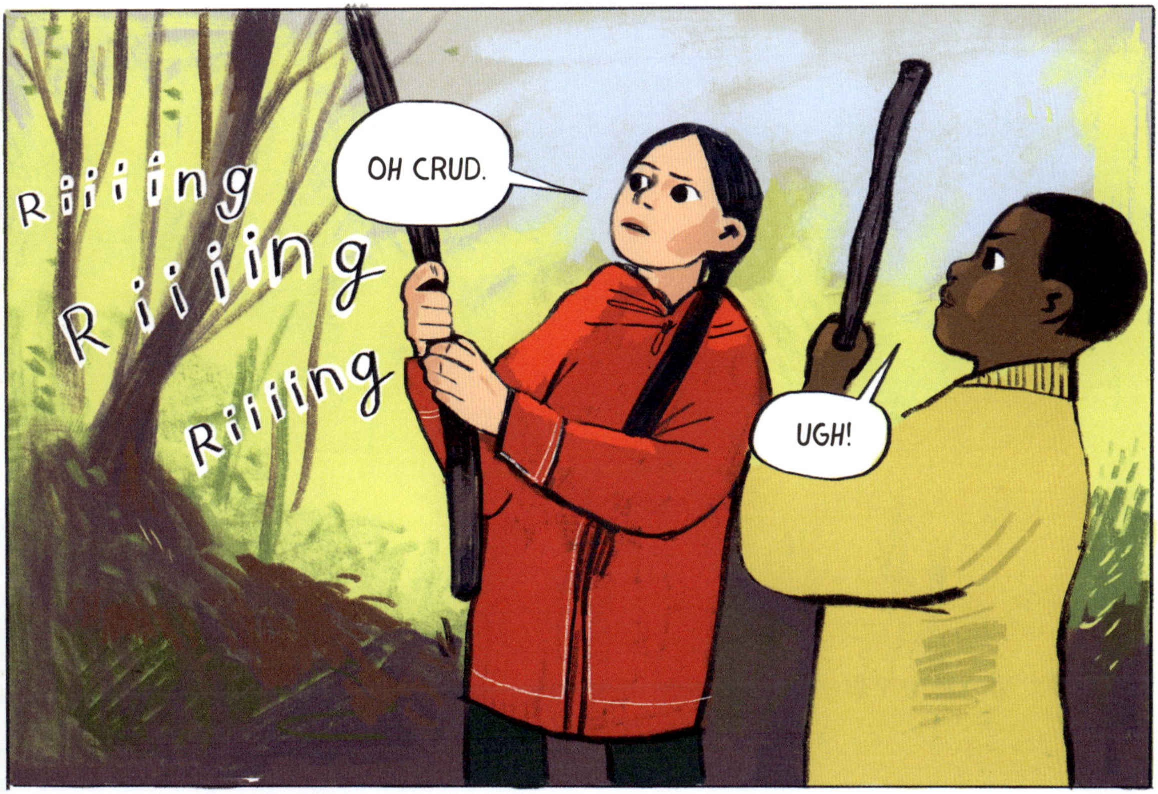
Riiiing
Riiiing
Riiiing
OH CRUD.
UGH!

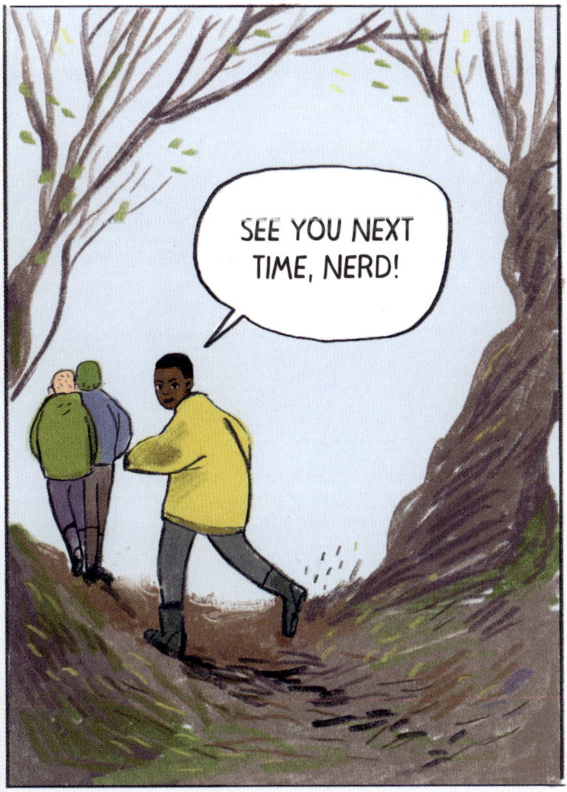
SEE YOU NEXT TIME, NERD!

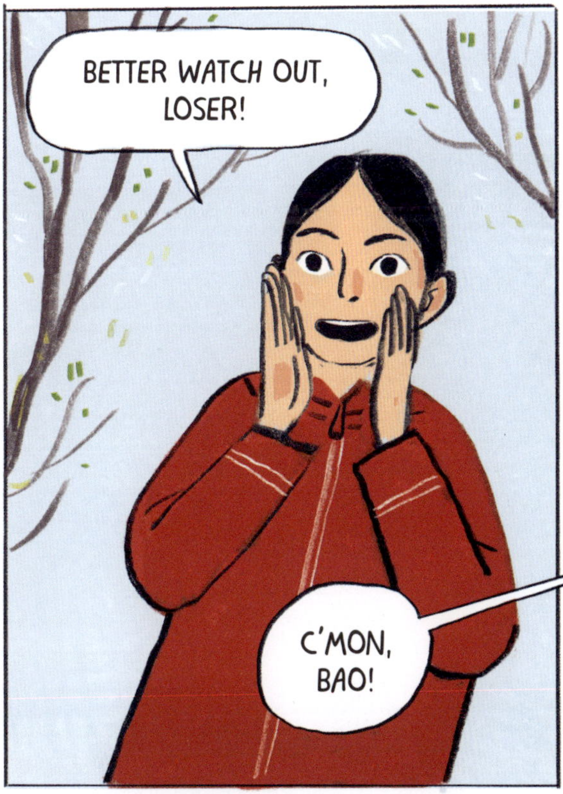
BETTER WATCH OUT, LOSER!
C'MON, BAO!

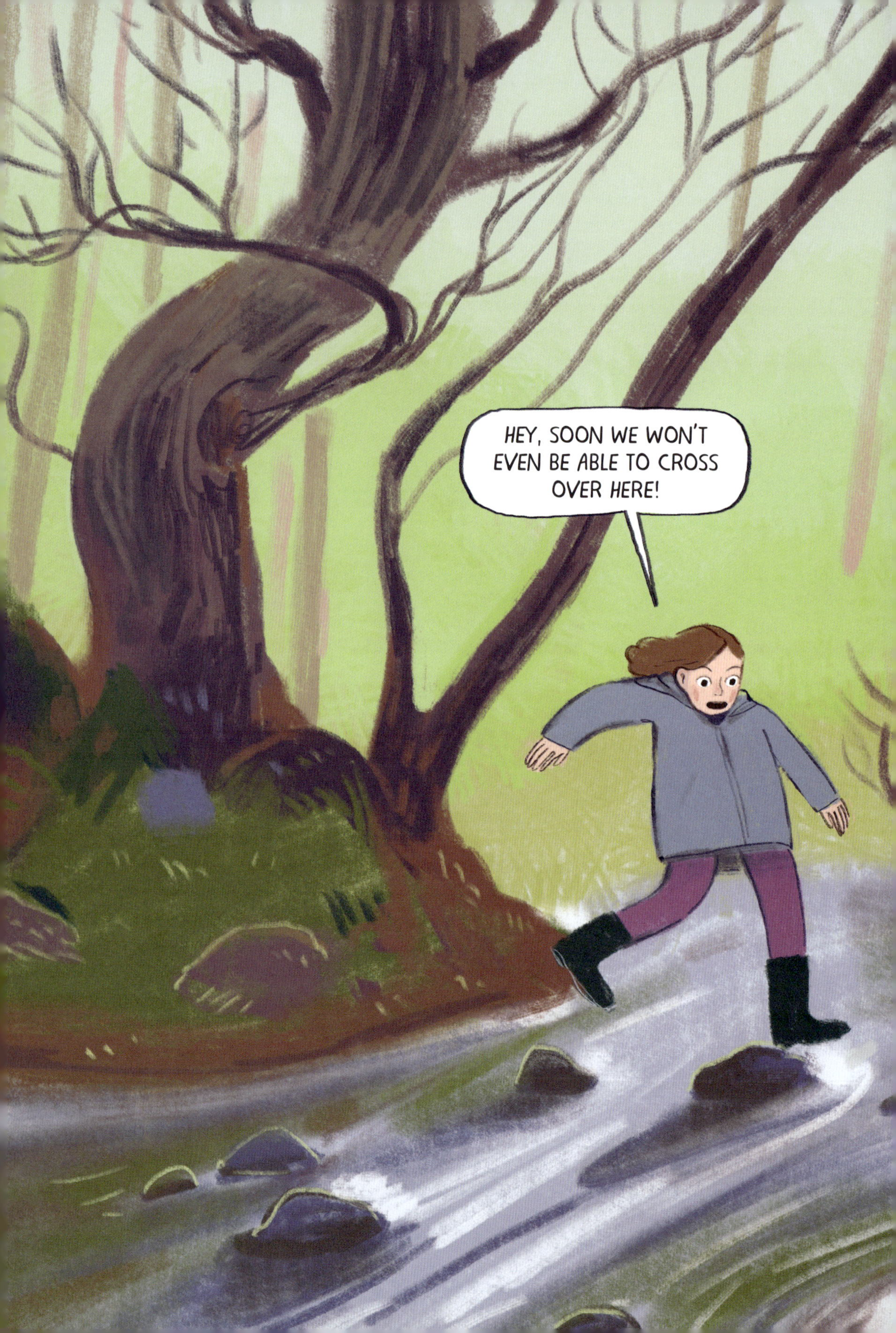
HEY, SOON WE WON'T EVEN BE ABLE TO CROSS OVER HERE!

PART 1: ADULTS DON'T GET CRAP

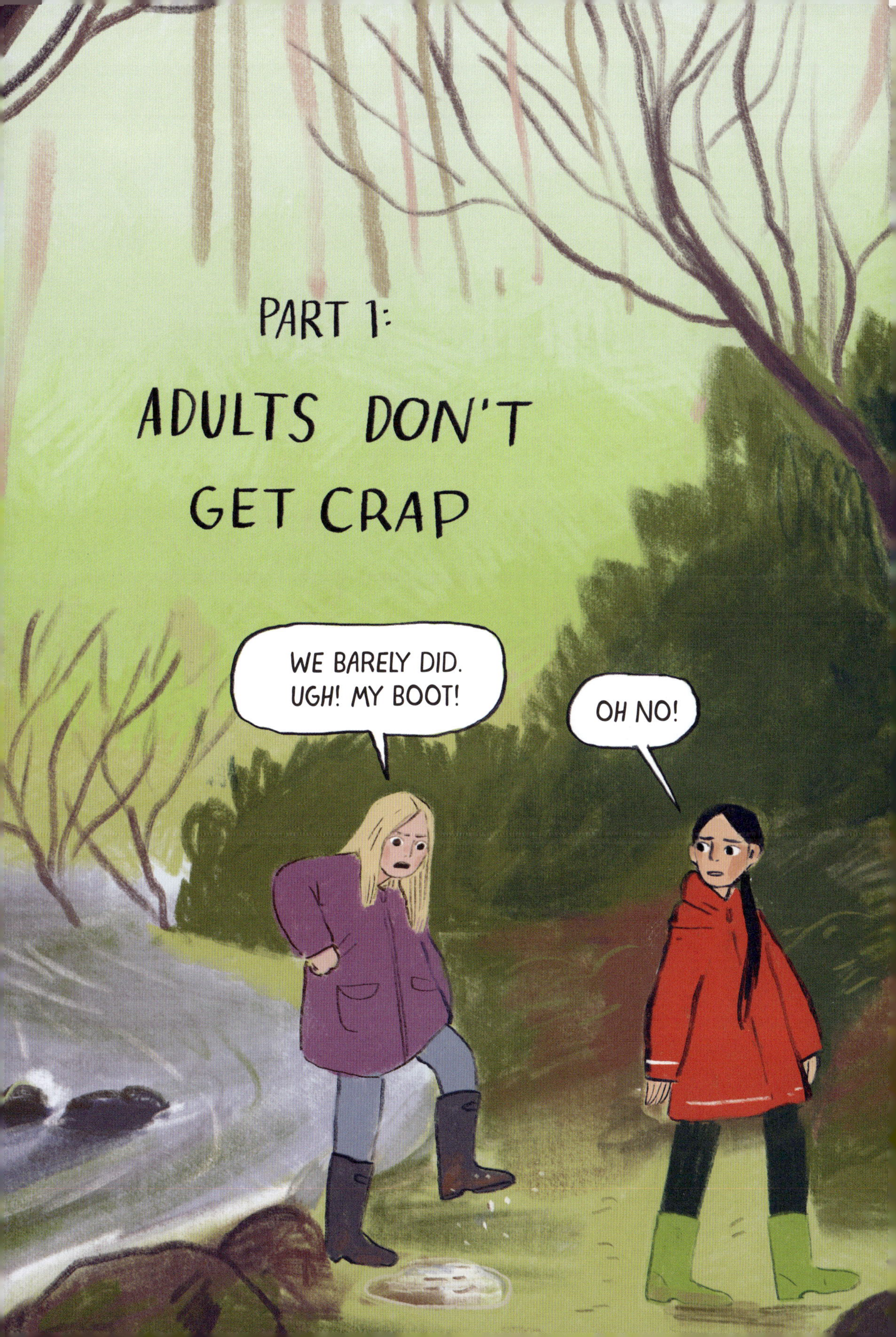
WE BARELY DID. UGH! MY BOOT!
OH NO!

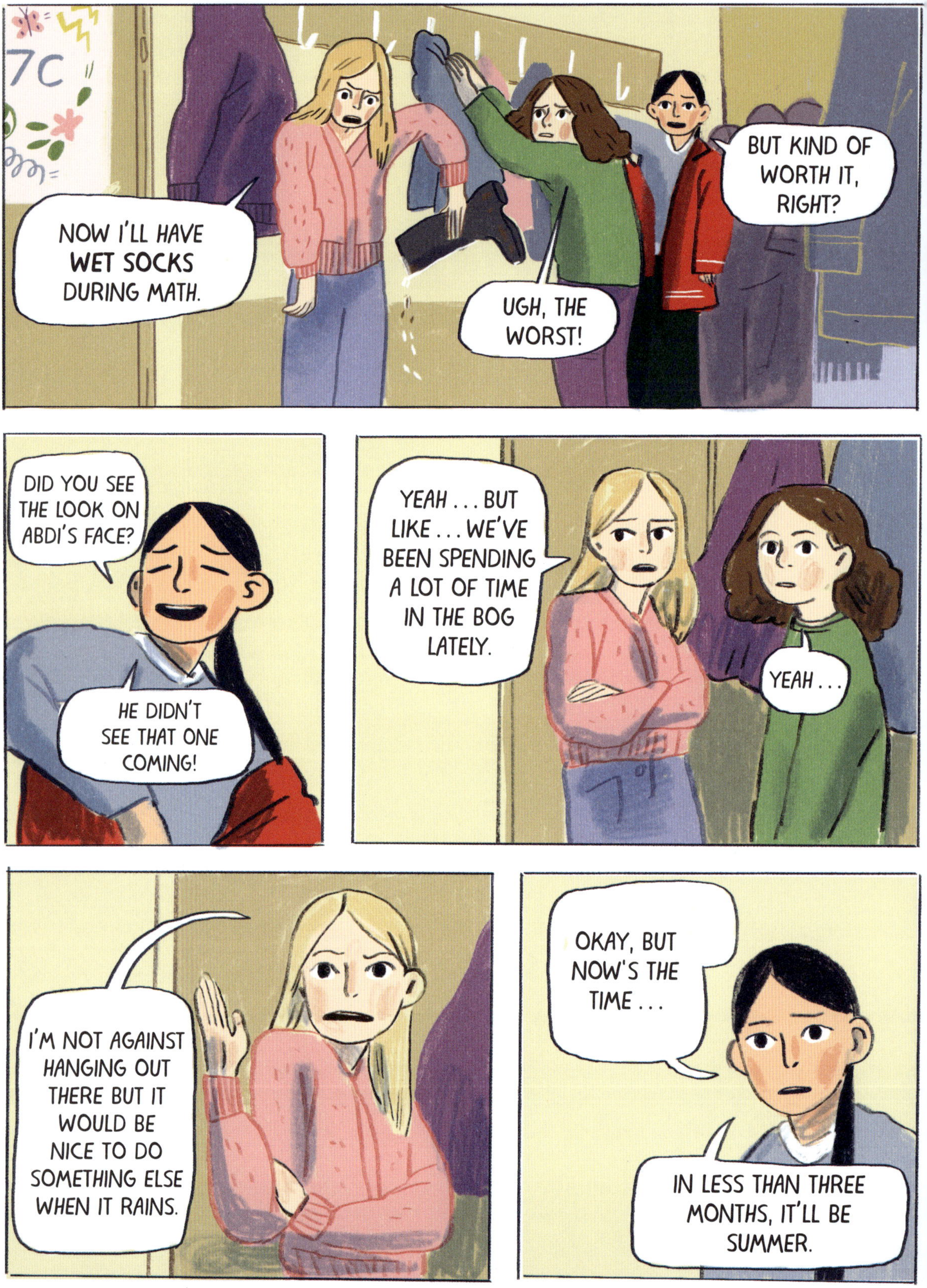
7C
NOW I'LL HAVE **WET SOCKS** DURING MATH.
UGH, THE WORST!
BUT KIND OF WORTH IT, RIGHT?
DID YOU SEE THE LOOK ON ABDI'S FACE?
HE DIDN'T SEE THAT ONE COMING!
YEAH . . . BUT LIKE . . . WE'VE BEEN SPENDING A LOT OF TIME IN THE BOG LATELY.
YEAH . . .
I'M NOT AGAINST HANGING OUT THERE BUT IT WOULD BE NICE TO DO SOMETHING ELSE WHEN IT RAINS.
OKAY, BUT NOW'S THE TIME . . .
IN LESS THAN THREE MONTHS, IT'LL BE SUMMER.

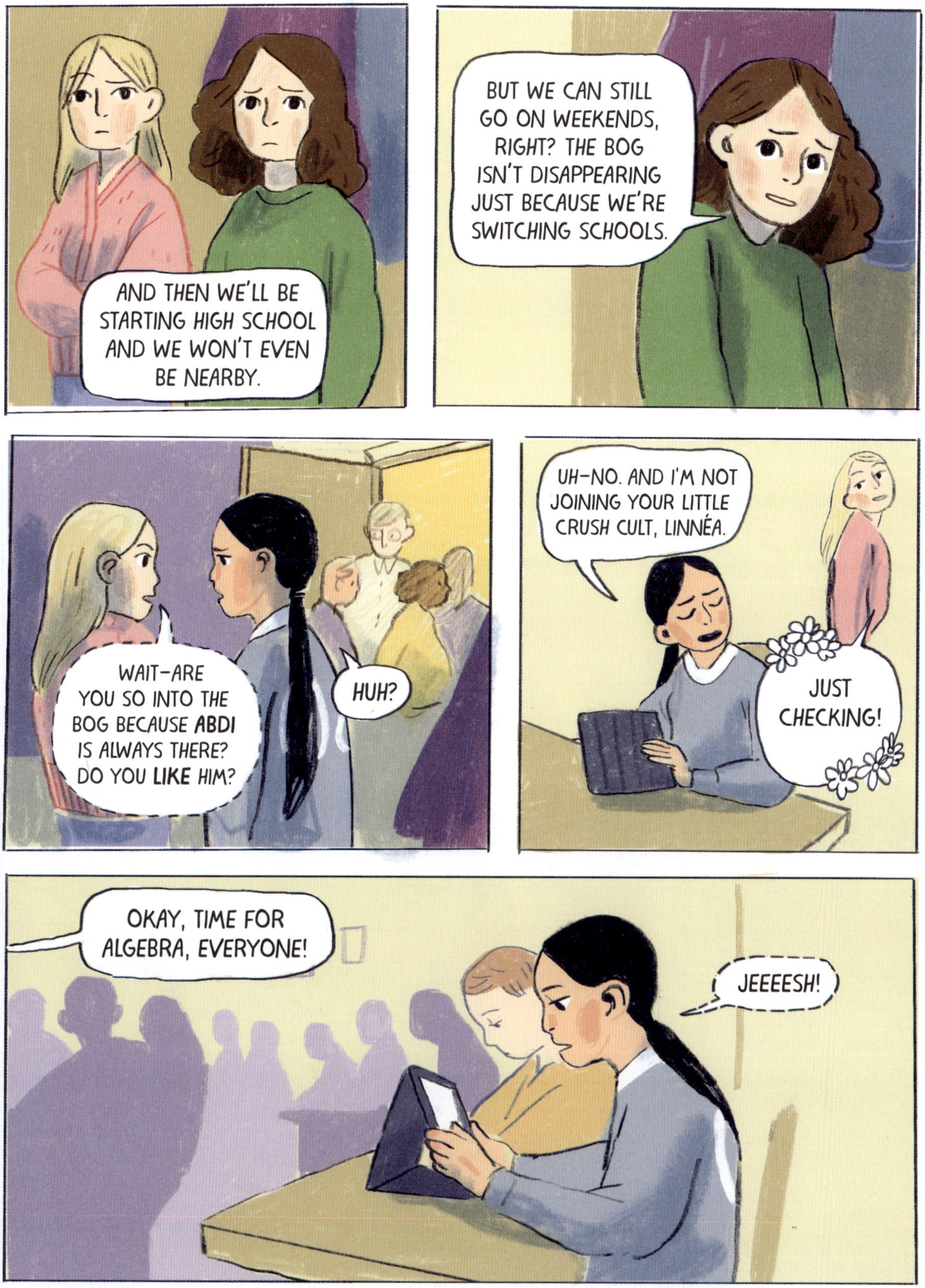
AND THEN WE'LL BE STARTING HIGH SCHOOL AND WE WON'T EVEN BE NEARBY.
BUT WE CAN STILL GO ON WEEKENDS, RIGHT? THE BOG ISN'T DISAPPEARING JUST BECAUSE WE'RE SWITCHING SCHOOLS.
WAIT—ARE YOU SO INTO THE BOG BECAUSE **ABDI** IS ALWAYS THERE? DO YOU **LIKE** HIM?
HUH?
UH—NO. AND I'M NOT JOINING YOUR LITTLE CRUSH CULT, LINNÉA.
JUST CHECKING!
OKAY, TIME FOR ALGEBRA, EVERYONE!
JEEEESH!

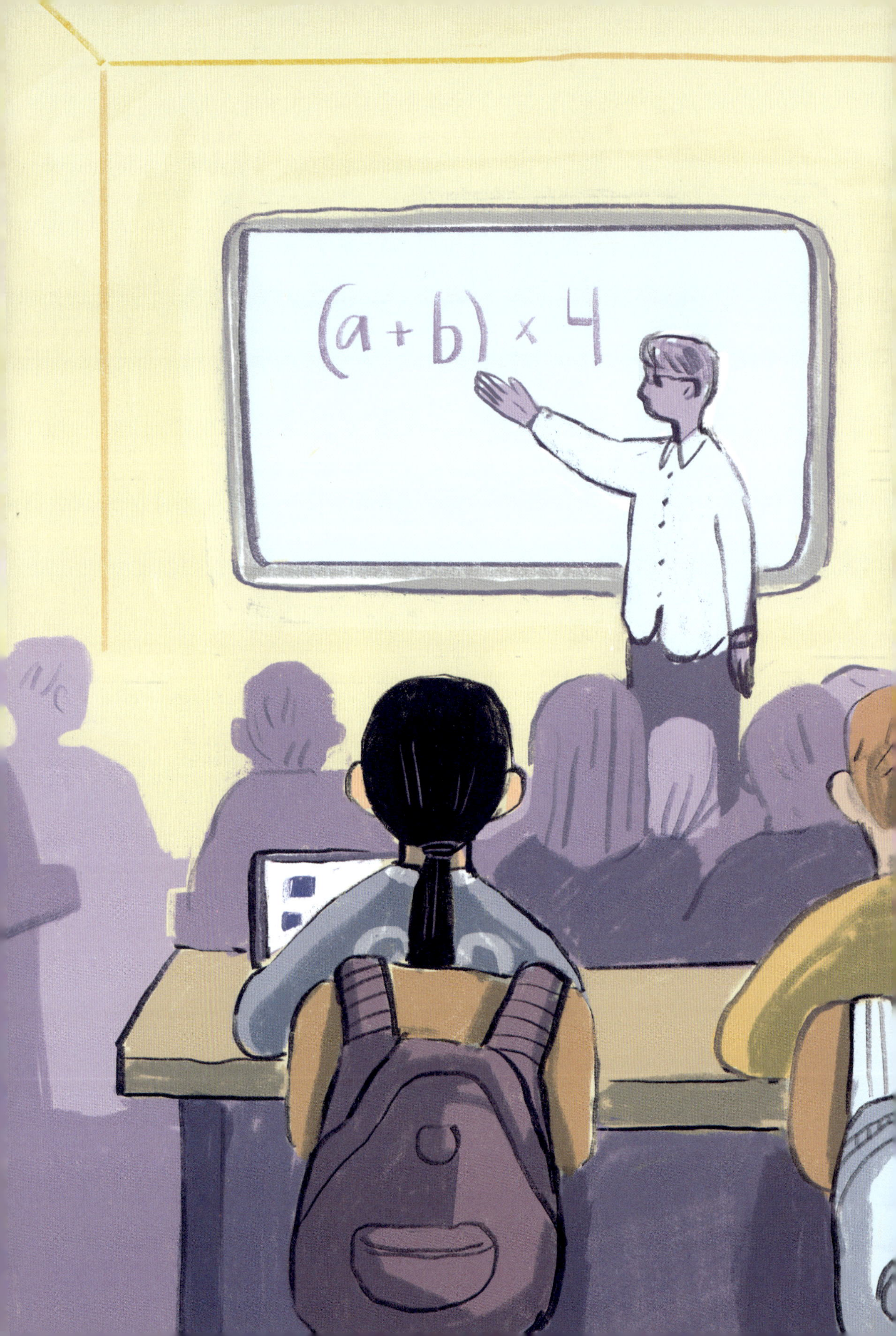
(a + b) × 4

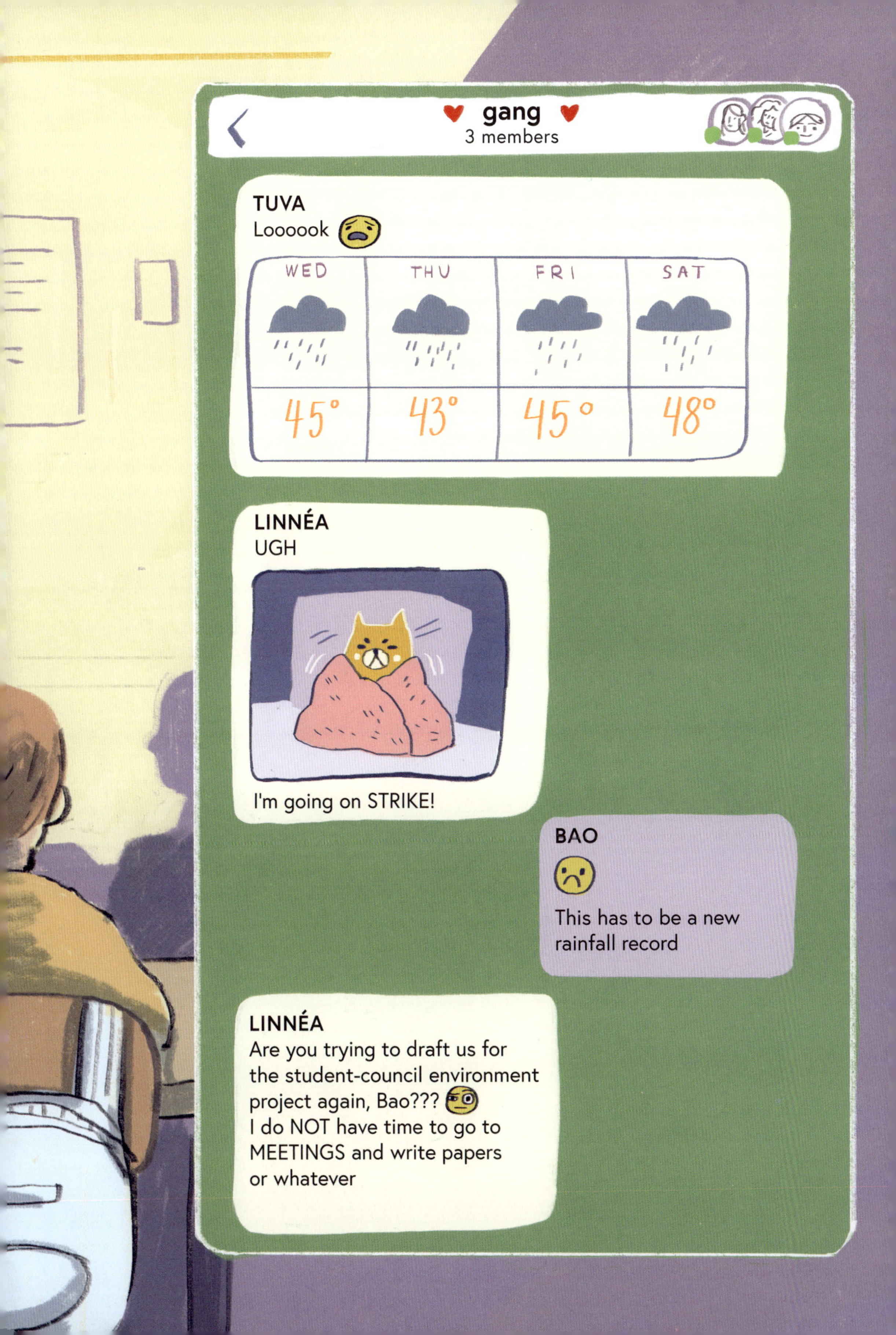
gang
3 members
TUVA
Loooook
WED
THU
FRI
SAT
45°
43°
45°
48°
LINNÉA
UGH
I'm going on STRIKE!
BAO
This has to be a new rainfall record
LINNÉA
Are you trying to draft us for the student-council environment project again, Bao???
I do NOT have time to go to MEETINGS and write papers or whatever

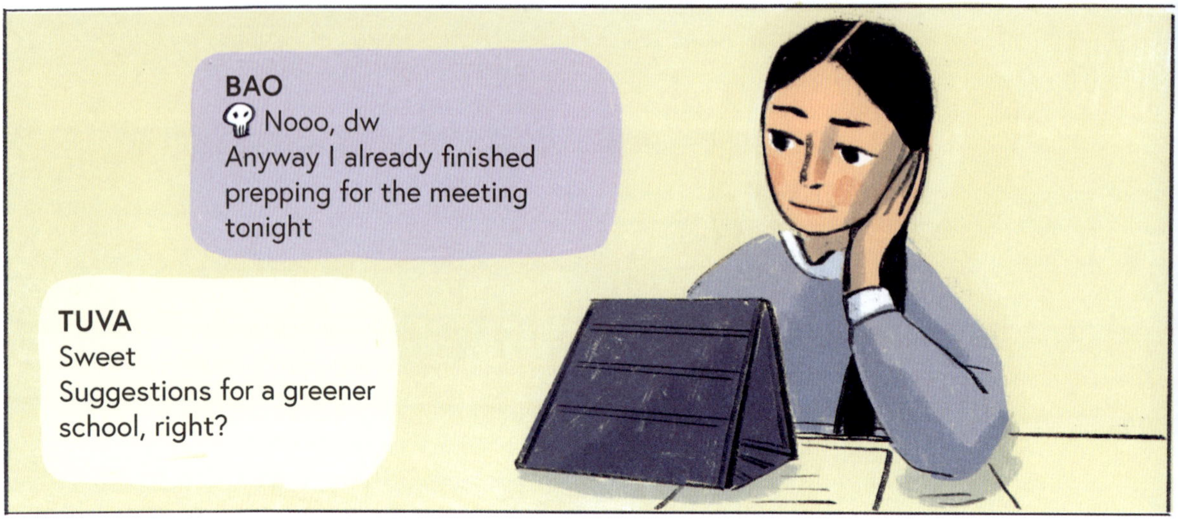
BAO
Nooo, dw
Anyway I already finished prepping for the meeting tonight
TUVA
Sweet
Suggestions for a greener school, right?

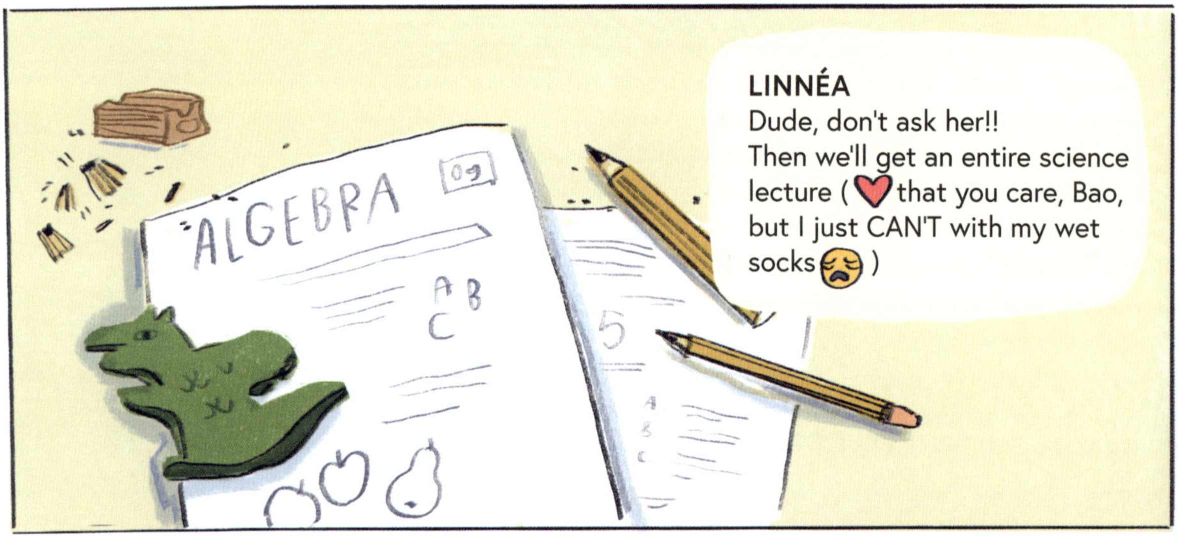
LINNÉA
Dude, don't ask her!!
Then we'll get an entire science lecture (that you care, Bao, but I just CAN'T with my wet socks)
ALGEBRA

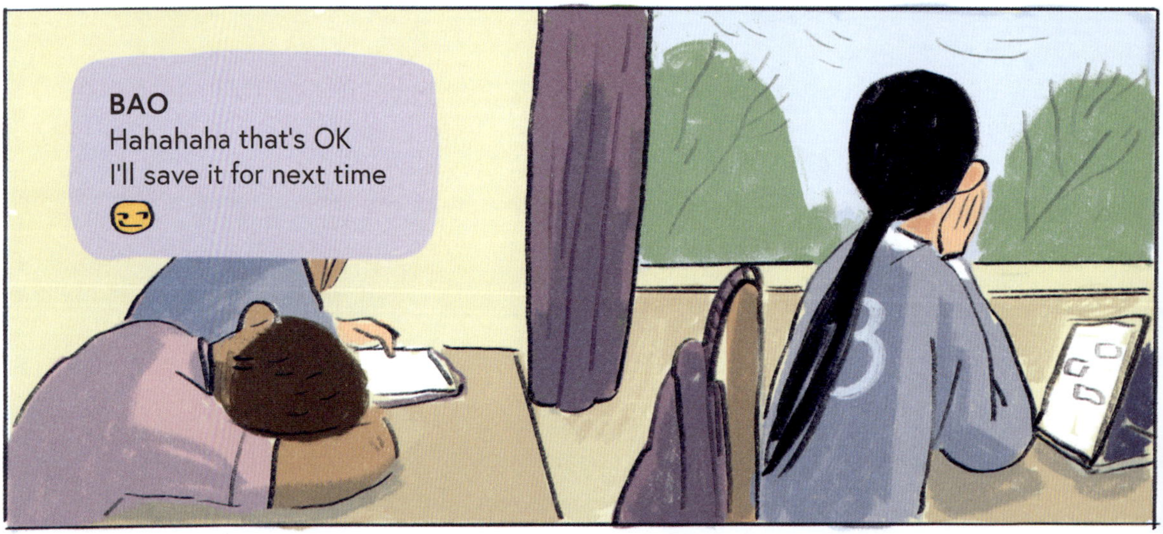
BAO
Hahahaha that's OK
I'll save it for next time

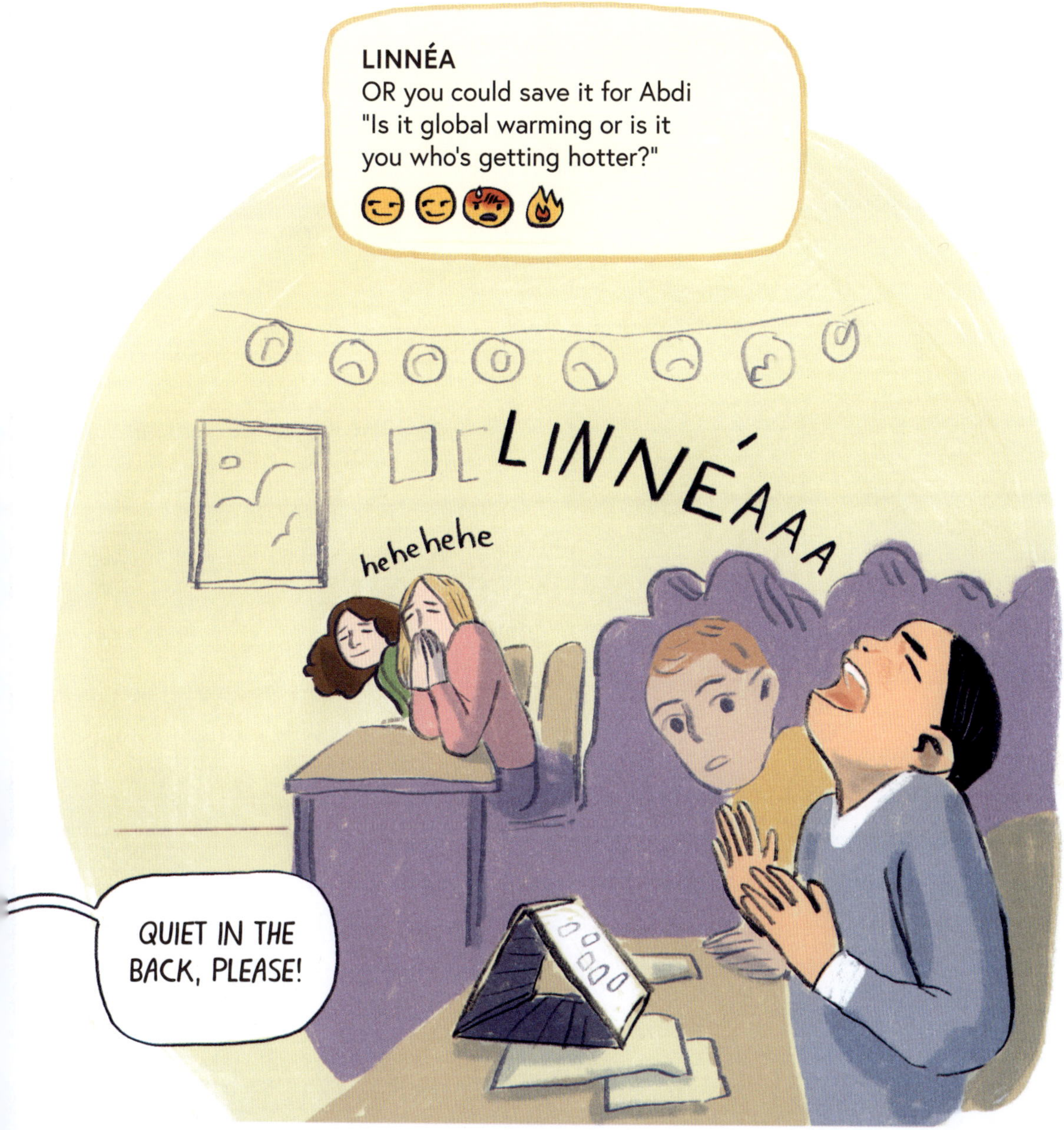
LINNÉA
OR you could save it for Abdi "Is it global warming or is it you who's getting hotter?"
LINNÉAAA
hehehehe
QUIET IN THE BACK, PLEASE!

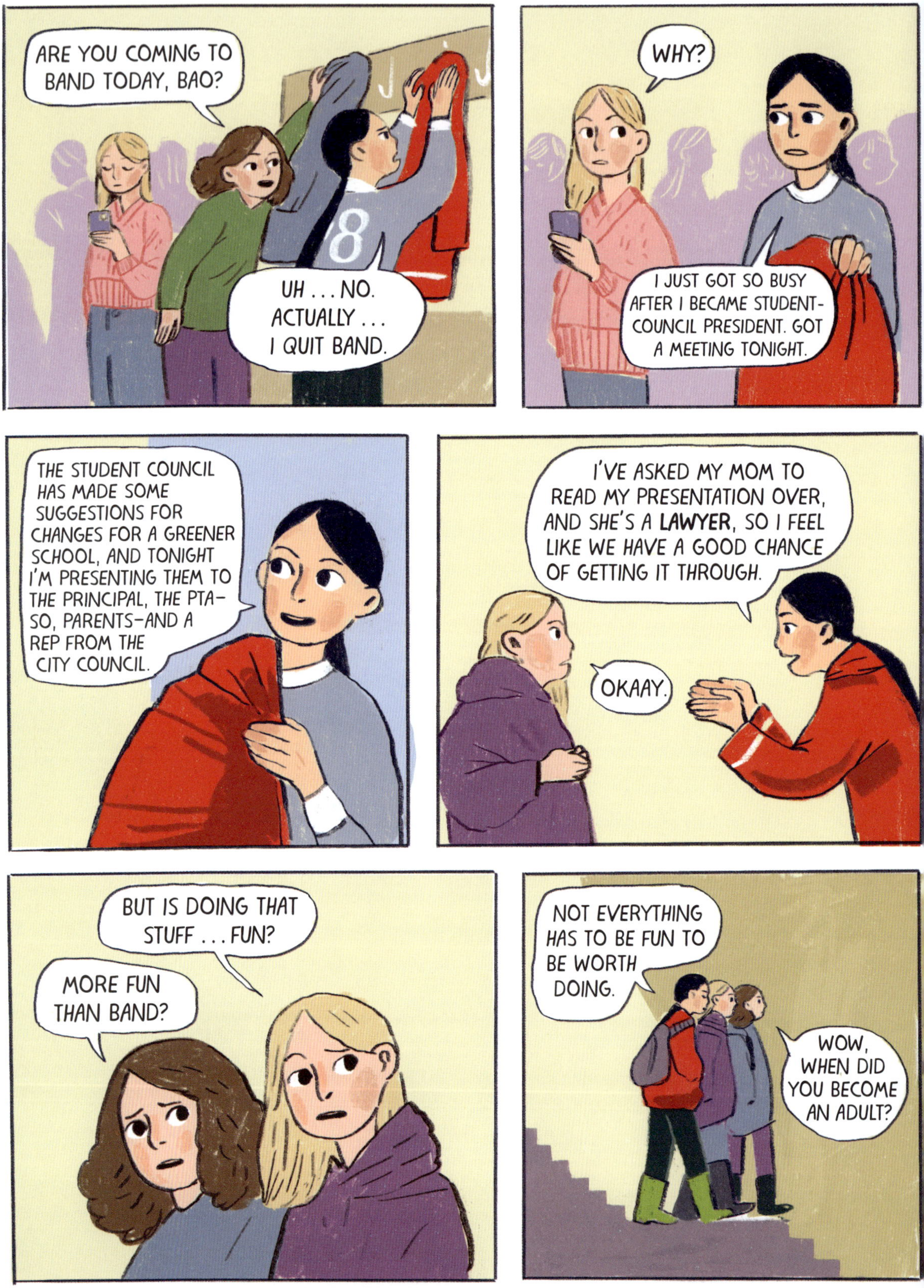
ARE YOU COMING TO BAND TODAY, BAO?
UH . . . NO. ACTUALLY . . . I QUIT BAND.
WHY?
I JUST GOT SO BUSY AFTER I BECAME STUDENT-COUNCIL PRESIDENT. GOT A MEETING TONIGHT.
THE STUDENT COUNCIL HAS MADE SOME SUGGESTIONS FOR CHANGES FOR A GREENER SCHOOL, AND TONIGHT I'M PRESENTING THEM TO THE PRINCIPAL, THE PTA–SO, PARENTS–AND A REP FROM THE CITY COUNCIL.
I'VE ASKED MY MOM TO READ MY PRESENTATION OVER, AND SHE'S A **LAWYER**, SO I FEEL LIKE WE HAVE A GOOD CHANCE OF GETTING IT THROUGH.
OKAAY.
BUT IS DOING THAT STUFF . . . FUN?
MORE FUN THAN BAND?
NOT EVERYTHING HAS TO BE FUN TO BE WORTH DOING.
WOW, WHEN DID YOU BECOME AN ADULT?

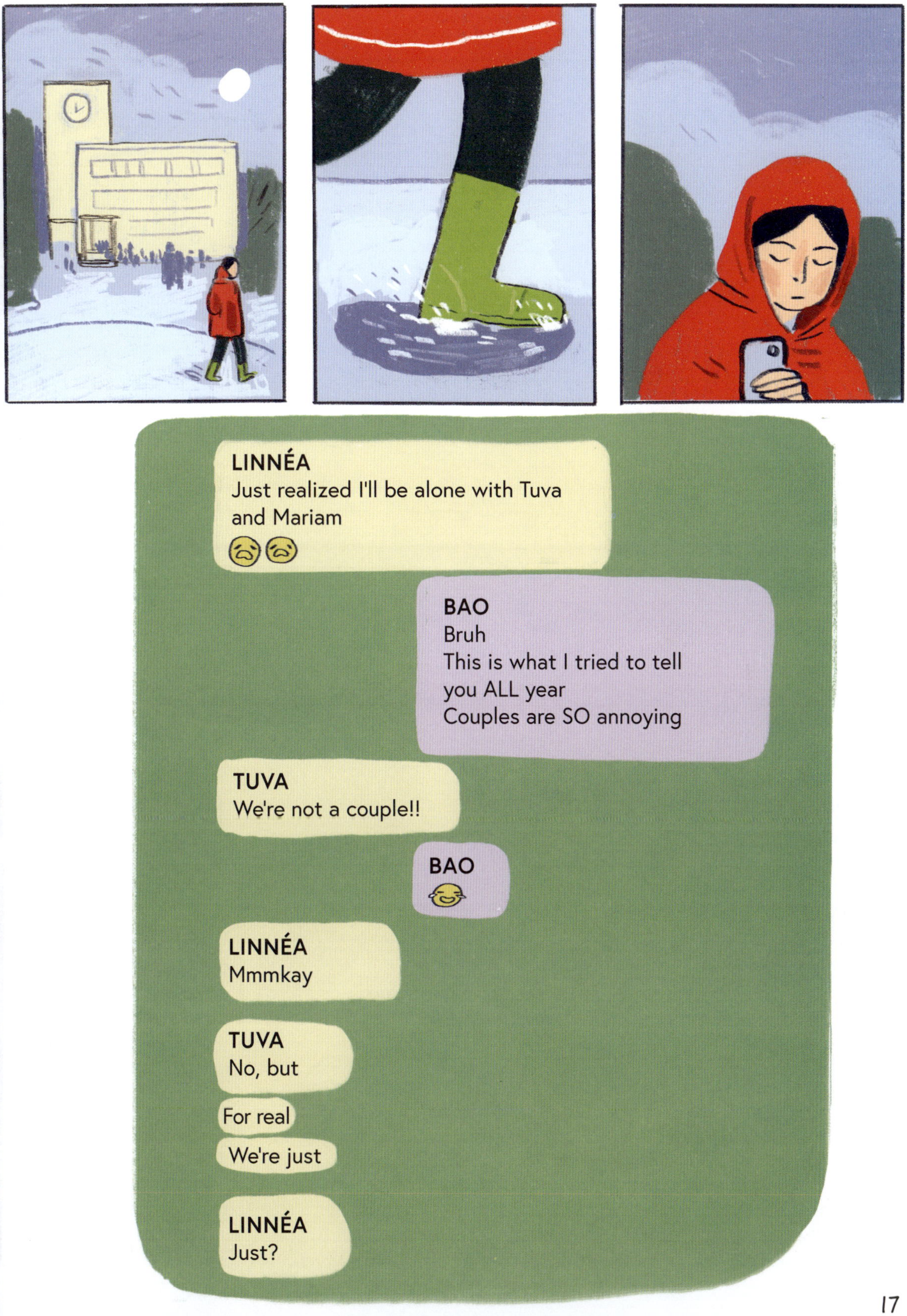
LINNÉA
Just realized I'll be alone with Tuva and Mariam
BAO
Bruh
This is what I tried to tell you ALL year
Couples are SO annoying
TUVA
We're not a couple!!
BAO
LINNÉA
Mmmkay
TUVA
No, but
For real
We're just
LINNÉA
Just?

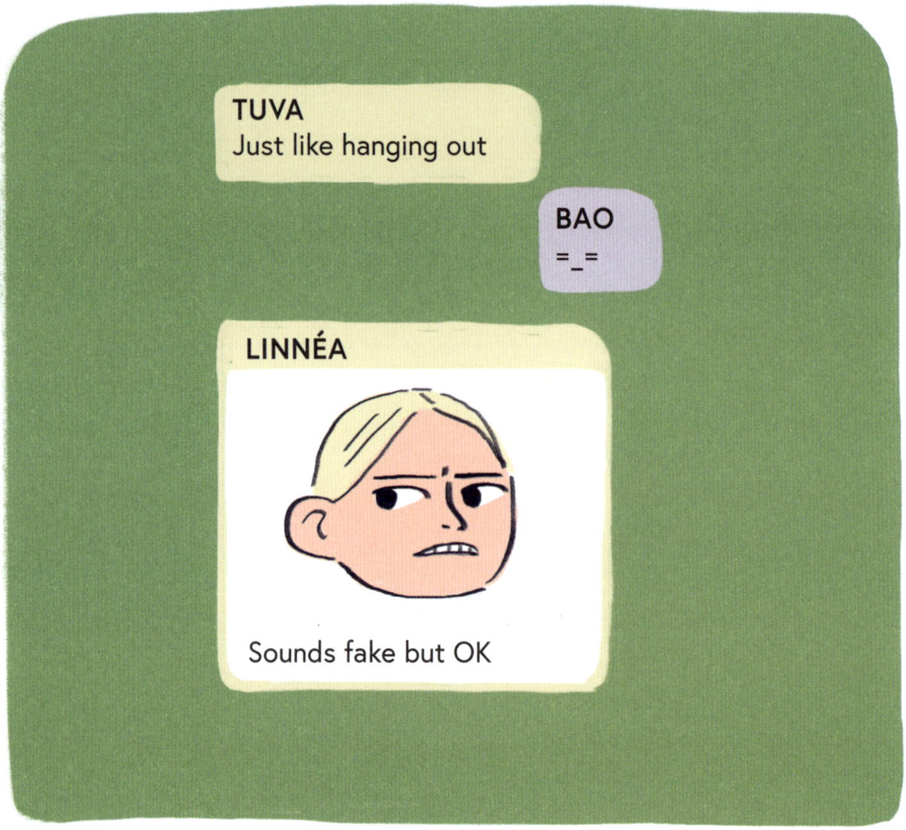
TUVA
Just like hanging out
BAO
=_=
LINNÉA
Sounds fake but OK

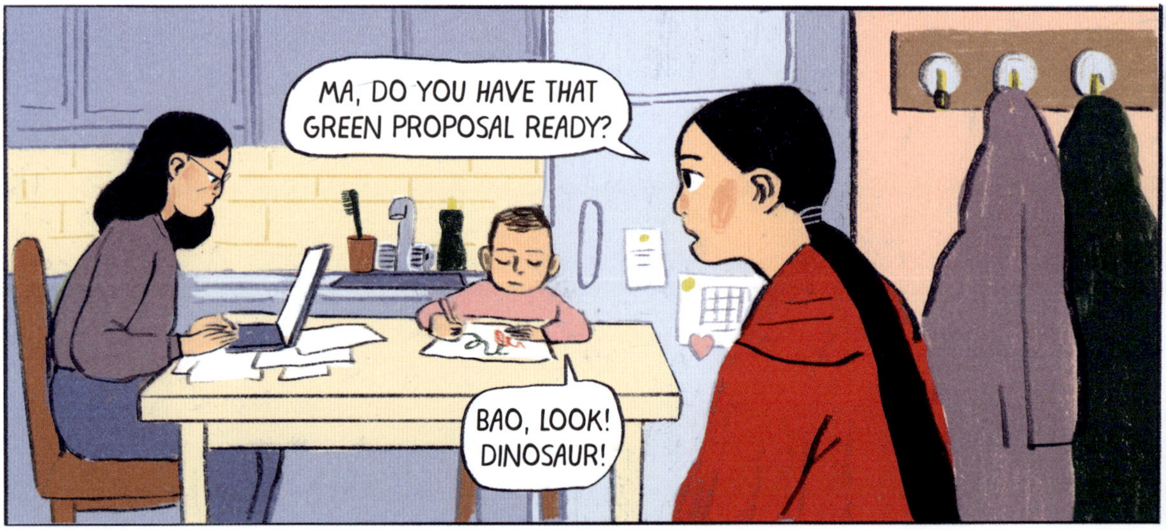
MA, DO YOU HAVE THAT GREEN PROPOSAL READY?
BAO, LOOK! DINOSAUR!

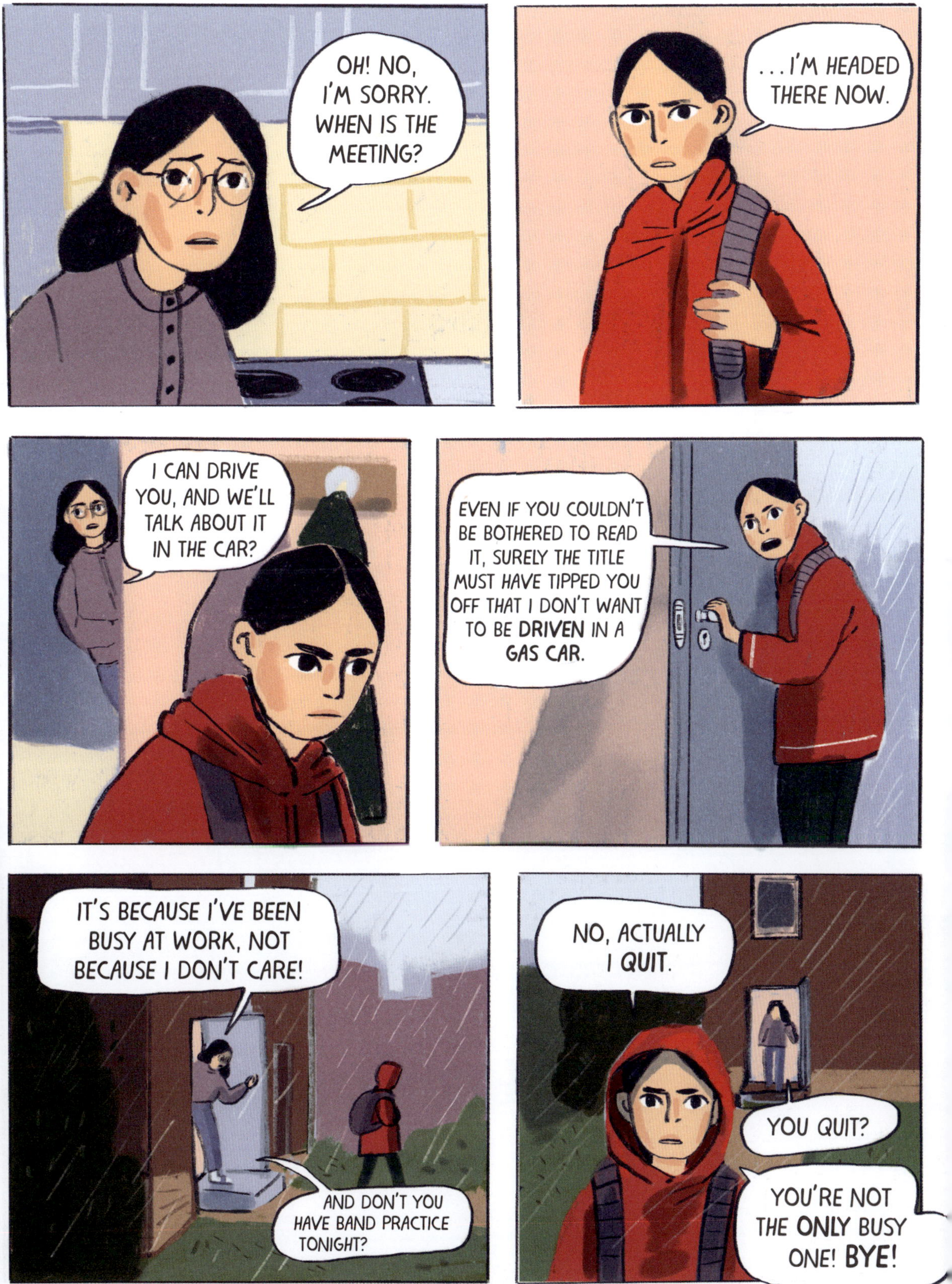
OH! NO, I'M SORRY. WHEN IS THE MEETING?
...I'M HEADED THERE NOW.
I CAN DRIVE YOU, AND WE'LL TALK ABOUT IT IN THE CAR?
EVEN IF YOU COULDN'T BE BOTHERED TO READ IT, SURELY THE TITLE MUST HAVE TIPPED YOU OFF THAT I DON'T WANT TO BE **DRIVEN** IN A **GAS CAR**.
IT'S BECAUSE I'VE BEEN BUSY AT WORK, NOT BECAUSE I DON'T CARE!
AND DON'T YOU HAVE BAND PRACTICE TONIGHT?
NO, ACTUALLY I **QUIT**.
YOU QUIT?
YOU'RE NOT THE **ONLY** BUSY ONE! **BYE!**

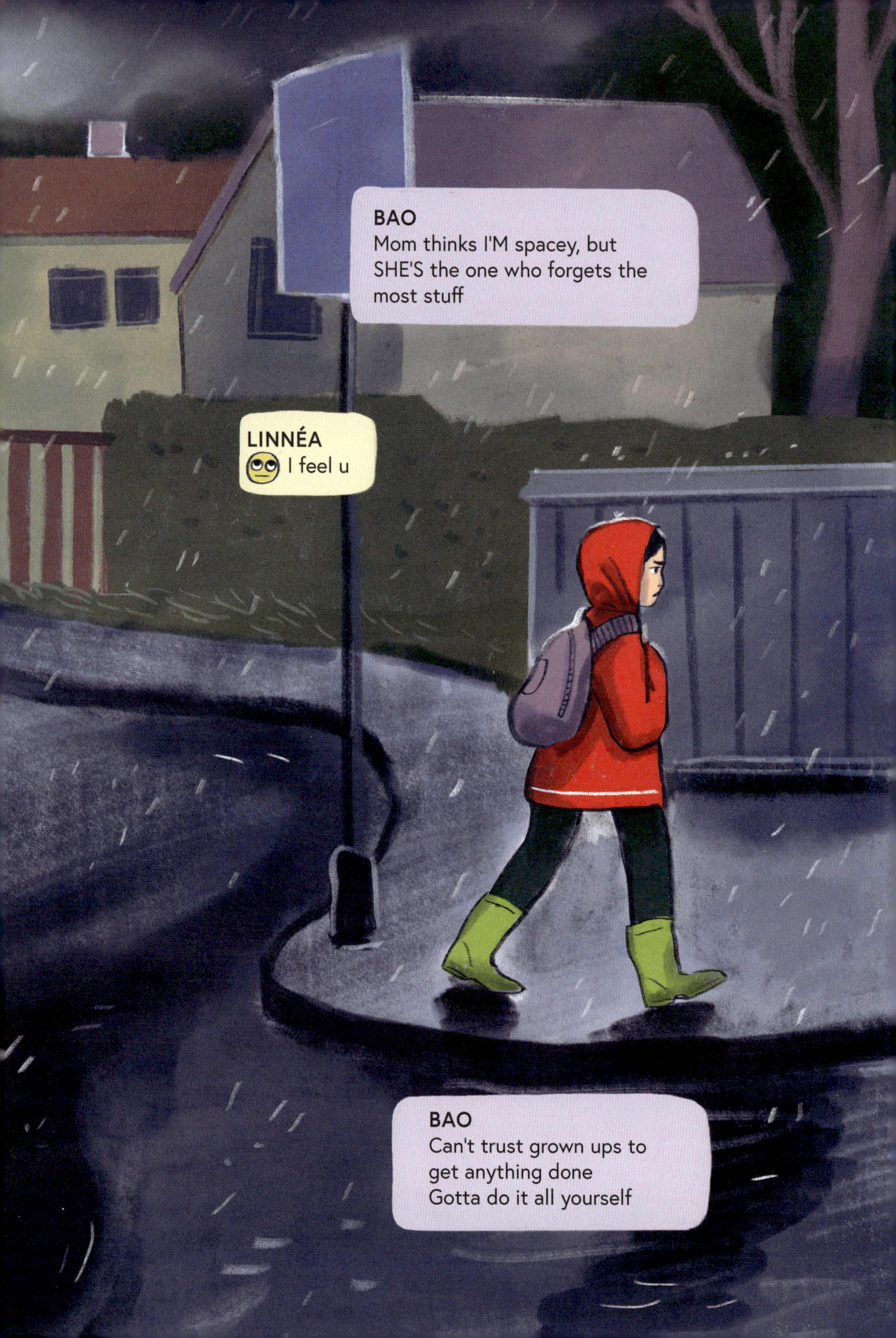
BAO
Mom thinks I'M spacey, but SHE'S the one who forgets the most stuff
LINNÉA
I feel u
BAO
Can't trust grown ups to get anything done
Gotta do it all yourself

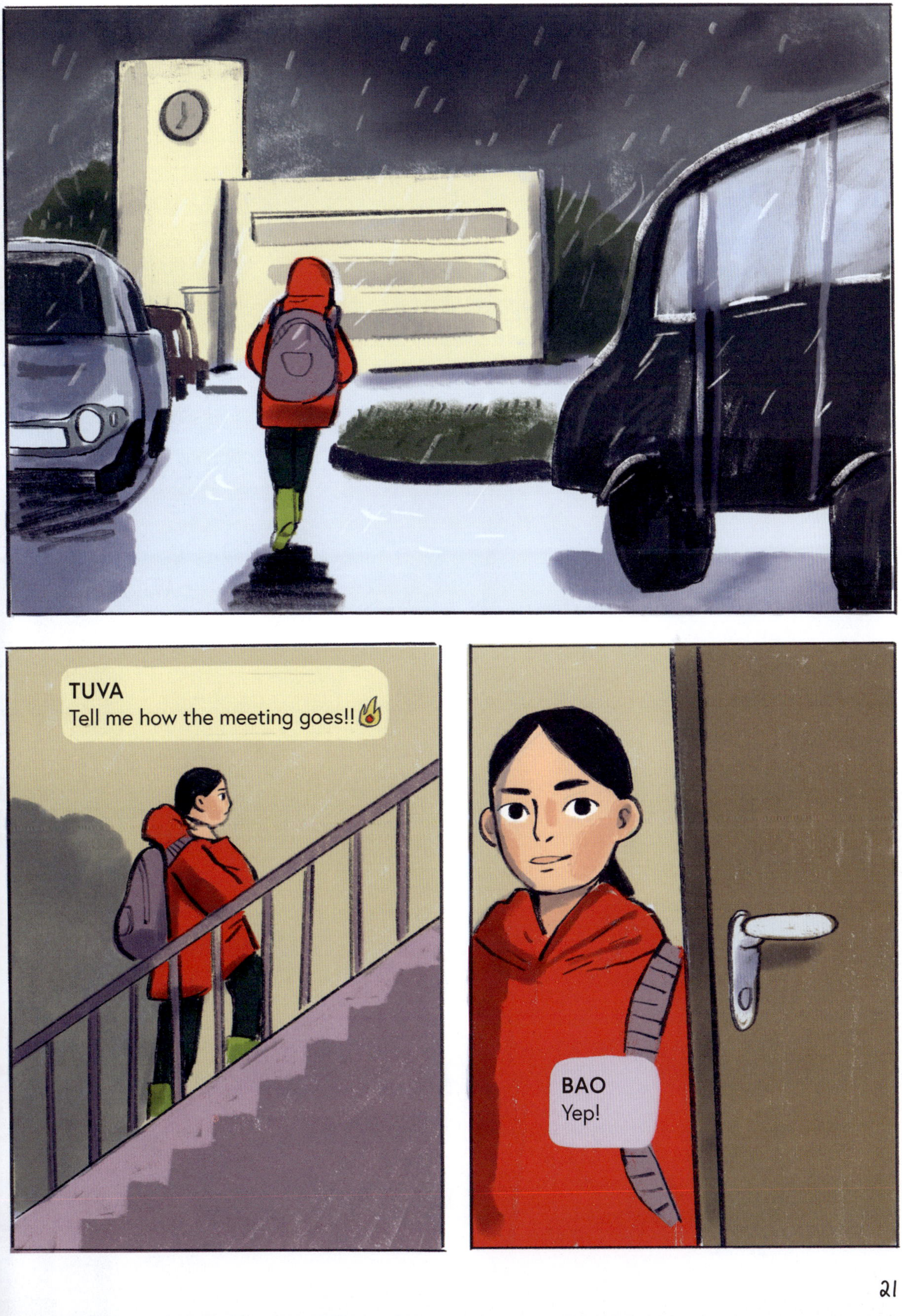
TUVA
Tell me how the meeting goes!!
BAO
Yep!

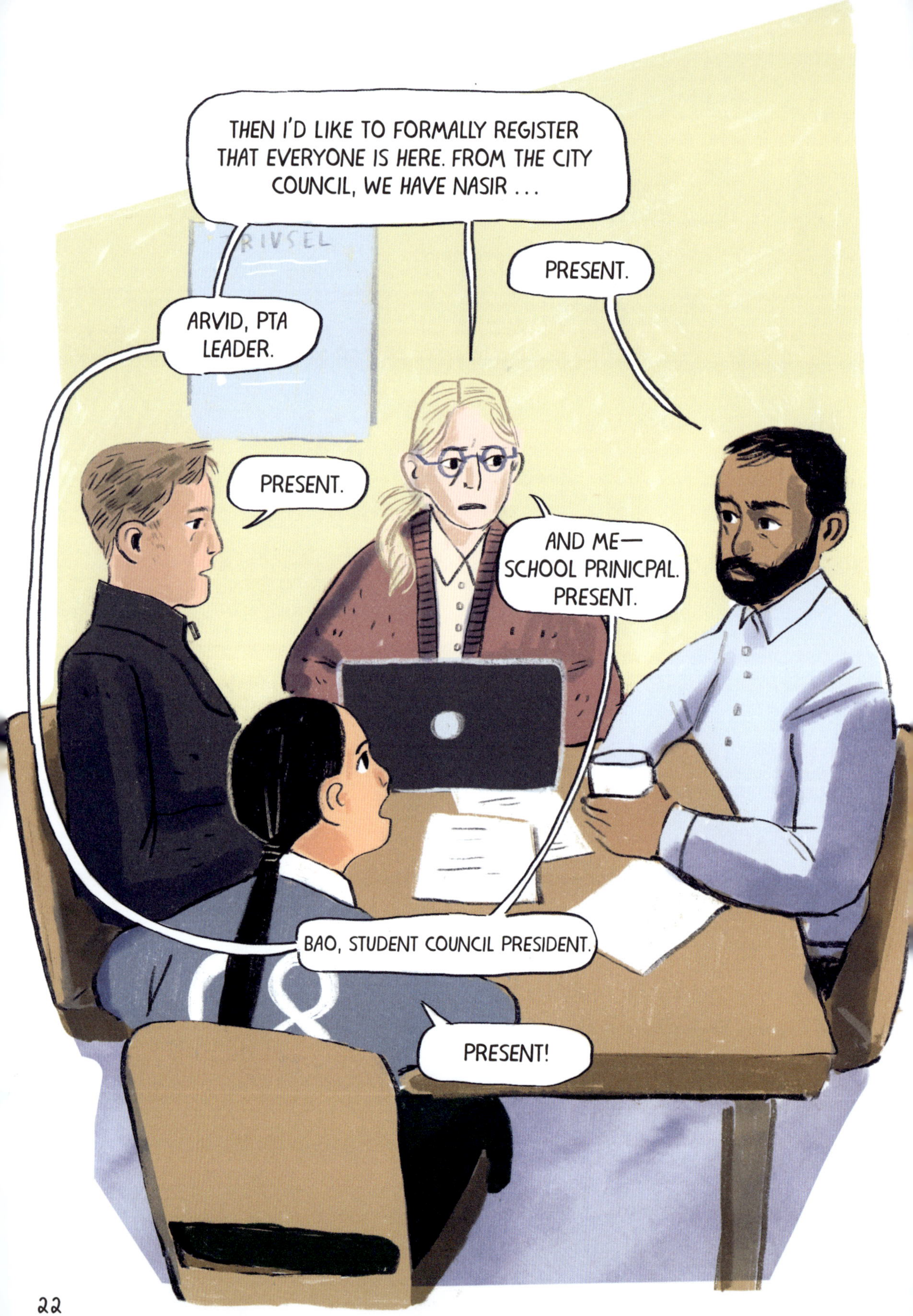
THEN I'D LIKE TO FORMALLY REGISTER THAT EVERYONE IS HERE. FROM THE CITY COUNCIL, WE HAVE NASIR . . .
PRESENT.
ARVID, PTA LEADER.
PRESENT.
AND ME— SCHOOL PRINICPAL. PRESENT.
BAO, STUDENT COUNCIL PRESIDENT.
PRESENT!

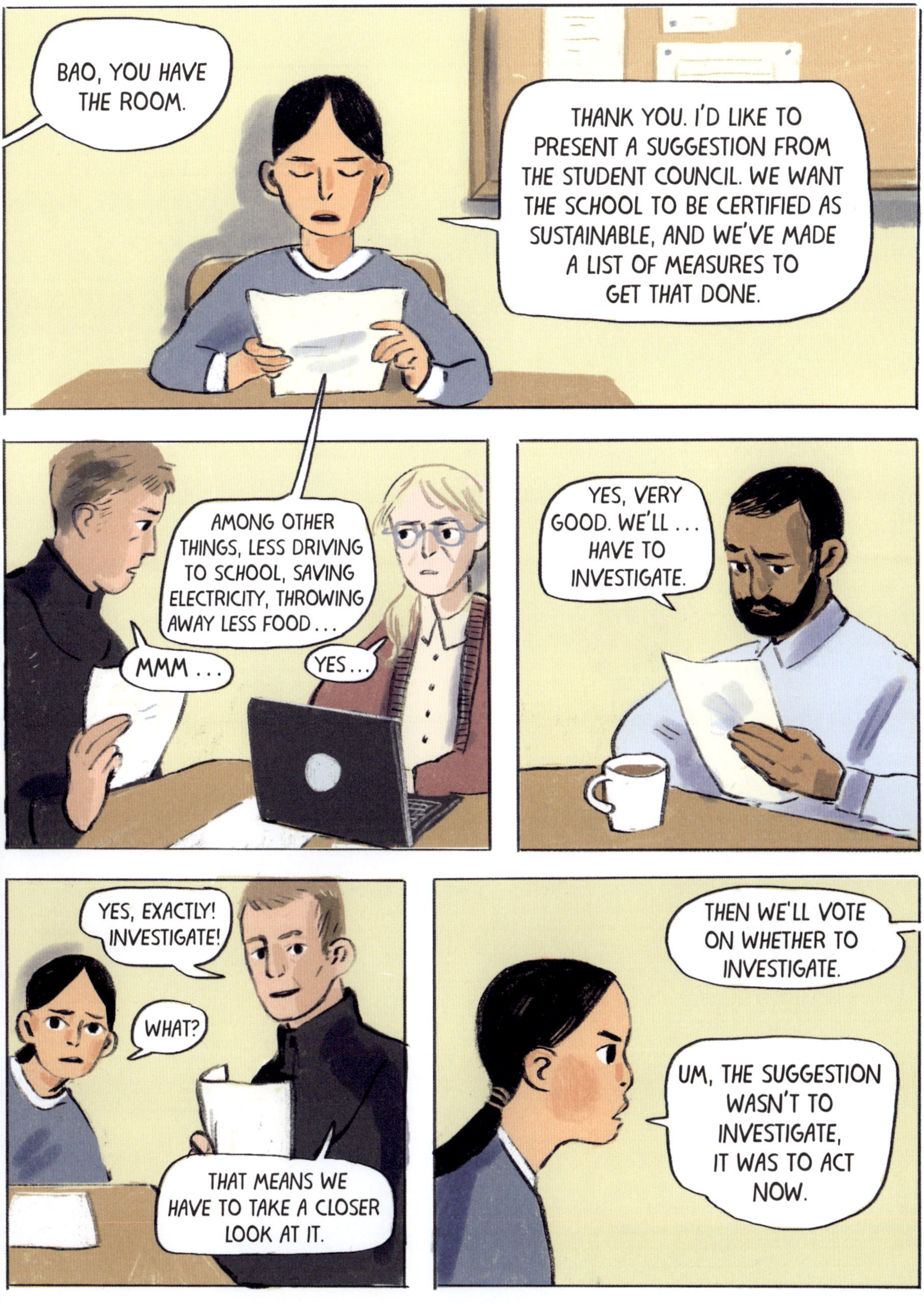

BAO, YOU HAVE THE ROOM.
THANK YOU. I'D LIKE TO PRESENT A SUGGESTION FROM THE STUDENT COUNCIL. WE WANT THE SCHOOL TO BE CERTIFIED AS SUSTAINABLE, AND WE'VE MADE A LIST OF MEASURES TO GET THAT DONE.
AMONG OTHER THINGS, LESS DRIVING TO SCHOOL, SAVING ELECTRICITY, THROWING AWAY LESS FOOD . . .
MMM . . .
YES . . .
YES, VERY GOOD. WE'LL . . . HAVE TO INVESTIGATE.
YES, EXACTLY! INVESTIGATE!
WHAT?
THAT MEANS WE HAVE TO TAKE A CLOSER LOOK AT IT.
THEN WE'LL VOTE ON WHETHER TO INVESTIGATE.
UM, THE SUGGESTION WASN'T TO INVESTIGATE, IT WAS TO ACT NOW.

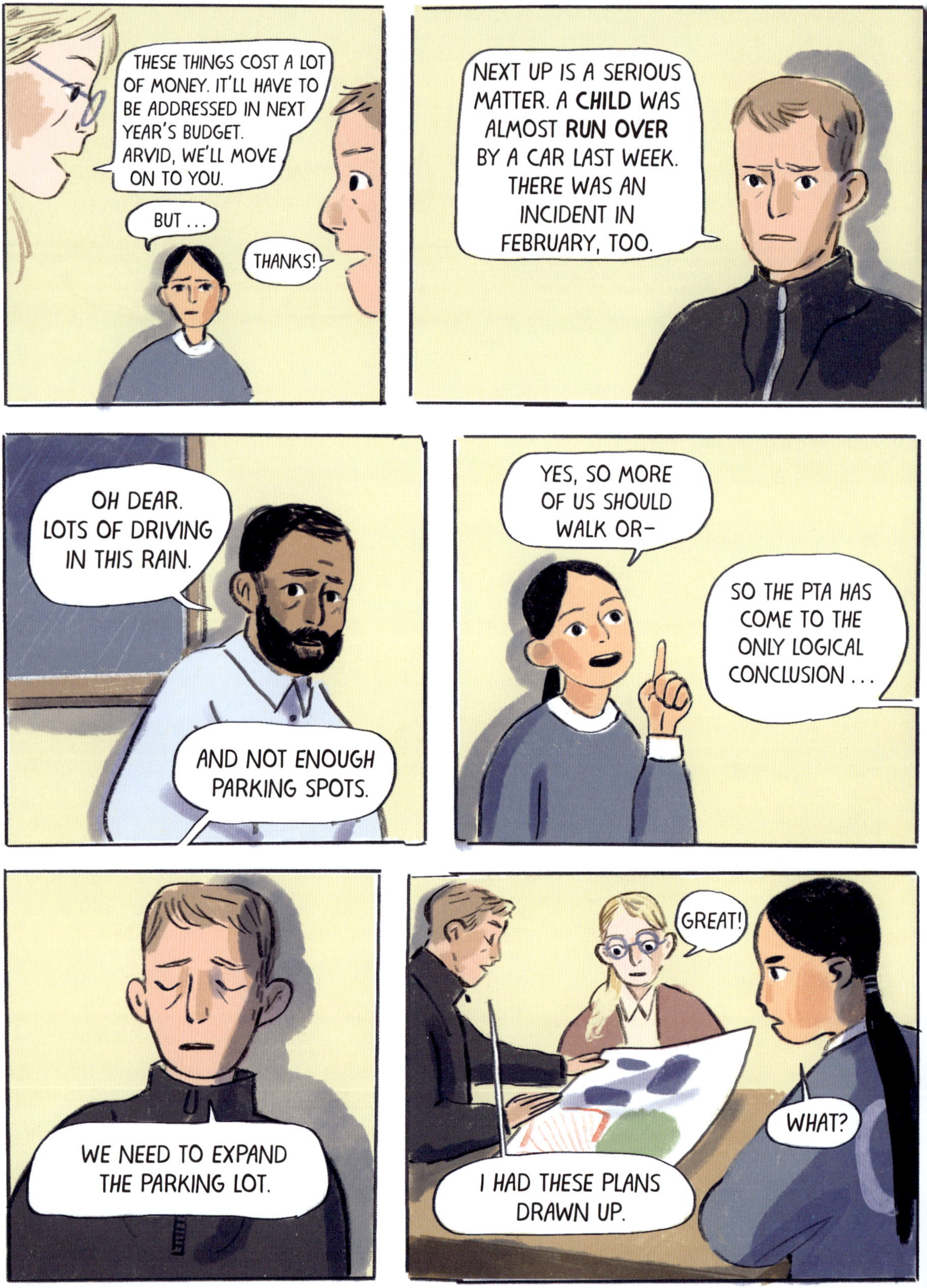
THESE THINGS COST A LOT OF MONEY. IT'LL HAVE TO BE ADDRESSED IN NEXT YEAR'S BUDGET. ARVID, WE'LL MOVE ON TO YOU.
BUT . . .
THANKS!
NEXT UP IS A SERIOUS MATTER. A **CHILD** WAS ALMOST **RUN OVER** BY A CAR LAST WEEK. THERE WAS AN INCIDENT IN FEBRUARY, TOO.
OH DEAR. LOTS OF DRIVING IN THIS RAIN.
AND NOT ENOUGH PARKING SPOTS.
YES, SO MORE OF US SHOULD WALK OR–
SO THE PTA HAS COME TO THE ONLY LOGICAL CONCLUSION . . .
WE NEED TO EXPAND THE PARKING LOT.
GREAT!
WHAT?
I HAD THESE PLANS DRAWN UP.

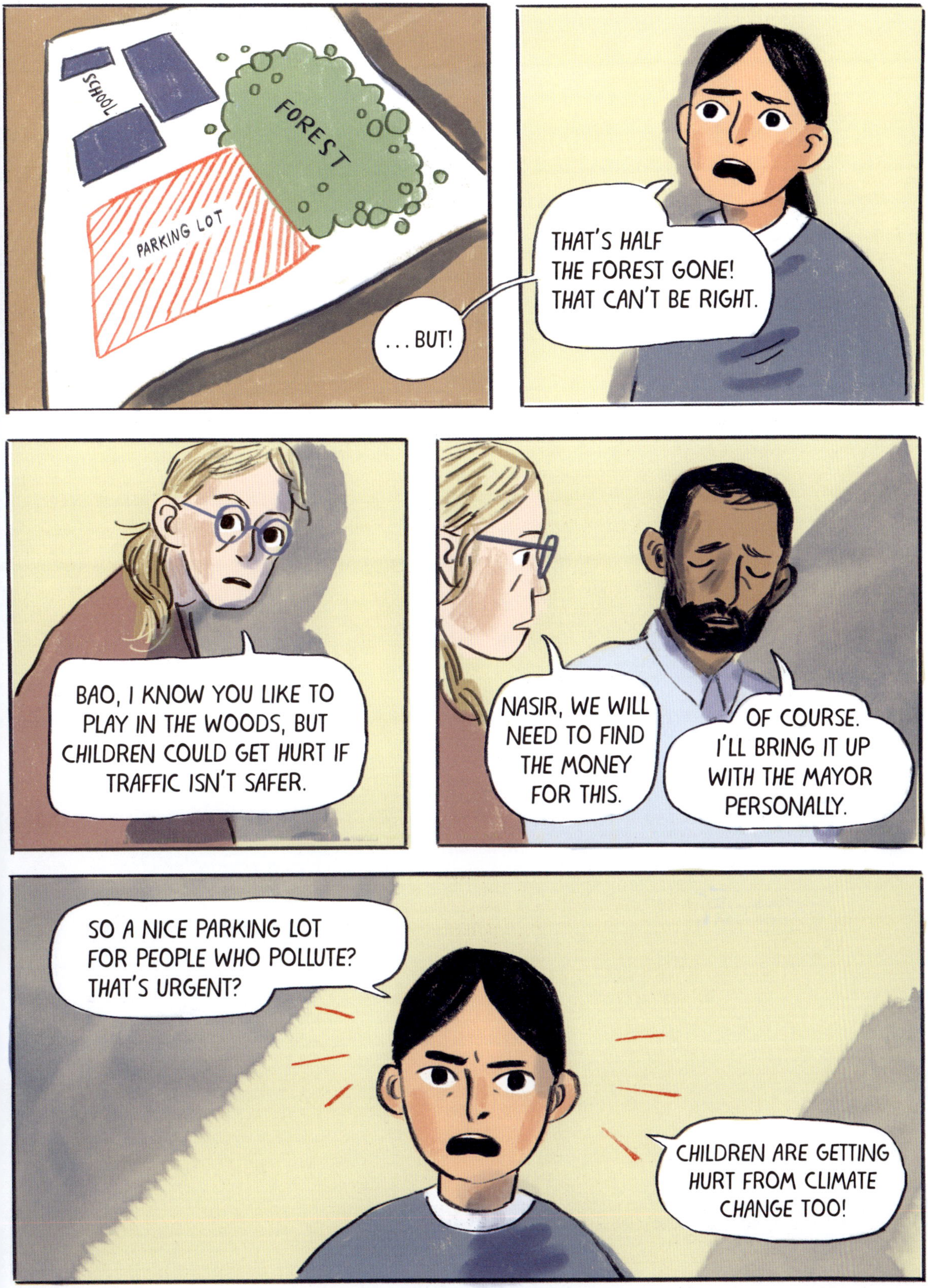
SCHOOL
FOREST
PARKING LOT
. . . BUT!
THAT'S HALF THE FOREST GONE! THAT CAN'T BE RIGHT.
BAO, I KNOW YOU LIKE TO PLAY IN THE WOODS, BUT CHILDREN COULD GET HURT IF TRAFFIC ISN'T SAFER.
NASIR, WE WILL NEED TO FIND THE MONEY FOR THIS.
OF COURSE. I'LL BRING IT UP WITH THE MAYOR PERSONALLY.
SO A NICE PARKING LOT FOR PEOPLE WHO POLLUTE? THAT'S URGENT?
CHILDREN ARE GETTING HURT FROM CLIMATE CHANGE TOO!

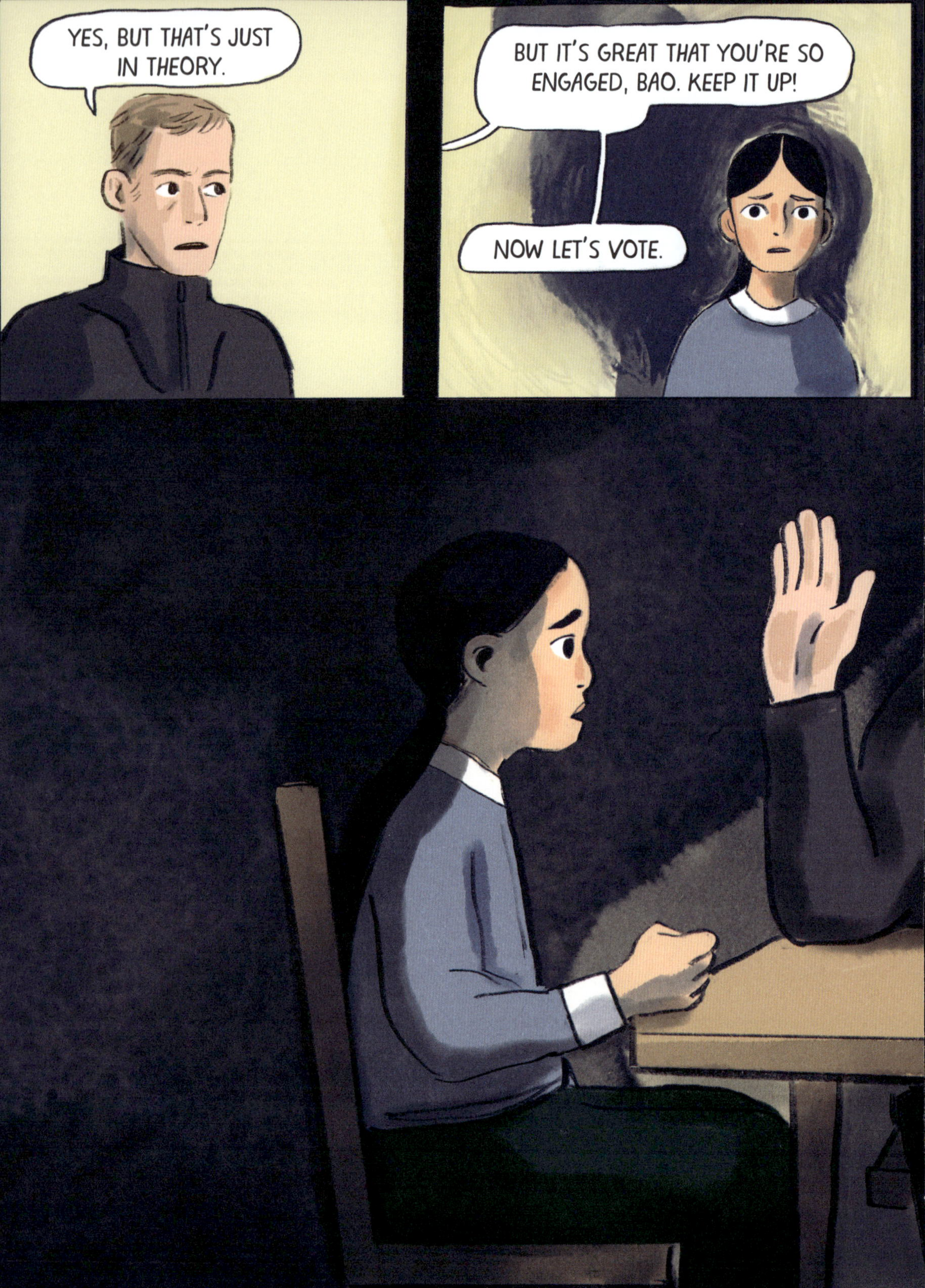
YES, BUT THAT'S JUST IN THEORY.
BUT IT'S GREAT THAT YOU'RE SO ENGAGED, BAO. KEEP IT UP!
NOW LET'S VOTE.

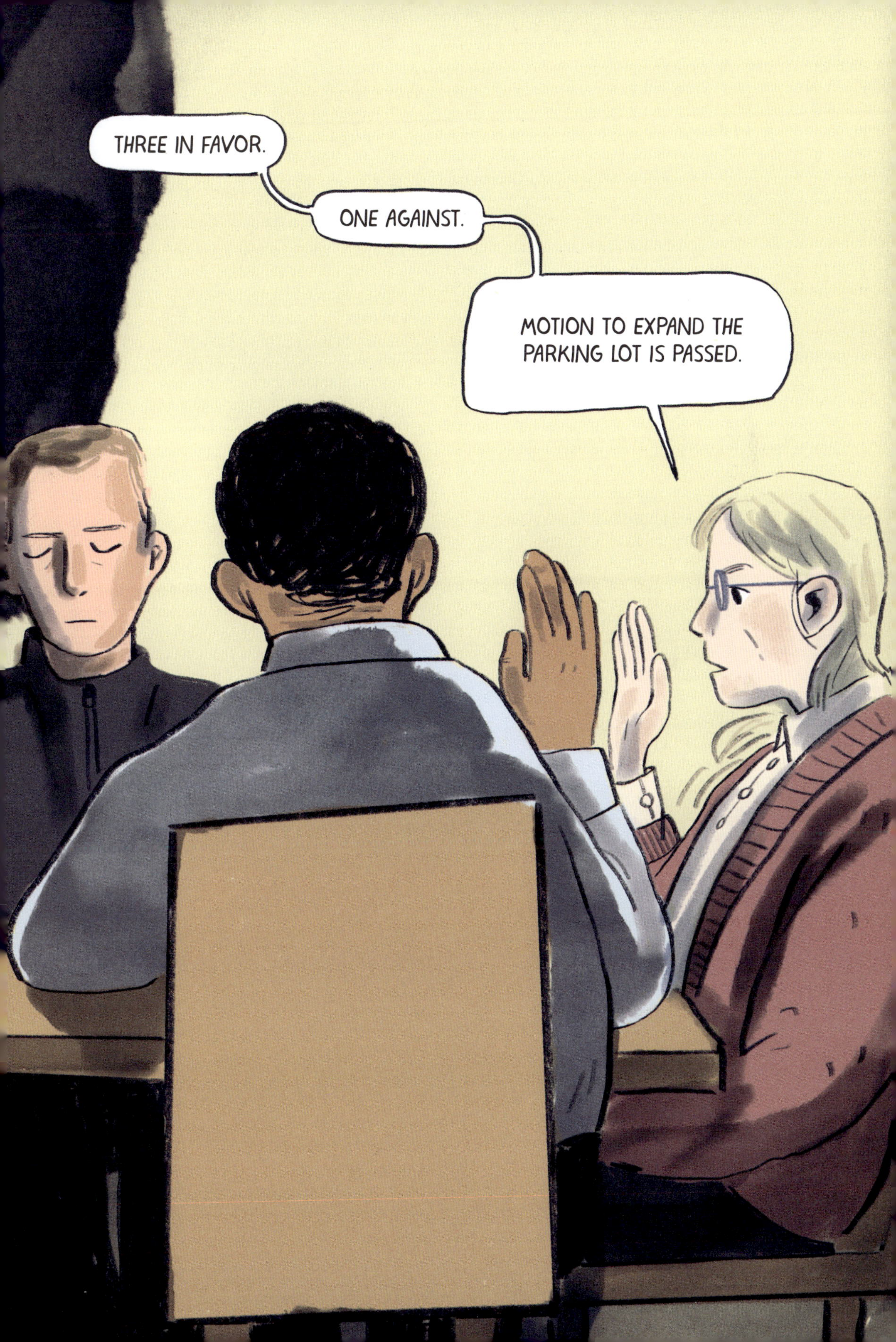
THREE IN FAVOR.
ONE AGAINST.
MOTION TO EXPAND THE PARKING LOT IS PASSED.

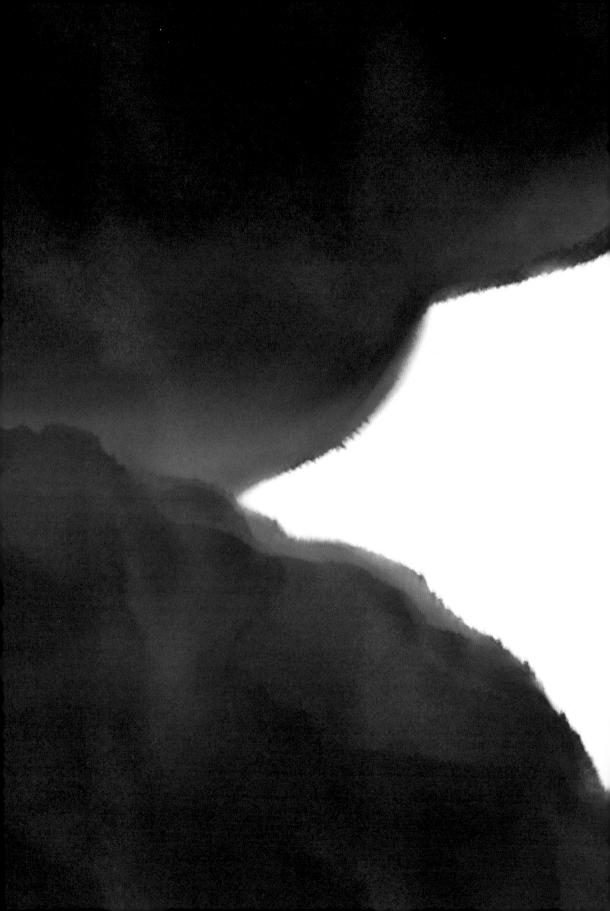

BAO
WTF

LINNÉA
Bao!! What's up??? Pls don't swear
btw

BAO
No
I won't stop actually
I CAN'T TAKE any more
of this

TUVA
What happened?? Smth go down at
the meeting with the PTA?

BAO
Yes
They don't understand crap
It's a crisis
I'm not kidding

TUVA

LINNÉA
  But what did they say?

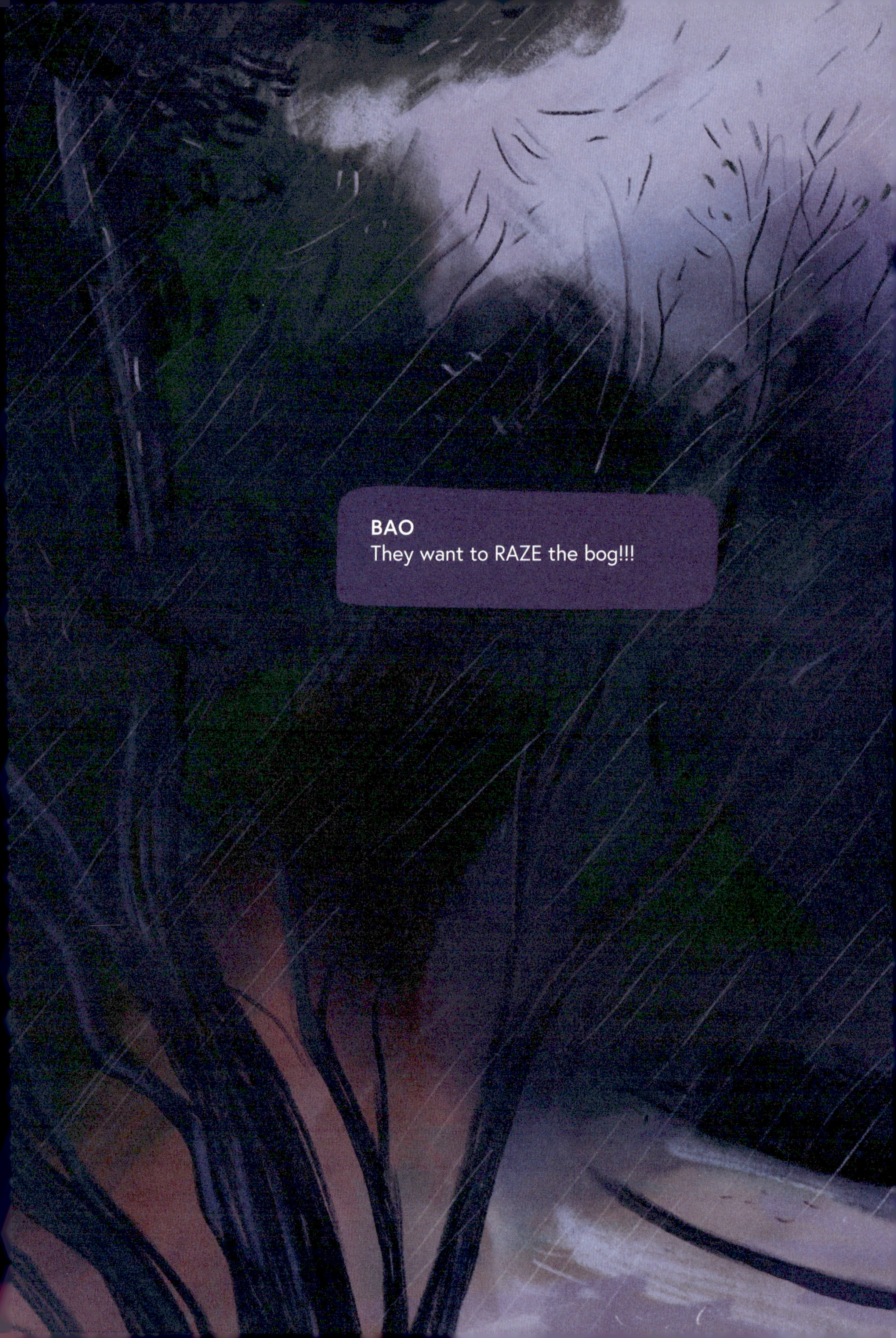
BAO
They want to RAZE the bog!!!

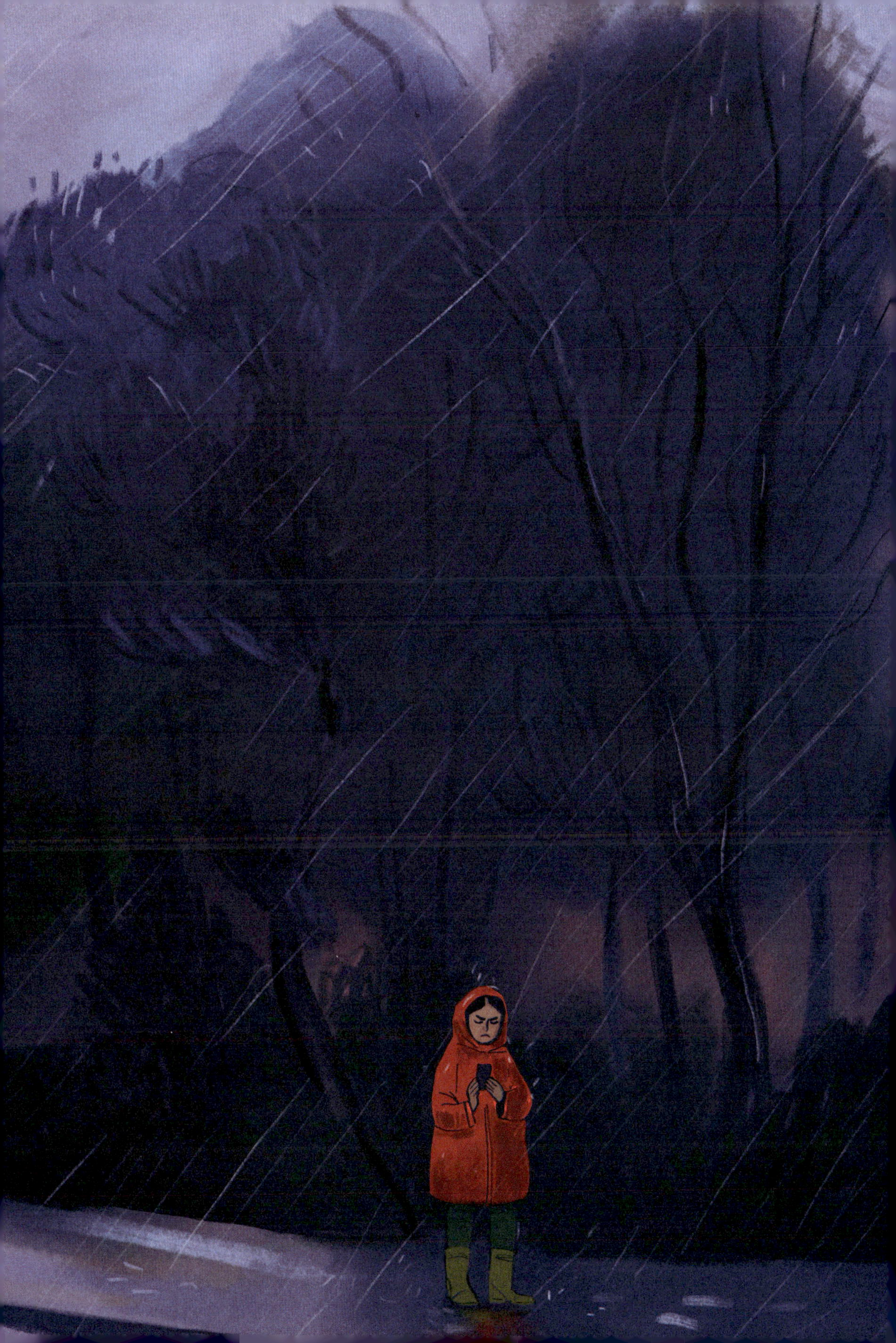

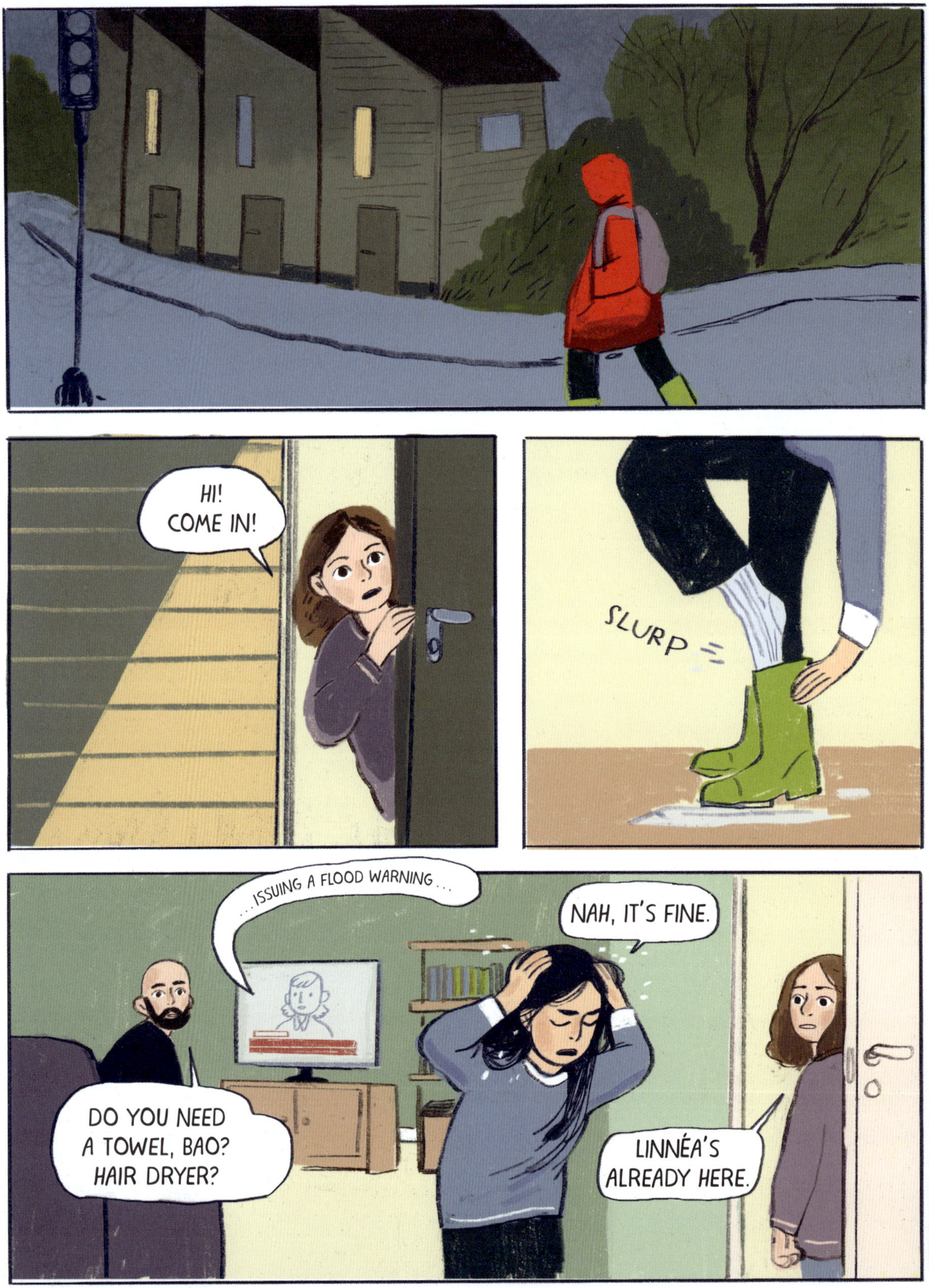
HI! COME IN!
SLURP
...ISSUING A FLOOD WARNING...
NAH, IT'S FINE.
DO YOU NEED A TOWEL, BAO? HAIR DRYER?
LINNÉA'S ALREADY HERE.

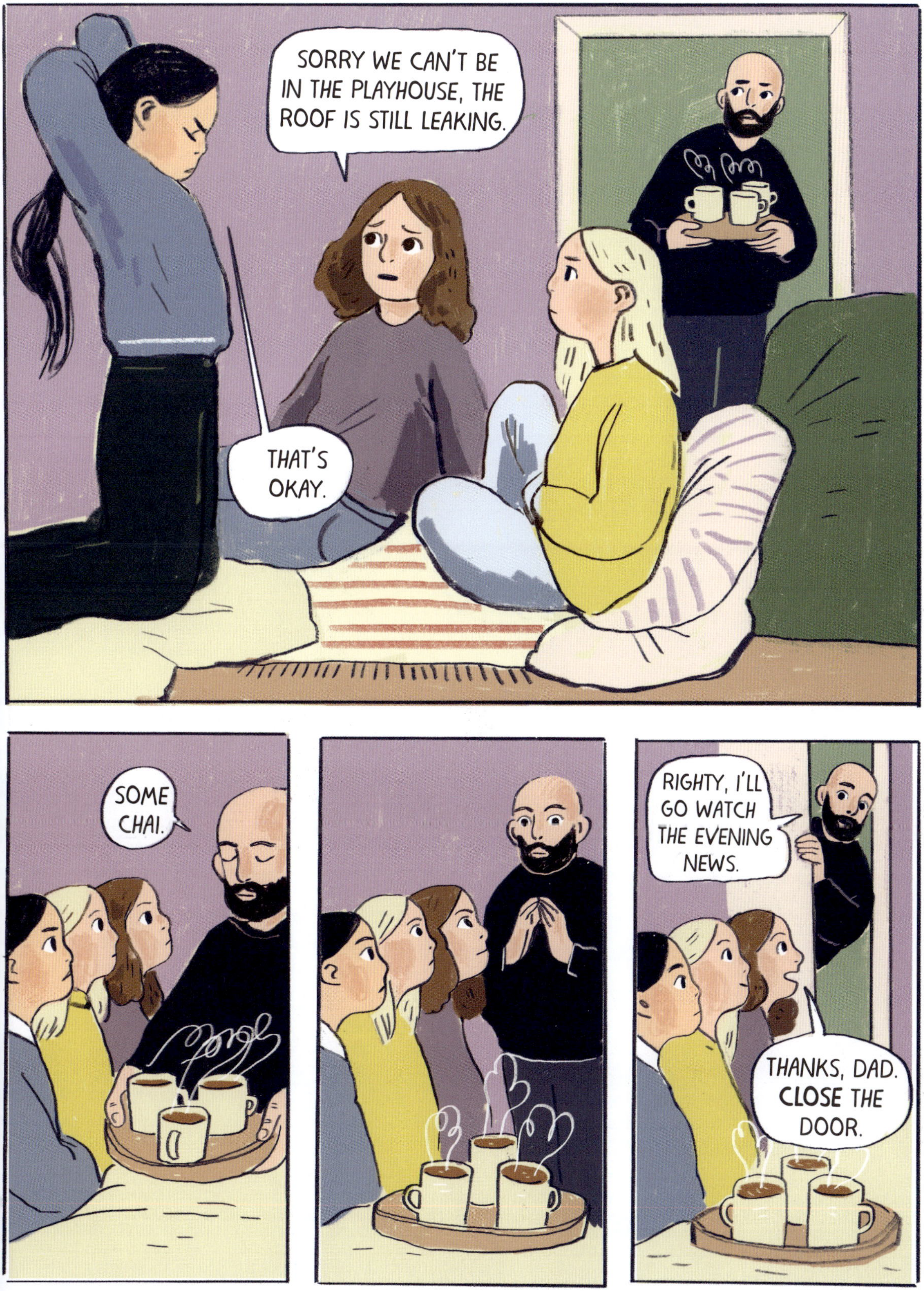
SORRY WE CAN'T BE IN THE PLAYHOUSE, THE ROOF IS STILL LEAKING.
THAT'S OKAY.
SOME CHAI.
RIGHTY, I'LL GO WATCH THE EVENING NEWS.
THANKS, DAD. **CLOSE** THE DOOR.

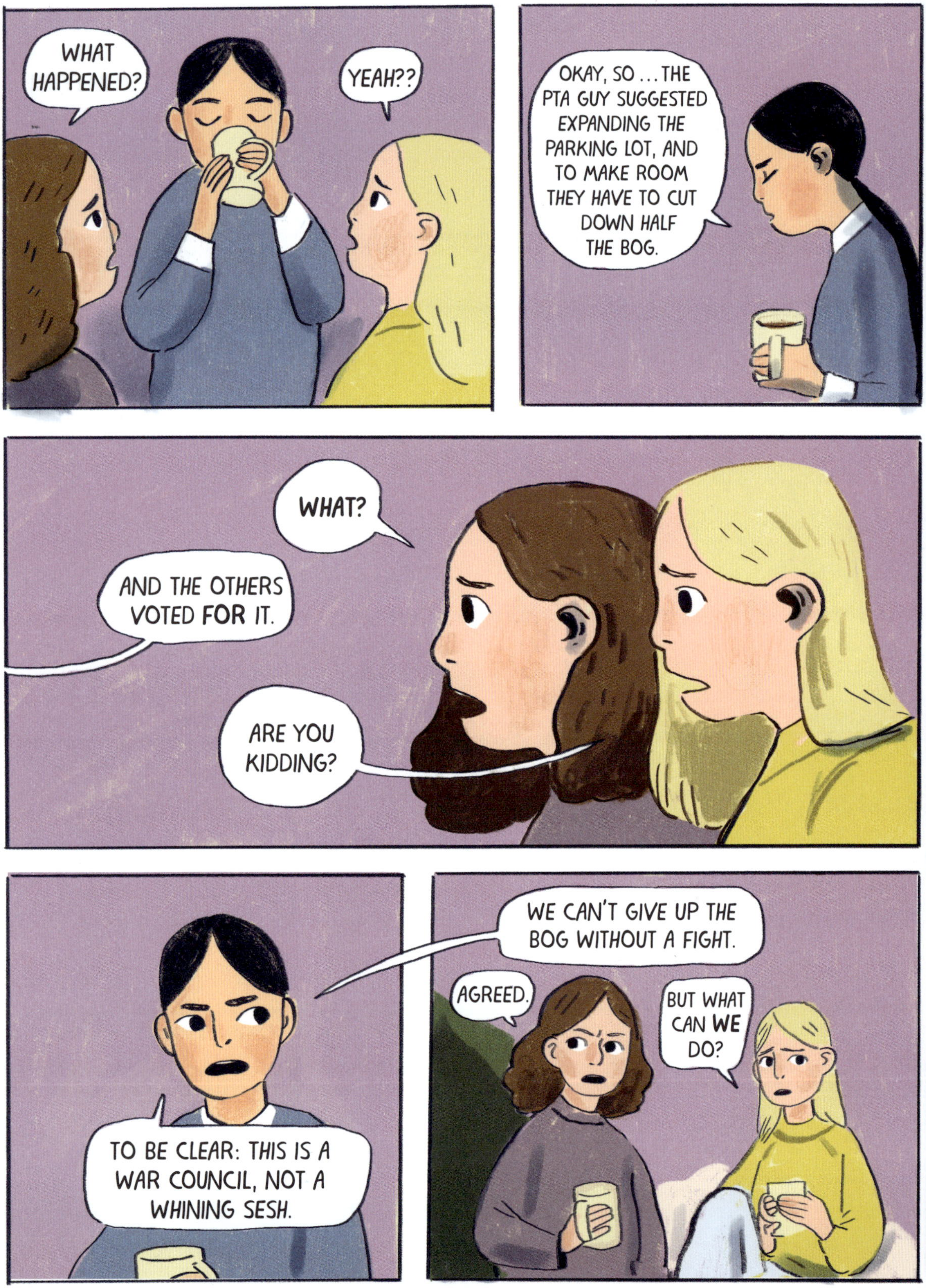
WHAT HAPPENED?
YEAH??
OKAY, SO ... THE PTA GUY SUGGESTED EXPANDING THE PARKING LOT, AND TO MAKE ROOM THEY HAVE TO CUT DOWN HALF THE BOG.
WHAT?
AND THE OTHERS VOTED FOR IT.
ARE YOU KIDDING?
TO BE CLEAR: THIS IS A WAR COUNCIL, NOT A WHINING SESH.
WE CAN'T GIVE UP THE BOG WITHOUT A FIGHT.
AGREED.
BUT WHAT CAN WE DO?

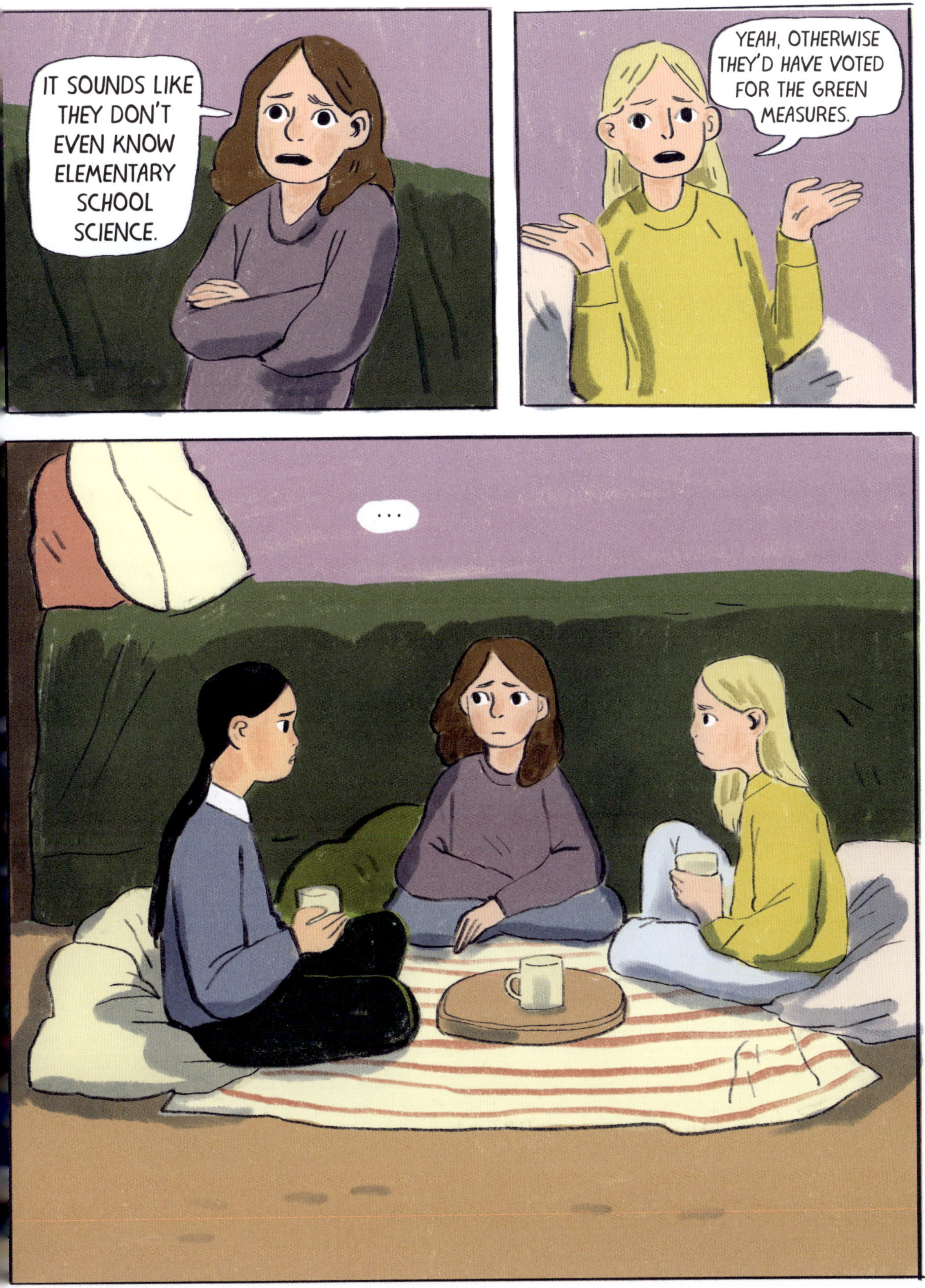
IT SOUNDS LIKE THEY DON'T EVEN KNOW ELEMENTARY SCHOOL SCIENCE.
YEAH, OTHERWISE THEY'D HAVE VOTED FOR THE GREEN MEASURES.
...

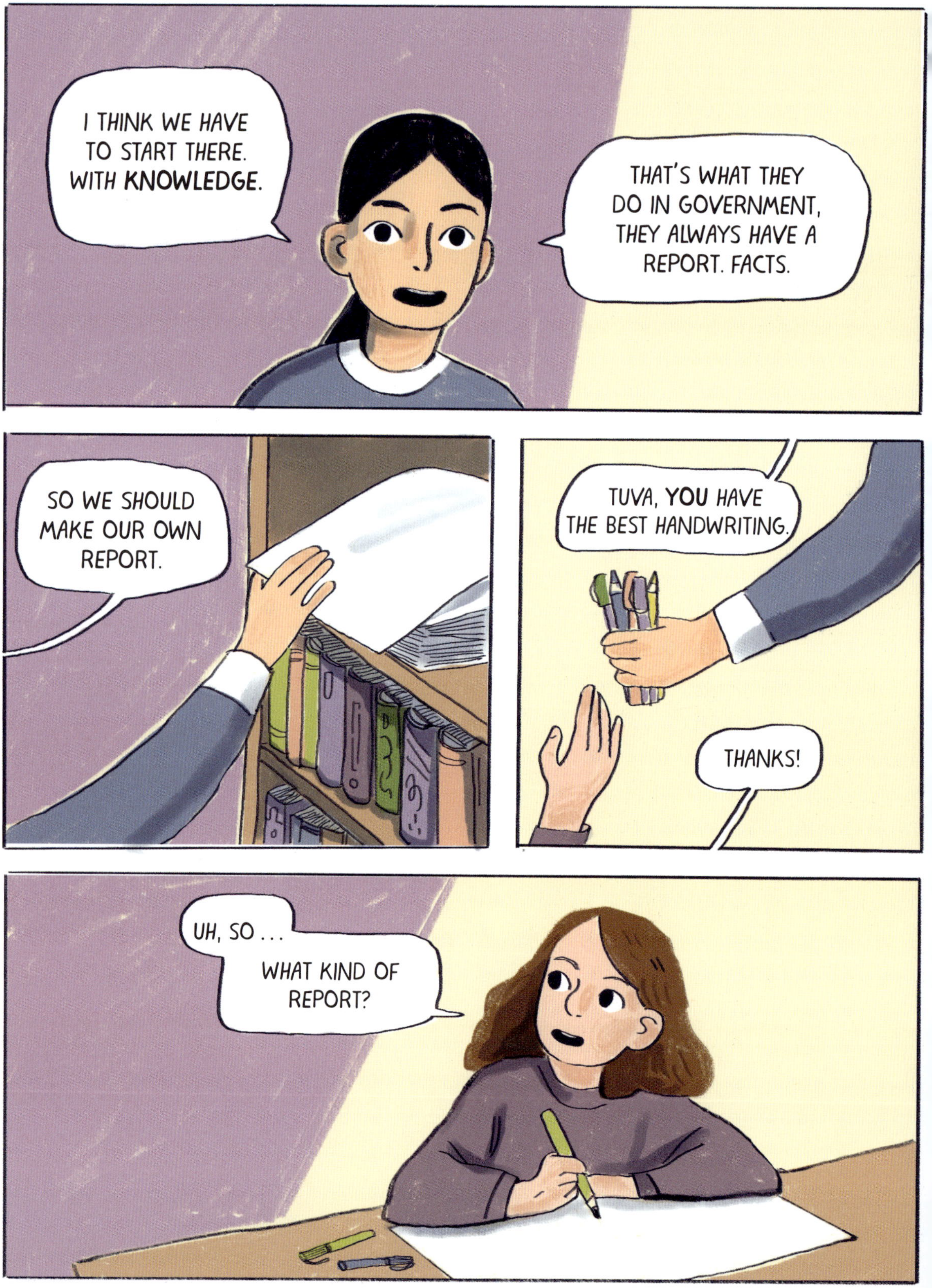
I THINK WE HAVE TO START THERE. WITH **KNOWLEDGE**.
THAT'S WHAT THEY DO IN GOVERNMENT, THEY ALWAYS HAVE A REPORT. FACTS.
SO WE SHOULD MAKE OUR OWN REPORT.
TUVA, **YOU** HAVE THE BEST HANDWRITING.
THANKS!
UH, SO . . .
WHAT KIND OF REPORT?

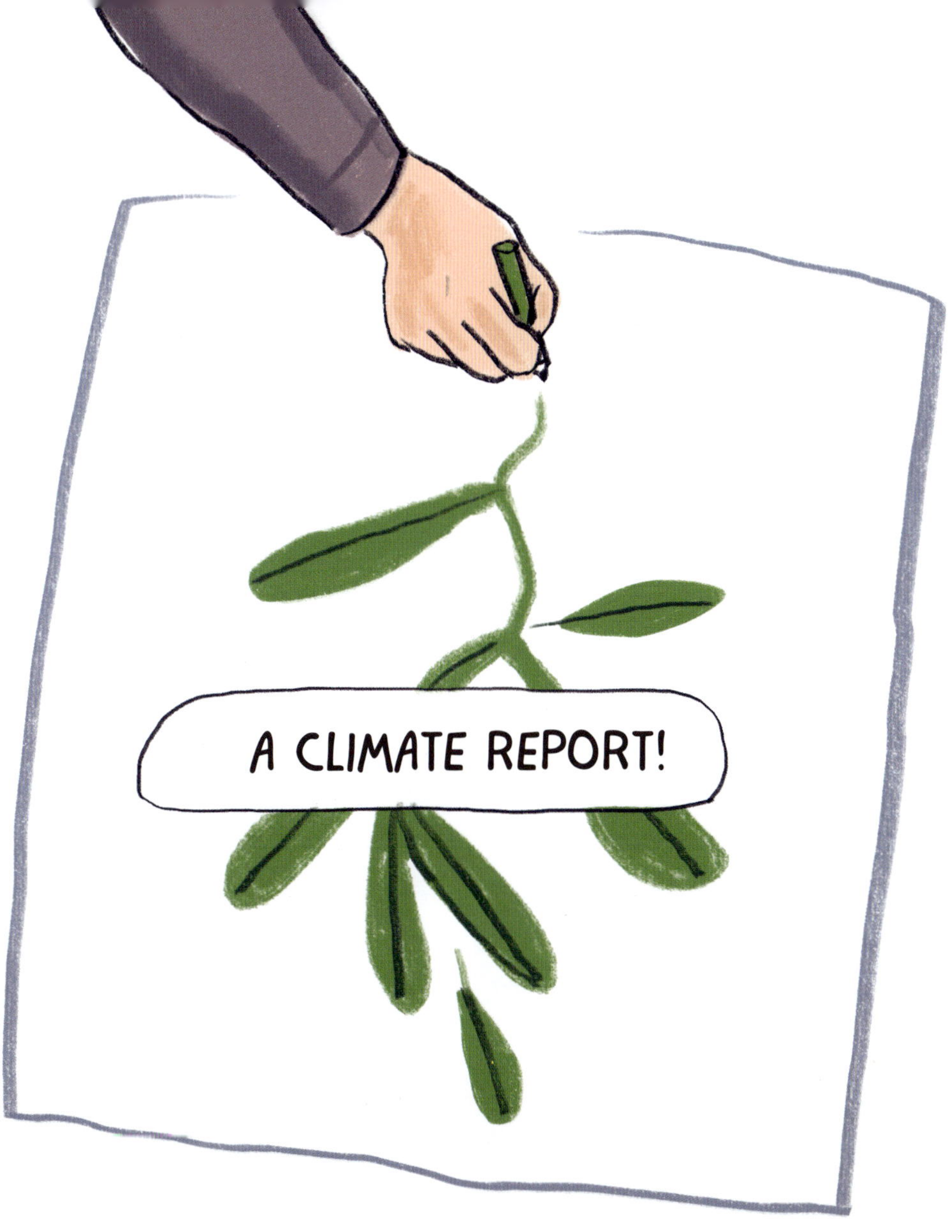
A CLIMATE REPORT!

CLIMATE REPORT

INTRODUCTION

Dear faculty and parents (PTA),

We have realized that you haven't yet learned what climate change is. That's the only explanation for why you would choose a parking lot over making the school greener, anyway.

We had originally planned on sending you a copy of the UN's climate report. But it's so long, the school printers won't print it. And really it's too complicated.

So here is a simplified version:

WHAT IS GLOBAL WARMING?

It's really embarrassing to be writing this to you, because this is old news. The first climate convention was in <u>1992</u>. That was LAST CENTURY and you already knew this then:

$\longrightarrow$

You extract lots of oil, coal, and gas from inside the Earth. You also have too much livestock farting methane.

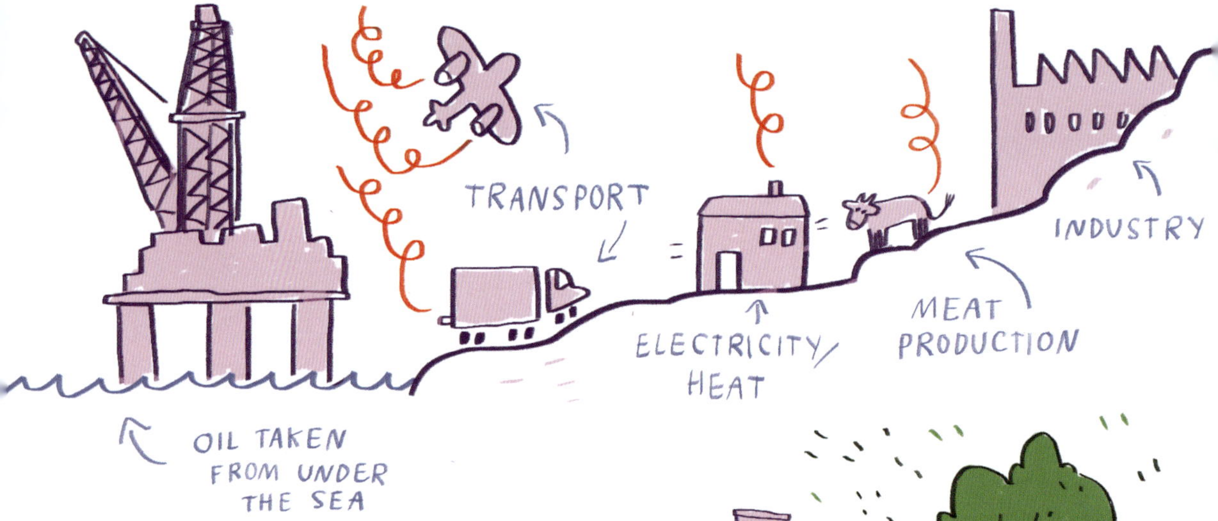
TRANSPORT
ELECTRICITY/HEAT
MEAT PRODUCTION
INDUSTRY
OIL TAKEN FROM UNDER THE SEA

And you destroyed forests, which store CO_2.

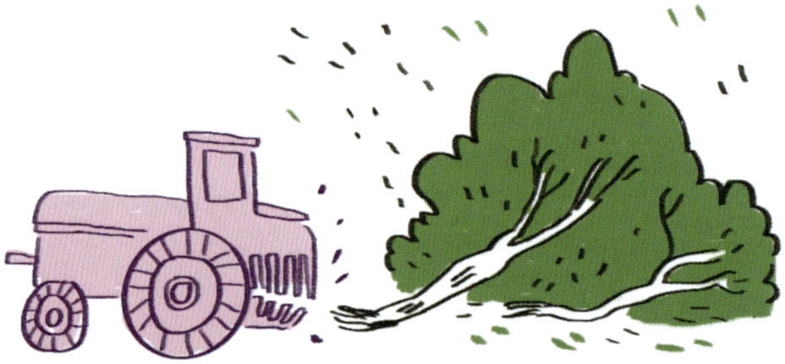

Greenhouse gases like methane and CO_2 make the atmosphere more dense.

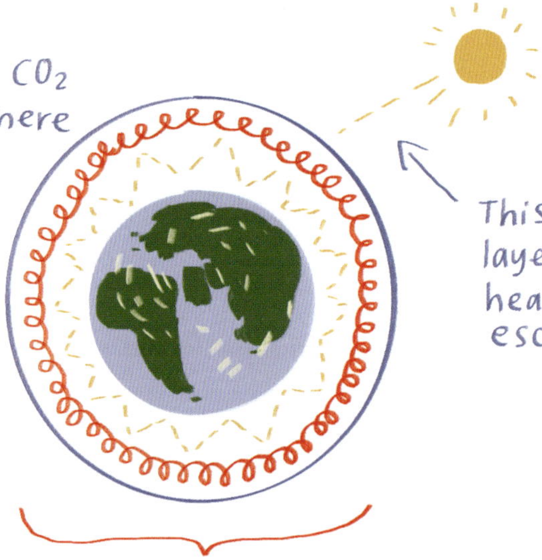

This thick layer prevents heat from escaping.

The Earth is warmed up, like a greenhouse.

Most people know that when the planet gets hotter, more of the _ice_ at the poles will melt, as well as the _glaciers_ in Greenland, which will melt into the sea.

Then sea levels will rise. Only a few feet, but those feet mean _a lot_ for the people who live close to the water.

"But us Norwegians live up high," you think. "And warmer weather would be nice!"

WELL...

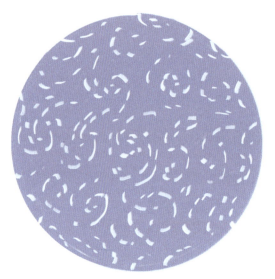

The Earth has a
WEATHER SYSTEM.
There are patterns for
the wind and rain that
are set by the temperature
in the air and the oceans.

A HURRICANE, for
example, is powered
by the heat of the
ocean. The warmer the
ocean, the more
powerful the
hurricane is.

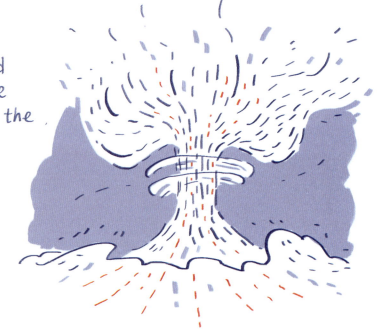

So what happens when temperatures rise?

The threat of EXTREME WEATHER increases. All over the world.

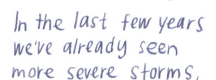

In the last few years we've already seen more severe storms,

more intense monsoons in Asia,

droughts in East Africa,

and enormous wildfires in California, Australia, and even Sweden.

All of that is bad enough.
But the changing weather and
seasons also affect all
living things.

IF SPRING COMES TOO EARLY...

Plants might flower
and die before the
insects wake up...

...insects who
live off of
pollen die...

...birds who
live off of insects
die.

Ecosystems

collapse.

And plants are our food. We need them to live,

Additionally, climate change will be most difficult for those who live in the Global South. This is very unfair, because it is us in the north who pollute the most, and Norway makes lots of money selling oil and gas,

Many people will have to move out of their countries because it will become impossible to live there.

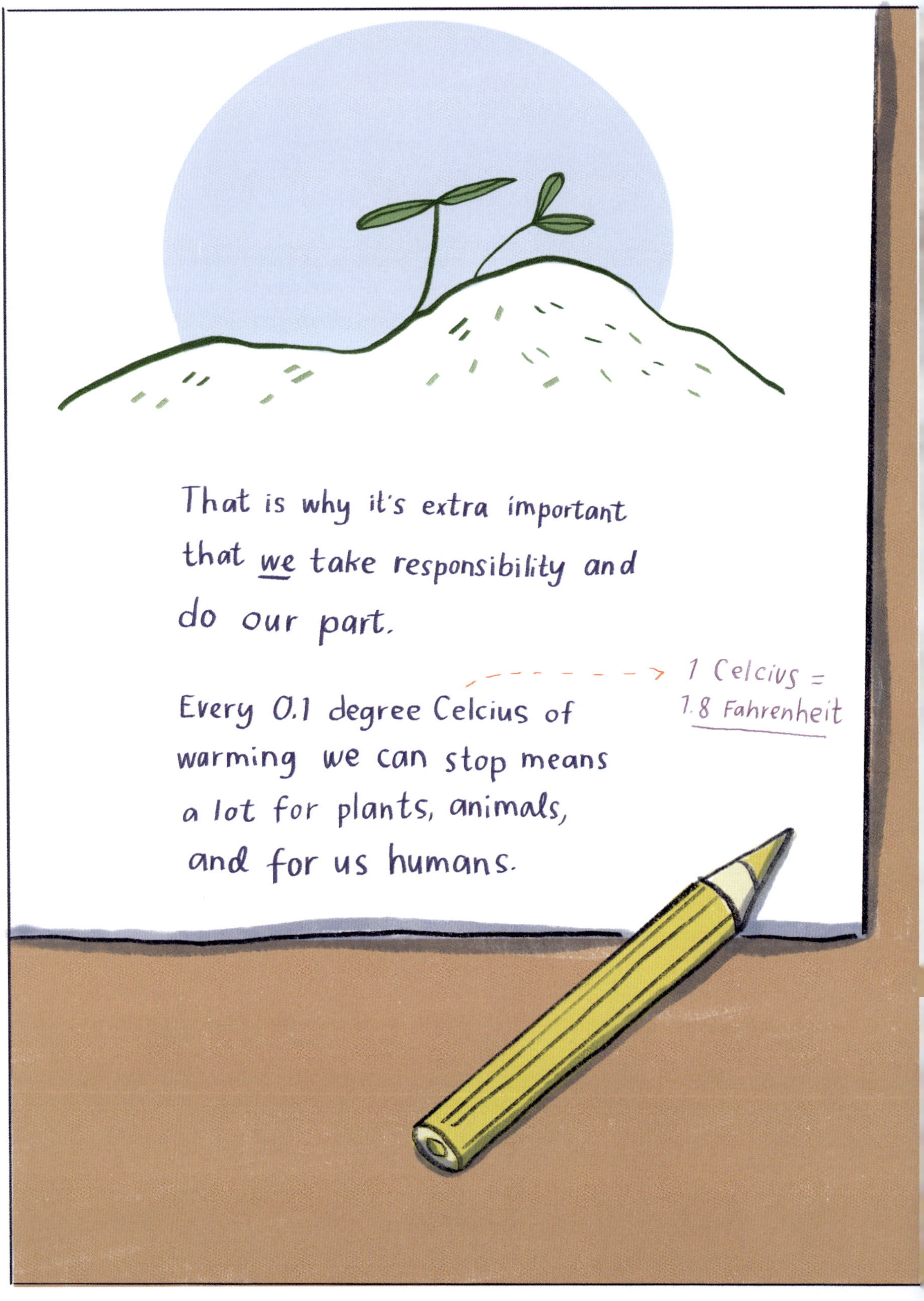
That is why it's extra important that we take responsibility and do our part.
Every 0.1 degree Celcius of warming we can stop means a lot for plants, animals, and for us humans.
1 Celcius = 1.8 Fahrenheit

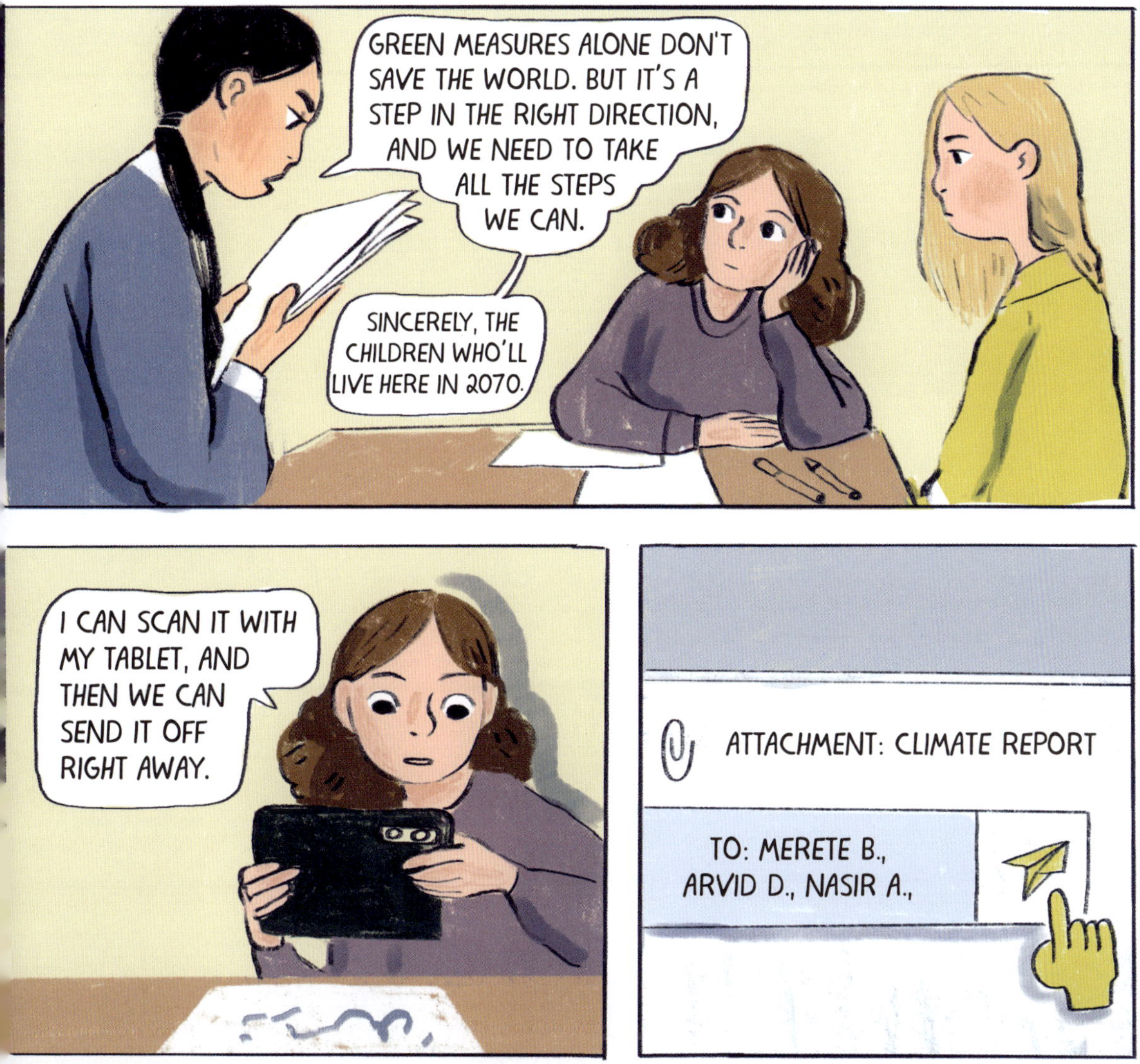
GREEN MEASURES ALONE DON'T SAVE THE WORLD. BUT IT'S A STEP IN THE RIGHT DIRECTION, AND WE NEED TO TAKE ALL THE STEPS WE CAN.
SINCERELY, THE CHILDREN WHO'LL LIVE HERE IN 2070.
I CAN SCAN IT WITH MY TABLET, AND THEN WE CAN SEND IT OFF RIGHT AWAY.
ATTACHMENT: CLIMATE REPORT
TO: MERETE B., ARVID D., NASIR A.,

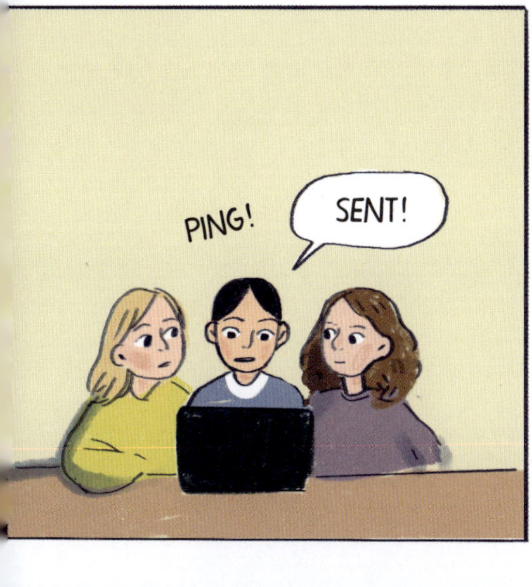
PING!
SENT!

MOM
When will you be home?

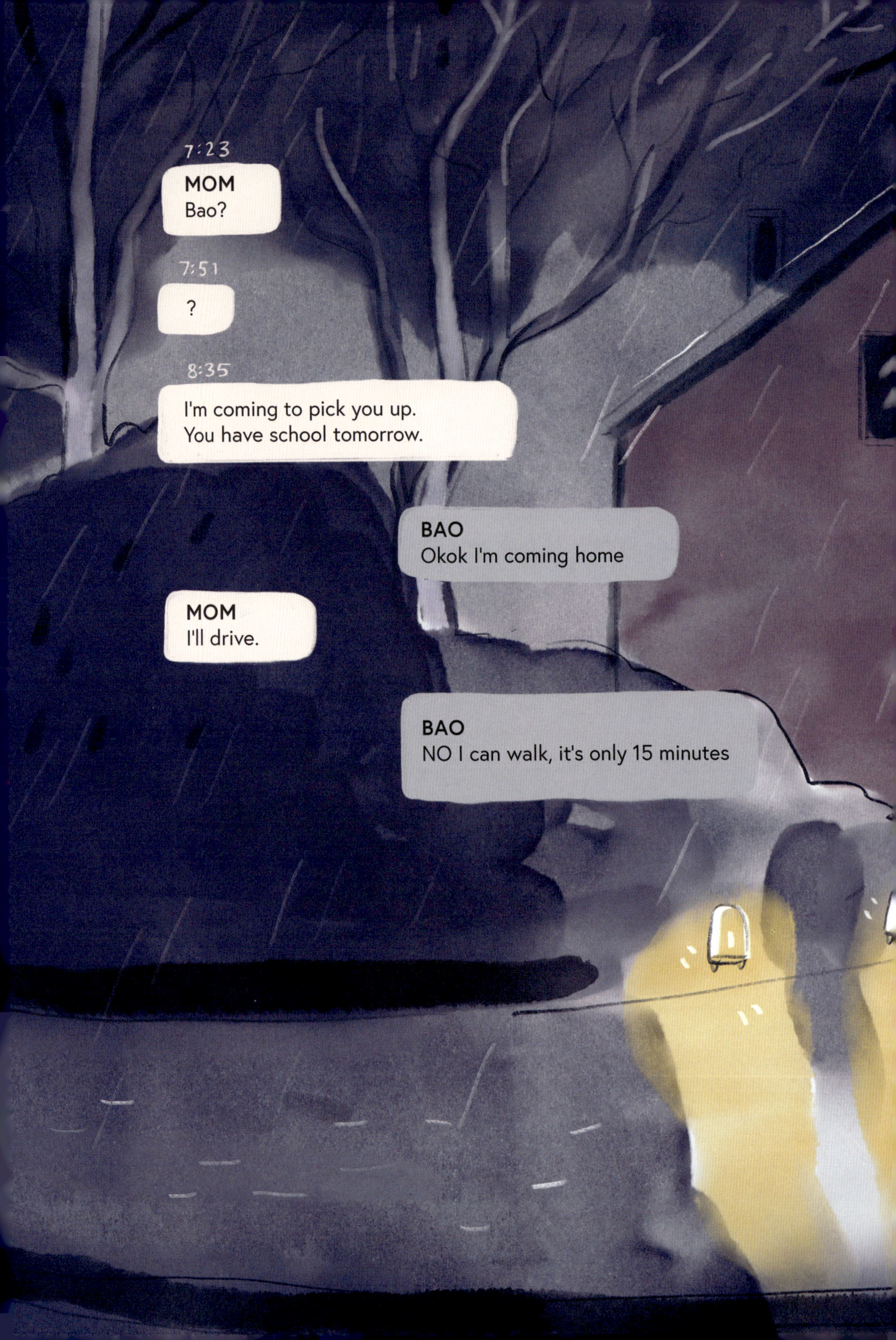
7:23
MOM
Bao?
7:51
?
8:35
I'm coming to pick you up.
You have school tomorrow.
BAO
Okok I'm coming home
MOM
I'll drive.
BAO
NO I can walk, it's only 15 minutes

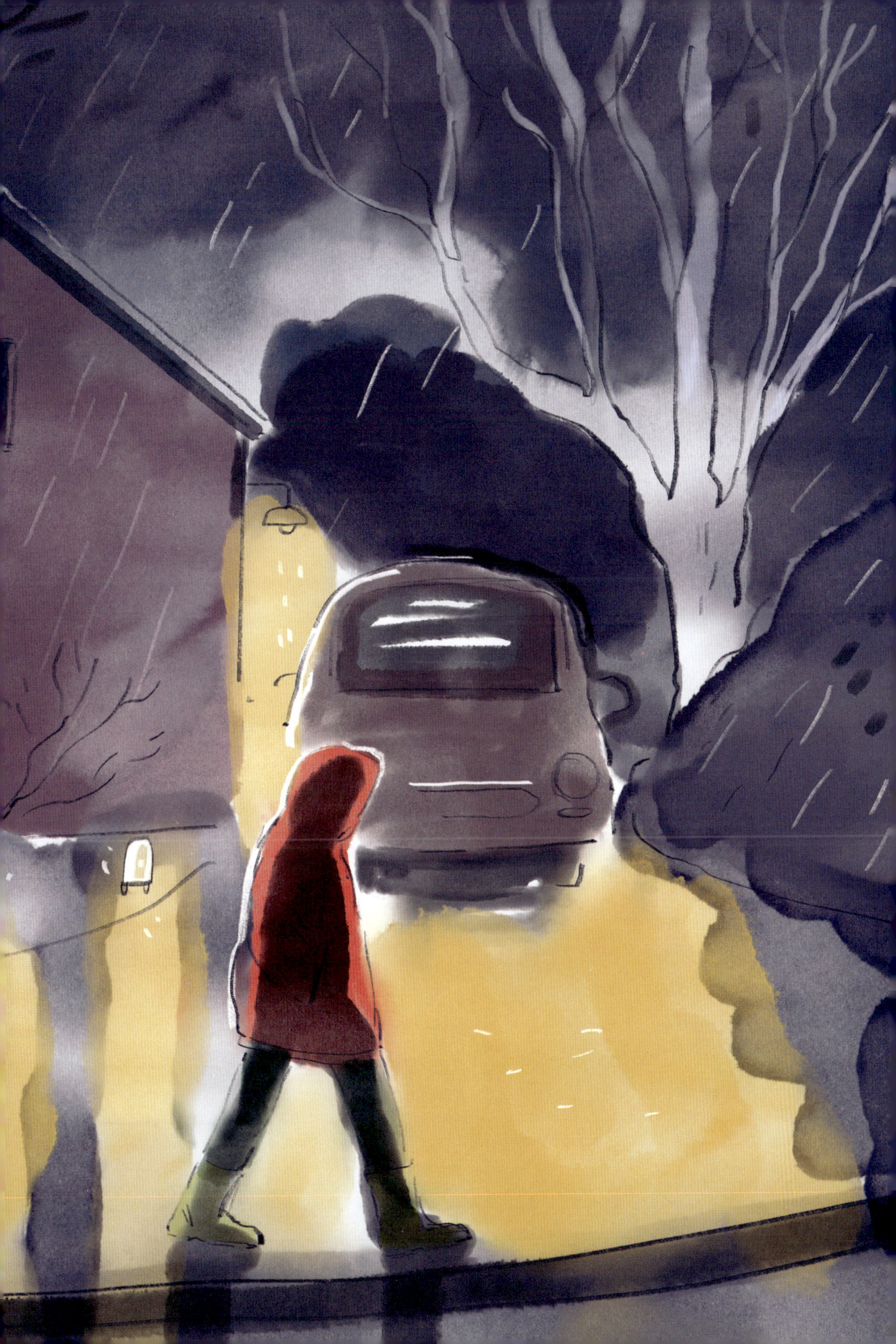

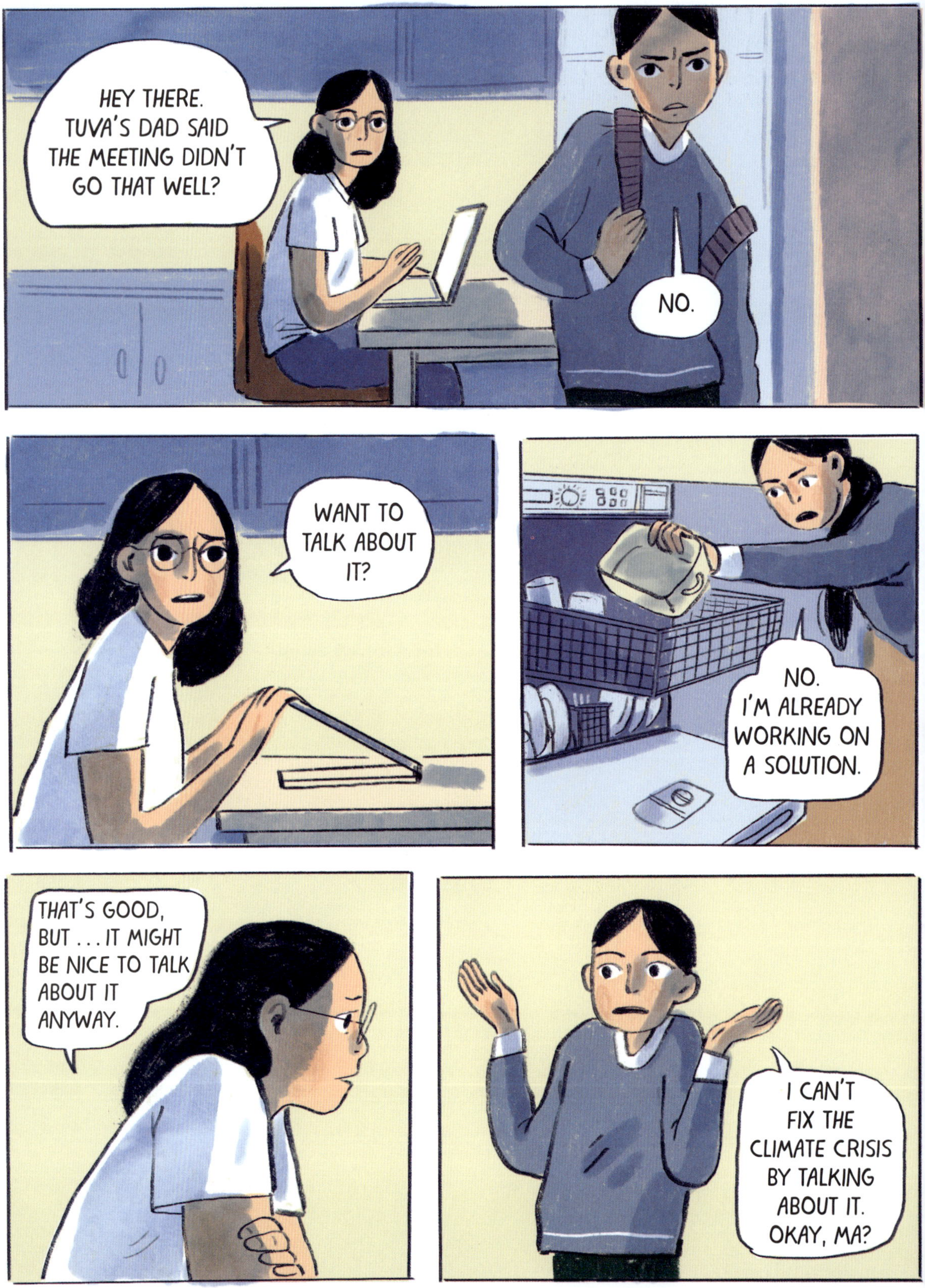
HEY THERE. TUVA'S DAD SAID THE MEETING DIDN'T GO THAT WELL?
NO.
WANT TO TALK ABOUT IT?
NO. I'M ALREADY WORKING ON A SOLUTION.
THAT'S GOOD, BUT . . . IT MIGHT BE NICE TO TALK ABOUT IT ANYWAY.
I CAN'T FIX THE CLIMATE CRISIS BY TALKING ABOUT IT. OKAY, MA?

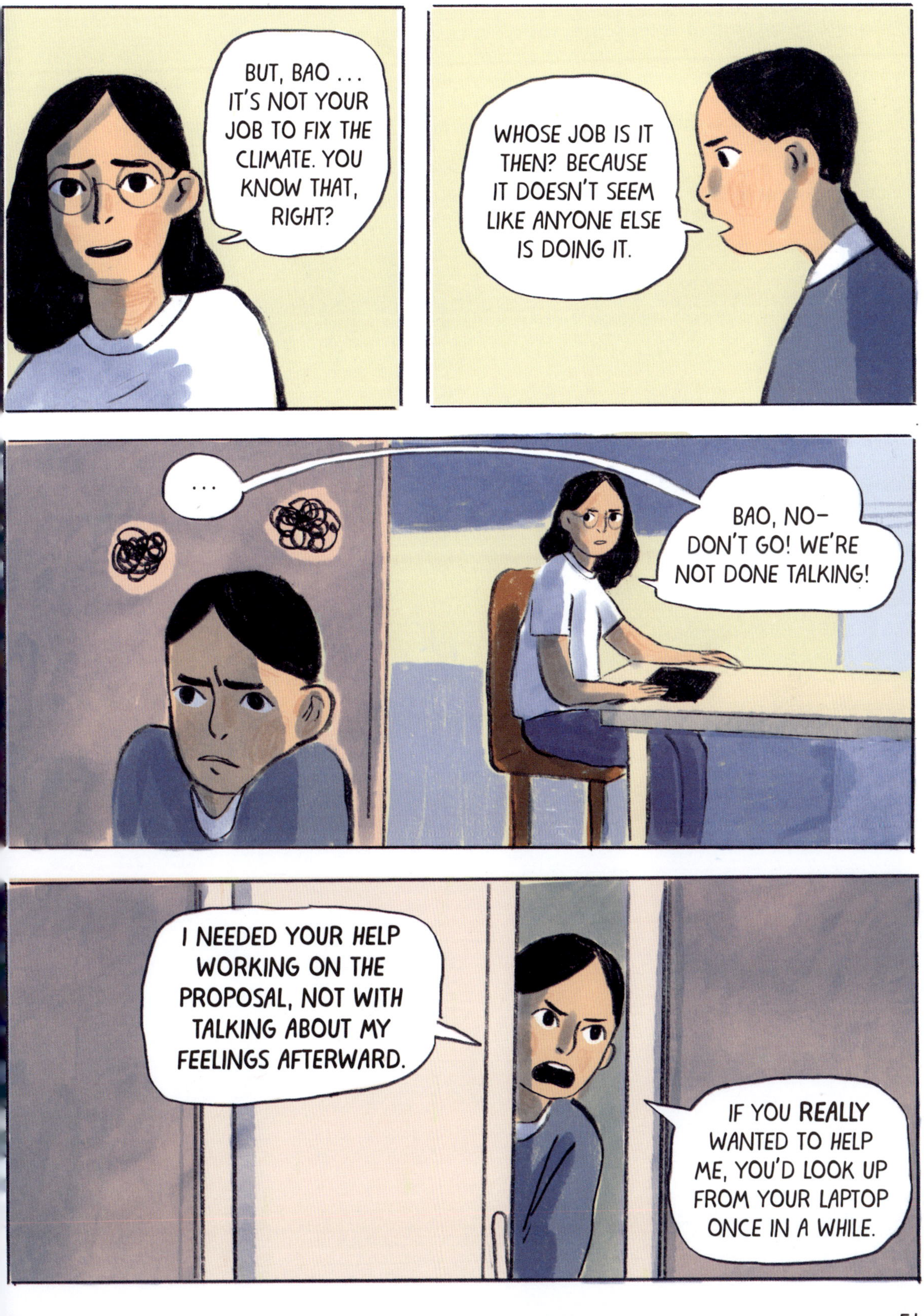
BUT, BAO . . . IT'S NOT YOUR JOB TO FIX THE CLIMATE. YOU KNOW THAT, RIGHT?
WHOSE JOB IS IT THEN? BECAUSE IT DOESN'T SEEM LIKE ANYONE ELSE IS DOING IT.
. . .
BAO, NO– DON'T GO! WE'RE NOT DONE TALKING!
I NEEDED YOUR HELP WORKING ON THE PROPOSAL, NOT WITH TALKING ABOUT MY FEELINGS AFTERWARD.
IF YOU **REALLY** WANTED TO HELP ME, YOU'D LOOK UP FROM YOUR LAPTOP ONCE IN A WHILE.

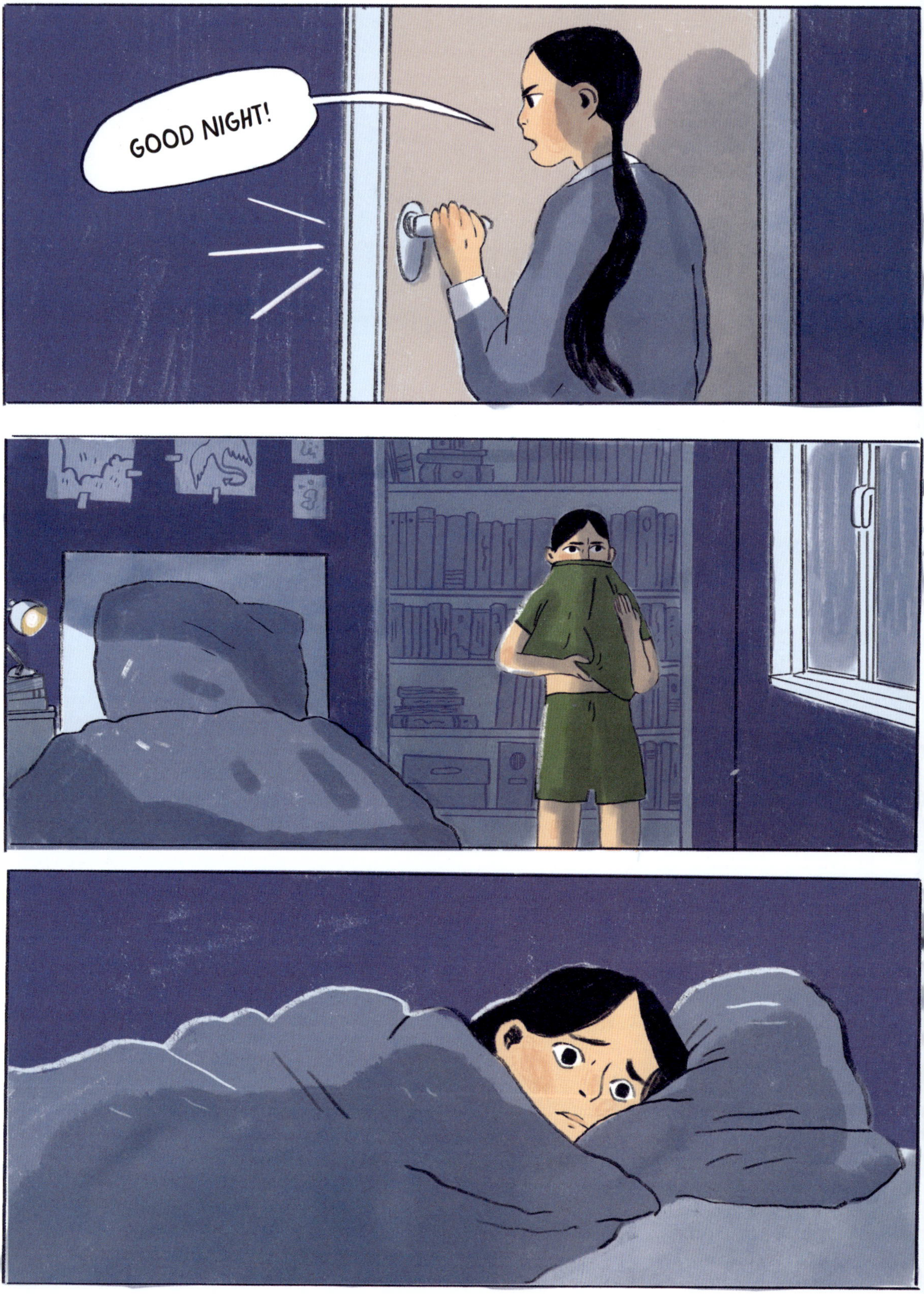
GOOD NIGHT!

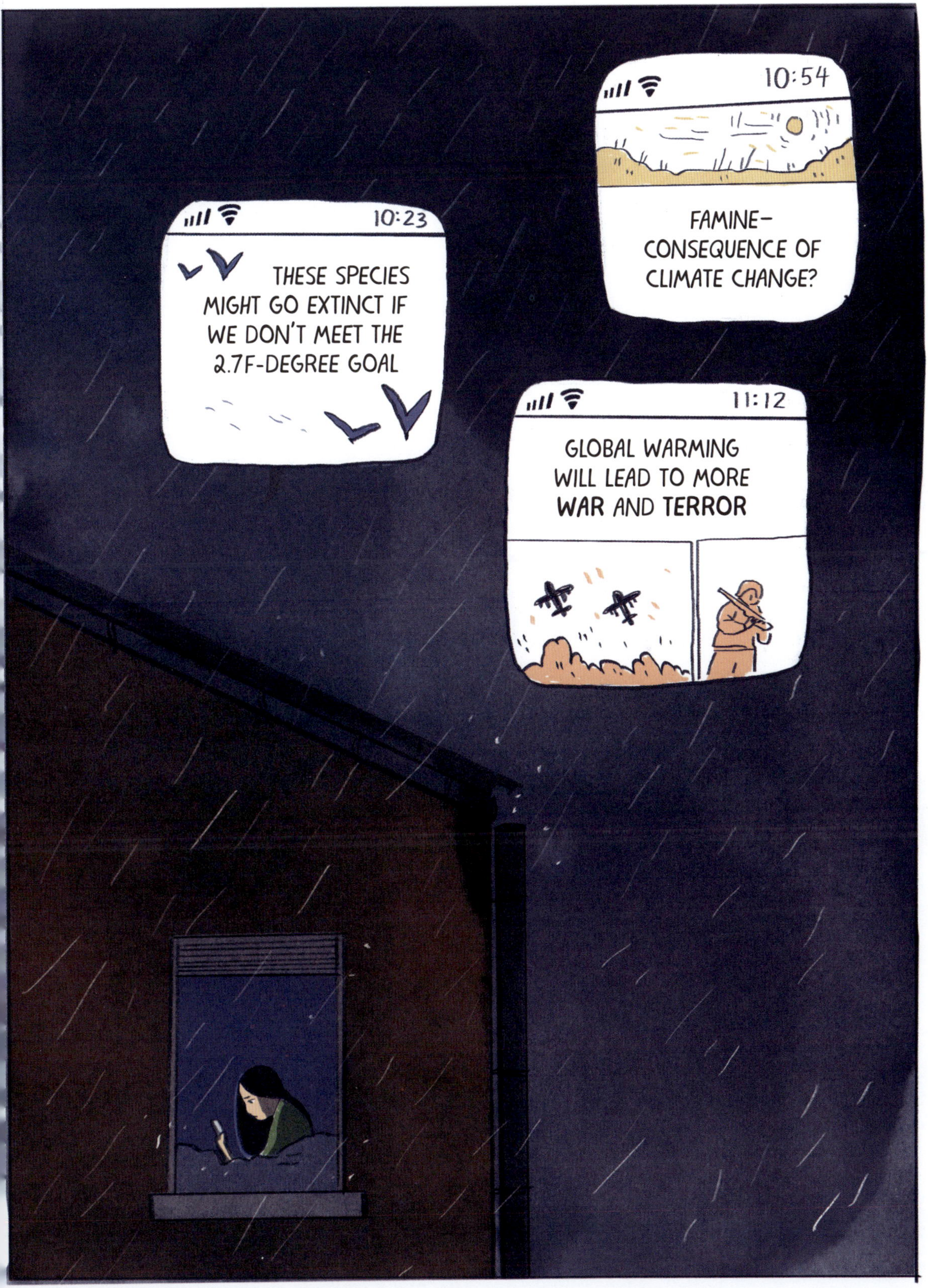
10:23
THESE SPECIES MIGHT GO EXTINCT IF WE DON'T MEET THE 2.7F-DEGREE GOAL
10:54
FAMINE– CONSEQUENCE OF CLIMATE CHANGE?
11:12
GLOBAL WARMING WILL LEAD TO MORE **WAR** AND **TERROR**

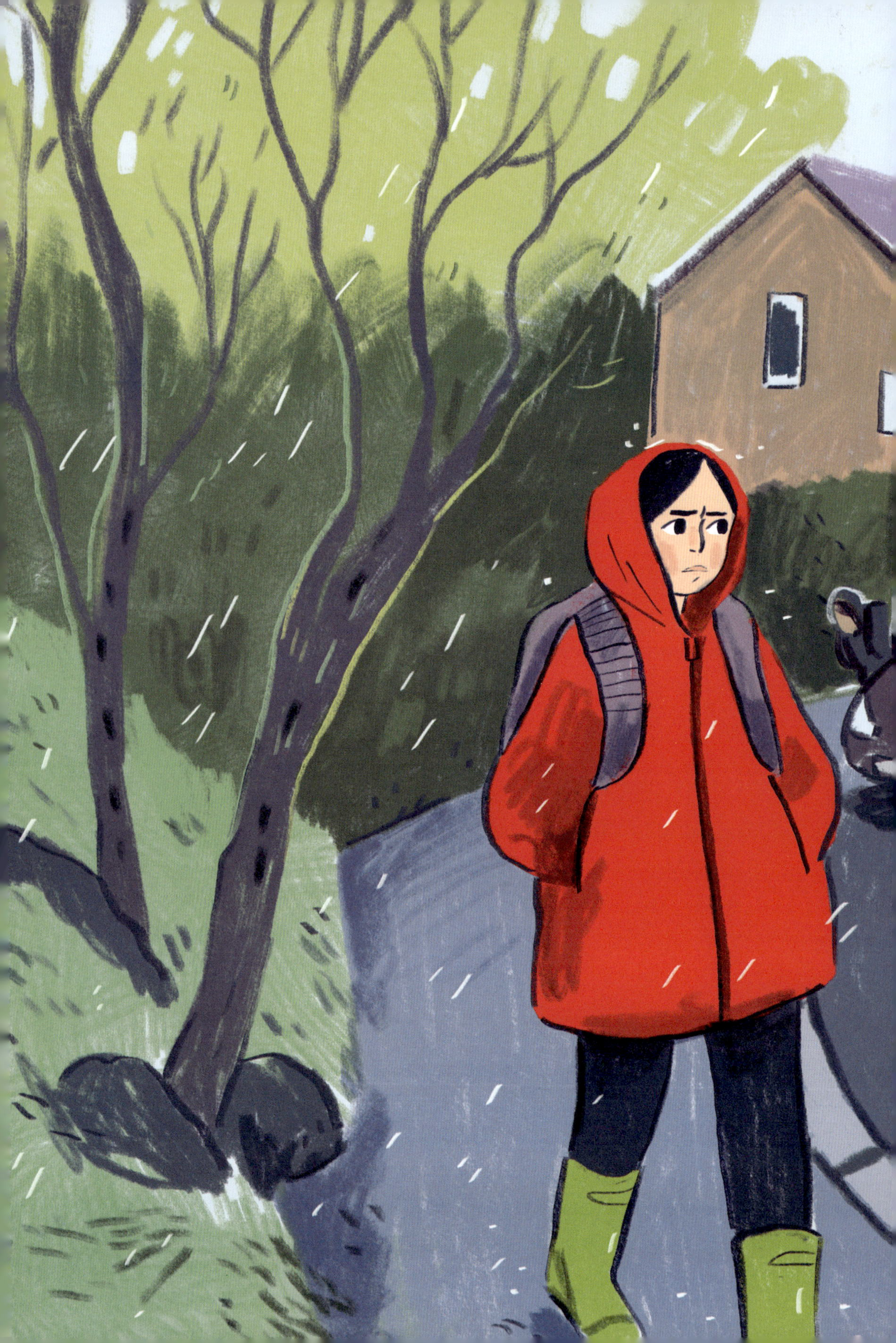

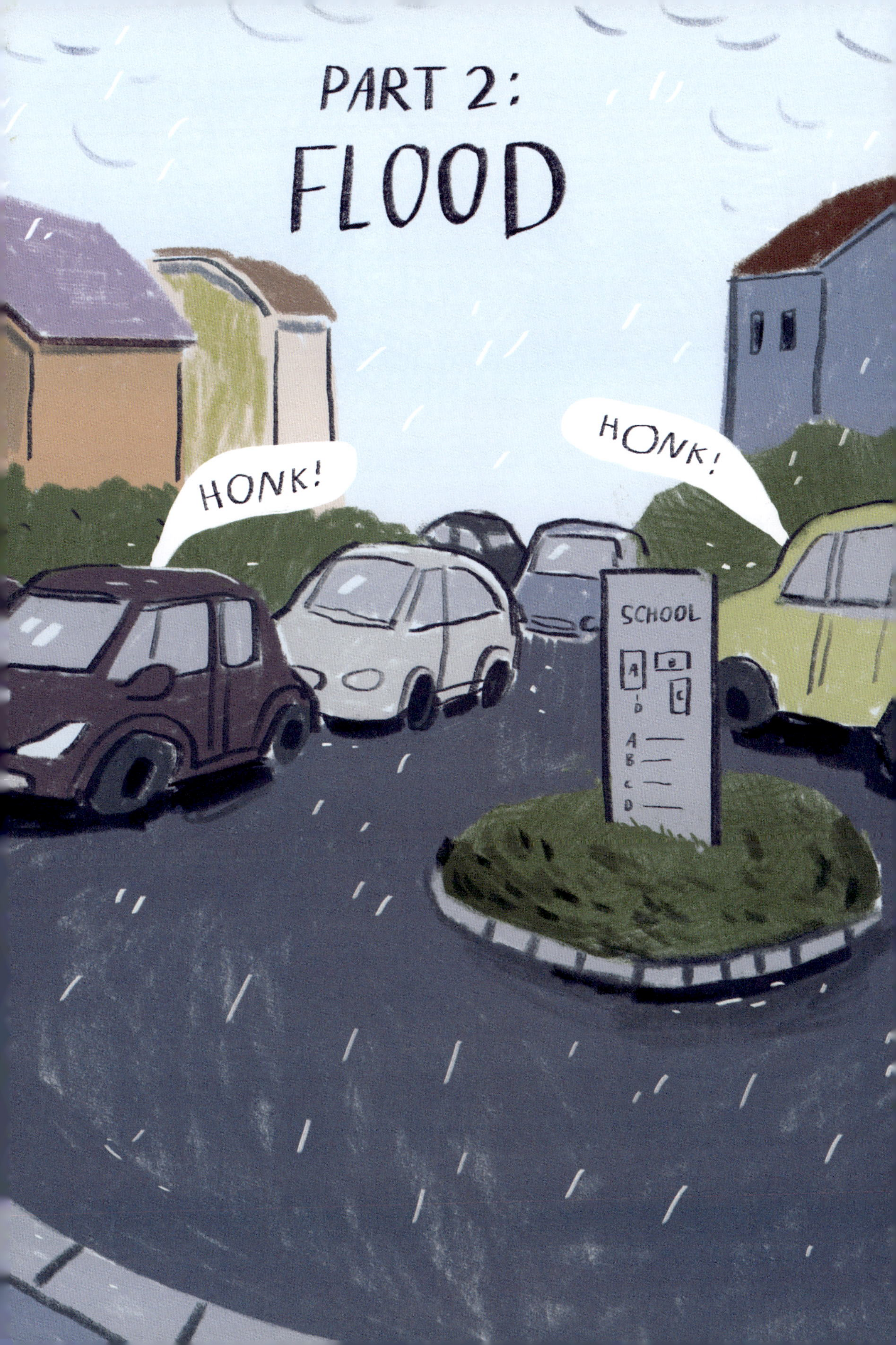
PART 2:
FLOOD
HONK!
HONK!
SCHOOL

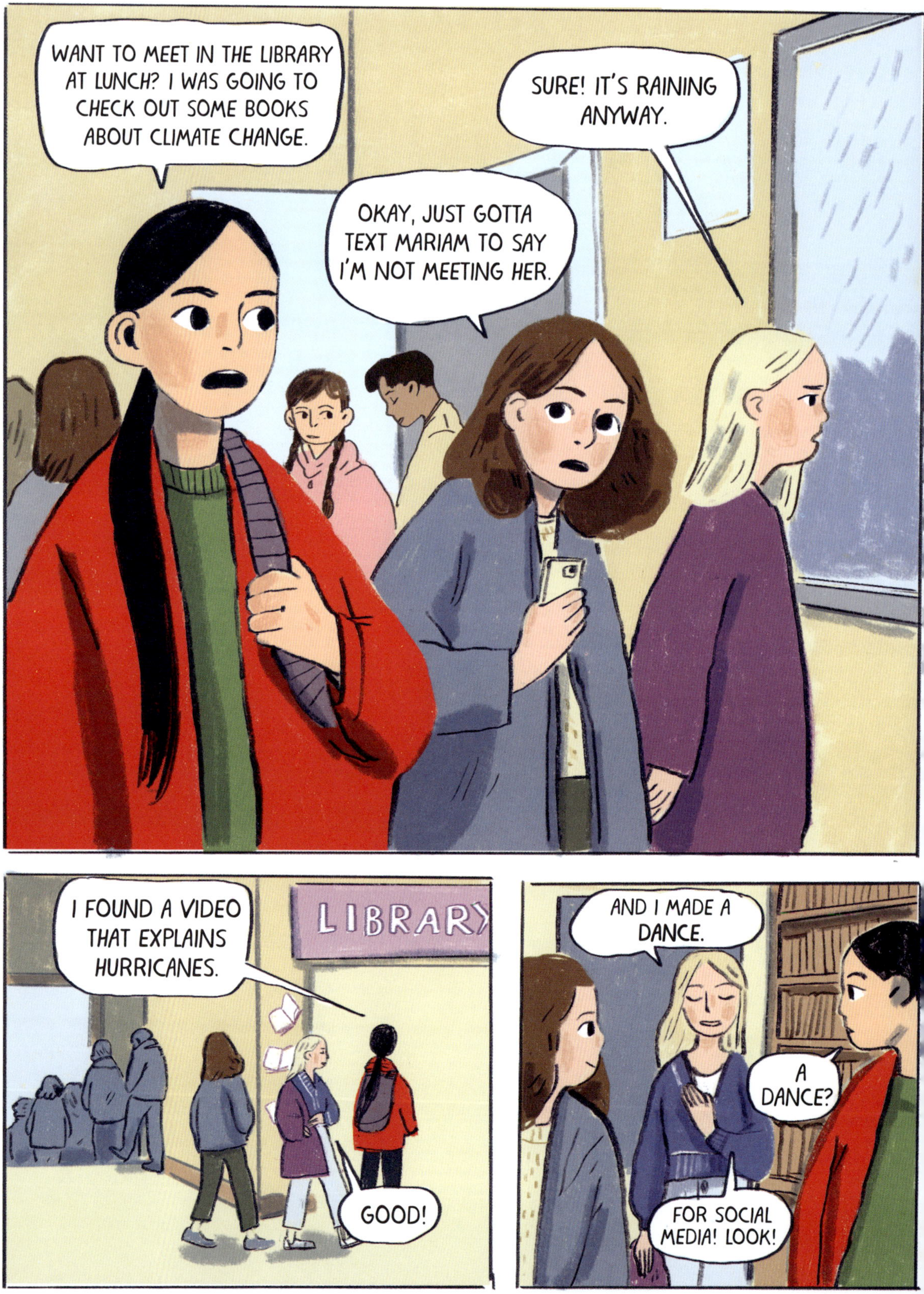
WANT TO MEET IN THE LIBRARY AT LUNCH? I WAS GOING TO CHECK OUT SOME BOOKS ABOUT CLIMATE CHANGE.
SURE! IT'S RAINING ANYWAY.
OKAY, JUST GOTTA TEXT MARIAM TO SAY I'M NOT MEETING HER.
I FOUND A VIDEO THAT EXPLAINS HURRICANES.
LIBRARY
GOOD!
AND I MADE A DANCE.
A DANCE?
FOR SOCIAL MEDIA! LOOK!

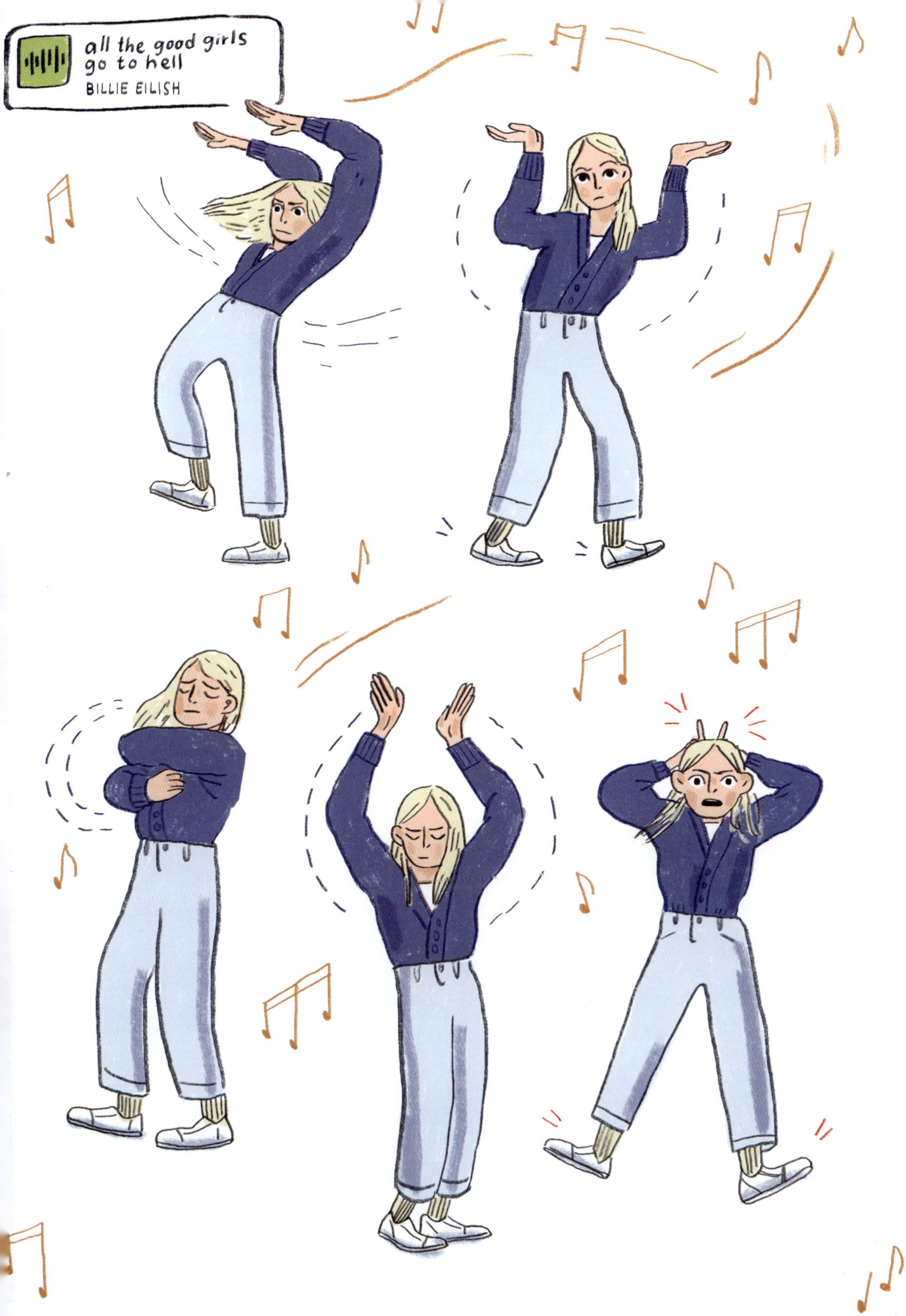
all the good girls go to hell
BILLIE EILISH

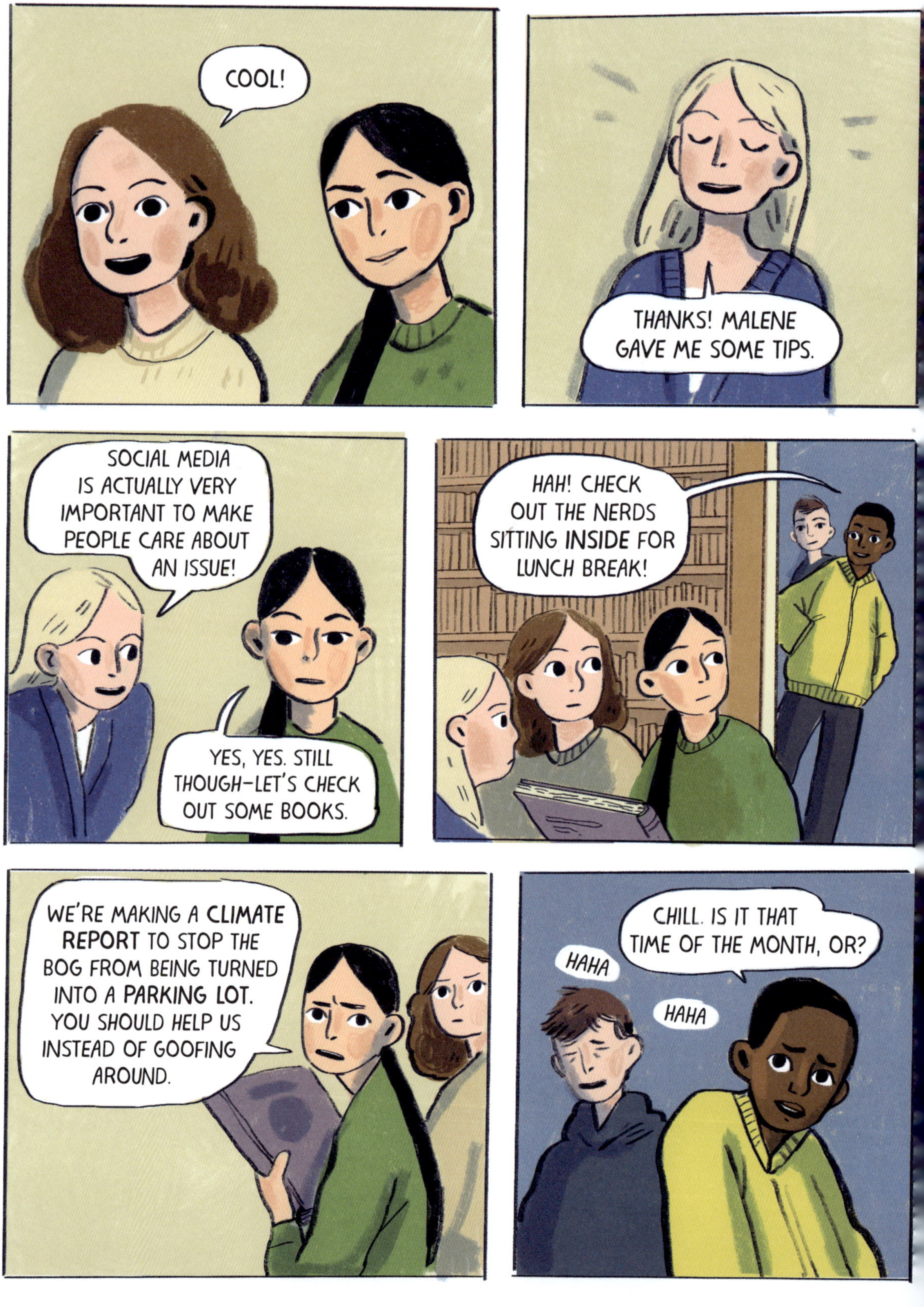
COOL!
THANKS! MALENE GAVE ME SOME TIPS.
SOCIAL MEDIA IS ACTUALLY VERY IMPORTANT TO MAKE PEOPLE CARE ABOUT AN ISSUE!
YES, YES. STILL THOUGH—LET'S CHECK OUT SOME BOOKS.
HAH! CHECK OUT THE NERDS SITTING **INSIDE** FOR LUNCH BREAK!
WE'RE MAKING A **CLIMATE REPORT** TO STOP THE BOG FROM BEING TURNED INTO A **PARKING LOT**. YOU SHOULD HELP US INSTEAD OF GOOFING AROUND.
CHILL. IS IT THAT TIME OF THE MONTH, OR?
HAHA
HAHA

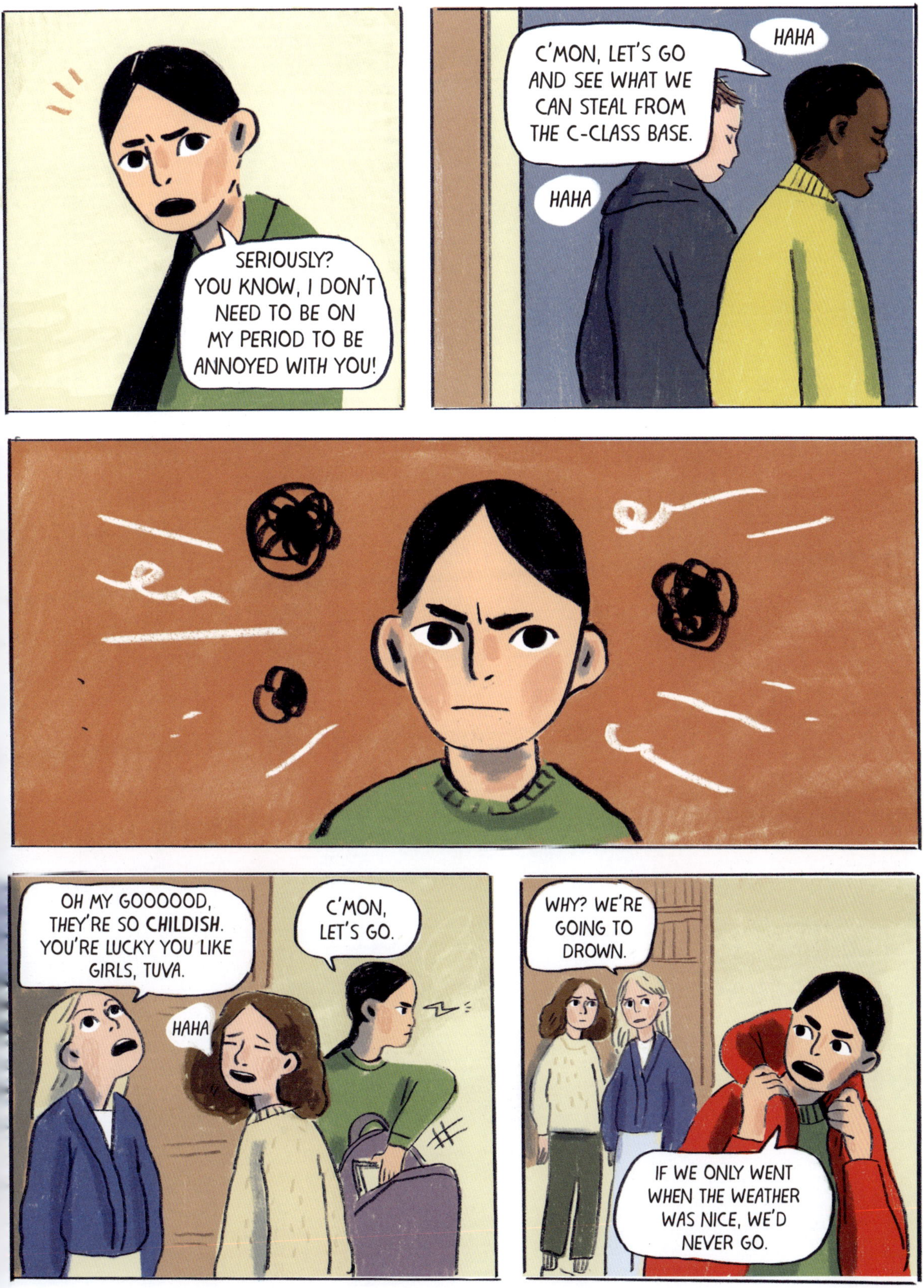
SERIOUSLY? YOU KNOW, I DON'T NEED TO BE ON MY PERIOD TO BE ANNOYED WITH YOU!
C'MON, LET'S GO AND SEE WHAT WE CAN STEAL FROM THE C-CLASS BASE.
HAHA
HAHA
OH MY GOOOOOD, THEY'RE SO **CHILDISH**. YOU'RE LUCKY YOU LIKE GIRLS, TUVA.
HAHA
C'MON, LET'S GO.
WHY? WE'RE GOING TO DROWN.
IF WE ONLY WENT WHEN THE WEATHER WAS NICE, WE'D NEVER GO.

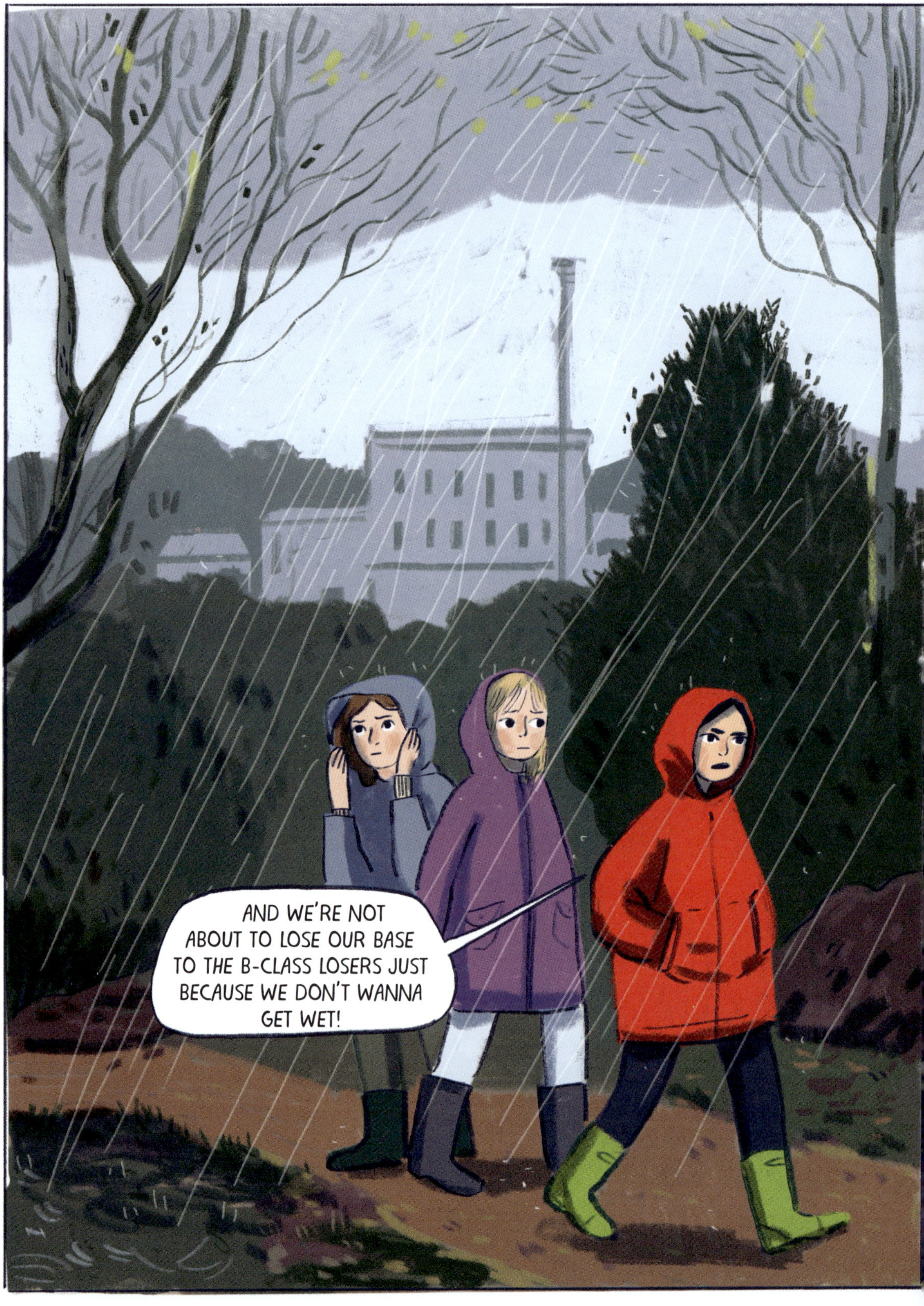
AND WE'RE NOT ABOUT TO LOSE OUR BASE TO THE B-CLASS LOSERS JUST BECAUSE WE DON'T WANNA GET WET!

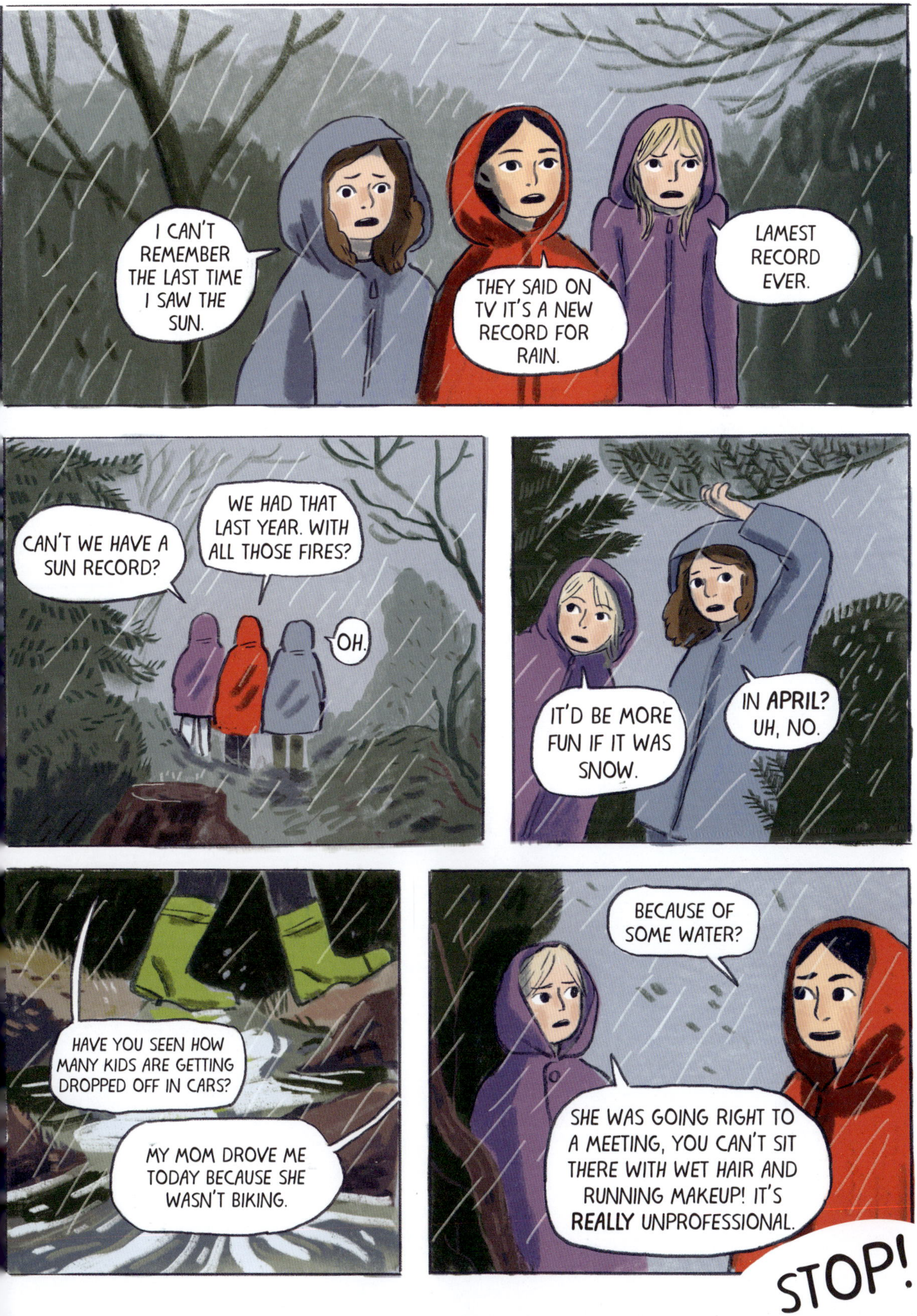
I CAN'T REMEMBER THE LAST TIME I SAW THE SUN.
THEY SAID ON TV IT'S A NEW RECORD FOR RAIN.
LAMEST RECORD EVER.
CAN'T WE HAVE A SUN RECORD?
WE HAD THAT LAST YEAR. WITH ALL THOSE FIRES?
OH.
IT'D BE MORE FUN IF IT WAS SNOW.
IN **APRIL?** UH, NO.
HAVE YOU SEEN HOW MANY KIDS ARE GETTING DROPPED OFF IN CARS?
MY MOM DROVE ME TODAY BECAUSE SHE WASN'T BIKING.
BECAUSE OF SOME WATER?
SHE WAS GOING RIGHT TO A MEETING, YOU CAN'T SIT THERE WITH WET HAIR AND RUNNING MAKEUP! IT'S **REALLY** UNPROFESSIONAL.
STOP!

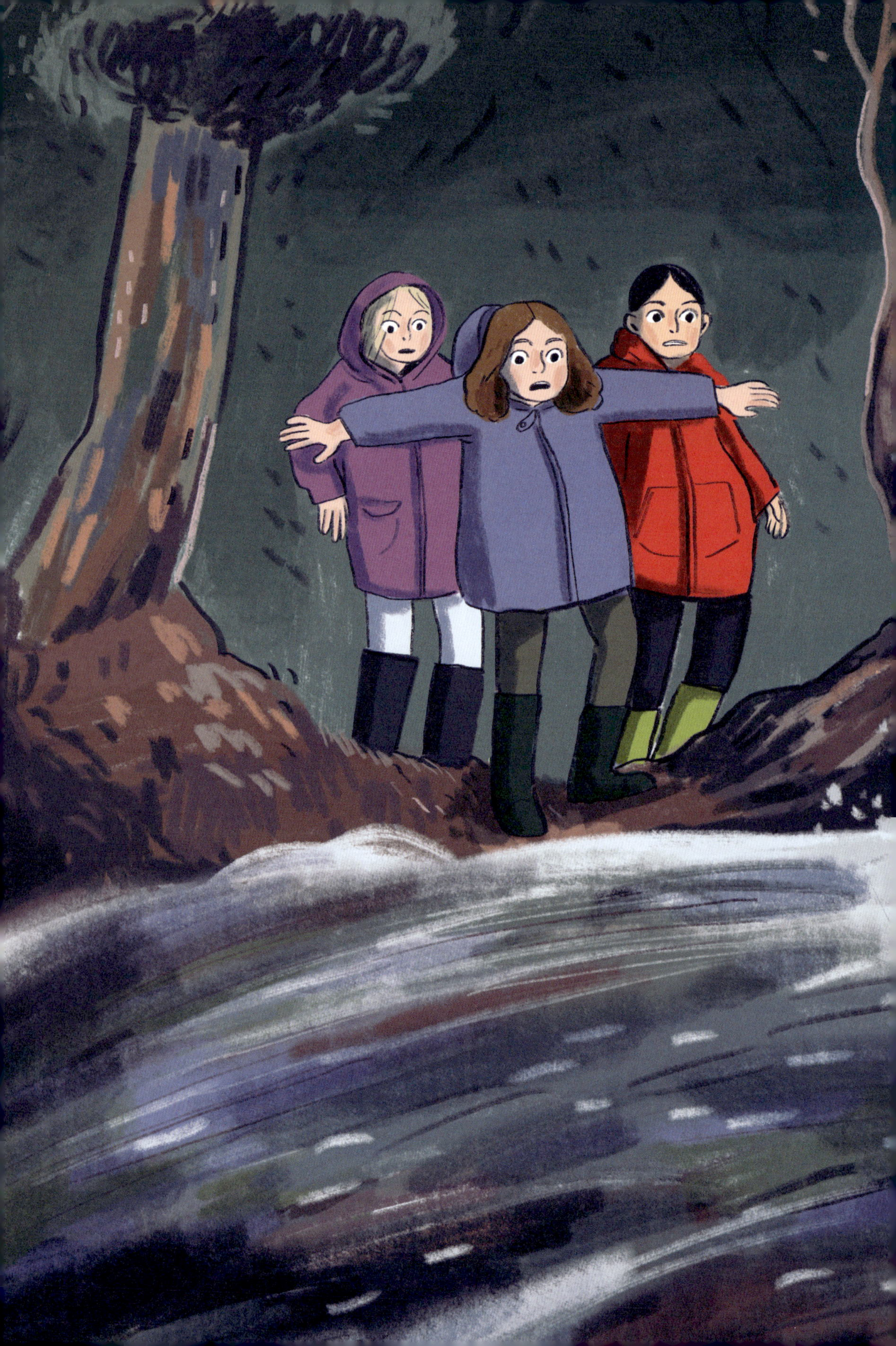

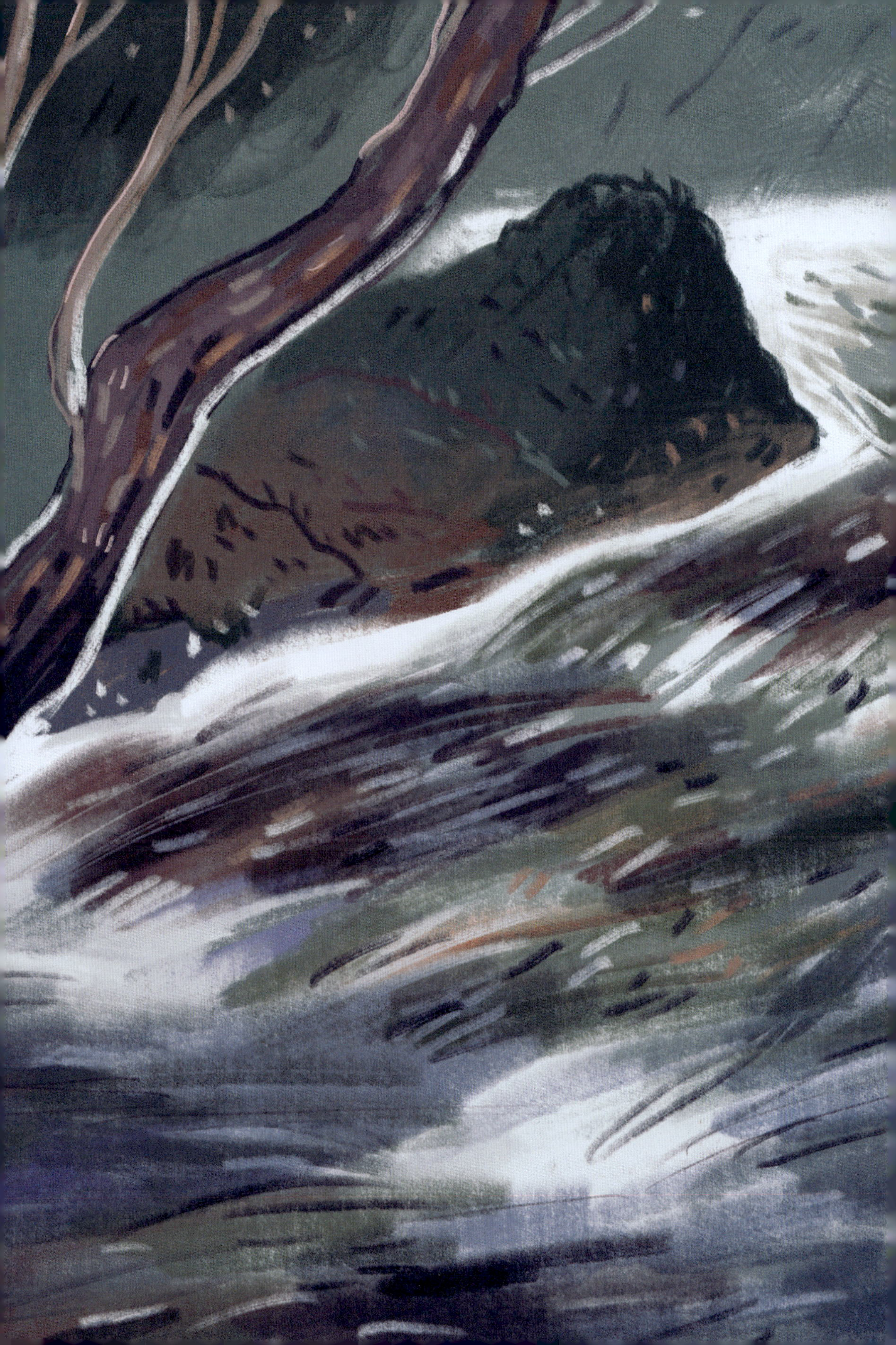

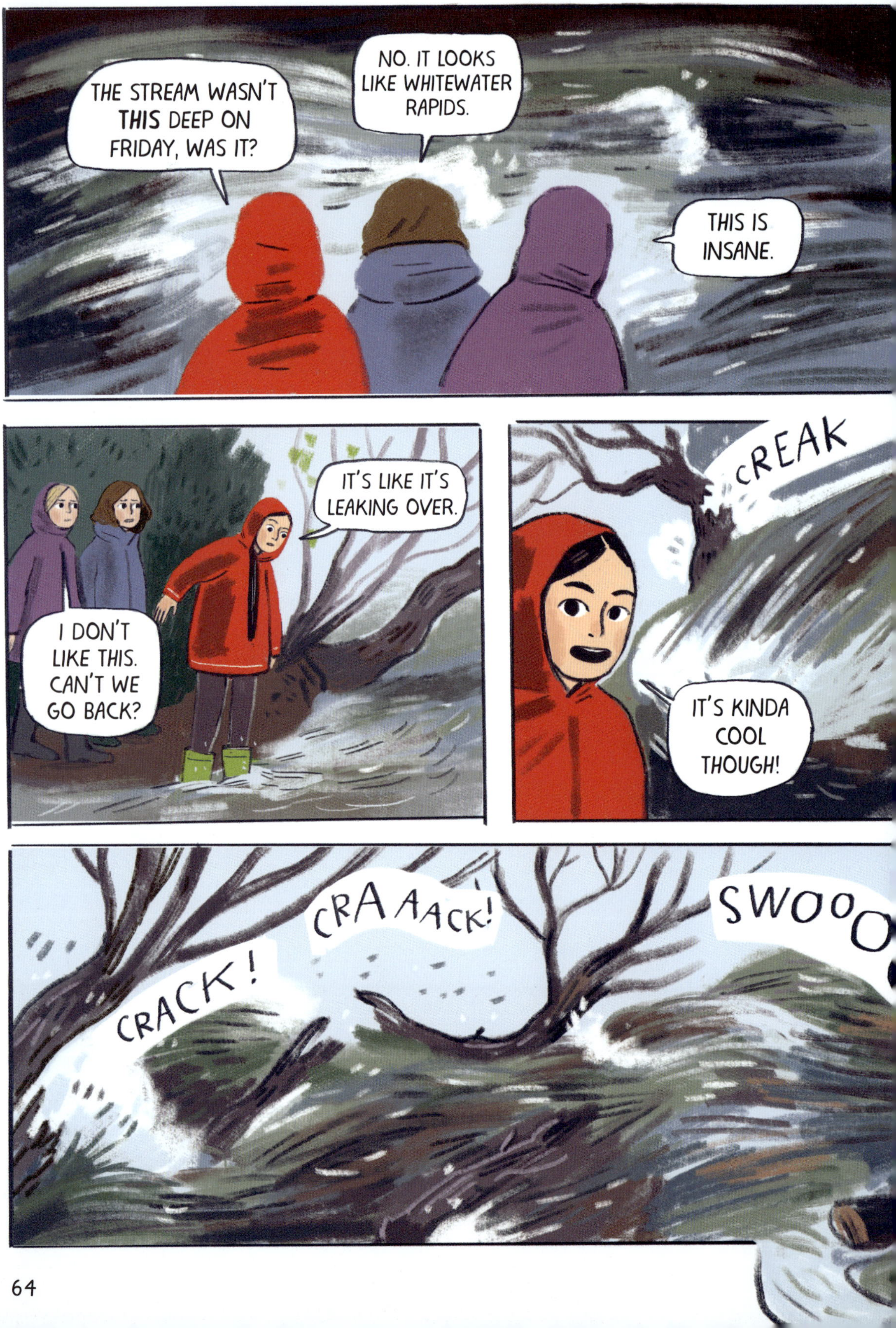
THE STREAM WASN'T **THIS** DEEP ON FRIDAY, WAS IT?
NO. IT LOOKS LIKE WHITEWATER RAPIDS.
THIS IS INSANE.
IT'S LIKE IT'S LEAKING OVER.
I DON'T LIKE THIS. CAN'T WE GO BACK?
CREAK
IT'S KINDA COOL THOUGH!
CRACK!
CRAAACK!
SWOOO

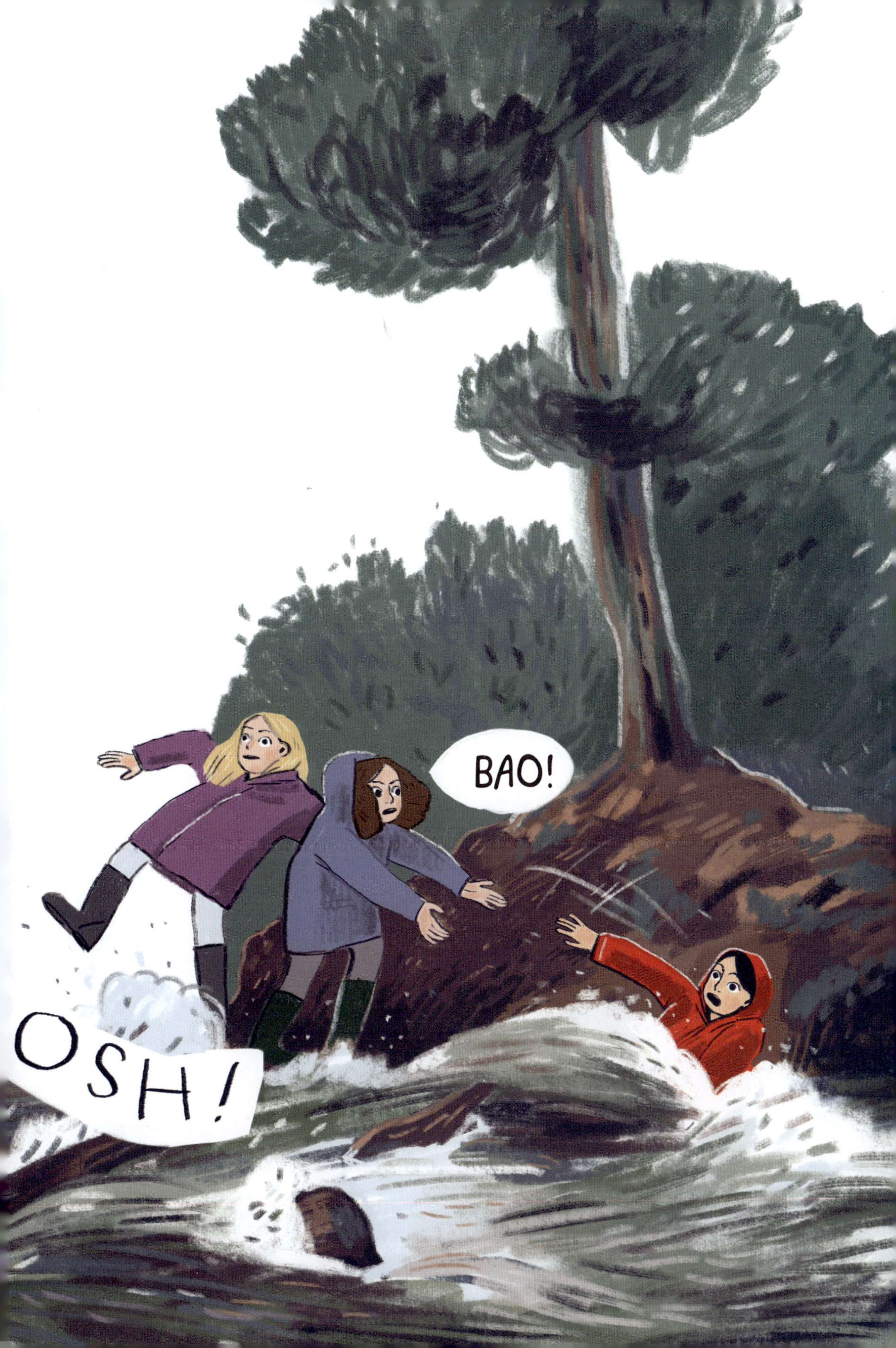
BAO!
OSH!

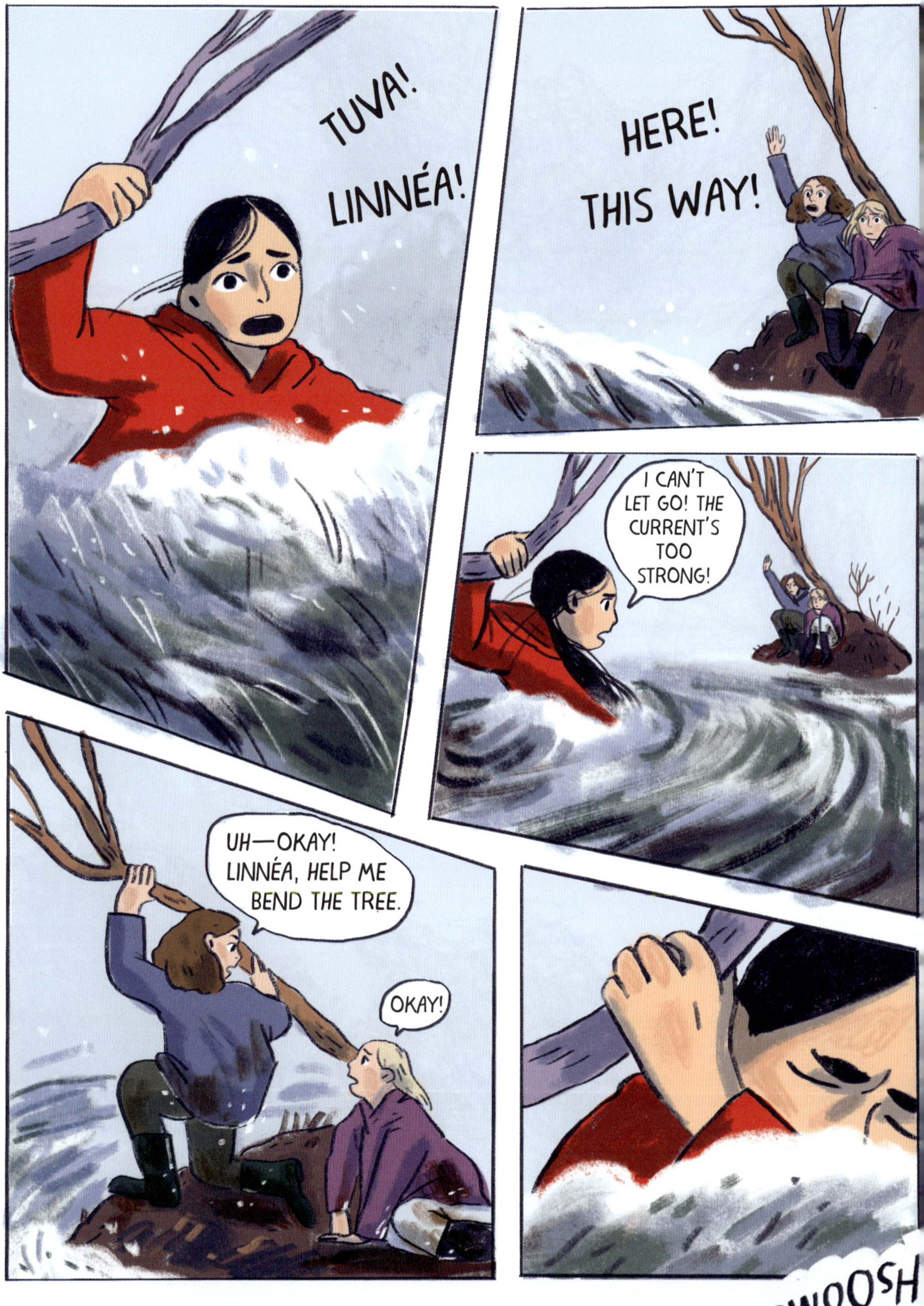
TUVA!
LINNÉA!
HERE! THIS WAY!
I CAN'T LET GO! THE CURRENT'S TOO STRONG!
UH—OKAY! LINNÉA, HELP ME BEND THE TREE.
OKAY!
SWOOSH

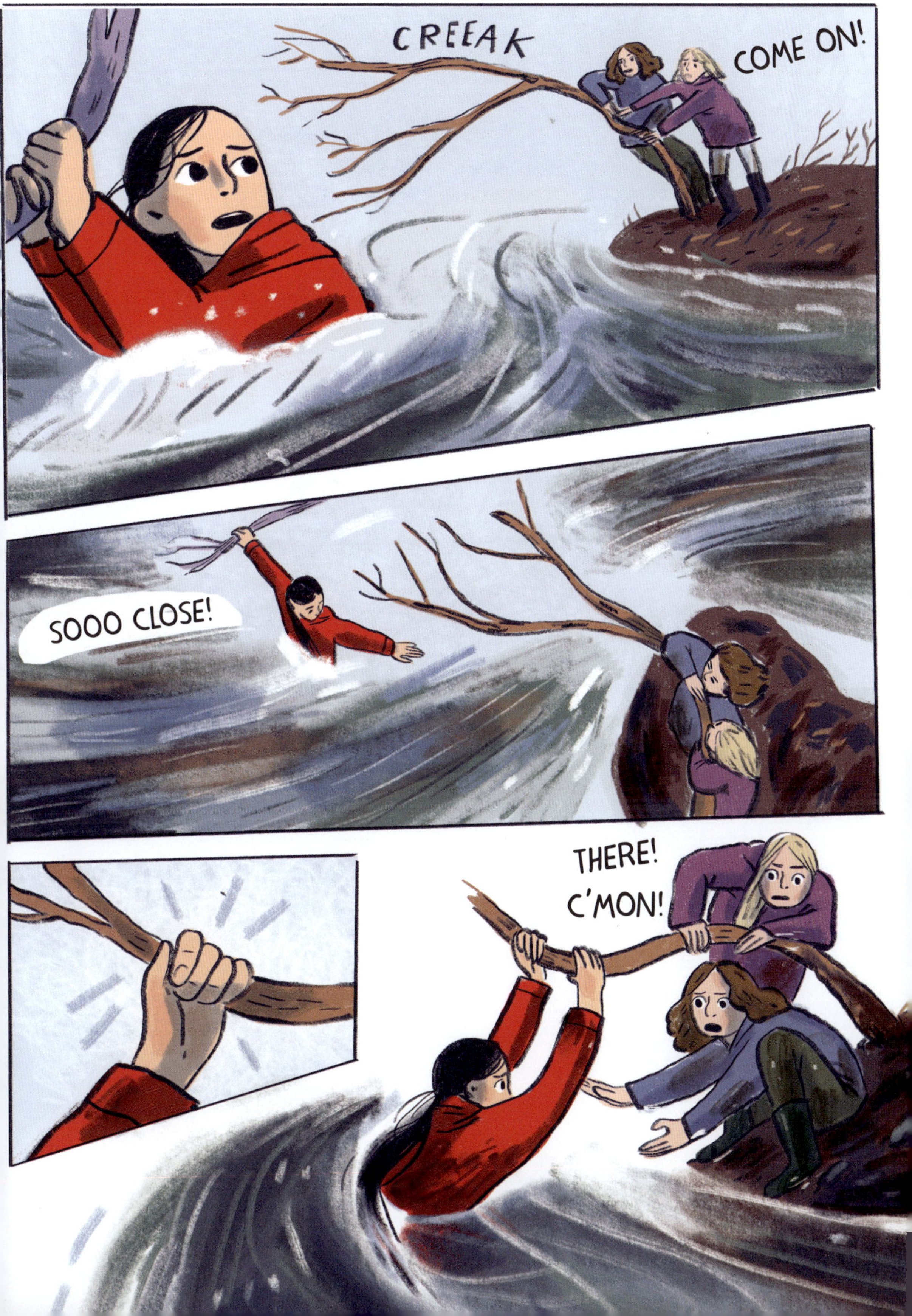
CREEAK
COME ON!
SOOO CLOSE!
THERE!
C'MON!

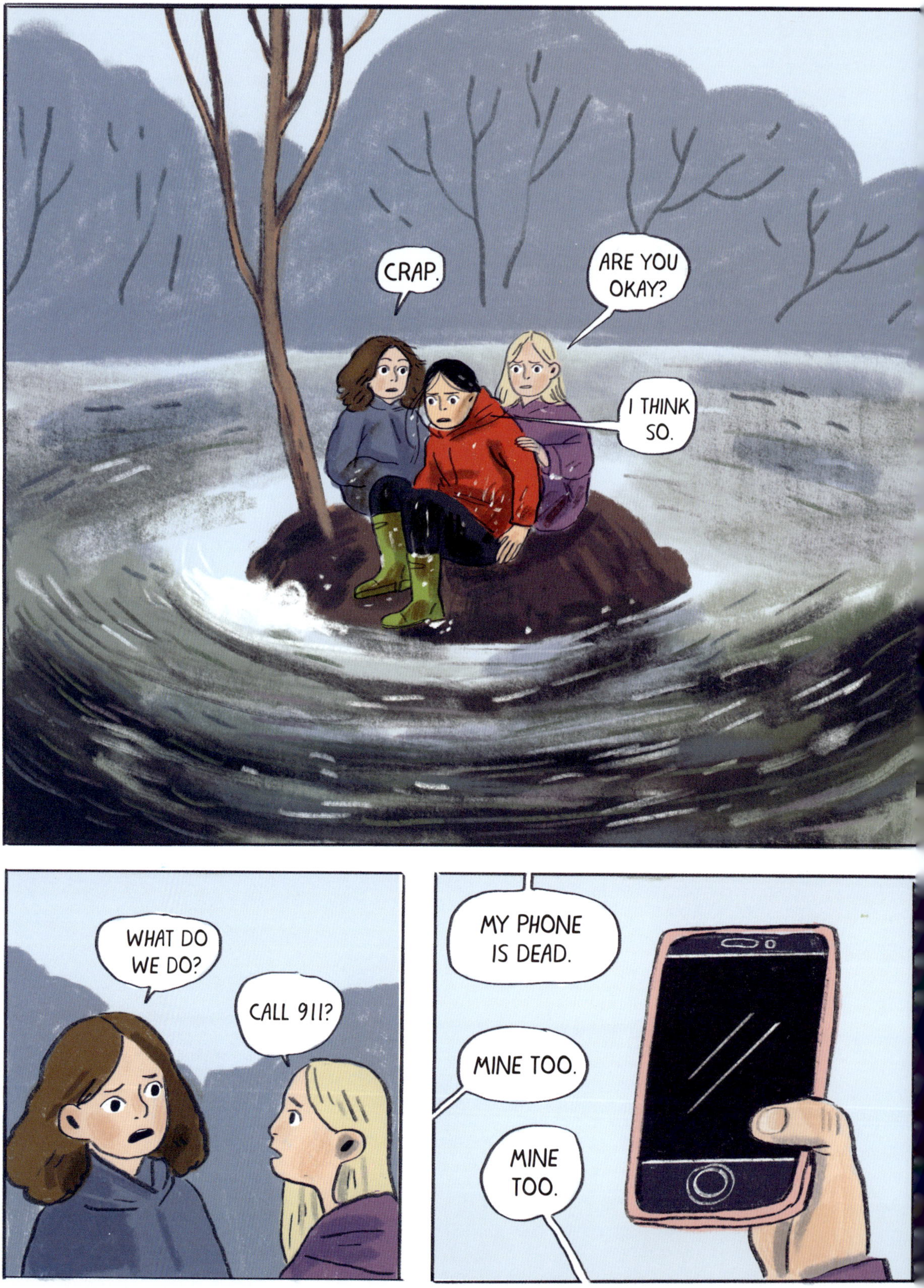
CRAP.
ARE YOU OKAY?
I THINK SO.
WHAT DO WE DO?
CALL 911?
MY PHONE IS DEAD.
MINE TOO.
MINE TOO.

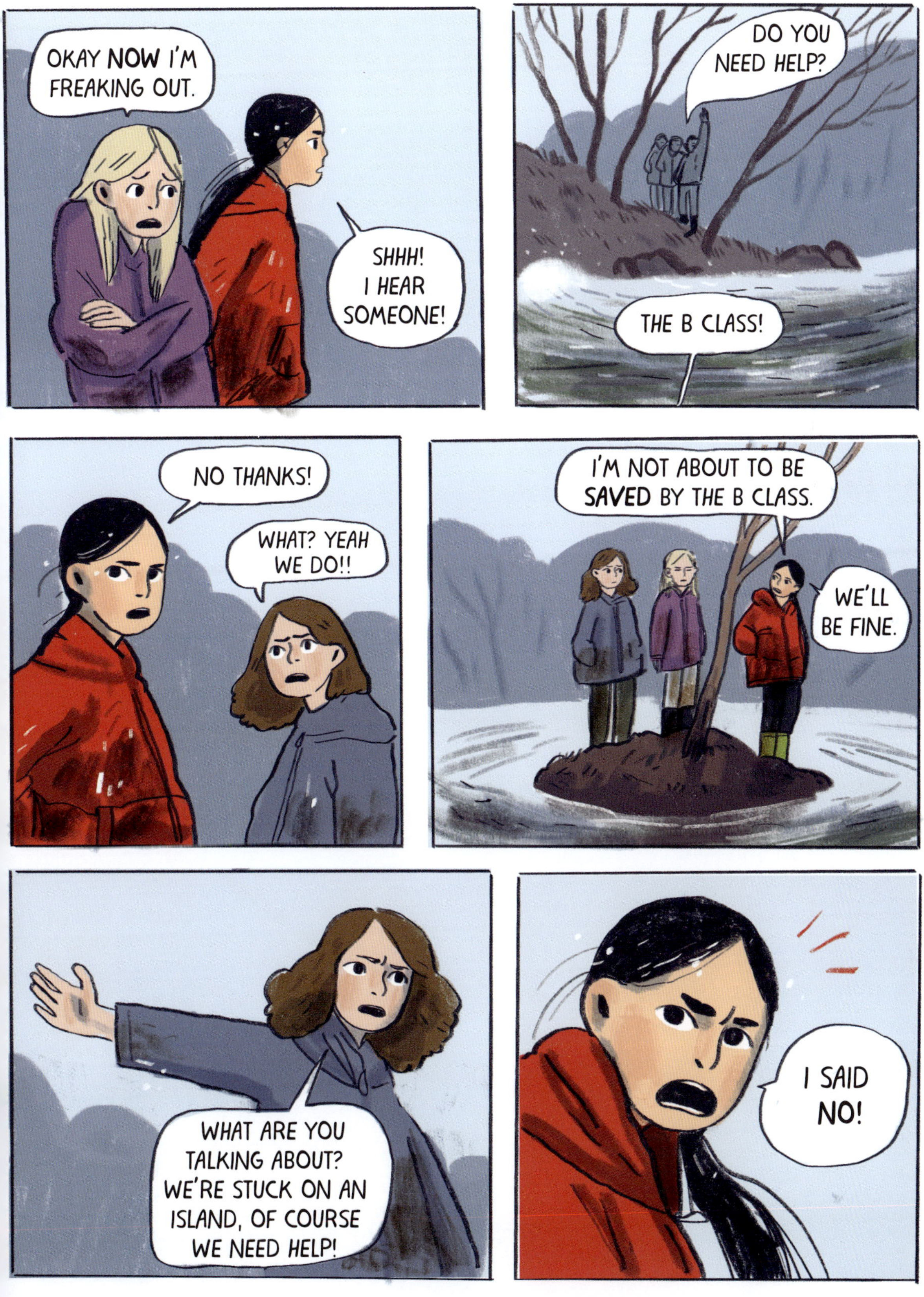
OKAY NOW I'M FREAKING OUT.
SHHH! I HEAR SOMEONE!
DO YOU NEED HELP?
THE B CLASS!
NO THANKS!
WHAT? YEAH WE DO!!
I'M NOT ABOUT TO BE SAVED BY THE B CLASS.
WE'LL BE FINE.
WHAT ARE YOU TALKING ABOUT? WE'RE STUCK ON AN ISLAND, OF COURSE WE NEED HELP!
I SAID NO!

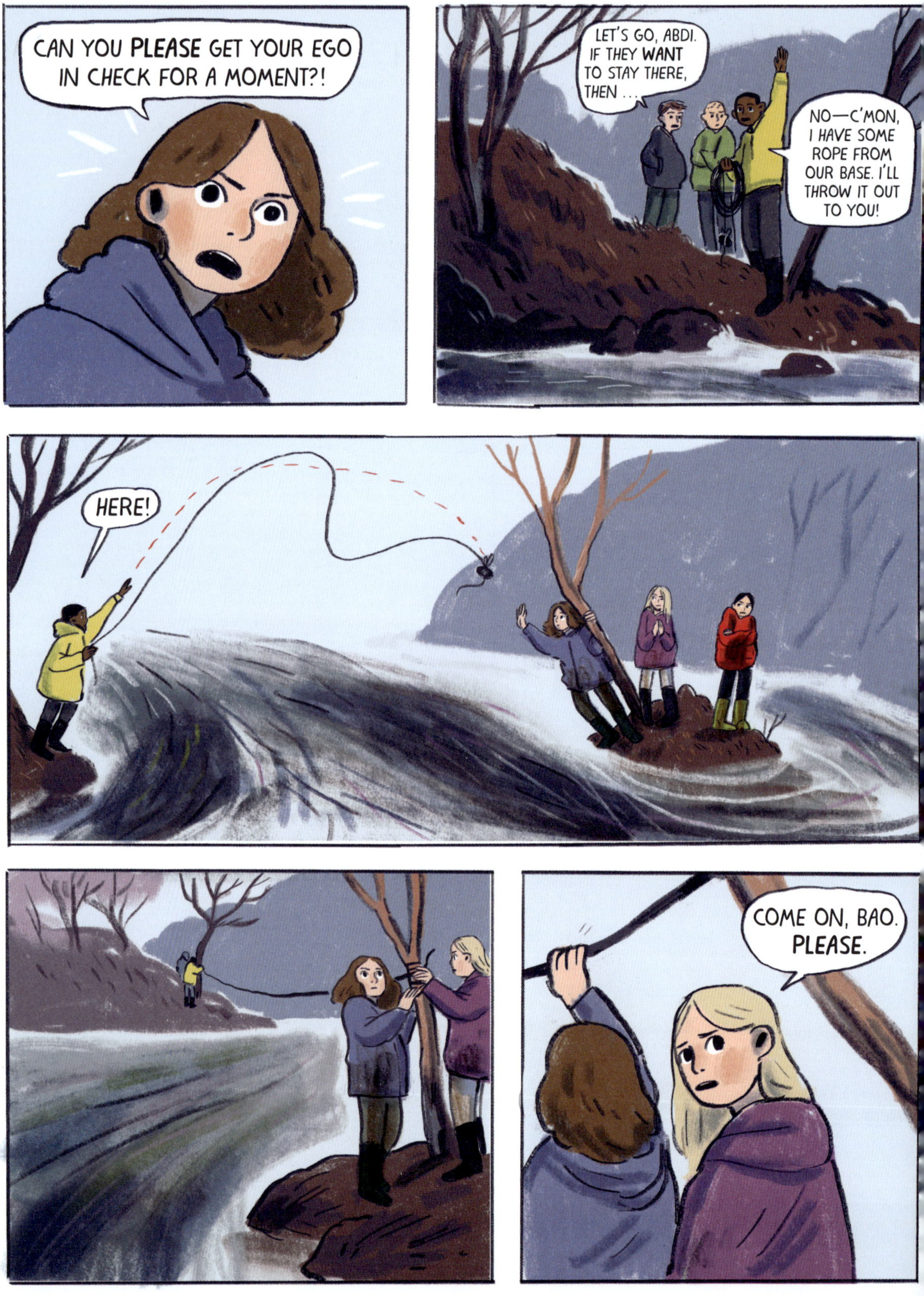

CAN YOU PLEASE GET YOUR EGO IN CHECK FOR A MOMENT?!
LET'S GO, ABDI. IF THEY WANT TO STAY THERE, THEN . . .
NO—C'MON, I HAVE SOME ROPE FROM OUR BASE. I'LL THROW IT OUT TO YOU!
HERE!
COME ON, BAO. PLEASE.

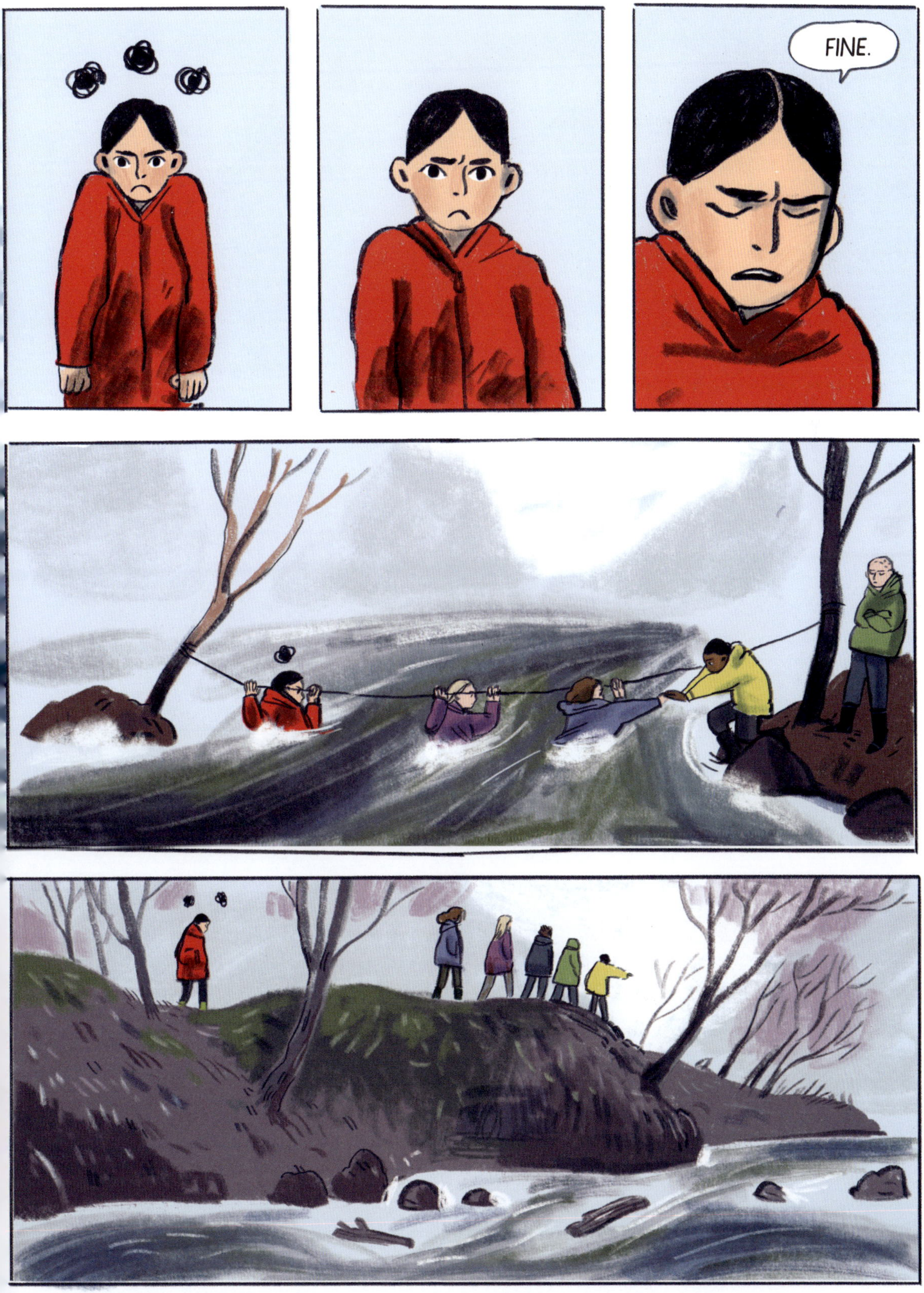
FINE.

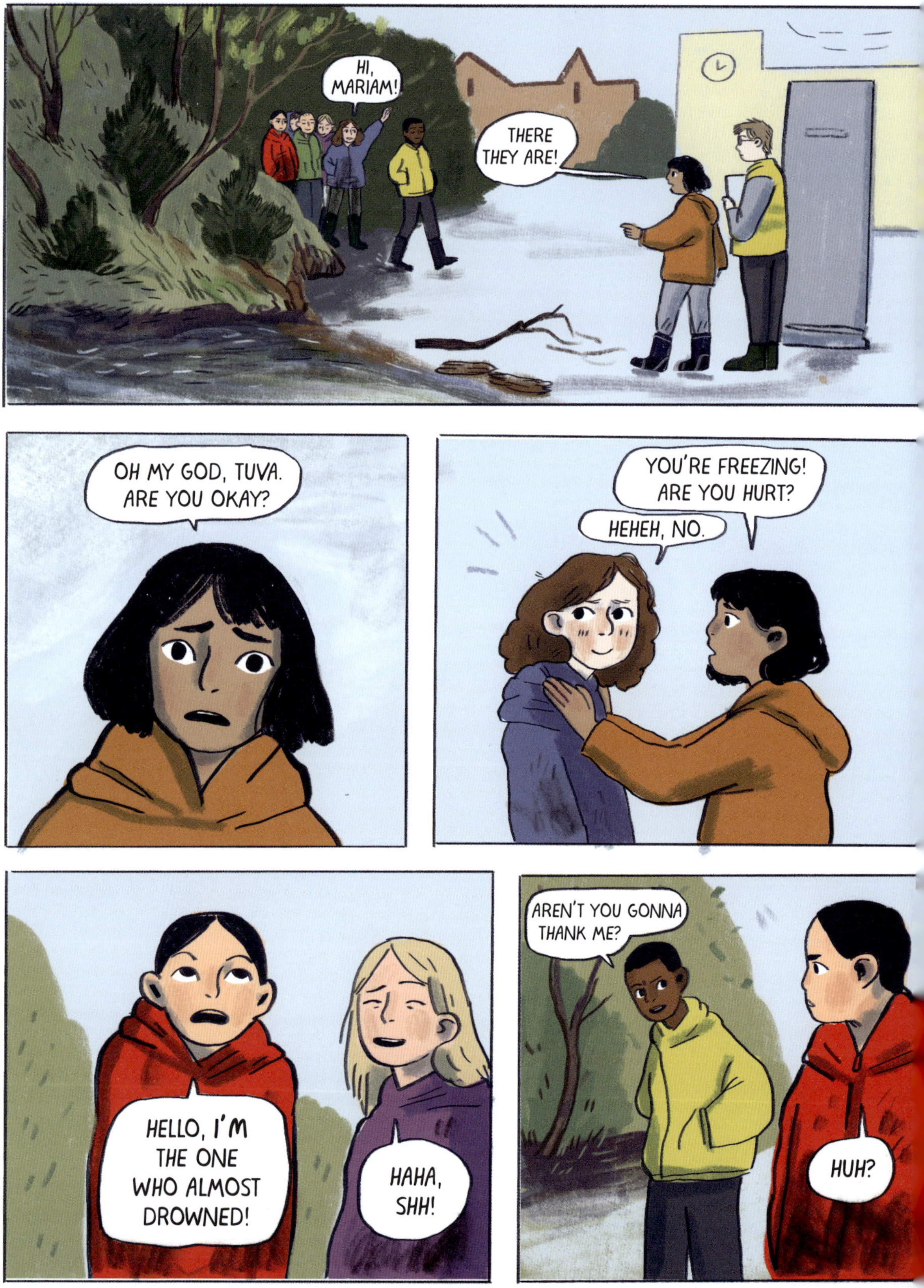
HI, MARIAM!
THERE THEY ARE!
OH MY GOD, TUVA. ARE YOU OKAY?
YOU'RE FREEZING! ARE YOU HURT?
HEHEH, NO.
HELLO, I'M THE ONE WHO ALMOST DROWNED!
HAHA, SHH!
AREN'T YOU GONNA THANK ME?
HUH?

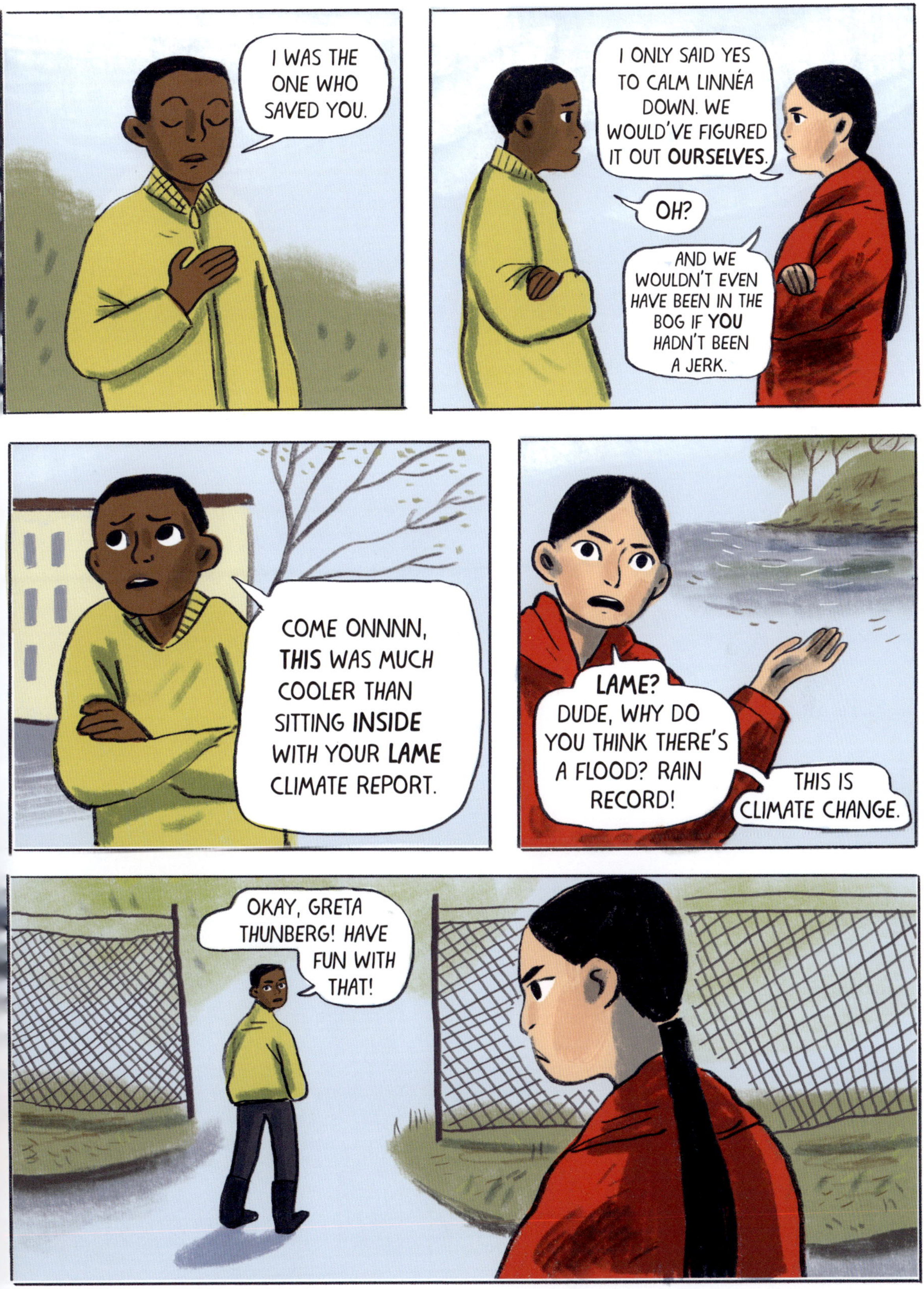
I WAS THE ONE WHO SAVED YOU.
I ONLY SAID YES TO CALM LINNÉA DOWN. WE WOULD'VE FIGURED IT OUT **OURSELVES**.
OH?
AND WE WOULDN'T EVEN HAVE BEEN IN THE BOG IF **YOU** HADN'T BEEN A JERK.
COME ONNNN, **THIS** WAS MUCH COOLER THAN SITTING **INSIDE** WITH YOUR **LAME** CLIMATE REPORT.
LAME? DUDE, WHY DO YOU THINK THERE'S A FLOOD? RAIN RECORD!
THIS IS CLIMATE CHANGE.
OKAY, GRETA THUNBERG! HAVE FUN WITH THAT!

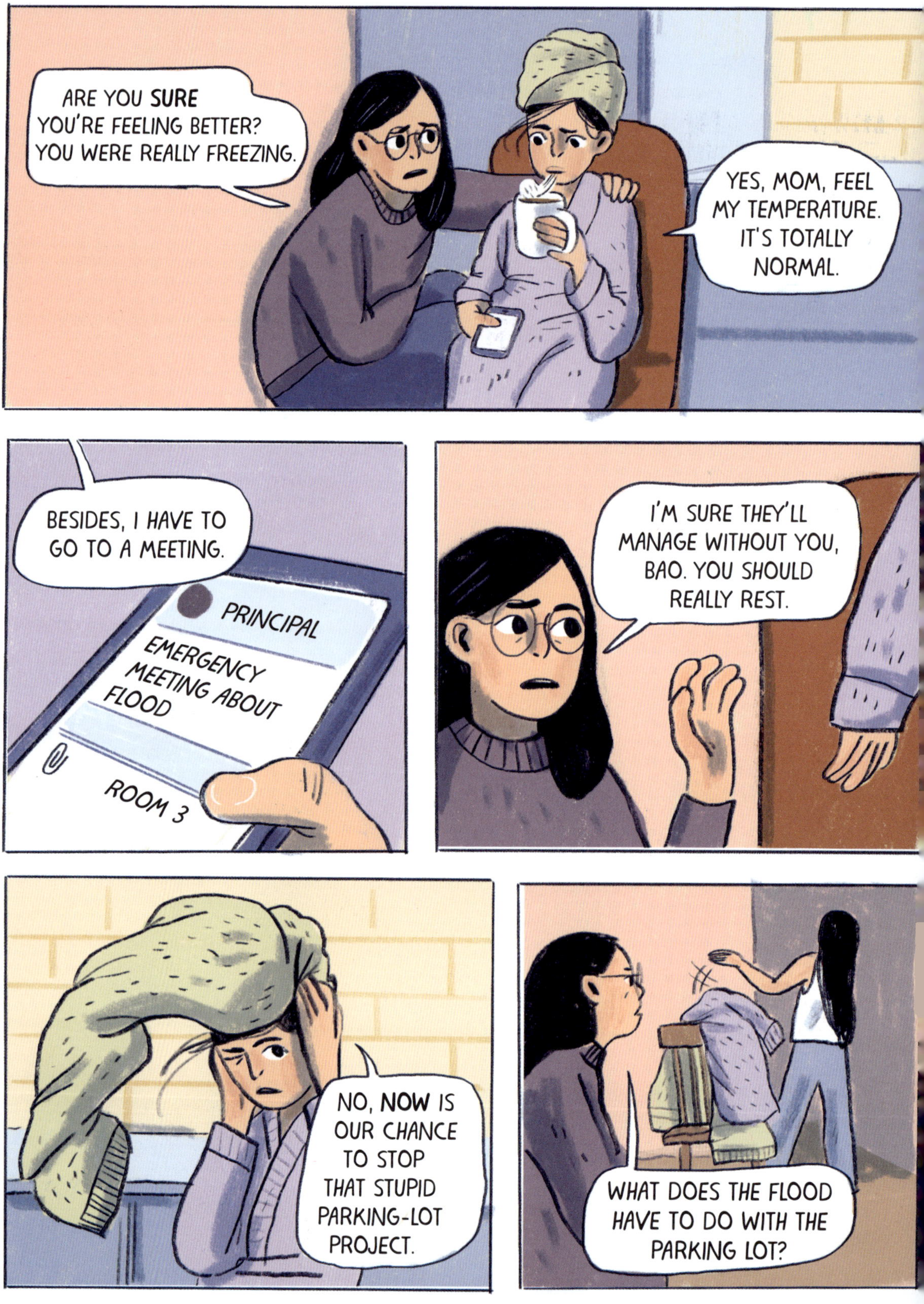
ARE YOU **SURE** YOU'RE FEELING BETTER? YOU WERE REALLY FREEZING.
YES, MOM, FEEL MY TEMPERATURE. IT'S TOTALLY NORMAL.
BESIDES, I HAVE TO GO TO A MEETING.
PRINCIPAL
EMERGENCY MEETING ABOUT FLOOD
ROOM 3
I'M SURE THEY'LL MANAGE WITHOUT YOU, BAO. YOU SHOULD REALLY REST.
NO, **NOW** IS OUR CHANCE TO STOP THAT STUPID PARKING-LOT PROJECT.
WHAT DOES THE FLOOD HAVE TO DO WITH THE PARKING LOT?

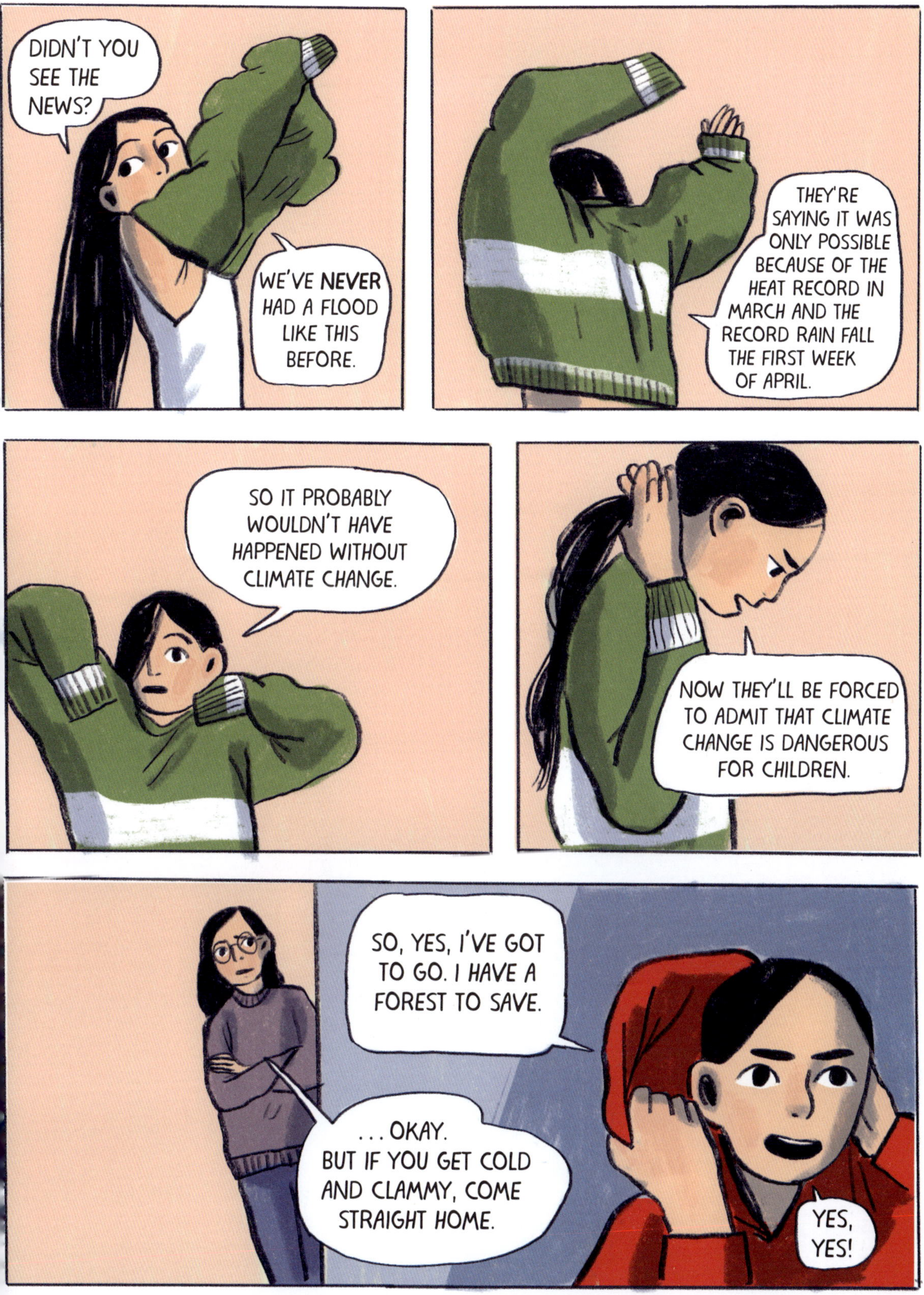
DIDN'T YOU SEE THE NEWS?
WE'VE **NEVER** HAD A FLOOD LIKE THIS BEFORE.
THEY'RE SAYING IT WAS ONLY POSSIBLE BECAUSE OF THE HEAT RECORD IN MARCH AND THE RECORD RAIN FALL THE FIRST WEEK OF APRIL.
SO IT PROBABLY WOULDN'T HAVE HAPPENED WITHOUT CLIMATE CHANGE.
NOW THEY'LL BE FORCED TO ADMIT THAT CLIMATE CHANGE IS DANGEROUS FOR CHILDREN.
SO, YES, I'VE GOT TO GO. I HAVE A FOREST TO SAVE.
. . . OKAY. BUT IF YOU GET COLD AND CLAMMY, COME STRAIGHT HOME.
YES, YES!

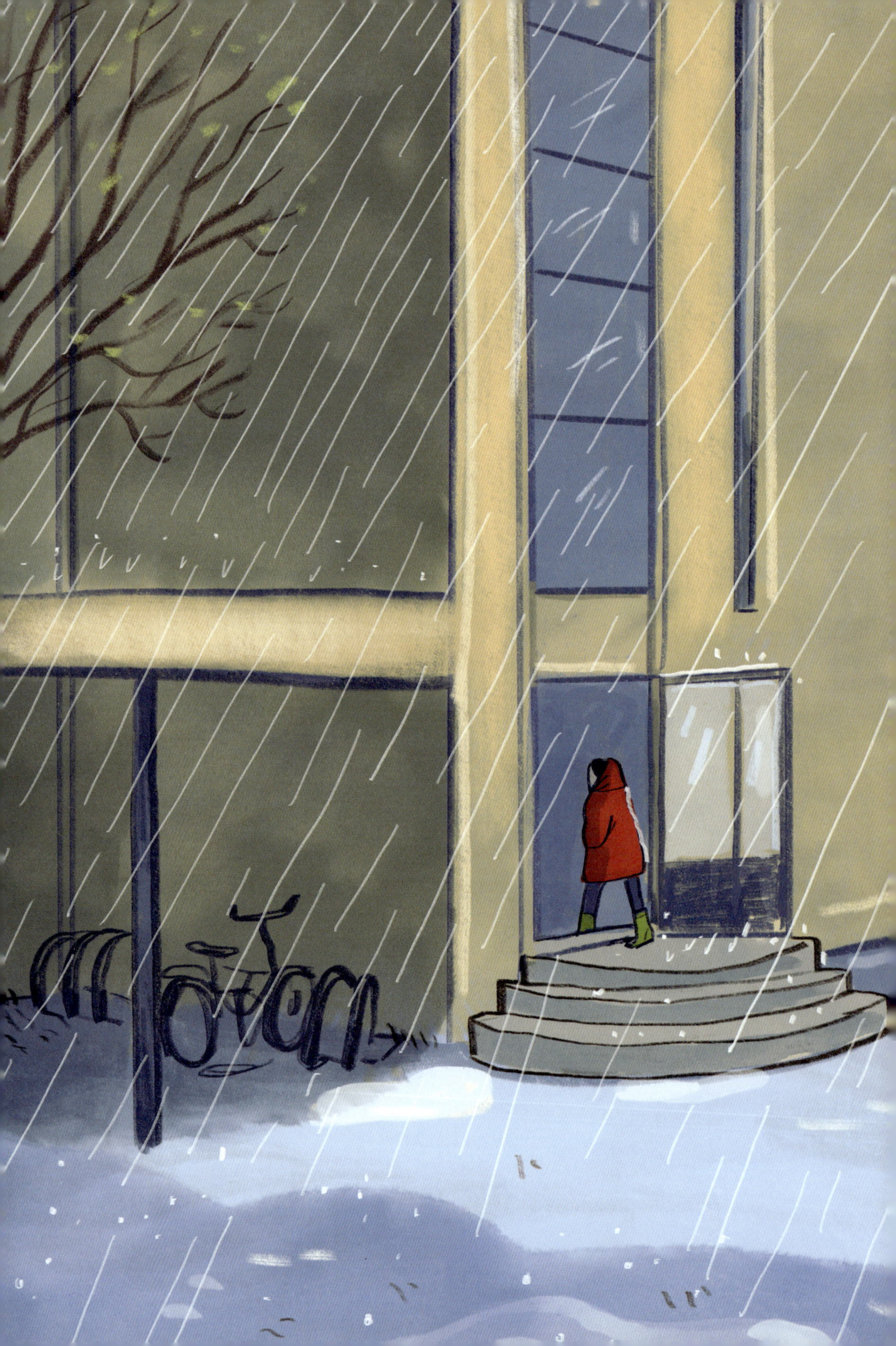

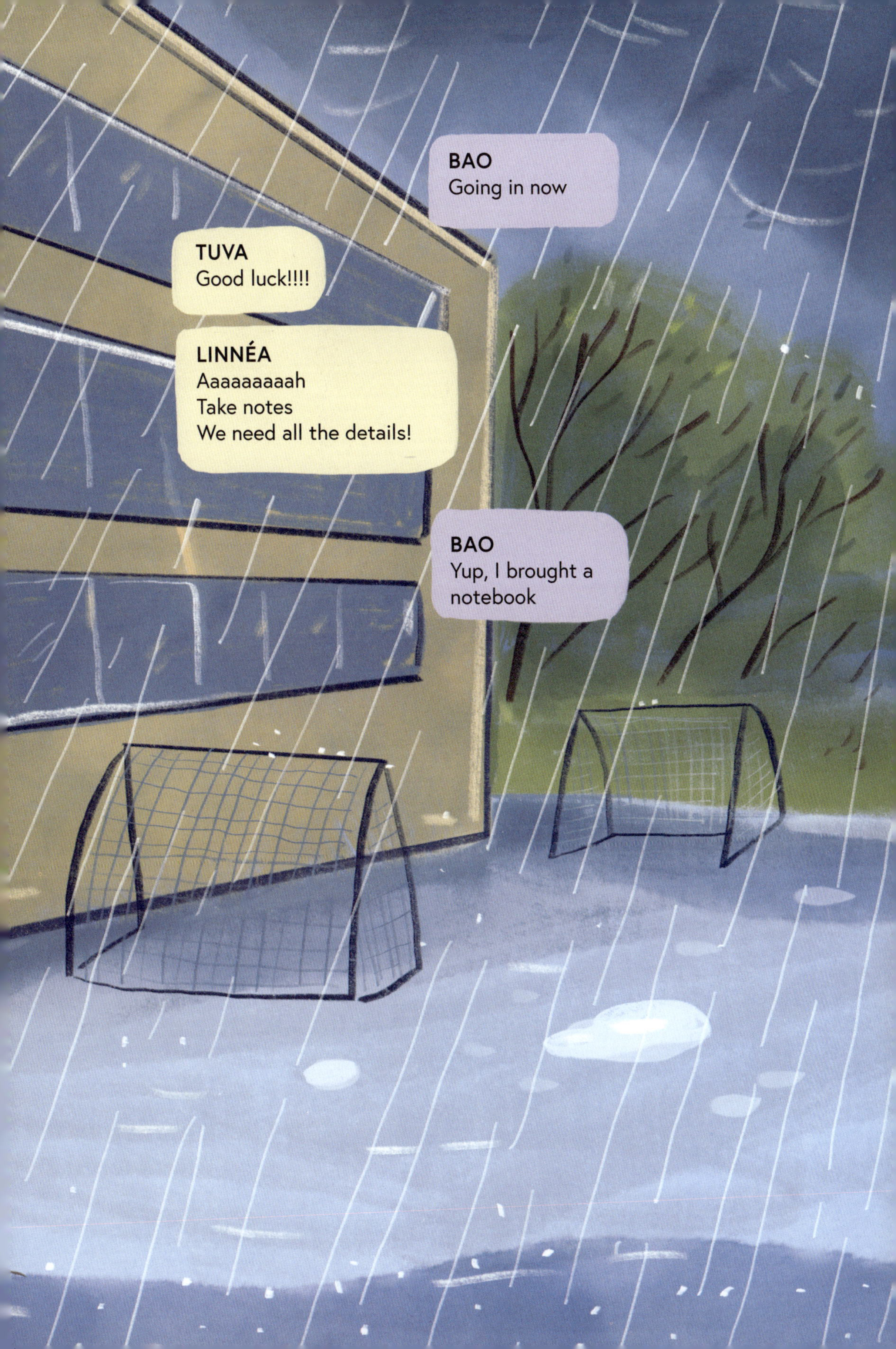
BAO
Going in now
TUVA
Good luck!!!!
LINNÉA
Aaaaaaaaah
Take notes
We need all the details!
BAO
Yup, I brought a notebook

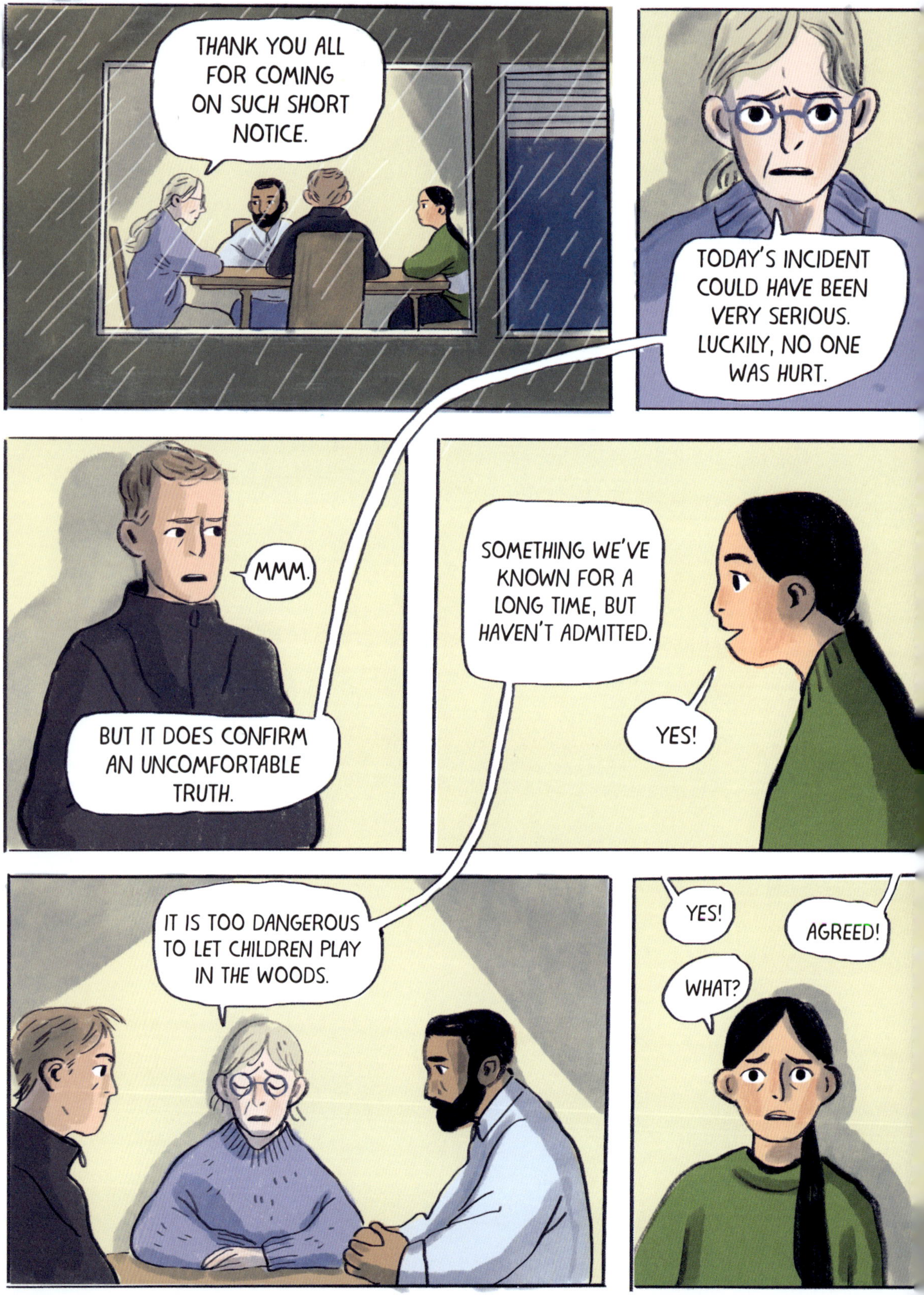

THANK YOU ALL FOR COMING ON SUCH SHORT NOTICE.
TODAY'S INCIDENT COULD HAVE BEEN VERY SERIOUS. LUCKILY, NO ONE WAS HURT.
MMM.
BUT IT DOES CONFIRM AN UNCOMFORTABLE TRUTH.
SOMETHING WE'VE KNOWN FOR A LONG TIME, BUT HAVEN'T ADMITTED.
YES!
IT IS TOO DANGEROUS TO LET CHILDREN PLAY IN THE WOODS.
YES!
AGREED!
WHAT?

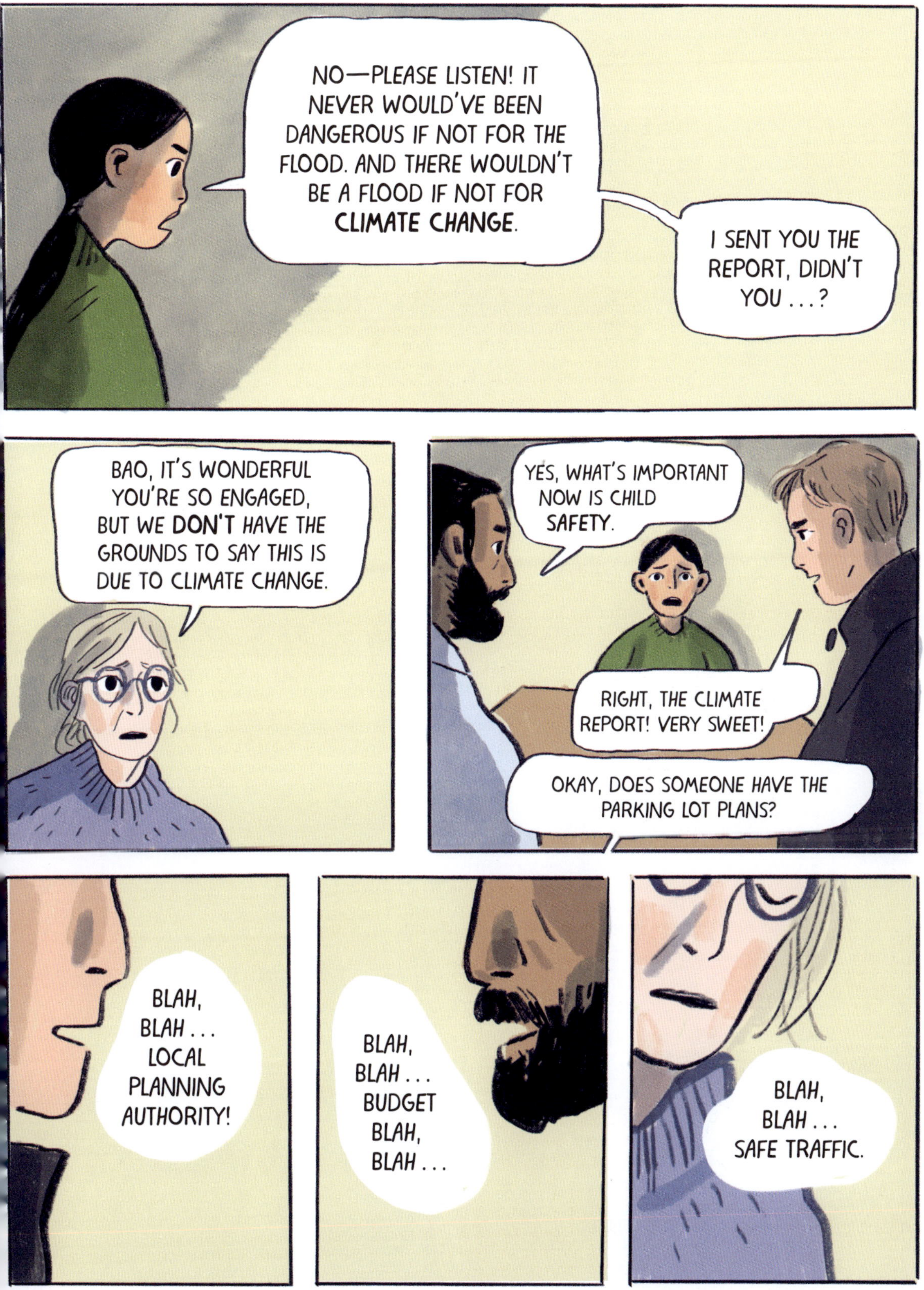
NO—PLEASE LISTEN! IT NEVER WOULD'VE BEEN DANGEROUS IF NOT FOR THE FLOOD. AND THERE WOULDN'T BE A FLOOD IF NOT FOR **CLIMATE CHANGE**.
I SENT YOU THE REPORT, DIDN'T YOU . . . ?
BAO, IT'S WONDERFUL YOU'RE SO ENGAGED, BUT WE **DON'T** HAVE THE GROUNDS TO SAY THIS IS DUE TO CLIMATE CHANGE.
YES, WHAT'S IMPORTANT NOW IS CHILD **SAFETY**.
RIGHT, THE CLIMATE REPORT! VERY SWEET!
OKAY, DOES SOMEONE HAVE THE PARKING LOT PLANS?
BLAH, BLAH . . . LOCAL PLANNING AUTHORITY!
BLAH, BLAH . . . BUDGET BLAH, BLAH . . .
BLAH, BLAH . . . SAFE TRAFFIC.

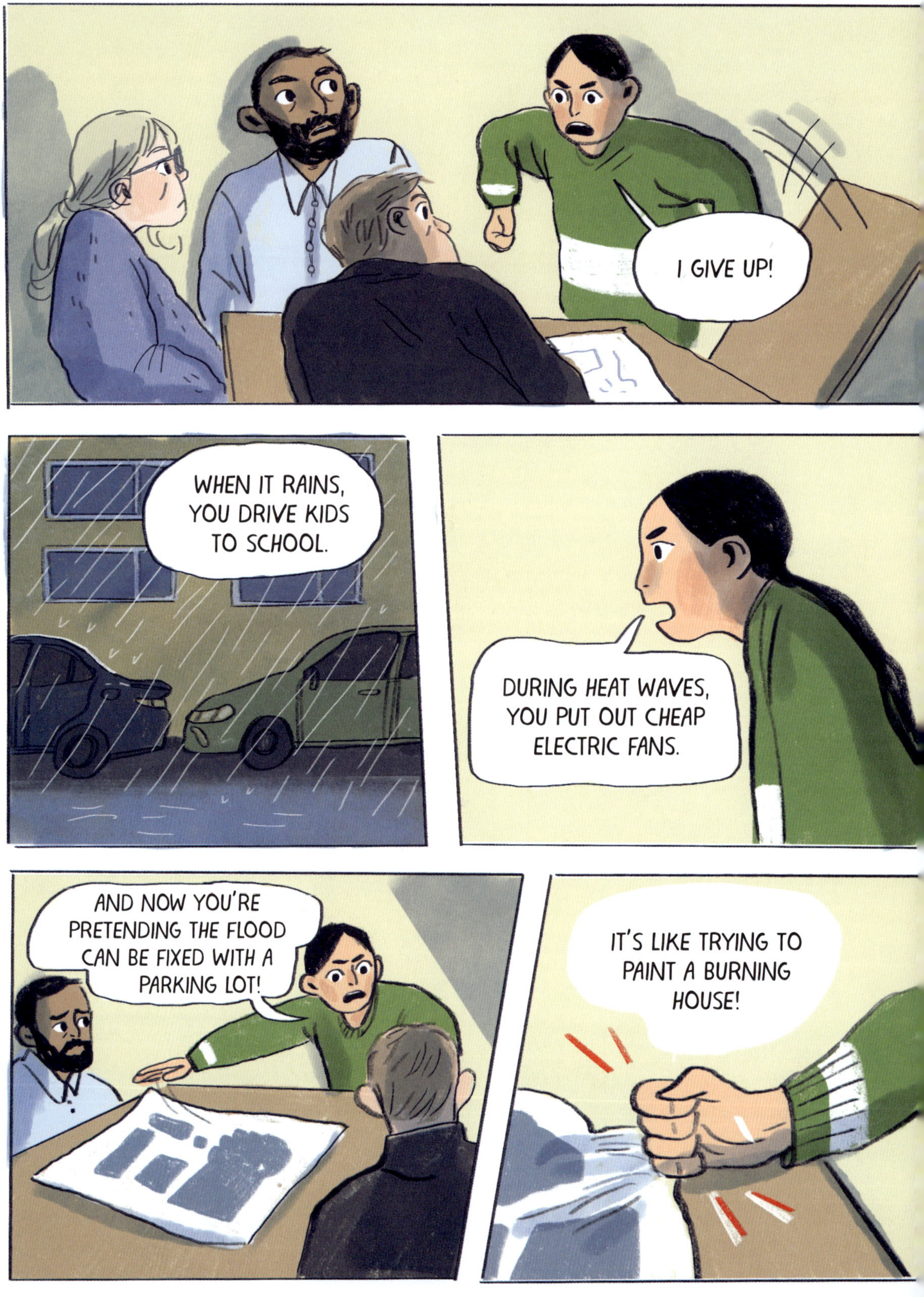
I GIVE UP!
WHEN IT RAINS, YOU DRIVE KIDS TO SCHOOL.
DURING HEAT WAVES, YOU PUT OUT CHEAP ELECTRIC FANS.
AND NOW YOU'RE PRETENDING THE FLOOD CAN BE FIXED WITH A PARKING LOT!
IT'S LIKE TRYING TO PAINT A BURNING HOUSE!

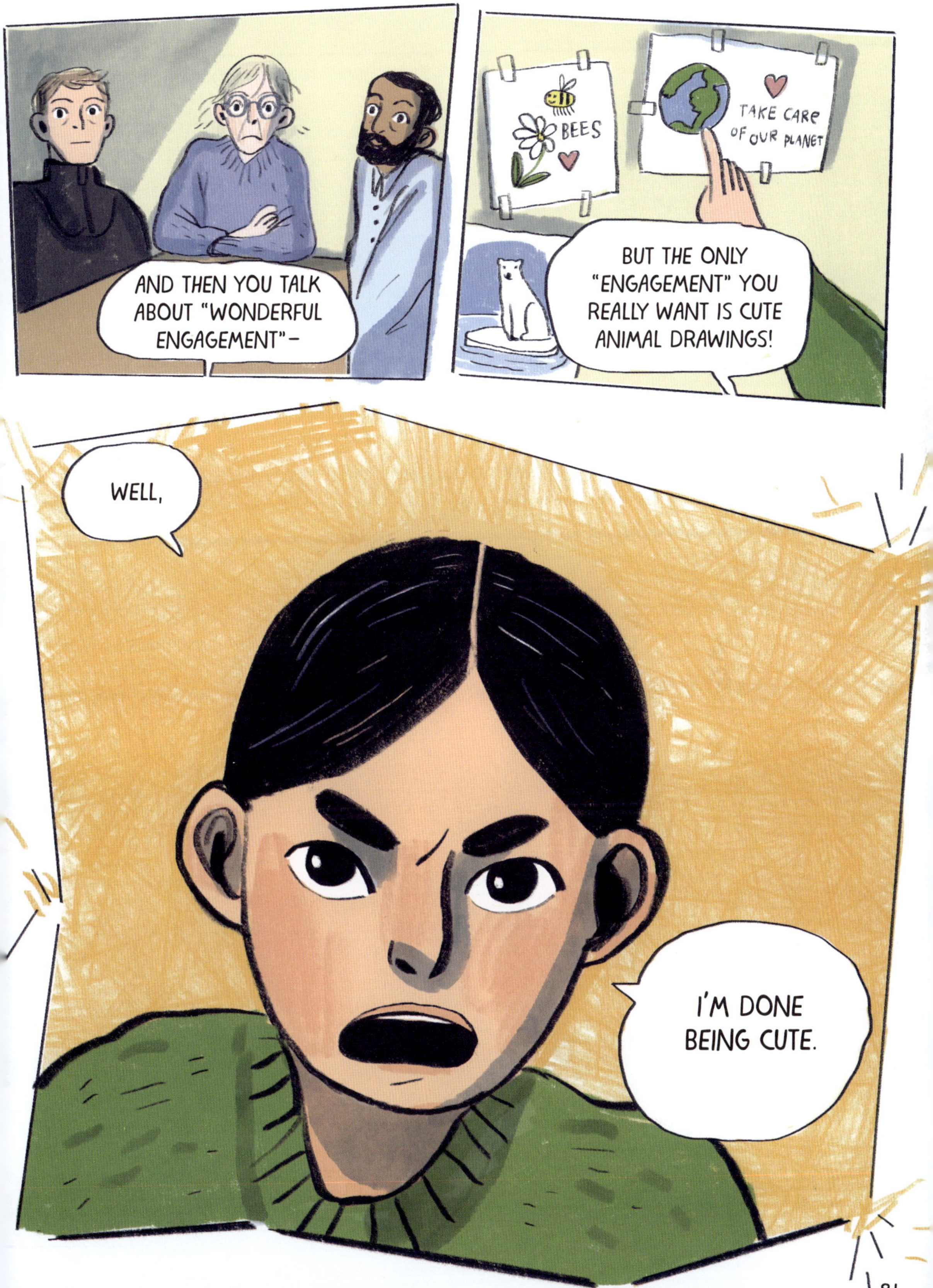
AND THEN YOU TALK ABOUT "WONDERFUL ENGAGEMENT"–
BEES
TAKE CARE OF OUR PLANET
BUT THE ONLY "ENGAGEMENT" YOU REALLY WANT IS CUTE ANIMAL DRAWINGS!
WELL,
I'M DONE BEING CUTE.

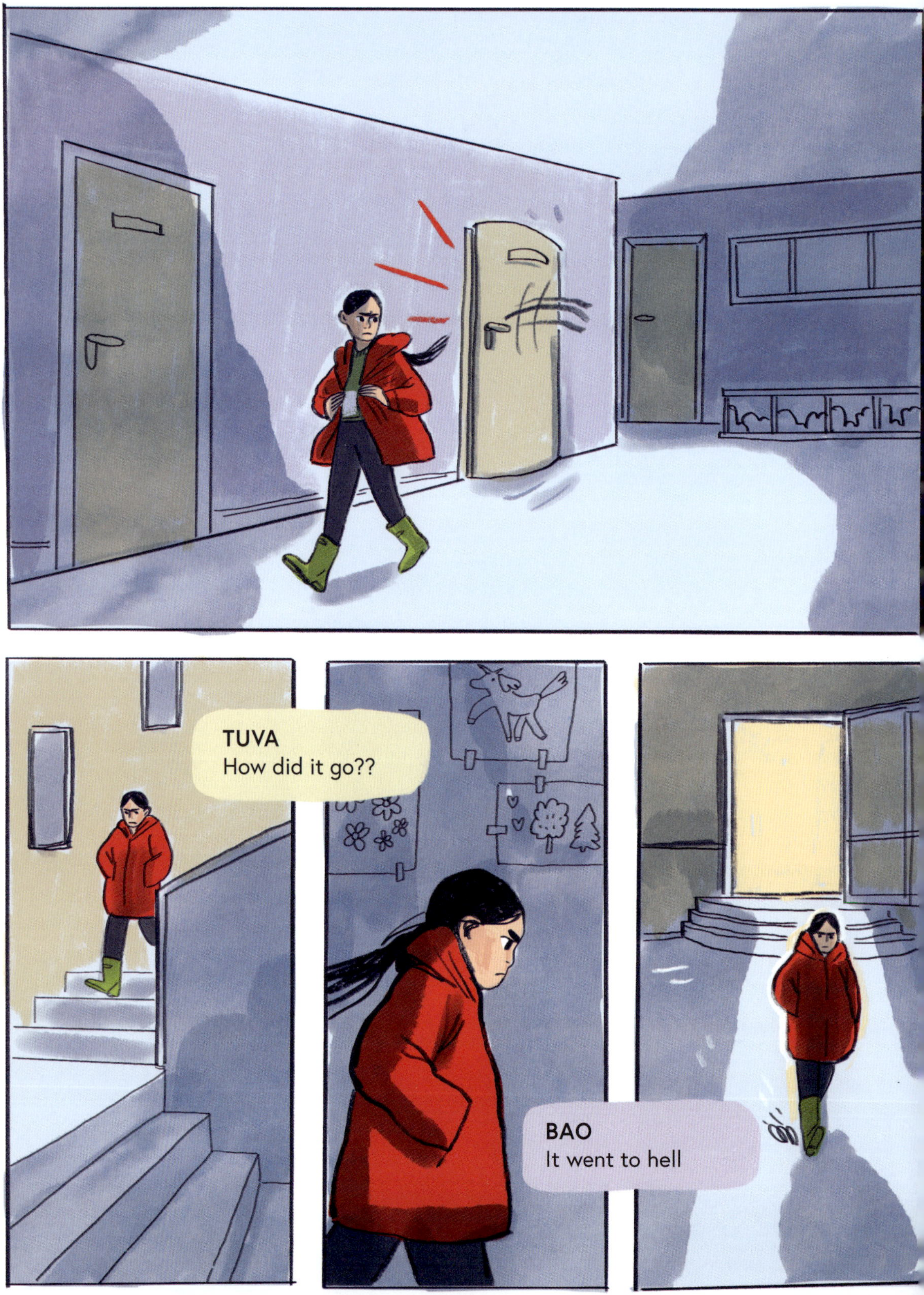
TUVA
How did it go??
BAO
It went to hell

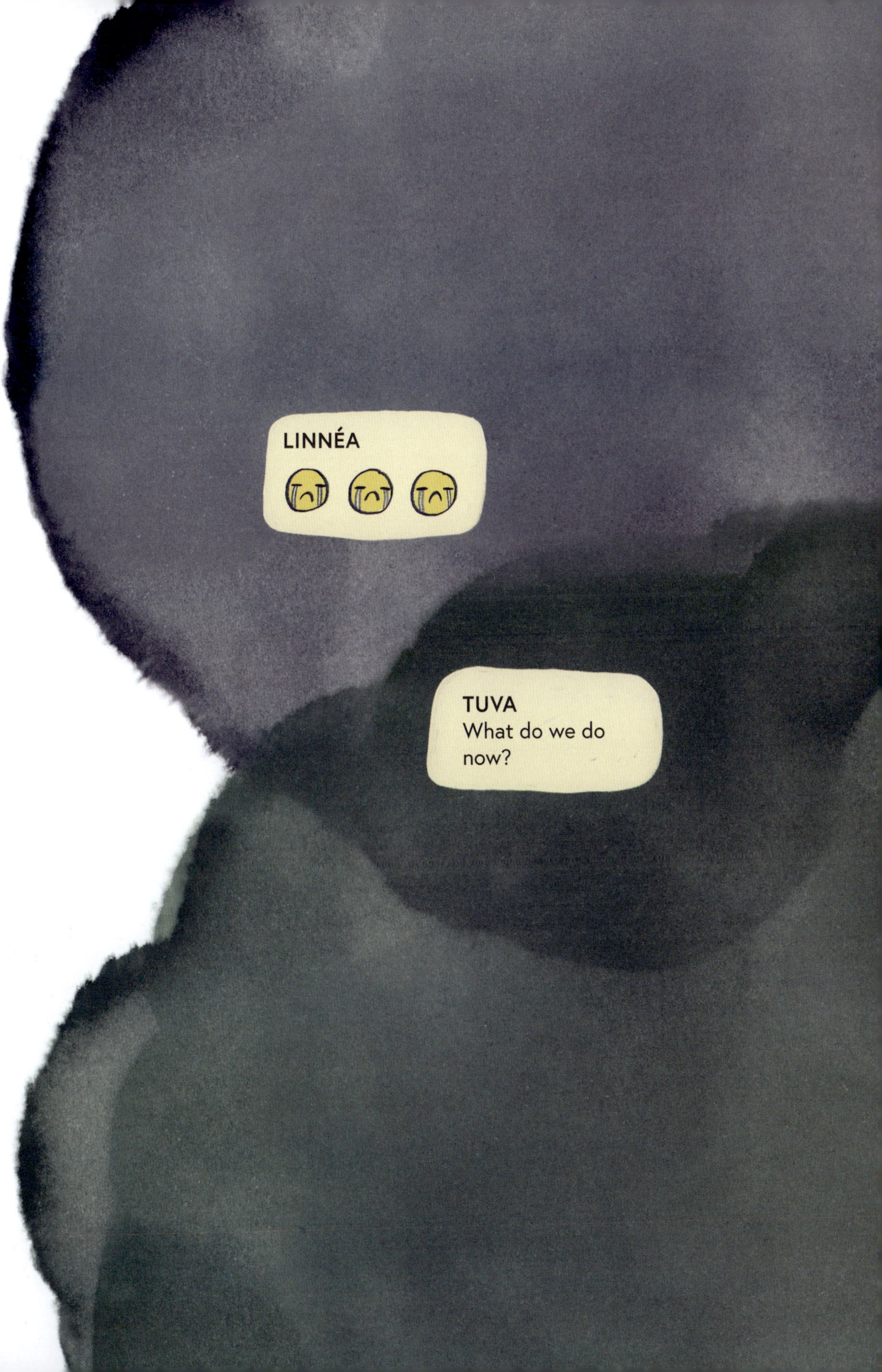
LINNÉA
TUVA
What do we do now?

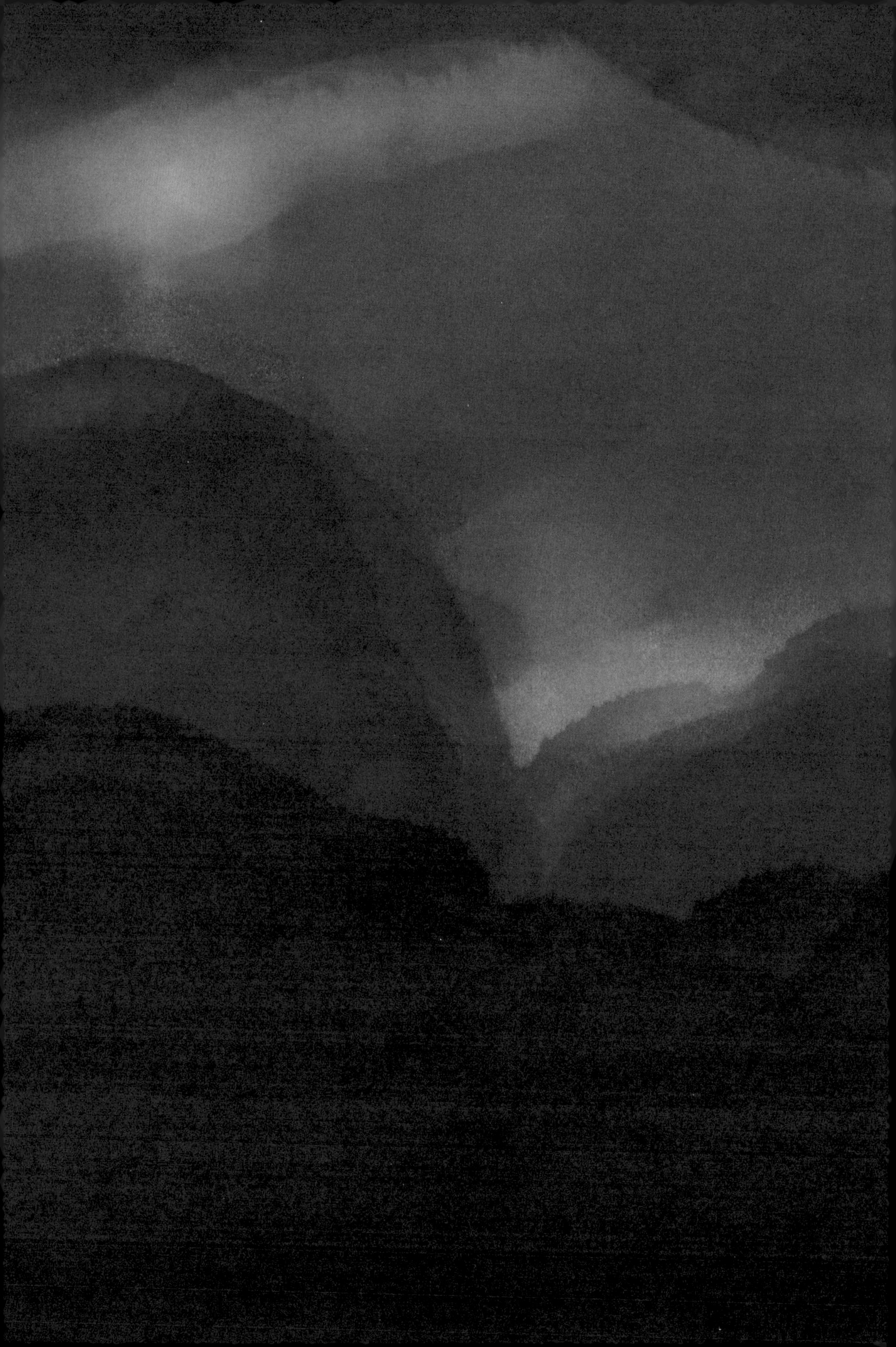

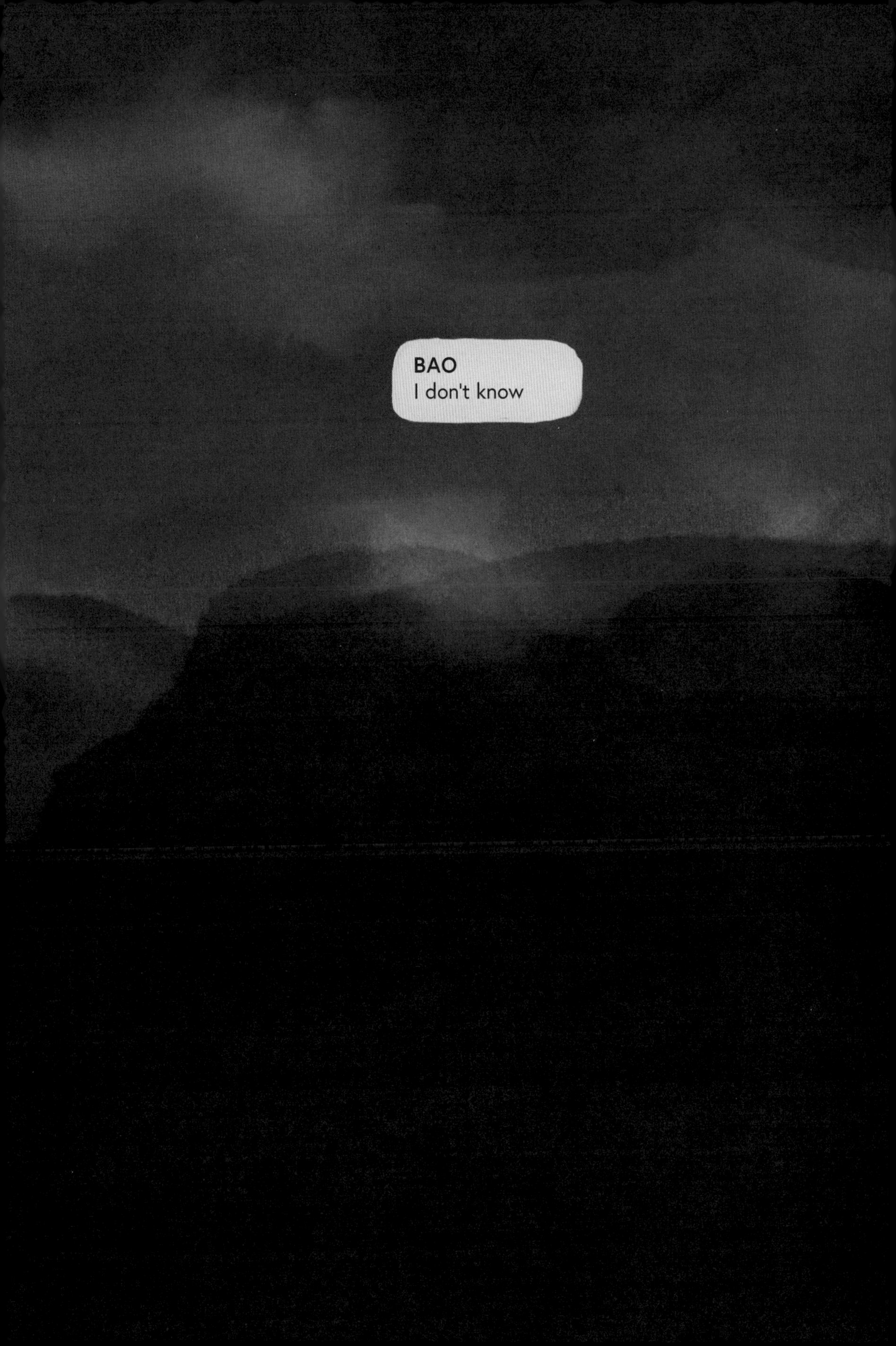
BAO
I don't know

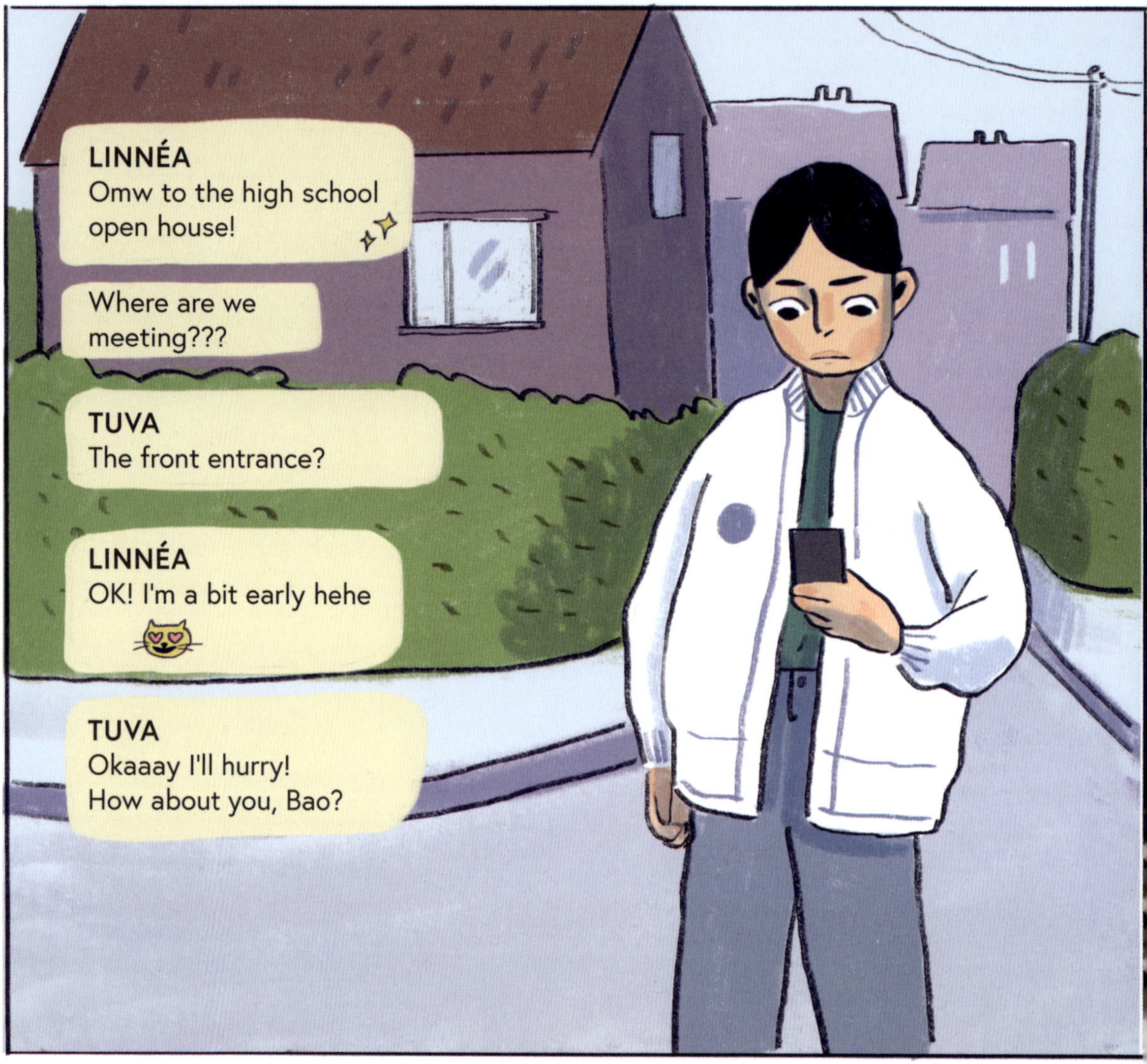
LINNÉA
Omw to the high school open house!
Where are we meeting???
TUVA
The front entrance?
LINNÉA
OK! I'm a bit early hehe
TUVA
Okaaay I'll hurry! How about you, Bao?

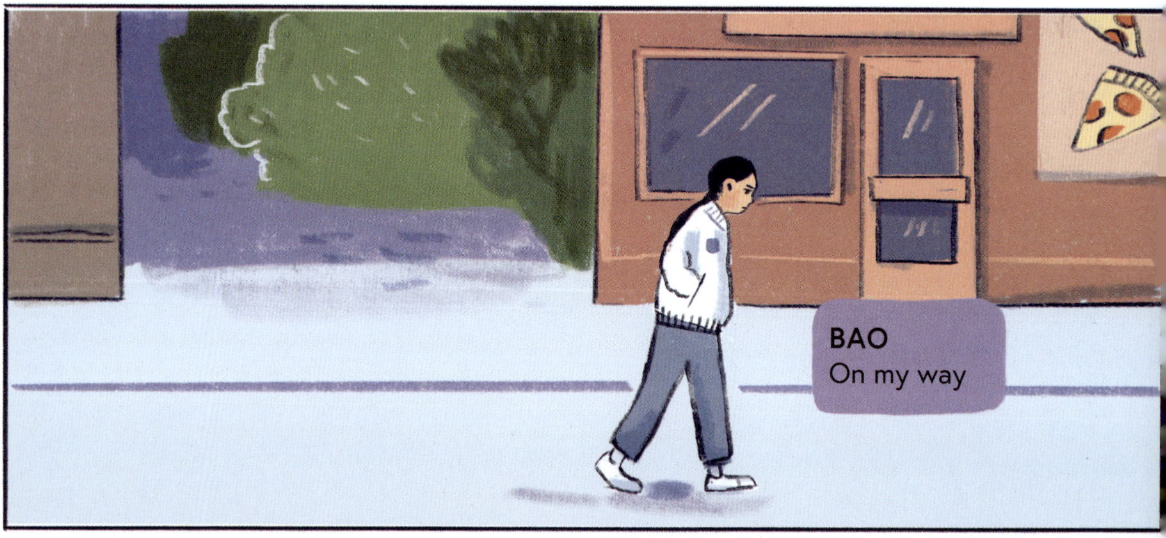
BAO
On my way

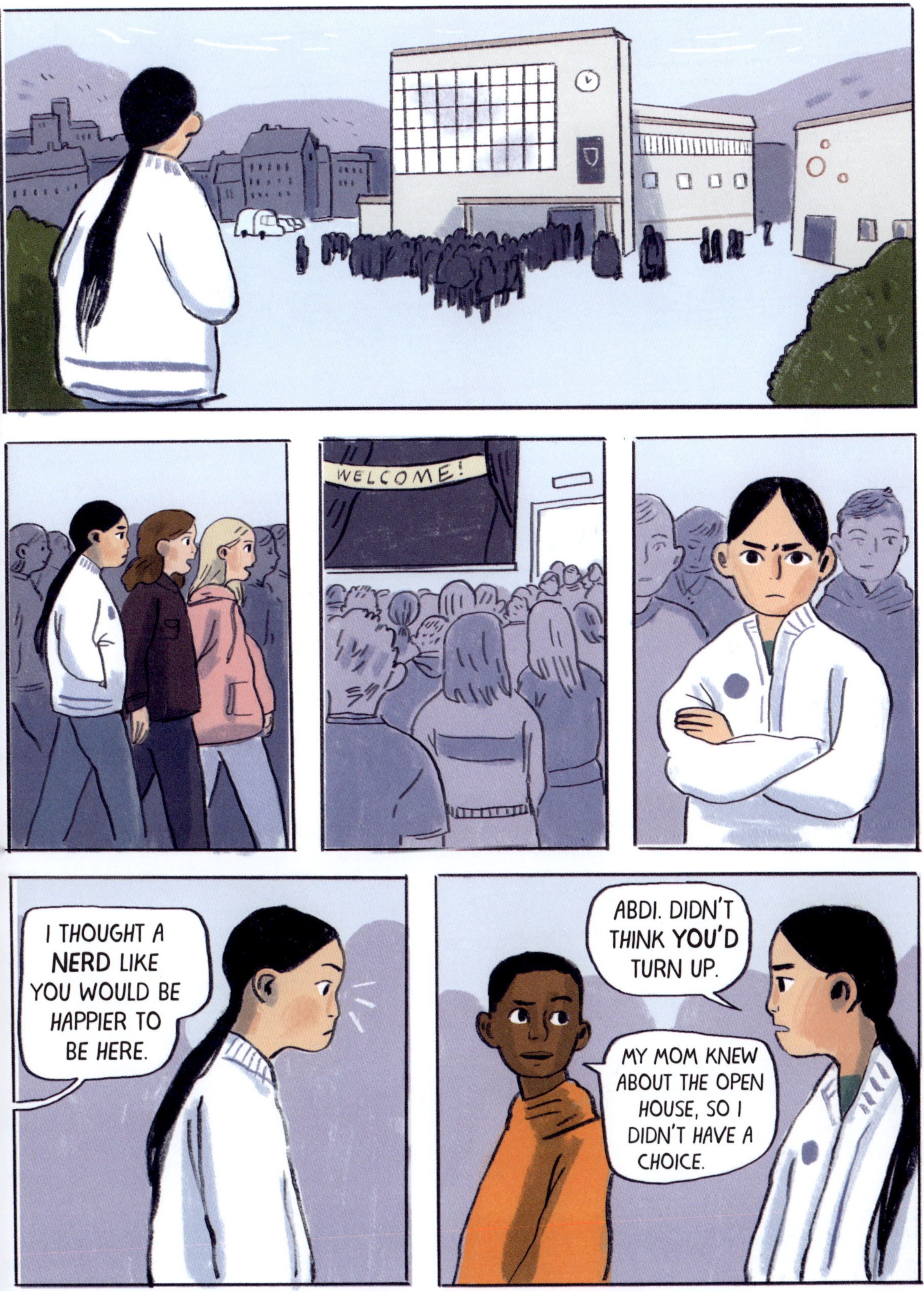
WELCOME!
I THOUGHT A NERD LIKE YOU WOULD BE HAPPIER TO BE HERE.
ABDI. DIDN'T THINK YOU'D TURN UP.
MY MOM KNEW ABOUT THE OPEN HOUSE, SO I DIDN'T HAVE A CHOICE.

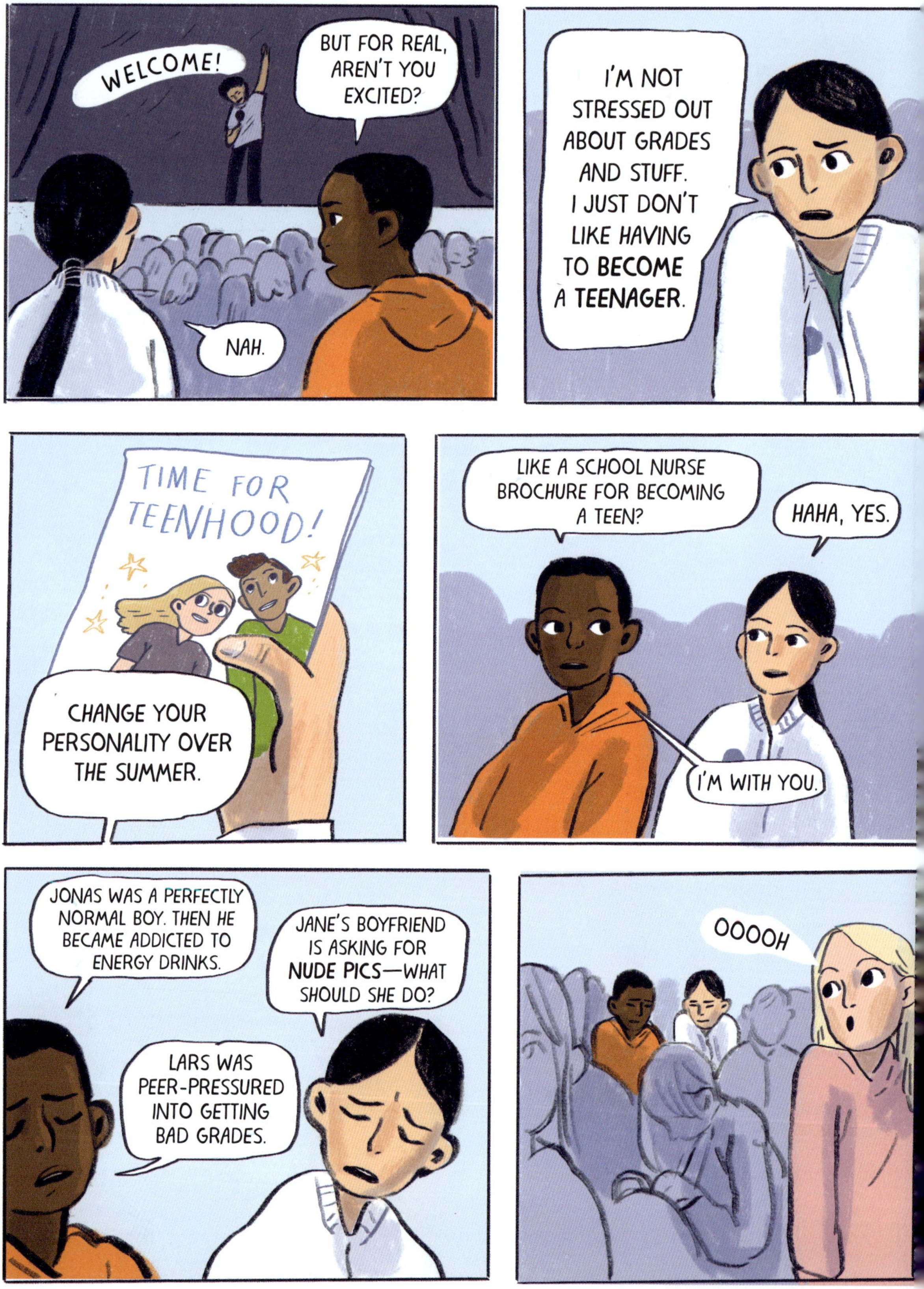
WELCOME!
BUT FOR REAL, AREN'T YOU EXCITED?
NAH.
I'M NOT STRESSED OUT ABOUT GRADES AND STUFF. I JUST DON'T LIKE HAVING TO **BECOME** A **TEENAGER**.
TIME FOR TEENHOOD!
CHANGE YOUR PERSONALITY OVER THE SUMMER.
LIKE A SCHOOL NURSE BROCHURE FOR BECOMING A TEEN?
HAHA, YES.
I'M WITH YOU.
JONAS WAS A PERFECTLY NORMAL BOY. THEN HE BECAME ADDICTED TO ENERGY DRINKS.
JANE'S BOYFRIEND IS ASKING FOR **NUDE PICS**—WHAT SHOULD SHE DO?
LARS WAS PEER-PRESSURED INTO GETTING BAD GRADES.
OOOOH

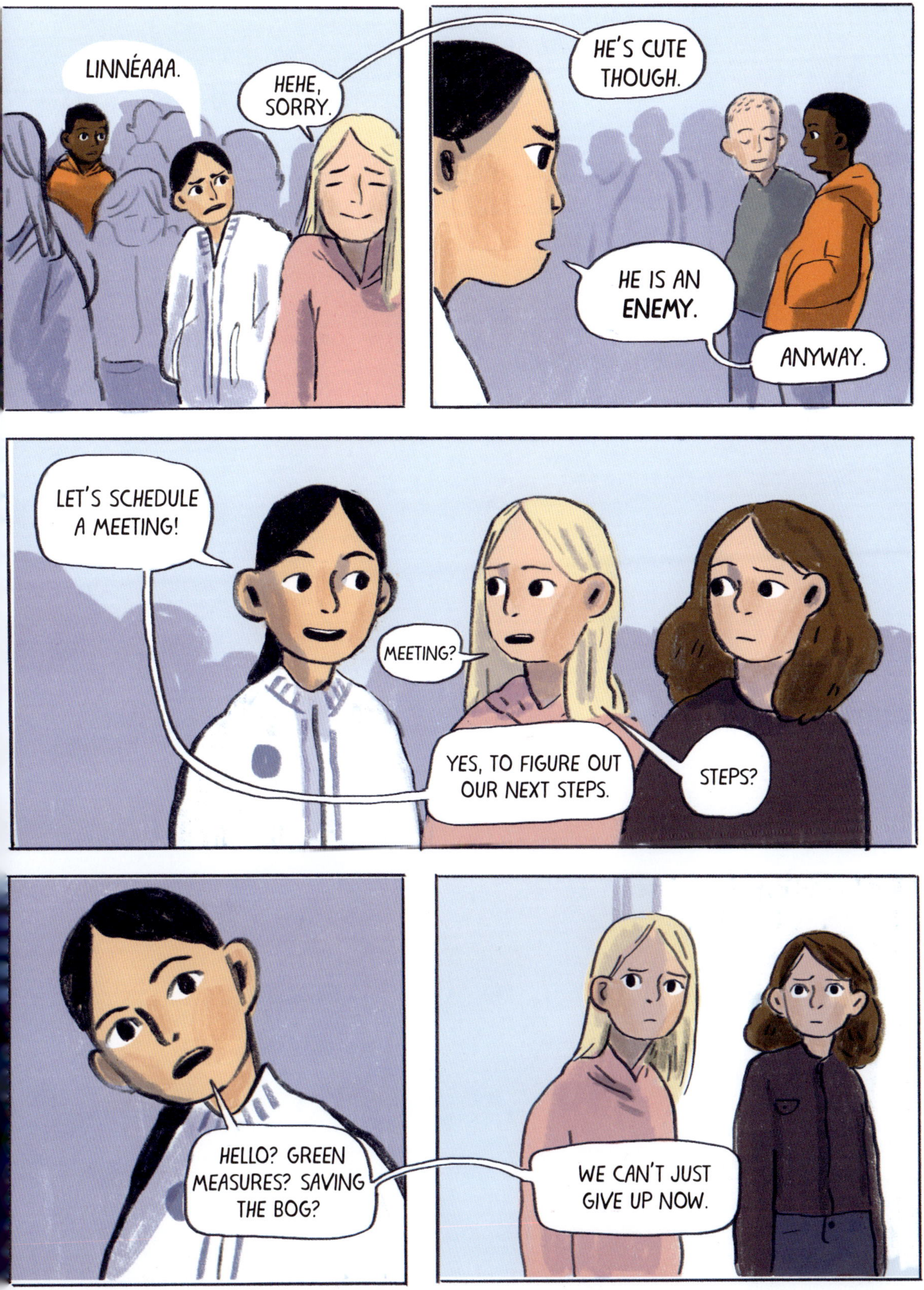
LINNÉAAA.
HEHE, SORRY.
HE'S CUTE THOUGH.
HE IS AN ENEMY.
ANYWAY.
LET'S SCHEDULE A MEETING!
MEETING?
YES, TO FIGURE OUT OUR NEXT STEPS.
STEPS?
HELLO? GREEN MEASURES? SAVING THE BOG?
WE CAN'T JUST GIVE UP NOW.

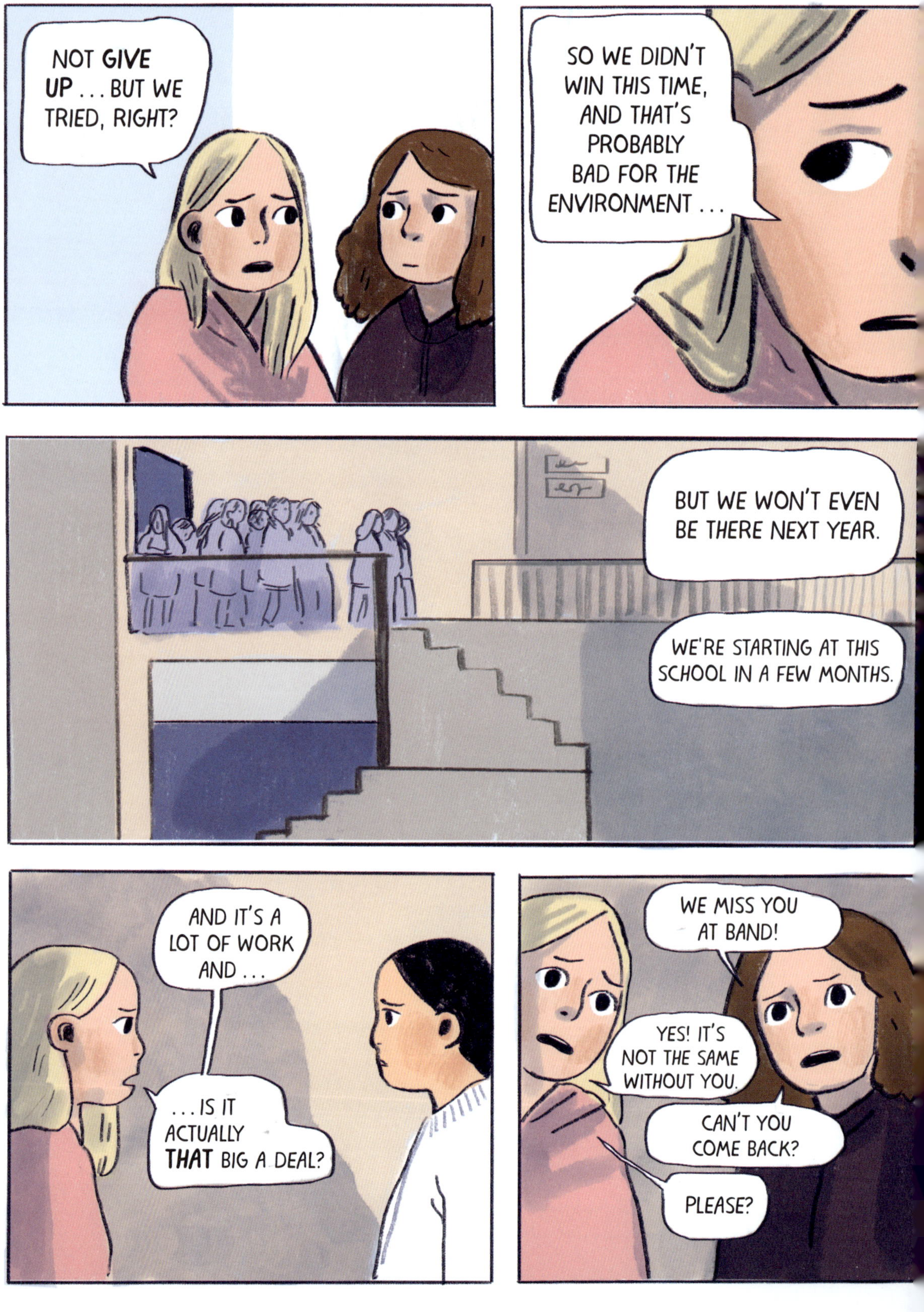
NOT GIVE UP ... BUT WE TRIED, RIGHT?
SO WE DIDN'T WIN THIS TIME, AND THAT'S PROBABLY BAD FOR THE ENVIRONMENT ...
BUT WE WON'T EVEN BE THERE NEXT YEAR.
WE'RE STARTING AT THIS SCHOOL IN A FEW MONTHS.
AND IT'S A LOT OF WORK AND ...
... IS IT ACTUALLY THAT BIG A DEAL?
WE MISS YOU AT BAND!
YES! IT'S NOT THE SAME WITHOUT YOU.
CAN'T YOU COME BACK?
PLEASE?

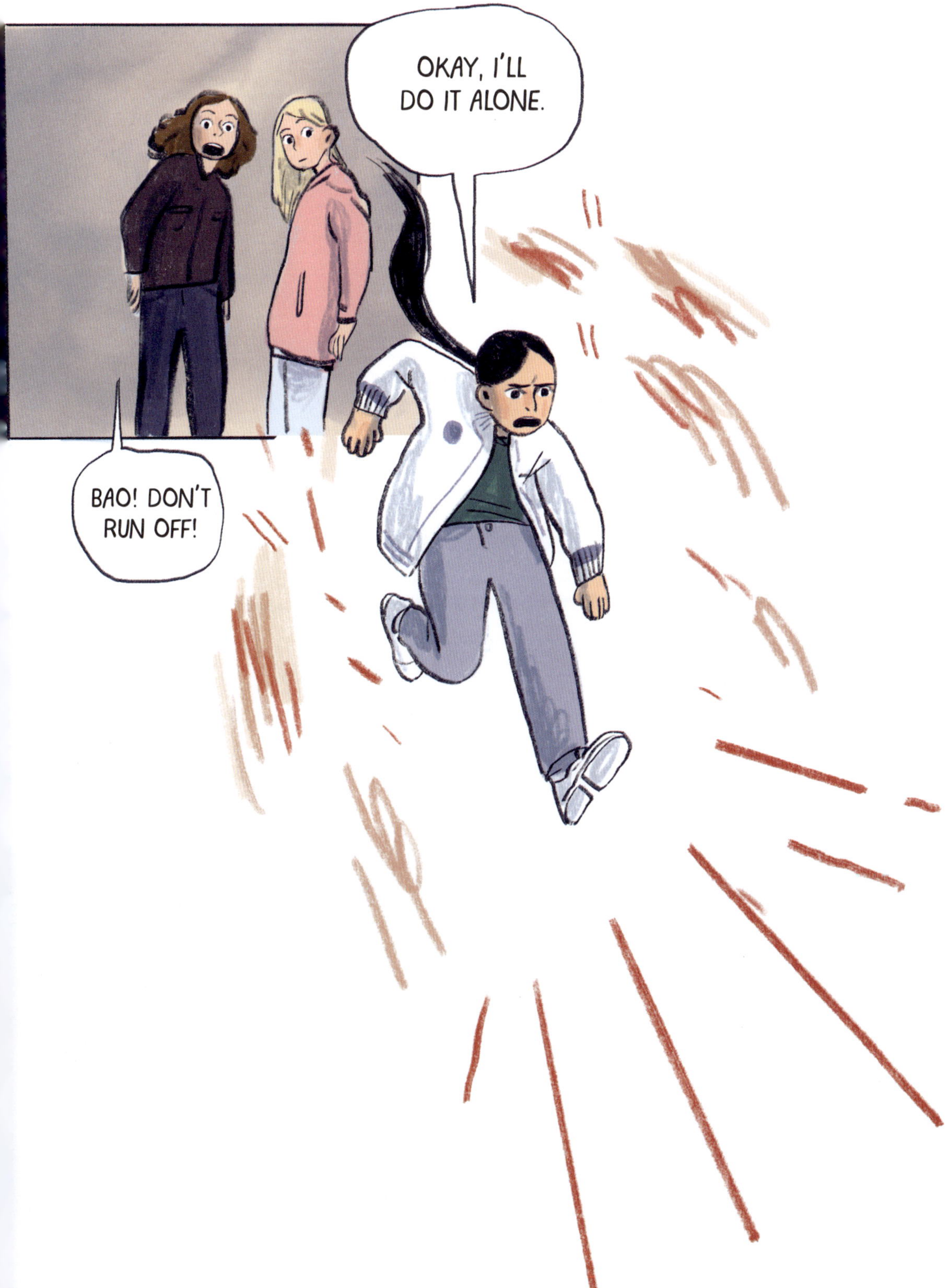
OKAY, I'LL DO IT ALONE.
BAO! DON'T RUN OFF!

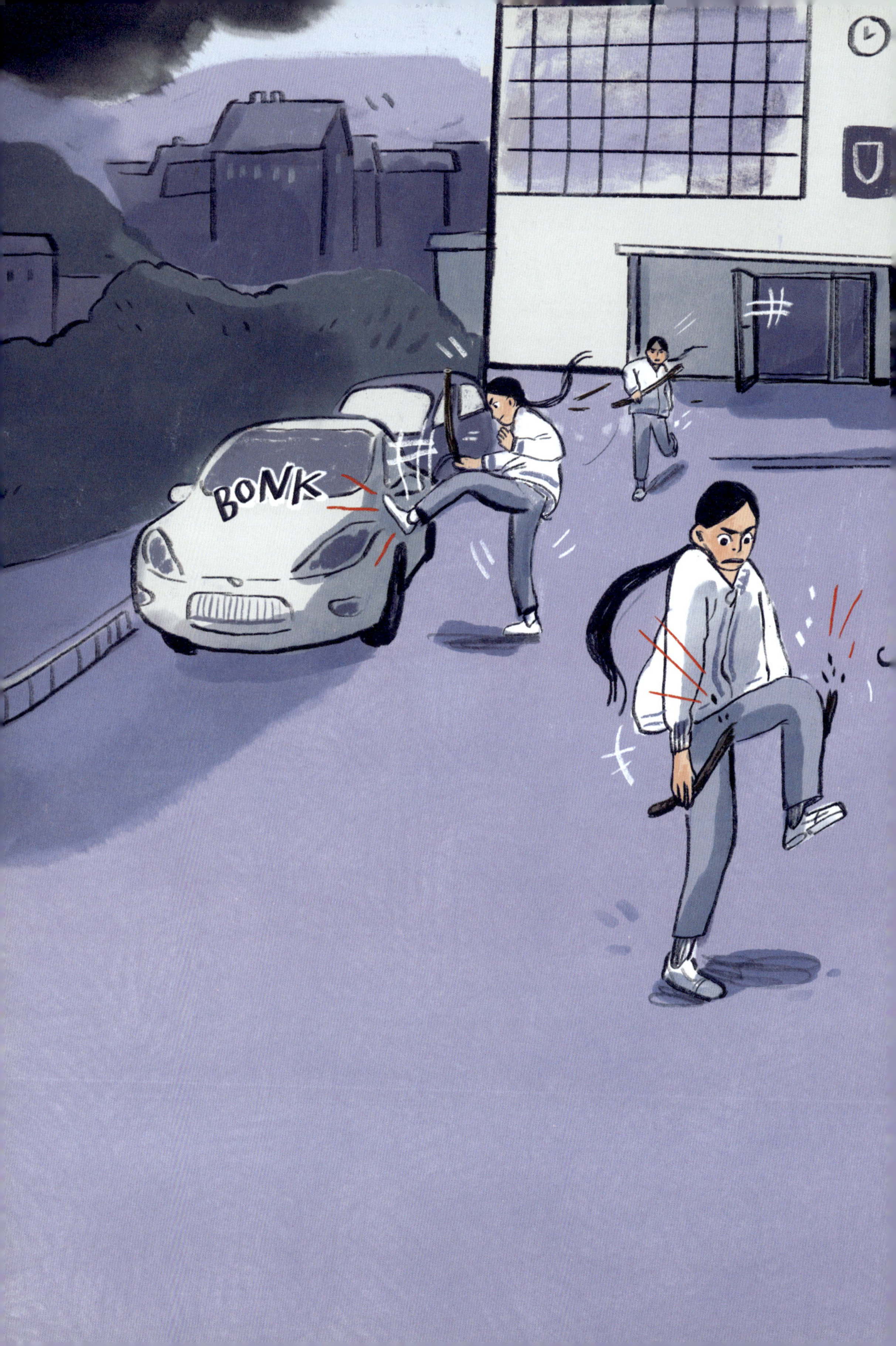
BONK

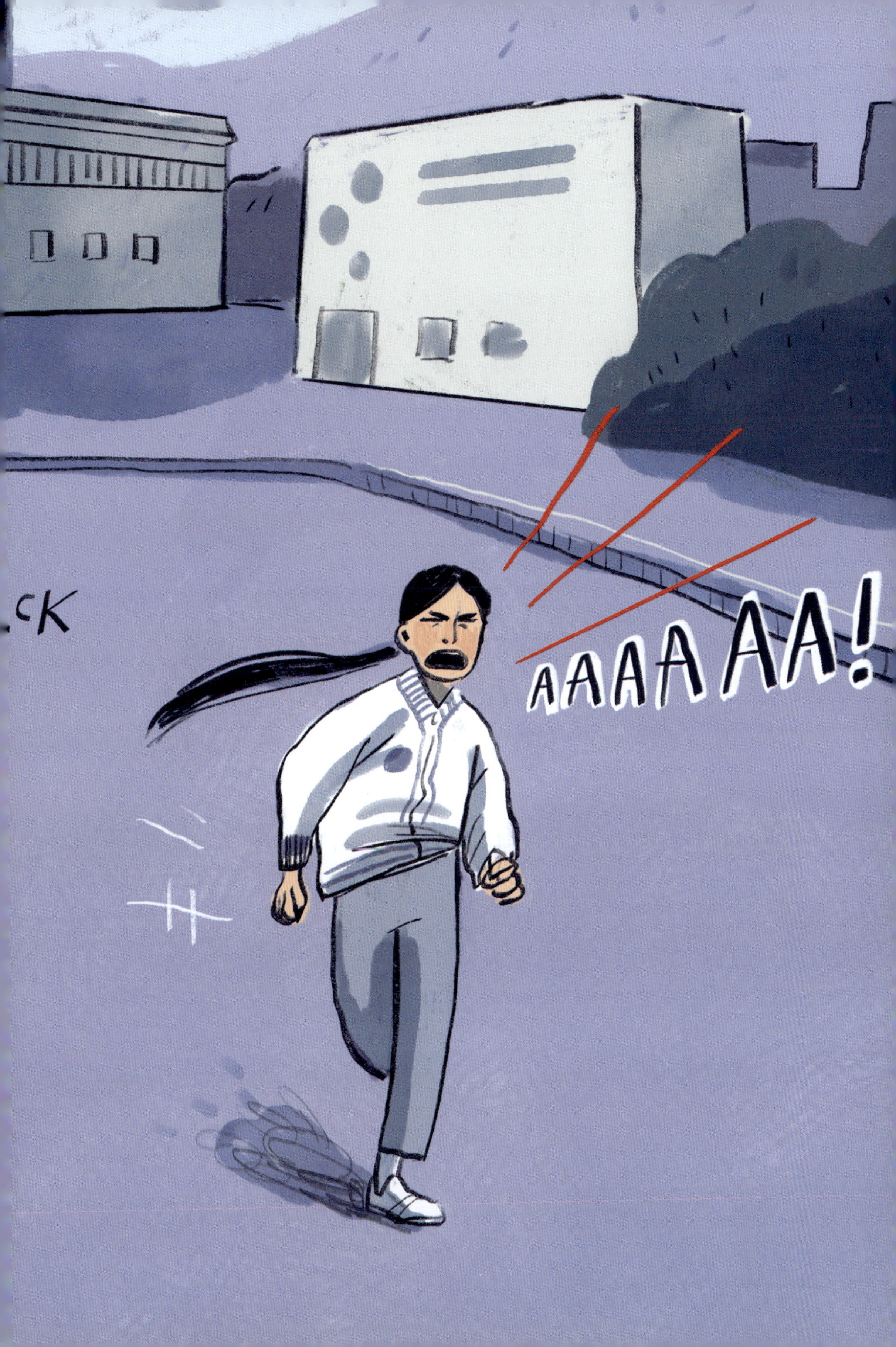
CK
AAAAAA!

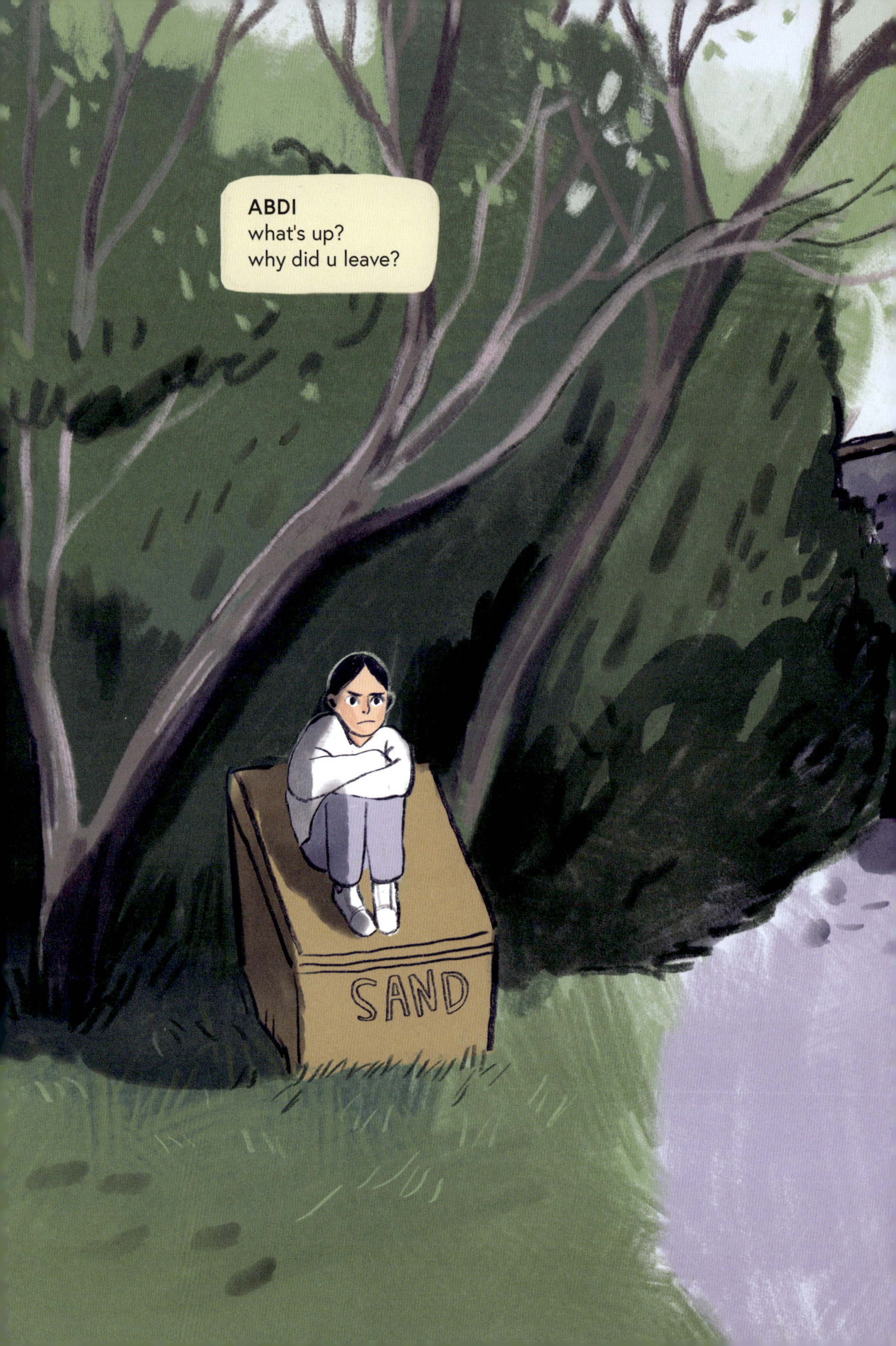
ABDI
what's up?
why did u leave?
SAND

PART 3: CIVIL DISOBEDIENCE

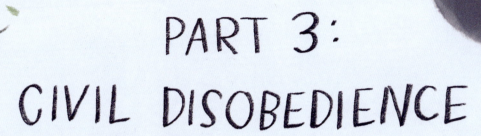

MOM
Coming to get you at the
high school now!
Excited to hear about it. 🩷

BAO
Don't wanna talk about it

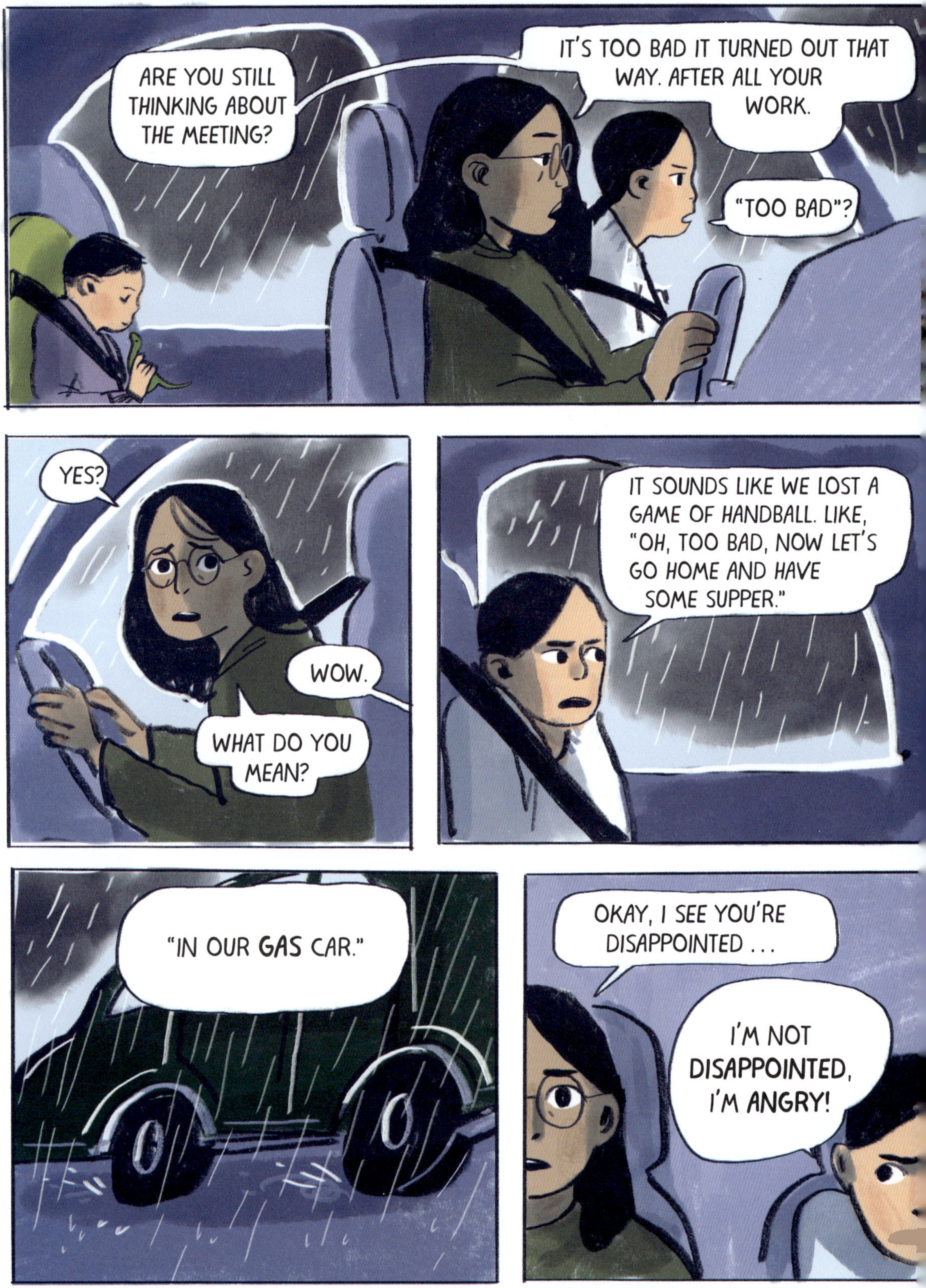
ARE YOU STILL THINKING ABOUT THE MEETING?
IT'S TOO BAD IT TURNED OUT THAT WAY. AFTER ALL YOUR WORK.
"TOO BAD"?
YES?
WOW.
WHAT DO YOU MEAN?
IT SOUNDS LIKE WE LOST A GAME OF HANDBALL. LIKE, "OH, TOO BAD, NOW LET'S GO HOME AND HAVE SOME SUPPER."
"IN OUR GAS CAR."
OKAY, I SEE YOU'RE DISAPPOINTED . . .
I'M NOT DISAPPOINTED, I'M ANGRY!

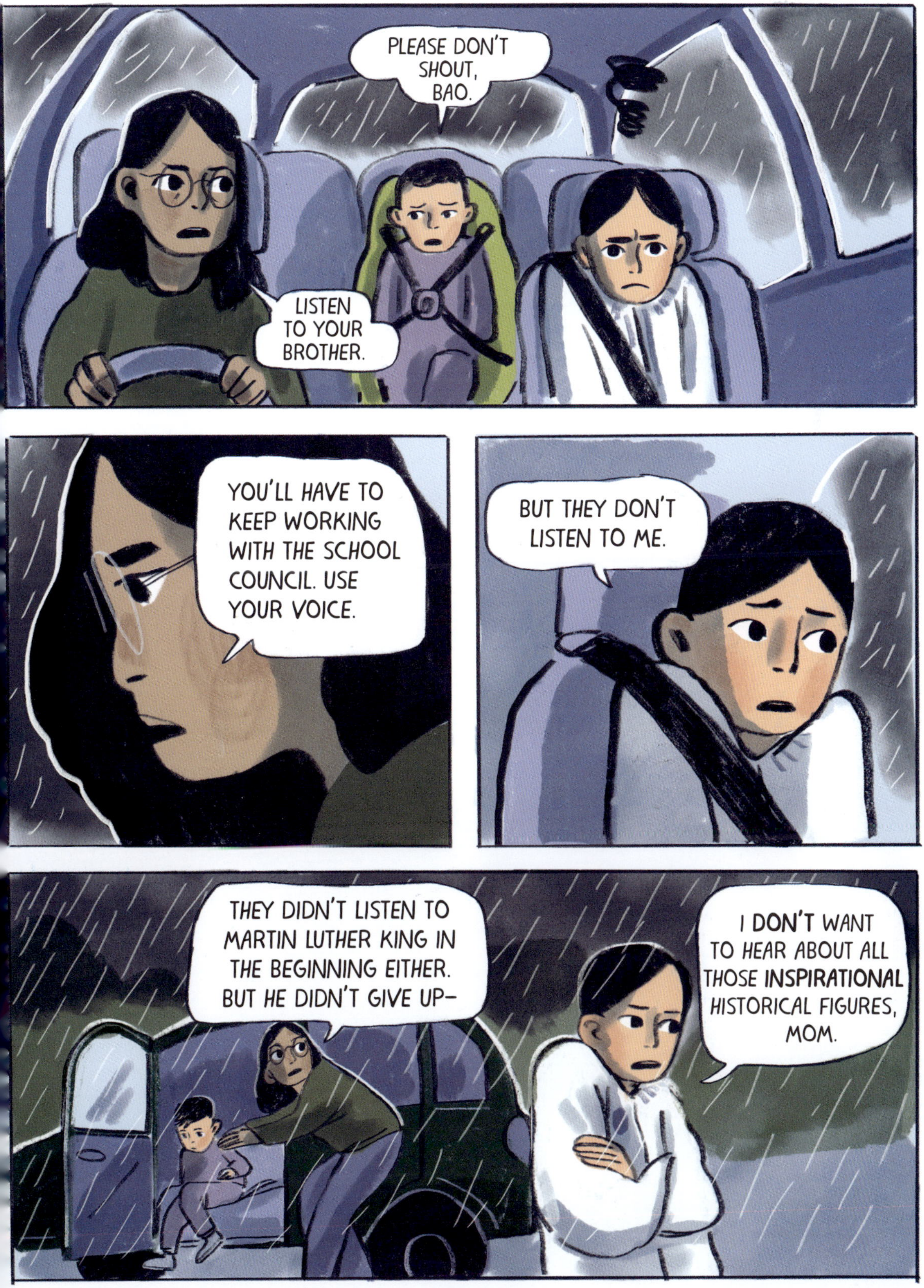
PLEASE DON'T SHOUT, BAO.
LISTEN TO YOUR BROTHER.
YOU'LL *HAVE* TO KEEP WORKING WITH THE SCHOOL COUNCIL. USE YOUR VOICE.
BUT THEY DON'T LISTEN TO ME.
THEY DIDN'T LISTEN TO MARTIN LUTHER KING IN THE BEGINNING EITHER. BUT *HE* DIDN'T GIVE UP–
I **DON'T** WANT TO HEAR ABOUT ALL THOSE **INSPIRATIONAL** HISTORICAL FIGURES, MOM.

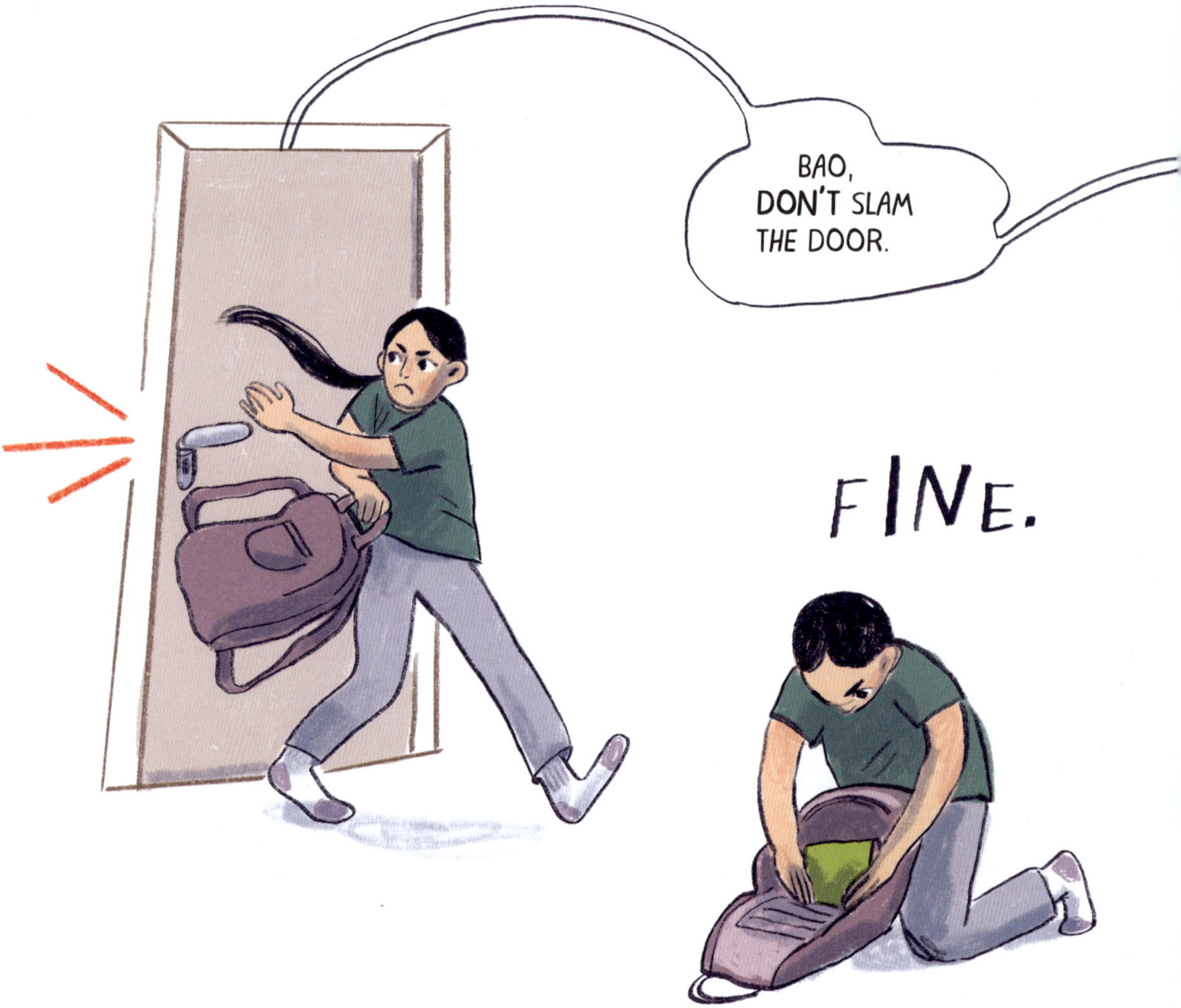
BAO, DON'T SLAM THE DOOR.
FINE.

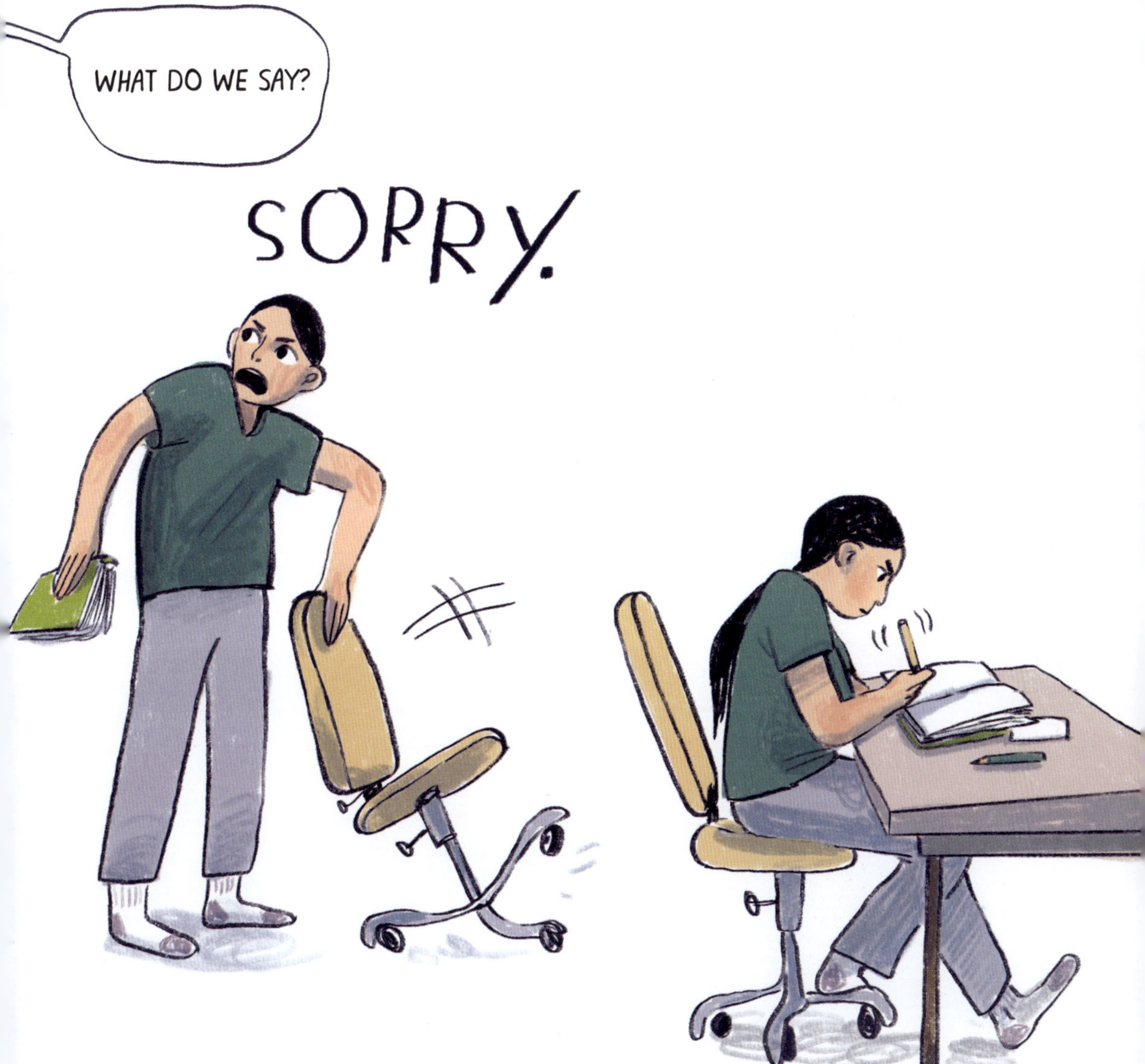
WHAT DO WE SAY?
SORRY.

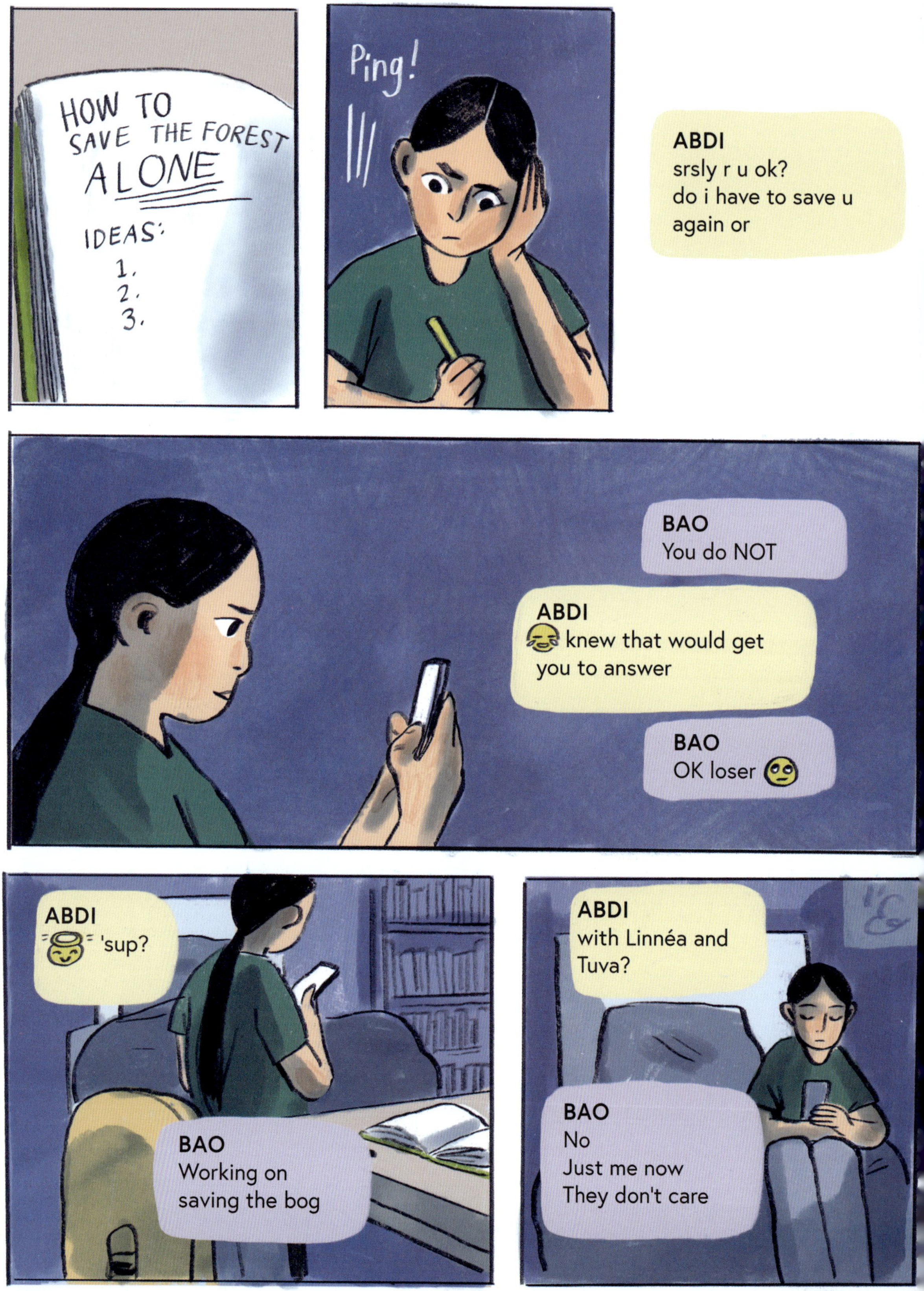
HOW TO SAVE THE FOREST ALONE
IDEAS:
1.
2.
3.
Ping!
ABDI
srsly r u ok?
do i have to save u again or
BAO
You do NOT
ABDI
knew that would get you to answer
BAO
OK loser
ABDI
'sup?
BAO
Working on saving the bog
ABDI
with Linnéa and Tuva?
BAO
No
Just me now
They don't care

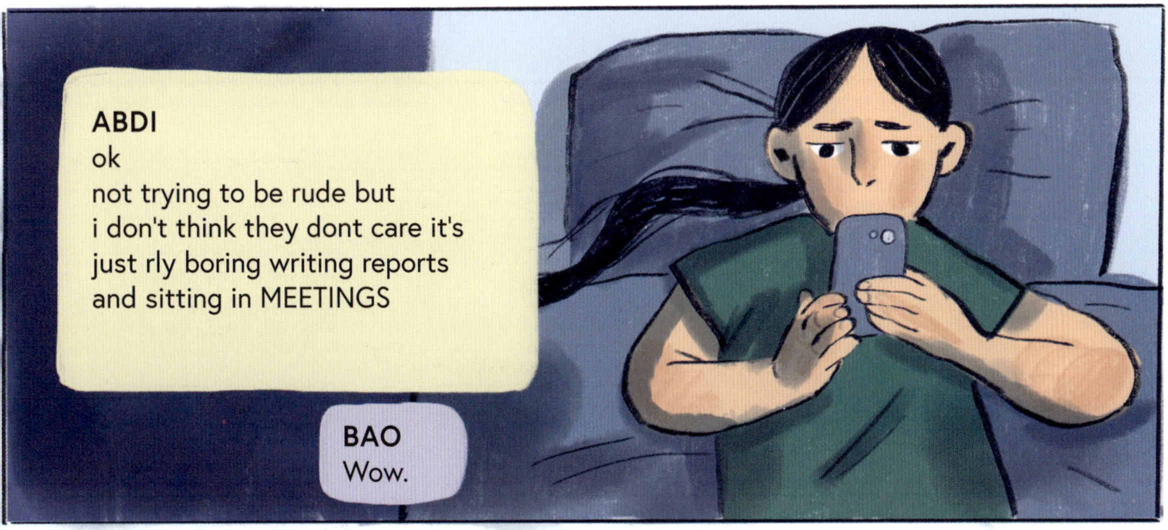
ABDI
ok
not trying to be rude but
i don't think they dont care it's
just rly boring writing reports
and sitting in MEETINGS
BAO
Wow.

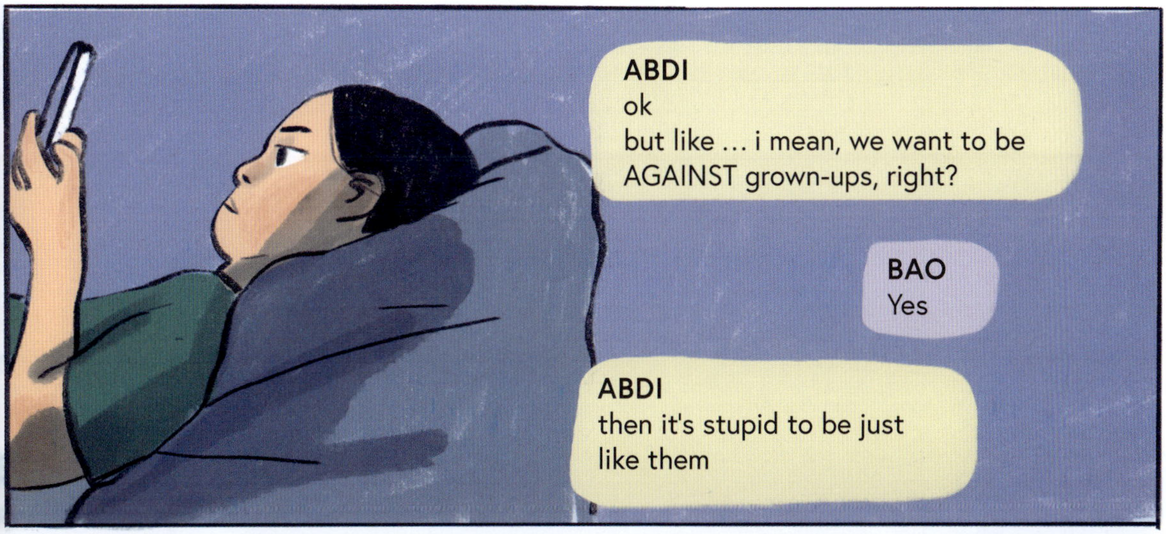
ABDI
ok
but like ... i mean, we want to be
AGAINST grown-ups, right?
BAO
Yes
ABDI
then it's stupid to be just
like them

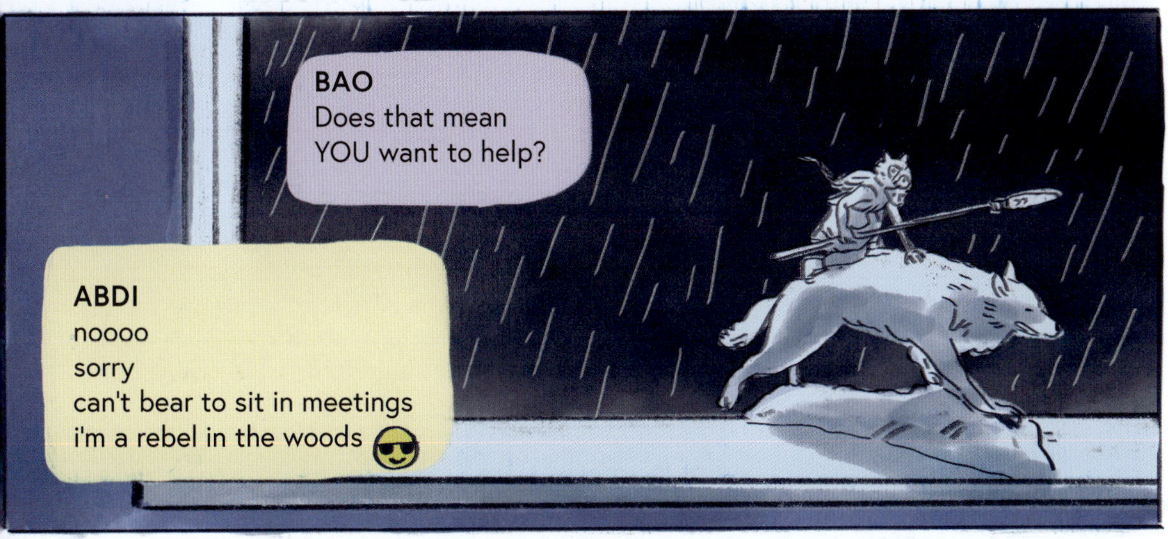
BAO
Does that mean
YOU want to help?
ABDI
noooo
sorry
can't bear to sit in meetings
i'm a rebel in the woods

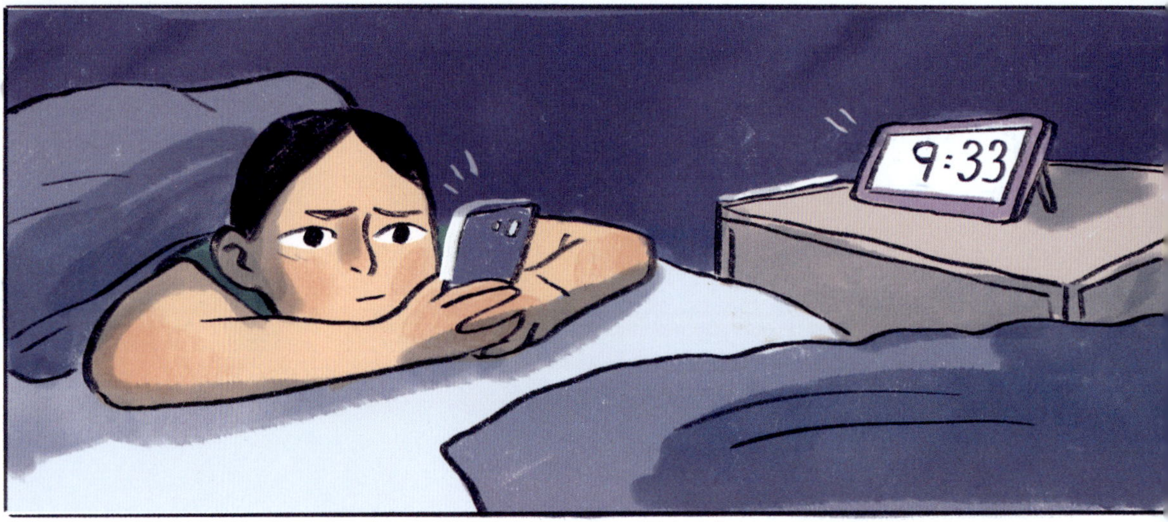
9:33

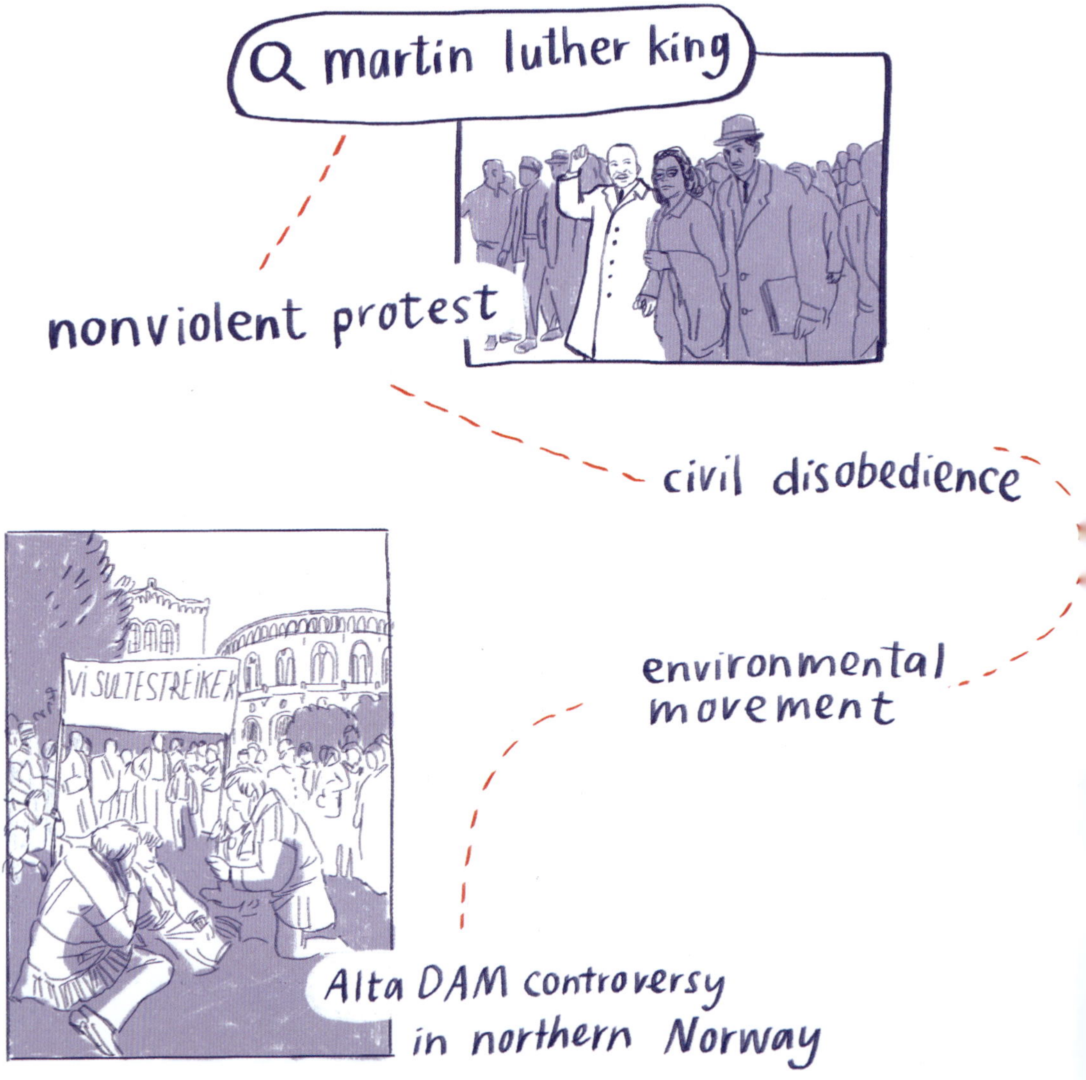
martin luther king
nonviolent protest
civil disobedience
environmental movement
VI SULTESTREIKER
Alta DAM controversy in northern Norway

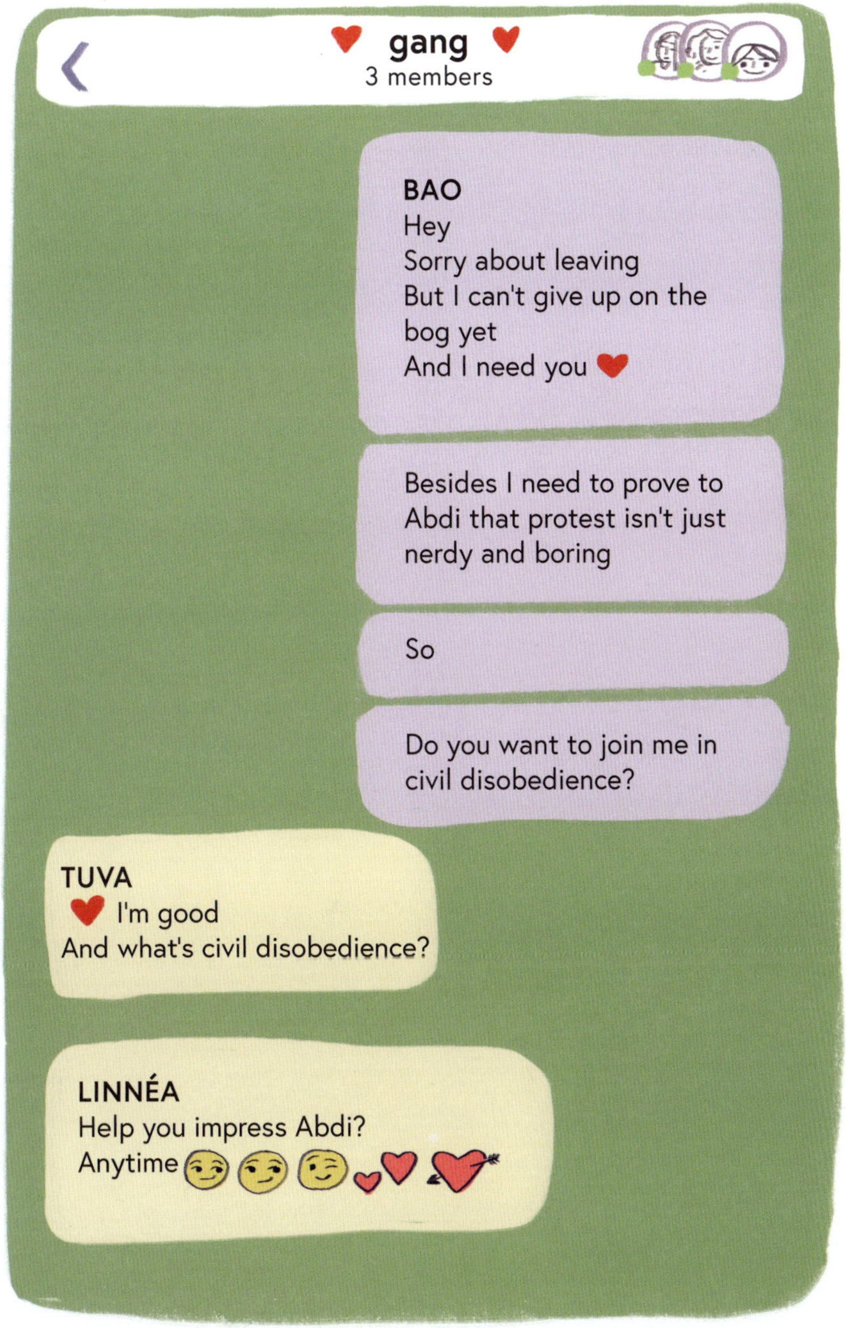
gang
3 members
BAO
Hey
Sorry about leaving
But I can't give up on the bog yet
And I need you
Besides I need to prove to Abdi that protest isn't just nerdy and boring
So
Do you want to join me in civil disobedience?
TUVA
I'm good
And what's civil disobedience?
LINNÉA
Help you impress Abdi?
Anytime

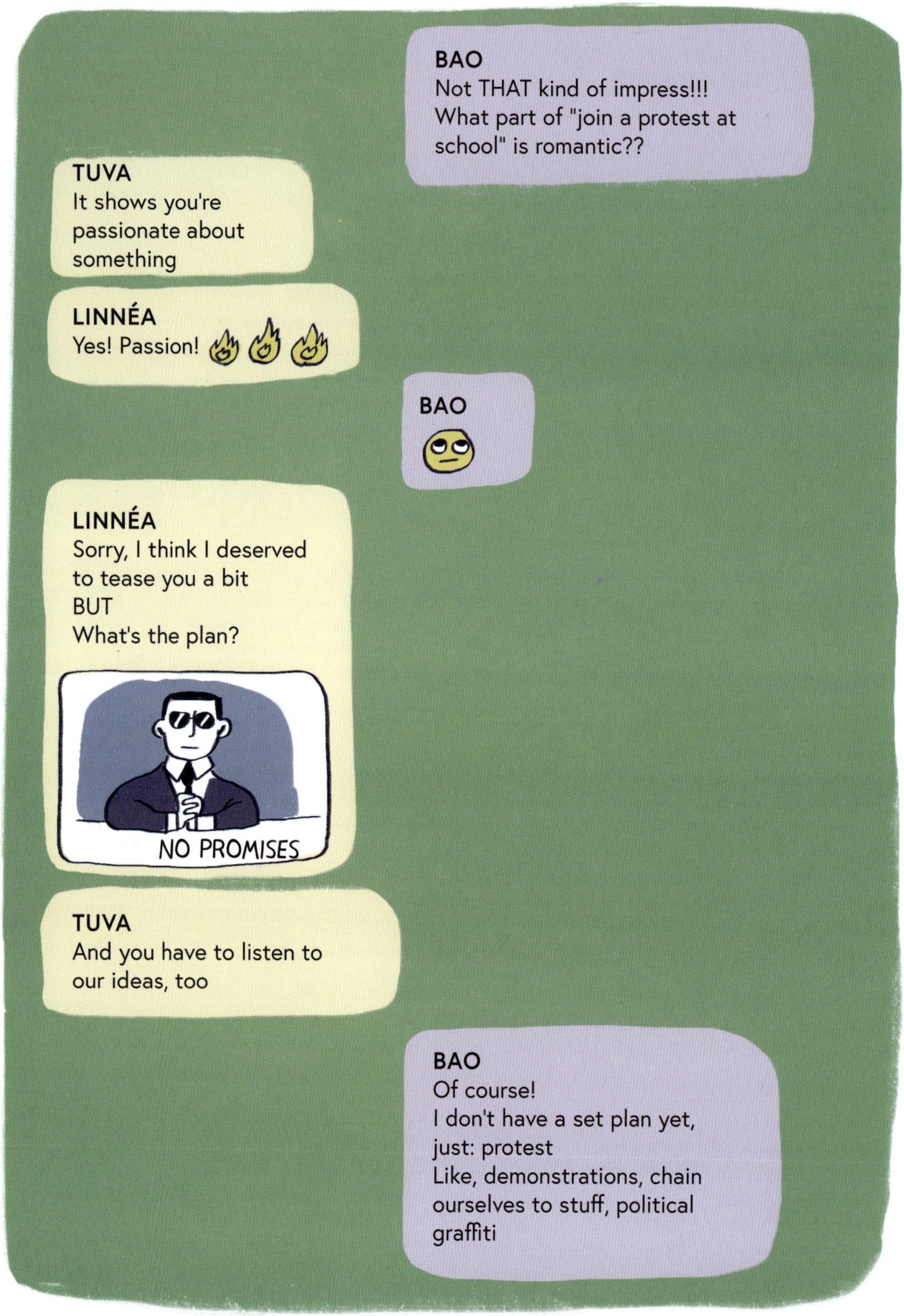
BAO
Not THAT kind of impress!!!
What part of "join a protest at school" is romantic??
TUVA
It shows you're passionate about something
LINNÉA
Yes! Passion!
BAO
LINNÉA
Sorry, I think I deserved to tease you a bit
BUT
What's the plan?
NO PROMISES
TUVA
And you have to listen to our ideas, too
BAO
Of course!
I don't have a set plan yet, just: protest
Like, demonstrations, chain ourselves to stuff, political graffiti

TUVA
But graffiti is illegal

BAO
That's the point! You have to break rules on purpose to get attention for a cause

LINNÉA
Oooh
Intriguing

Stalking Greenpeace on IG now

Okok: idea!
V basic, but it looks cool and is something the three of us can do

BAO
 What?

LINNÉA
Put up a banner, but in a really high up and annoying place, so they can't take it down right away and then I'll stream it live on IG

TUVA
Ooooooooh

LINNÉA
But uh
Someone has to climb
Really high

BAO

Don't you worry about that

LINNÉA
WHAT is that

BAO
My alter ego Red Squirrel!
Can climb anything, always fights
for the trees 🍃🥦✨

TUVA

BAO
So they won't recognize me

LINNÉA
... It will be MEMORABLE for sure

TUVA
Hahaha

TUVA
I asked Dad about protest and stuff
(he revealed nothing)

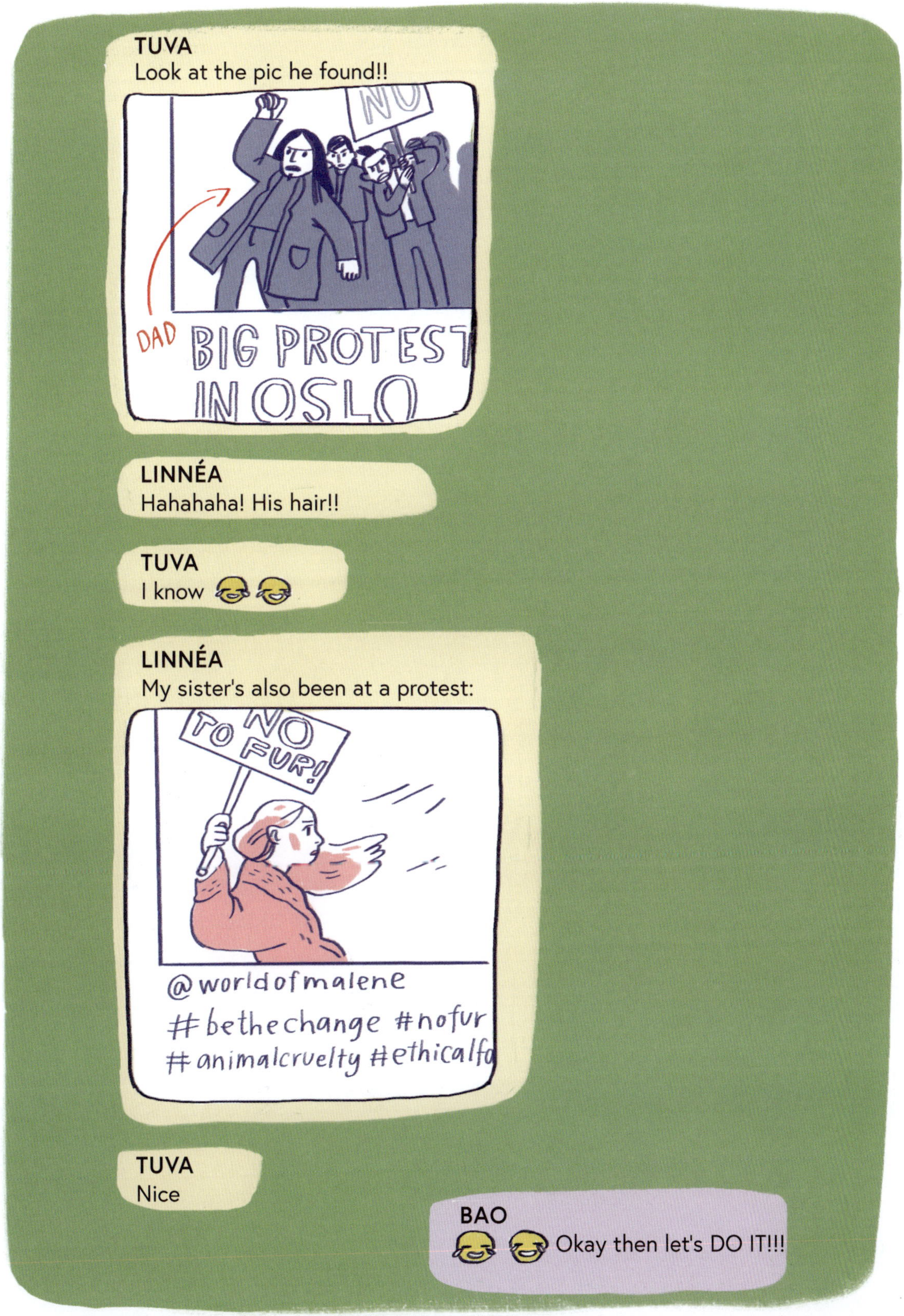
TUVA
Look at the pic he found!!
NO
DAD
BIG PROTEST
IN OSLO
LINNÉA
Hahahaha! His hair!!
TUVA
I know
LINNÉA
My sister's also been at a protest:
NO TO FUR!
@worldofmalene
#bethechange #nofur
#animalcruelty #ethicalfa
TUVA
Nice
BAO
Okay then let's DO IT!!!

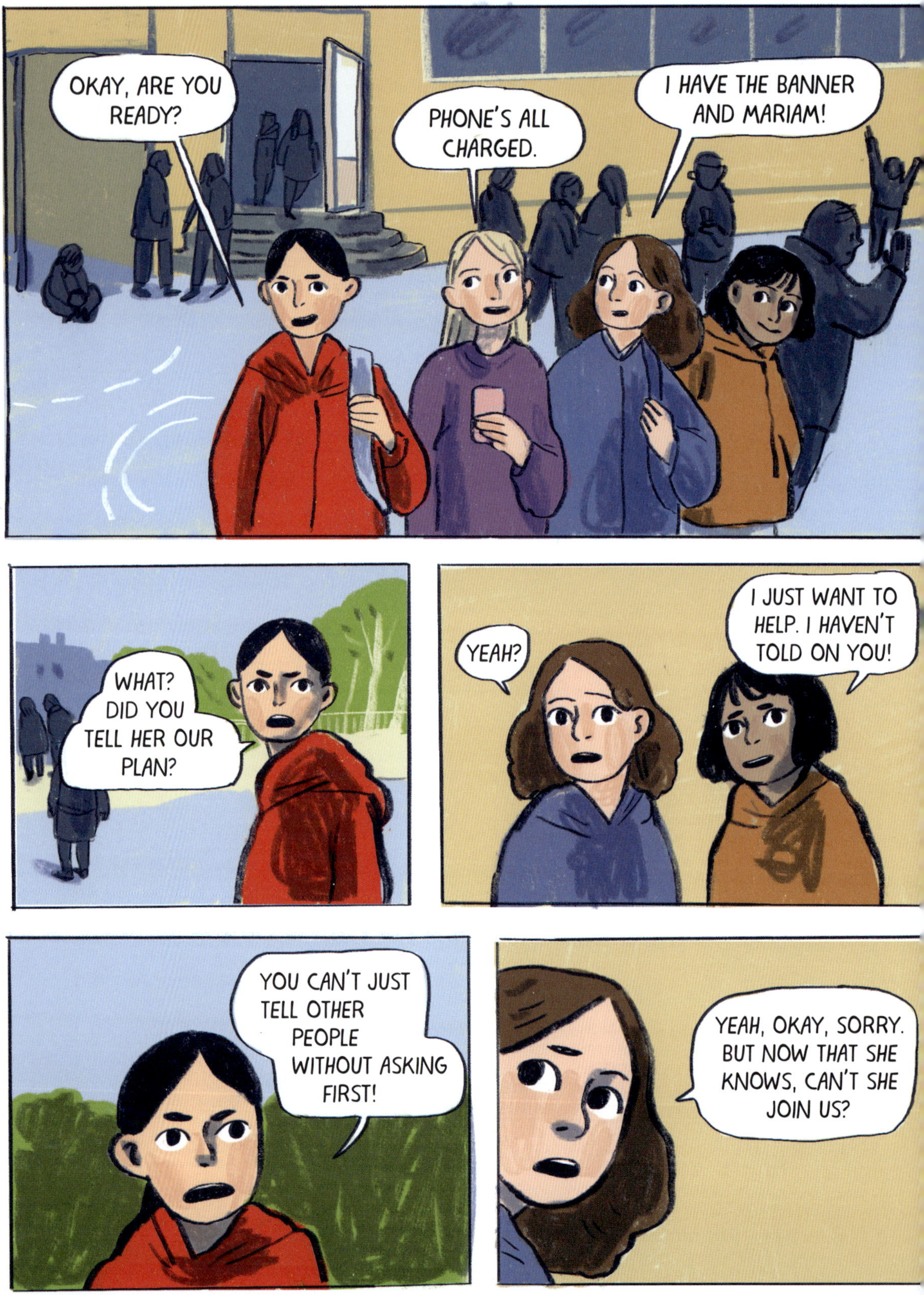
OKAY, ARE YOU READY?
PHONE'S ALL CHARGED.
I HAVE THE BANNER AND MARIAM!
WHAT? DID YOU TELL HER OUR PLAN?
YEAH?
I JUST WANT TO HELP. I HAVEN'T TOLD ON YOU!
YOU CAN'T JUST TELL OTHER PEOPLE WITHOUT ASKING FIRST!
YEAH, OKAY, SORRY. BUT NOW THAT SHE KNOWS, CAN'T SHE JOIN US?

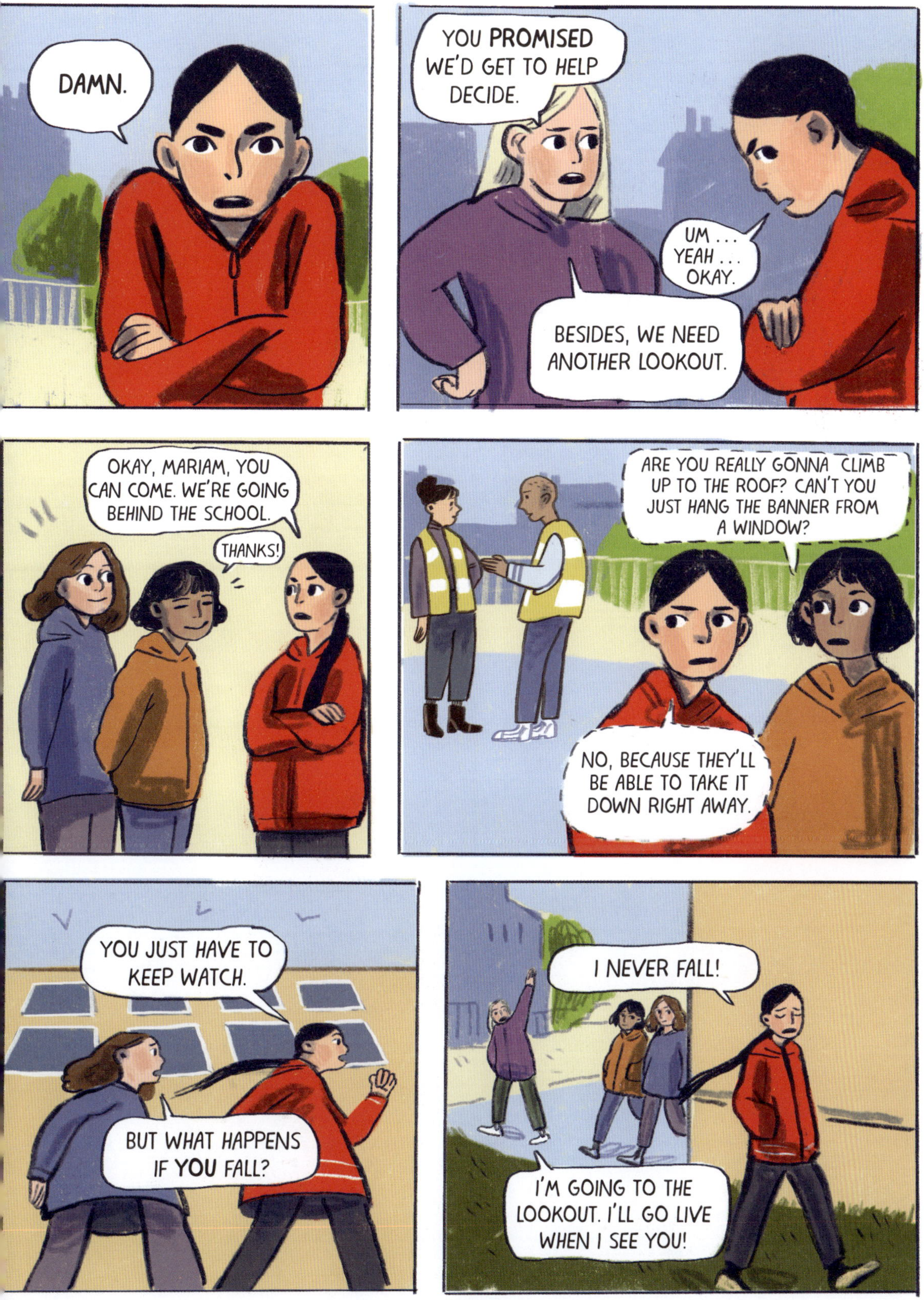
DAMN.
YOU PROMISED WE'D GET TO HELP DECIDE.
UM . . . YEAH . . . OKAY.
BESIDES, WE NEED ANOTHER LOOKOUT.
OKAY, MARIAM, YOU CAN COME. WE'RE GOING BEHIND THE SCHOOL.
THANKS!
ARE YOU REALLY GONNA CLIMB UP TO THE ROOF? CAN'T YOU JUST HANG THE BANNER FROM A WINDOW?
NO, BECAUSE THEY'LL BE ABLE TO TAKE IT DOWN RIGHT AWAY.
YOU JUST HAVE TO KEEP WATCH.
BUT WHAT HAPPENS IF YOU FALL?
I NEVER FALL!
I'M GOING TO THE LOOKOUT. I'LL GO LIVE WHEN I SEE YOU!

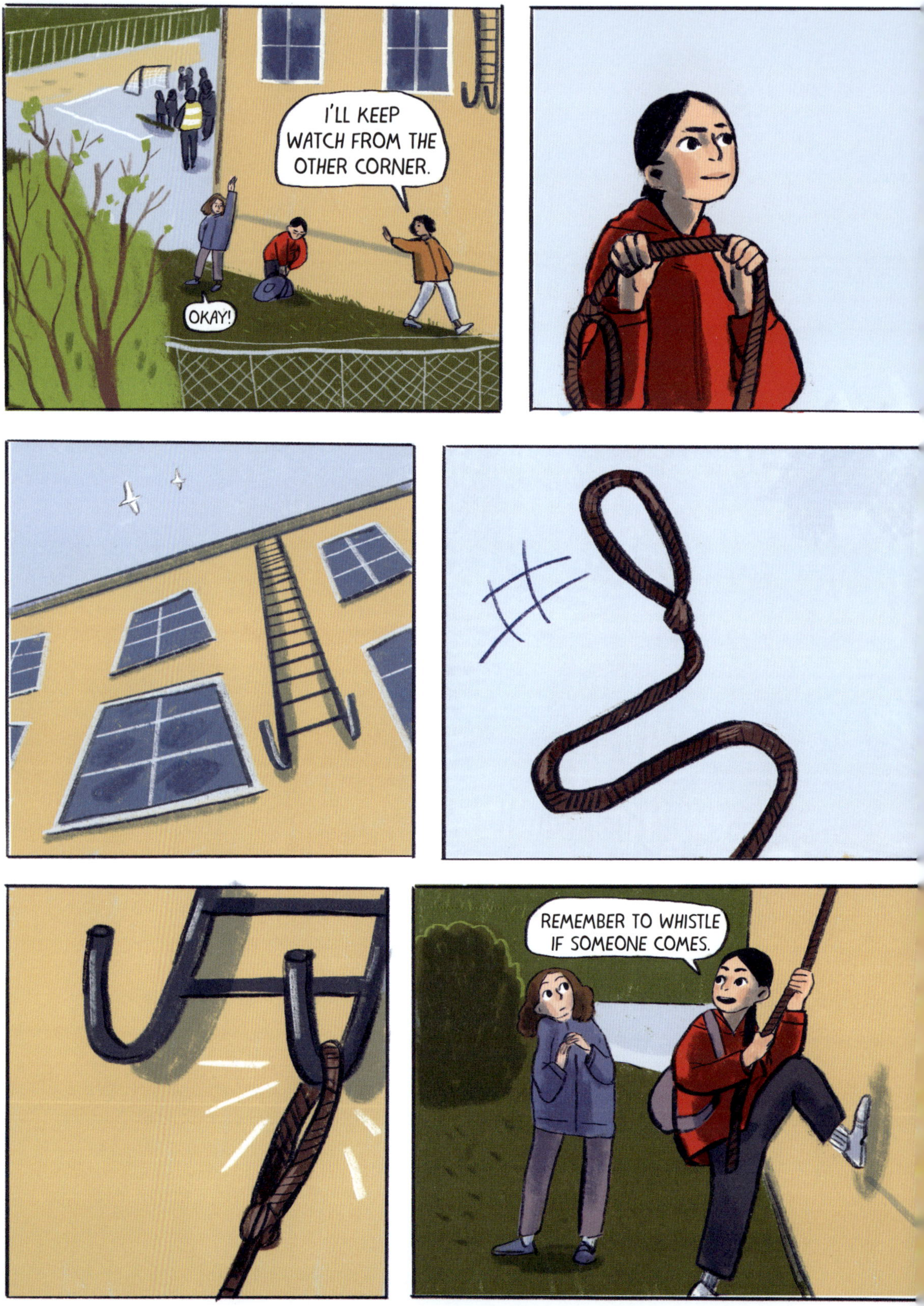
I'LL KEEP WATCH FROM THE OTHER CORNER.
OKAY!
REMEMBER TO WHISTLE IF SOMEONE COMES.

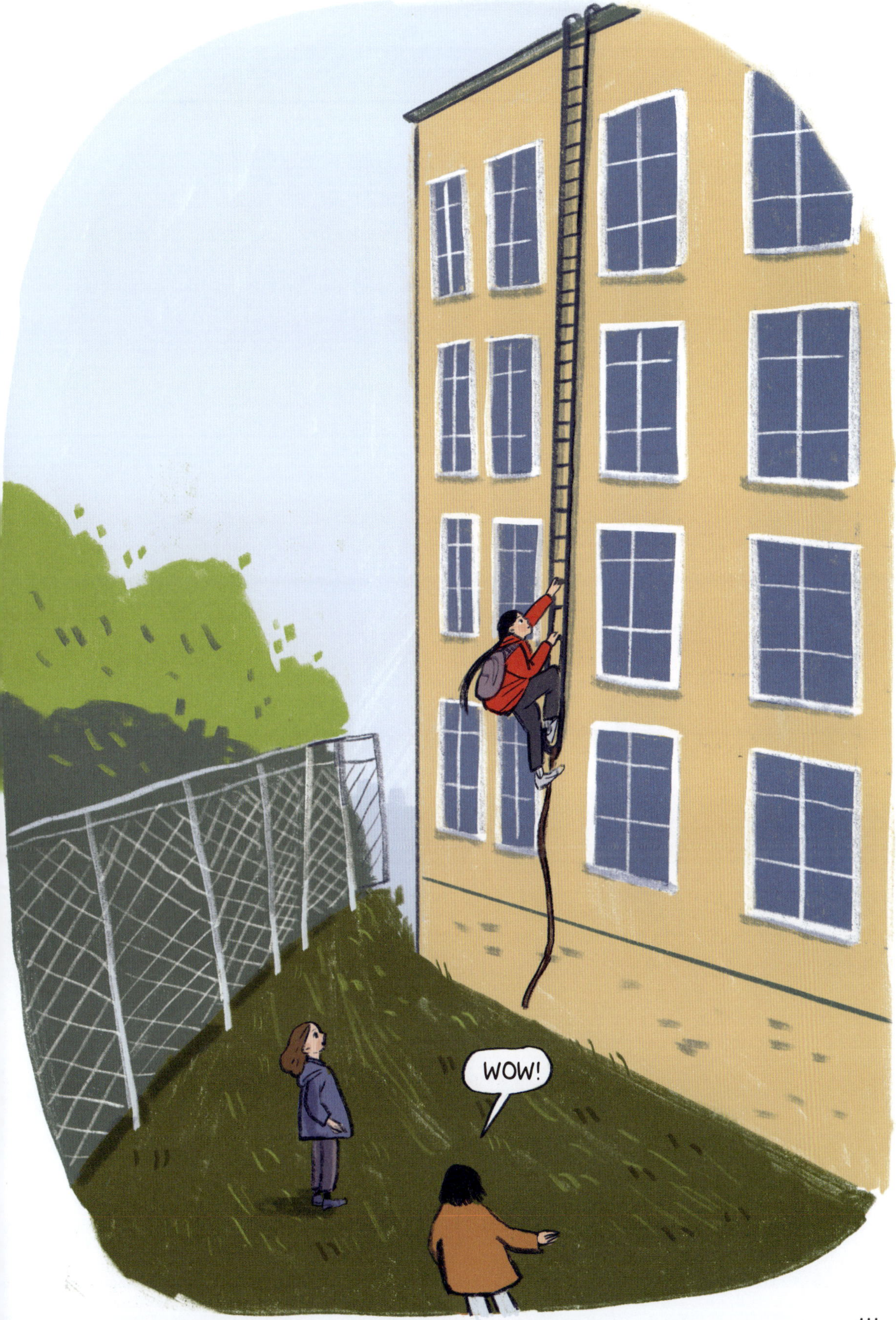
WOW!

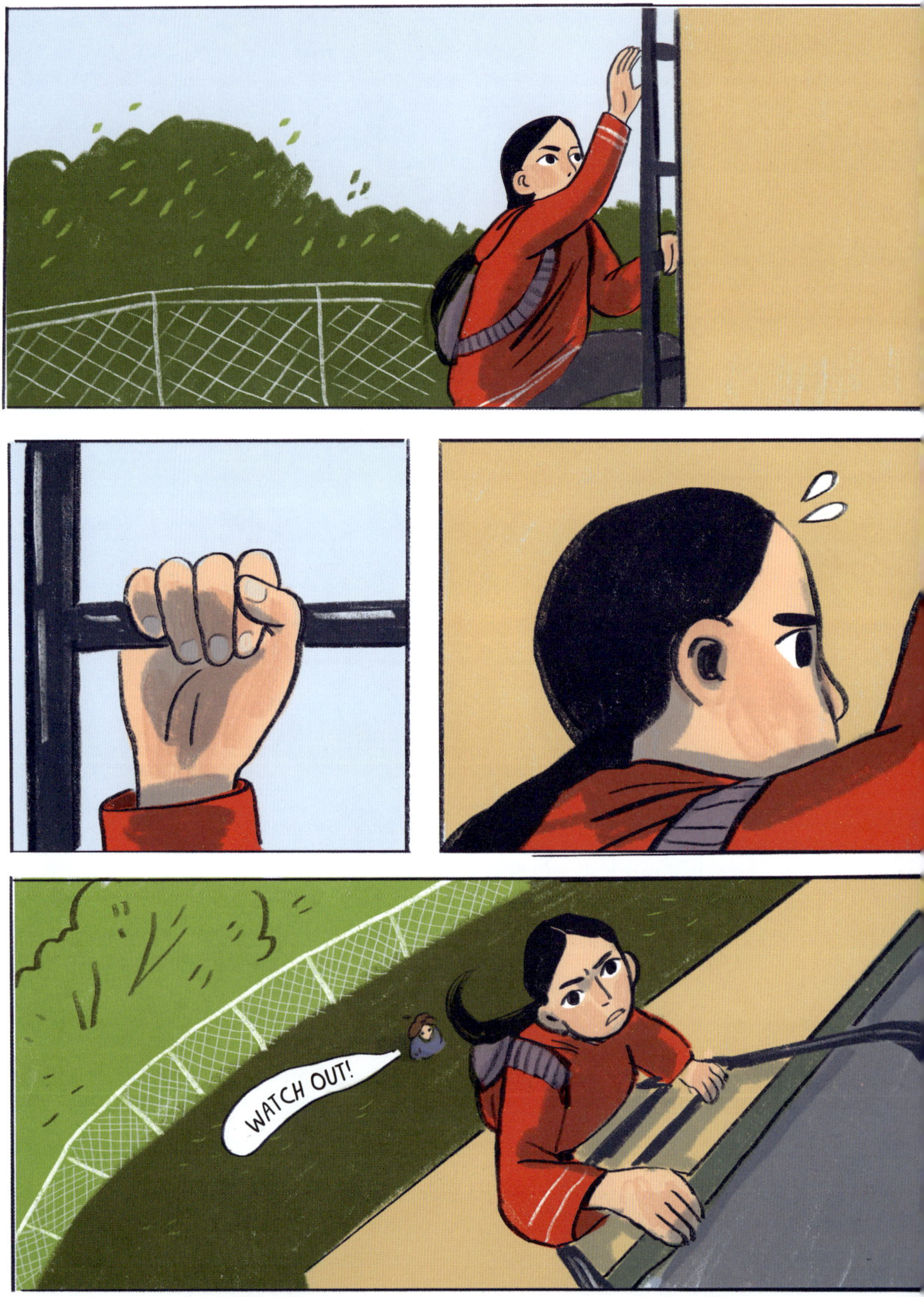
WATCH OUT!

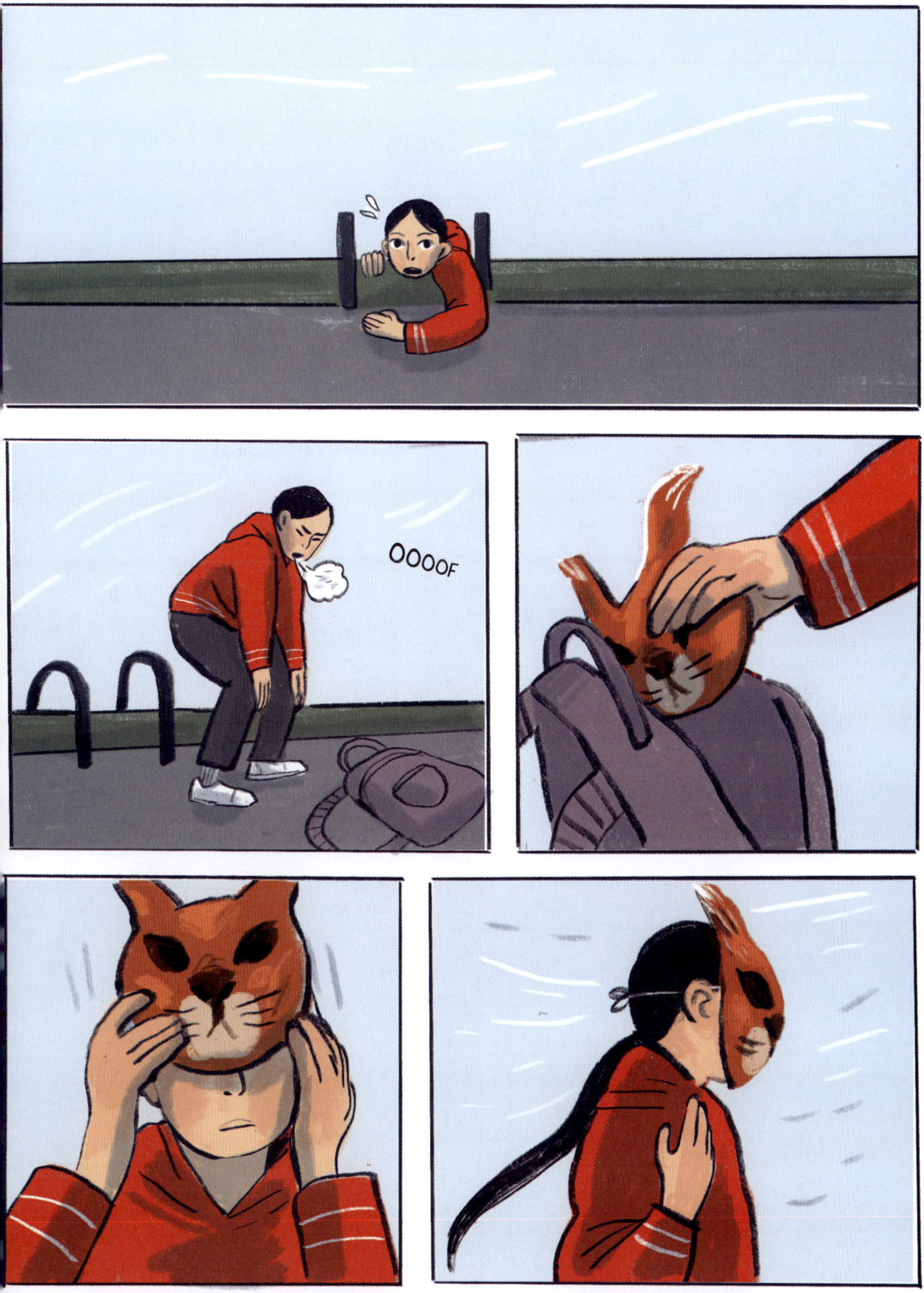
OOOOF

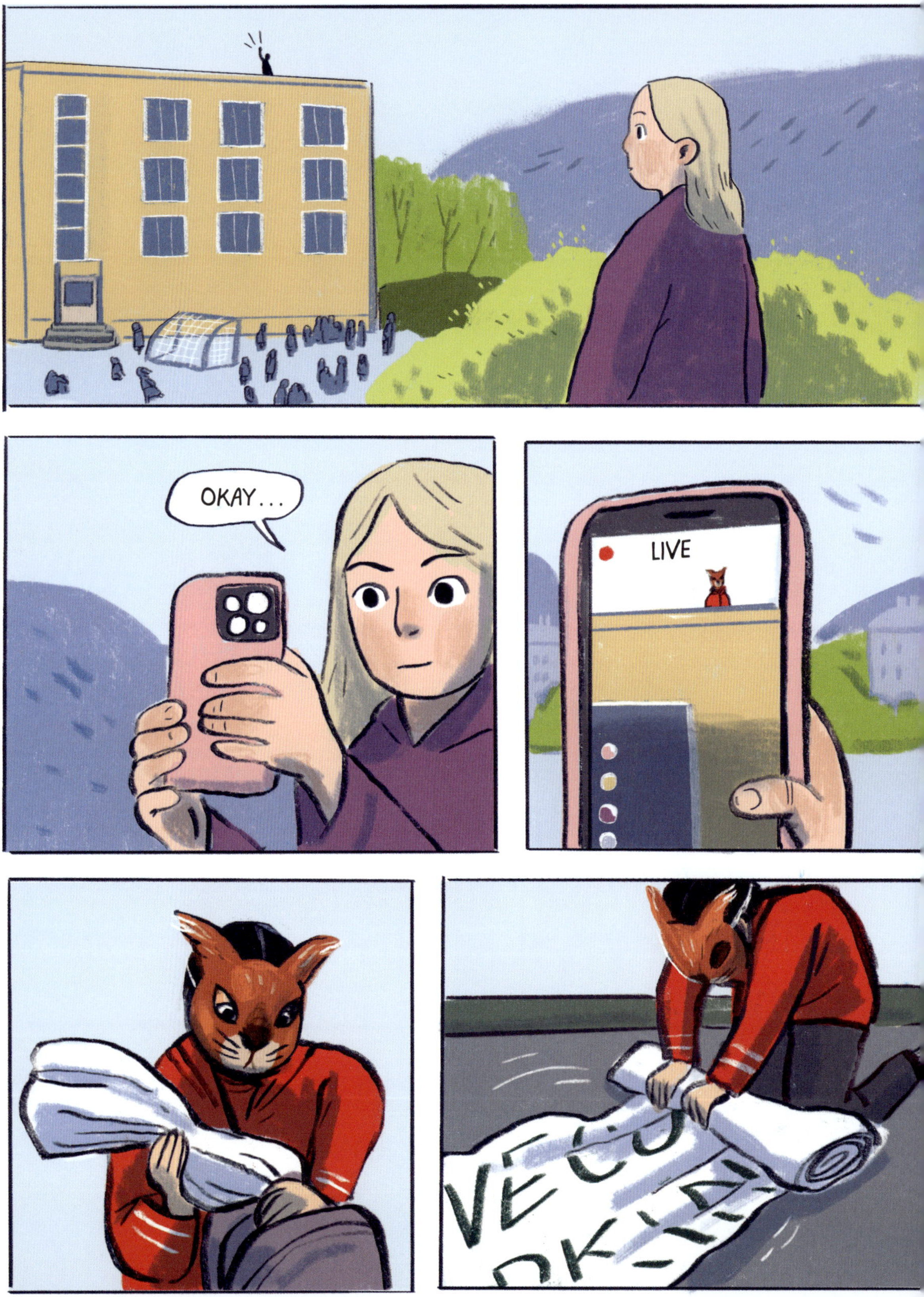
OKAY...
LIVE

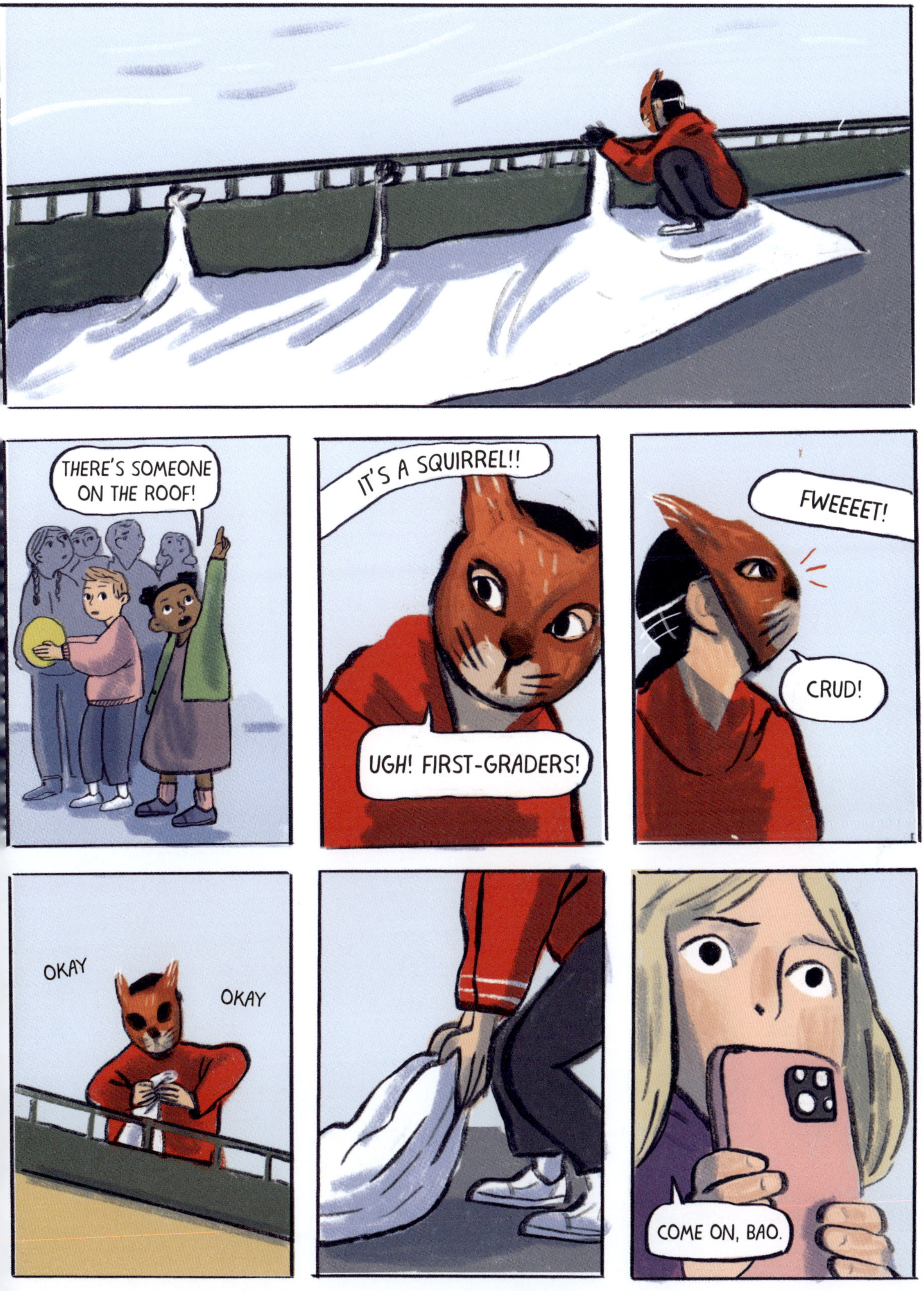
THERE'S SOMEONE ON THE ROOF!
IT'S A SQUIRREL!!
UGH! FIRST-GRADERS!
FWEEEET!
CRUD!
OKAY
OKAY
COME ON, BAO.

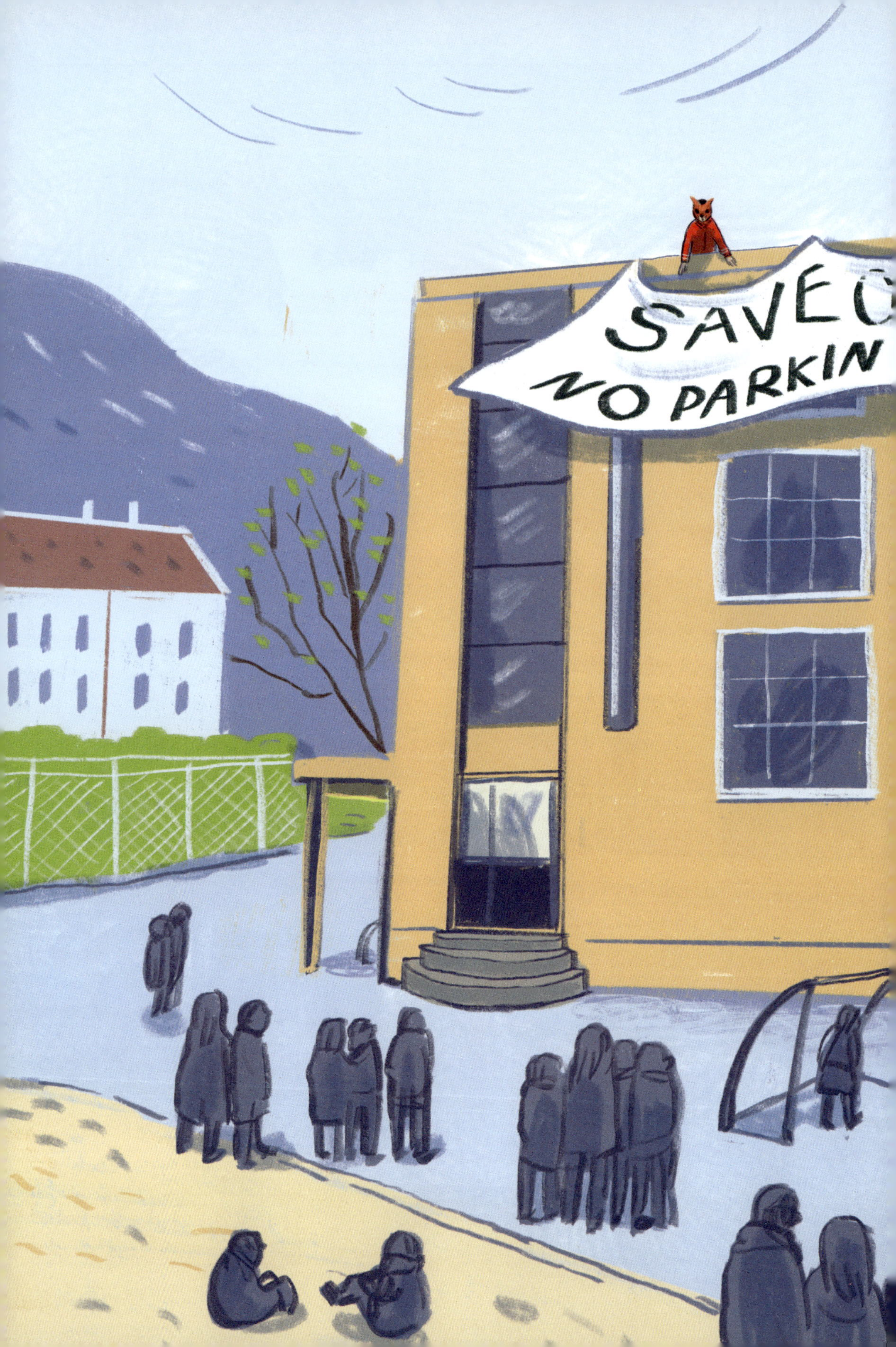
SAVE
NO PARKIN

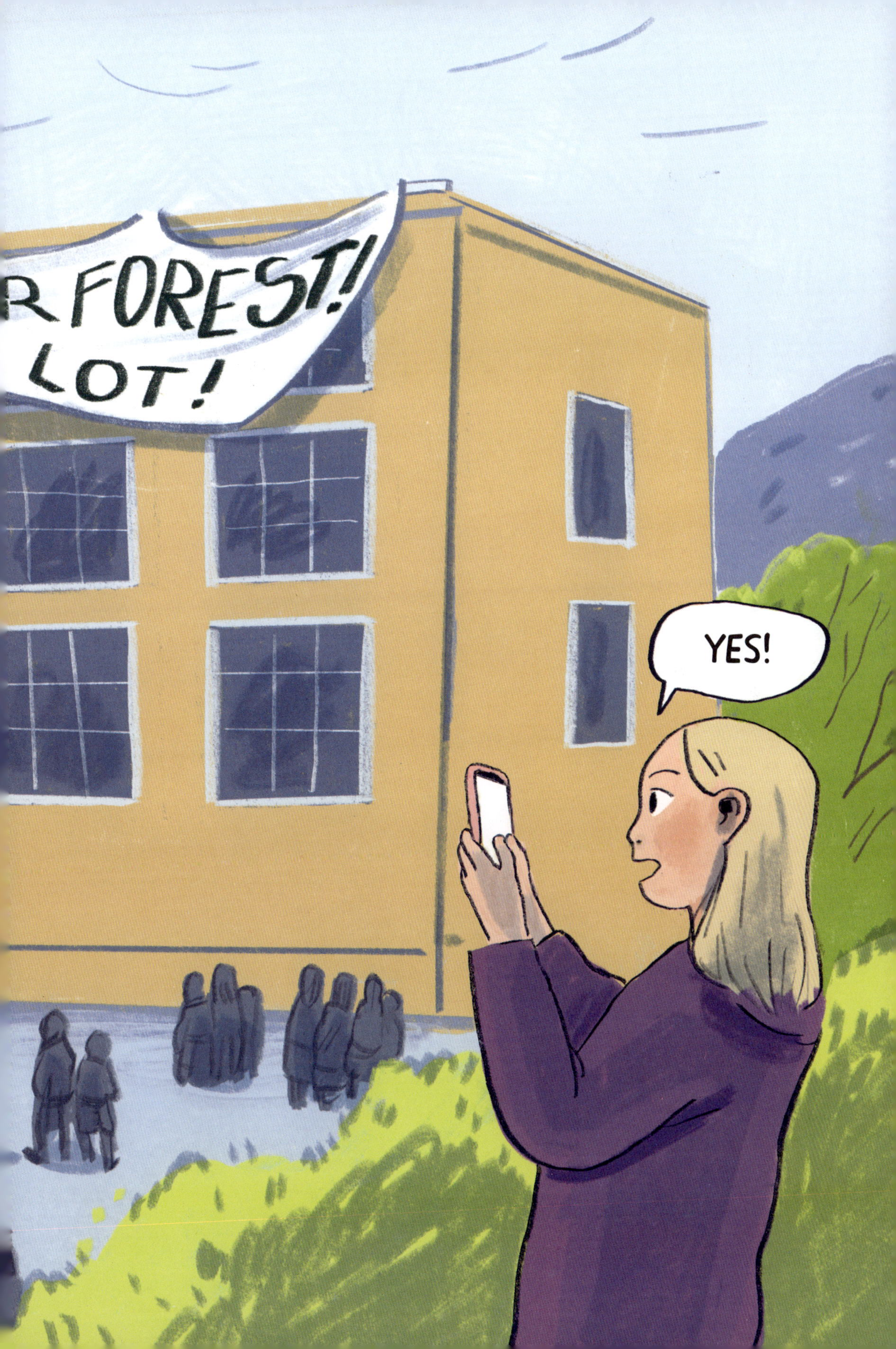
R FOREST!
LOT!
YES!

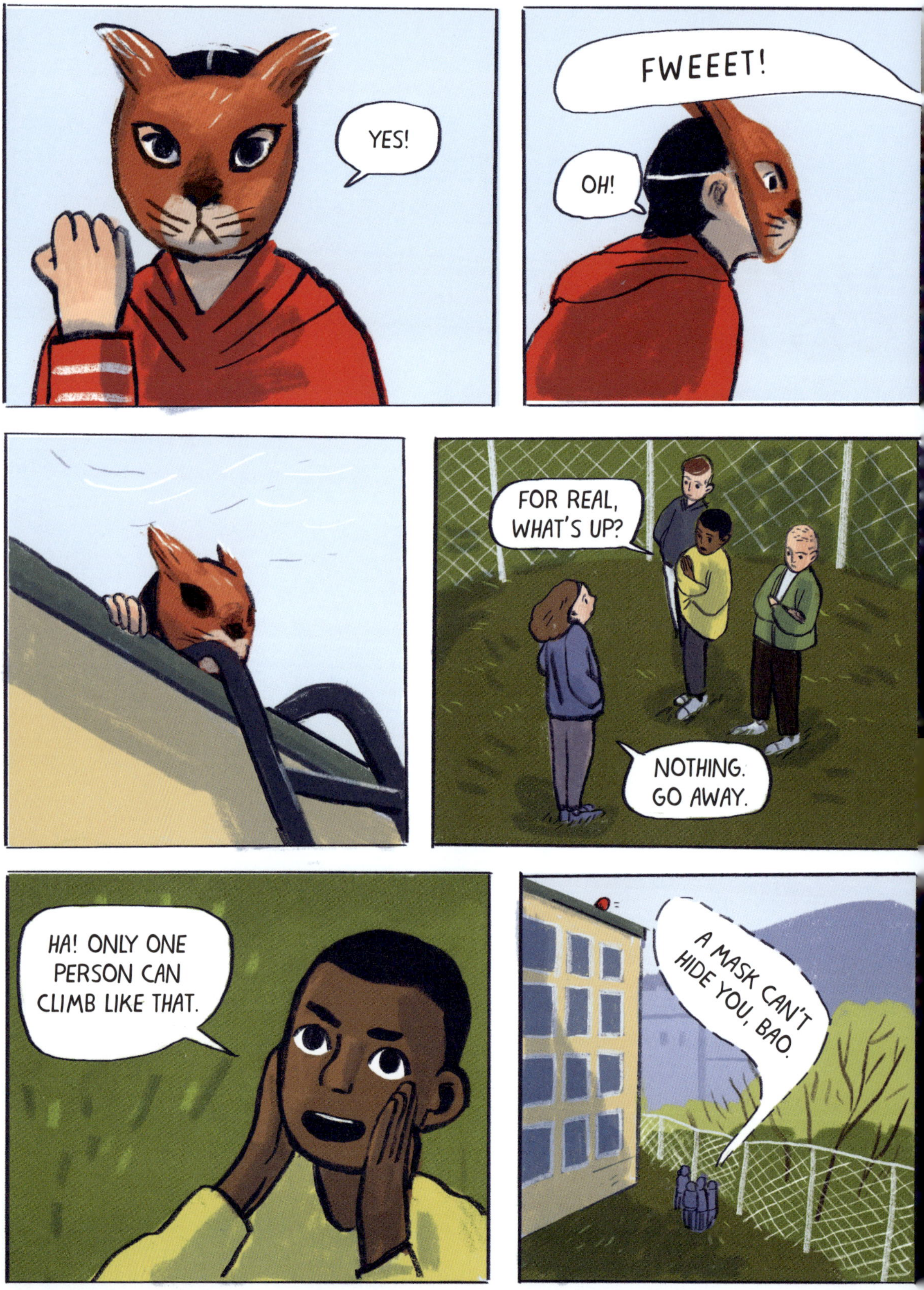
YES!
FWEEET!
OH!
FOR REAL, WHAT'S UP?
NOTHING. GO AWAY.
HA! ONLY ONE PERSON CAN CLIMB LIKE THAT.
A MASK CAN'T HIDE YOU, BAO.

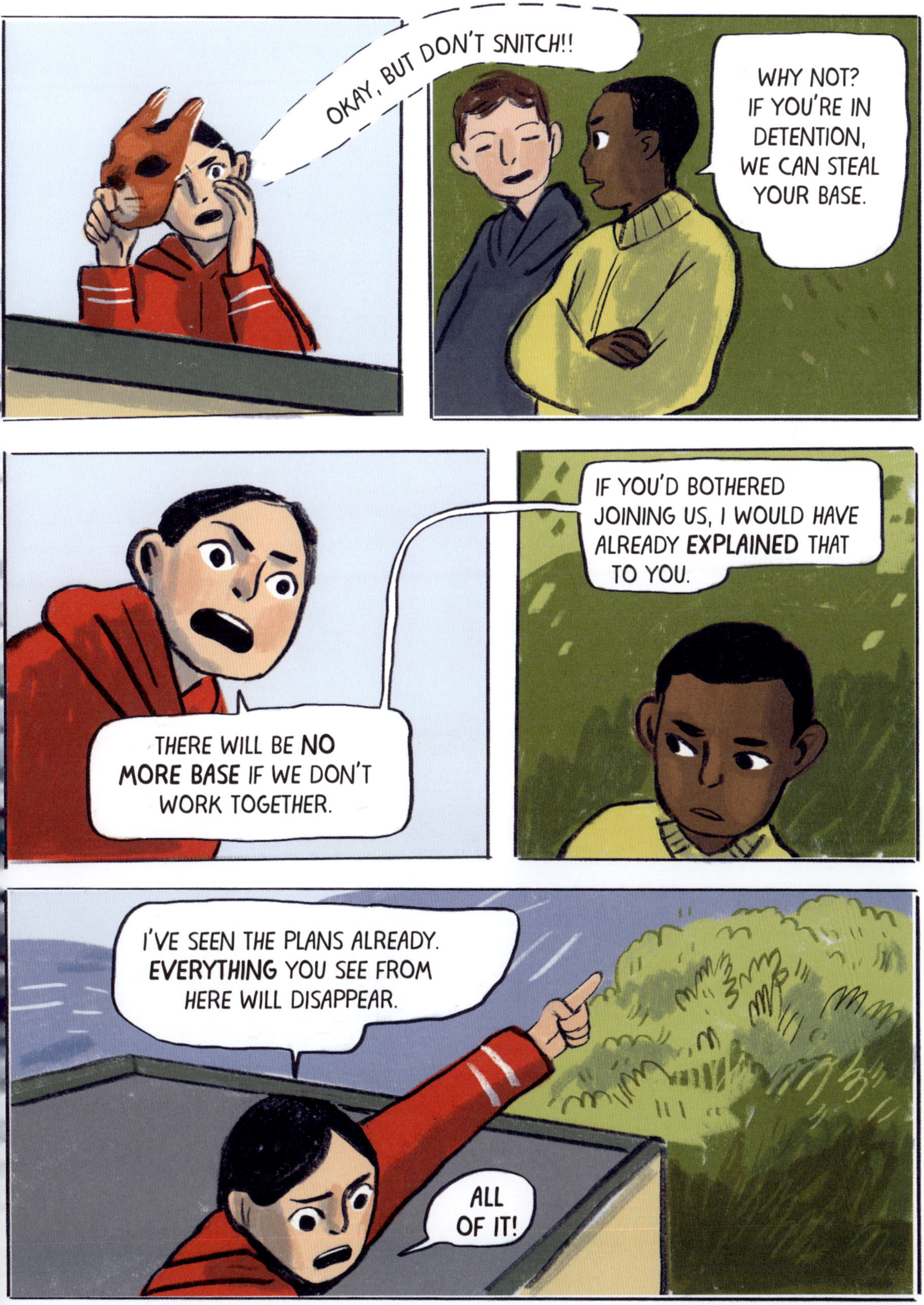
OKAY, BUT DON'T SNITCH!!
WHY NOT? IF YOU'RE IN DETENTION, WE CAN STEAL YOUR BASE.
THERE WILL BE **NO MORE BASE** IF WE DON'T WORK TOGETHER.
IF YOU'D BOTHERED JOINING US, I WOULD HAVE ALREADY **EXPLAINED** THAT TO YOU.
I'VE SEEN THE PLANS ALREADY. **EVERYTHING** YOU SEE FROM HERE WILL DISAPPEAR.
ALL OF IT!

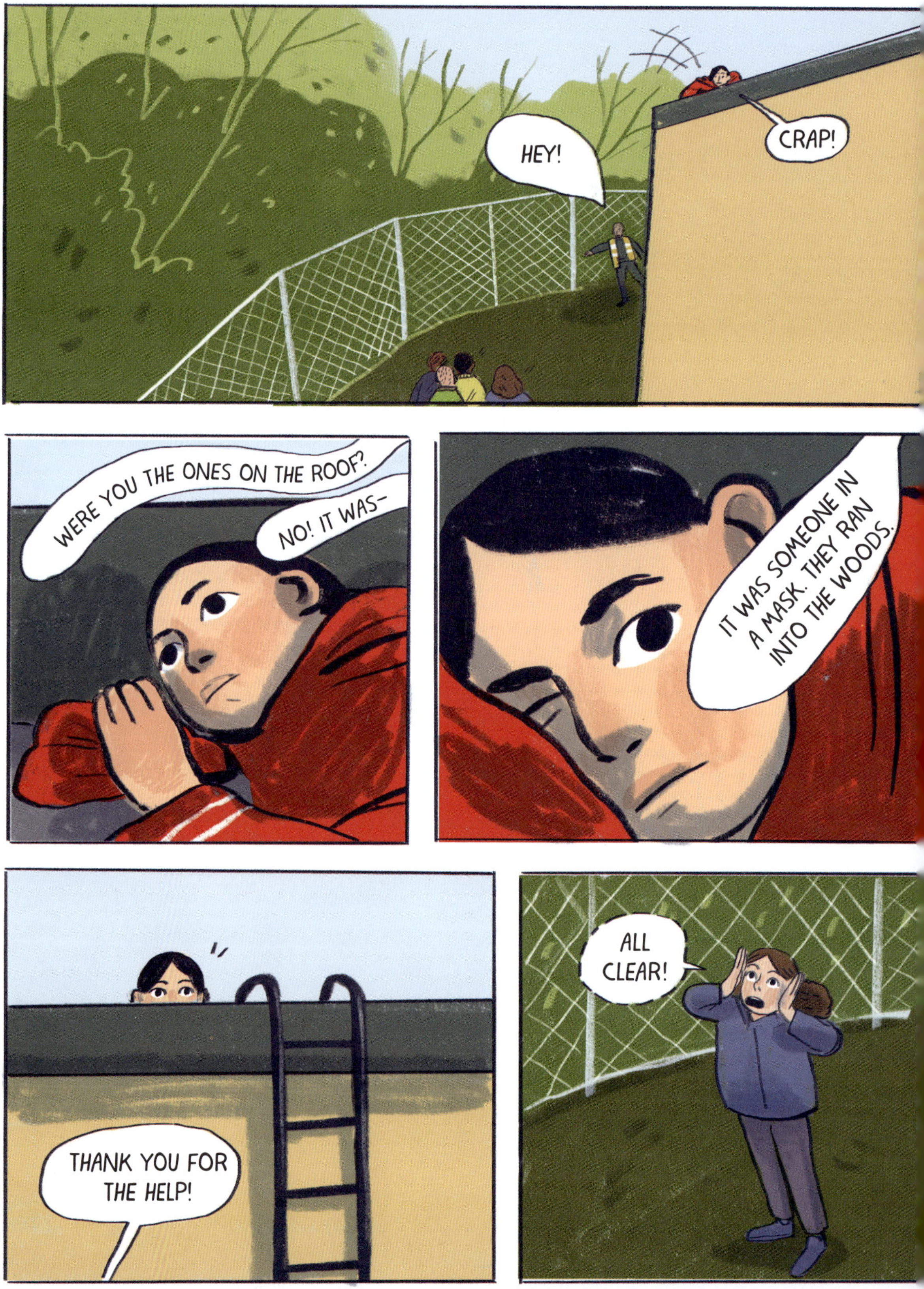
HEY!
CRAP!
WERE YOU THE ONES ON THE ROOF?
NO! IT WAS-
IT WAS SOMEONE IN A MASK. THEY RAN INTO THE WOODS.
THANK YOU FOR THE HELP!
ALL CLEAR!

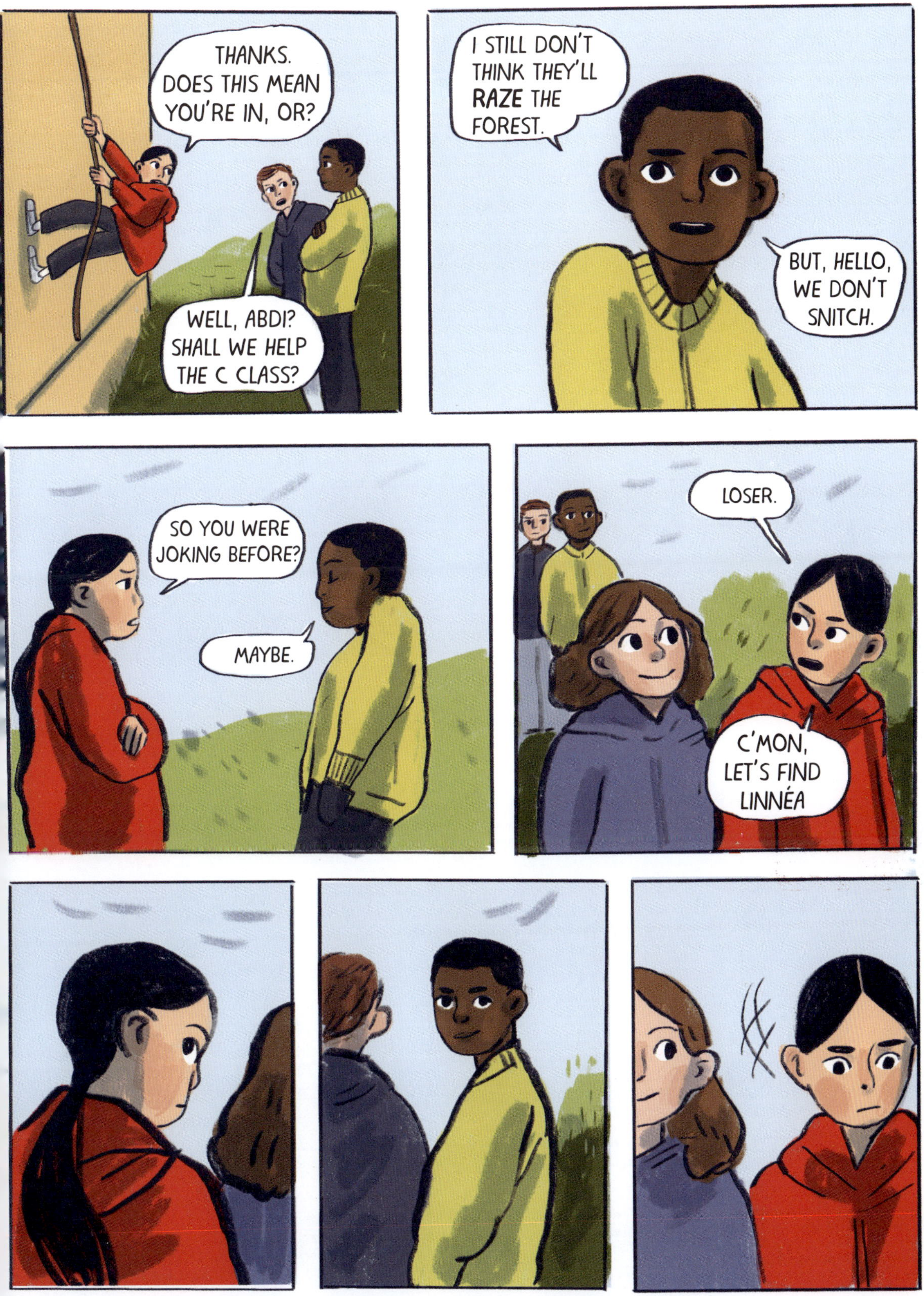
THANKS. DOES THIS MEAN YOU'RE IN, OR?
WELL, ABDI? SHALL WE HELP THE C CLASS?
I STILL DON'T THINK THEY'LL **RAZE** THE FOREST.
BUT, HELLO, WE DON'T SNITCH.
SO YOU WERE JOKING BEFORE?
MAYBE.
LOSER.
C'MON, LET'S FIND LINNÉA

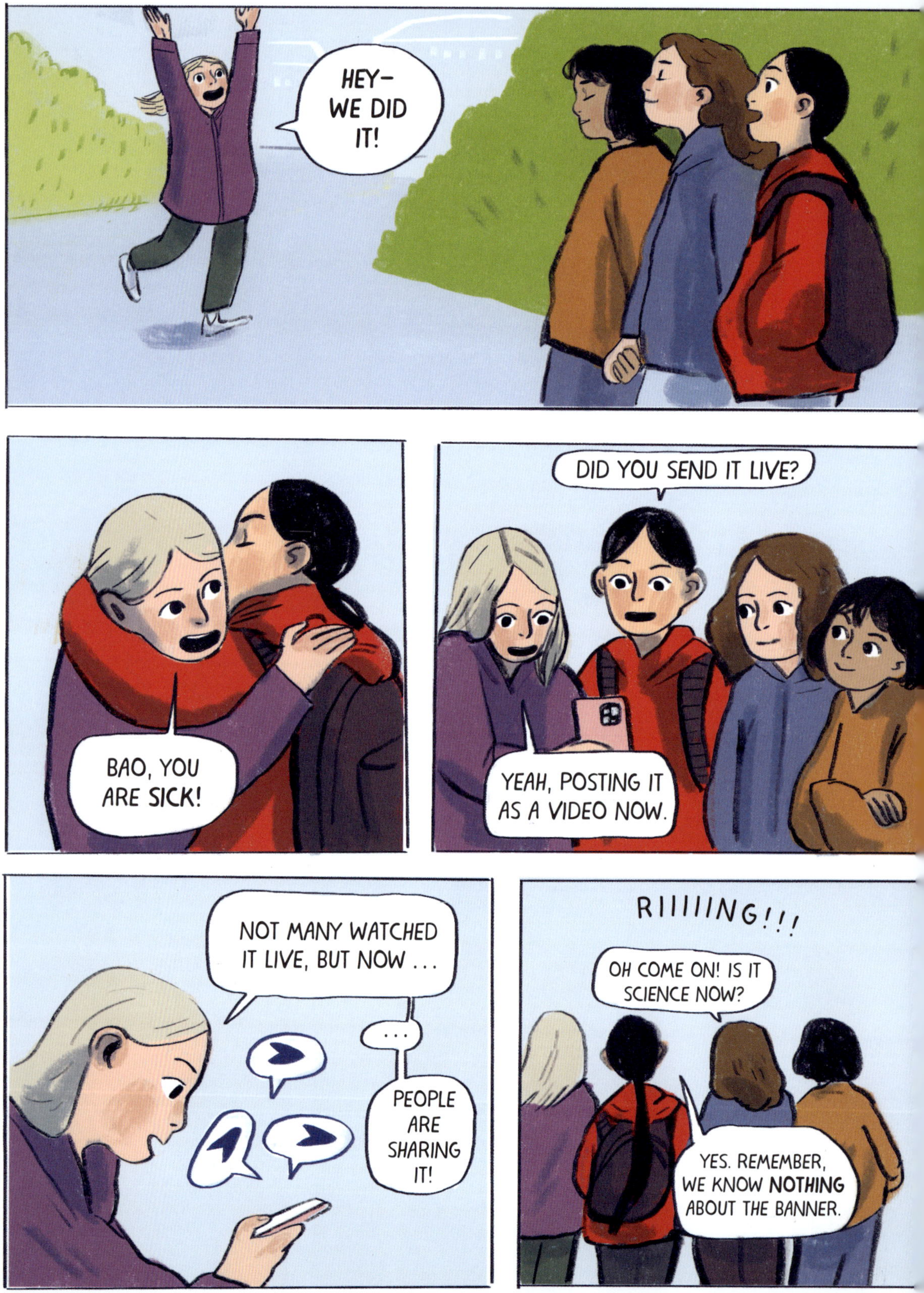
HEY—
WE DID
IT!
BAO, YOU
ARE **SICK**!
DID YOU SEND IT LIVE?
YEAH, POSTING IT
AS A VIDEO NOW.
NOT MANY WATCHED
IT LIVE, BUT NOW . . .
. . .
PEOPLE
ARE
SHARING
IT!
RIIIIING!!!
OH COME ON! IS IT
SCIENCE NOW?
YES. REMEMBER,
WE KNOW **NOTHING**
ABOUT THE BANNER.

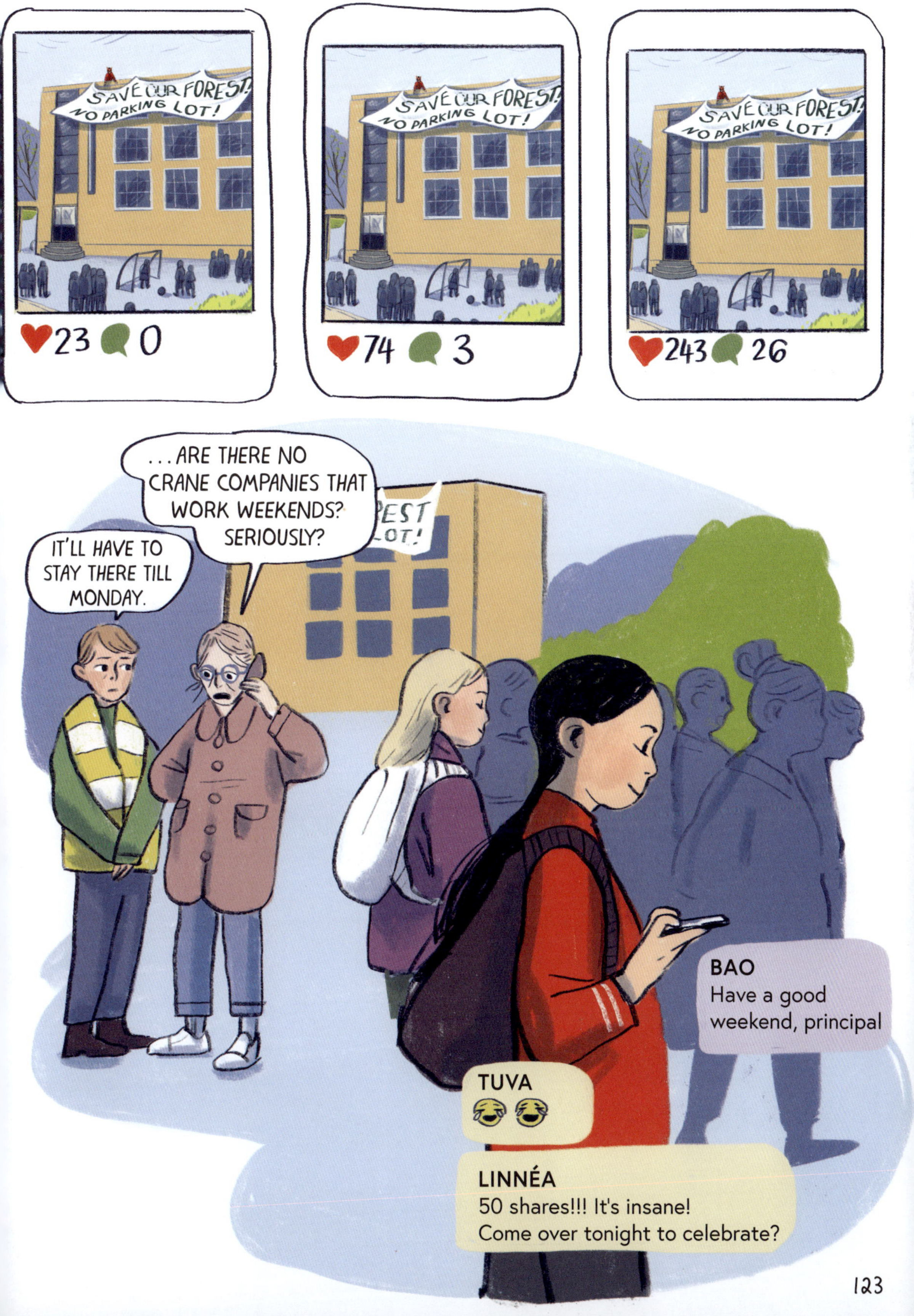
SAVE OUR FOREST! NO PARKING LOT!
23 0
SAVE OUR FOREST! NO PARKING LOT!
74 3
SAVE OUR FOREST! NO PARKING LOT!
243 26
...ARE THERE NO CRANE COMPANIES THAT WORK WEEKENDS? SERIOUSLY?
IT'LL HAVE TO STAY THERE TILL MONDAY.
BAO
Have a good weekend, principal
TUVA
LINNÉA
50 shares!!! It's insane!
Come over tonight to celebrate?

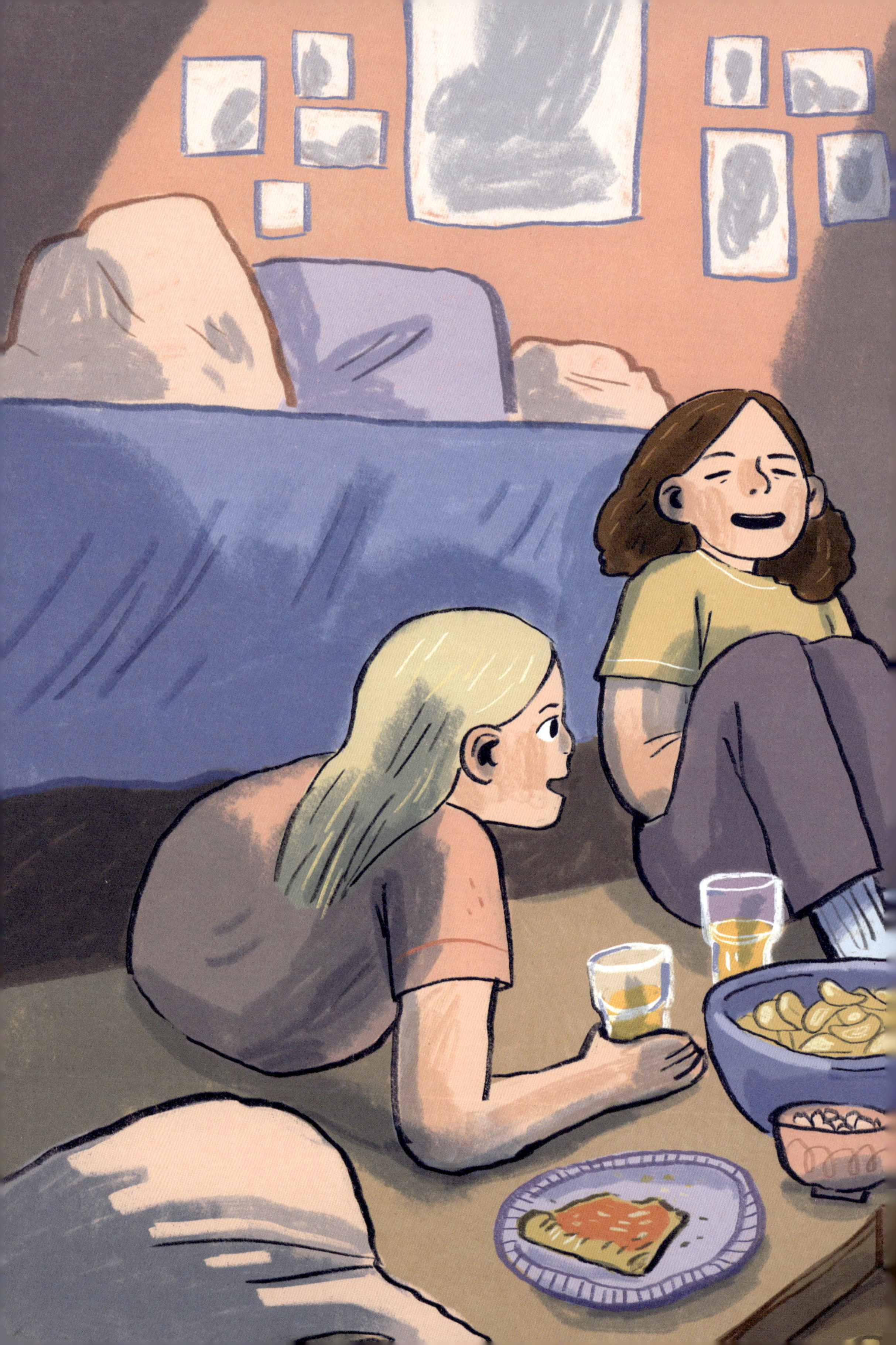

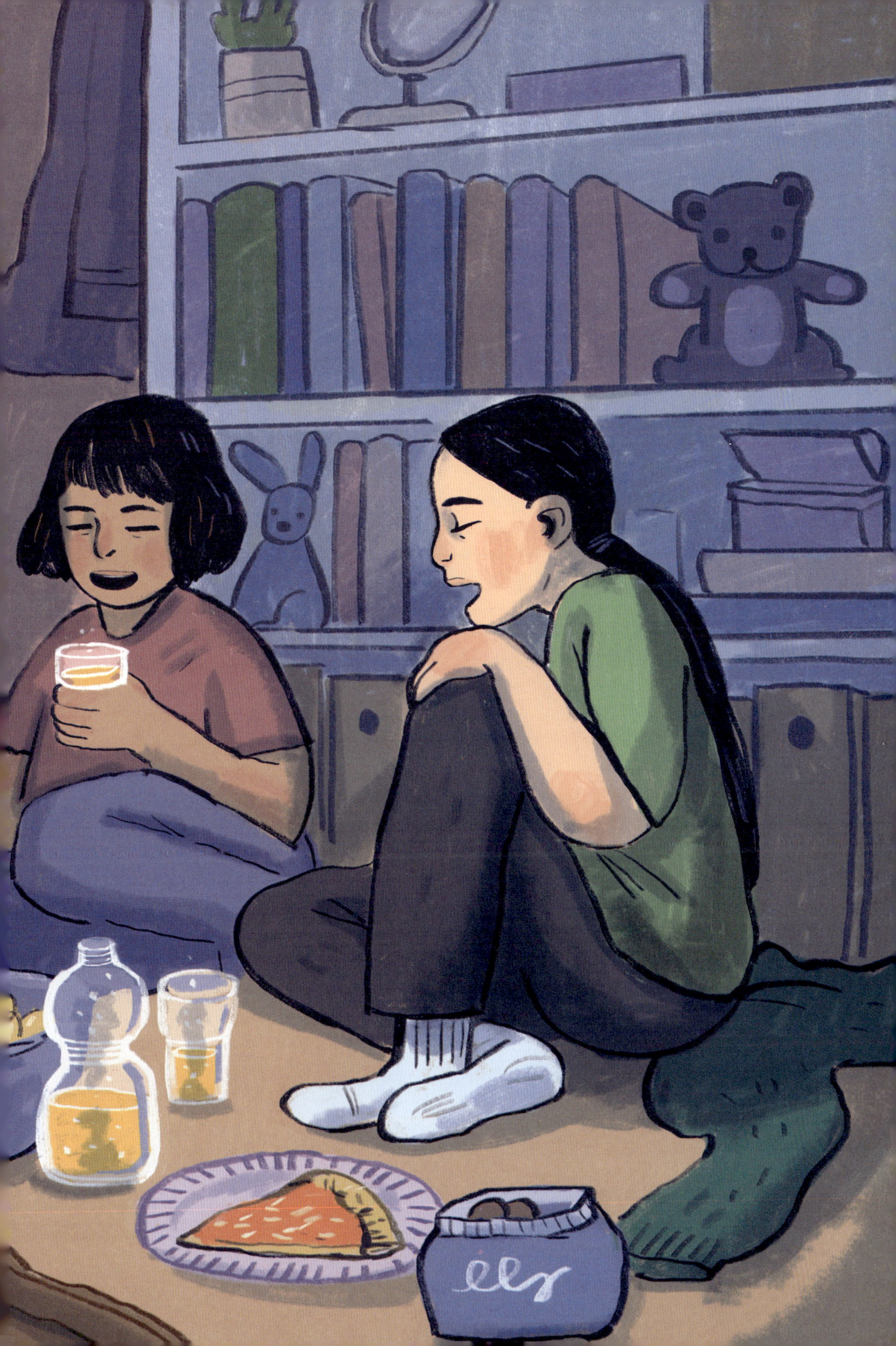

gang
3 members

BAO
Ugh
My mom realized it was me who climbed onto the roof and put up the banner

LINNÉA
Is she telling the principal?

BAO
No, thankfully
But she is MAD
Anyway, the MOST important thing is that we did it!!

TUVA
Yes!!!

LINNÉA
Yesssss
And the video is still being shared

BAO
Awesome!
The question is what now?

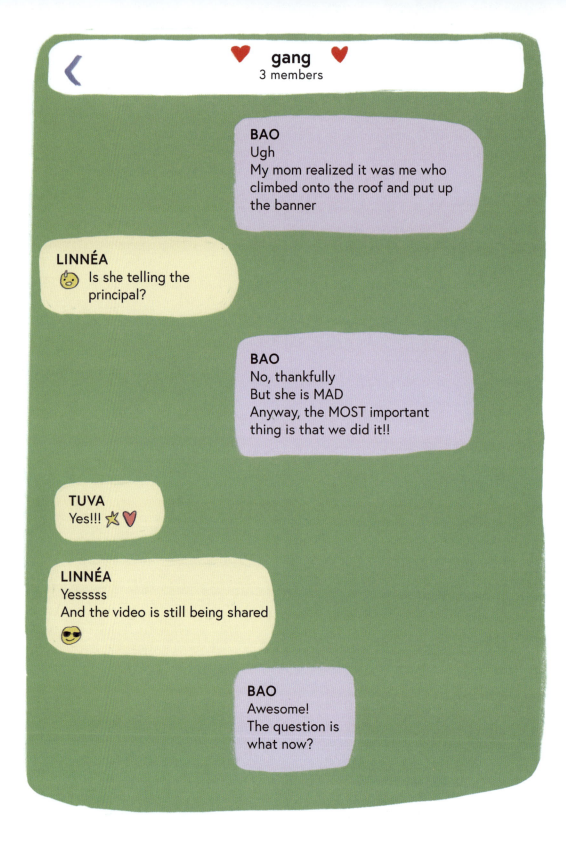

LINNÉA
Hmmm
Is there smthg we can
boycott?
 Maybe not

TUVA
We could start a petition?

BAO
Ooh
Yes?
Do you think we'll be able to
get enough people?

LINNÉA
Yes! Because we can ask people at school
And that's the most important

BAO
Ooh
Agreed! OK then we'll have
to find a website to start a
petition that students can use
We can still save the forest!

TUVA
Yess
I'll google tomorrow
Falling asleep now
Good night

LINNÉA
Yesss

Night girls

BAO
Night 🐱ᶻᶻ

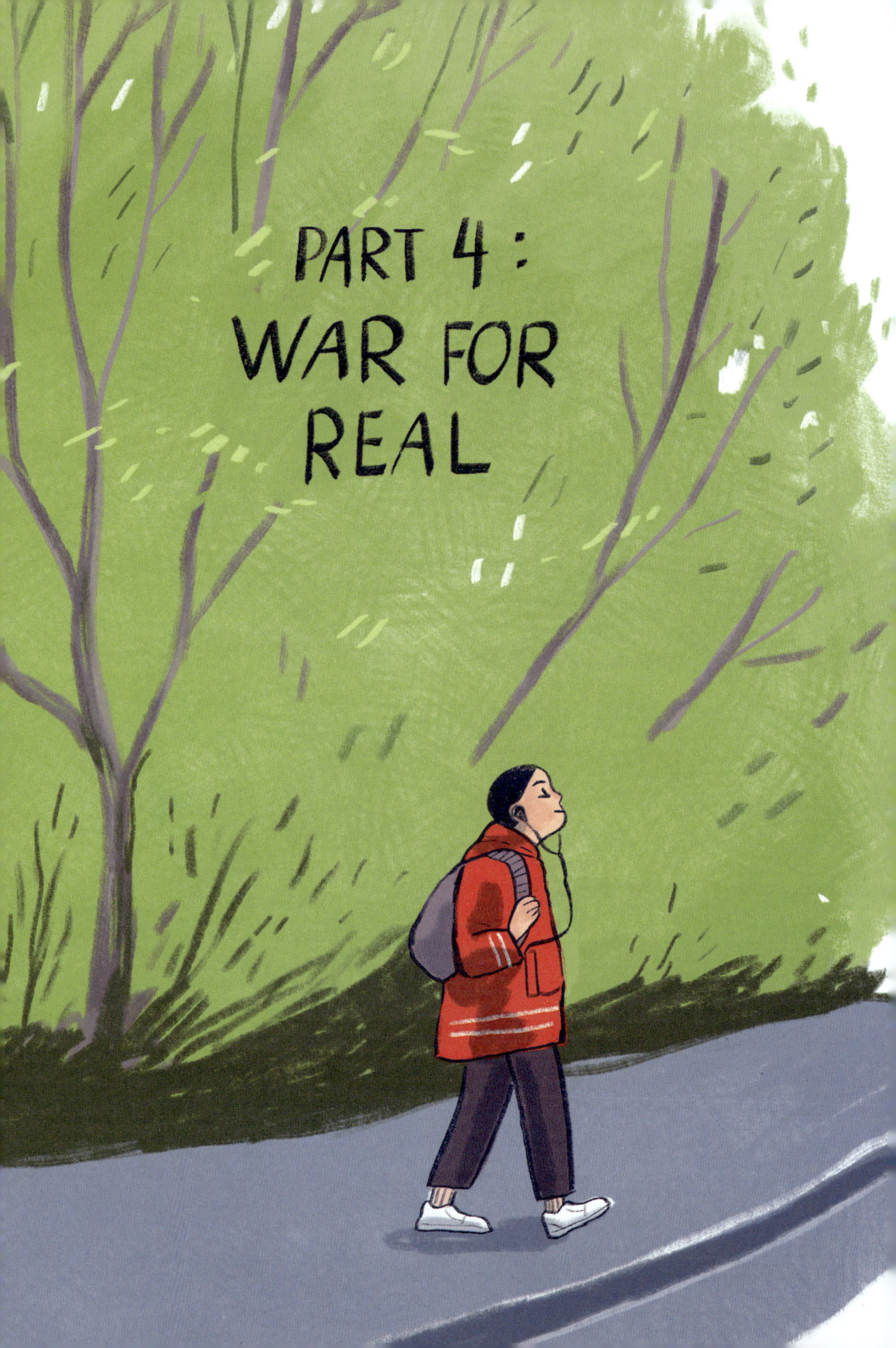
PART 4 :
WAR FOR
REAL

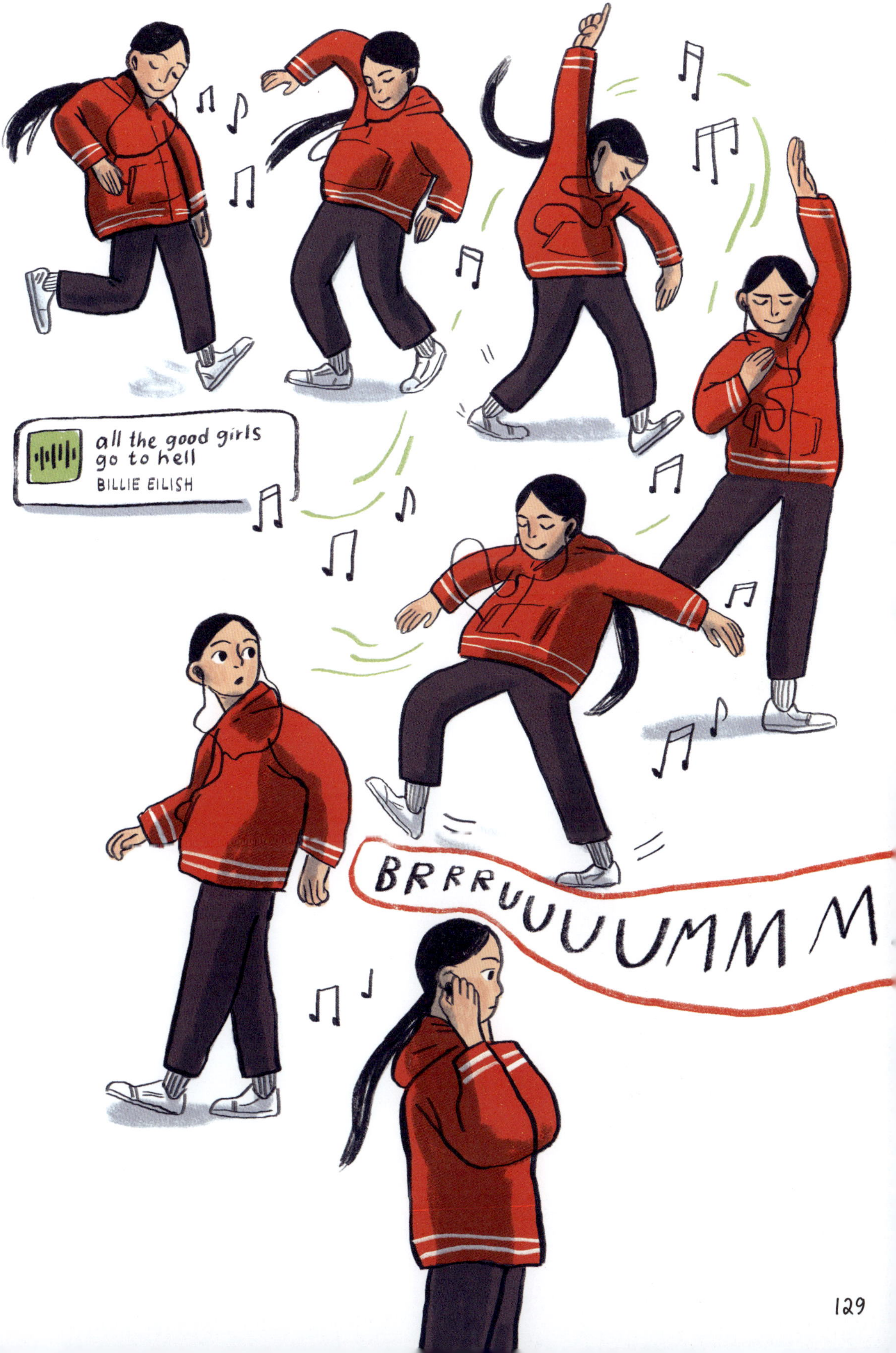
all the good girls go to hell
BILLIE EILISH
BRRRRUUUUUMMM

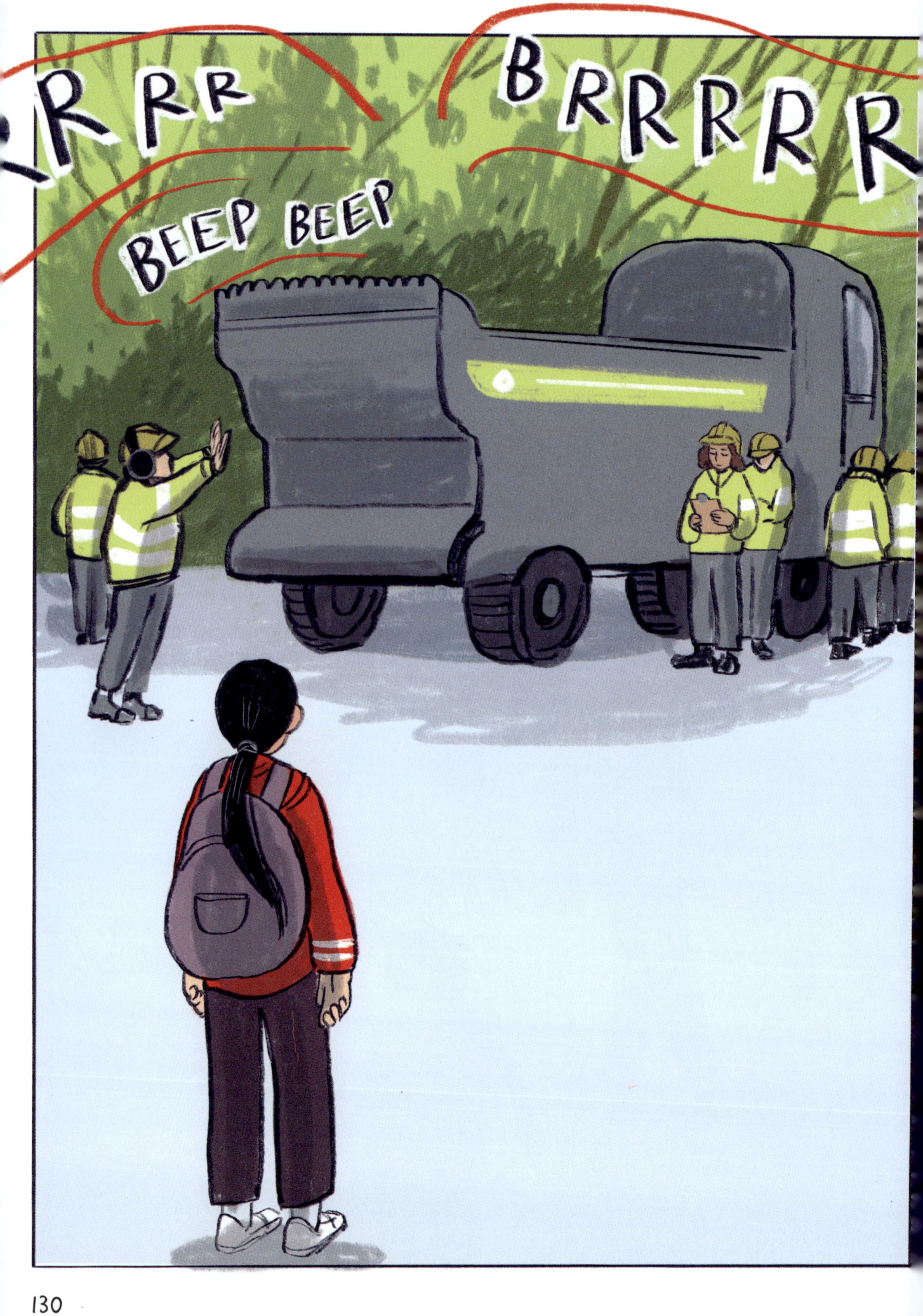
RRRR
BRRRRRR
BEEP BEEP

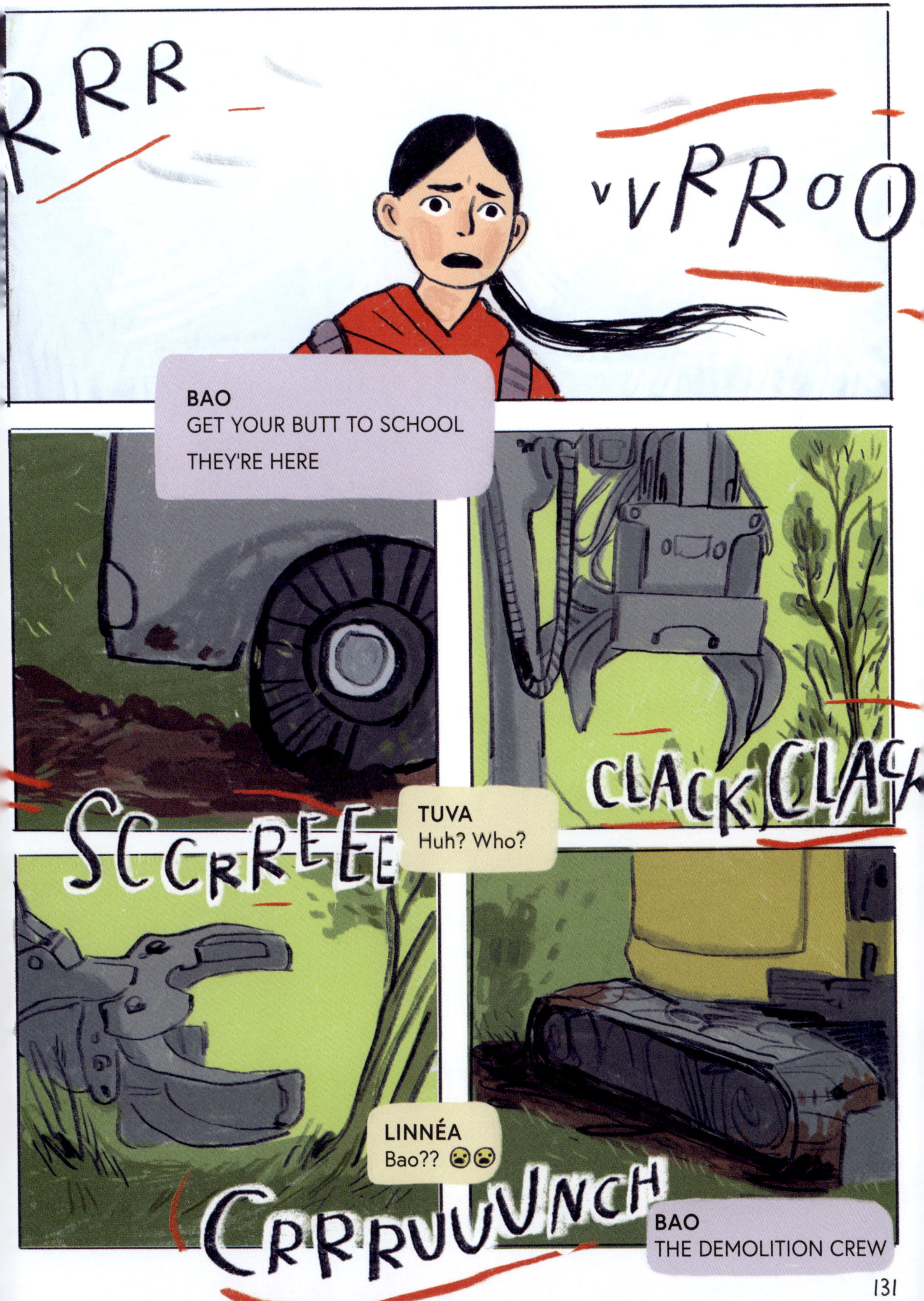
RRR
VVRROO
BAO
GET YOUR BUTT TO SCHOOL
THEY'RE HERE
SCCRREEE
TUVA
Huh? Who?
CLACK CLAC
LINNÉA
Bao??
CRRRUUUNCH
BAO
THE DEMOLITION CREW

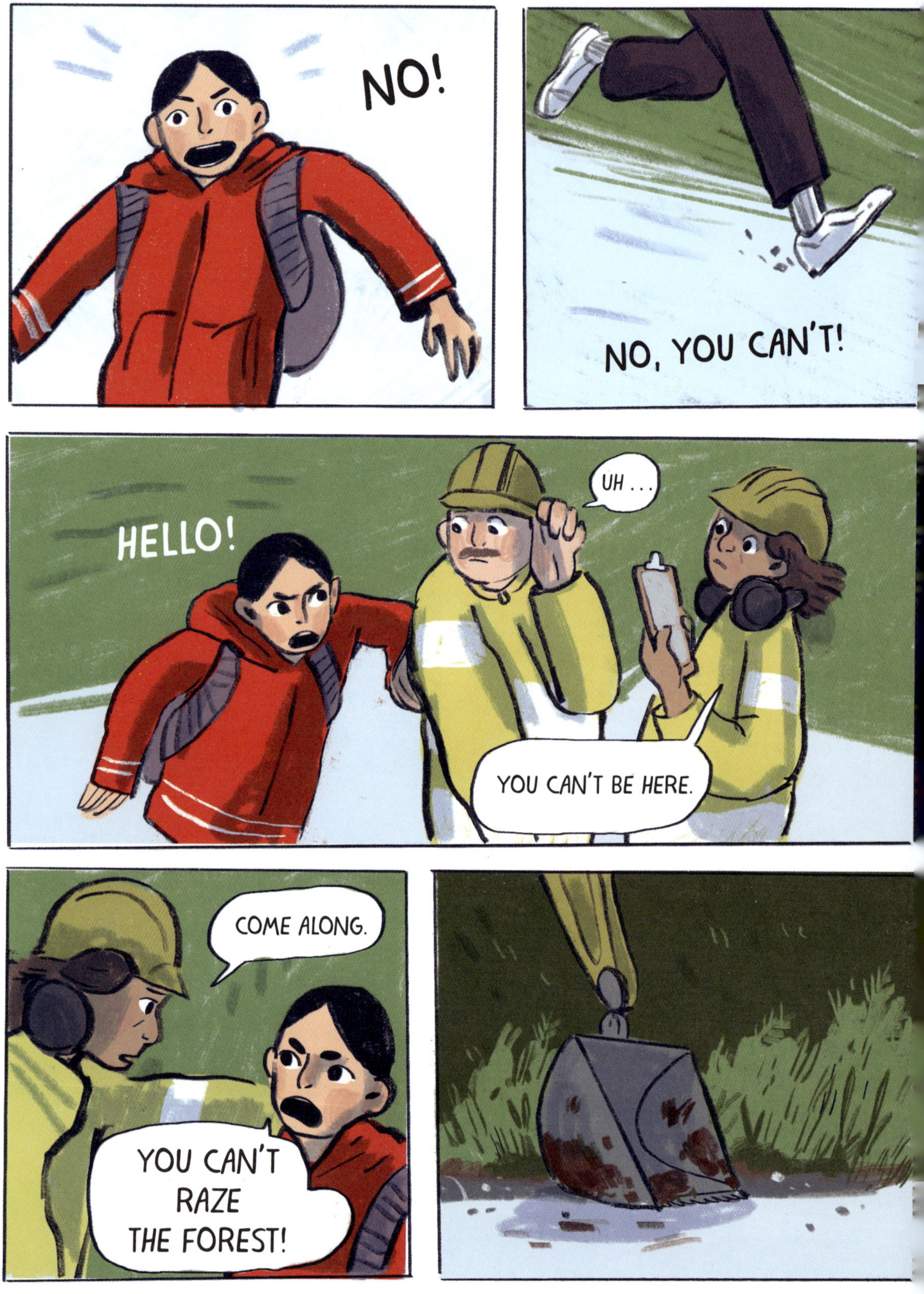
NO!
NO, YOU CAN'T!
HELLO!
UH . . .
YOU CAN'T BE HERE.
COME ALONG.
YOU CAN'T RAZE THE FOREST!

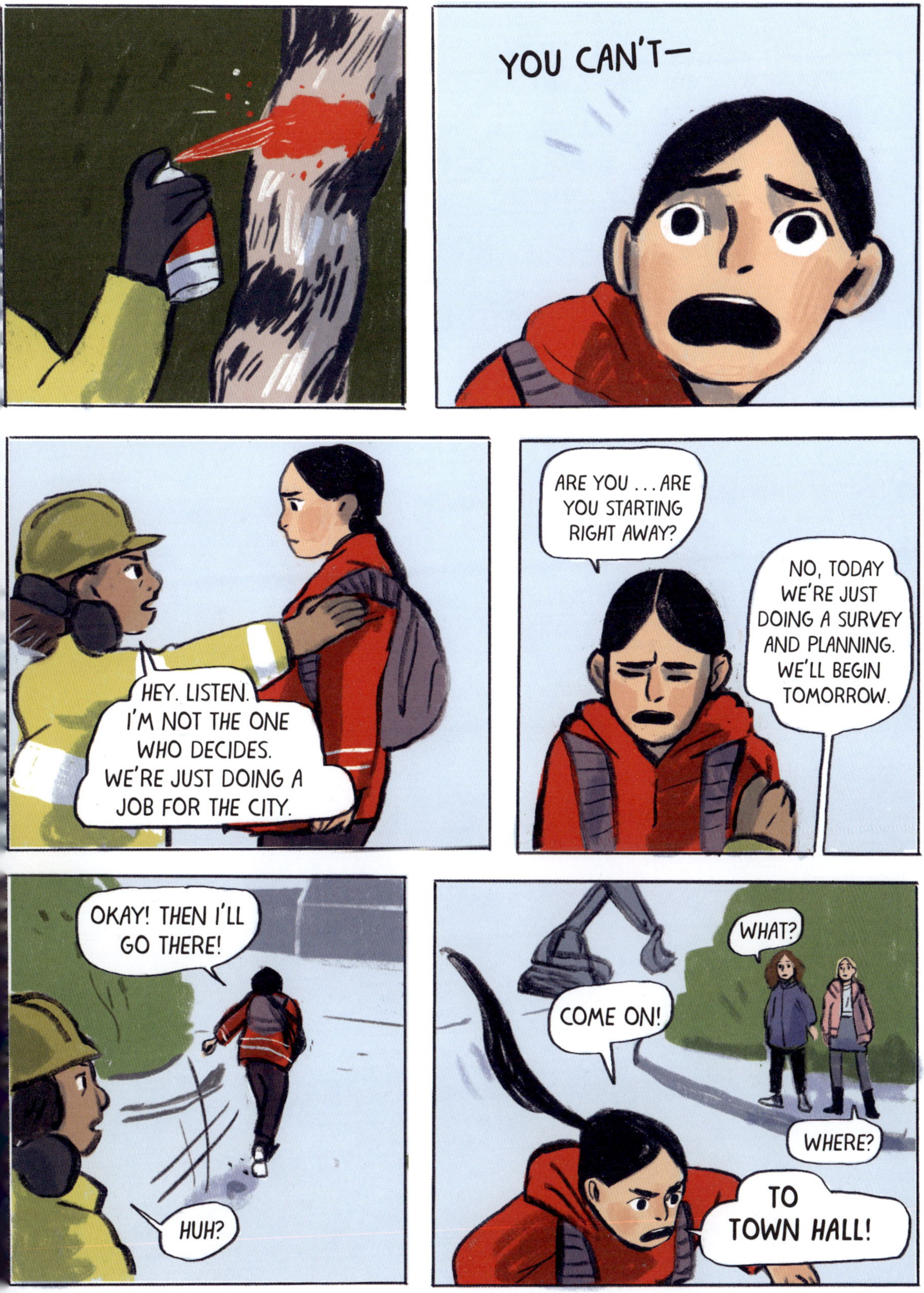
YOU CAN'T—
HEY. LISTEN. I'M NOT THE ONE WHO DECIDES. WE'RE JUST DOING A JOB FOR THE CITY.
ARE YOU . . . ARE YOU STARTING RIGHT AWAY?
NO, TODAY WE'RE JUST DOING A SURVEY AND PLANNING. WE'LL BEGIN TOMORROW.
OKAY! THEN I'LL GO THERE!
HUH?
WHAT?
COME ON!
WHERE?
TO TOWN HALL!

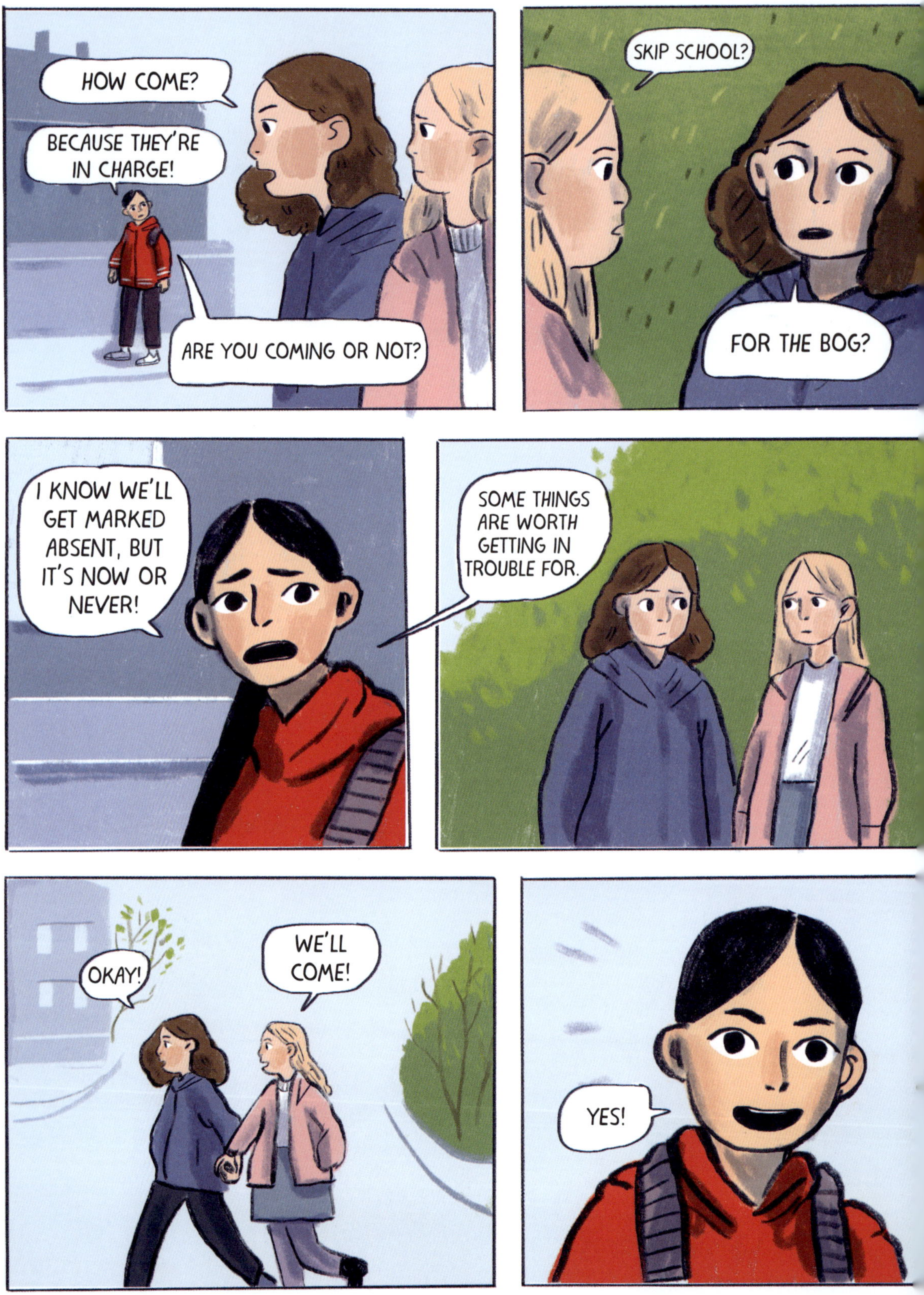
HOW COME?
BECAUSE THEY'RE IN CHARGE!
ARE YOU COMING OR NOT?
SKIP SCHOOL?
FOR THE BOG?
I KNOW WE'LL GET MARKED ABSENT, BUT IT'S NOW OR NEVER!
SOME THINGS ARE WORTH GETTING IN TROUBLE FOR.
OKAY!
WE'LL COME!
YES!

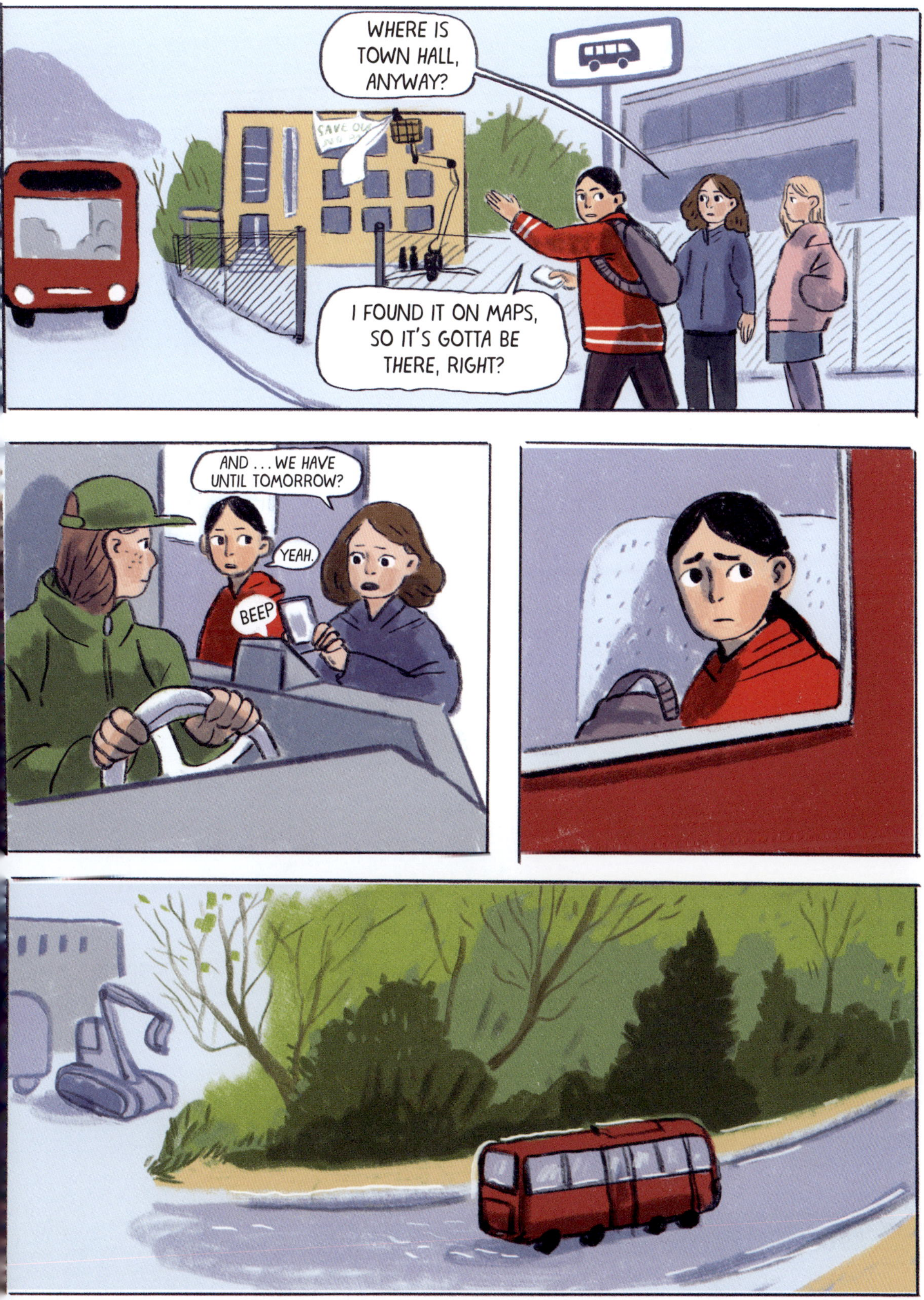
WHERE IS TOWN HALL, ANYWAY?
I FOUND IT ON MAPS, SO IT'S GOTTA BE THERE, RIGHT?
AND . . . WE HAVE UNTIL TOMORROW?
YEAH.
BEEP

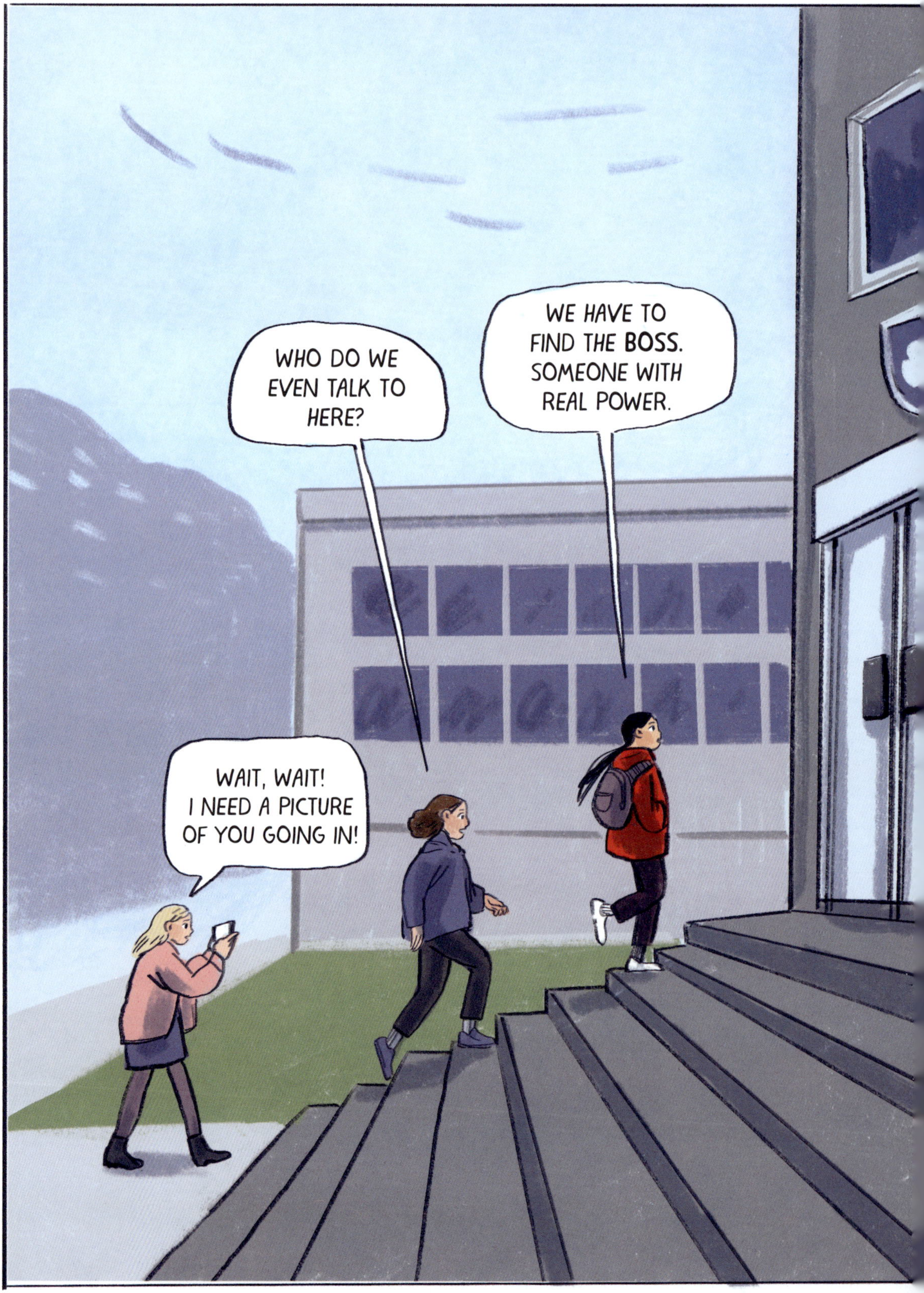
WAIT, WAIT! I NEED A PICTURE OF YOU GOING IN!
WHO DO WE EVEN TALK TO HERE?
WE HAVE TO FIND THE **BOSS.** SOMEONE WITH REAL POWER.

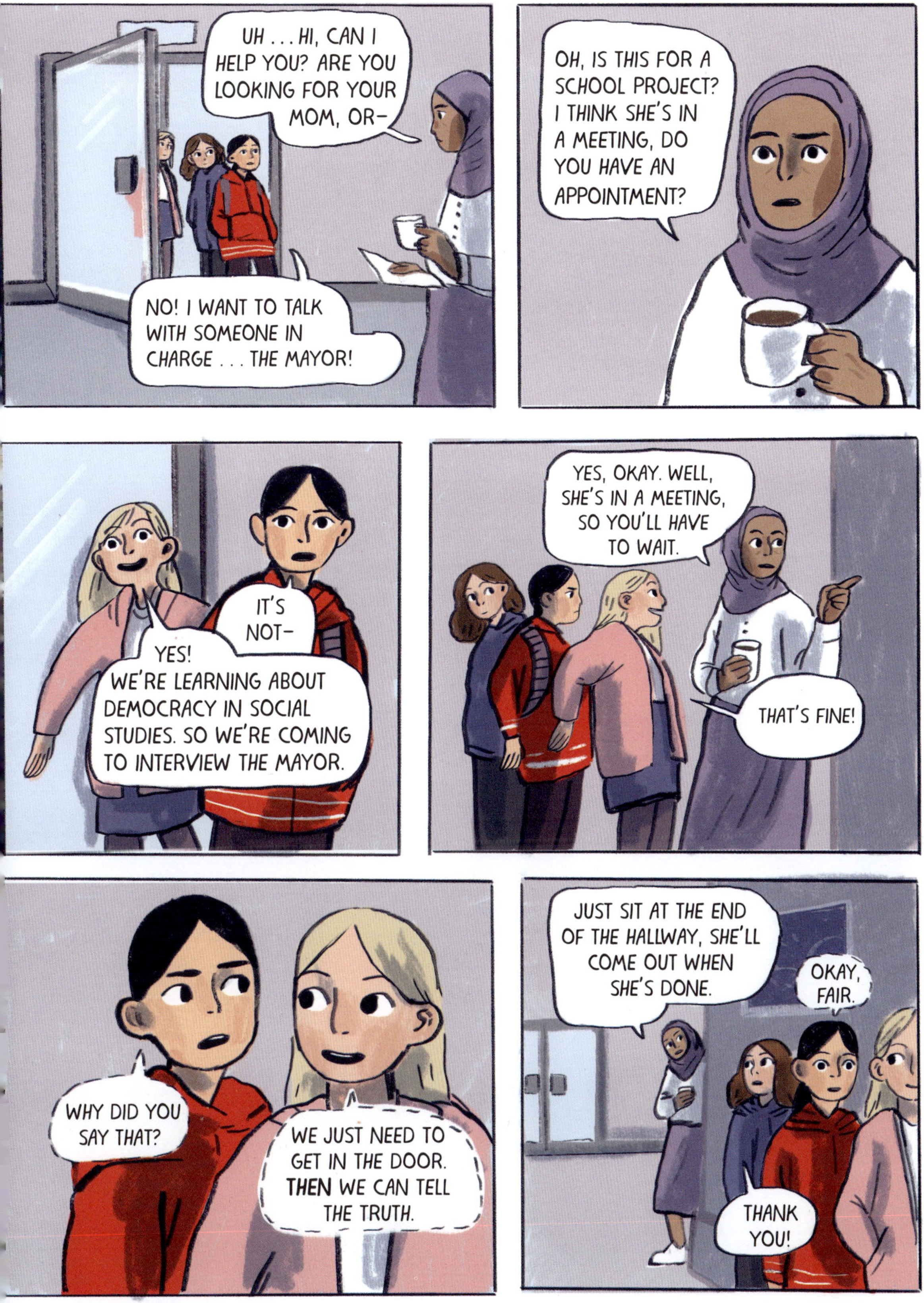
UH . . . HI, CAN I HELP YOU? ARE YOU LOOKING FOR YOUR MOM, OR–
NO! I WANT TO TALK WITH SOMEONE IN CHARGE . . . THE MAYOR!
OH, IS THIS FOR A SCHOOL PROJECT? I THINK SHE'S IN A MEETING, DO YOU HAVE AN APPOINTMENT?
IT'S NOT–
YES! WE'RE LEARNING ABOUT DEMOCRACY IN SOCIAL STUDIES. SO WE'RE COMING TO INTERVIEW THE MAYOR.
YES, OKAY. WELL, SHE'S IN A MEETING, SO YOU'LL HAVE TO WAIT.
THAT'S FINE!
WHY DID YOU SAY THAT?
WE JUST NEED TO GET IN THE DOOR. **THEN** WE CAN TELL THE TRUTH.
JUST SIT AT THE END OF THE HALLWAY, SHE'LL COME OUT WHEN SHE'S DONE.
OKAY, FAIR.
THANK YOU!

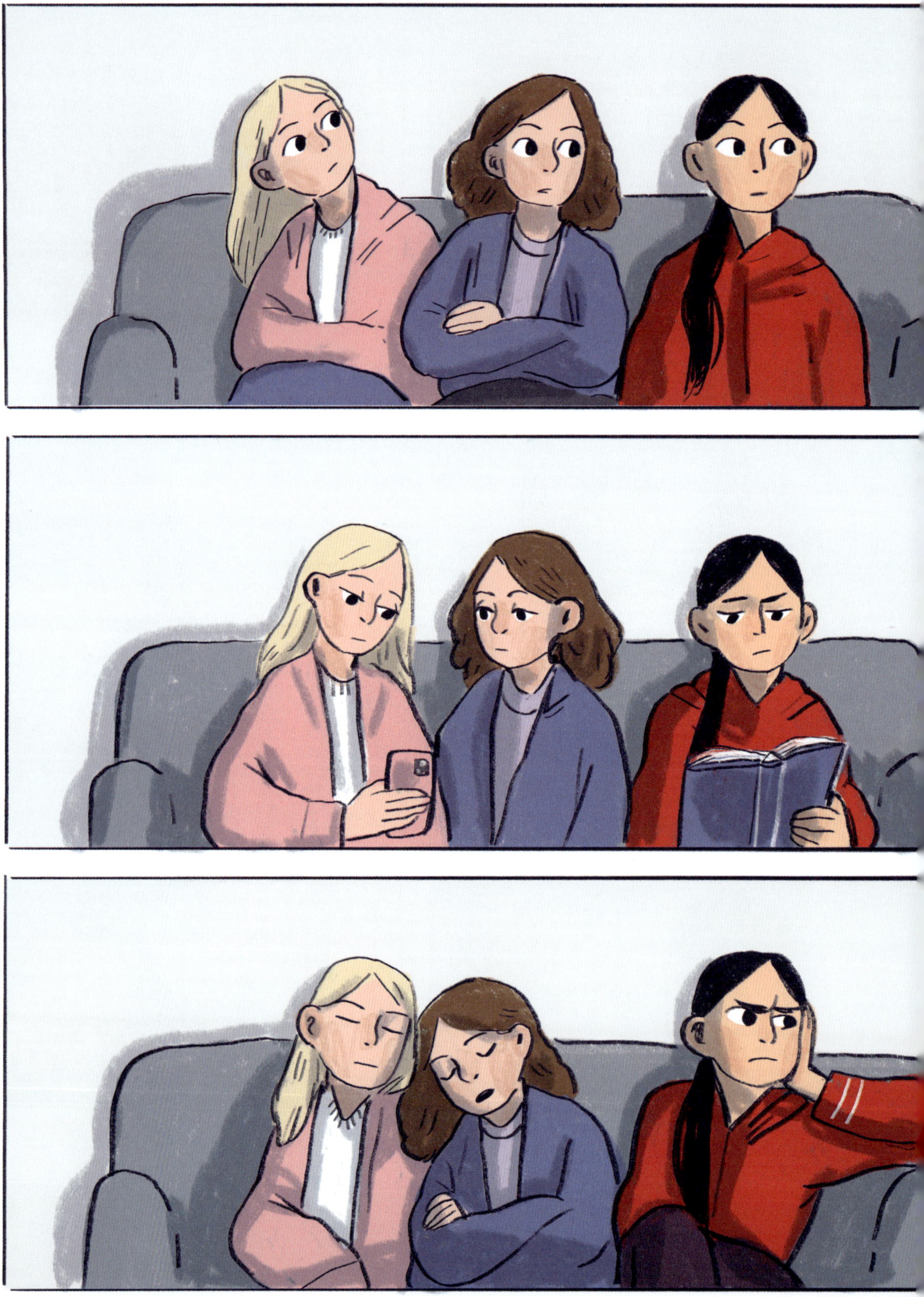

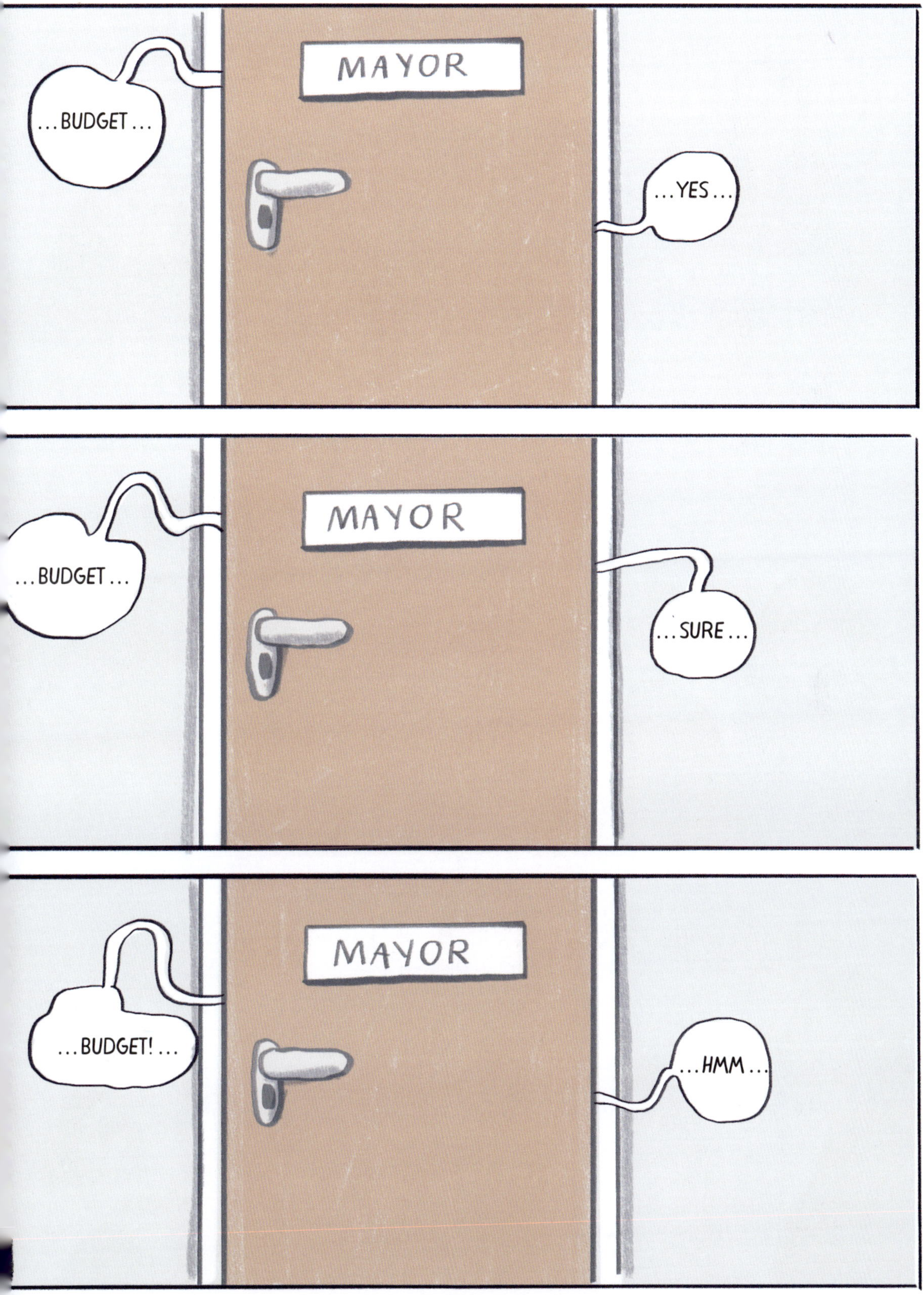
MAYOR
...BUDGET...
...YES...
MAYOR
...BUDGET...
...SURE...
MAYOR
...BUDGET!...
...HMM...

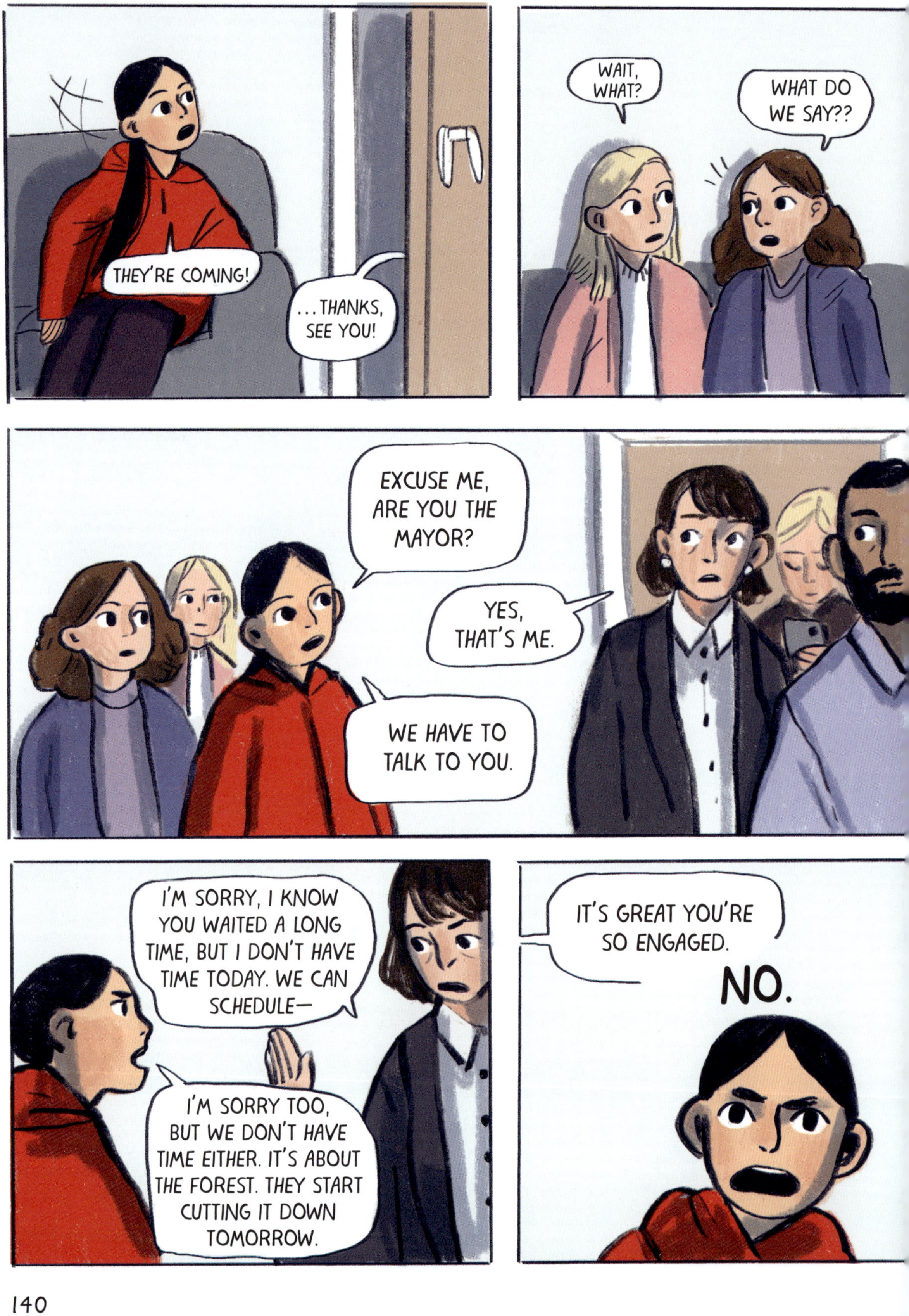
THEY'RE COMING!
...THANKS, SEE YOU!
WAIT, WHAT?
WHAT DO WE SAY??
EXCUSE ME, ARE YOU THE MAYOR?
YES, THAT'S ME.
WE HAVE TO TALK TO YOU.
I'M SORRY, I KNOW YOU WAITED A LONG TIME, BUT I DON'T HAVE TIME TODAY. WE CAN SCHEDULE—
I'M SORRY TOO, BUT WE DON'T HAVE TIME EITHER. IT'S ABOUT THE FOREST. THEY START CUTTING IT DOWN TOMORROW.
IT'S GREAT YOU'RE SO ENGAGED.
NO.

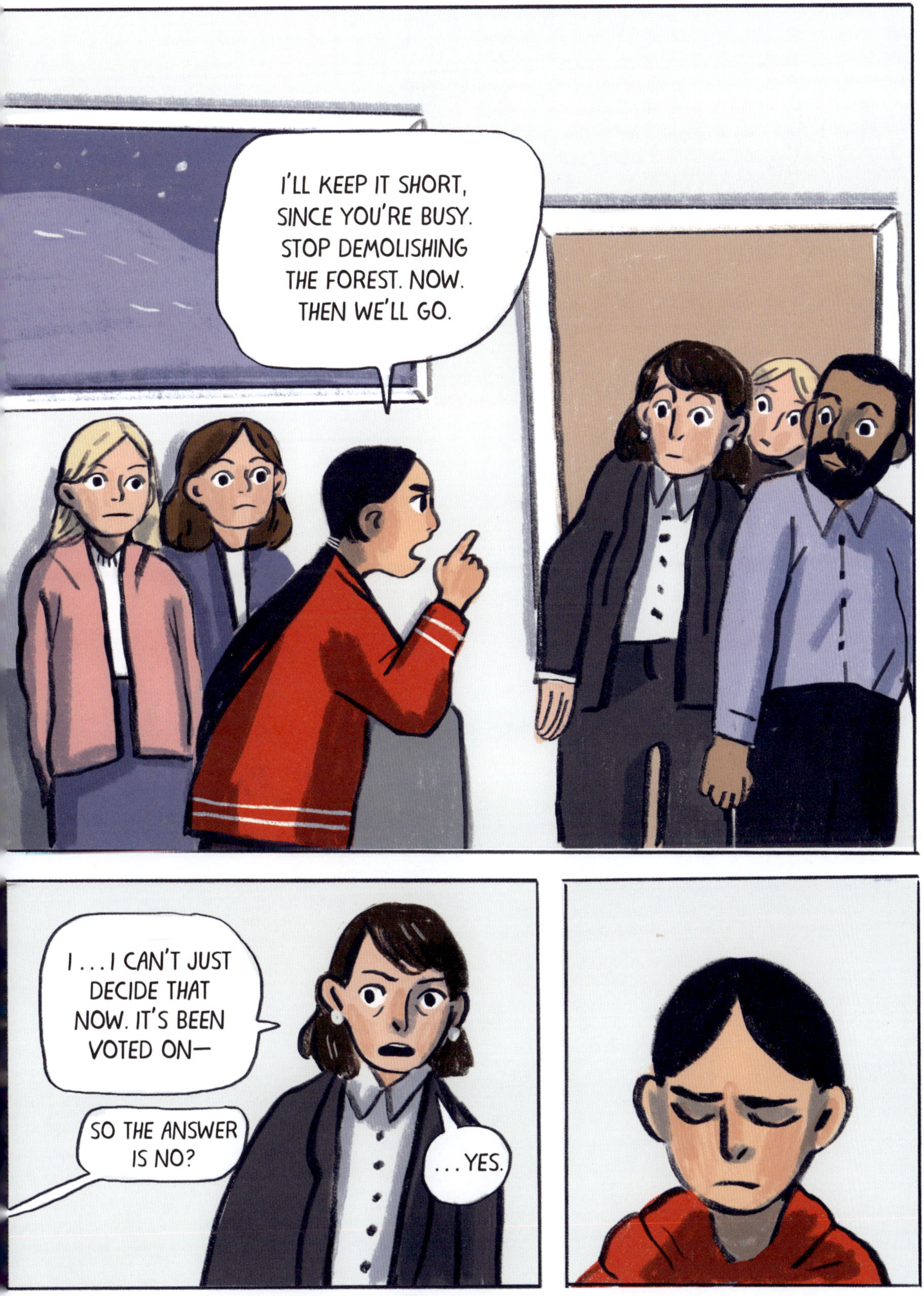
I'LL KEEP IT SHORT, SINCE YOU'RE BUSY. STOP DEMOLISHING THE FOREST. NOW. THEN WE'LL GO.
I . . . I CAN'T JUST DECIDE THAT NOW. IT'S BEEN VOTED ON—
SO THE ANSWER IS NO?
. . . YES.

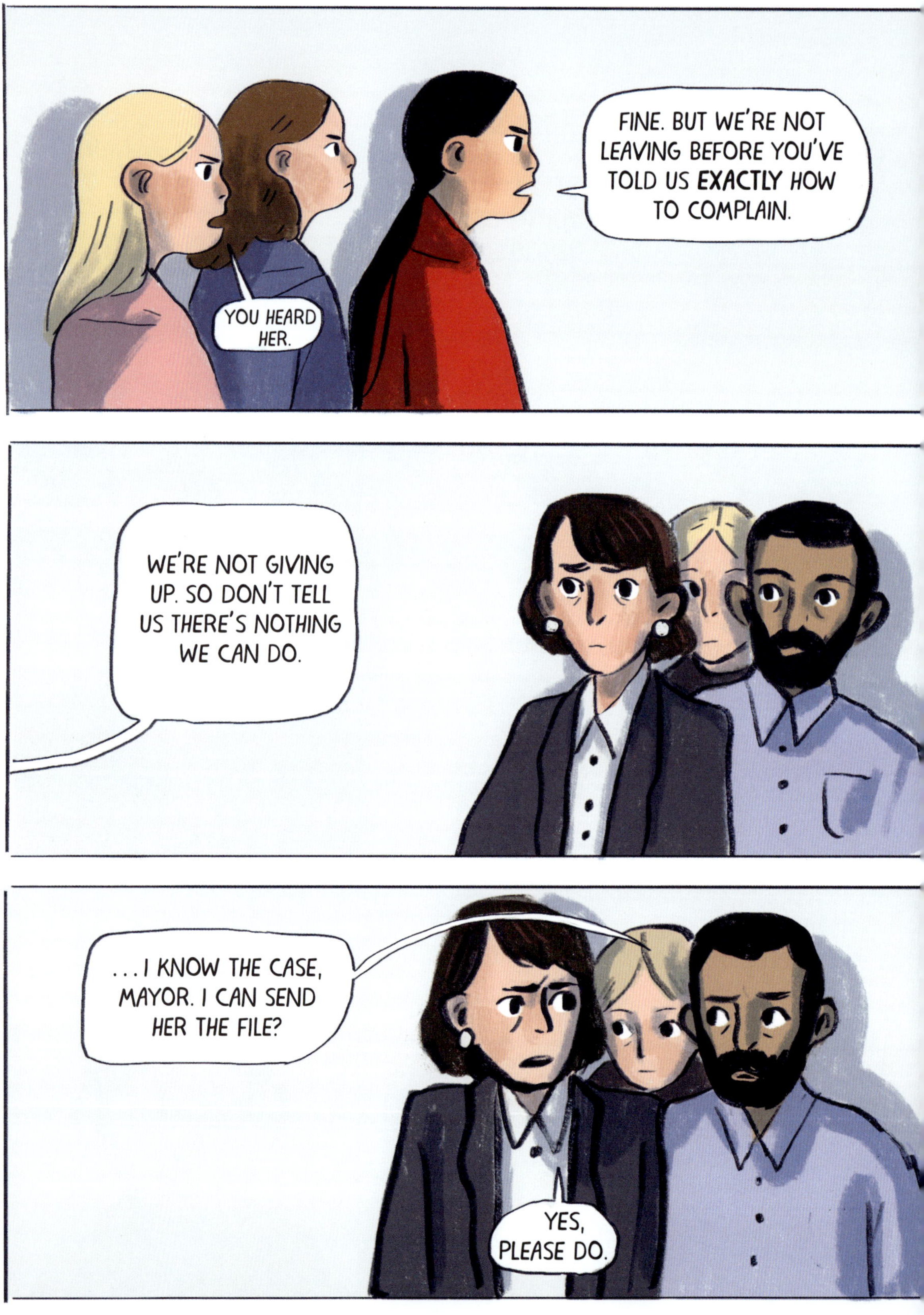
FINE. BUT WE'RE NOT LEAVING BEFORE YOU'VE TOLD US **EXACTLY** HOW TO COMPLAIN.
YOU HEARD HER.
WE'RE NOT GIVING UP. SO DON'T TELL US THERE'S NOTHING WE CAN DO.
. . . I KNOW THE CASE, MAYOR. I CAN SEND HER THE FILE?
YES, PLEASE DO.

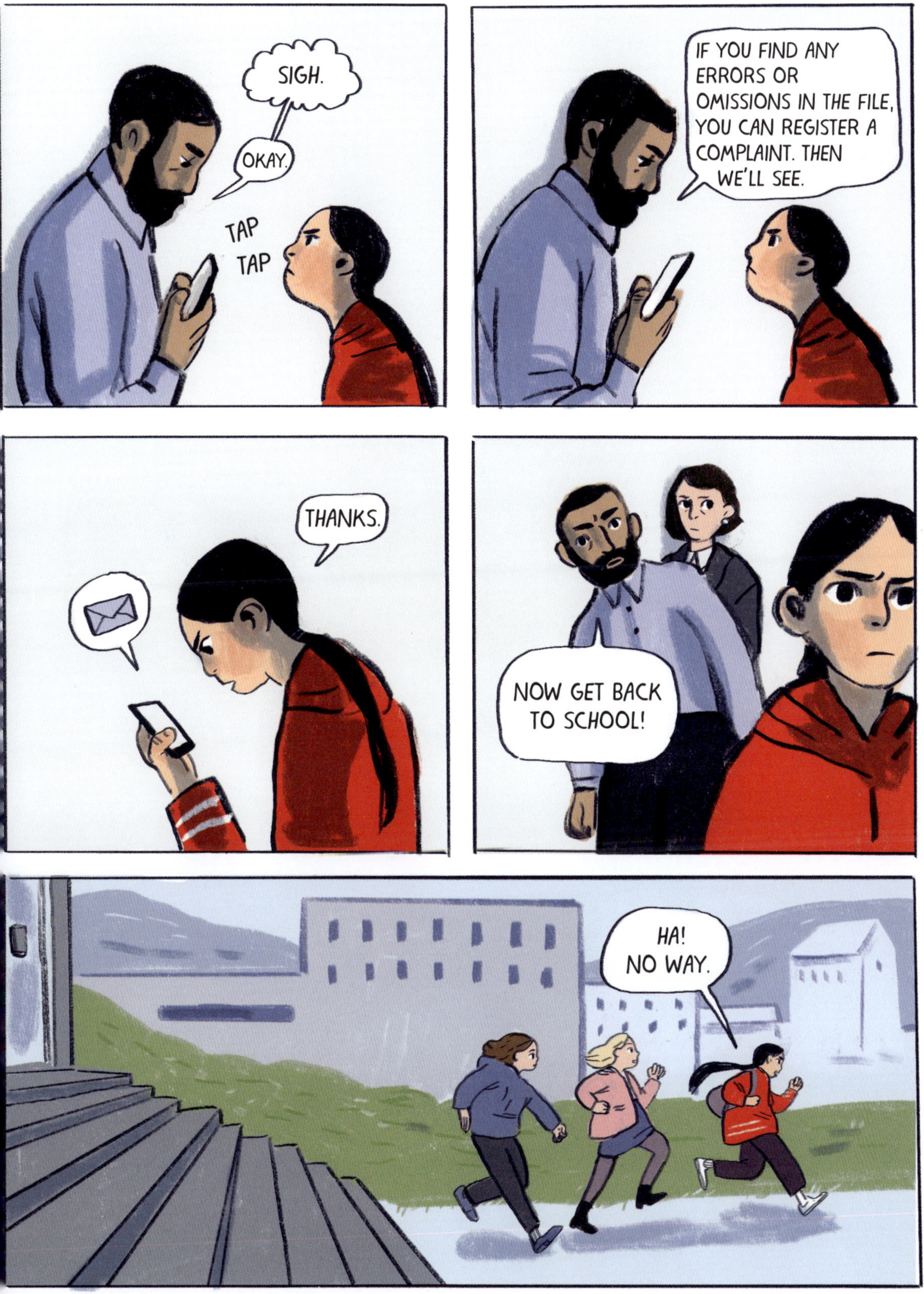
SIGH.
OKAY.
TAP
TAP
IF YOU FIND ANY ERRORS OR OMISSIONS IN THE FILE, YOU CAN REGISTER A COMPLAINT. THEN WE'LL SEE.
THANKS.
NOW GET BACK TO SCHOOL!
HA! NO WAY.

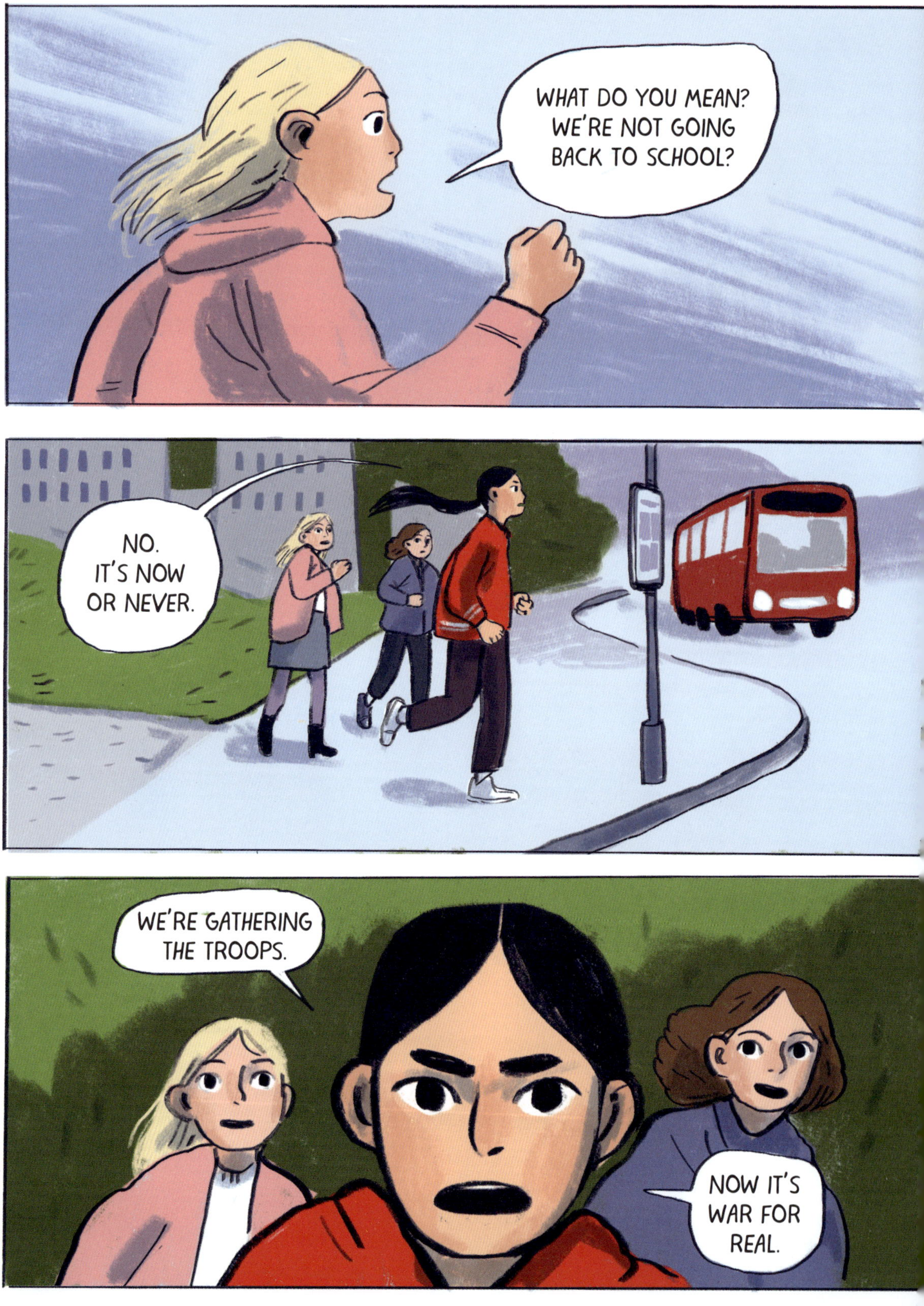
WHAT DO YOU MEAN? WE'RE NOT GOING BACK TO SCHOOL?
NO. IT'S NOW OR NEVER.
WE'RE GATHERING THE TROOPS.
NOW IT'S WAR FOR REAL.

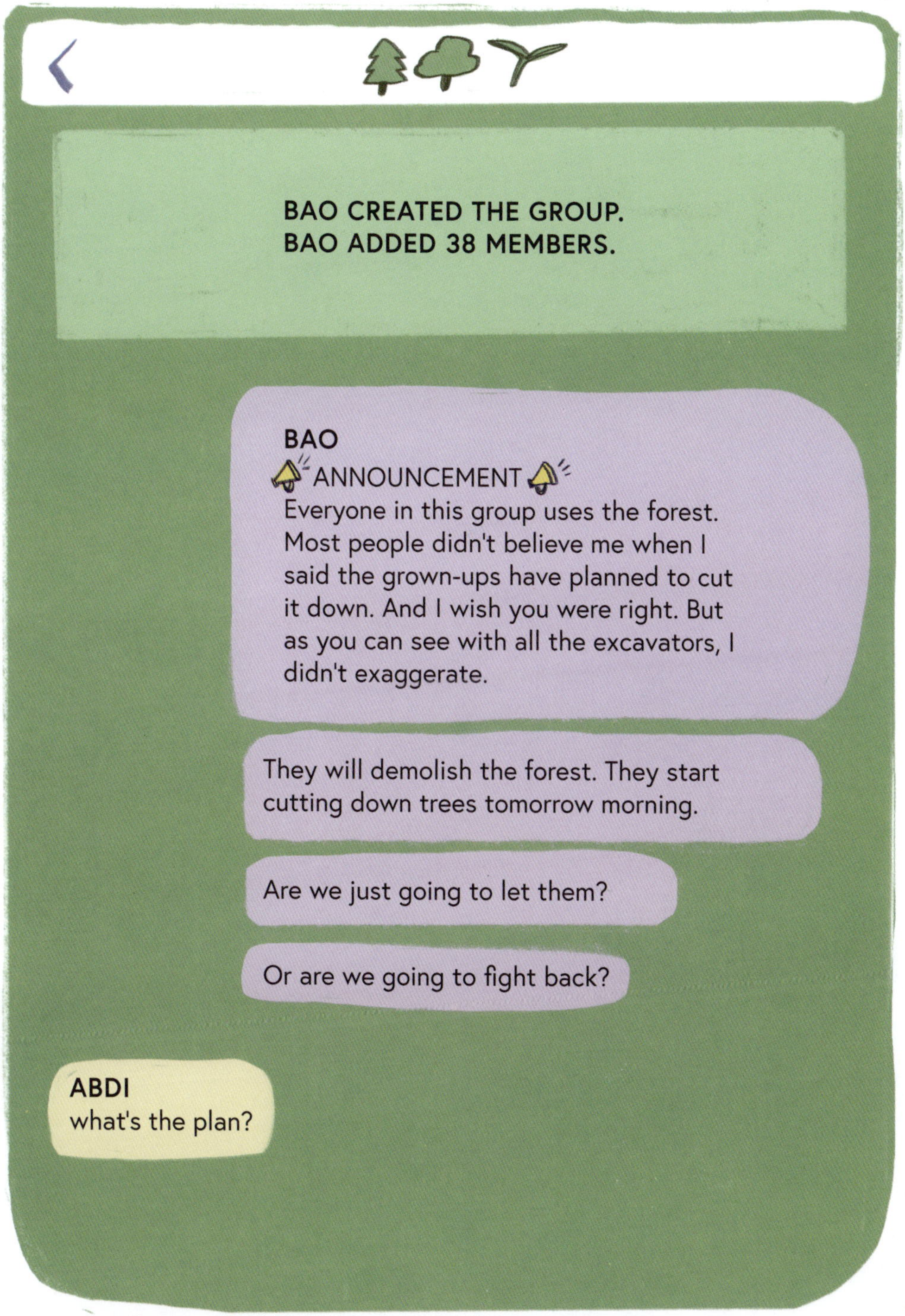
BAO CREATED THE GROUP.
BAO ADDED 38 MEMBERS.
BAO
ANNOUNCEMENT
Everyone in this group uses the forest. Most people didn't believe me when I said the grown-ups have planned to cut it down. And I wish you were right. But as you can see with all the excavators, I didn't exaggerate.
They will demolish the forest. They start cutting down trees tomorrow morning.
Are we just going to let them?
Or are we going to fight back?
ABDI
what's the plan?

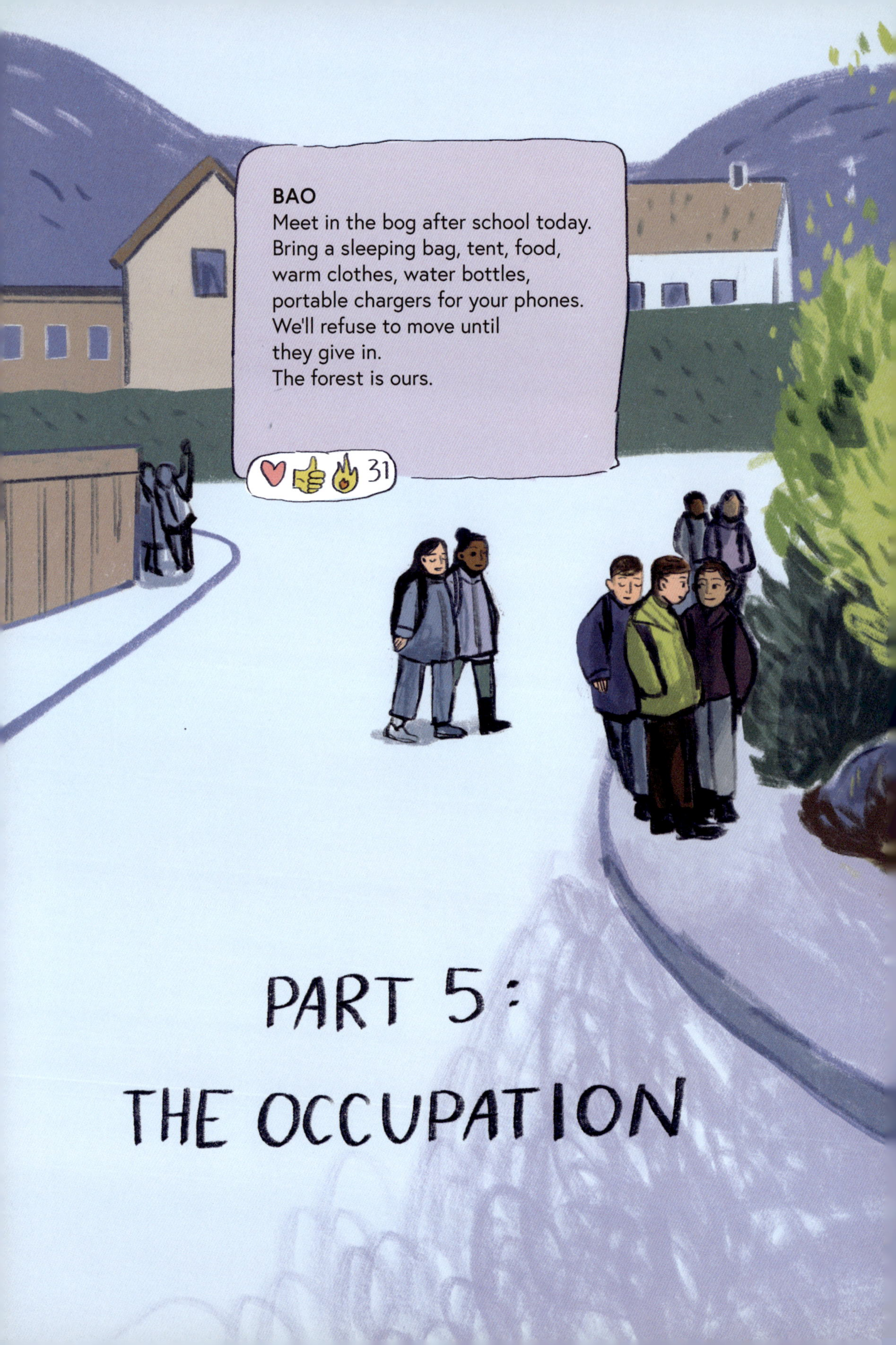
BAO
Meet in the bog after school today.
Bring a sleeping bag, tent, food,
warm clothes, water bottles,
portable chargers for your phones.
We'll refuse to move until
they give in.
The forest is ours.
31

PART 5: THE OCCUPATION

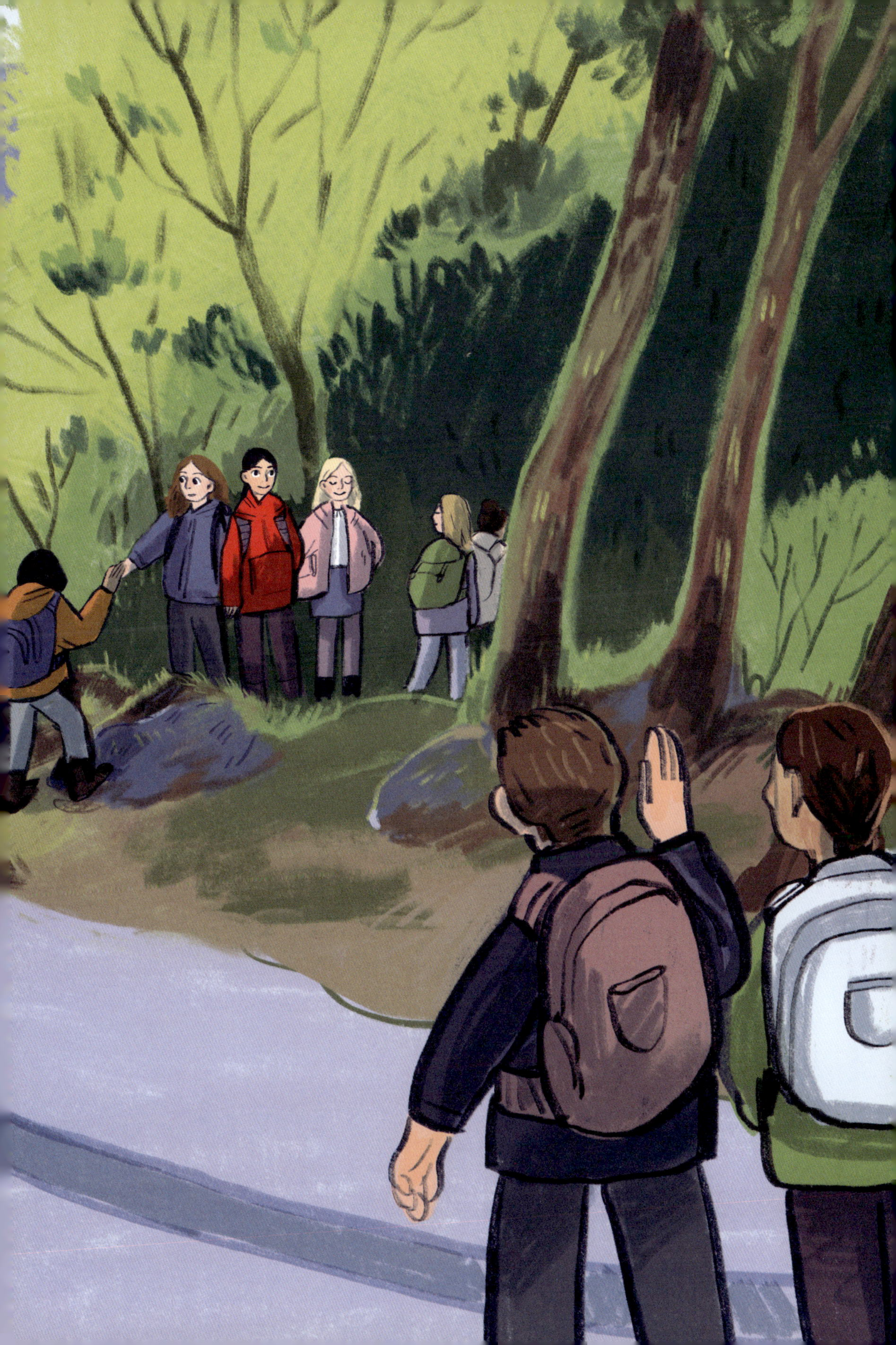

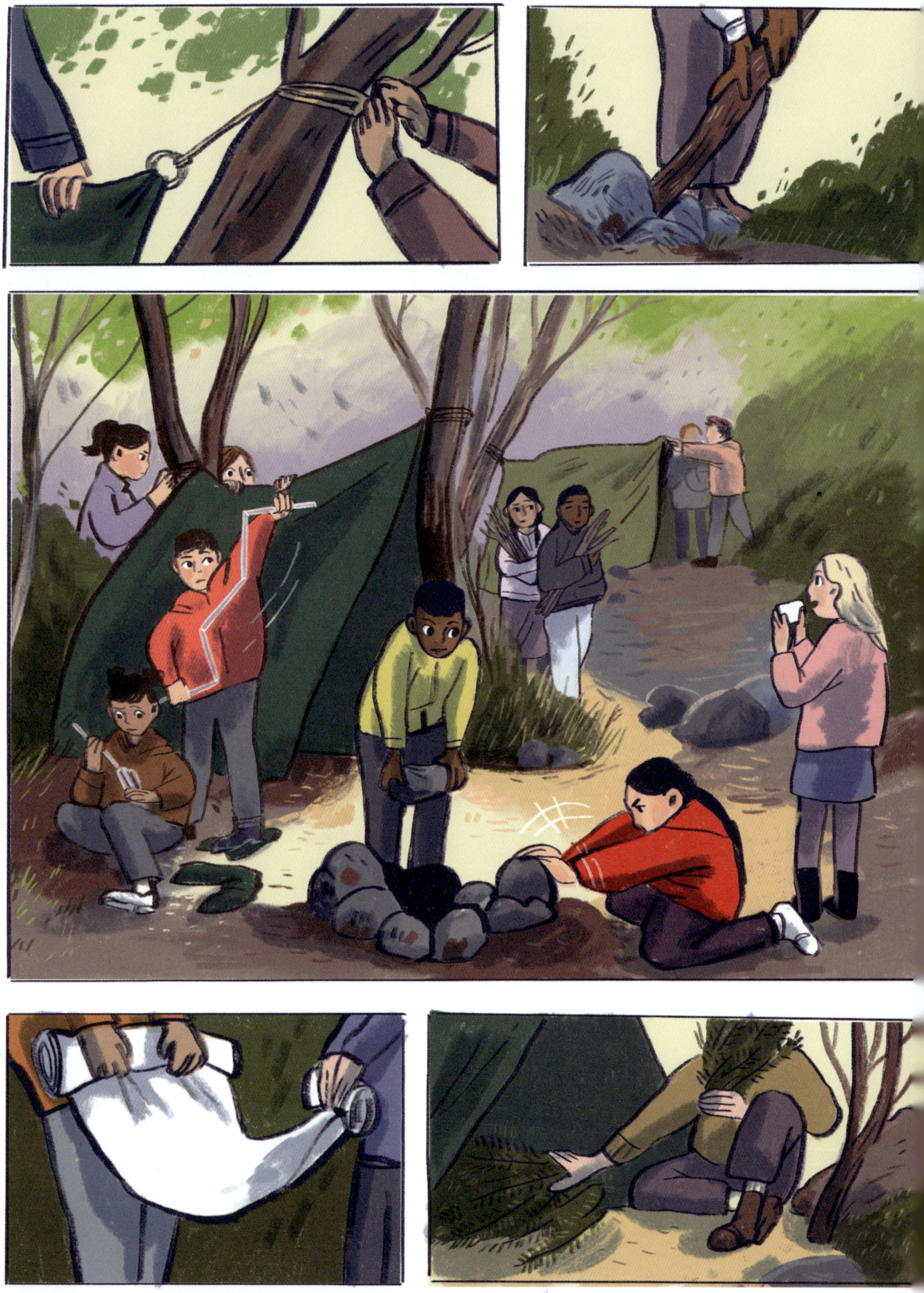

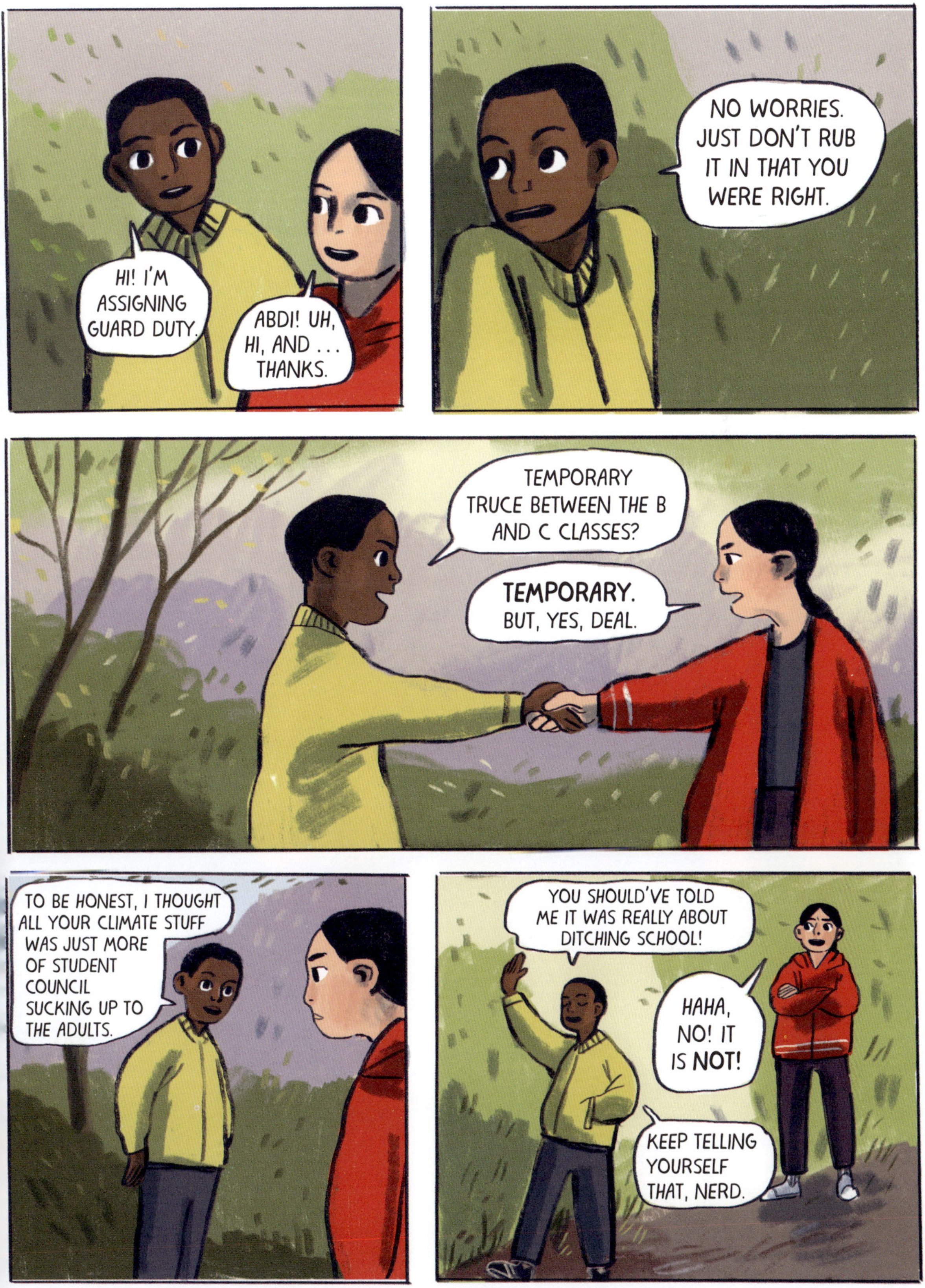
HI! I'M ASSIGNING GUARD DUTY.
ABDI! UH, HI, AND . . . THANKS.
NO WORRIES. JUST DON'T RUB IT IN THAT YOU WERE RIGHT.
TEMPORARY TRUCE BETWEEN THE B AND C CLASSES?
TEMPORARY. BUT, YES, DEAL.
TO BE HONEST, I THOUGHT ALL YOUR CLIMATE STUFF WAS JUST MORE OF STUDENT COUNCIL SUCKING UP TO THE ADULTS.
YOU SHOULD'VE TOLD ME IT WAS REALLY ABOUT DITCHING SCHOOL!
HAHA, NO! IT IS **NOT**!
KEEP TELLING YOURSELF THAT, NERD.

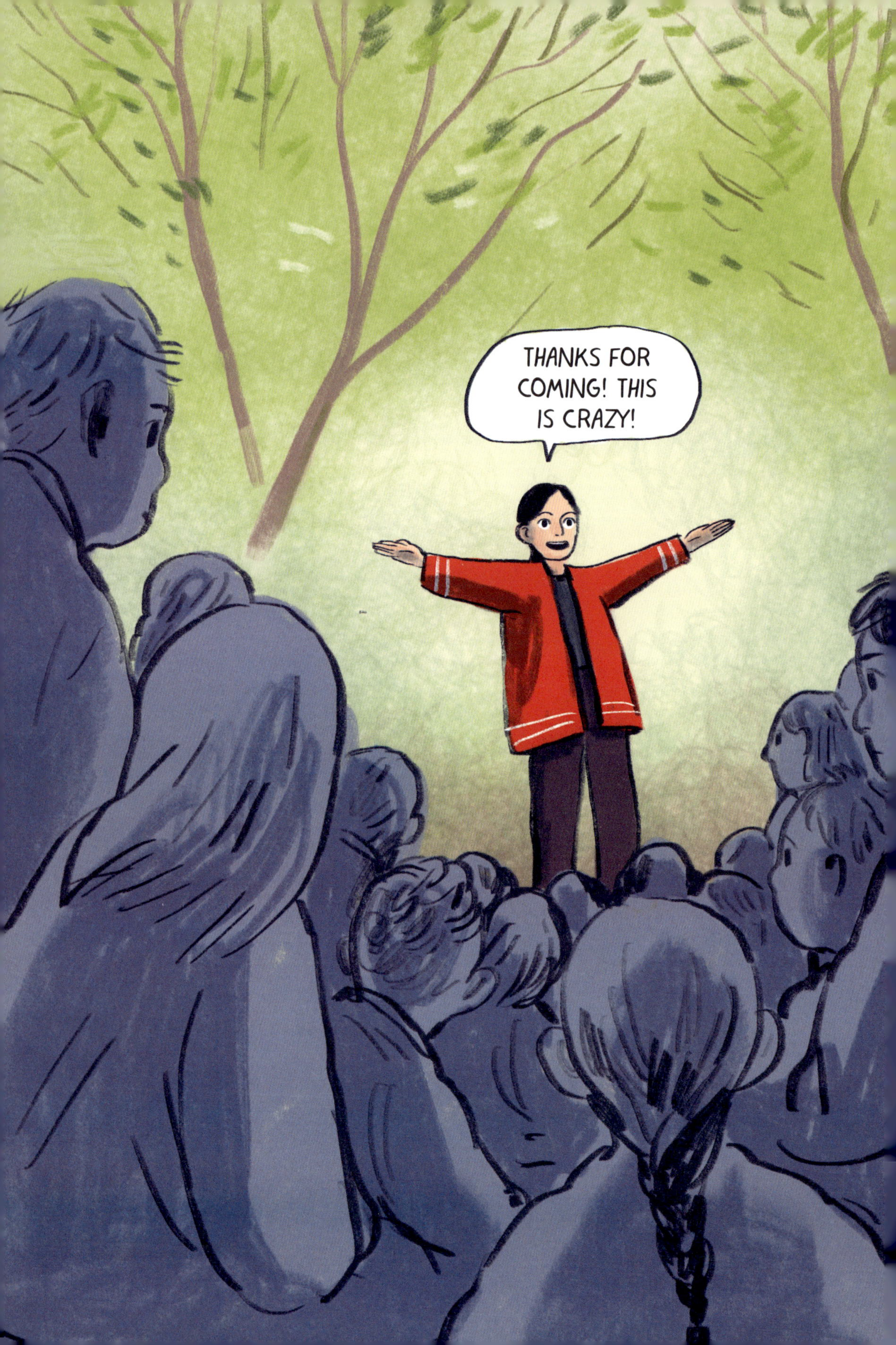
THANKS FOR COMING! THIS IS CRAZY!

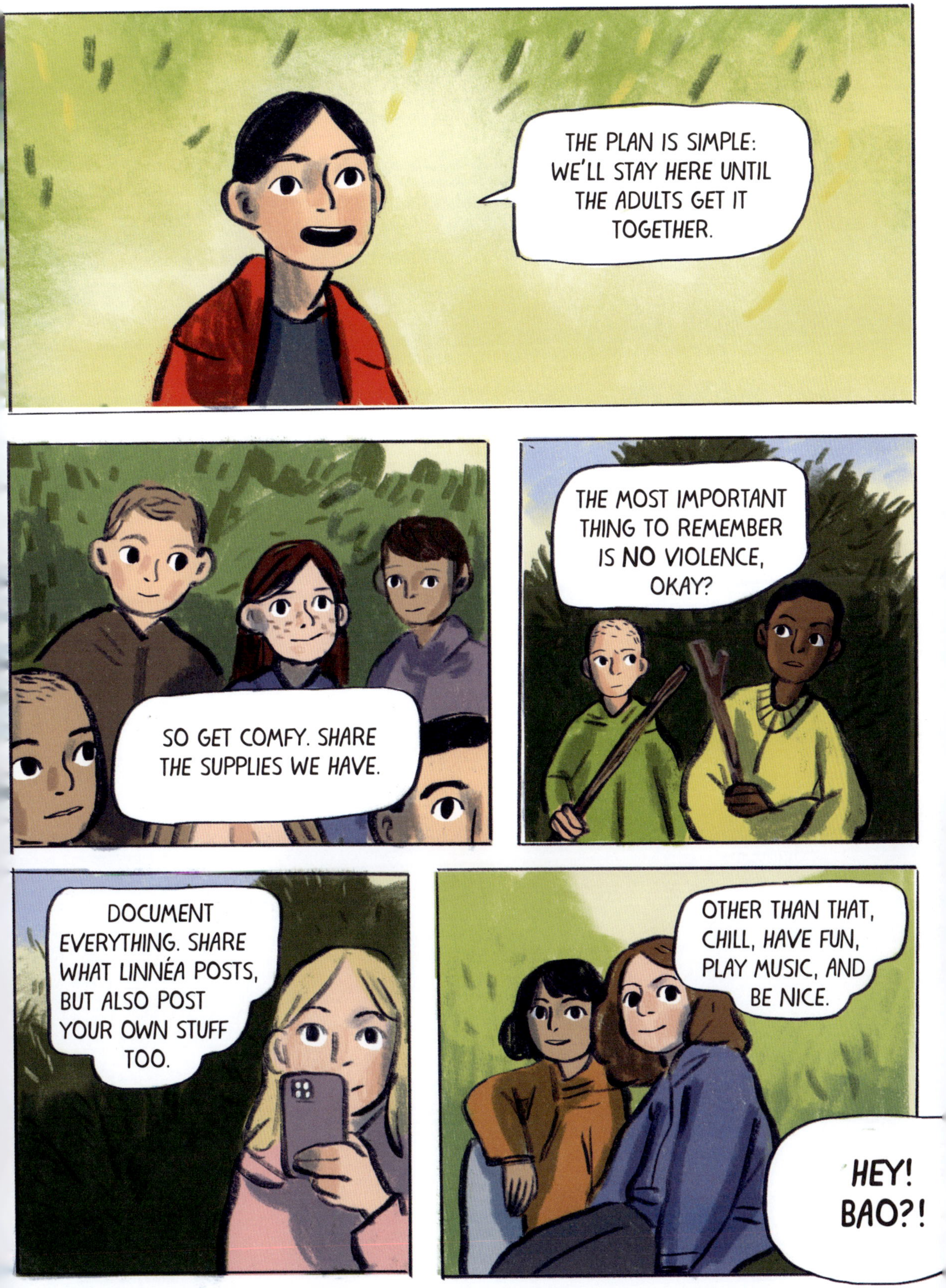
THE PLAN IS SIMPLE: WE'LL STAY HERE UNTIL THE ADULTS GET IT TOGETHER.
SO GET COMFY. SHARE THE SUPPLIES WE HAVE.
THE MOST IMPORTANT THING TO REMEMBER IS NO VIOLENCE, OKAY?
DOCUMENT EVERYTHING. SHARE WHAT LINNÉA POSTS, BUT ALSO POST YOUR OWN STUFF TOO.
OTHER THAN THAT, CHILL, HAVE FUN, PLAY MUSIC, AND BE NICE.
HEY! BAO?!

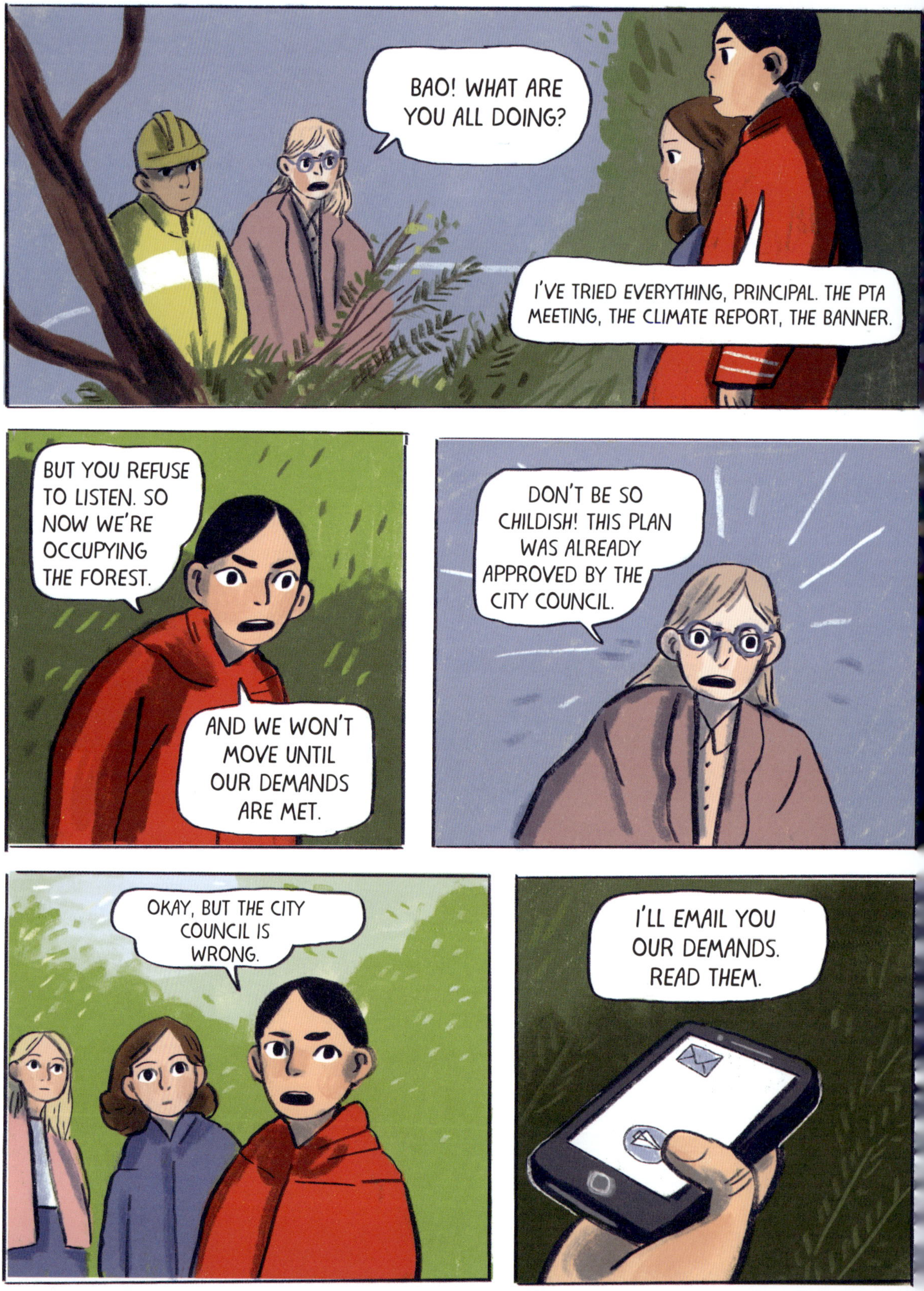
BAO! WHAT ARE YOU ALL DOING?
I'VE TRIED EVERYTHING, PRINCIPAL. THE PTA MEETING, THE CLIMATE REPORT, THE BANNER.
BUT YOU REFUSE TO LISTEN. SO NOW WE'RE OCCUPYING THE FOREST.
AND WE WON'T MOVE UNTIL OUR DEMANDS ARE MET.
DON'T BE SO CHILDISH! THIS PLAN WAS ALREADY APPROVED BY THE CITY COUNCIL.
OKAY, BUT THE CITY COUNCIL IS WRONG.
I'LL EMAIL YOU OUR DEMANDS. READ THEM.

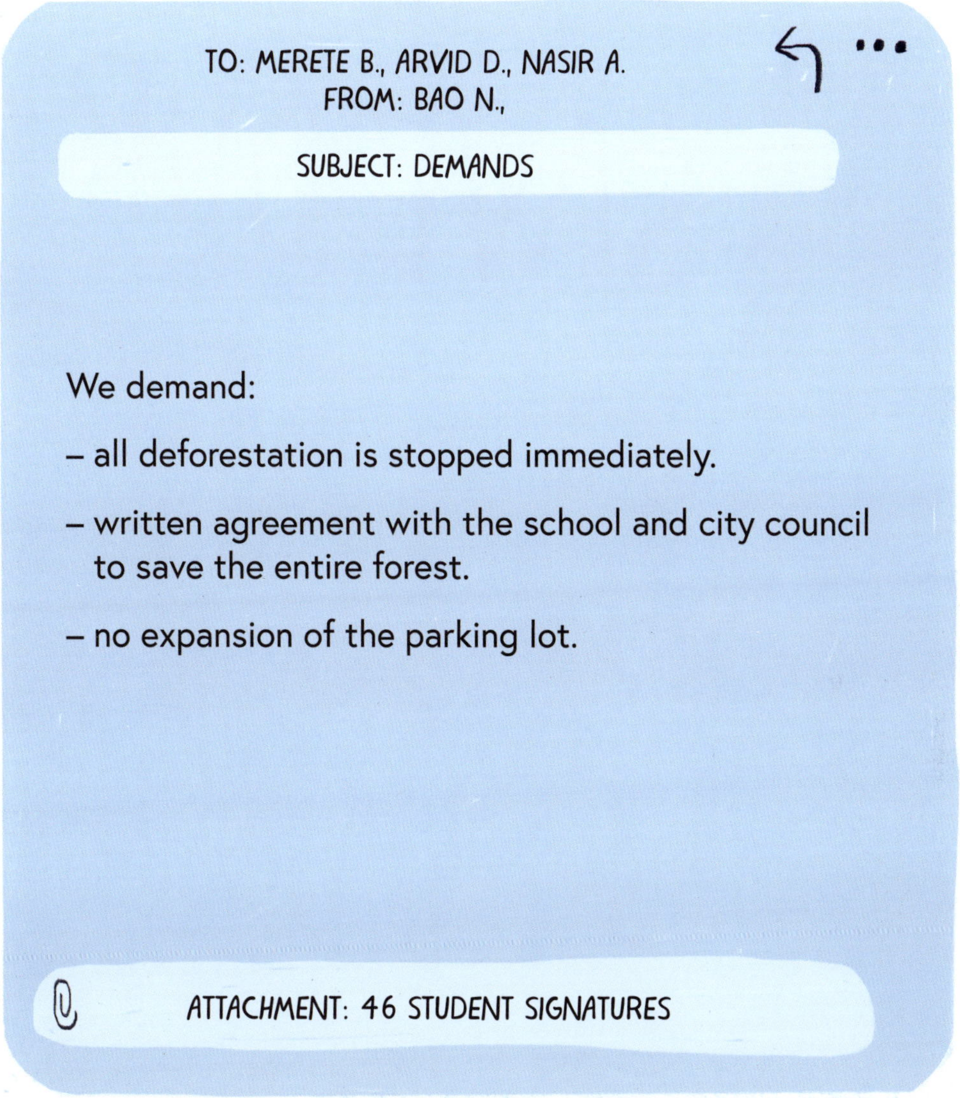
TO: MERETE B., ARVID D., NASIR A.
FROM: BAO N.,
SUBJECT: DEMANDS
We demand:
– all deforestation is stopped immediately.
– written agreement with the school and city council to save the entire forest.
– no expansion of the parking lot.
ATTACHMENT: 46 STUDENT SIGNATURES

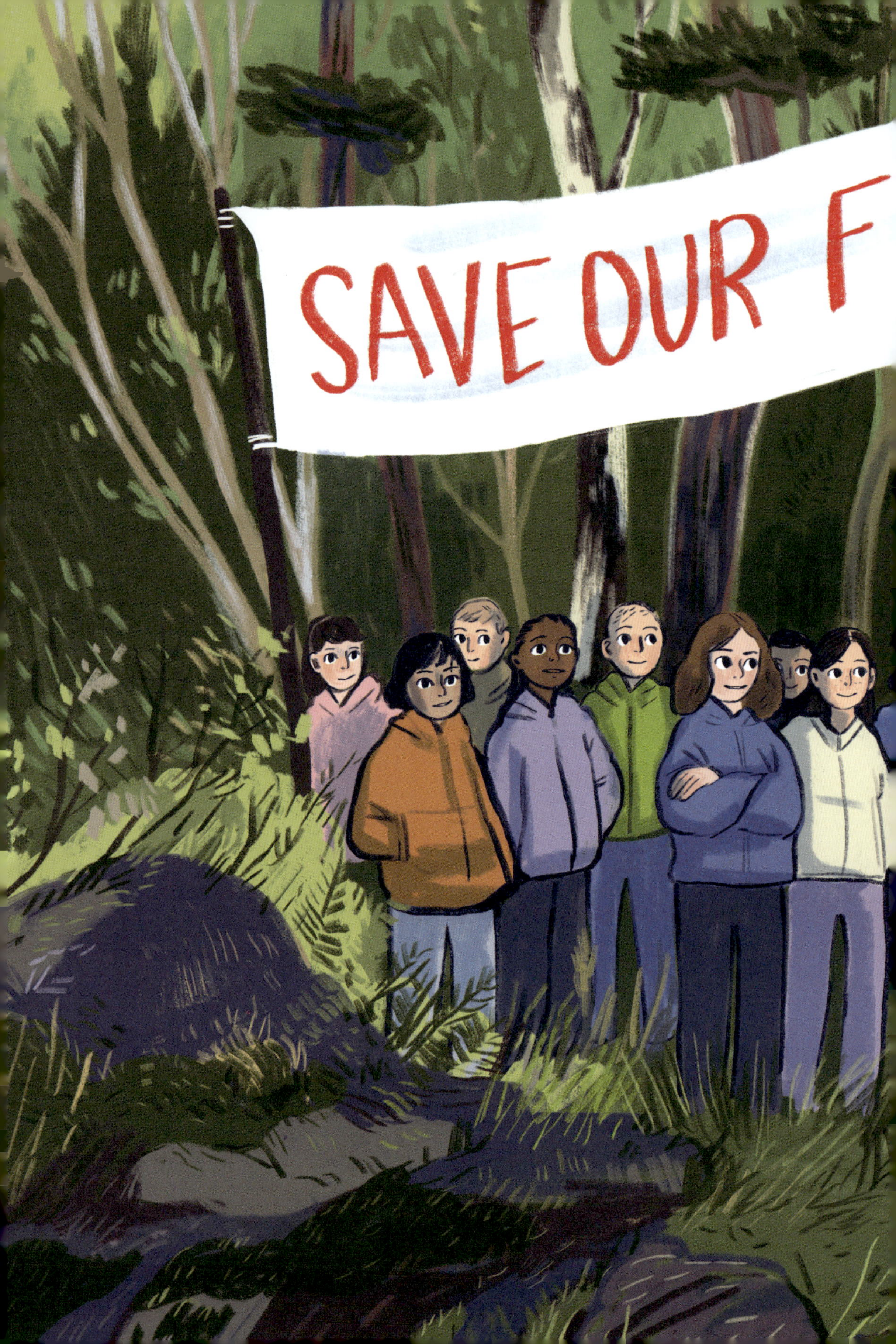
SAVE OUR F

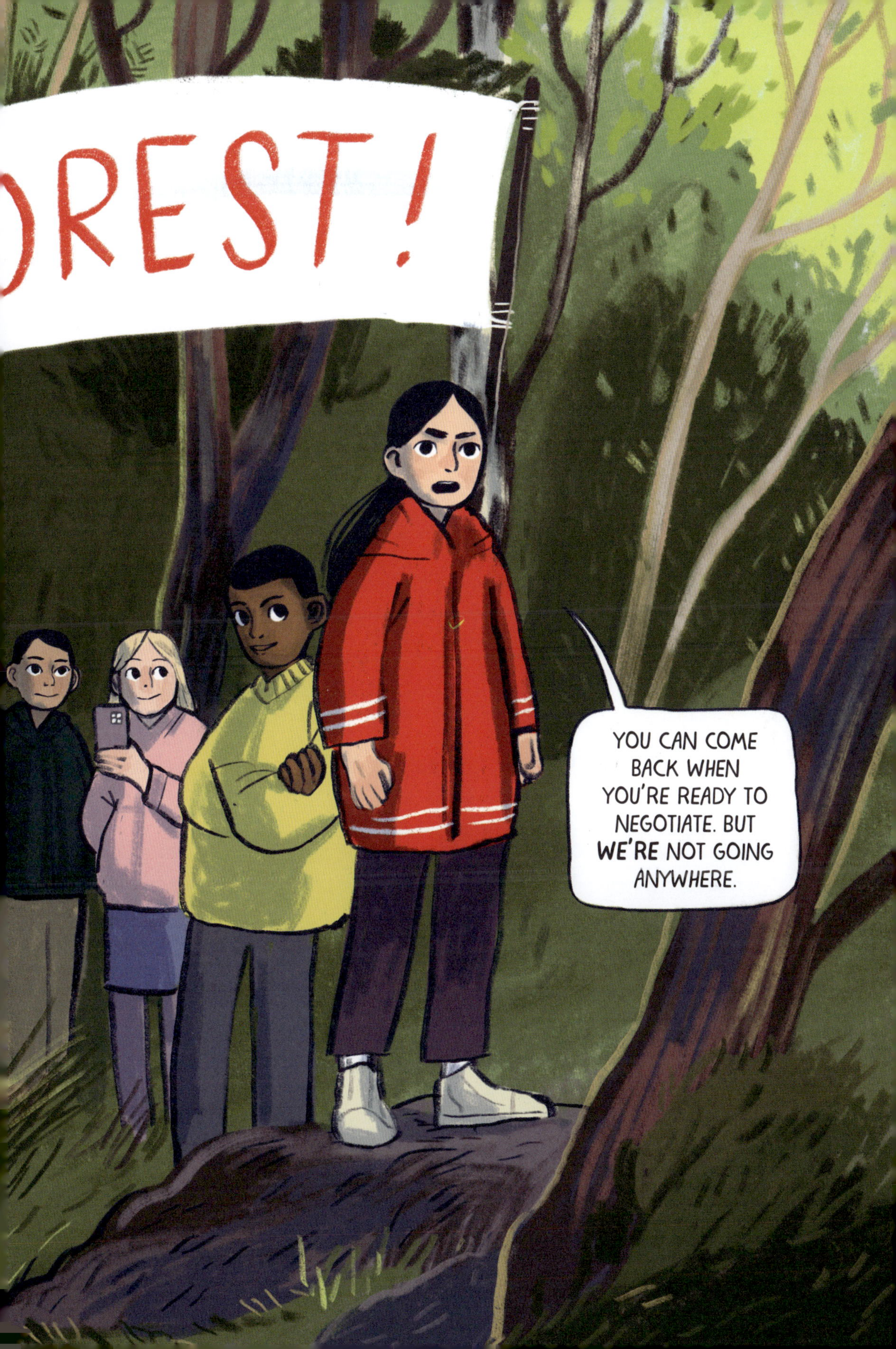
OREST!
YOU CAN COME BACK WHEN YOU'RE READY TO NEGOTIATE. BUT WE'RE NOT GOING ANYWHERE.

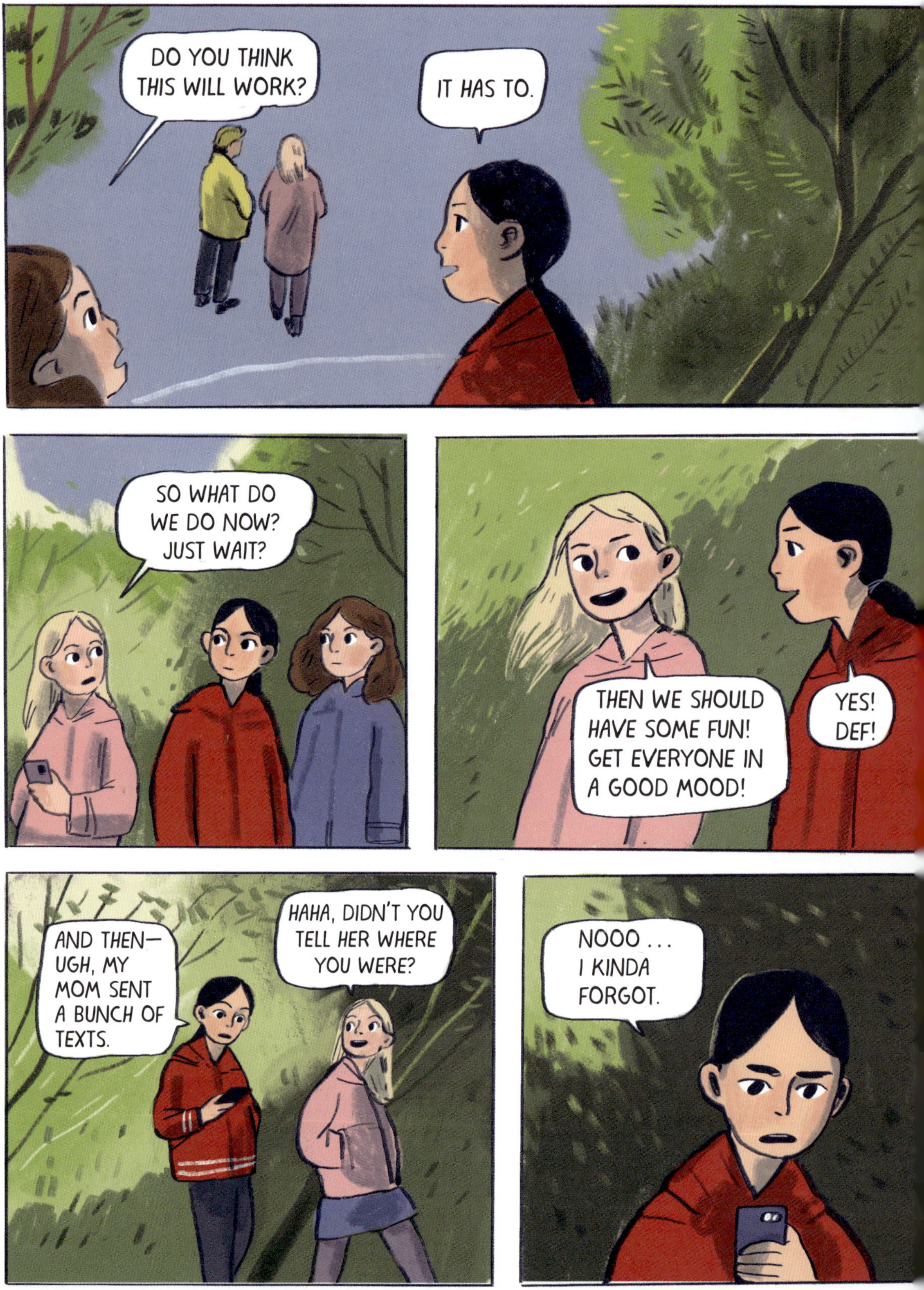
DO YOU THINK THIS WILL WORK?
IT HAS TO.
SO WHAT DO WE DO NOW? JUST WAIT?
THEN WE SHOULD HAVE SOME FUN! GET EVERYONE IN A GOOD MOOD!
YES! DEF!
AND THEN— UGH, MY MOM SENT A BUNCH OF TEXTS.
HAHA, DIDN'T YOU TELL HER WHERE YOU WERE?
NOOO . . . I KINDA FORGOT.

MOM
Bao, I just got a message from the principal. Is it true that you're occupying the forest?

Can you call me?

Bao, are you in the forest?

Call me.

I'll be there in 30 min if I don't hear from you.

BAO
Sorry I forgot to tell you I'm in the bog

MOM
????

BAO
It's a protest, mom!
It's important
And we have a first aid kit
And sleeping bags
And food
It's fine
I'll be home in a few days
and I'm 13 now, I can take care of myself

MOM
We have to talk.
I'm calling you.

BAO
NO time RN
Maybe tomorrow

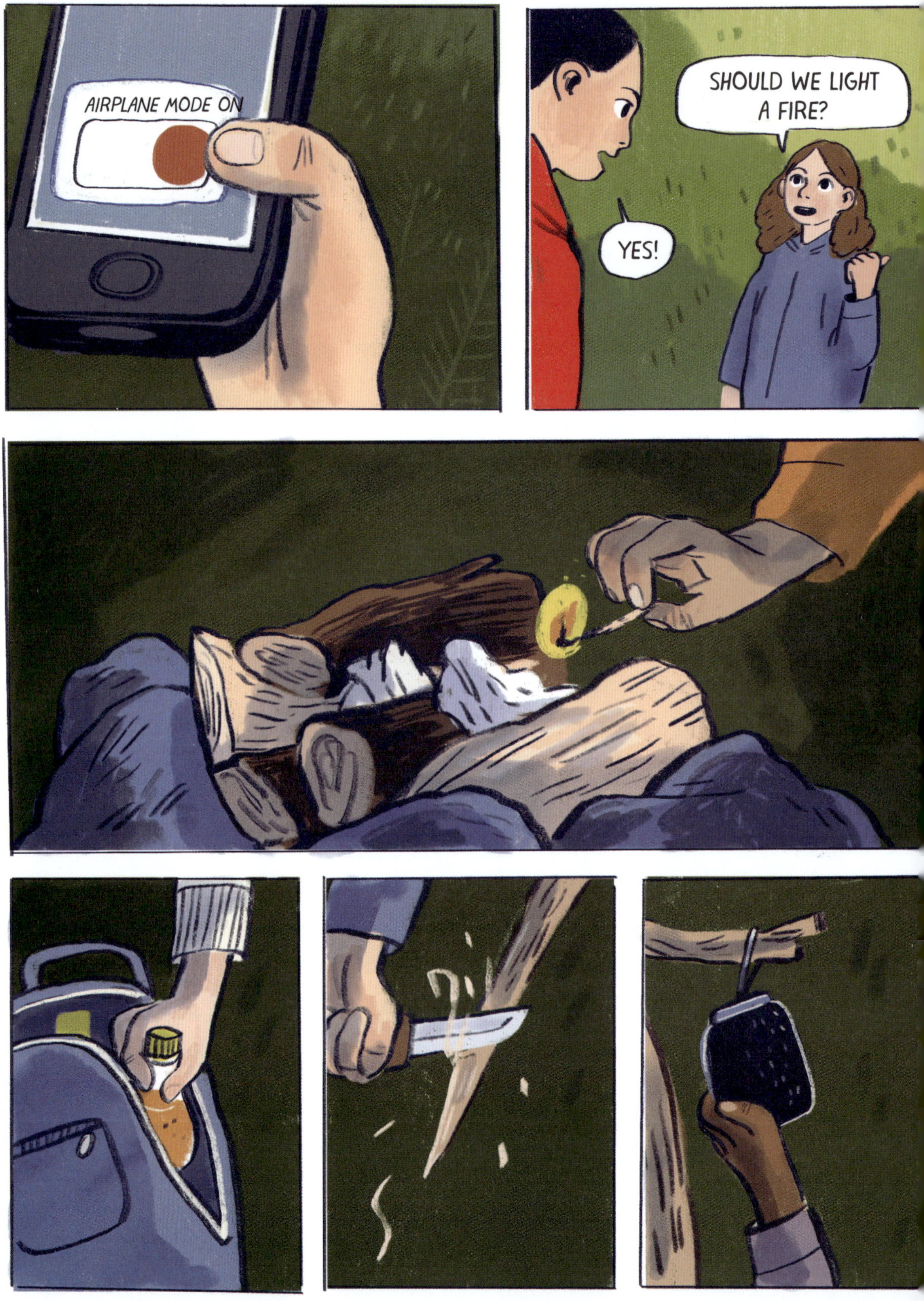
AIRPLANE MODE ON
SHOULD WE LIGHT A FIRE?
YES!

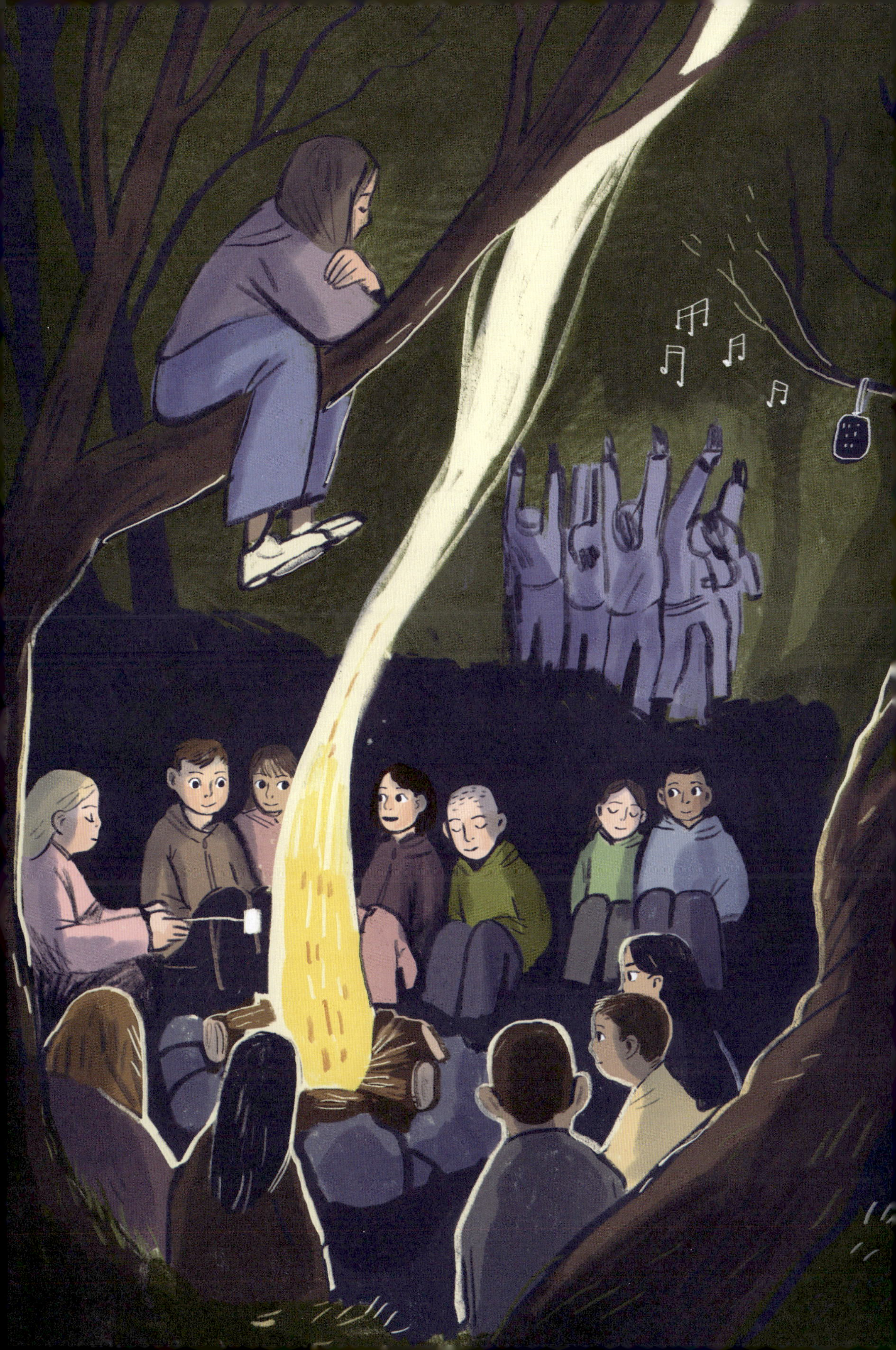

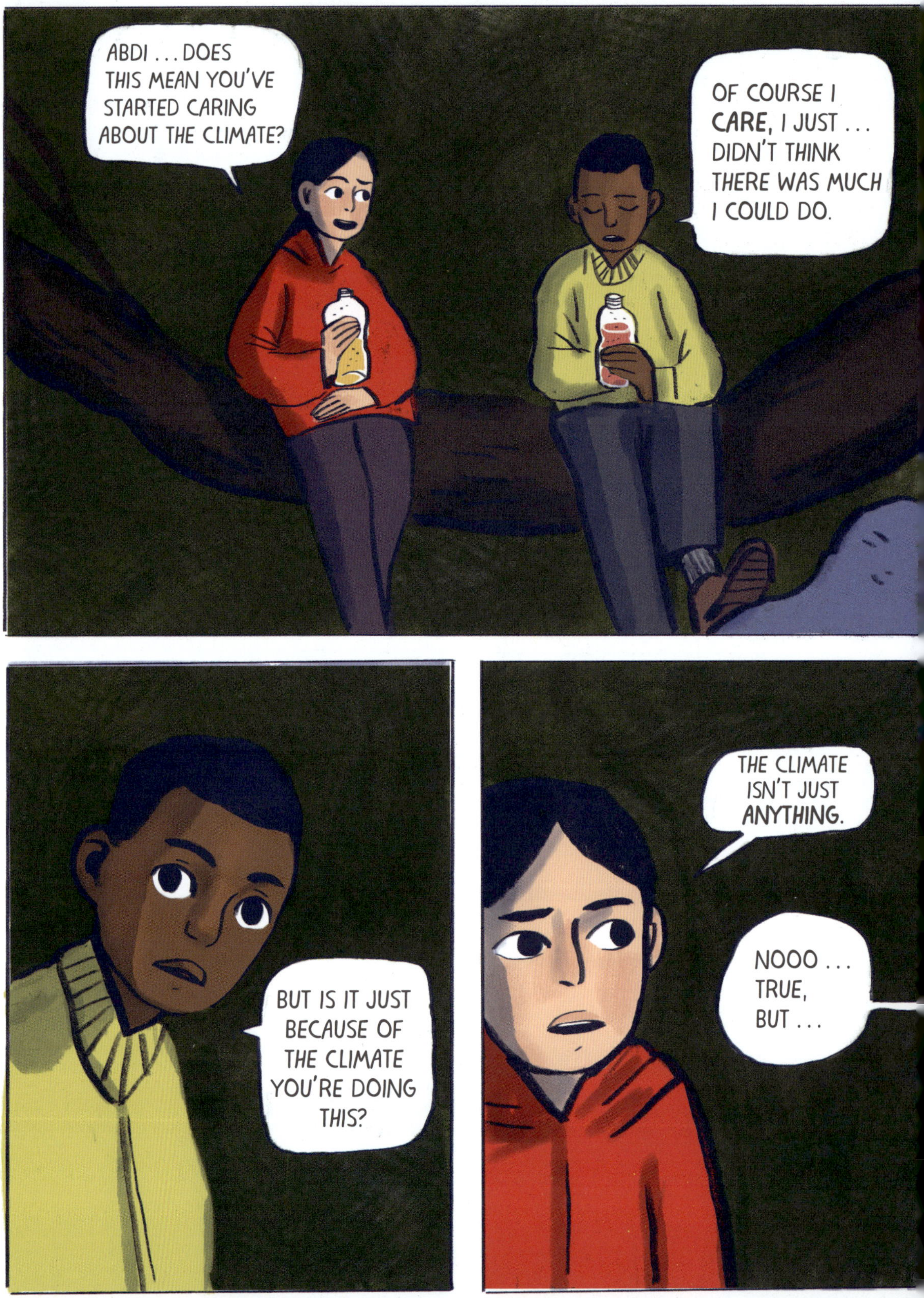
ABDI . . . DOES THIS MEAN YOU'VE STARTED CARING ABOUT THE CLIMATE?
OF COURSE I **CARE**, I JUST . . . DIDN'T THINK THERE WAS MUCH I COULD DO.
BUT IS IT JUST BECAUSE OF THE CLIMATE YOU'RE DOING THIS?
THE CLIMATE ISN'T JUST **ANYTHING**.
NOOO . . . TRUE, BUT . . .

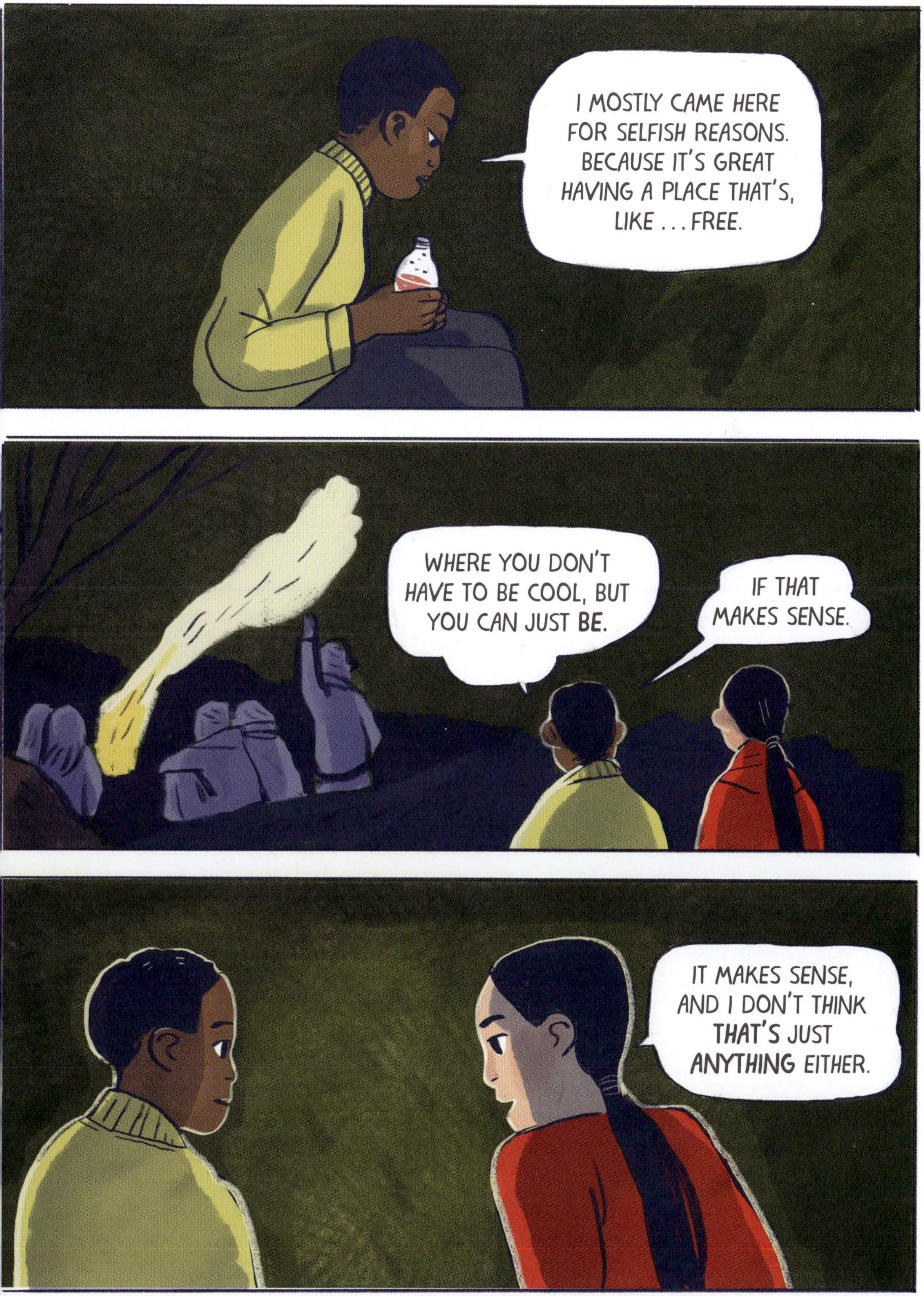
I MOSTLY CAME HERE FOR SELFISH REASONS. BECAUSE IT'S GREAT HAVING A PLACE THAT'S, LIKE . . . FREE.
WHERE YOU DON'T HAVE TO BE COOL, BUT YOU CAN JUST **BE**.
IF THAT MAKES SENSE.
IT MAKES SENSE, AND I DON'T THINK **THAT'S** JUST **ANYTHING** EITHER.

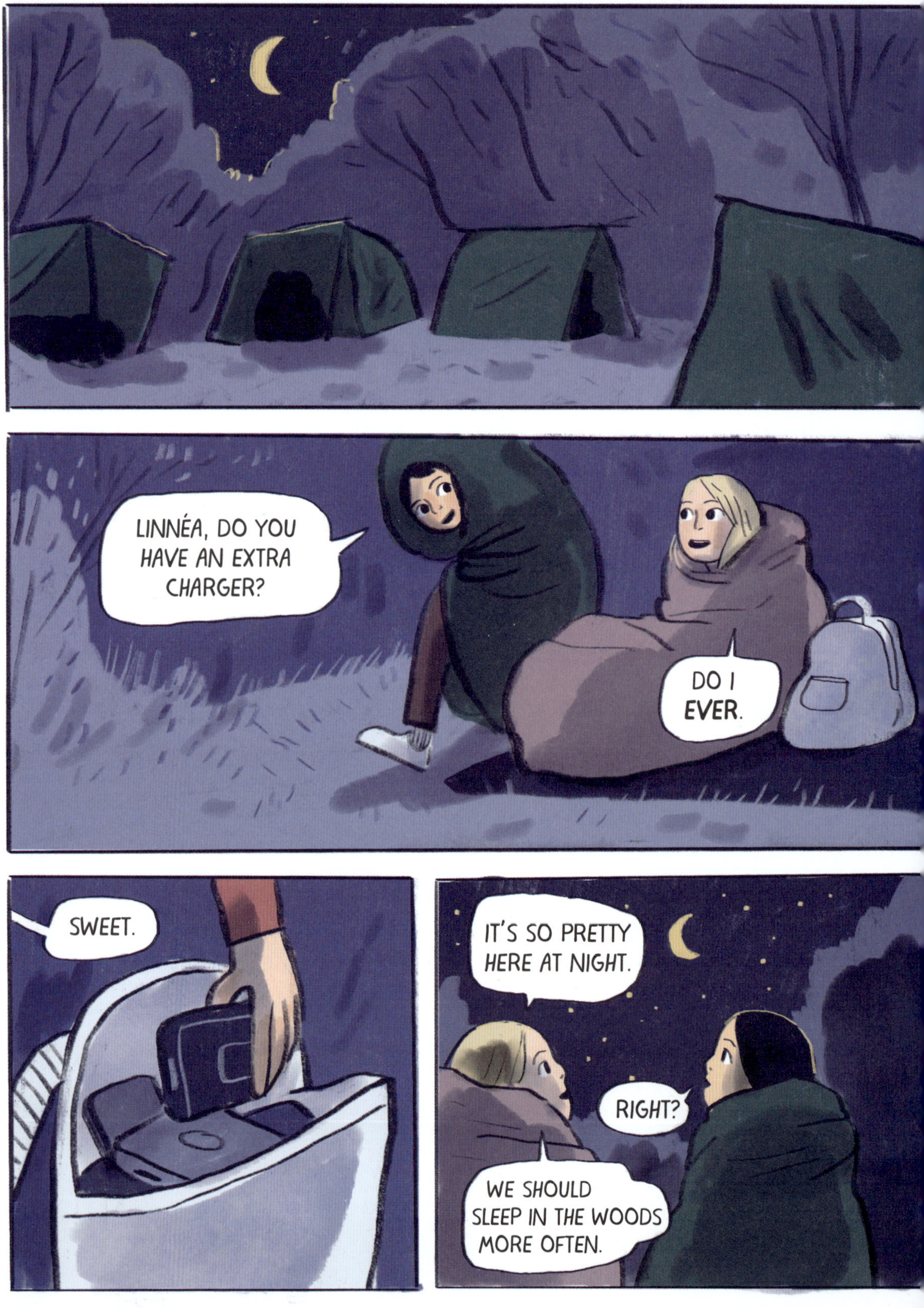
LINNÉA, DO YOU HAVE AN EXTRA CHARGER?
DO I EVER.
SWEET.
IT'S SO PRETTY HERE AT NIGHT.
RIGHT?
WE SHOULD SLEEP IN THE WOODS MORE OFTEN.

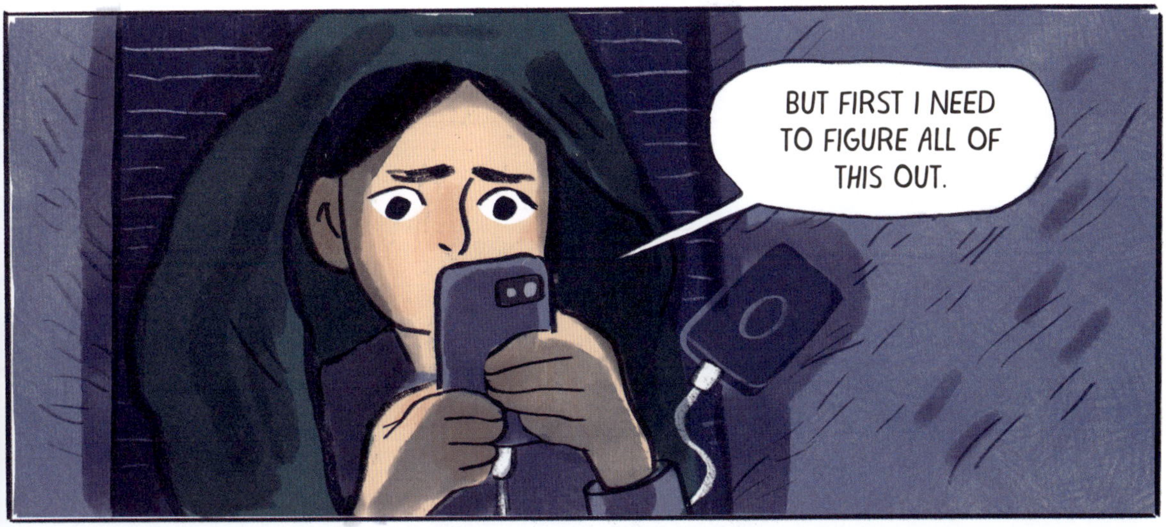
BUT FIRST I NEED TO FIGURE ALL OF THIS OUT.

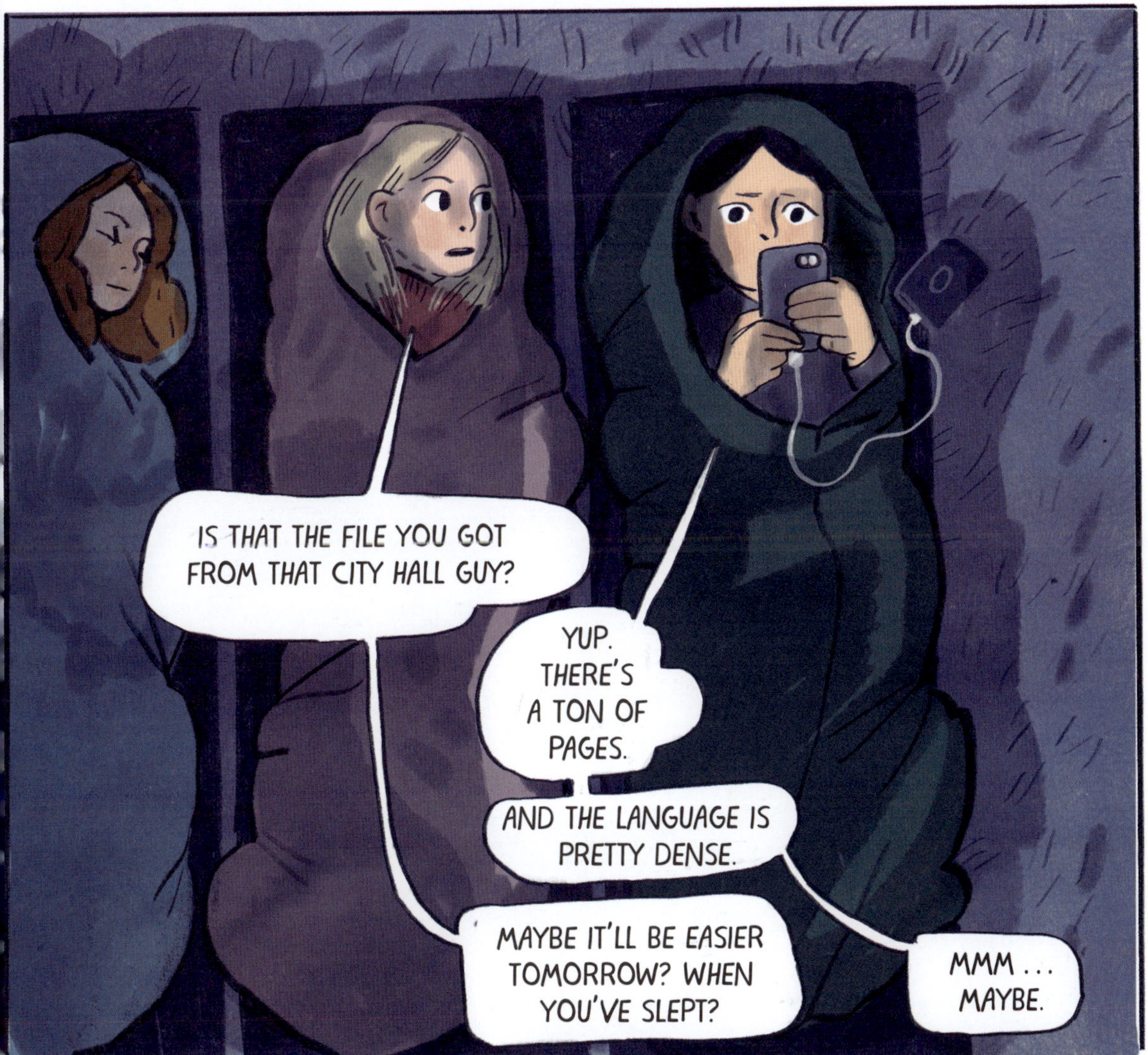
IS THAT THE FILE YOU GOT FROM THAT CITY HALL GUY?
YUP. THERE'S A TON OF PAGES.
AND THE LANGUAGE IS PRETTY DENSE.
MAYBE IT'LL BE EASIER TOMORROW? WHEN YOU'VE SLEPT?
MMM . . . MAYBE.

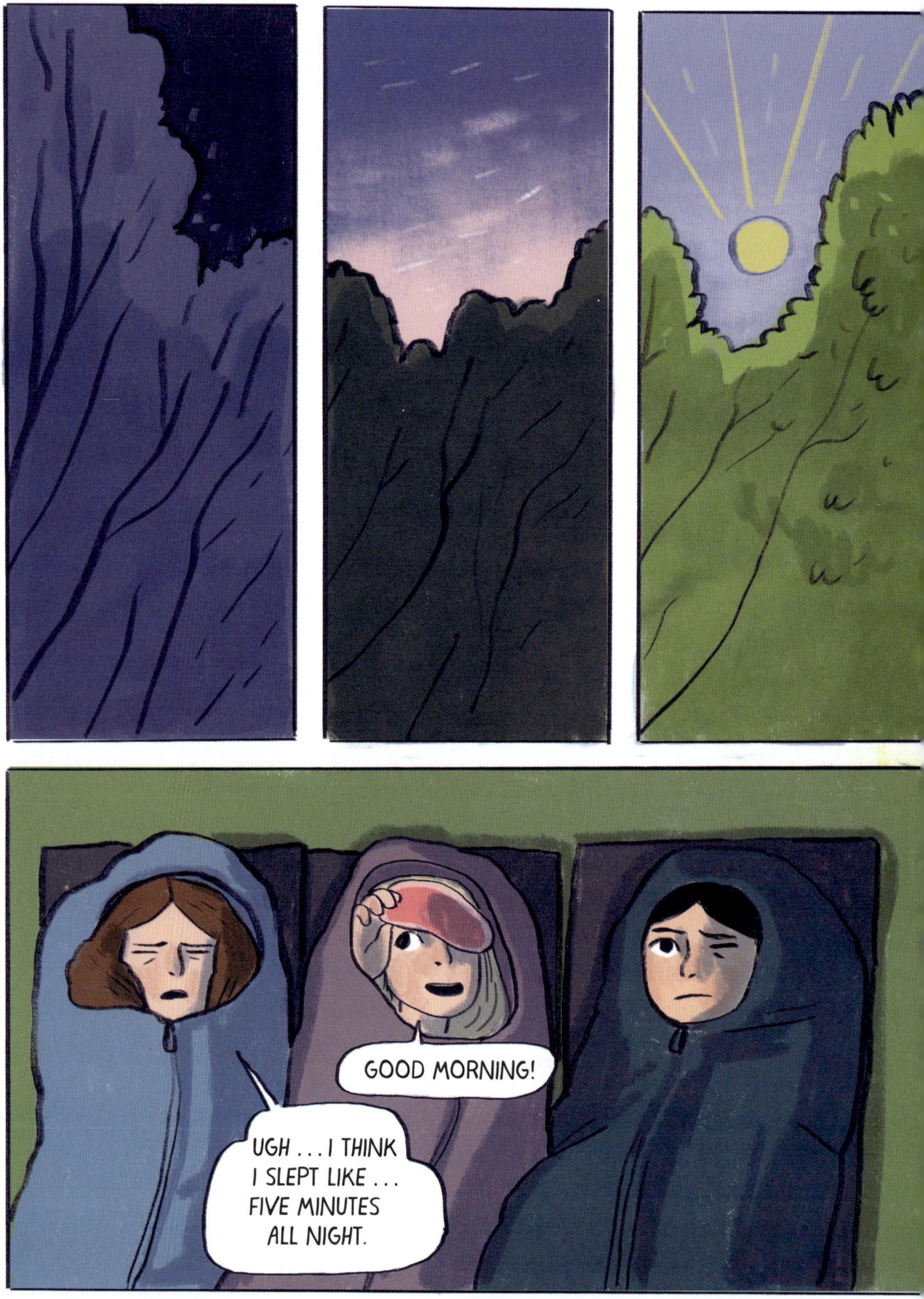
GOOD MORNING!
UGH . . . I THINK I SLEPT LIKE . . . FIVE MINUTES ALL NIGHT.

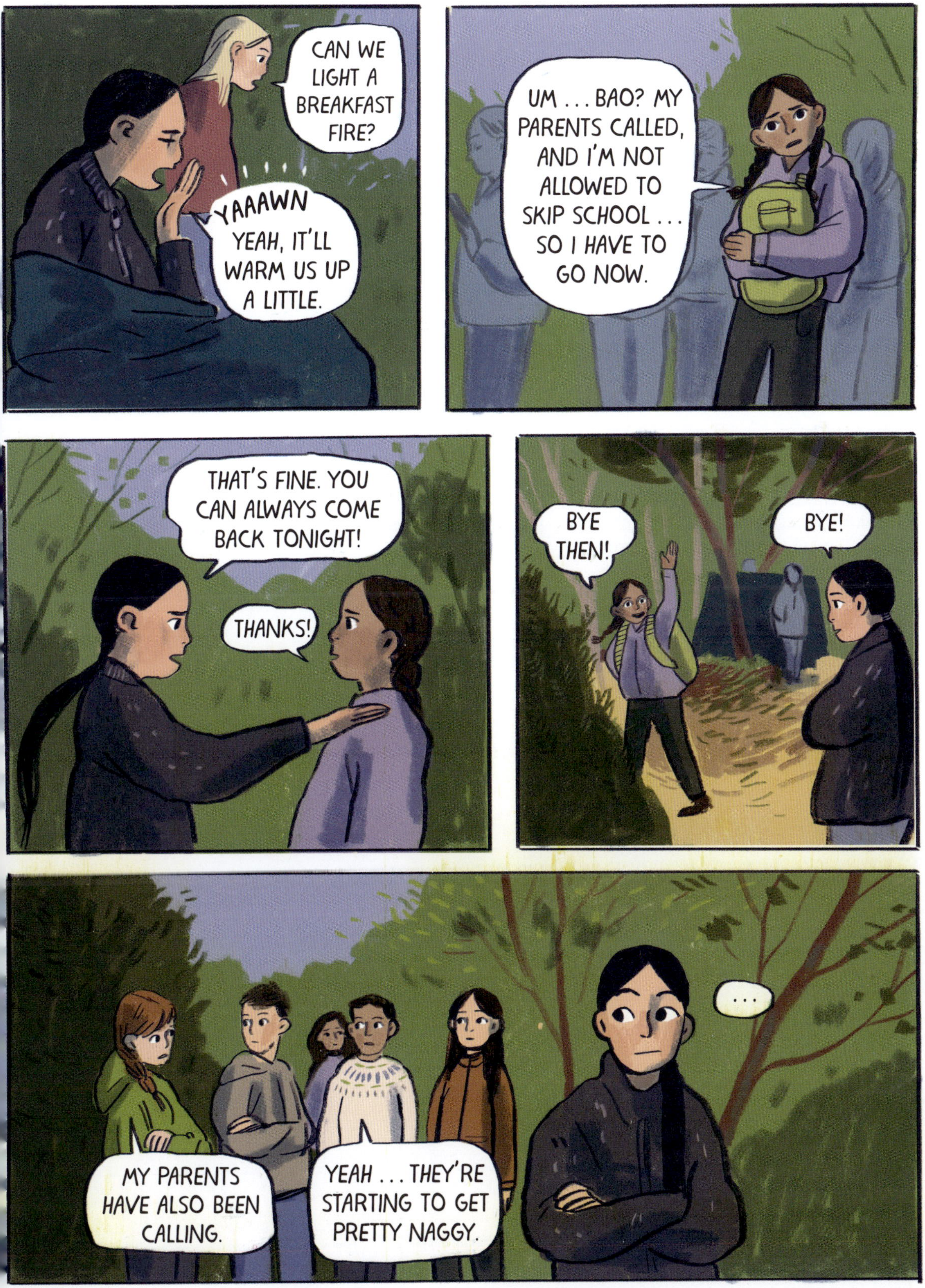
CAN WE LIGHT A BREAKFAST FIRE?
YAAAWN
YEAH, IT'LL WARM US UP A LITTLE.
UM ... BAO? MY PARENTS CALLED, AND I'M NOT ALLOWED TO SKIP SCHOOL ... SO I HAVE TO GO NOW.
THAT'S FINE. YOU CAN ALWAYS COME BACK TONIGHT!
THANKS!
BYE THEN!
BYE!
...
MY PARENTS HAVE ALSO BEEN CALLING.
YEAH ... THEY'RE STARTING TO GET PRETTY NAGGY.

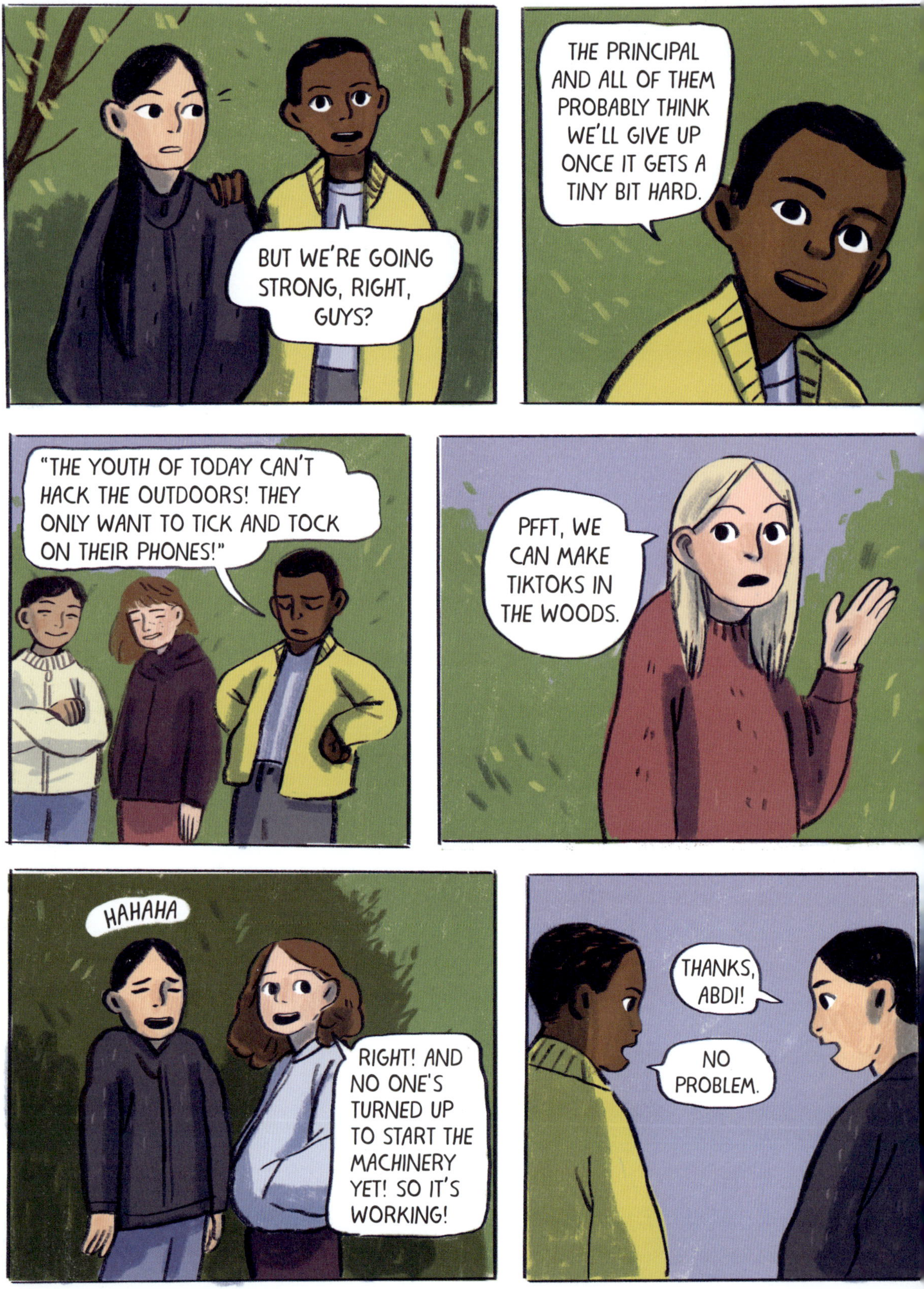
BUT WE'RE GOING STRONG, RIGHT, GUYS?
THE PRINCIPAL AND ALL OF THEM PROBABLY THINK WE'LL GIVE UP ONCE IT GETS A TINY BIT HARD.
"THE YOUTH OF TODAY CAN'T HACK THE OUTDOORS! THEY ONLY WANT TO TICK AND TOCK ON THEIR PHONES!"
PFFT, WE CAN MAKE TIKTOKS IN THE WOODS.
HAHAHA
RIGHT! AND NO ONE'S TURNED UP TO START THE MACHINERY YET! SO IT'S WORKING!
THANKS, ABDI!
NO PROBLEM.

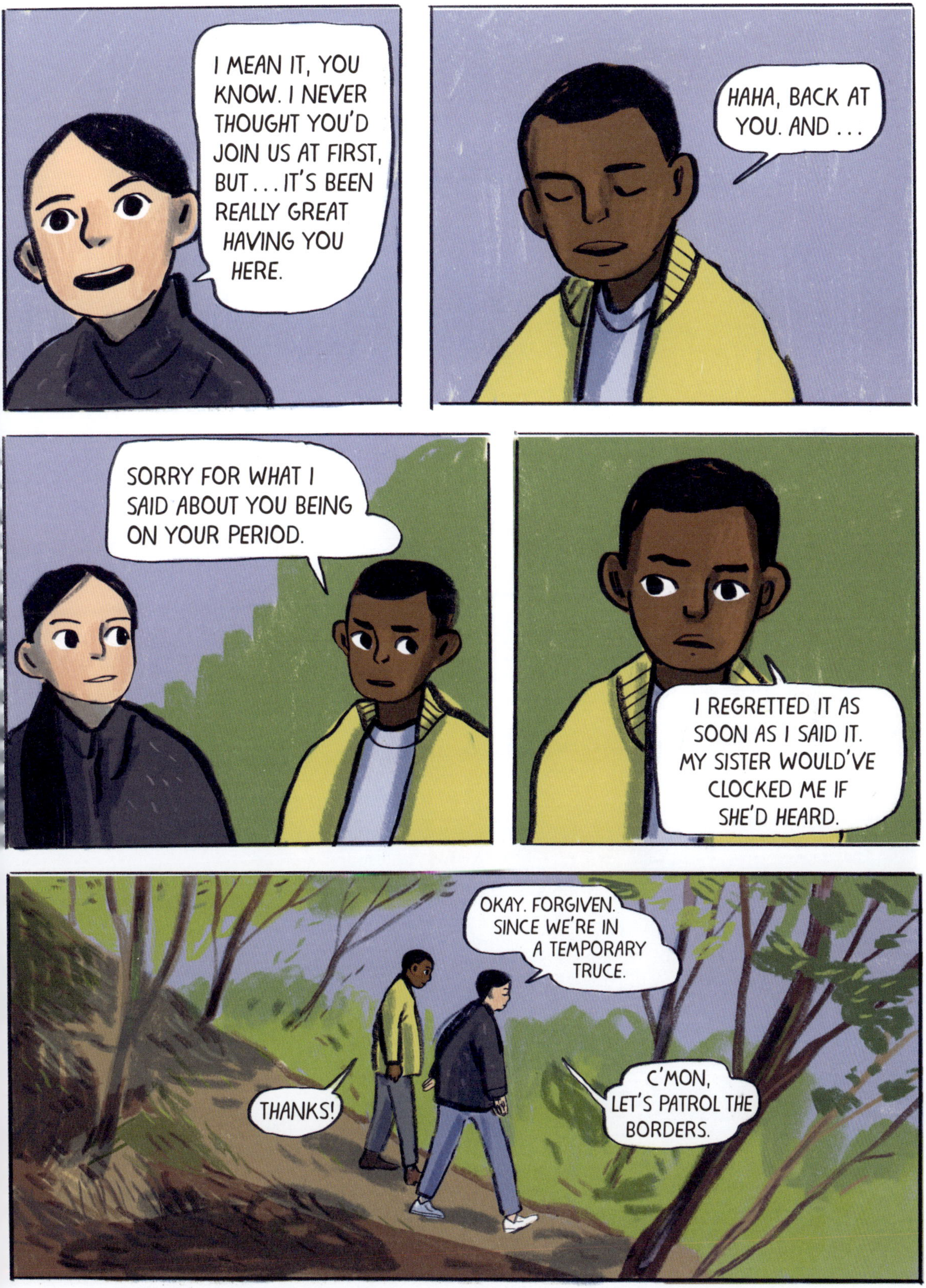
I MEAN IT, YOU KNOW. I NEVER THOUGHT YOU'D JOIN US AT FIRST, BUT . . . IT'S BEEN REALLY GREAT HAVING YOU HERE.
HAHA, BACK AT YOU. AND . . .
SORRY FOR WHAT I SAID ABOUT YOU BEING ON YOUR PERIOD.
I REGRETTED IT AS SOON AS I SAID IT. MY SISTER WOULD'VE CLOCKED ME IF SHE'D HEARD.
OKAY. FORGIVEN. SINCE WE'RE IN A TEMPORARY TRUCE.
THANKS!
C'MON, LET'S PATROL THE BORDERS.

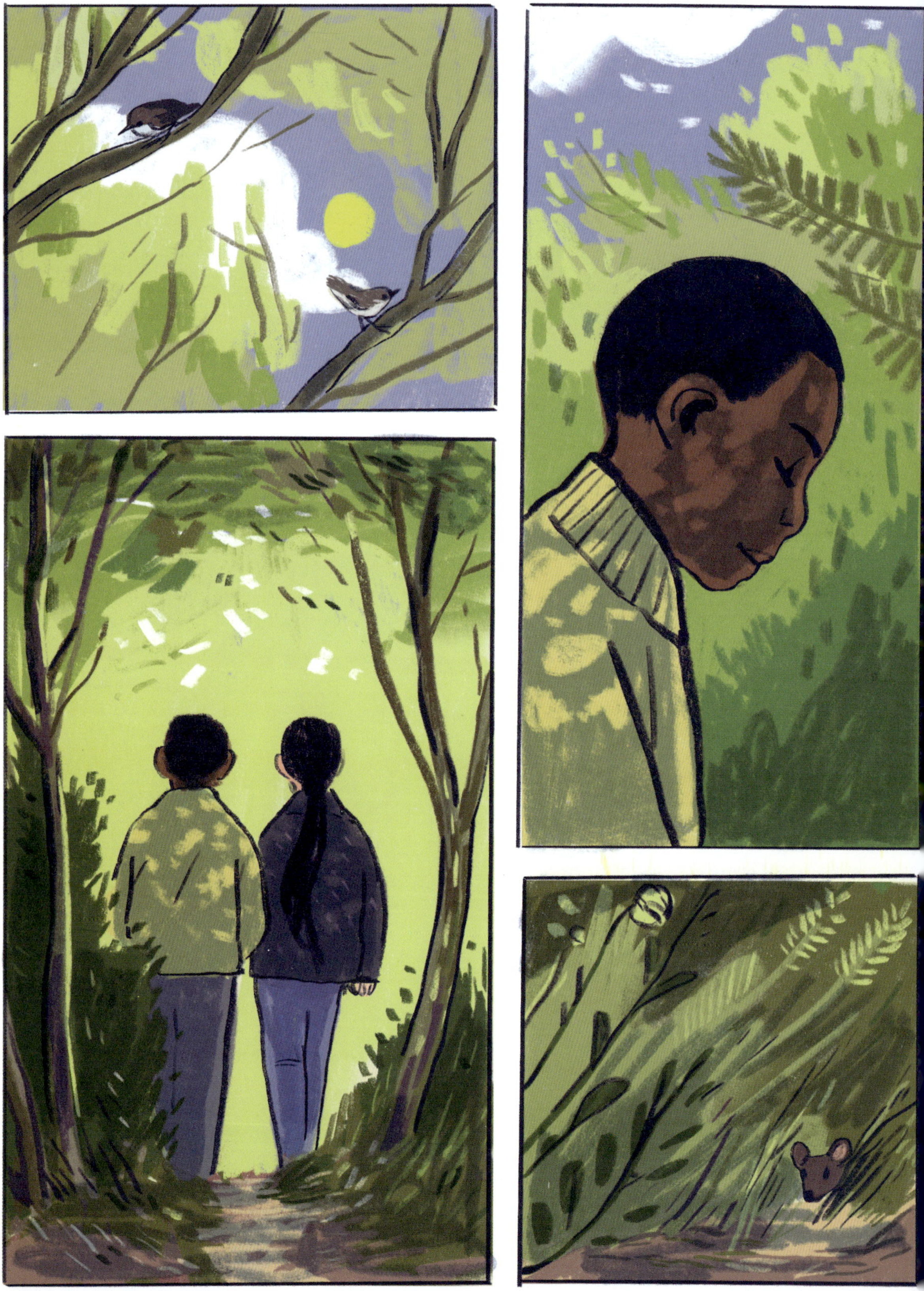

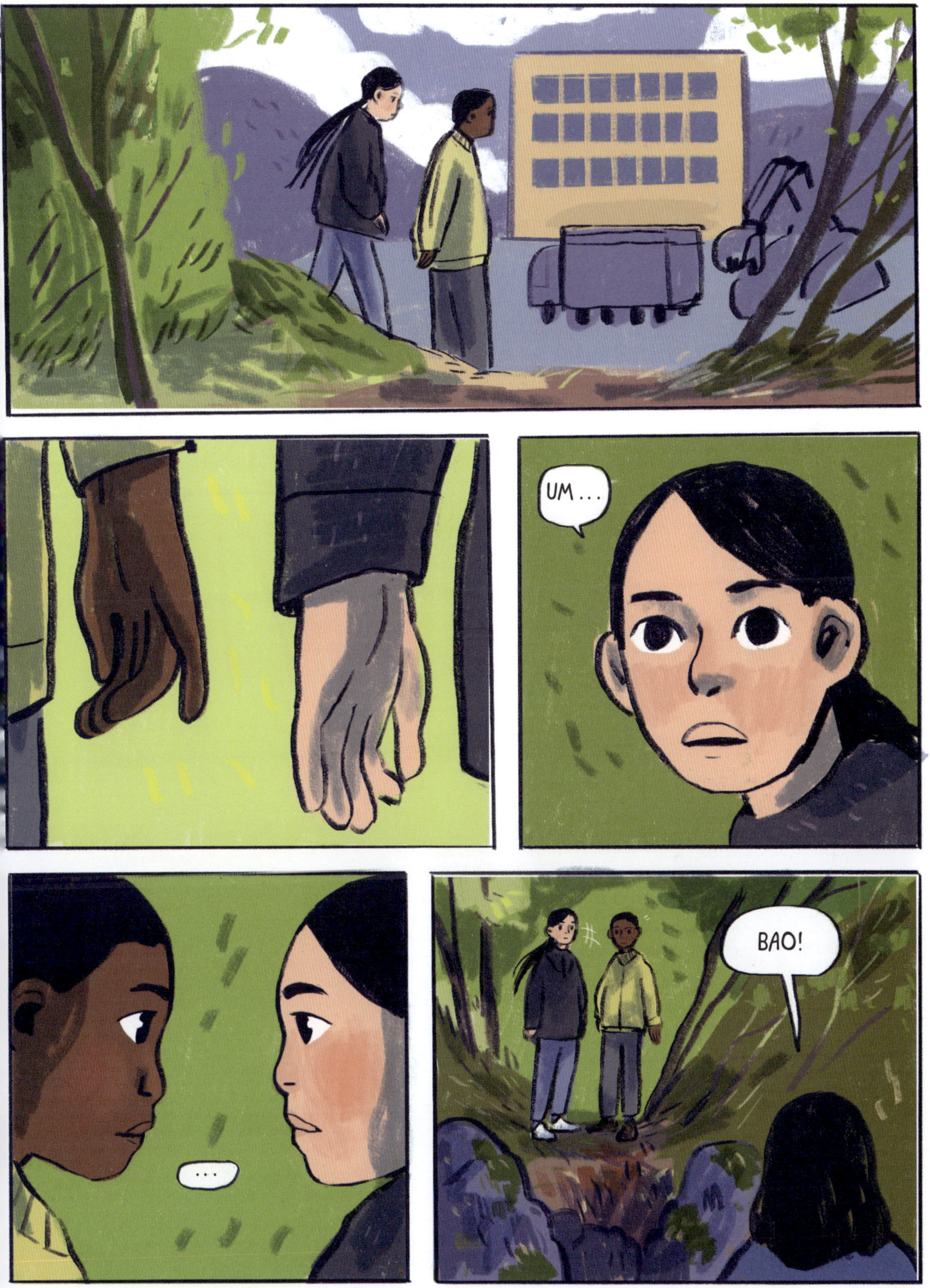
UM...
...
BAO!

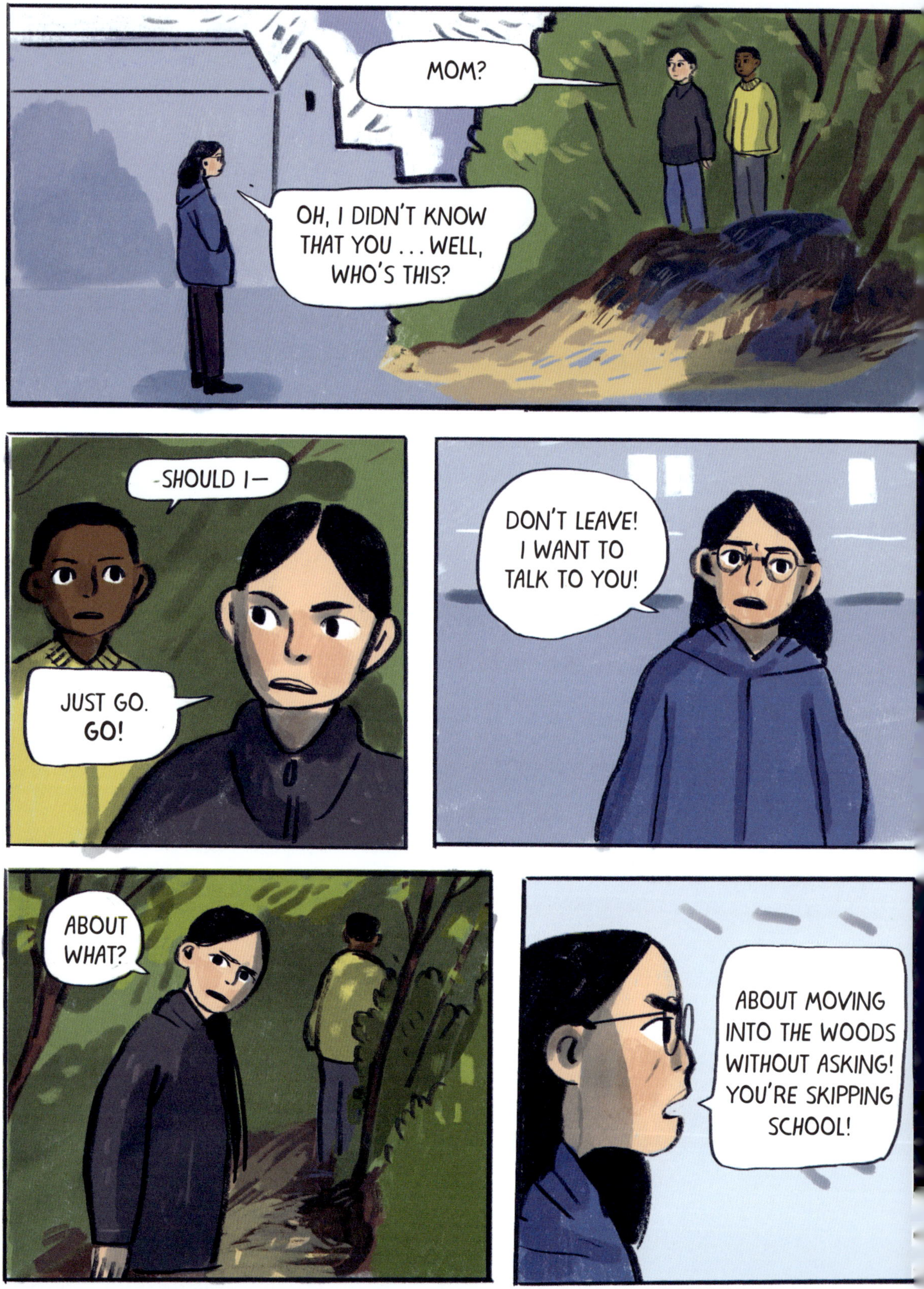
MOM?
OH, I DIDN'T KNOW THAT YOU . . . WELL, WHO'S THIS?
-SHOULD I—
JUST GO. GO!
DON'T LEAVE! I WANT TO TALK TO YOU!
ABOUT WHAT?
ABOUT MOVING INTO THE WOODS WITHOUT ASKING! YOU'RE SKIPPING SCHOOL!

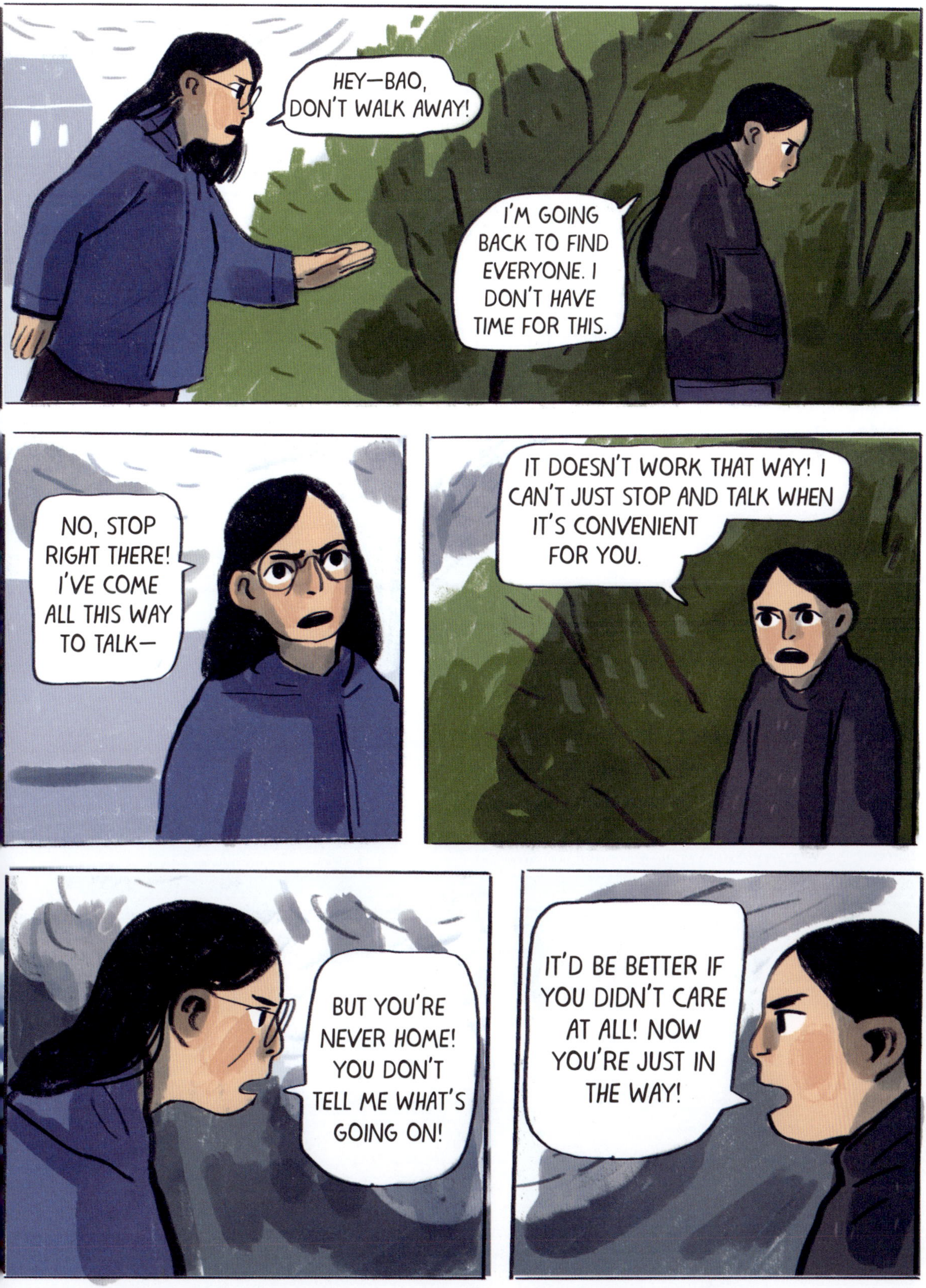
HEY—BAO, DON'T WALK AWAY!
I'M GOING BACK TO FIND EVERYONE. I DON'T HAVE TIME FOR THIS.
NO, STOP RIGHT THERE! I'VE COME ALL THIS WAY TO TALK—
IT DOESN'T WORK THAT WAY! I CAN'T JUST STOP AND TALK WHEN IT'S CONVENIENT FOR YOU.
BUT YOU'RE NEVER HOME! YOU DON'T TELL ME WHAT'S GOING ON!
IT'D BE BETTER IF YOU DIDN'T CARE AT ALL! NOW YOU'RE JUST IN THE WAY!

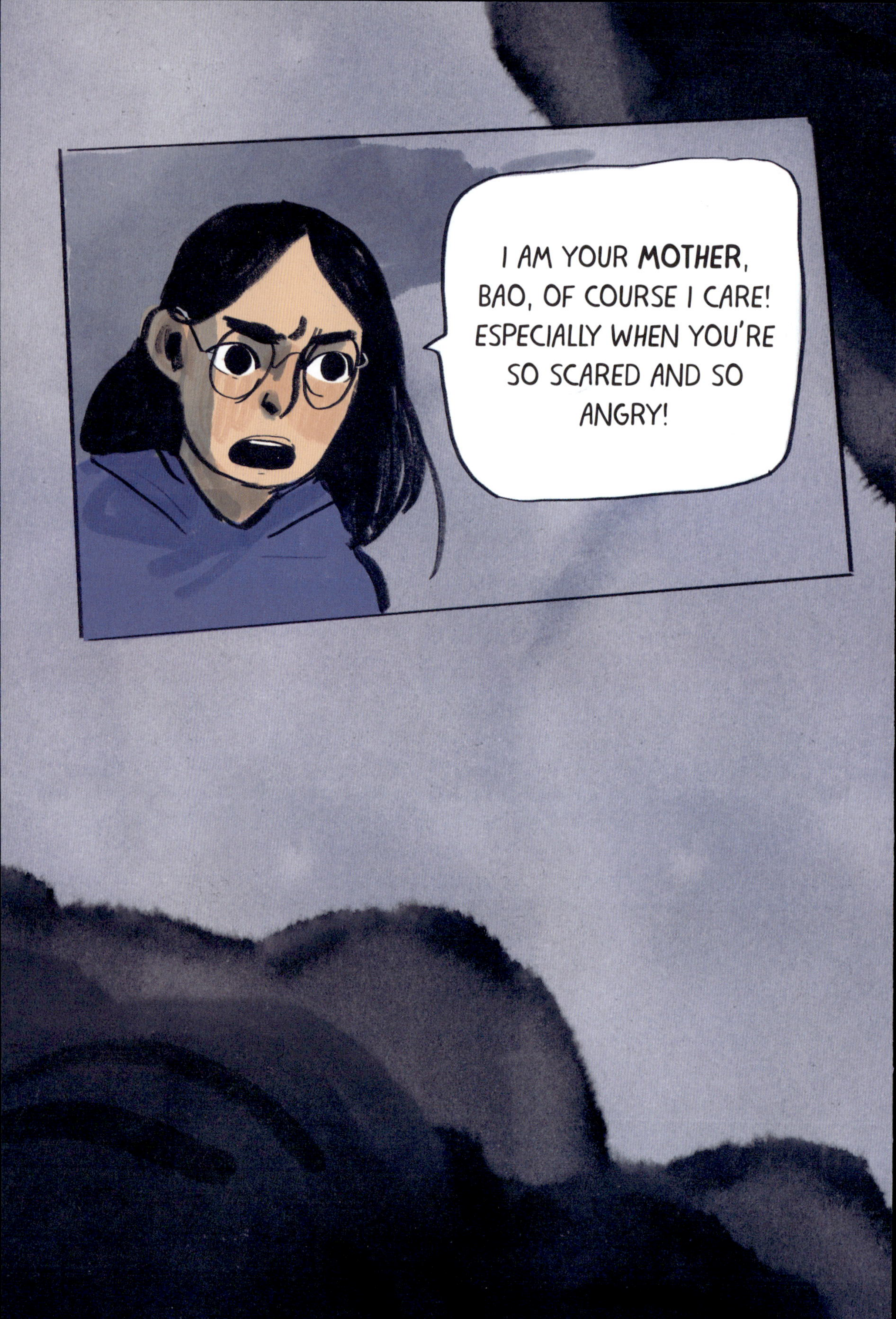
I AM YOUR **MOTHER**, BAO, OF COURSE I CARE! ESPECIALLY WHEN YOU'RE SO SCARED AND SO ANGRY!

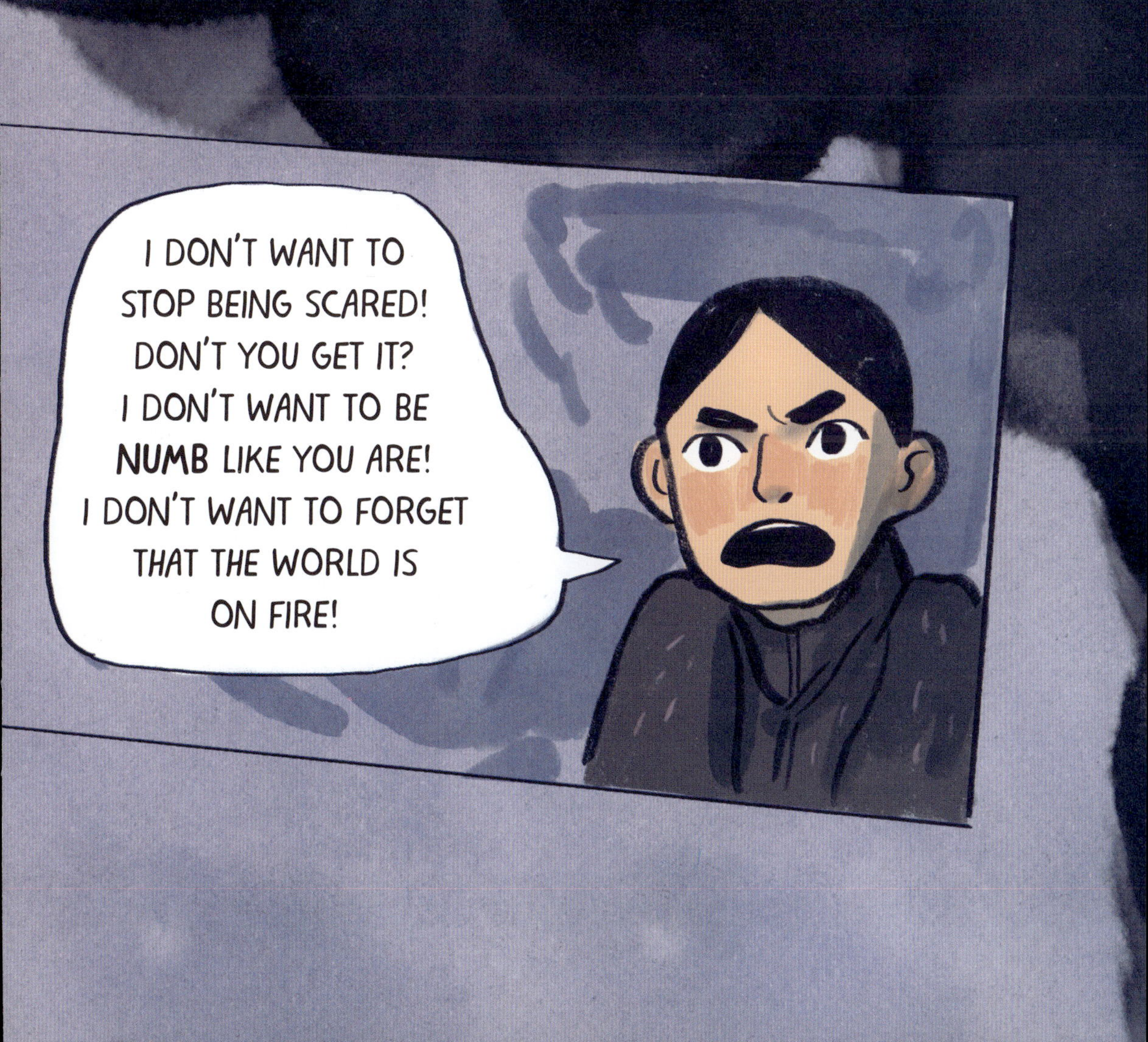
I DON'T WANT TO STOP BEING SCARED! DON'T YOU GET IT? I DON'T WANT TO BE **NUMB** LIKE YOU ARE! I DON'T WANT TO FORGET THAT THE WORLD IS ON FIRE!

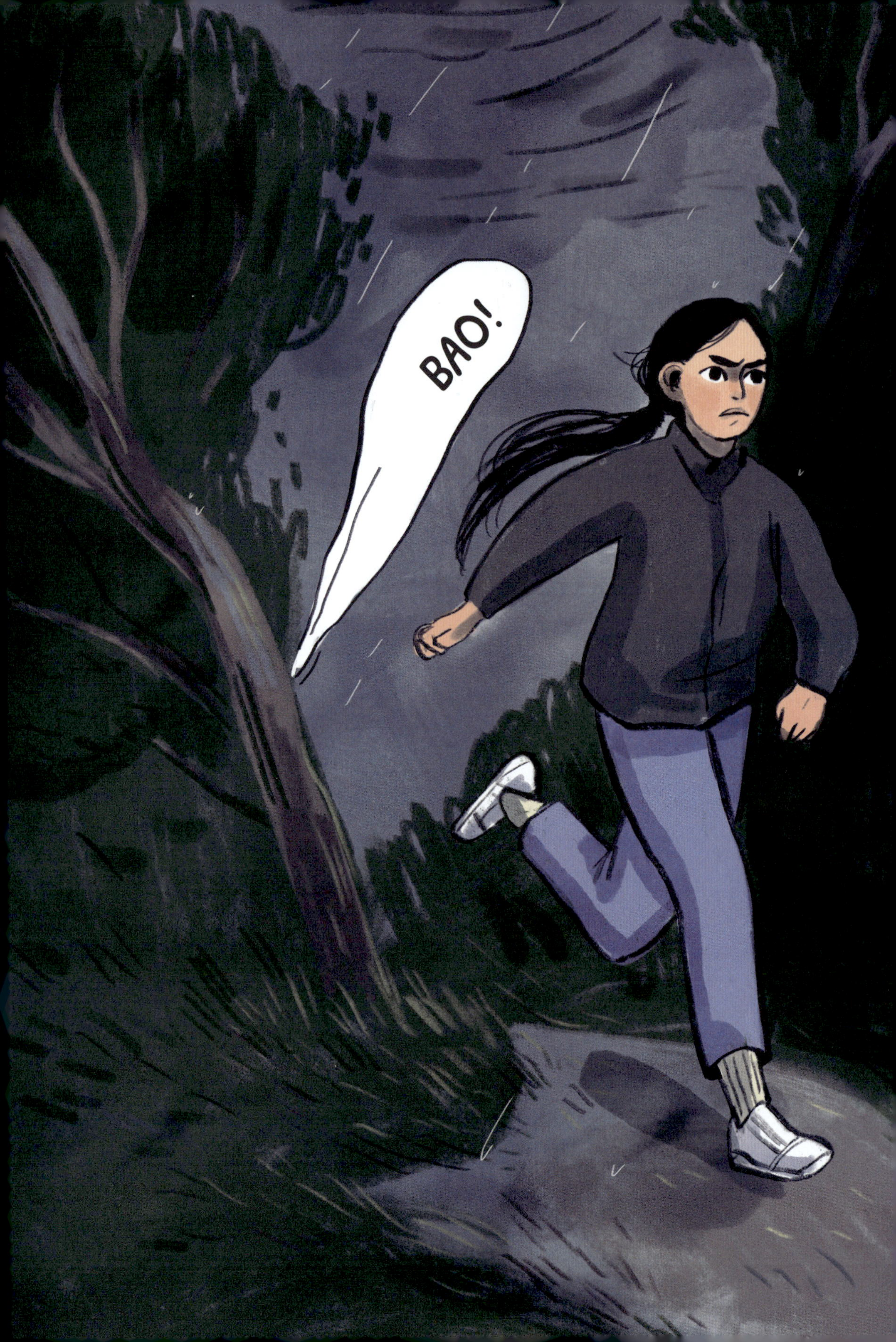
BAO!

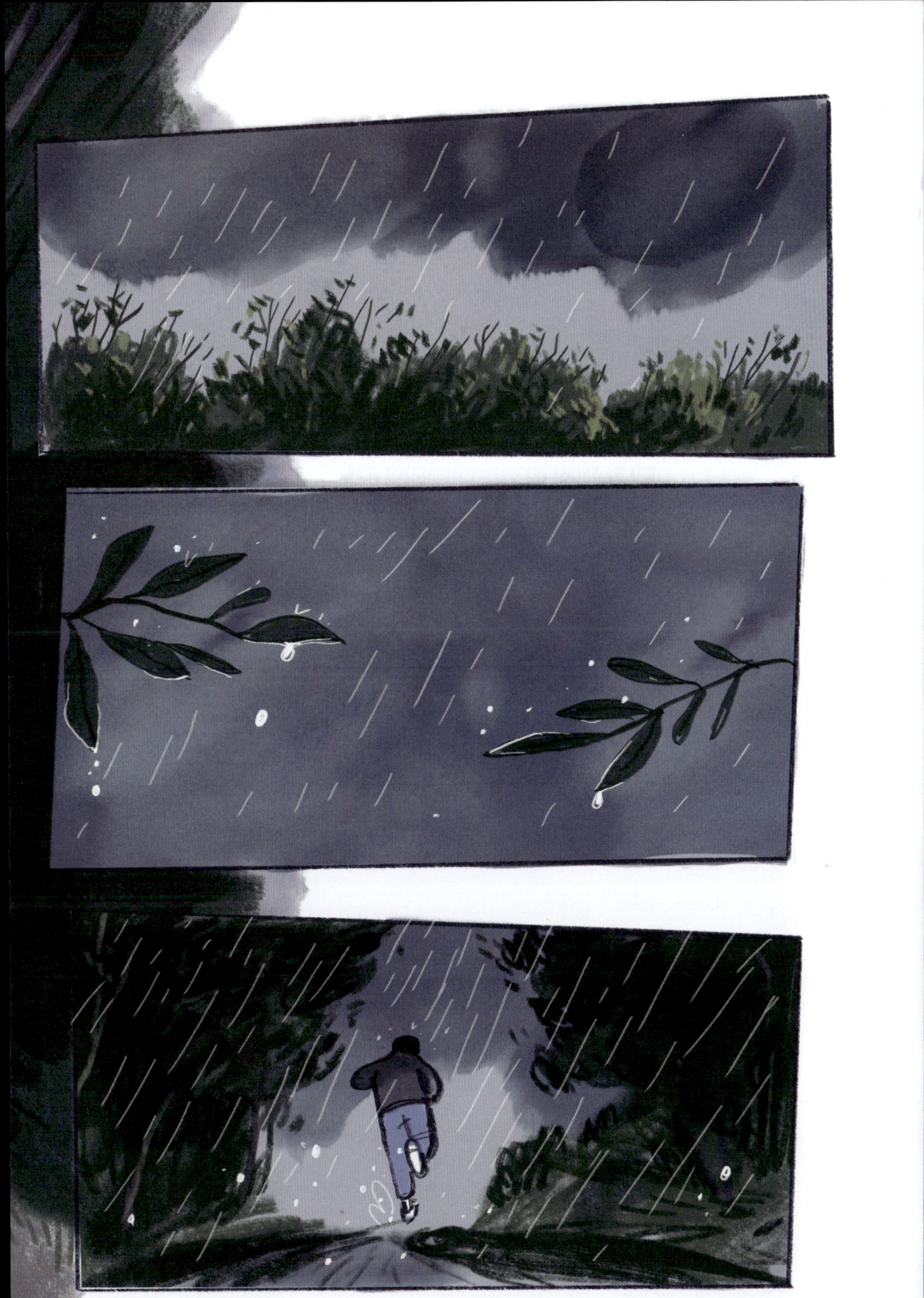

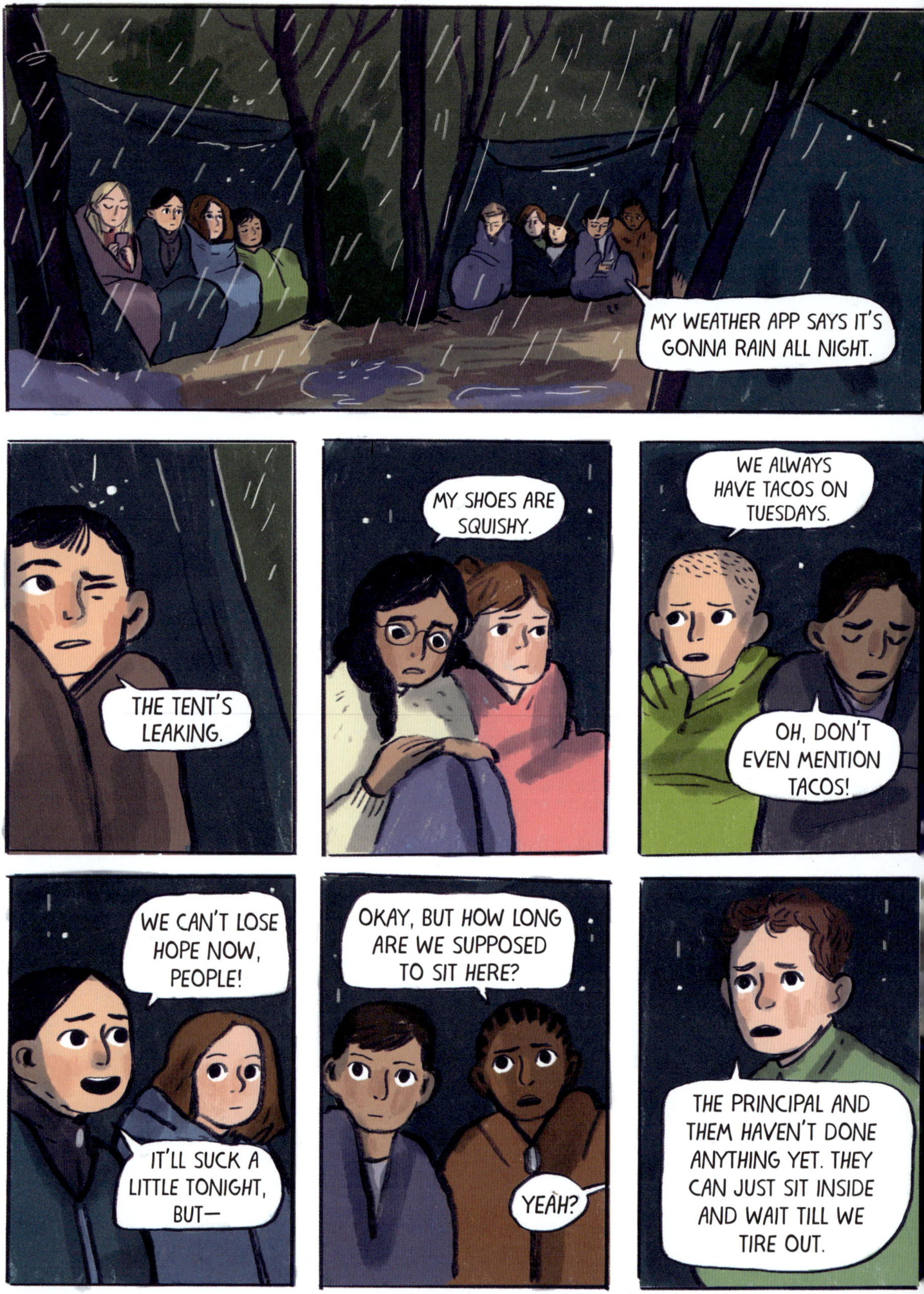
MY WEATHER APP SAYS IT'S GONNA RAIN ALL NIGHT.
THE TENT'S LEAKING.
MY SHOES ARE SQUISHY.
WE ALWAYS HAVE TACOS ON TUESDAYS.
OH, DON'T EVEN MENTION TACOS!
WE CAN'T LOSE HOPE NOW, PEOPLE!
IT'LL SUCK A LITTLE TONIGHT, BUT—
OKAY, BUT HOW LONG ARE WE SUPPOSED TO SIT HERE?
YEAH?
THE PRINCIPAL AND THEM HAVEN'T DONE ANYTHING YET. THEY CAN JUST SIT INSIDE AND WAIT TILL WE TIRE OUT.

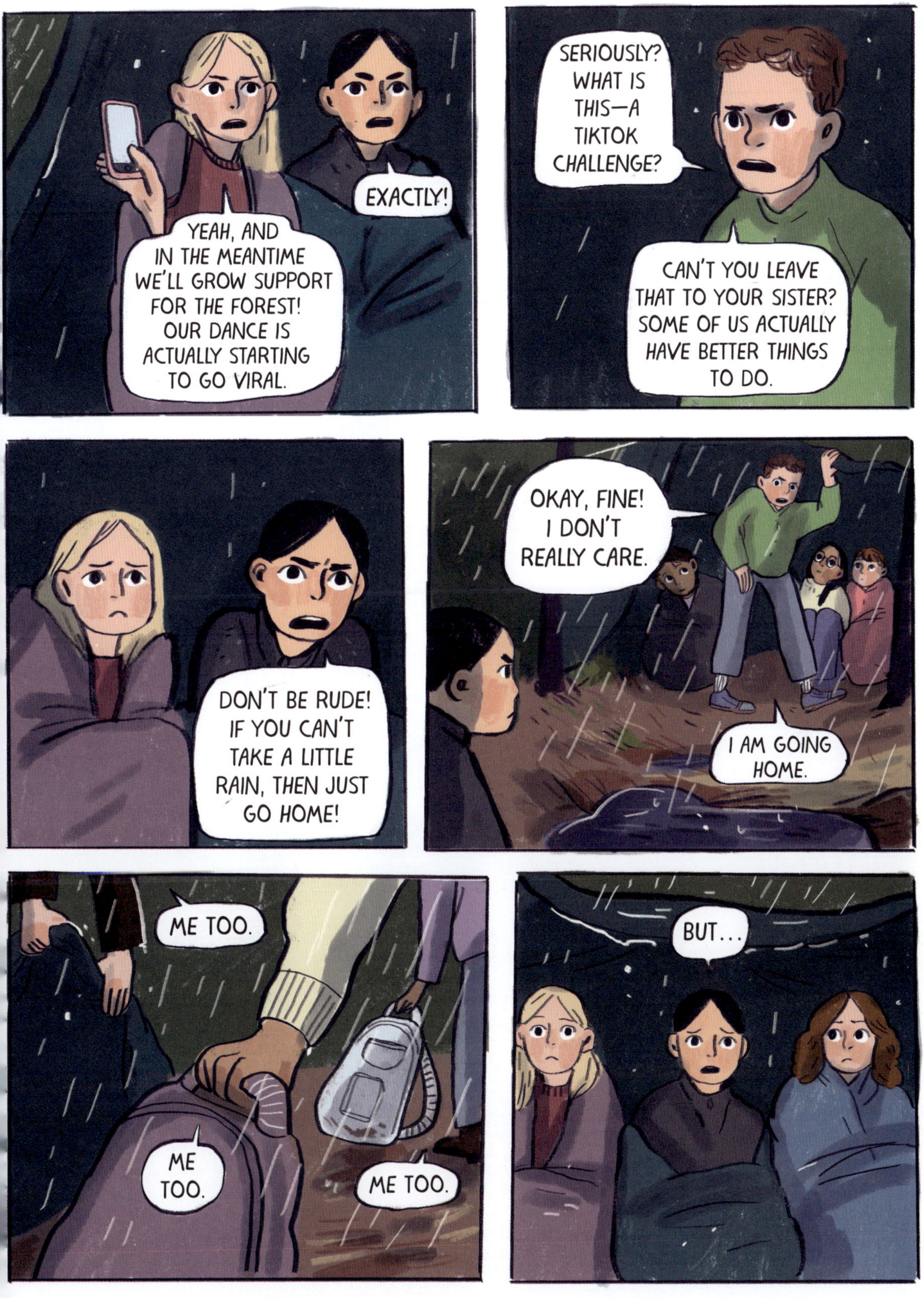
YEAH, AND IN THE MEANTIME WE'LL GROW SUPPORT FOR THE FOREST! OUR DANCE IS ACTUALLY STARTING TO GO VIRAL.
EXACTLY!
SERIOUSLY? WHAT IS THIS—A TIKTOK CHALLENGE?
CAN'T YOU LEAVE THAT TO YOUR SISTER? SOME OF US ACTUALLY HAVE BETTER THINGS TO DO.
DON'T BE RUDE! IF YOU CAN'T TAKE A LITTLE RAIN, THEN JUST GO HOME!
OKAY, FINE! I DON'T REALLY CARE.
I AM GOING HOME.
ME TOO.
ME TOO.
ME TOO.
BUT...

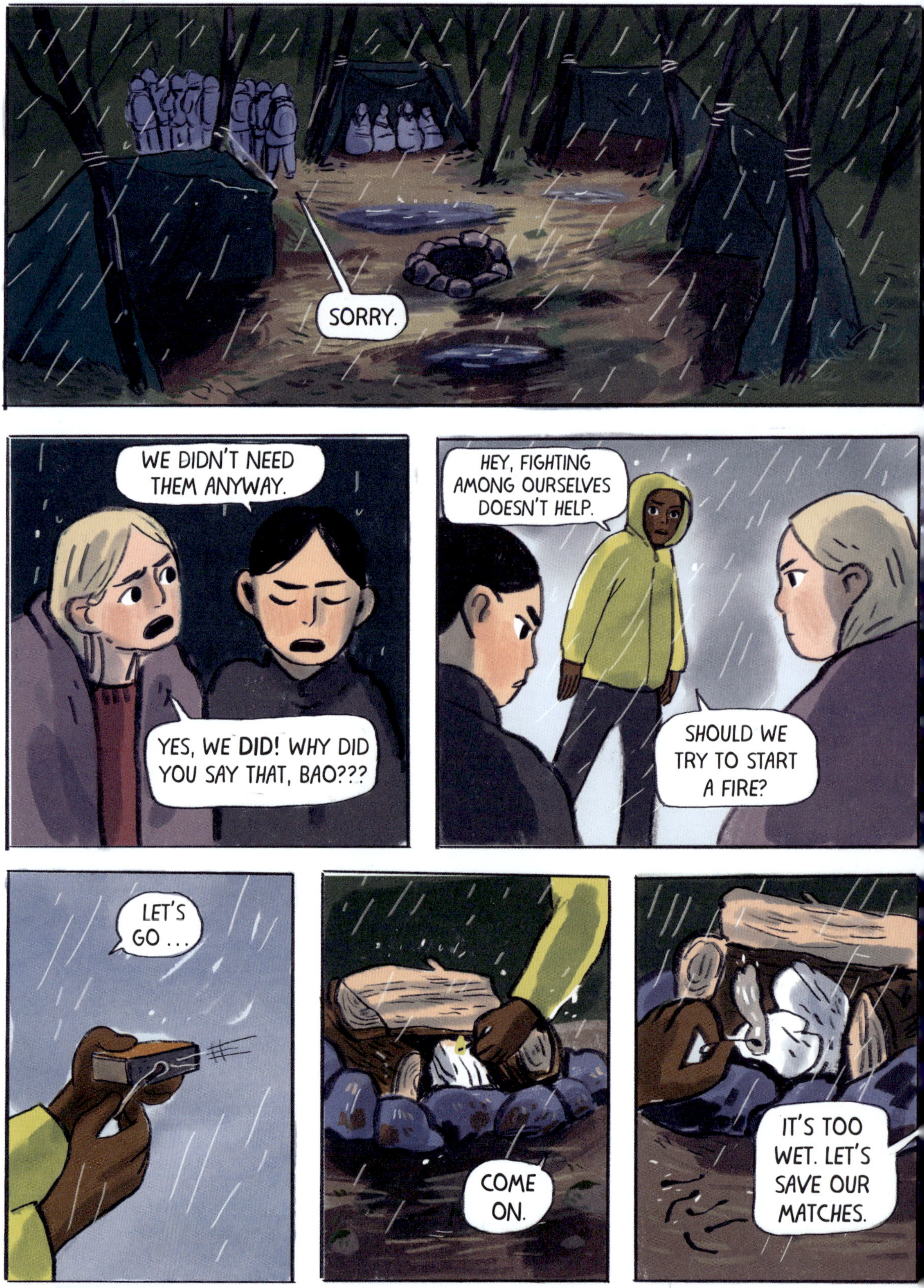
SORRY.
WE DIDN'T NEED THEM ANYWAY.
YES, WE DID! WHY DID YOU SAY THAT, BAO???
HEY, FIGHTING AMONG OURSELVES DOESN'T HELP.
SHOULD WE TRY TO START A FIRE?
LET'S GO ...
COME ON.
IT'S TOO WET. LET'S SAVE OUR MATCHES.

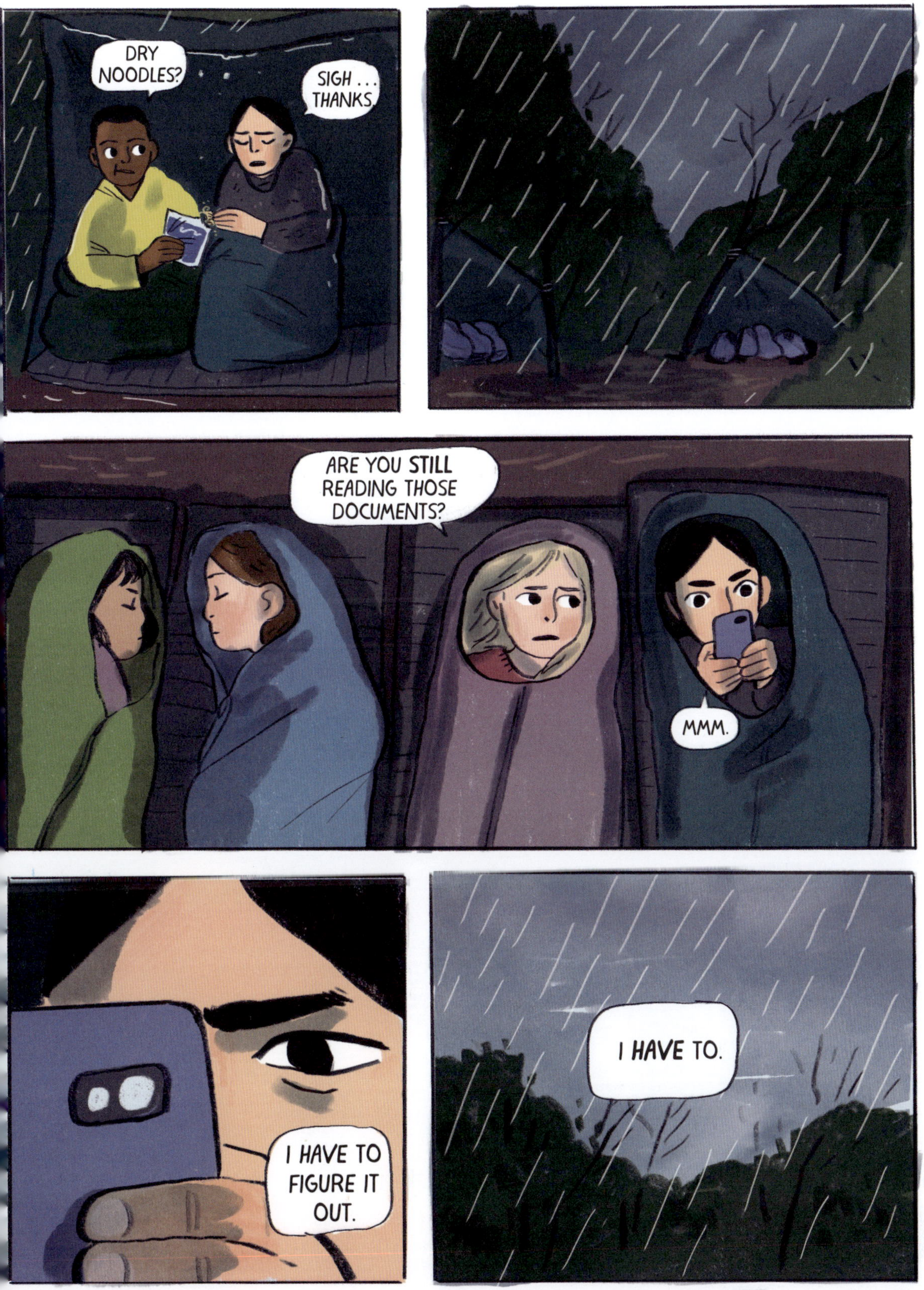
DRY NOODLES?
SIGH . . . THANKS.
ARE YOU STILL READING THOSE DOCUMENTS?
MMM.
I HAVE TO FIGURE IT OUT.
I HAVE TO.

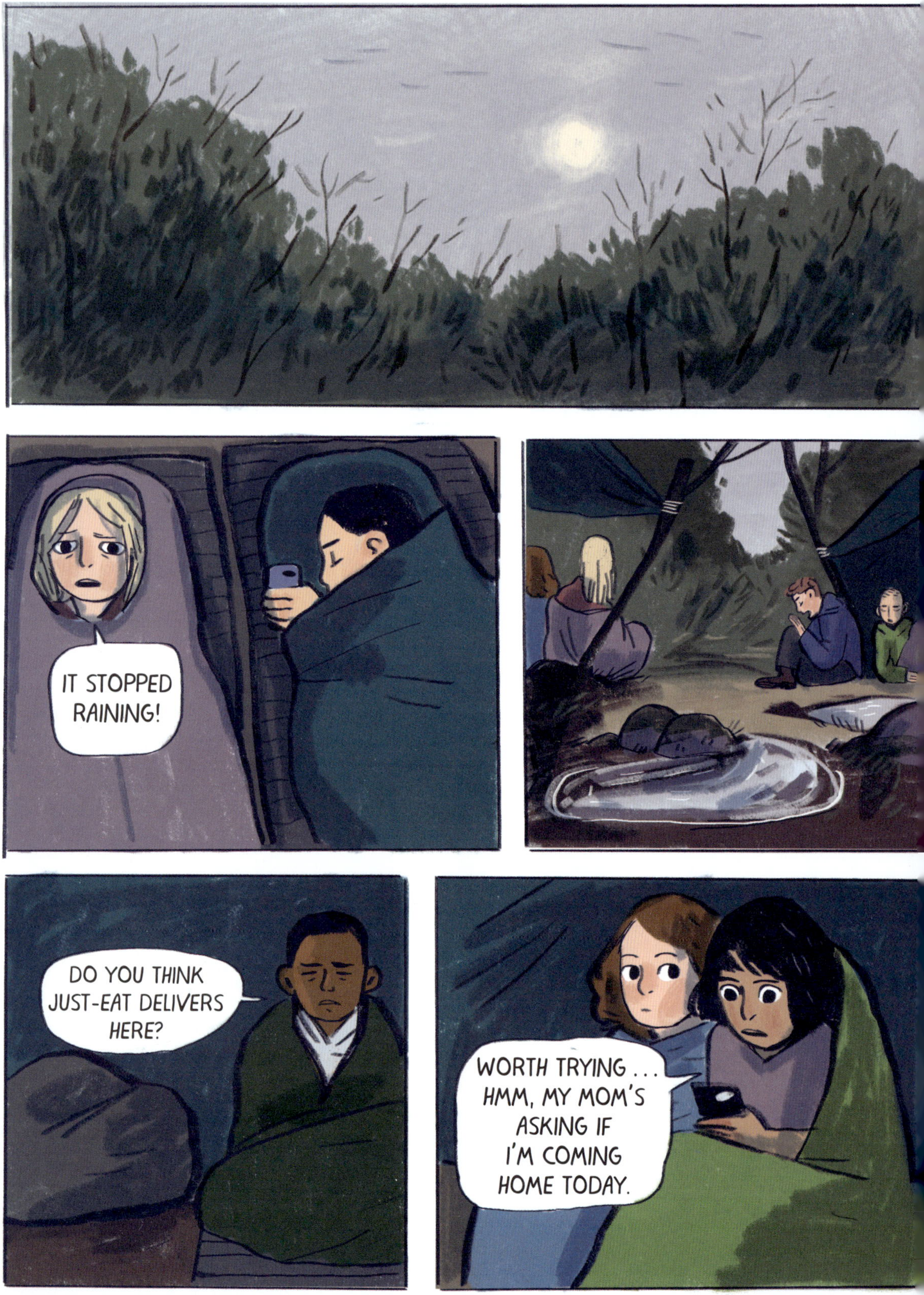
IT STOPPED RAINING!
DO YOU THINK JUST-EAT DELIVERS HERE?
WORTH TRYING . . . HMM, MY MOM'S ASKING IF I'M COMING HOME TODAY.

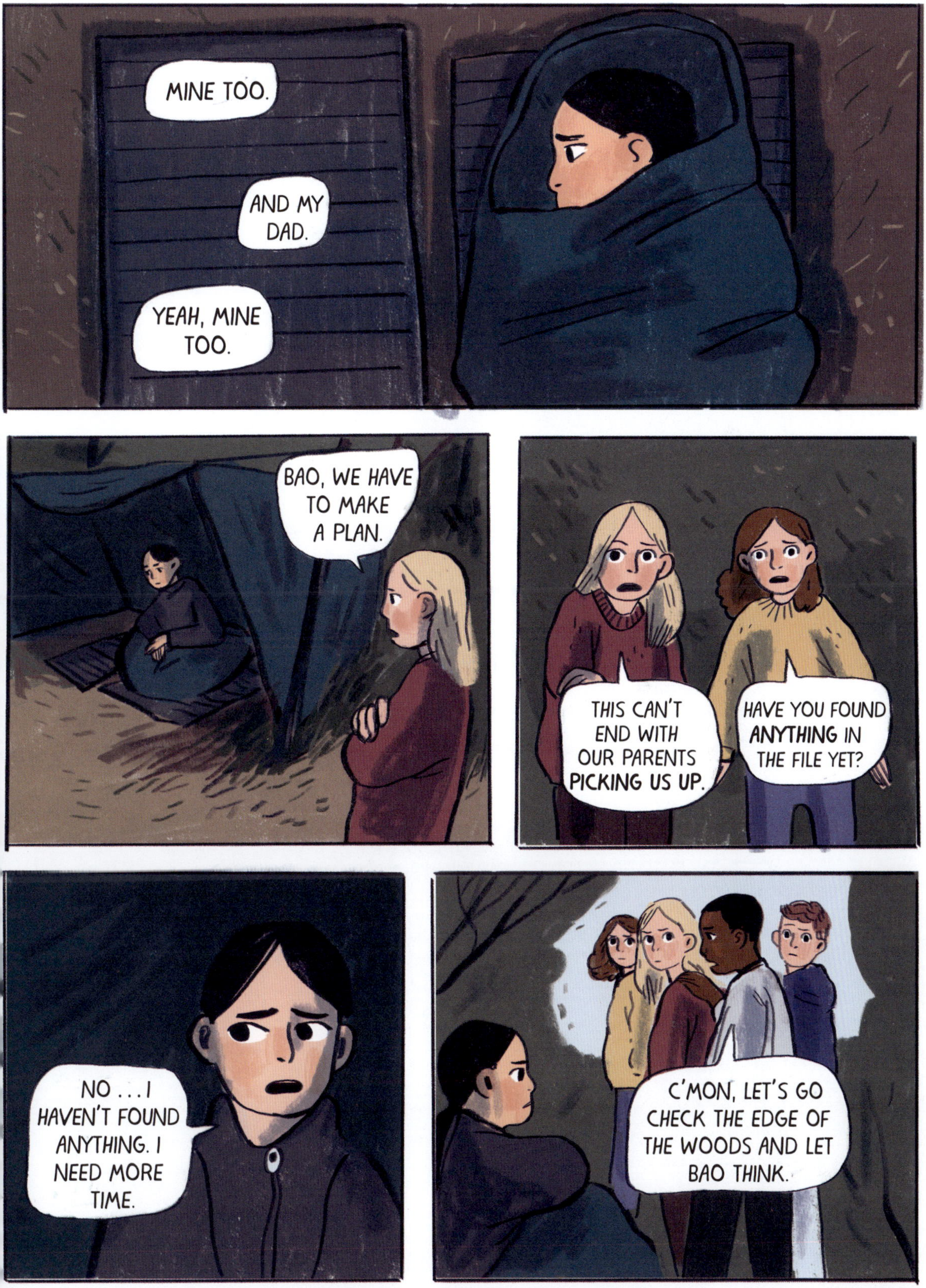
MINE TOO.
AND MY DAD.
YEAH, MINE TOO.
BAO, WE HAVE TO MAKE A PLAN.
THIS CAN'T END WITH OUR PARENTS PICKING US UP.
HAVE YOU FOUND ANYTHING IN THE FILE YET?
NO . . . I HAVEN'T FOUND ANYTHING. I NEED MORE TIME.
C'MON, LET'S GO CHECK THE EDGE OF THE WOODS AND LET BAO THINK.

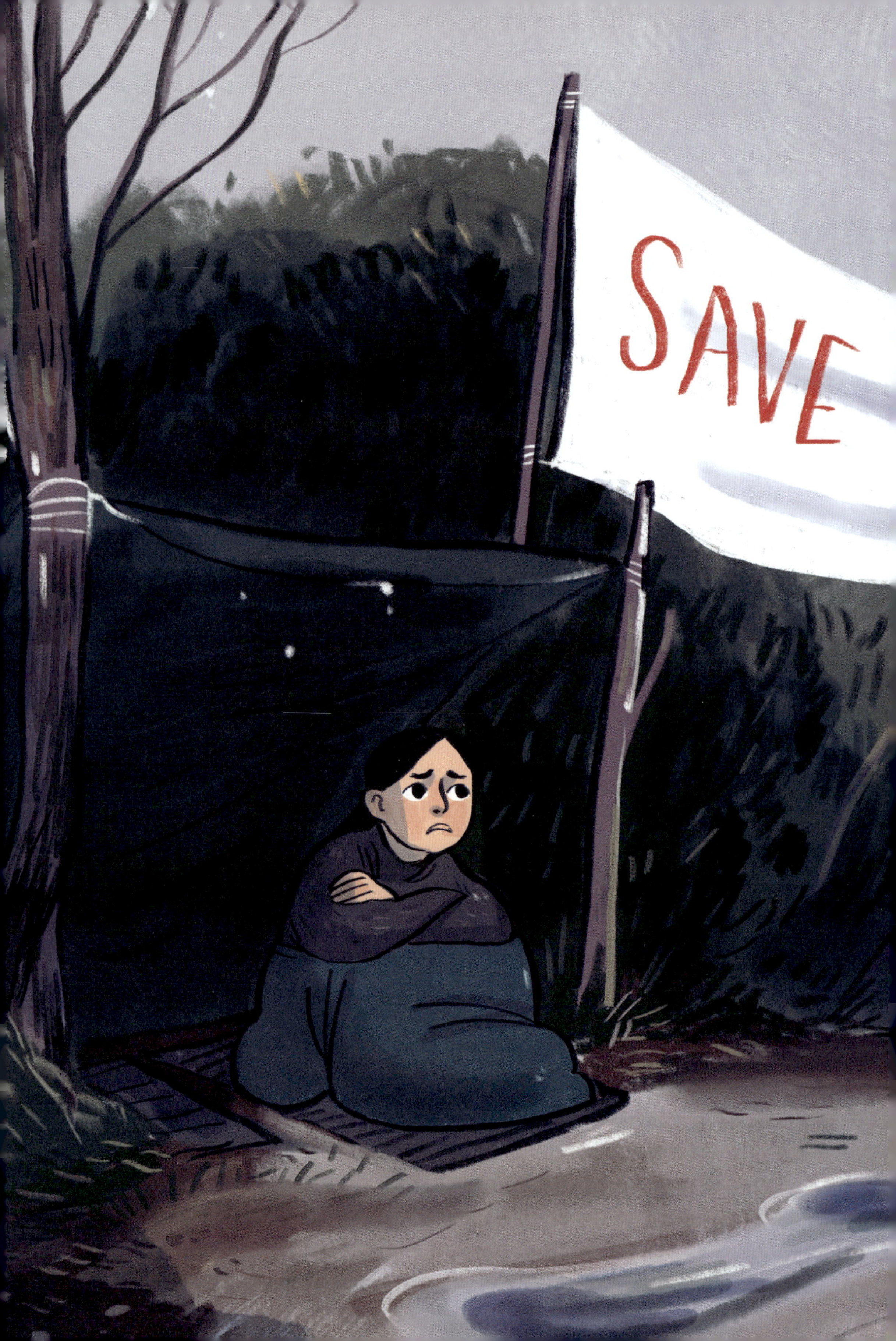
SAVE

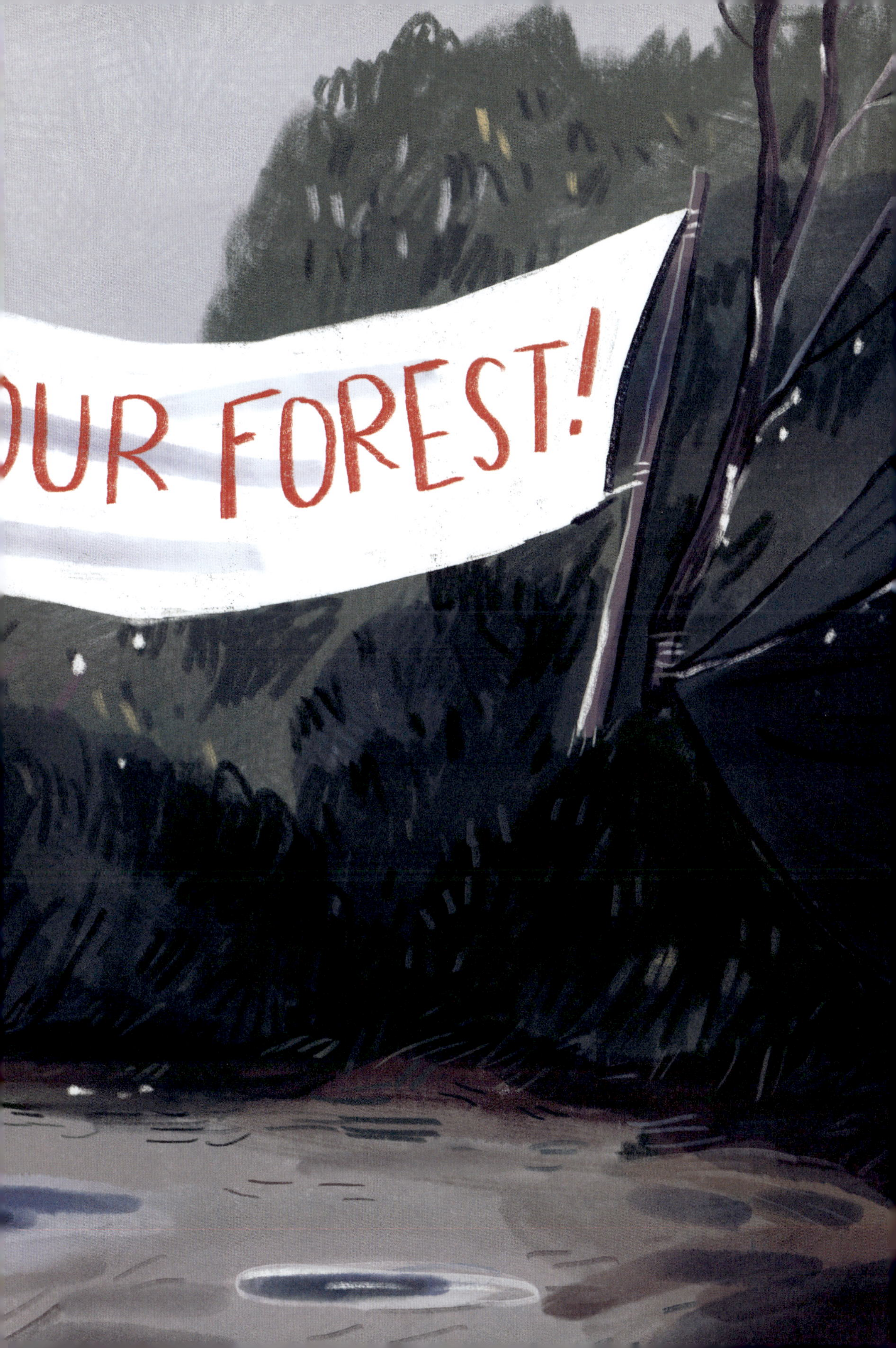
OUR FOREST!

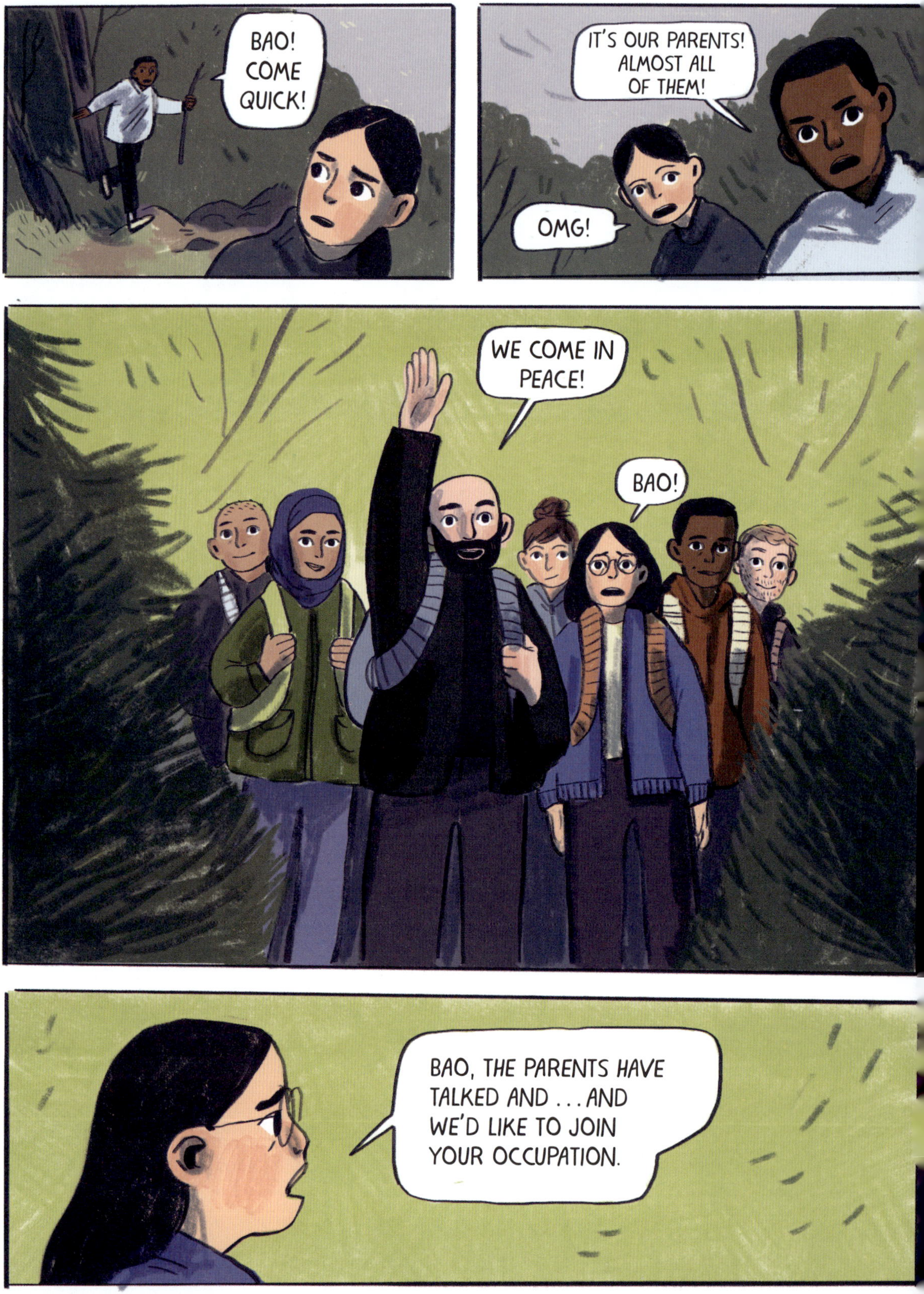
BAO! COME QUICK!
IT'S OUR PARENTS! ALMOST ALL OF THEM!
OMG!
WE COME IN PEACE!
BAO!
BAO, THE PARENTS HAVE TALKED AND . . . AND WE'D LIKE TO JOIN YOUR OCCUPATION.

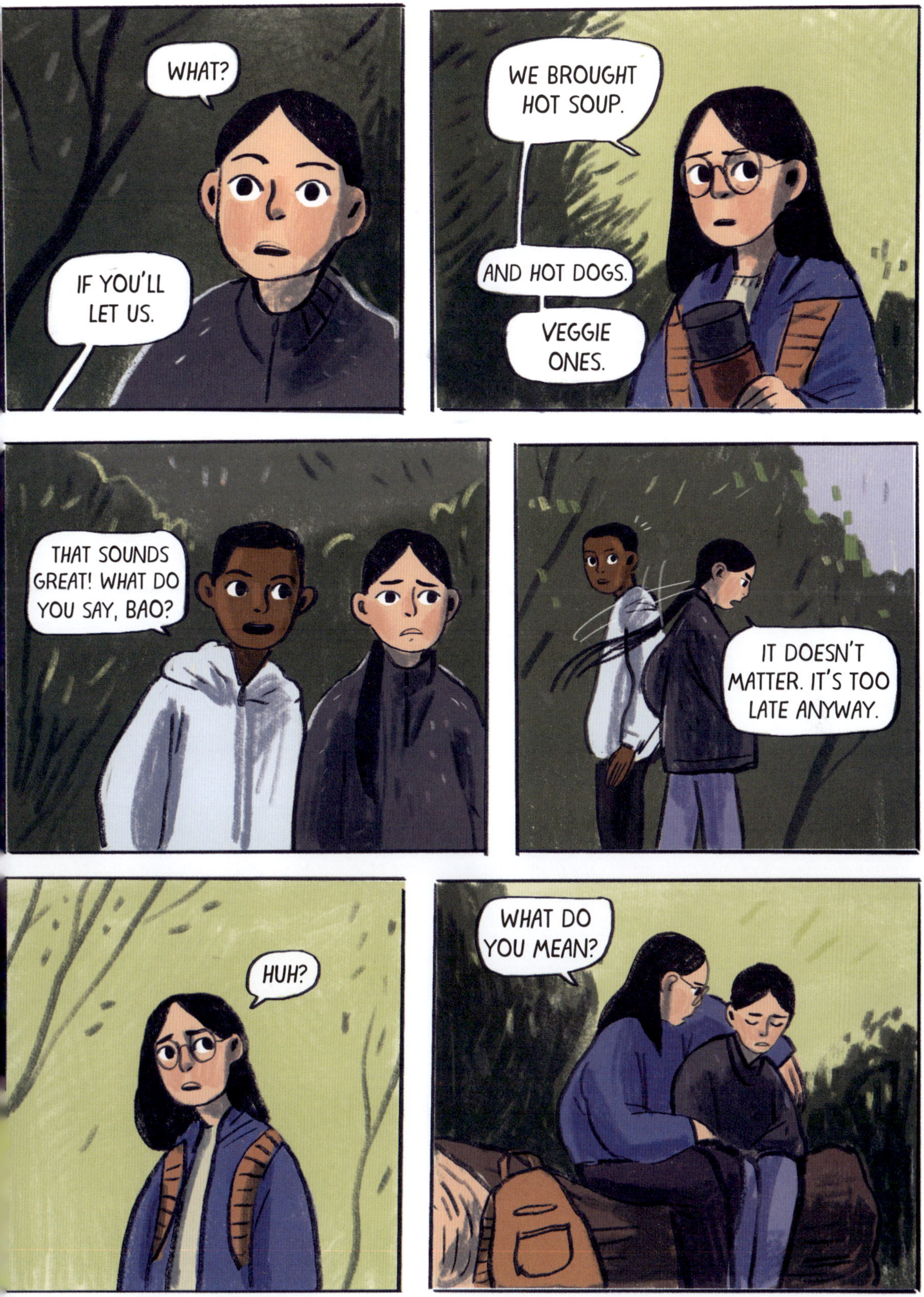
WHAT?
IF YOU'LL LET US.
WE BROUGHT HOT SOUP.
AND HOT DOGS.
VEGGIE ONES.
THAT SOUNDS GREAT! WHAT DO YOU SAY, BAO?
IT DOESN'T MATTER. IT'S TOO LATE ANYWAY.
HUH?
WHAT DO YOU MEAN?

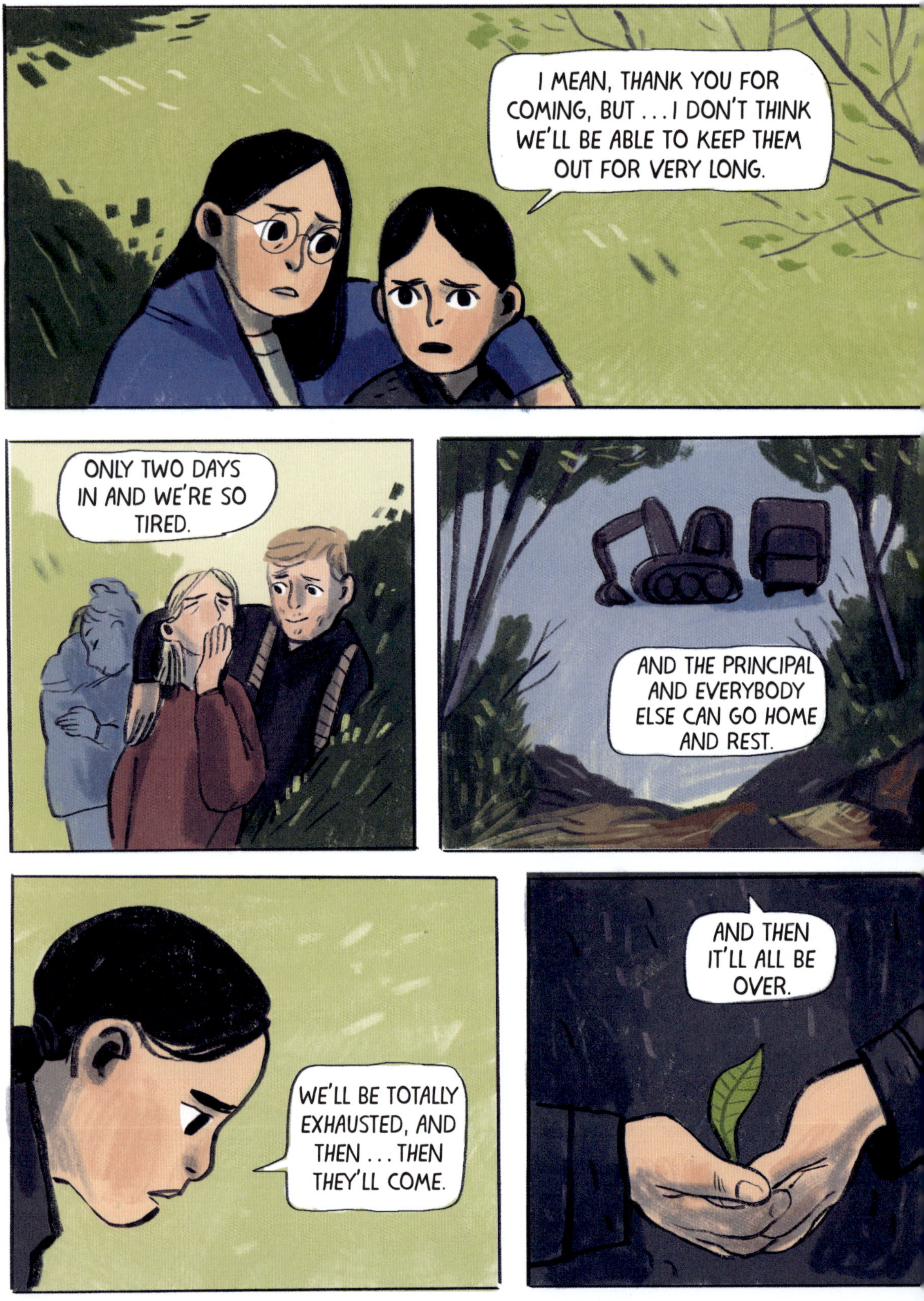
I MEAN, THANK YOU FOR COMING, BUT . . . I DON'T THINK WE'LL BE ABLE TO KEEP THEM OUT FOR VERY LONG.
ONLY TWO DAYS IN AND WE'RE SO TIRED.
AND THE PRINCIPAL AND EVERYBODY ELSE CAN GO HOME AND REST.
WE'LL BE TOTALLY EXHAUSTED, AND THEN . . . THEN THEY'LL COME.
AND THEN IT'LL ALL BE OVER.

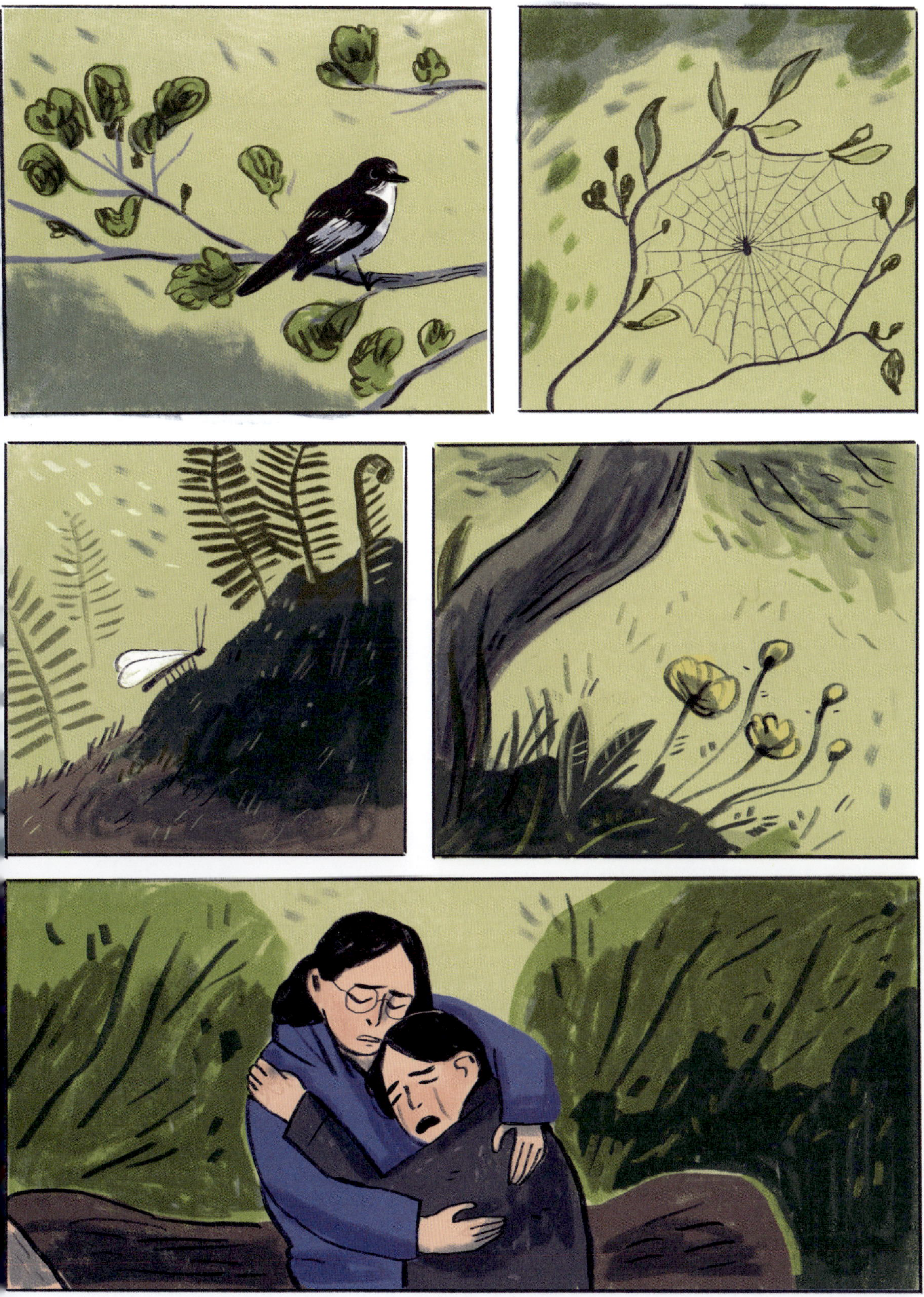

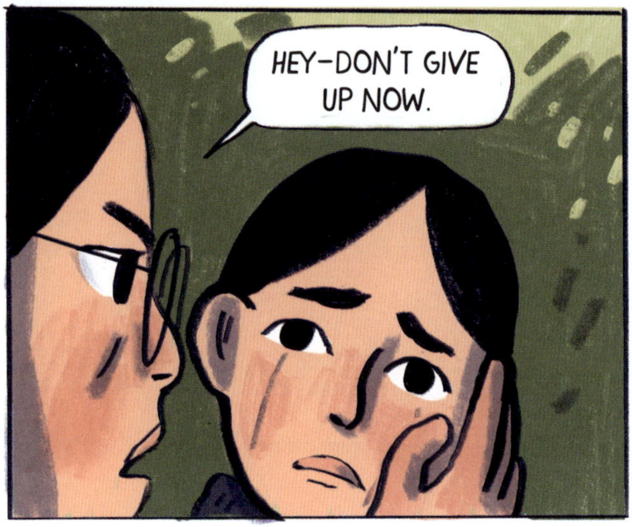
HEY—DON'T GIVE UP NOW.

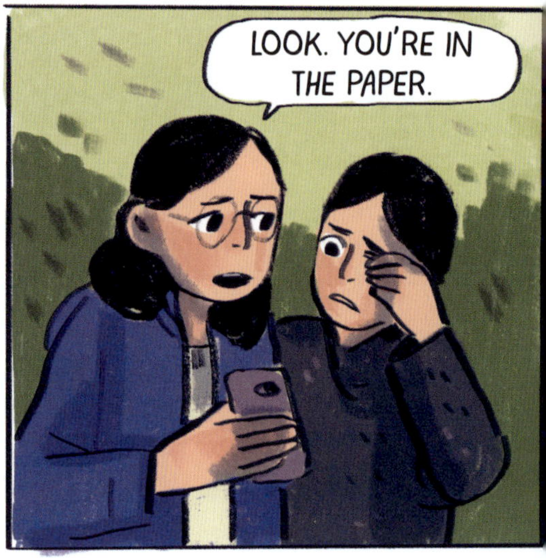
LOOK. YOU'RE IN THE PAPER.

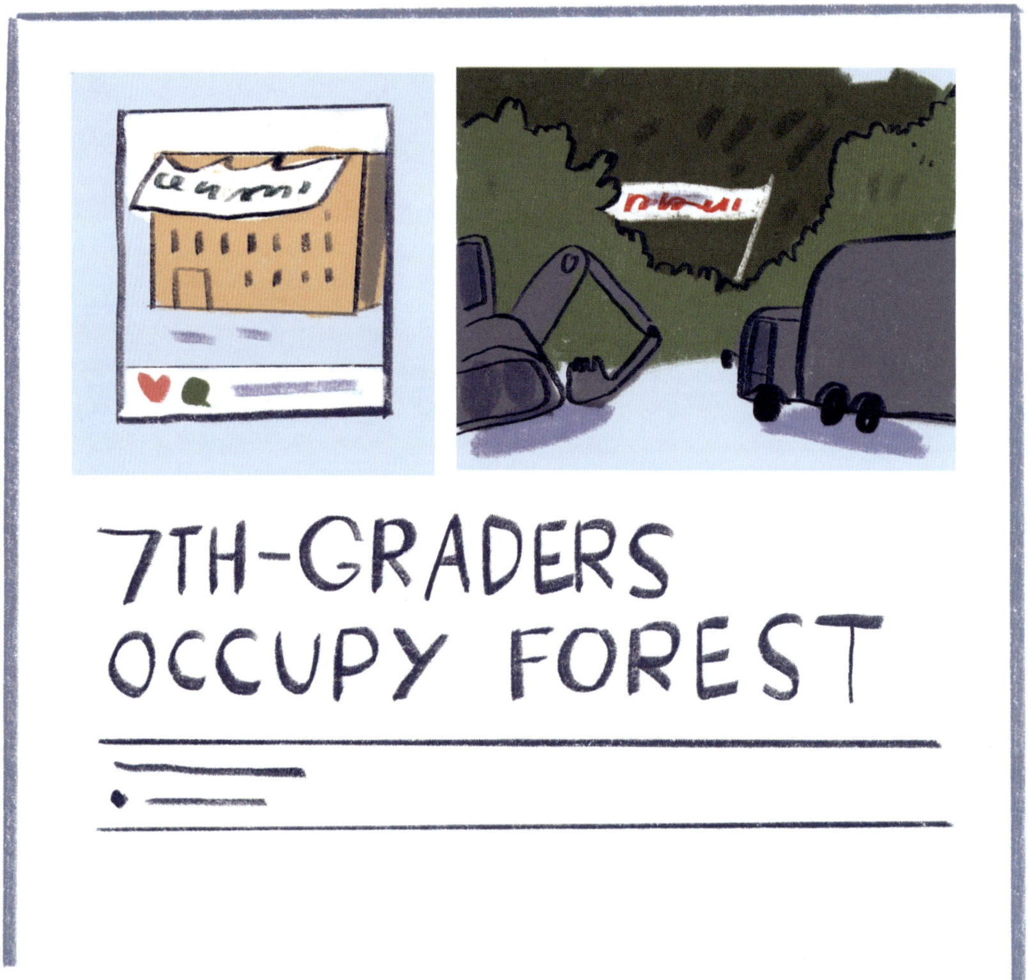
7TH-GRADERS OCCUPY FOREST

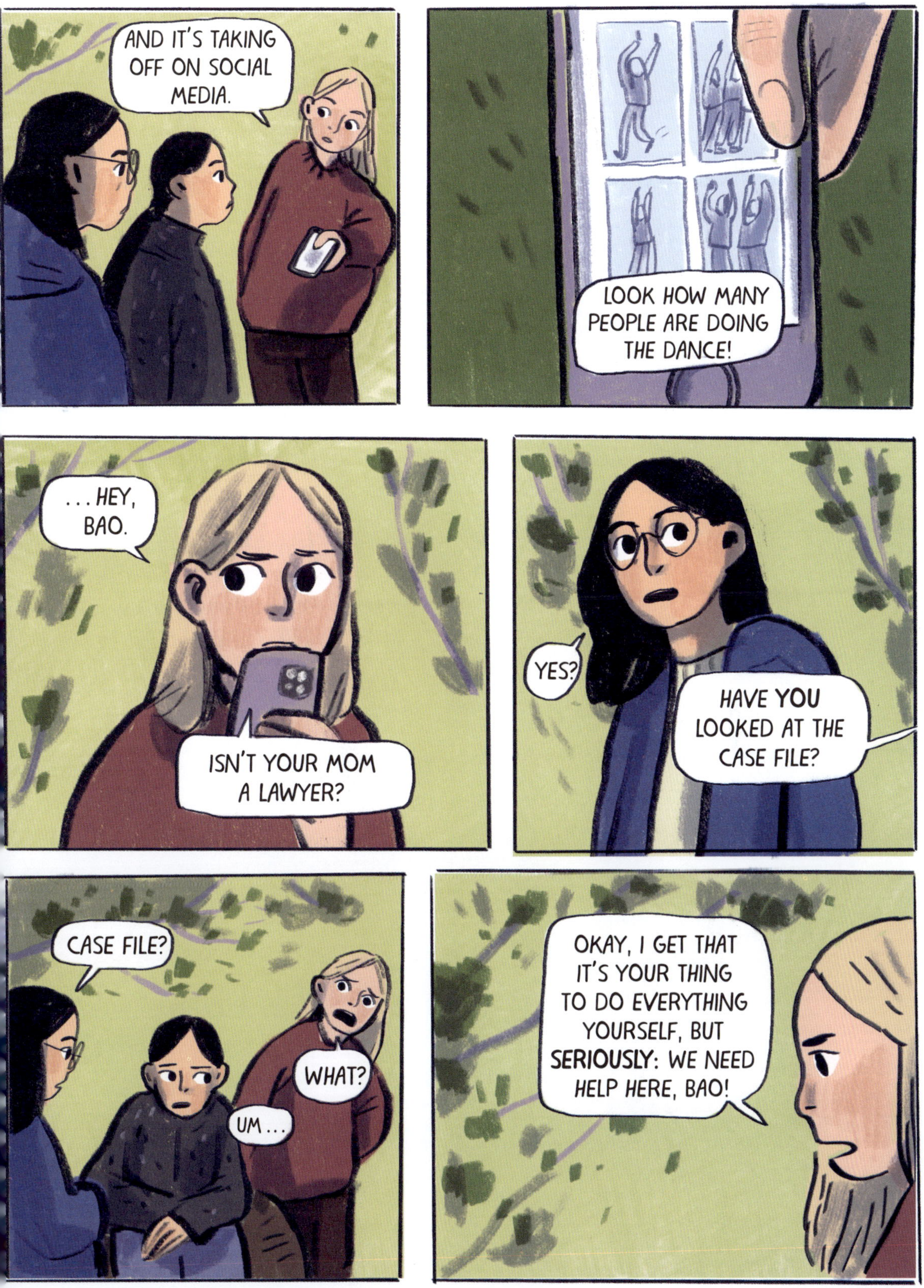
AND IT'S TAKING OFF ON SOCIAL MEDIA.
LOOK HOW MANY PEOPLE ARE DOING THE DANCE!
. . . HEY, BAO.
ISN'T YOUR MOM A LAWYER?
YES?
HAVE **YOU** LOOKED AT THE CASE FILE?
CASE FILE?
WHAT?
UM . . .
OKAY, I GET THAT IT'S YOUR THING TO DO EVERYTHING YOURSELF, BUT **SERIOUSLY**: WE NEED HELP HERE, BAO!

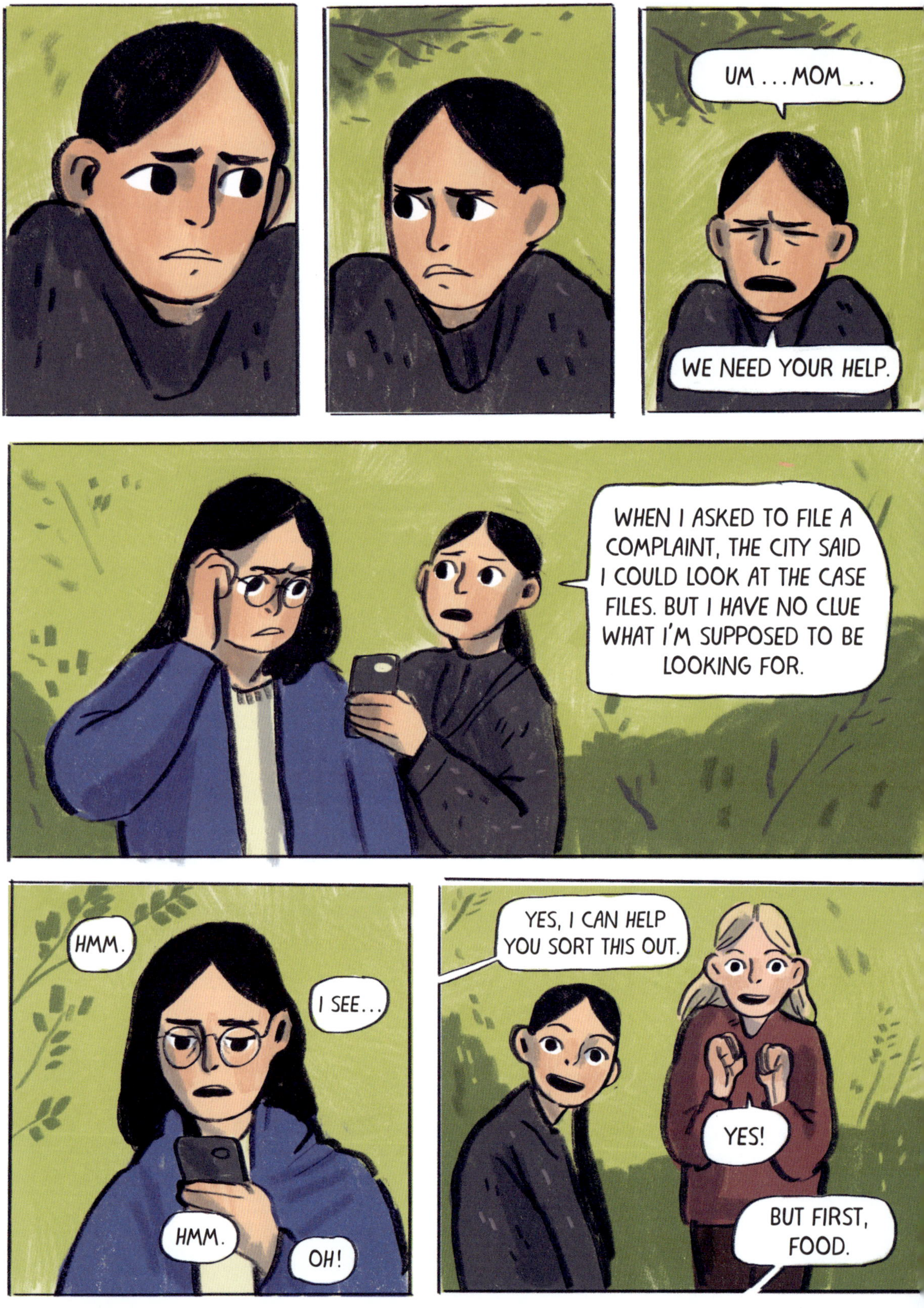

UM . . . MOM . . .
WE NEED YOUR HELP.
WHEN I ASKED TO FILE A COMPLAINT, THE CITY SAID I COULD LOOK AT THE CASE FILES. BUT I HAVE NO CLUE WHAT I'M SUPPOSED TO BE LOOKING FOR.
HMM.
I SEE. . .
HMM.
OH!
YES, I CAN HELP YOU SORT THIS OUT.
YES!
BUT FIRST, FOOD.

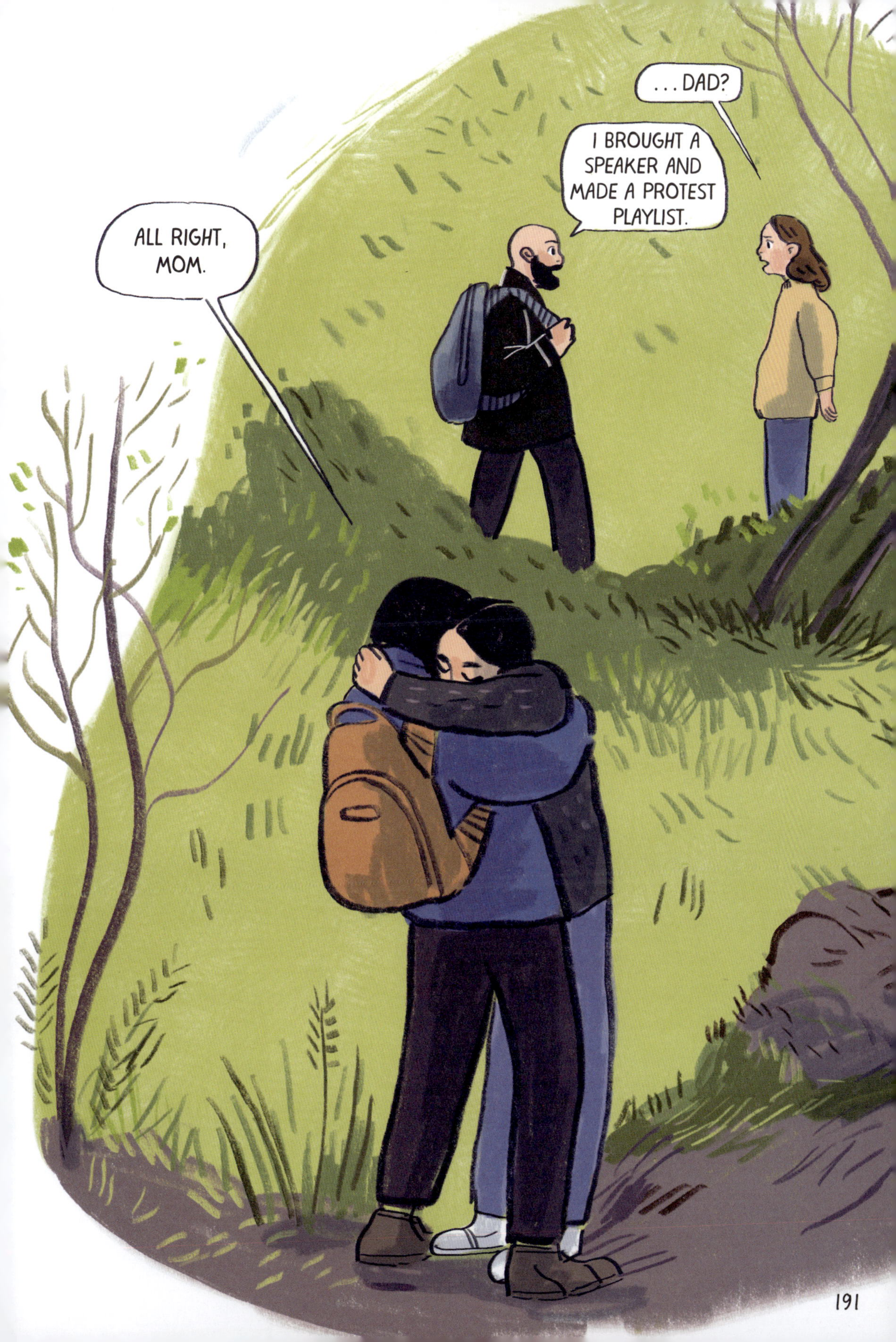
...DAD?
I BROUGHT A SPEAKER AND MADE A PROTEST PLAYLIST.
ALL RIGHT, MOM.

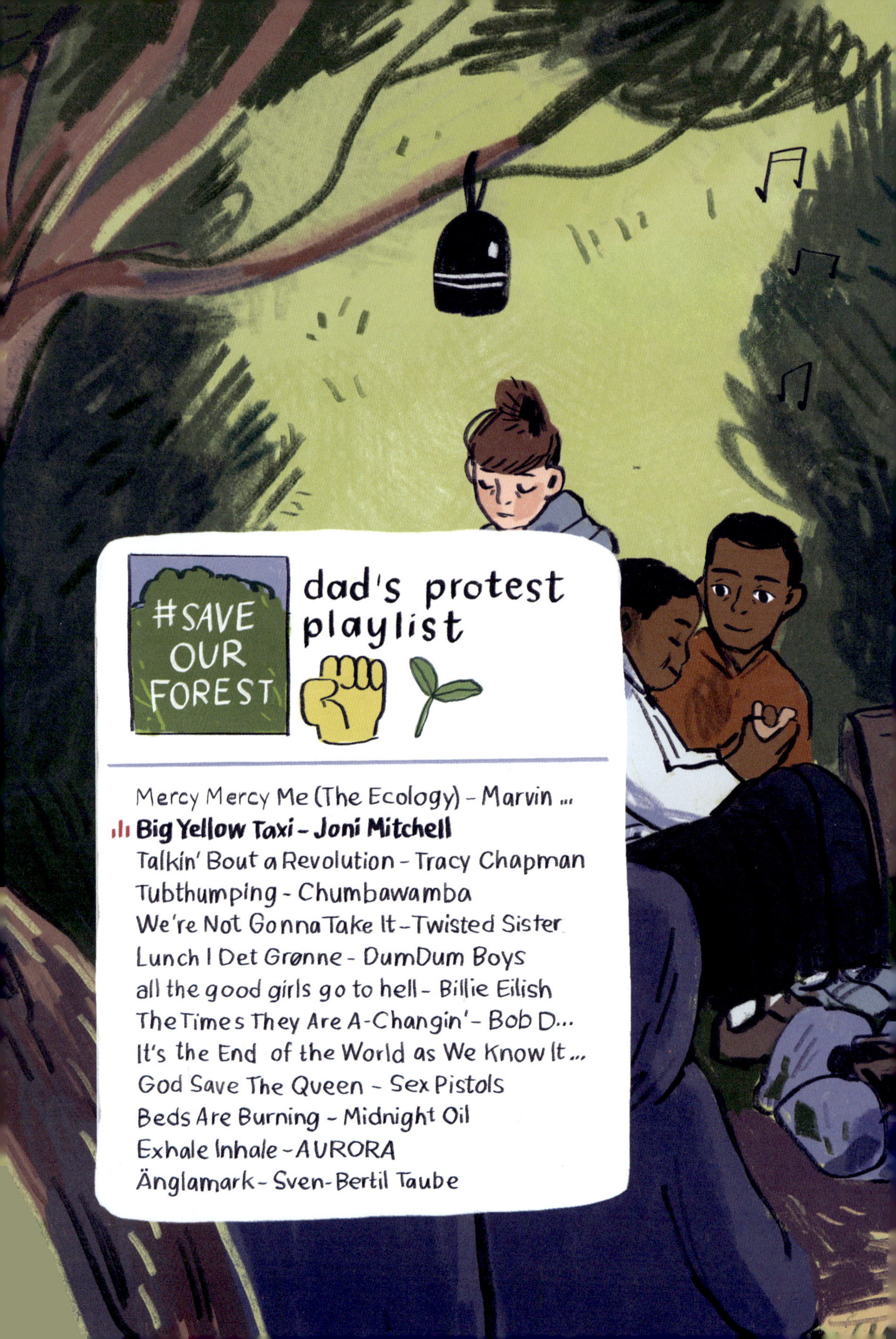
#SAVE OUR FOREST
dad's protest playlist
Mercy Mercy Me (The Ecology) - Marvin ...
Big Yellow Taxi - Joni Mitchell
Talkin' Bout a Revolution - Tracy Chapman
Tubthumping - Chumbawamba
We're Not Gonna Take It - Twisted Sister
Lunch I Det Grønne - DumDum Boys
all the good girls go to hell - Billie Eilish
The Times They Are A-Changin' - Bob D...
It's the End of the World as We Know It ...
God Save The Queen - Sex Pistols
Beds Are Burning - Midnight Oil
Exhale Inhale - AURORA
Änglamark - Sven-Bertil Taube

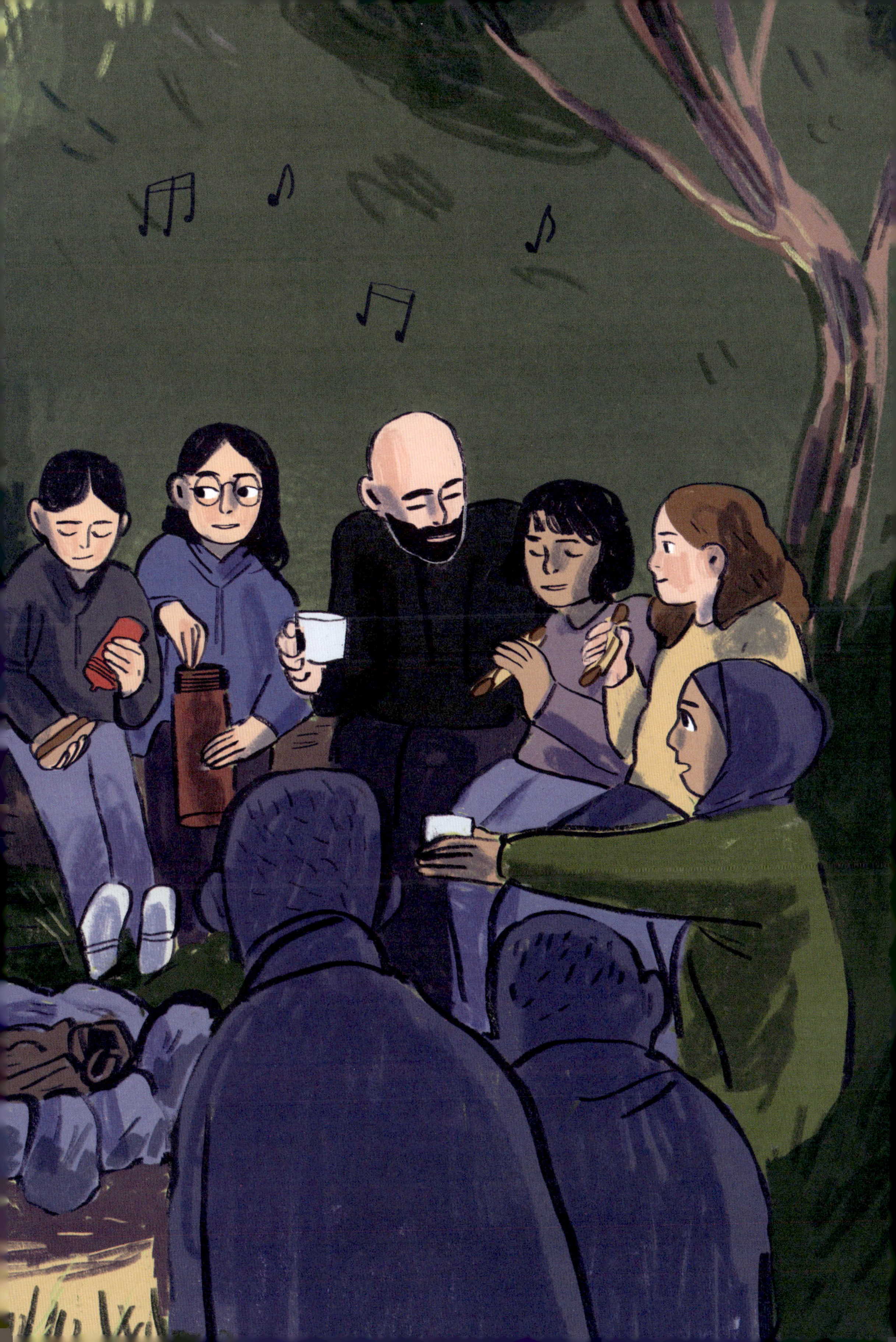

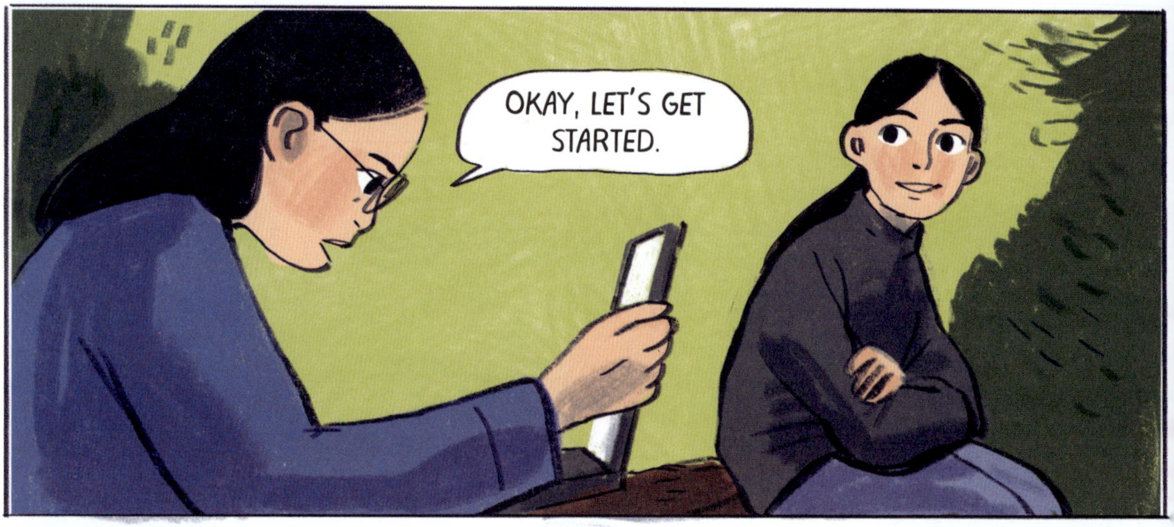
OKAY, LET'S GET STARTED.

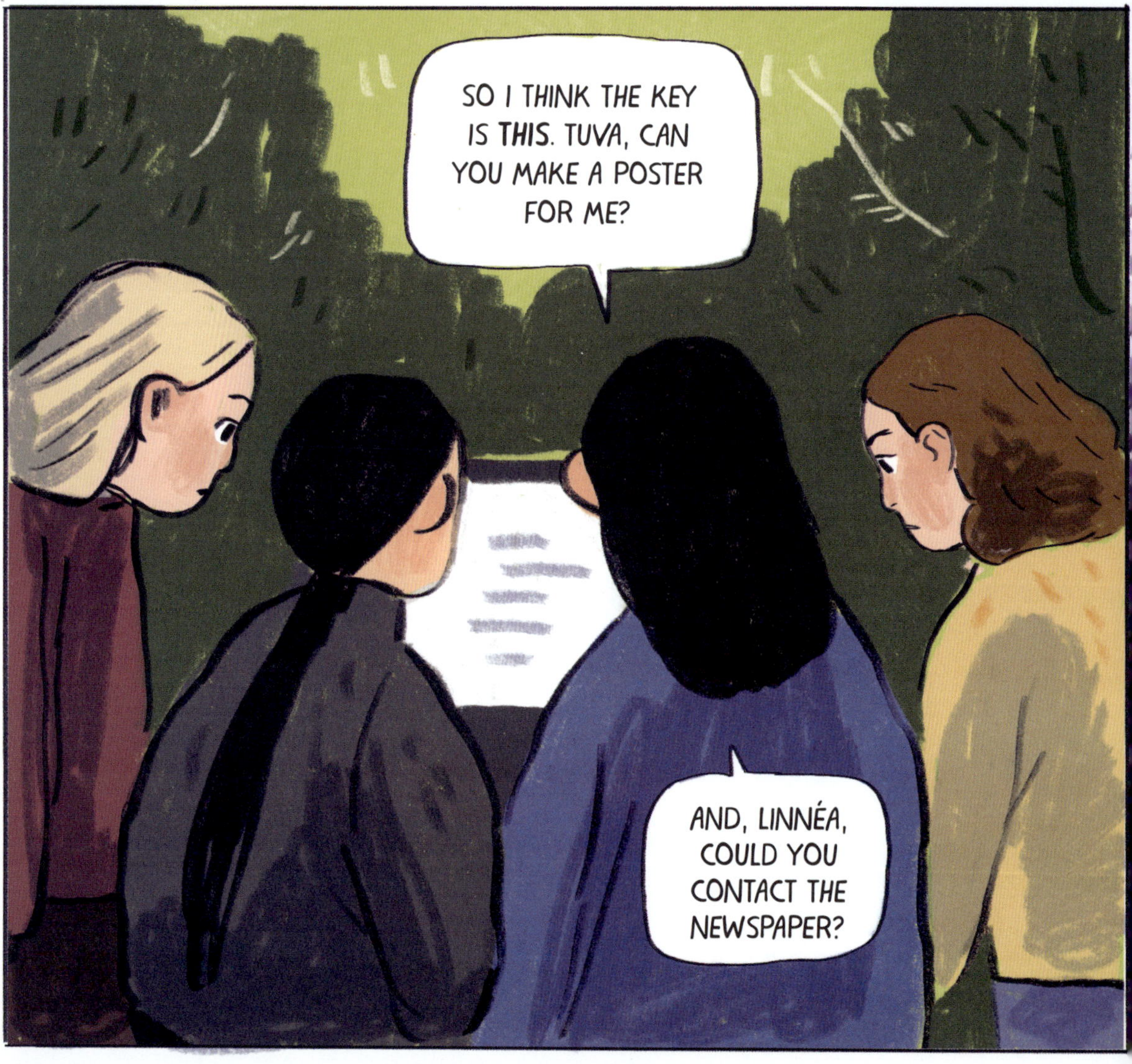
SO I THINK THE KEY IS **THIS**. TUVA, CAN YOU MAKE A POSTER FOR ME?
AND, LINNÉA, COULD YOU CONTACT THE NEWSPAPER?

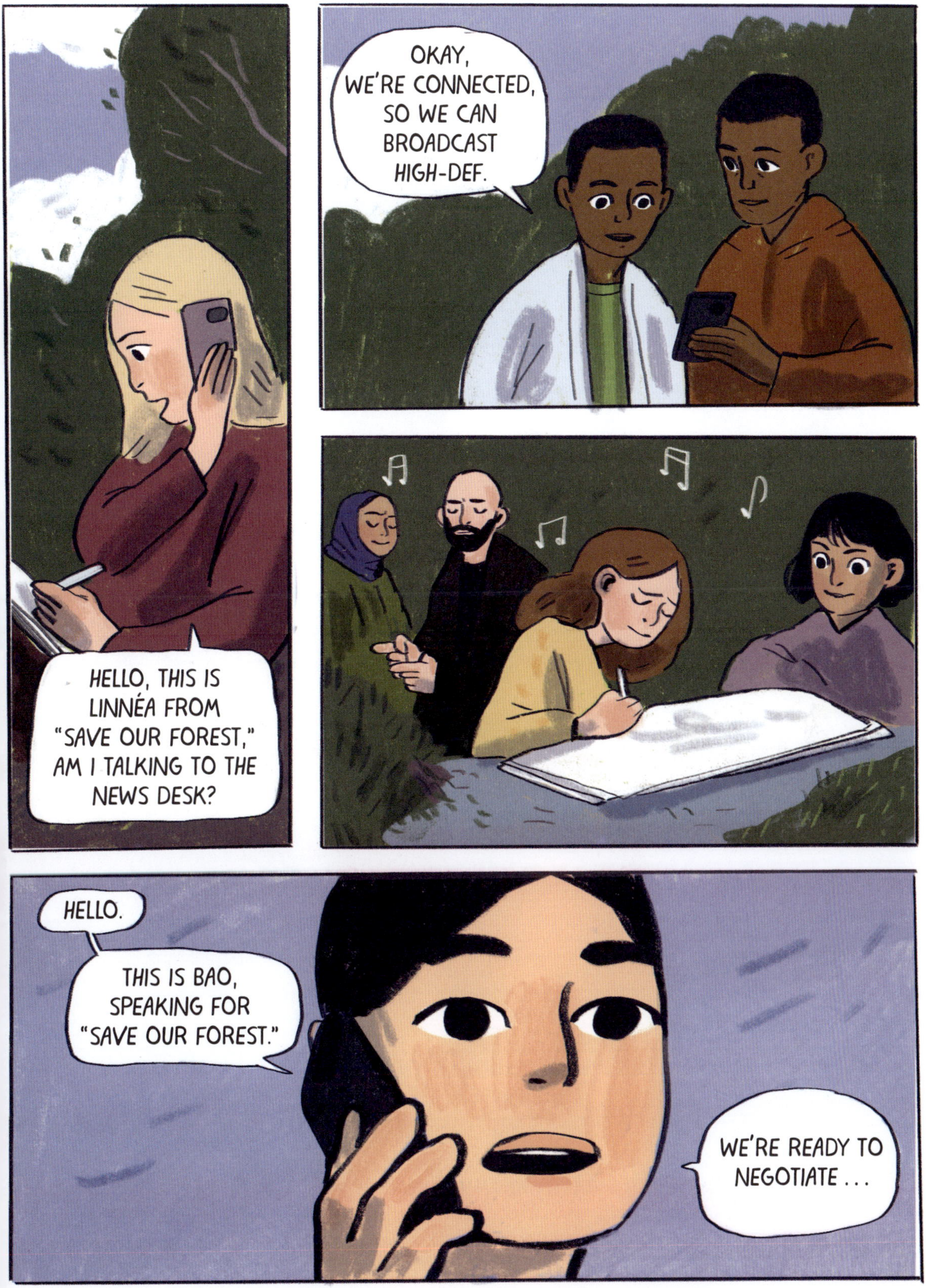
HELLO, THIS IS LINNÉA FROM "SAVE OUR FOREST," AM I TALKING TO THE NEWS DESK?
OKAY, WE'RE CONNECTED, SO WE CAN BROADCAST HIGH-DEF.
HELLO.
THIS IS BAO, SPEAKING FOR "SAVE OUR FOREST."
WE'RE READY TO NEGOTIATE . . .

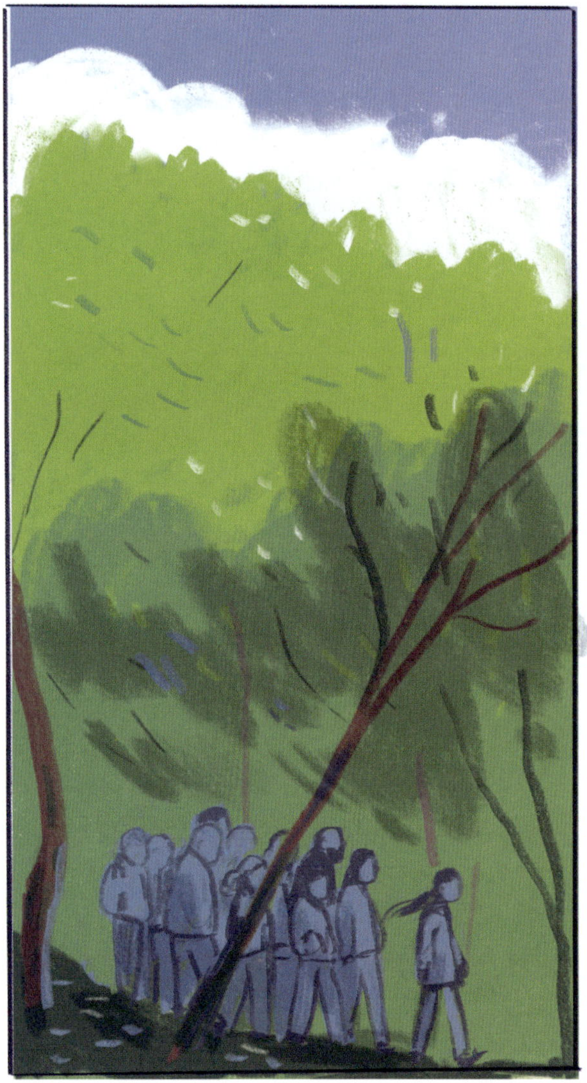

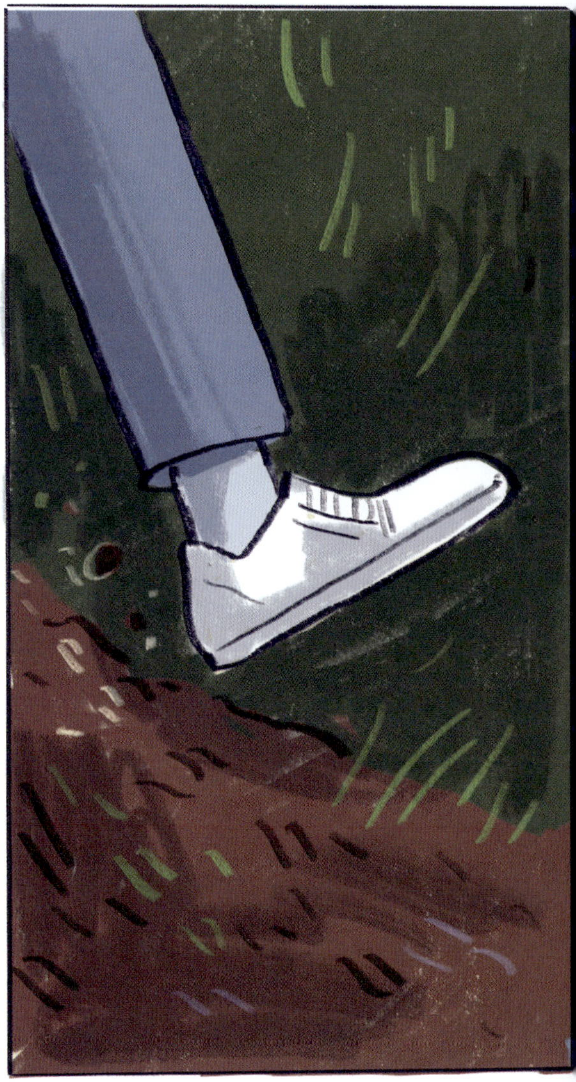

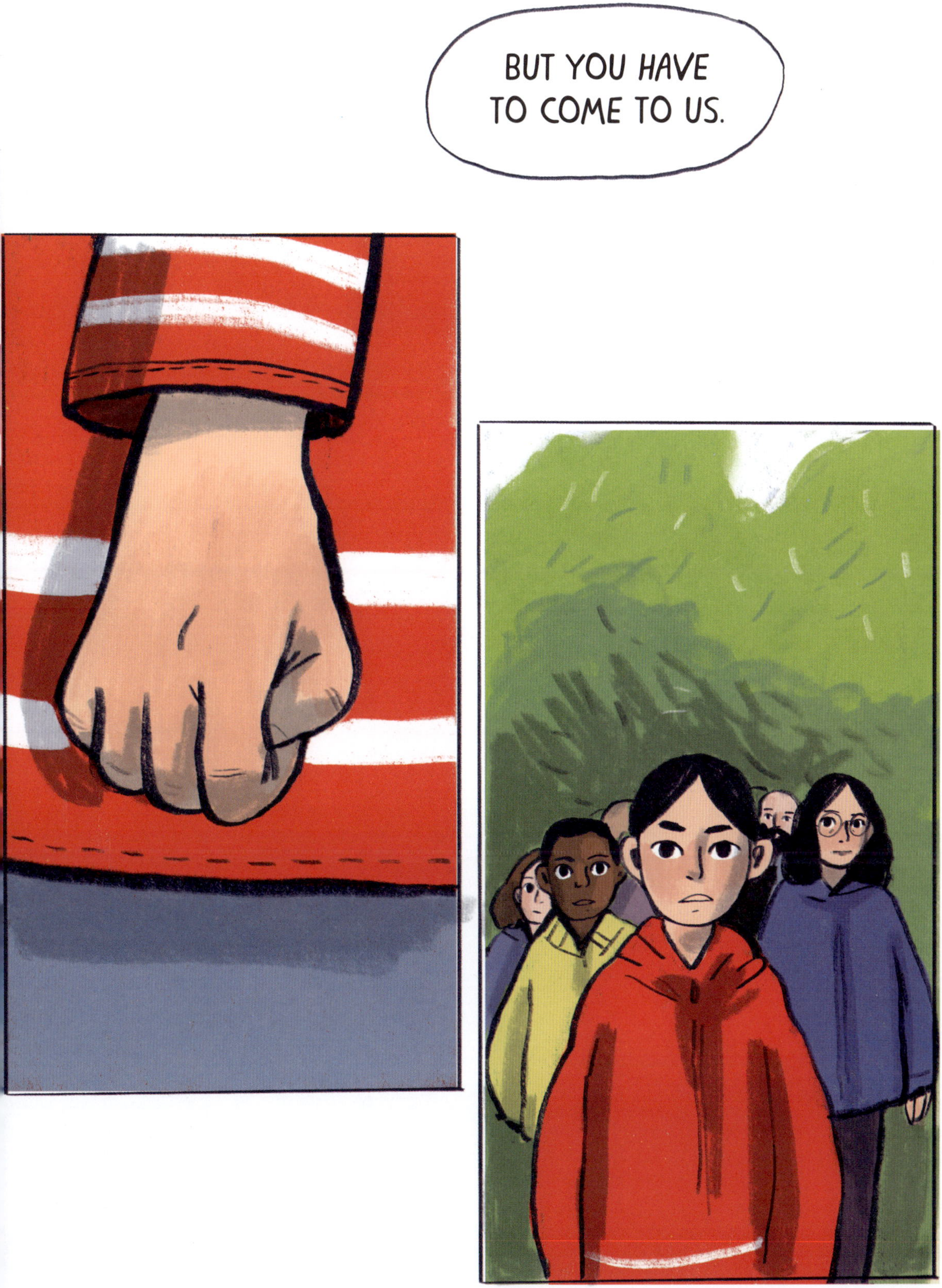
BUT YOU HAVE TO COME TO US.

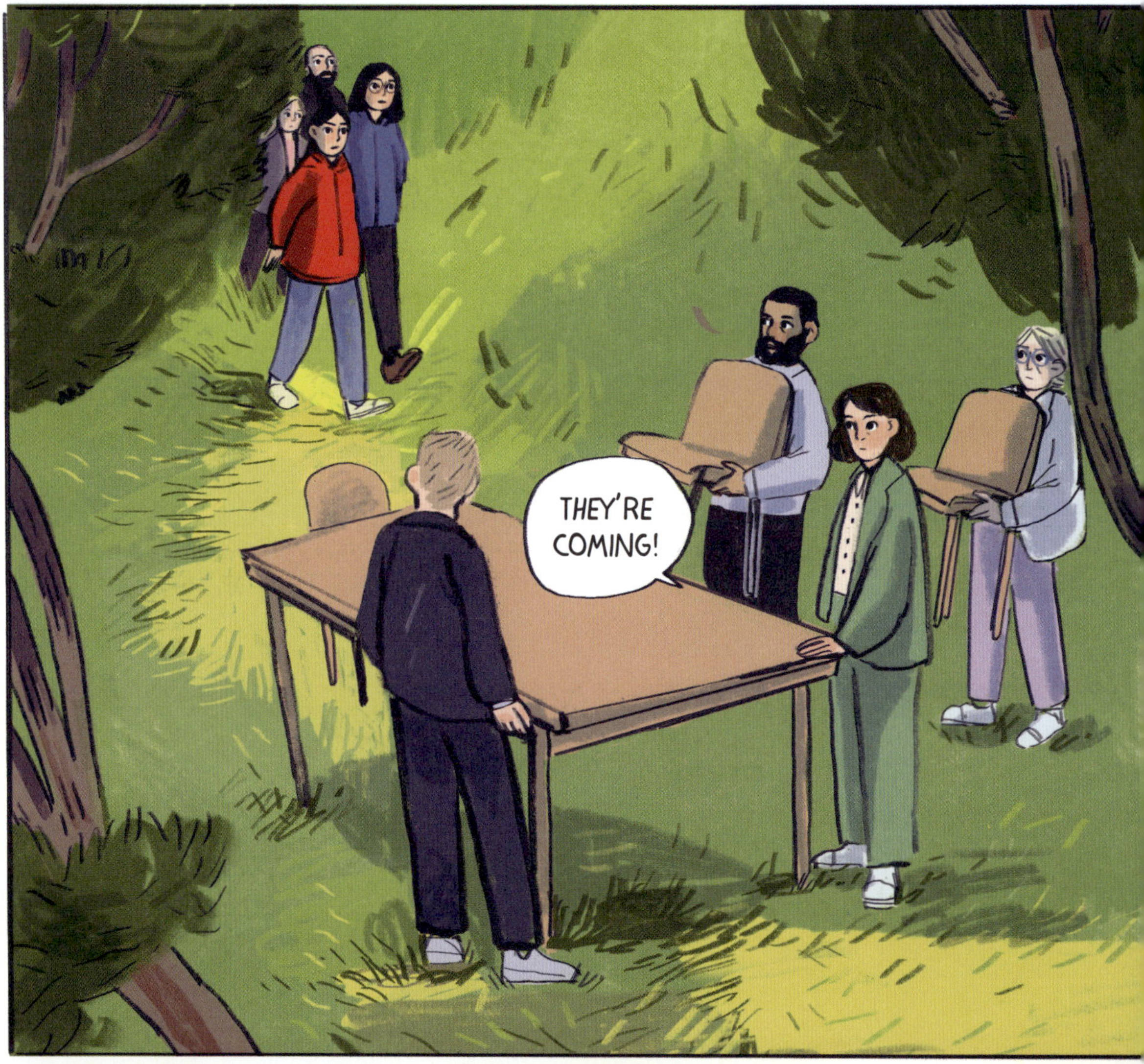
THEY'RE COMING!

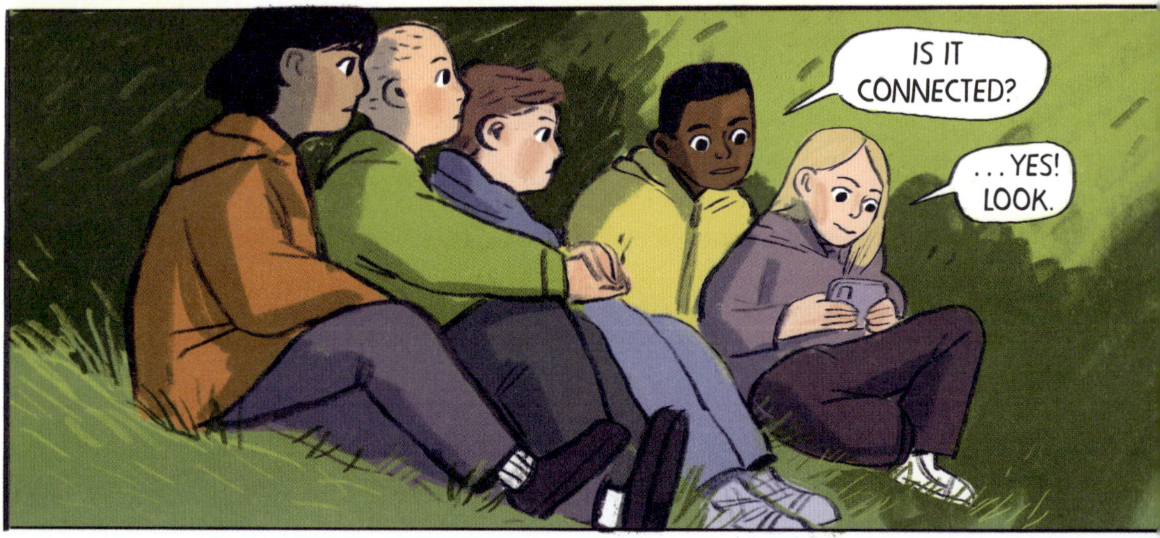
IS IT CONNECTED?
...YES! LOOK.

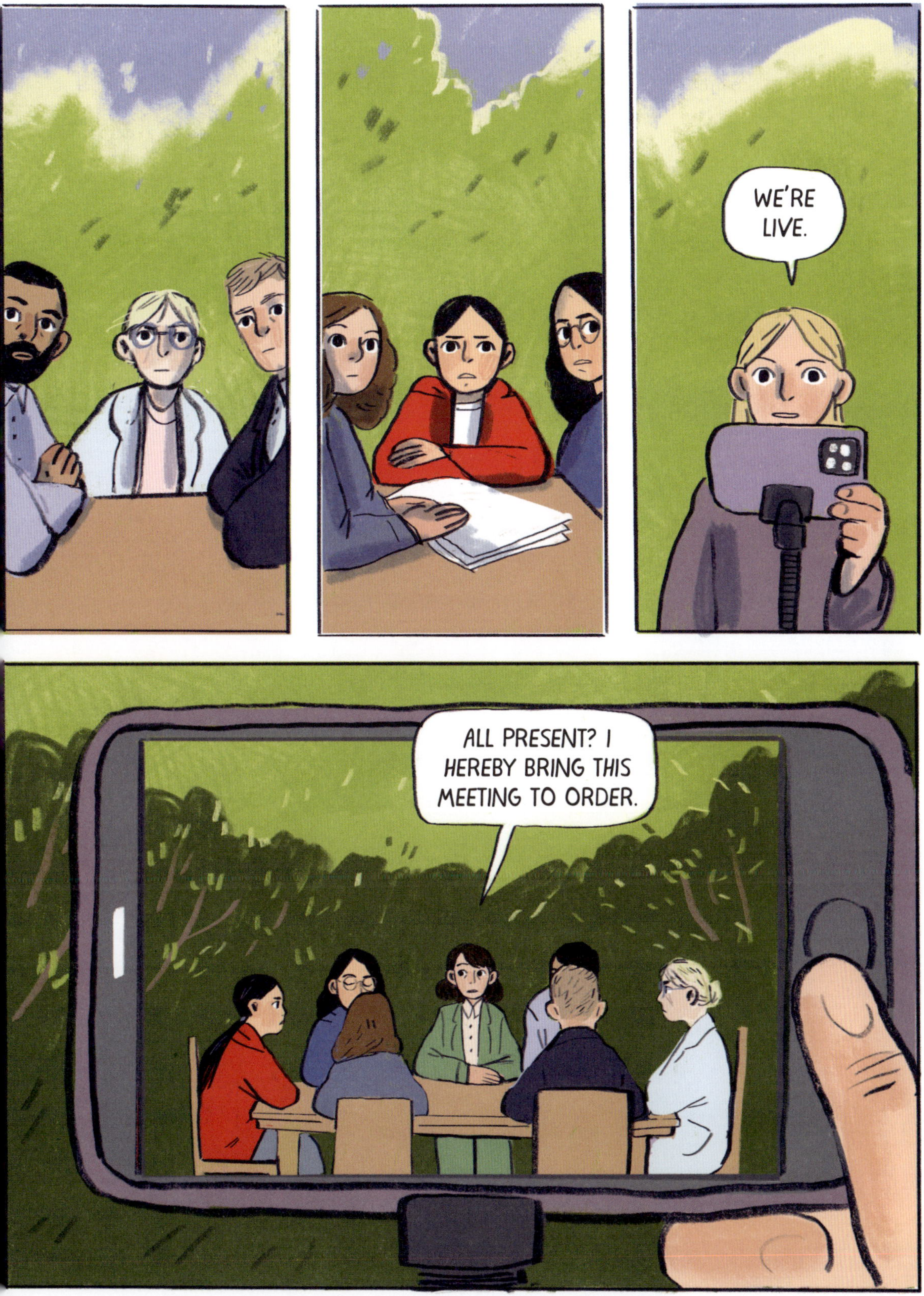
WE'RE LIVE.
ALL PRESENT? I HEREBY BRING THIS MEETING TO ORDER.

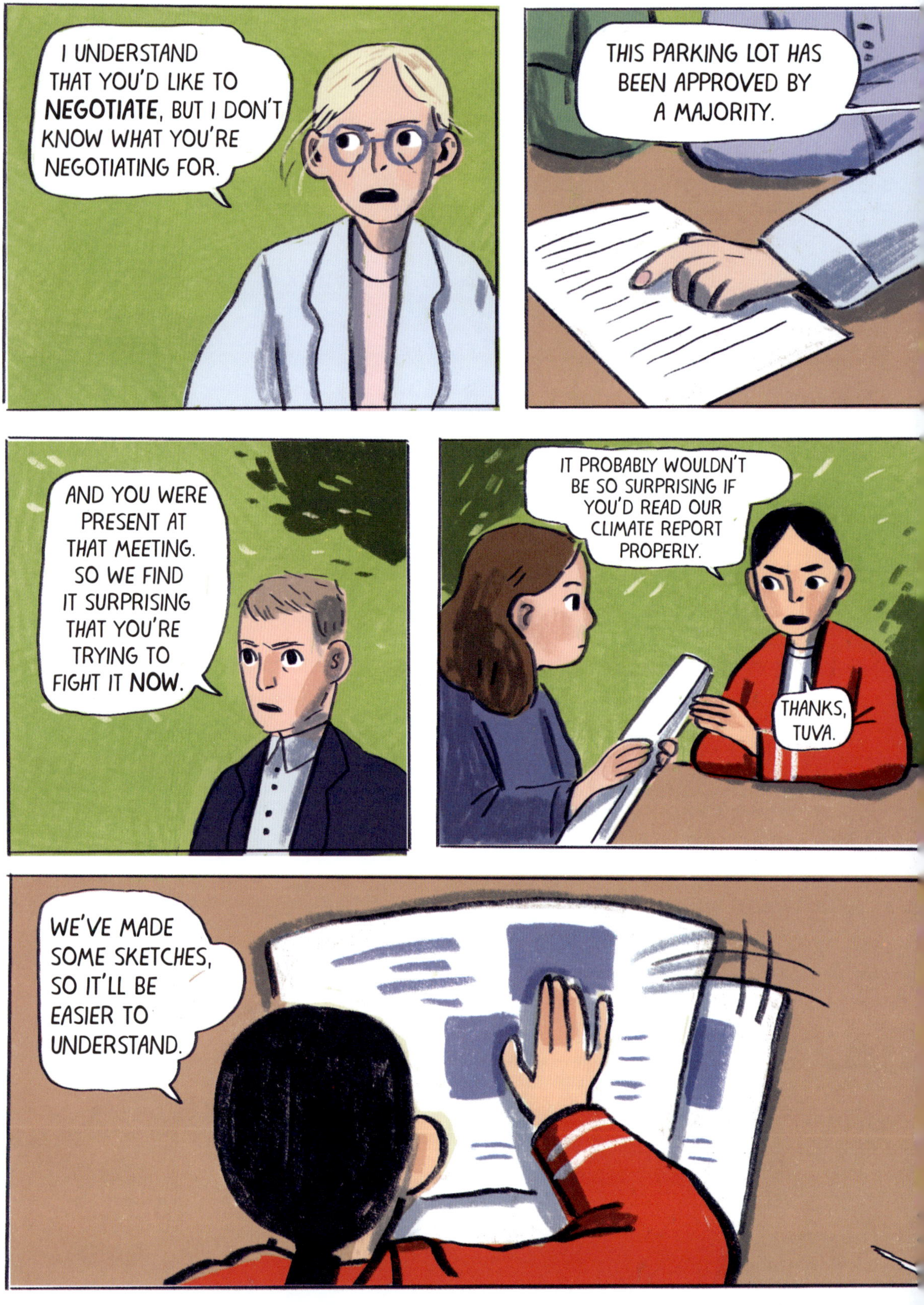
I UNDERSTAND THAT YOU'D LIKE TO **NEGOTIATE**, BUT I DON'T KNOW WHAT YOU'RE NEGOTIATING FOR.
THIS PARKING LOT HAS BEEN APPROVED BY A MAJORITY.
AND YOU WERE PRESENT AT THAT MEETING. SO WE FIND IT SURPRISING THAT YOU'RE TRYING TO FIGHT IT **NOW**.
IT PROBABLY WOULDN'T BE SO SURPRISING IF YOU'D READ OUR CLIMATE REPORT PROPERLY.
THANKS, TUVA.
WE'VE MADE SOME SKETCHES, SO IT'LL BE EASIER TO UNDERSTAND.

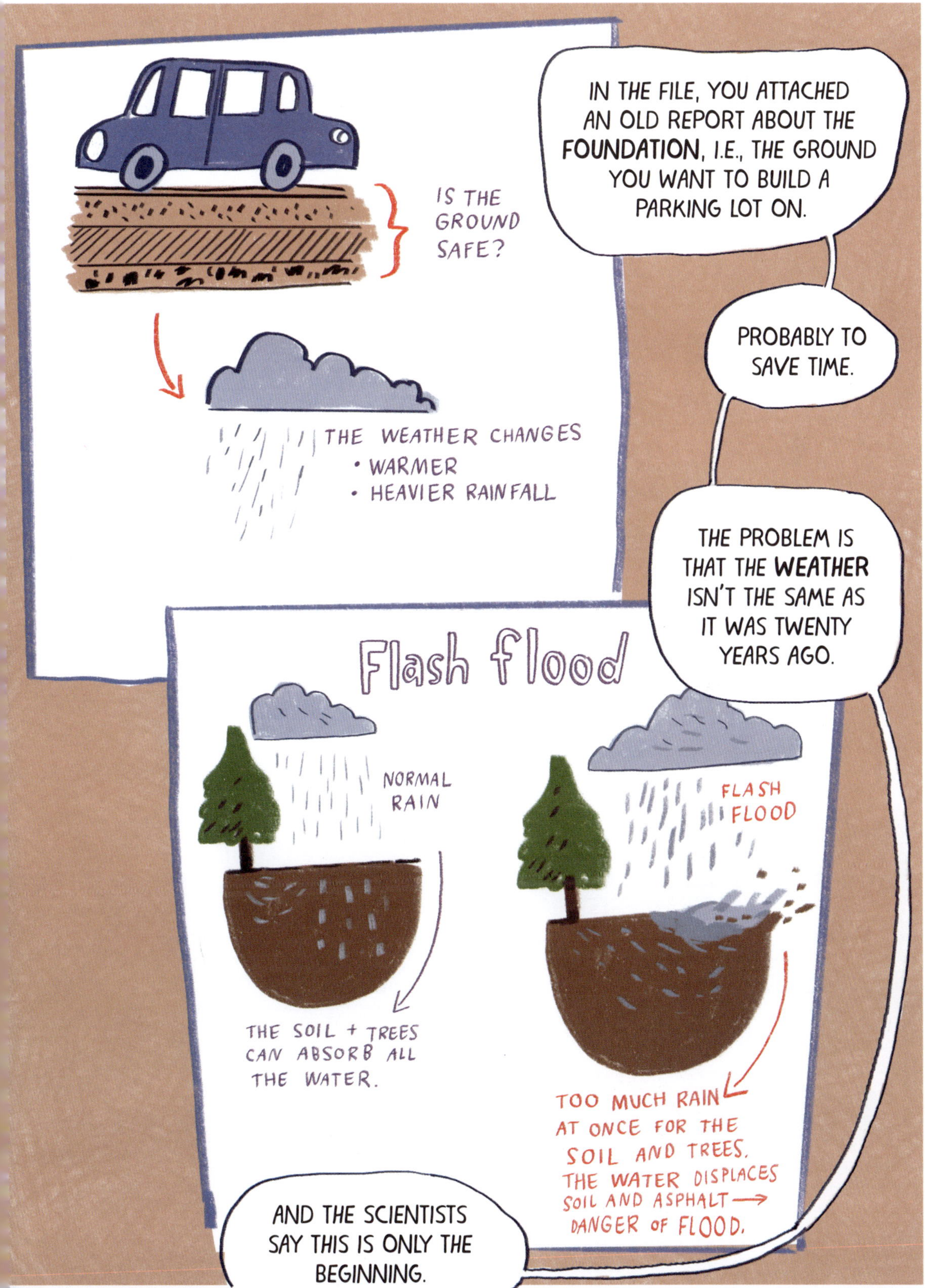
IS THE GROUND SAFE?
THE WEATHER CHANGES
• WARMER
• HEAVIER RAINFALL
IN THE FILE, YOU ATTACHED AN OLD REPORT ABOUT THE **FOUNDATION**, I.E., THE GROUND YOU WANT TO BUILD A PARKING LOT ON.
PROBABLY TO SAVE TIME.
THE PROBLEM IS THAT THE **WEATHER** ISN'T THE SAME AS IT WAS TWENTY YEARS AGO.
Flash flood
NORMAL RAIN
THE SOIL + TREES CAN ABSORB ALL THE WATER.
FLASH FLOOD
TOO MUCH RAIN AT ONCE FOR THE SOIL AND TREES. THE WATER DISPLACES SOIL AND ASPHALT → DANGER OF FLOOD.
AND THE SCIENTISTS SAY THIS IS ONLY THE BEGINNING.

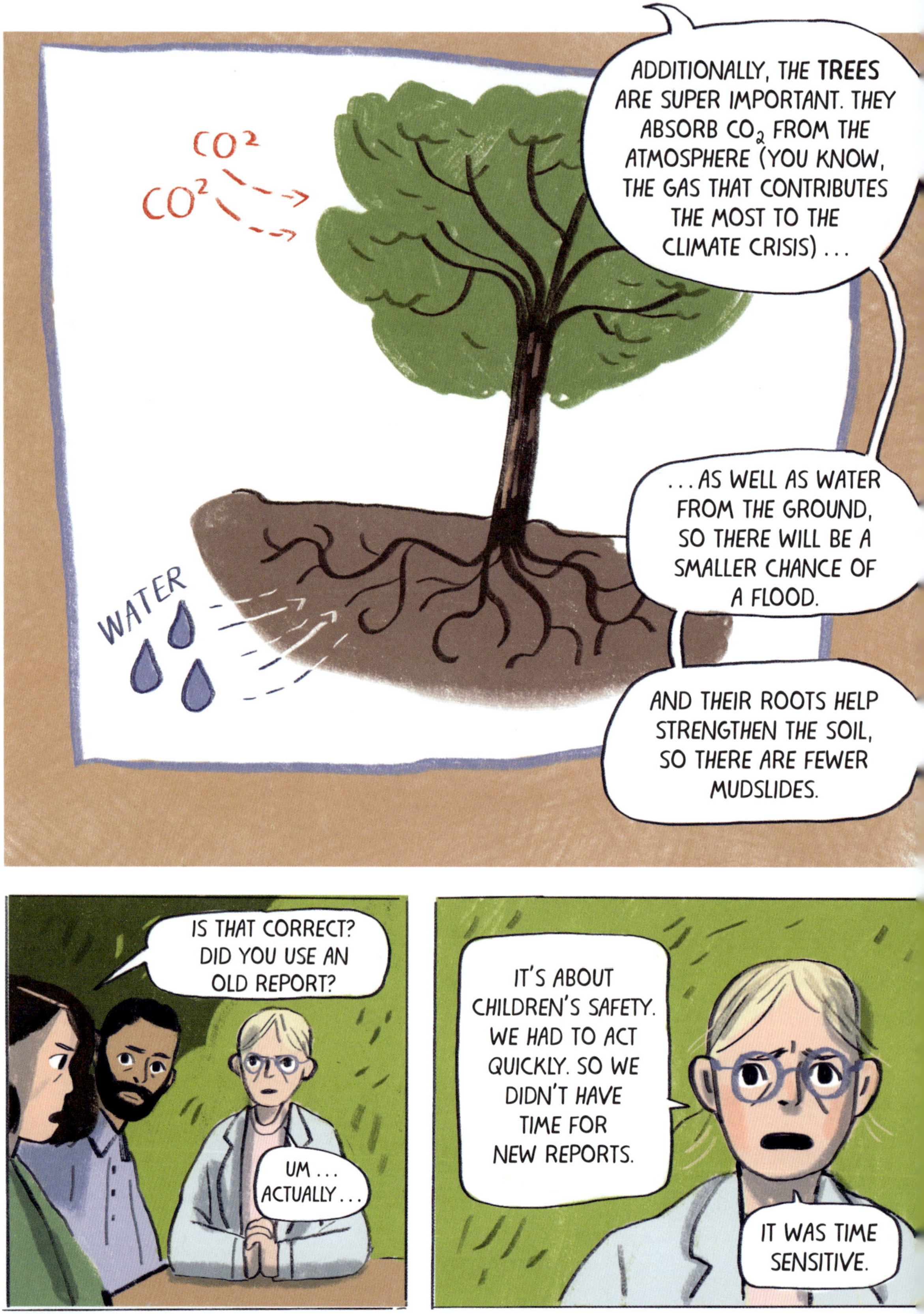

ADDITIONALLY, THE **TREES** ARE SUPER IMPORTANT. THEY ABSORB CO_2 FROM THE ATMOSPHERE (YOU KNOW, THE GAS THAT CONTRIBUTES THE MOST TO THE CLIMATE CRISIS) . . .
CO2
CO2
WATER
. . . AS WELL AS WATER FROM THE GROUND, SO THERE WILL BE A SMALLER CHANCE OF A FLOOD.
AND THEIR ROOTS HELP STRENGTHEN THE SOIL, SO THERE ARE FEWER MUDSLIDES.
IS THAT CORRECT? DID YOU USE AN OLD REPORT?
UM . . . ACTUALLY . . .
IT'S ABOUT CHILDREN'S SAFETY. WE HAD TO ACT QUICKLY. SO WE DIDN'T HAVE TIME FOR NEW REPORTS.
IT WAS TIME SENSITIVE.

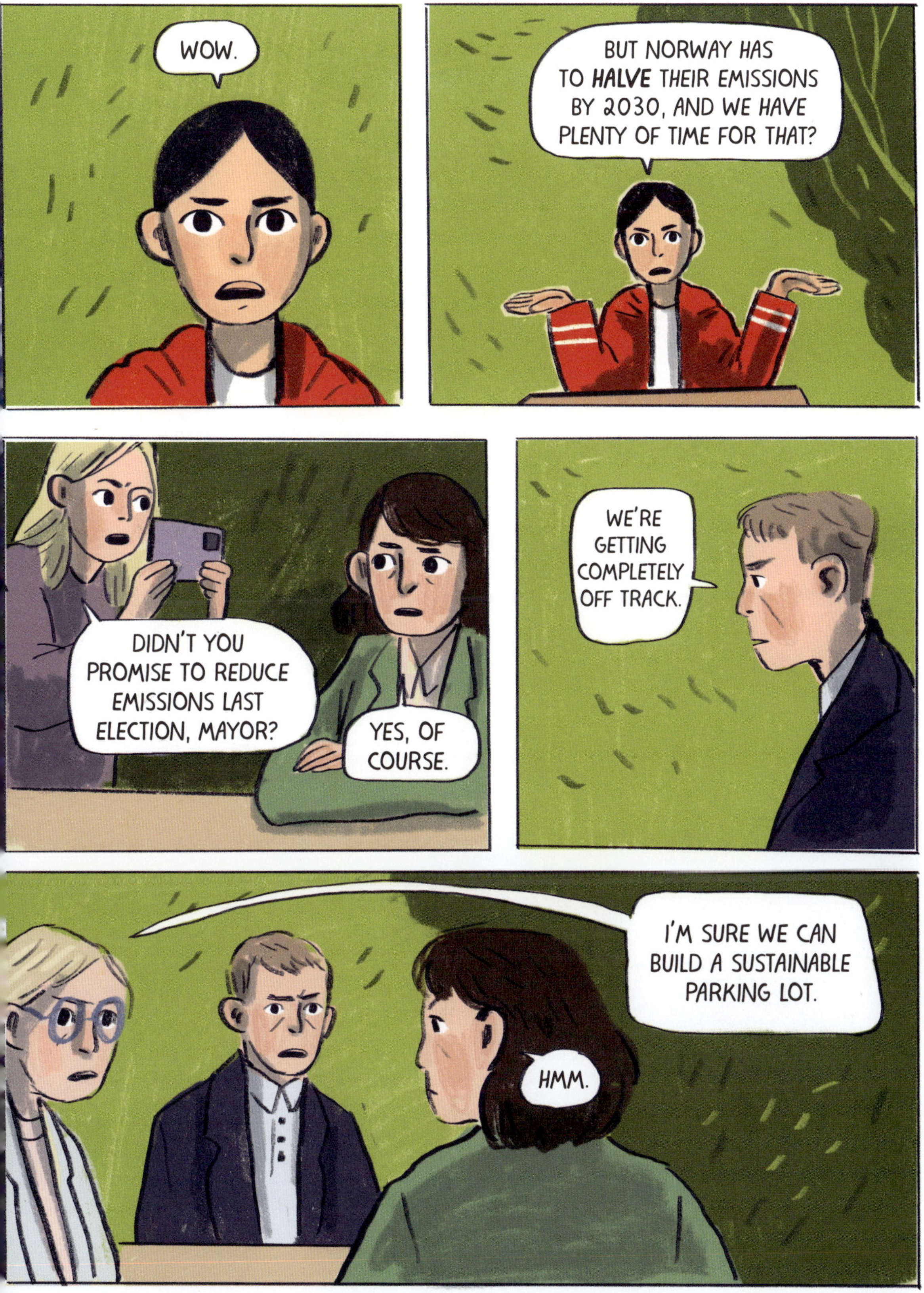
WOW.
BUT NORWAY HAS TO **HALVE** THEIR EMISSIONS BY 2030, AND WE HAVE PLENTY OF TIME FOR THAT?
DIDN'T YOU PROMISE TO REDUCE EMISSIONS LAST ELECTION, MAYOR?
YES, OF COURSE.
WE'RE GETTING COMPLETELY OFF TRACK.
I'M SURE WE CAN BUILD A SUSTAINABLE PARKING LOT.
HMM.

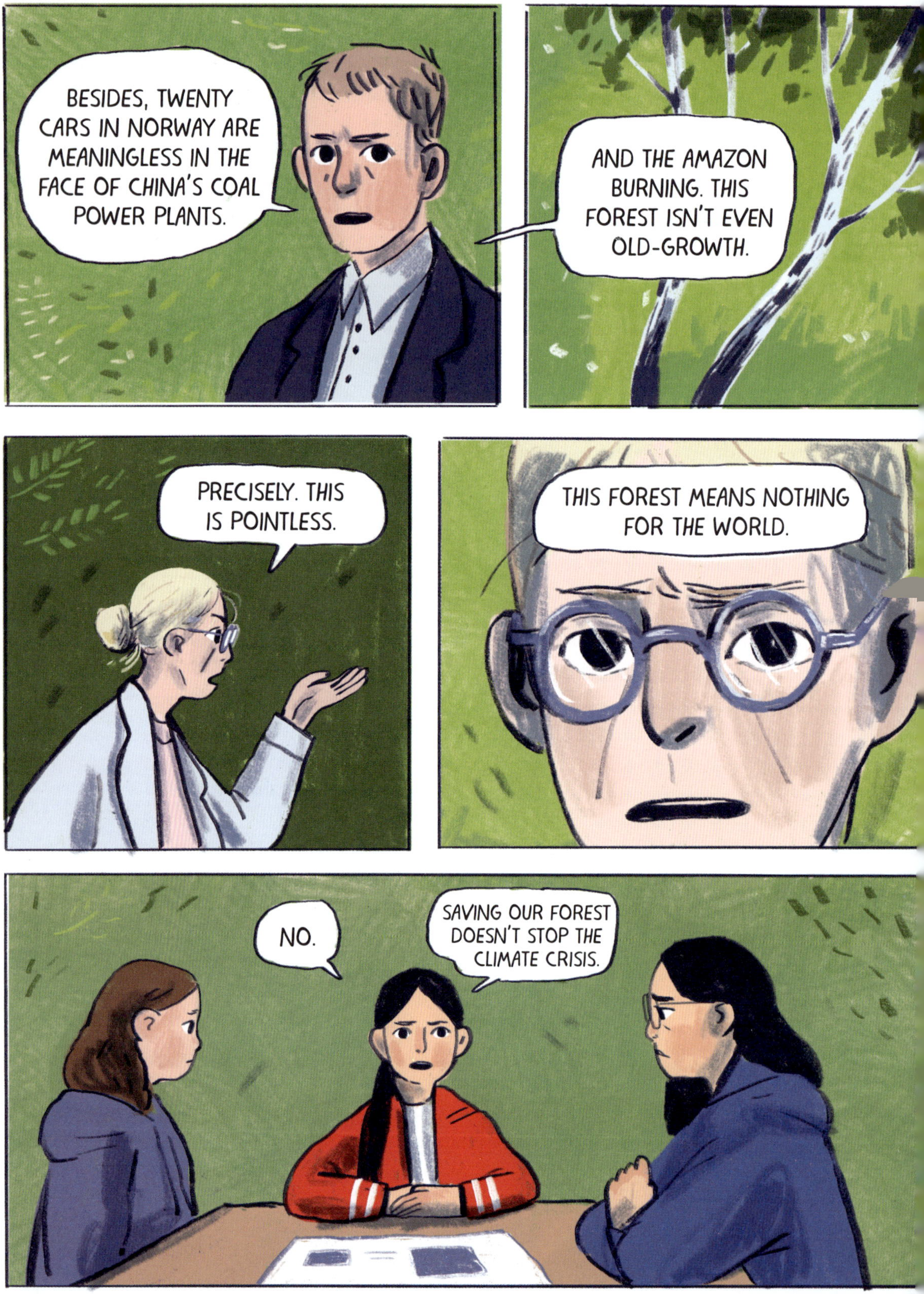

BESIDES, TWENTY CARS IN NORWAY ARE MEANINGLESS IN THE FACE OF CHINA'S COAL POWER PLANTS.
AND THE AMAZON BURNING. THIS FOREST ISN'T EVEN OLD-GROWTH.
PRECISELY. THIS IS POINTLESS.
THIS FOREST MEANS NOTHING FOR THE WORLD.
NO.
SAVING OUR FOREST DOESN'T STOP THE CLIMATE CRISIS.

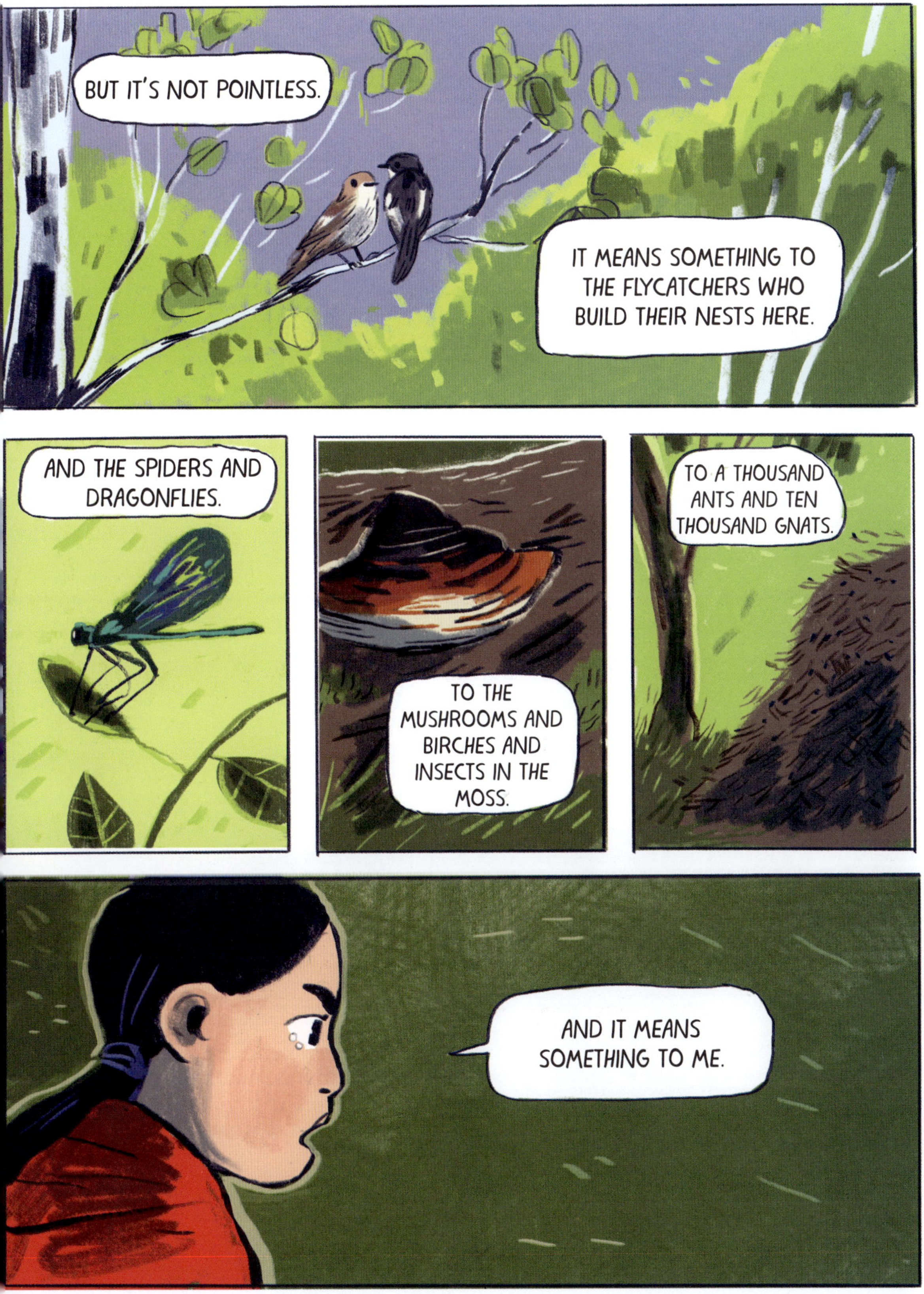
BUT IT'S NOT POINTLESS.
IT MEANS SOMETHING TO THE FLYCATCHERS WHO BUILD THEIR NESTS HERE.
AND THE SPIDERS AND DRAGONFLIES.
TO THE MUSHROOMS AND BIRCHES AND INSECTS IN THE MOSS.
TO A THOUSAND ANTS AND TEN THOUSAND GNATS.
AND IT MEANS SOMETHING TO ME.

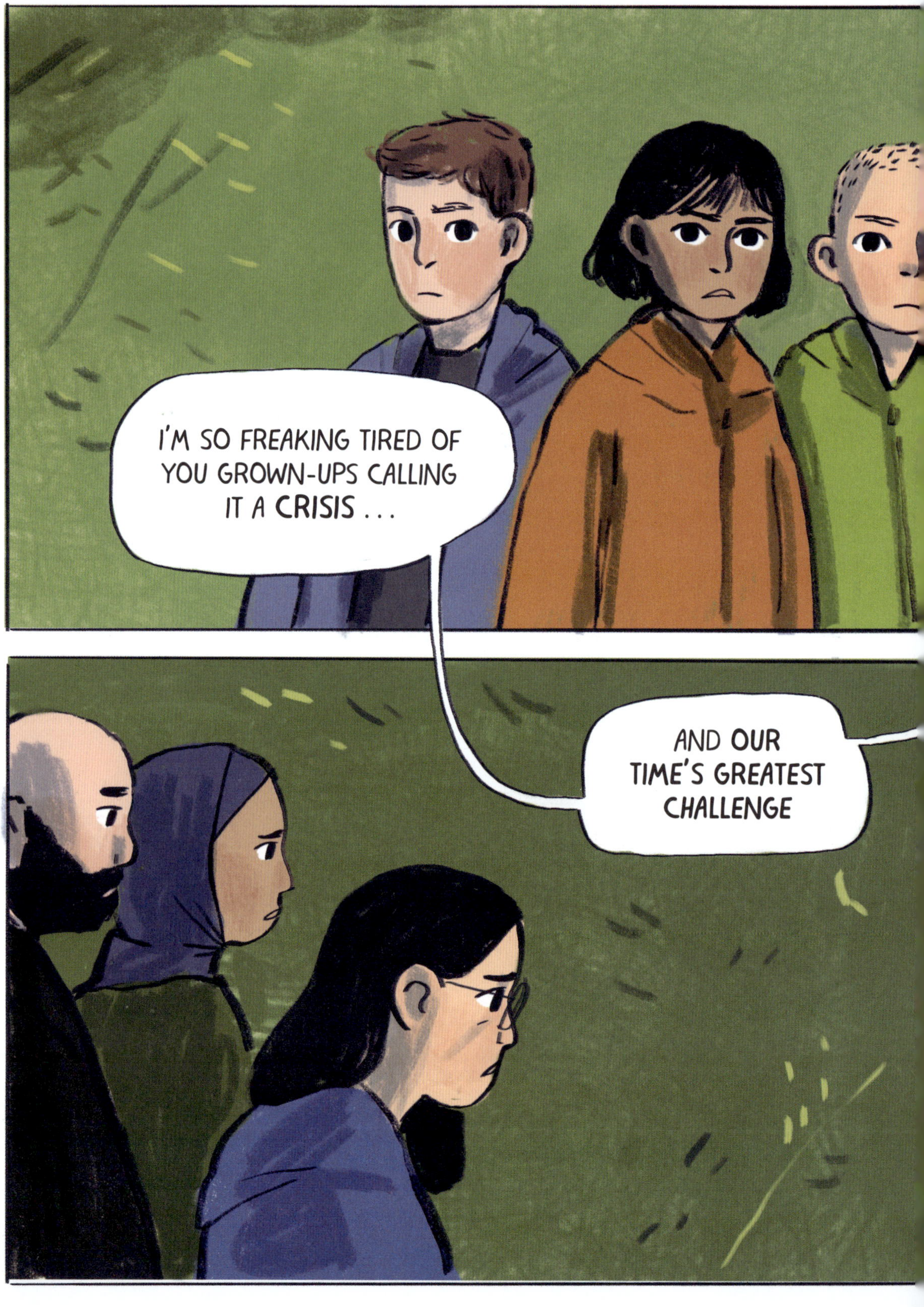
I'M SO FREAKING TIRED OF YOU GROWN-UPS CALLING IT A CRISIS . . .
AND OUR TIME'S GREATEST CHALLENGE

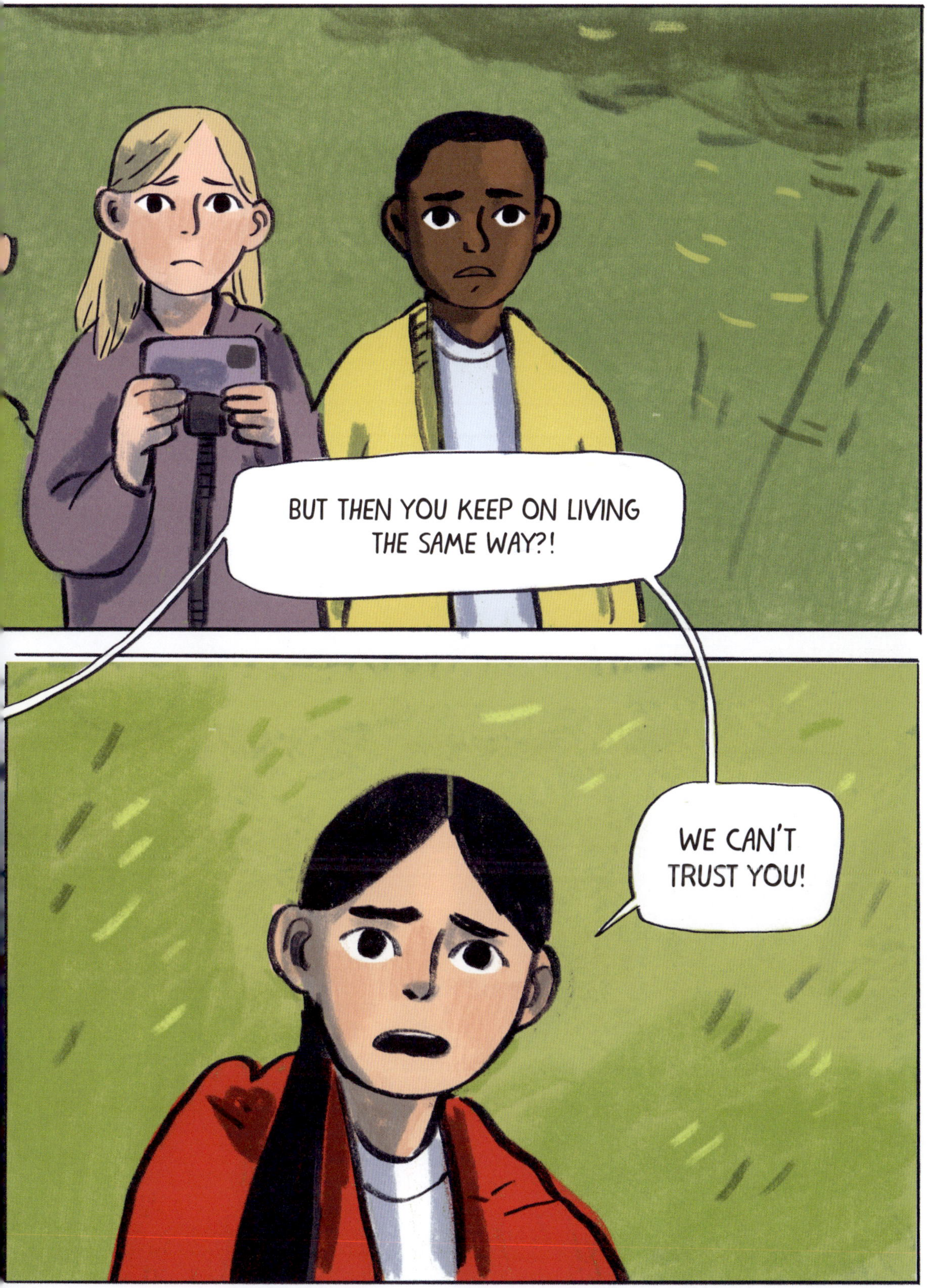
BUT THEN YOU KEEP ON LIVING THE SAME WAY?!
WE CAN'T TRUST YOU!

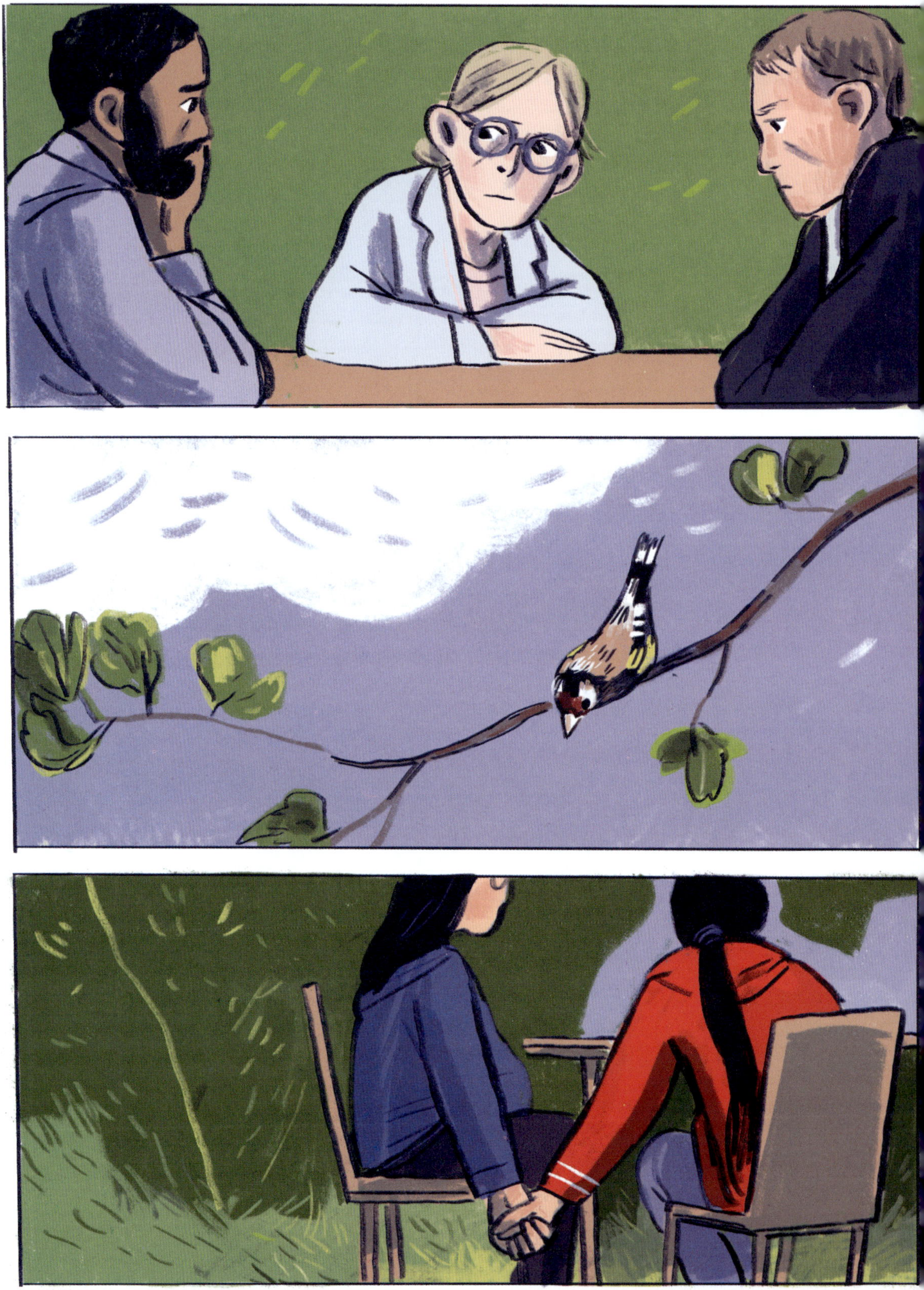

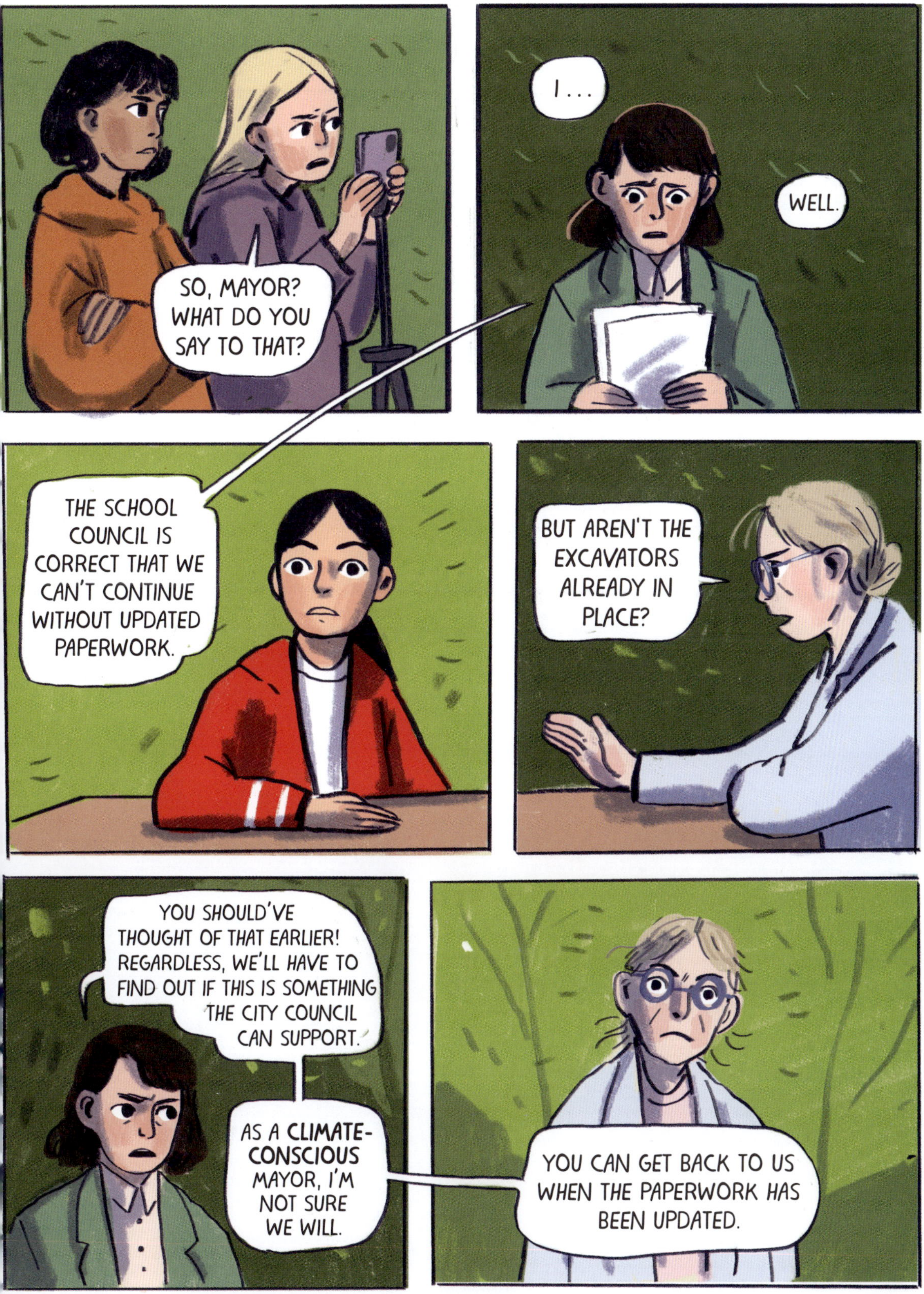
SO, MAYOR? WHAT DO YOU SAY TO THAT?
I...
WELL.
THE SCHOOL COUNCIL IS CORRECT THAT WE CAN'T CONTINUE WITHOUT UPDATED PAPERWORK.
BUT AREN'T THE EXCAVATORS ALREADY IN PLACE?
YOU SHOULD'VE THOUGHT OF THAT EARLIER! REGARDLESS, WE'LL HAVE TO FIND OUT IF THIS IS SOMETHING THE CITY COUNCIL CAN SUPPORT.
AS A **CLIMATE-CONSCIOUS** MAYOR, I'M NOT SURE WE WILL.
YOU CAN GET BACK TO US WHEN THE PAPERWORK HAS BEEN UPDATED.

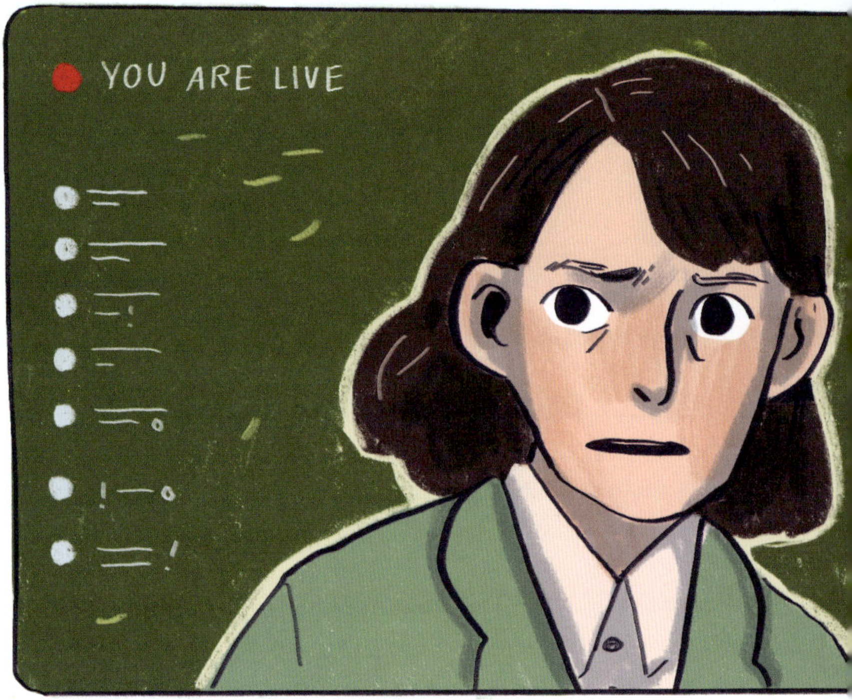
YOU ARE LIVE

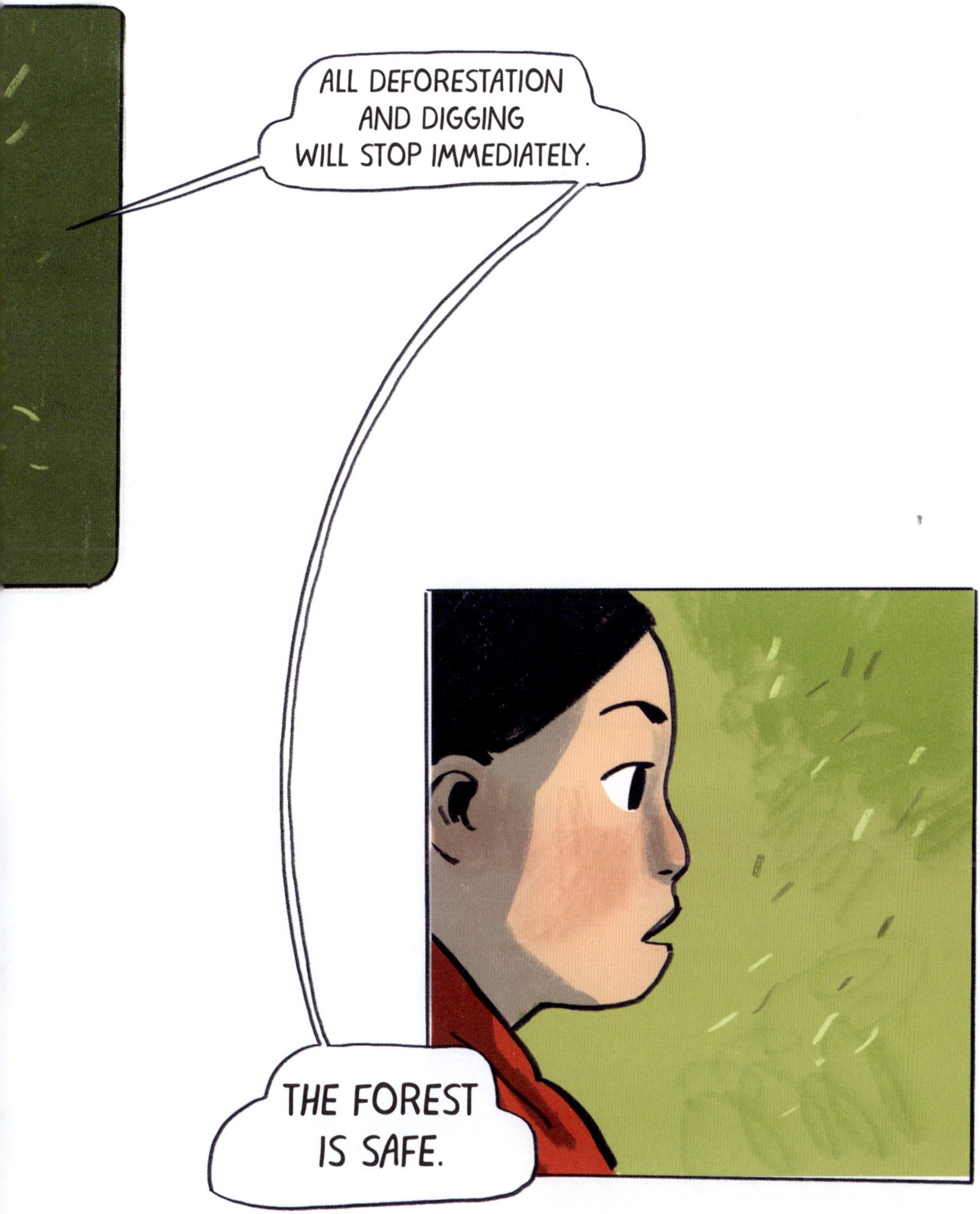
ALL DEFORESTATION AND DIGGING WILL STOP IMMEDIATELY.
THE FOREST IS SAFE.

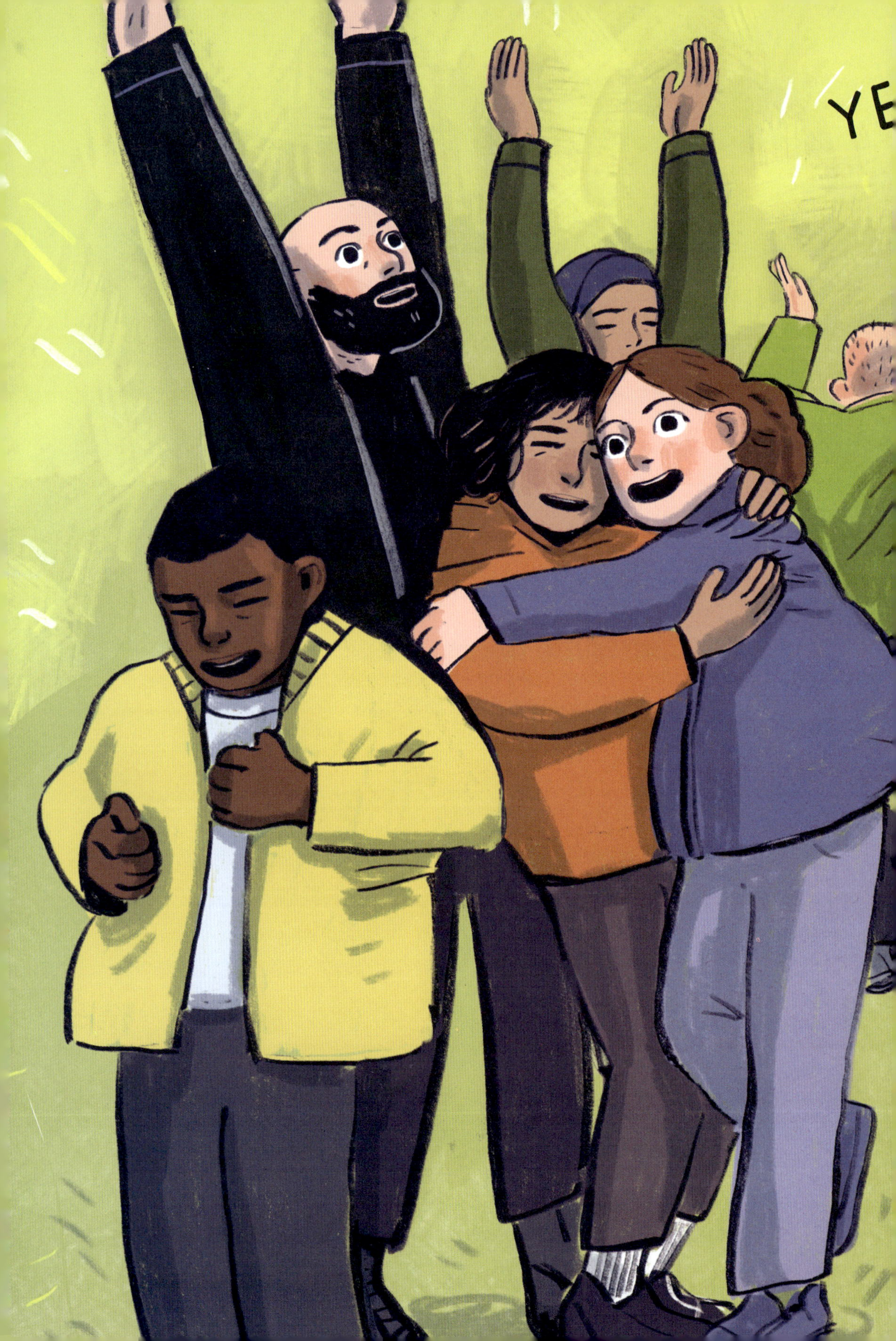
YE

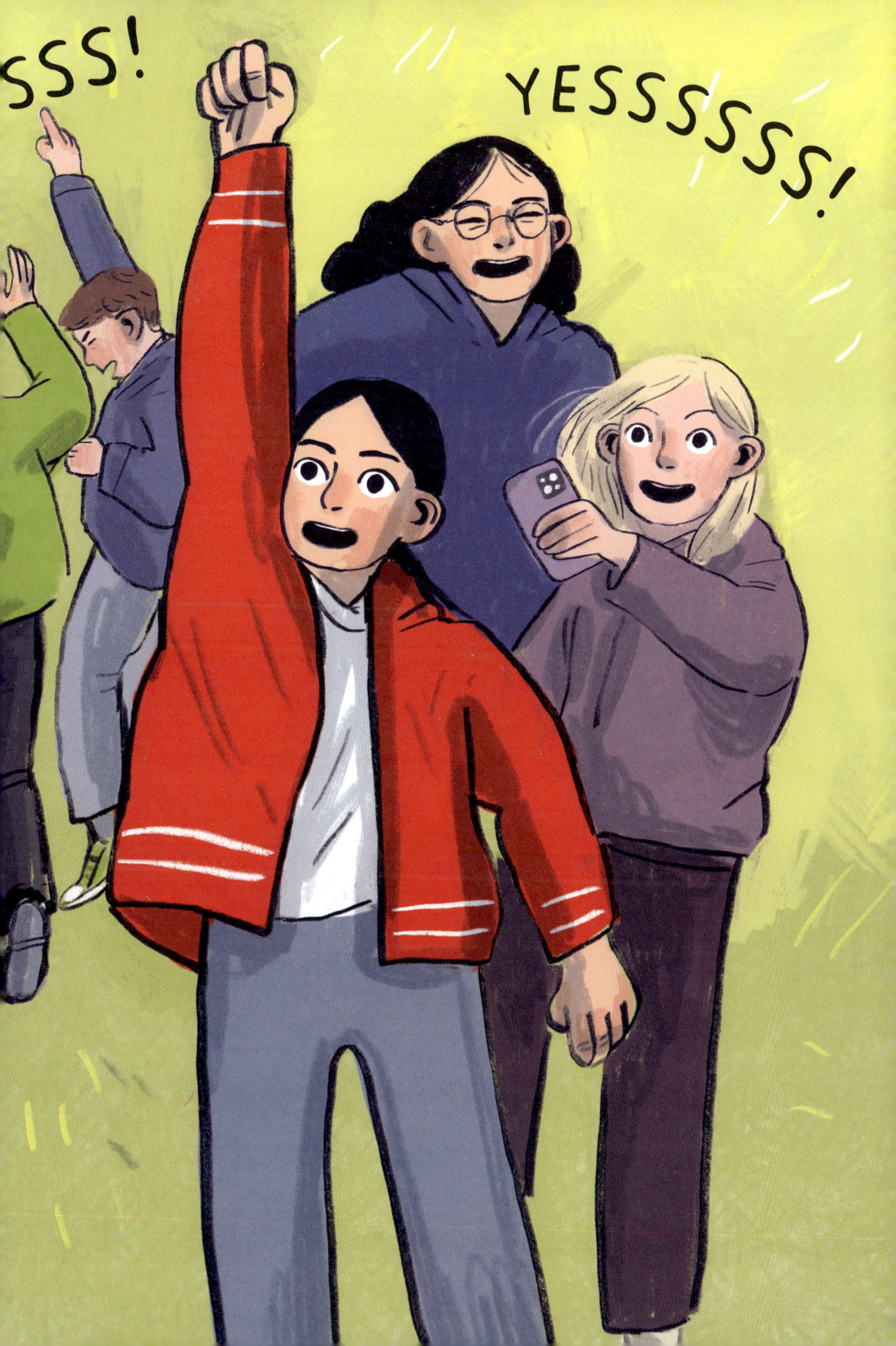
SSS!
YESSSSSS!

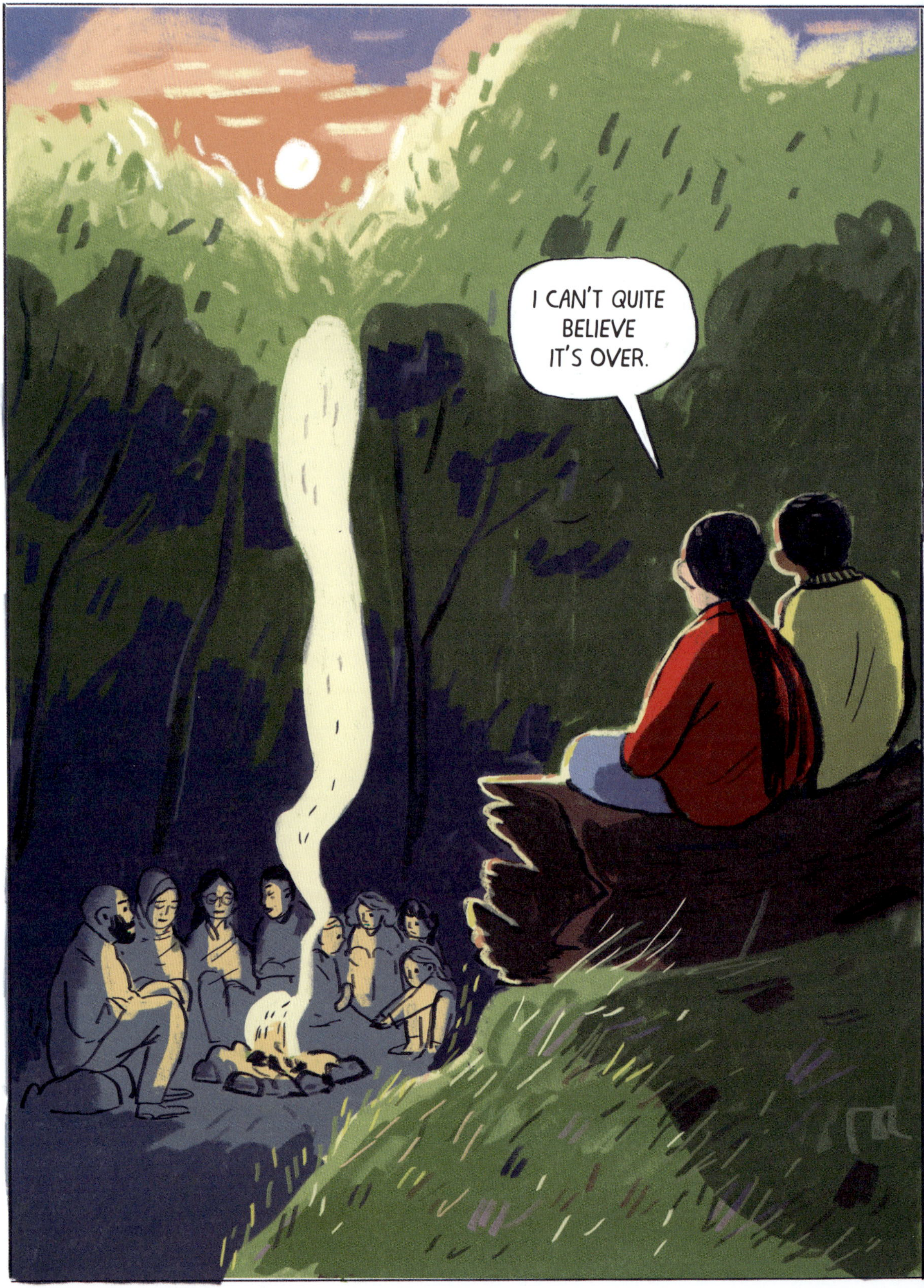
I CAN'T QUITE BELIEVE IT'S OVER.

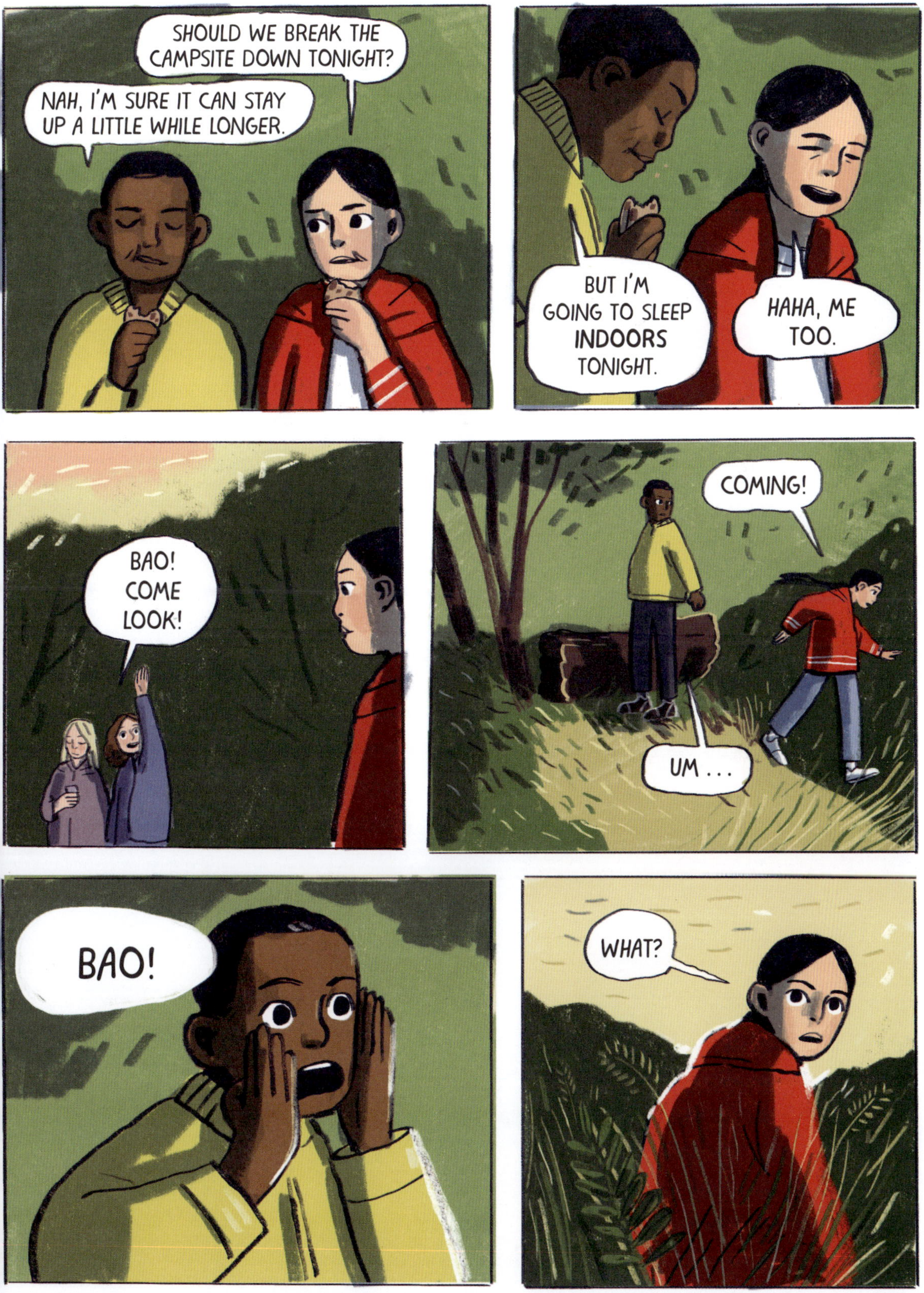
SHOULD WE BREAK THE CAMPSITE DOWN TONIGHT?
NAH, I'M SURE IT CAN STAY UP A LITTLE WHILE LONGER.
BUT I'M GOING TO SLEEP INDOORS TONIGHT.
HAHA, ME TOO.
BAO! COME LOOK!
COMING!
UM . . .
BAO!
WHAT?

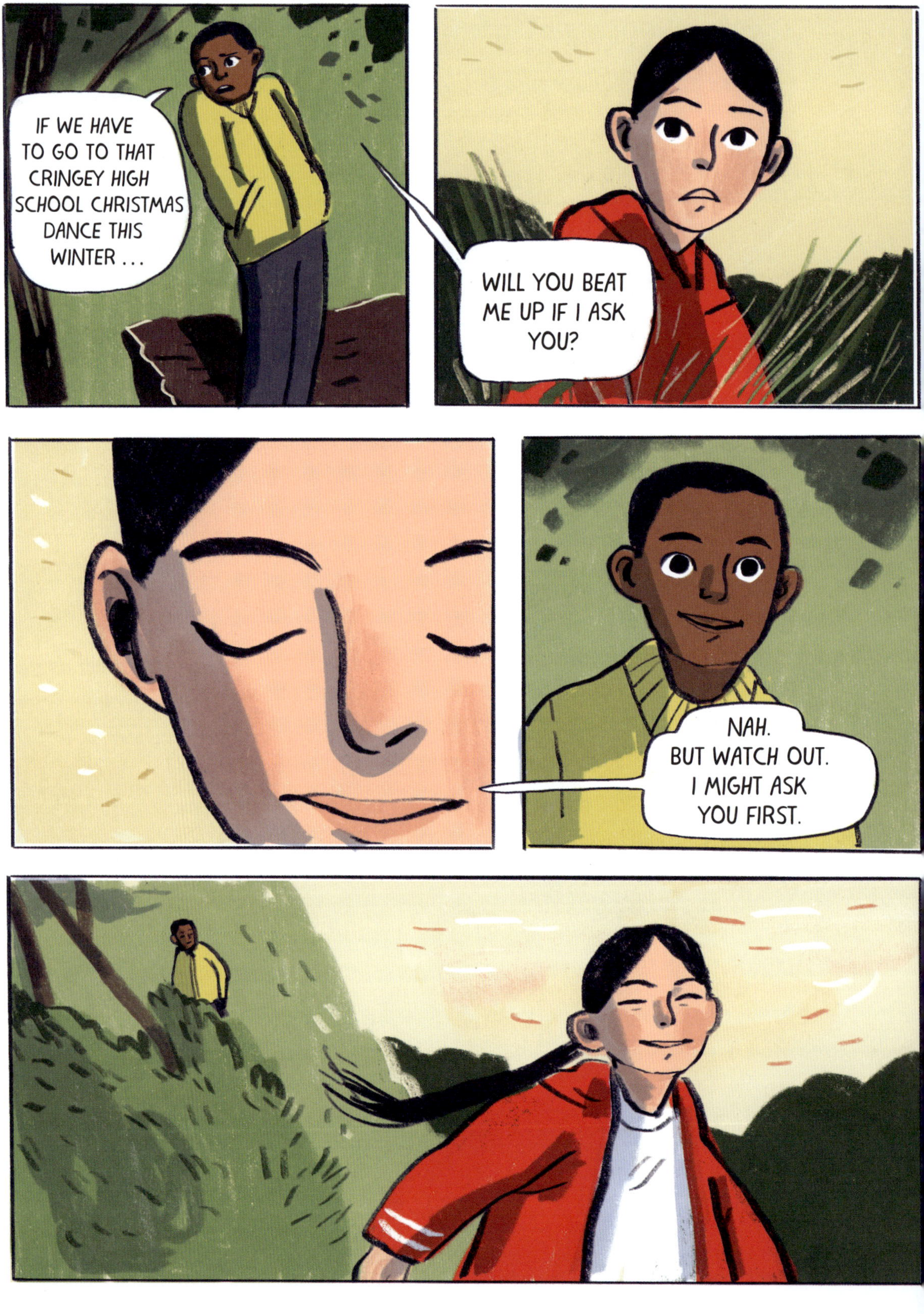
IF WE HAVE TO GO TO THAT CRINGEY HIGH SCHOOL CHRISTMAS DANCE THIS WINTER . . .
WILL YOU BEAT ME UP IF I ASK YOU?
NAH. BUT WATCH OUT. I MIGHT ASK YOU FIRST.

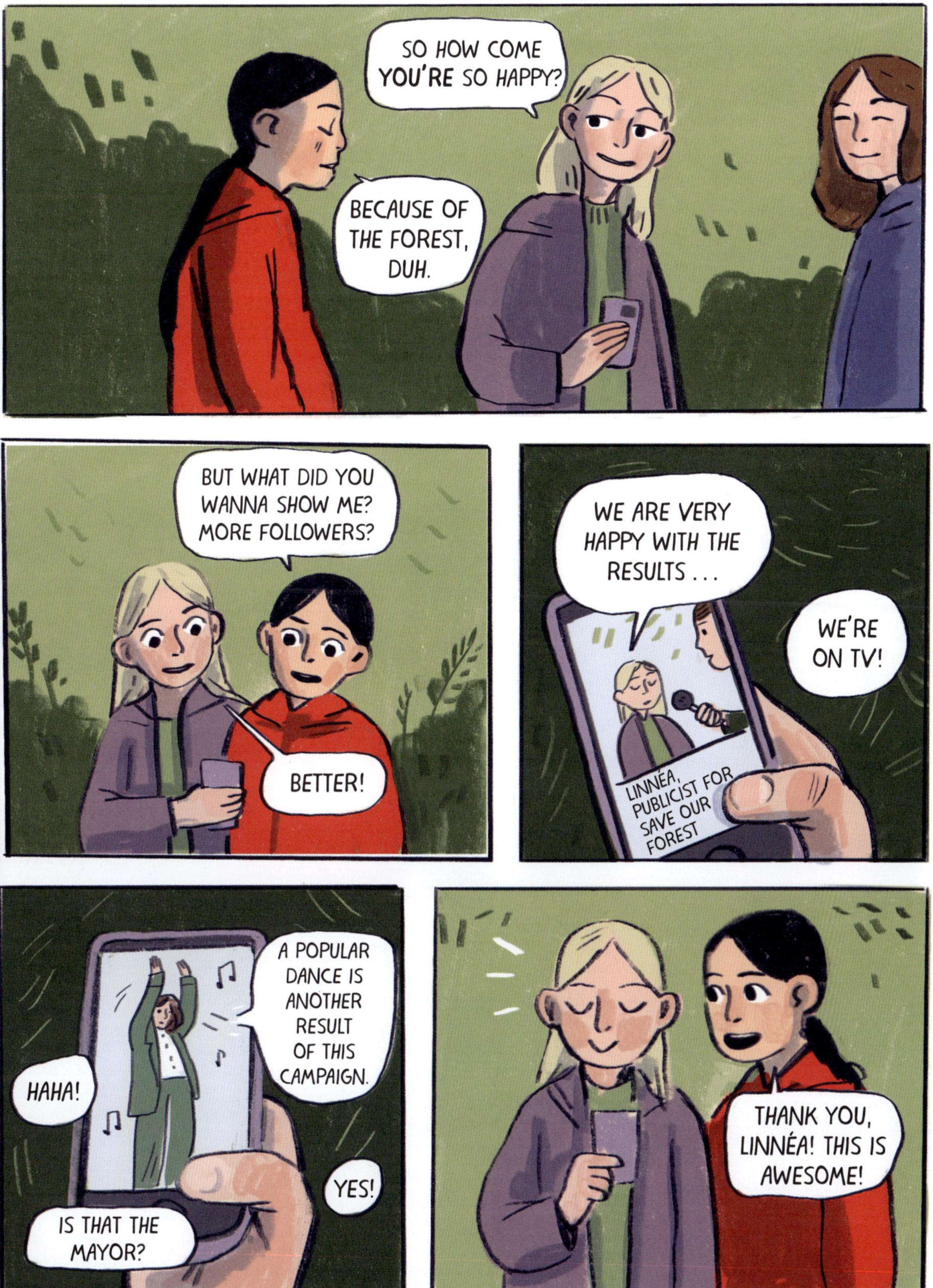
SO HOW COME YOU'RE SO HAPPY?
BECAUSE OF THE FOREST, DUH.
BUT WHAT DID YOU WANNA SHOW ME? MORE FOLLOWERS?
BETTER!
WE ARE VERY HAPPY WITH THE RESULTS . . .
LINNÉA, PUBLICIST FOR SAVE OUR FOREST
WE'RE ON TV!
A POPULAR DANCE IS ANOTHER RESULT OF THIS CAMPAIGN.
HAHA!
YES!
IS THAT THE MAYOR?
THANK YOU, LINNÉA! THIS IS AWESOME!

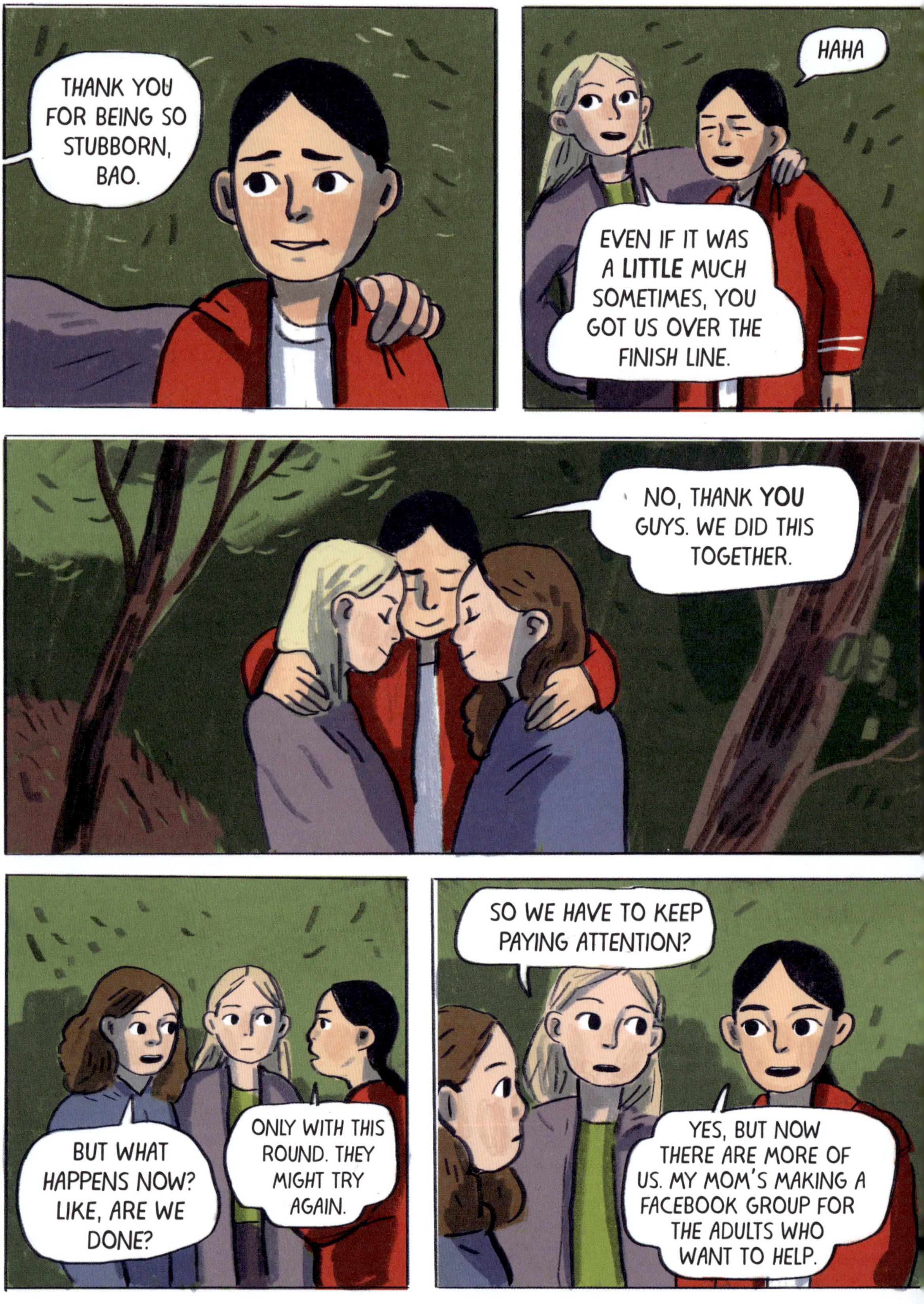
THANK YOU FOR BEING SO STUBBORN, BAO.
HAHA
EVEN IF IT WAS A **LITTLE** MUCH SOMETIMES, YOU GOT US OVER THE FINISH LINE.
NO, THANK **YOU** GUYS. WE DID THIS TOGETHER.
BUT WHAT HAPPENS NOW? LIKE, ARE WE DONE?
ONLY WITH THIS ROUND. THEY MIGHT TRY AGAIN.
SO WE HAVE TO KEEP PAYING ATTENTION?
YES, BUT NOW THERE ARE MORE OF US. MY MOM'S MAKING A FACEBOOK GROUP FOR THE ADULTS WHO WANT TO HELP.

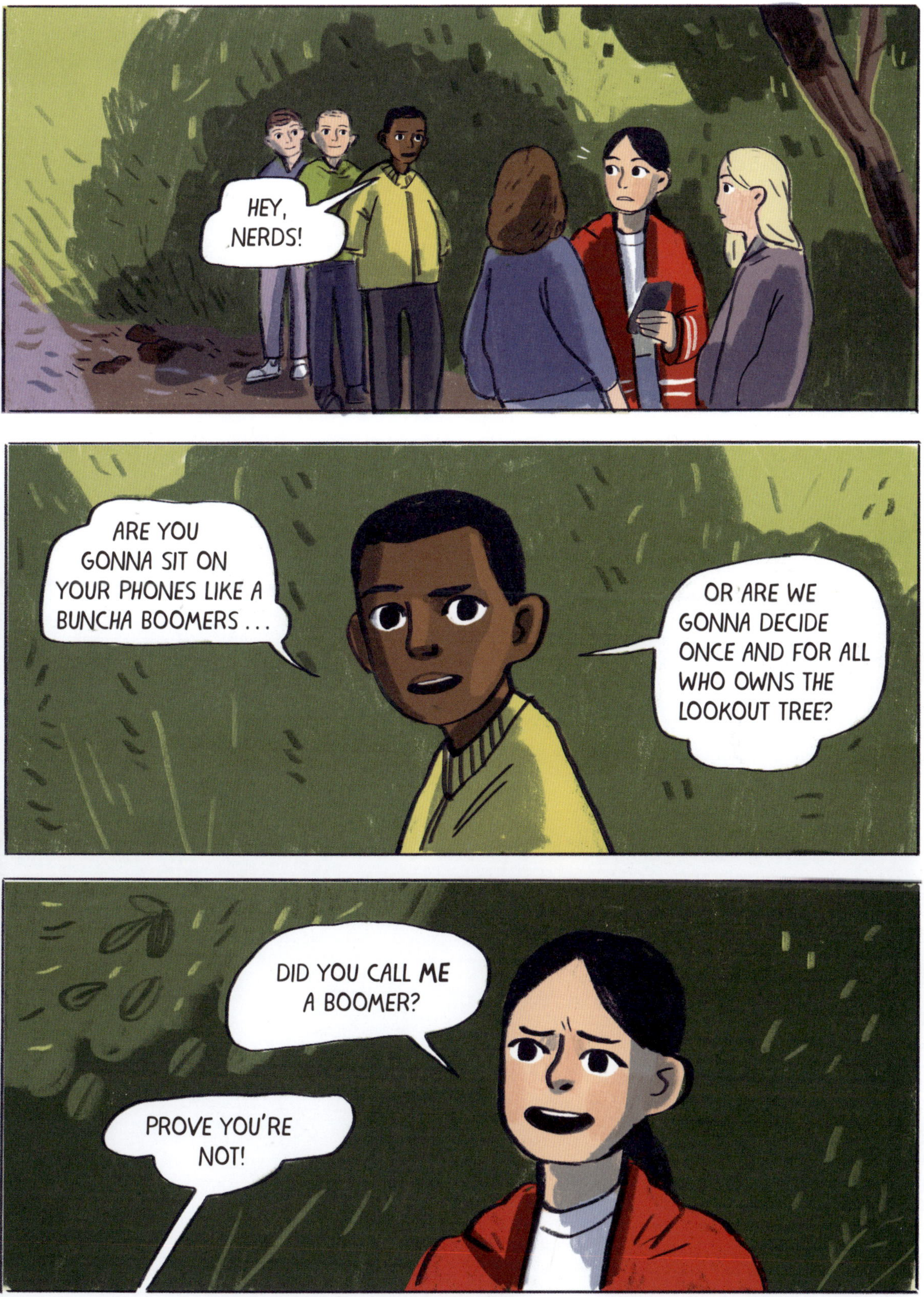
HEY, NERDS!
ARE YOU GONNA SIT ON YOUR PHONES LIKE A BUNCHA BOOMERS . . .
OR ARE WE GONNA DECIDE ONCE AND FOR ALL WHO OWNS THE LOOKOUT TREE?
DID YOU CALL **ME** A BOOMER?
PROVE YOU'RE NOT!

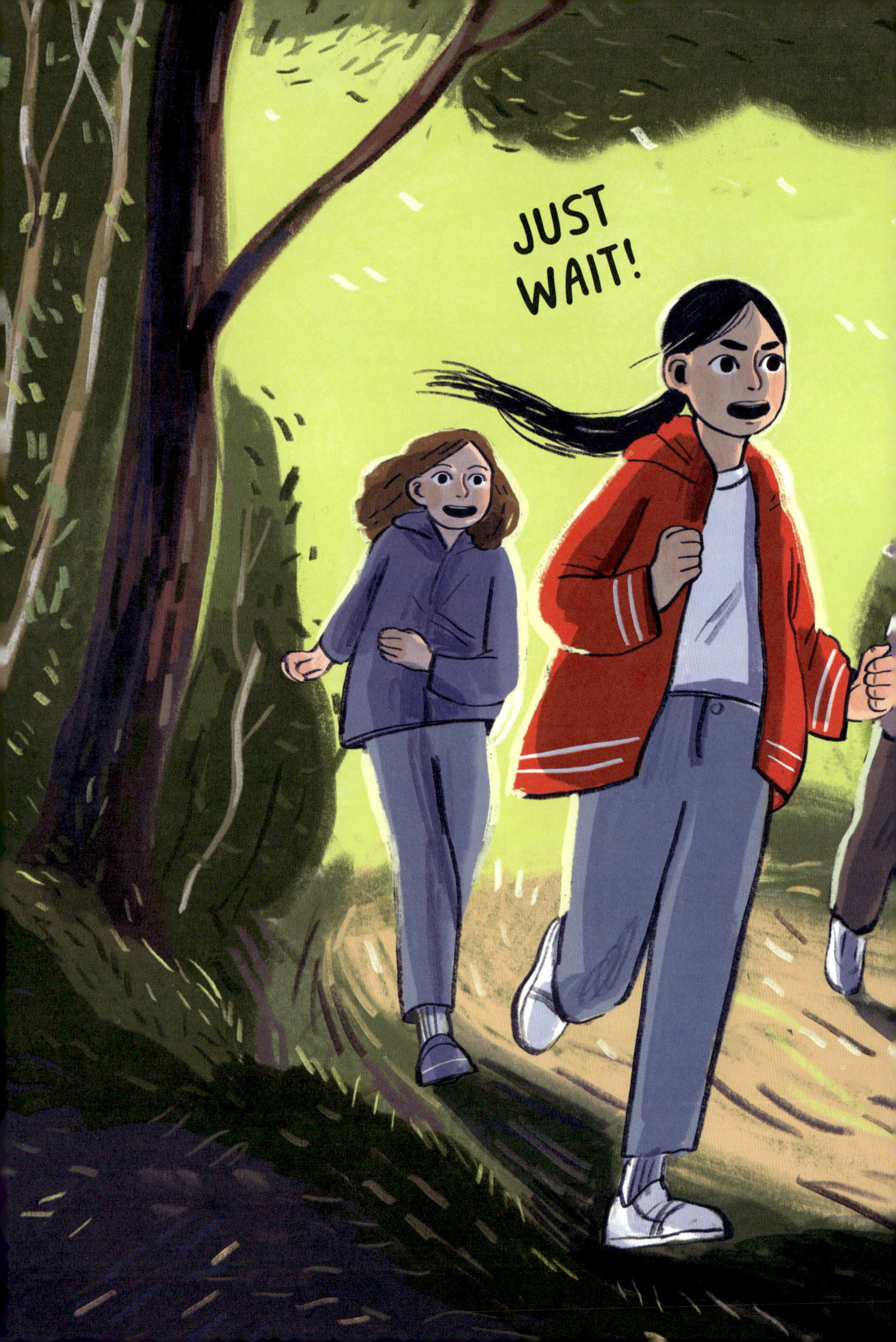
JUST WAIT!

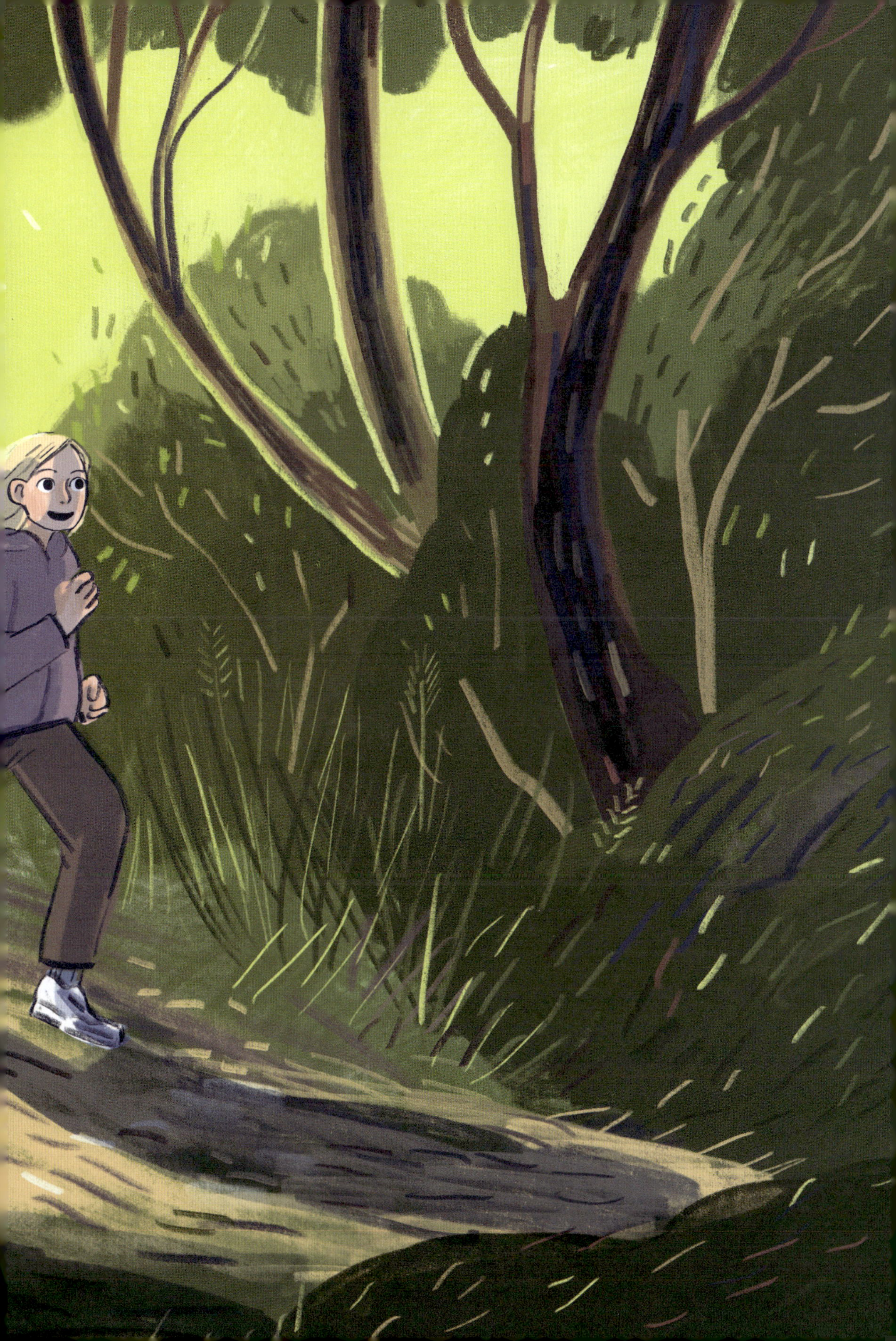

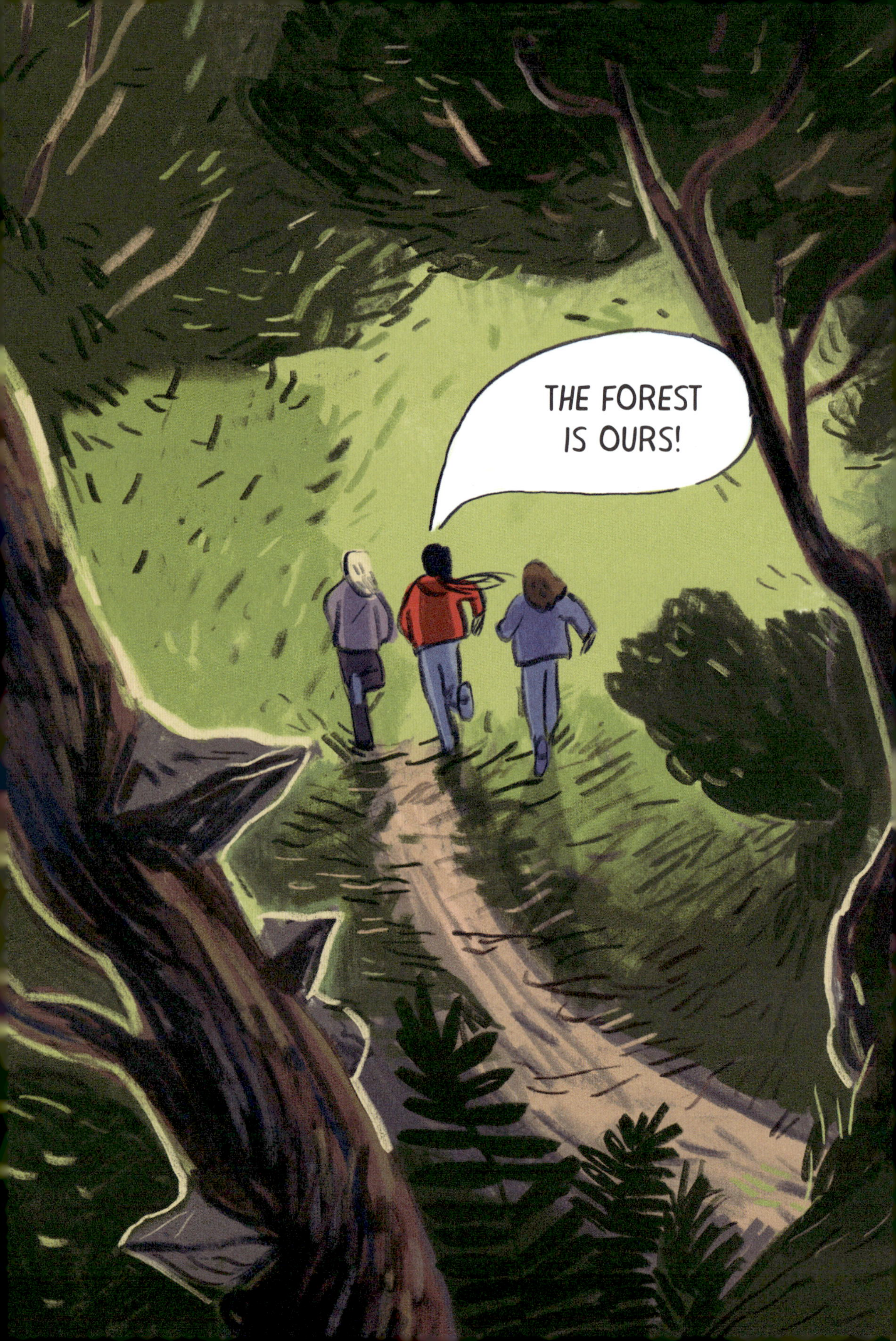
THE FOREST IS OURS!

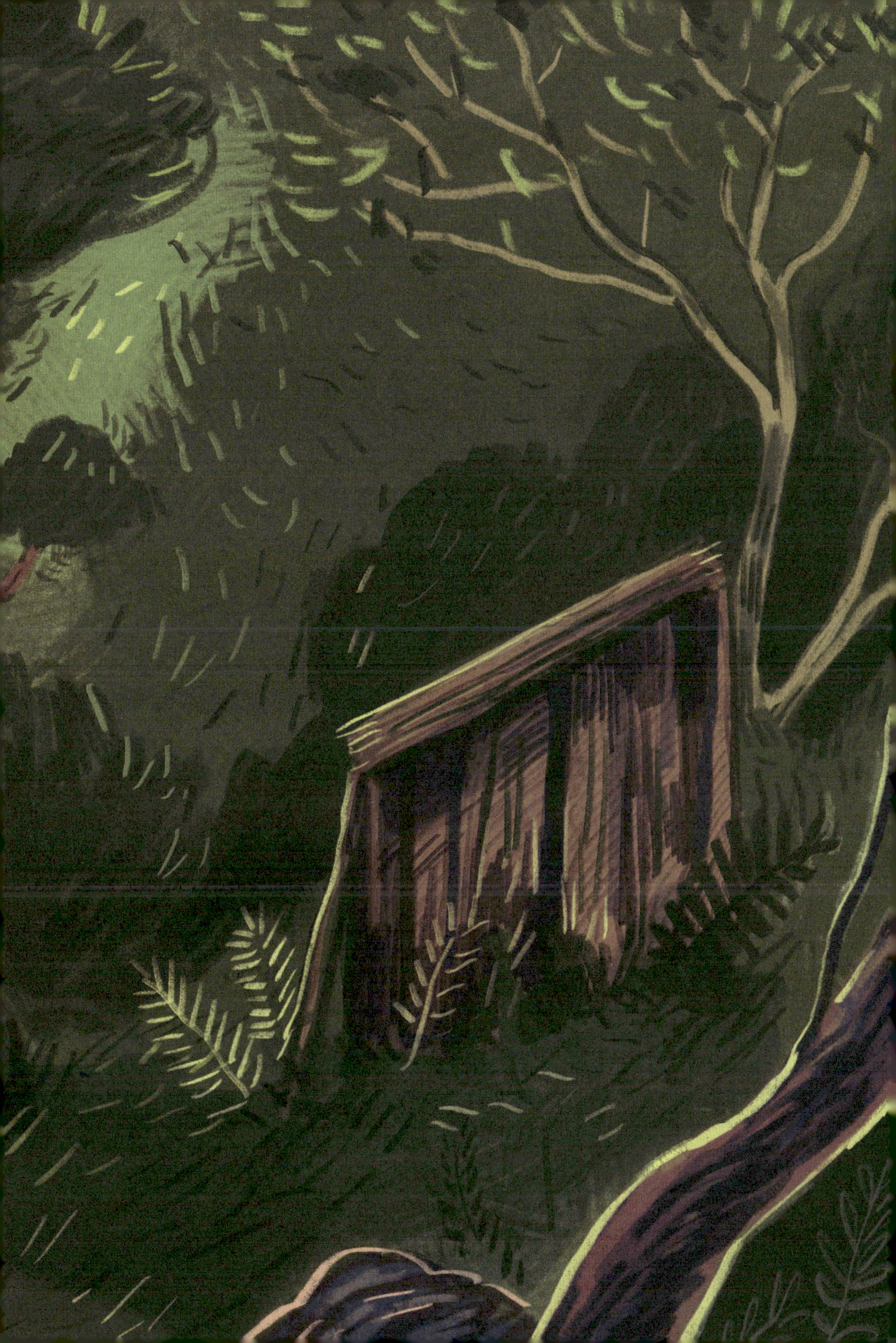

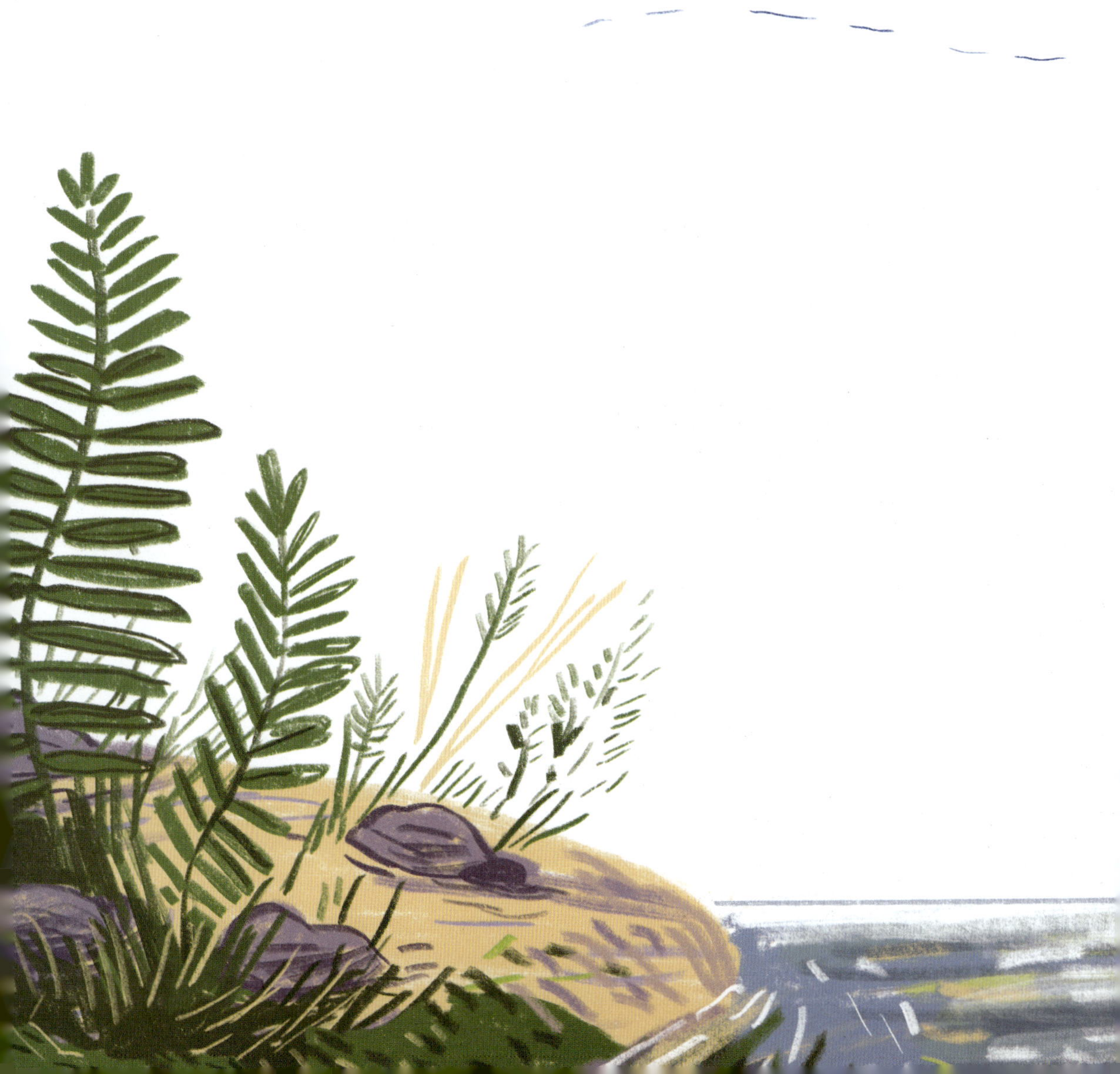

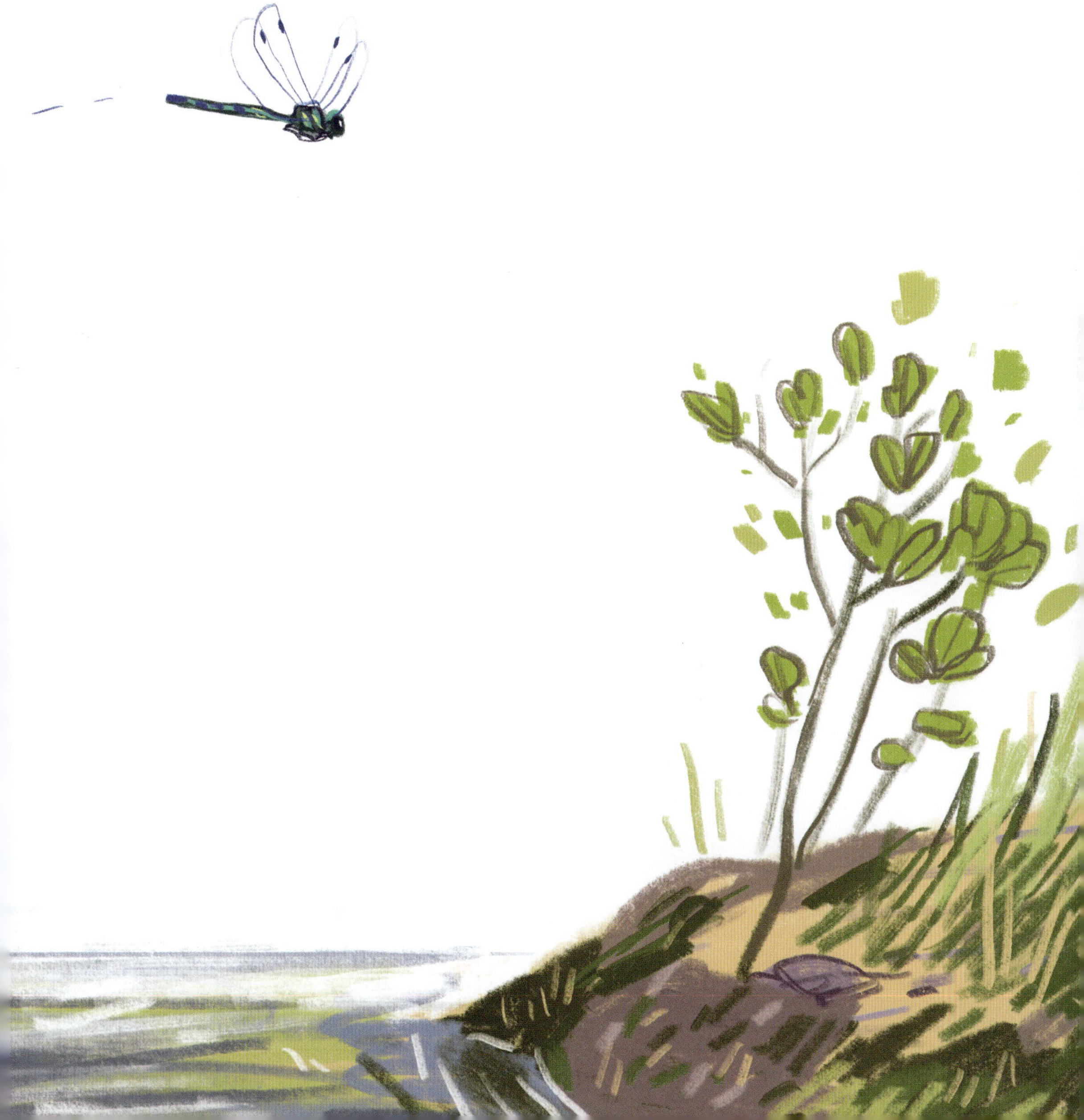

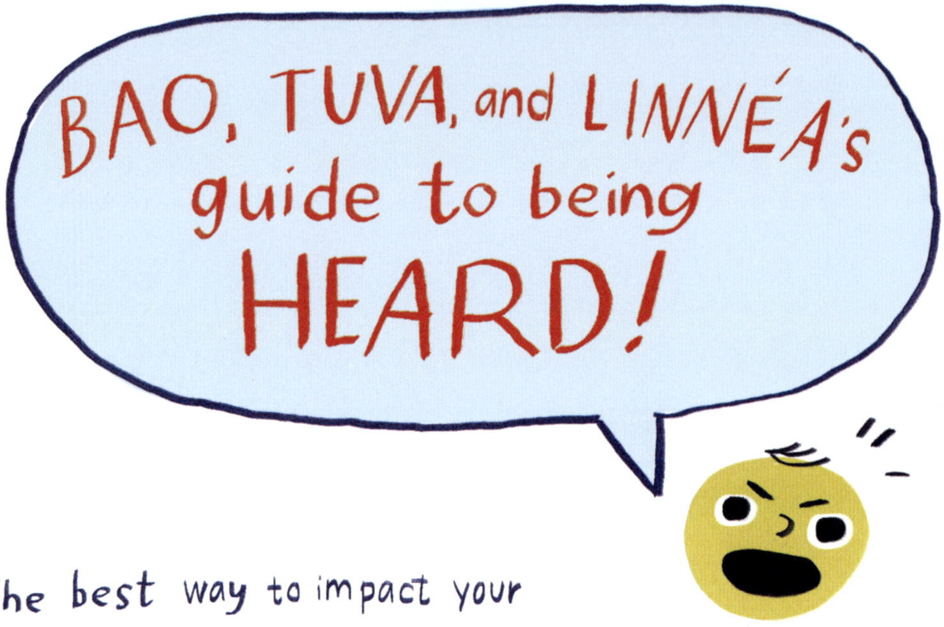
BAO, TUVA, and LINNÉA's guide to being HEARD!

The best way to impact your country is to vote in elections.

But to do that, you have to be at least eighteen years old.

So what do you do before then?

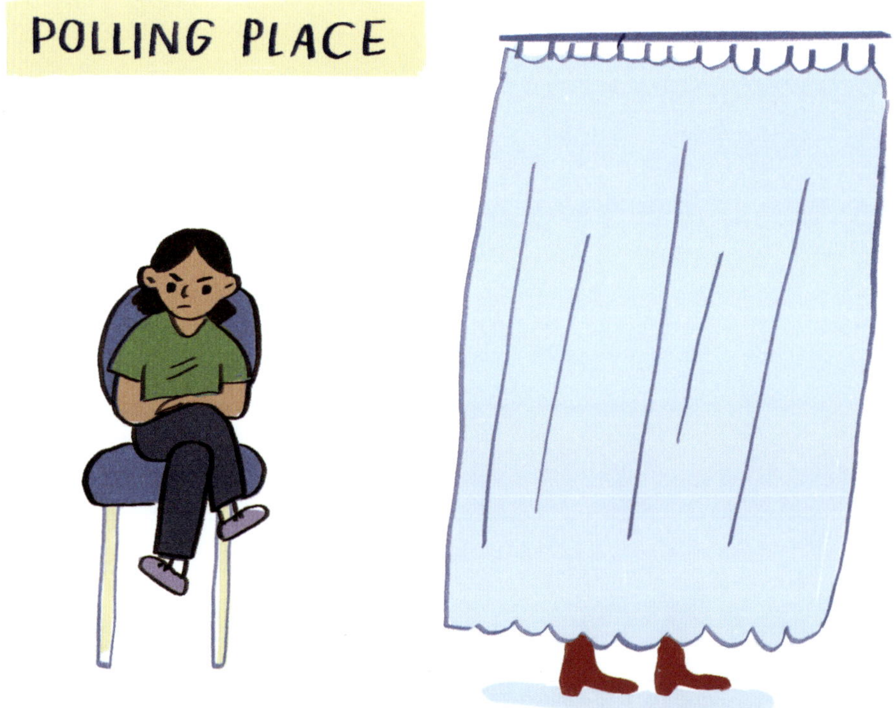
POLLING PLACE

Luckily, everyone in Norway is allowed to say whatever they want about issues.

BUT WHERE SHOULD YOU SHARE YOUR OPINION TO ACTUALLY HELP CHANGE SOCIETY?

OPINION!

STUDENT COUNCIL

Here you can change things at your school.

MEDIA
(newspapers, TV, radio)

They can spread your cause to more people. Everyone can call tip lines about breaking news and send letters to the editor with their opinions.

an
ORGANIZATION
you agree with

They can give you more information about your cause and how to contribute.

your
TOWN COUNCIL
or the
NEIGHBORHOOD
You live in

They decide what happens in your local area, such as parks, schools, sports, culture (and much more).

Your local
GOVERNMENT
REPRESENTATIVE

They decide on things that affect the entire country, such as laws, taxes, and how your government should act with other countries. They also decide how much money should be used, and for what.

It's smart to GET ORGANIZED

Join an organization that already exists, or start your own. You need a group of people to work with, including different people with various expertise.

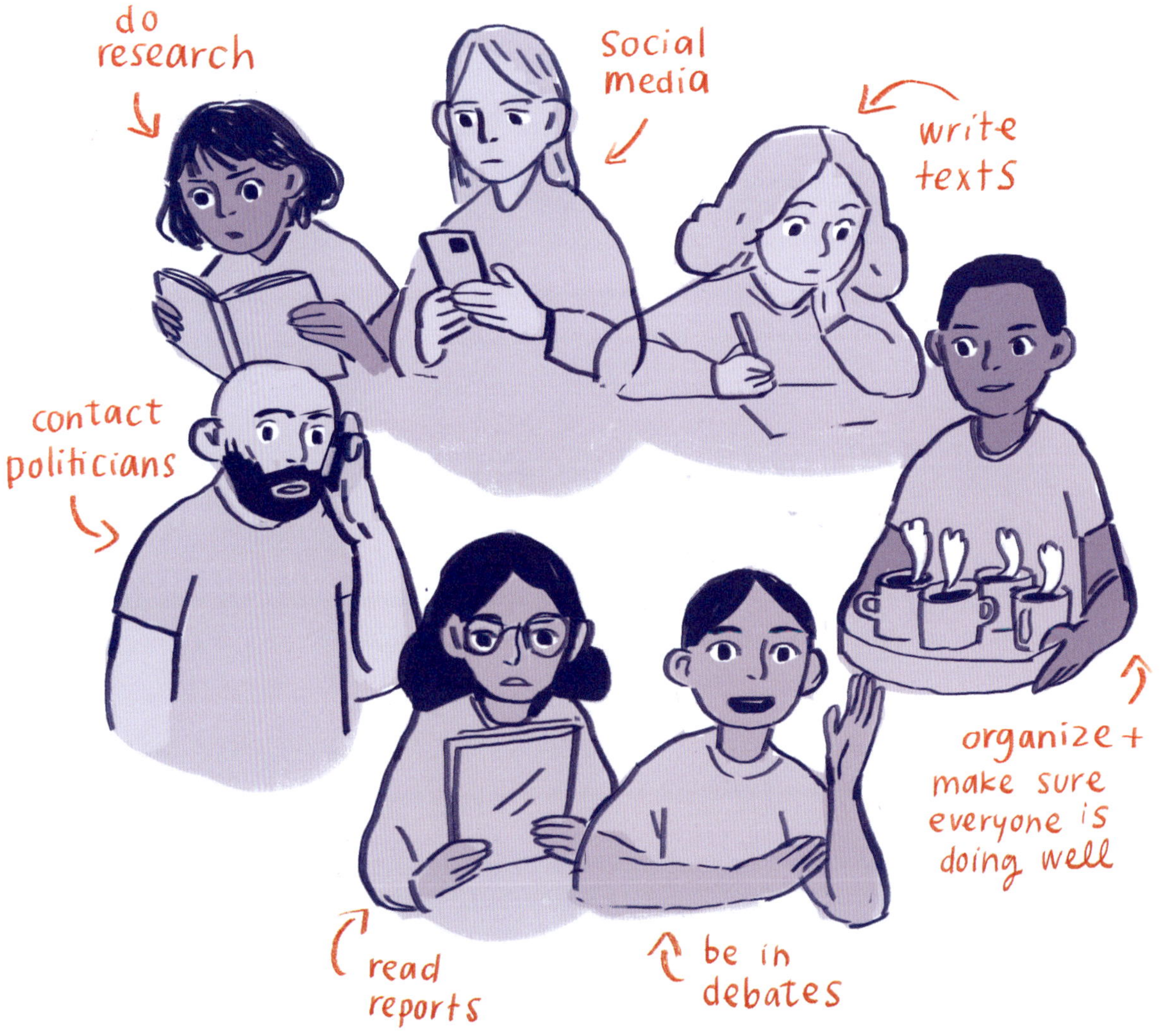

do research
social media
write texts
contact politicians
organize + make sure everyone is doing well
read reports
be in debates

Sometimes you have to **TAKE ACTION**

Then your cause will get more attention, and you can share your opinion with those who make the decisions.

A **PROTEST** CAN BE:

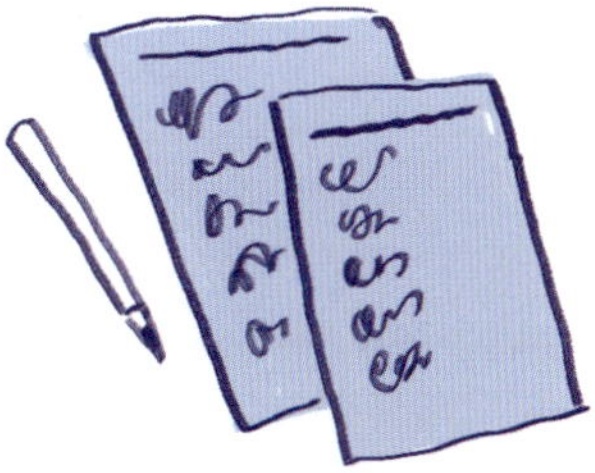

A PETITION

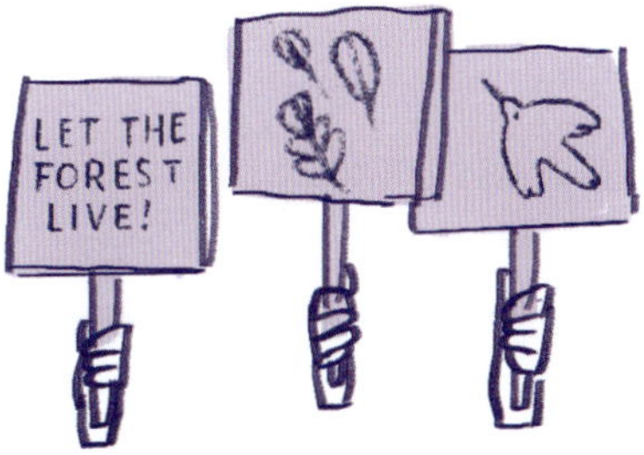
LET THE FOREST LIVE!

A DEMONSTRATION

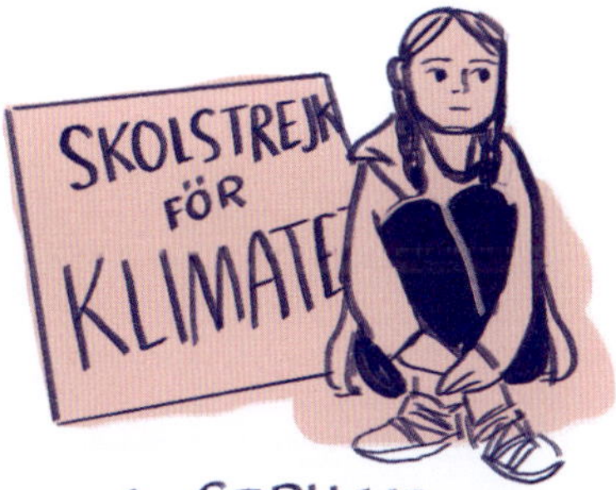
SKOLSTREJK
FÖR
KLIMATE

A STRIKE

Greta Thunberg became famous for school strikes on Fridays. She wants politicians to do more for the climate.

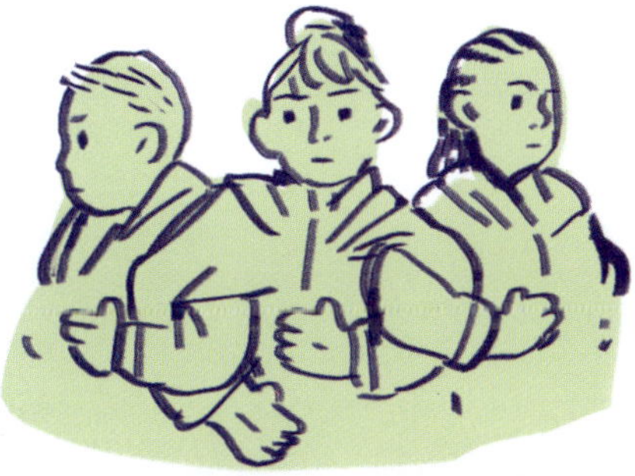

CIVIL DISOBEDIENCE

That is, breaking the law on purpose to protest. For example, blocking a road or occupying an area.

The police might show up. That's why you should do it with an organization that knows how to be safe.

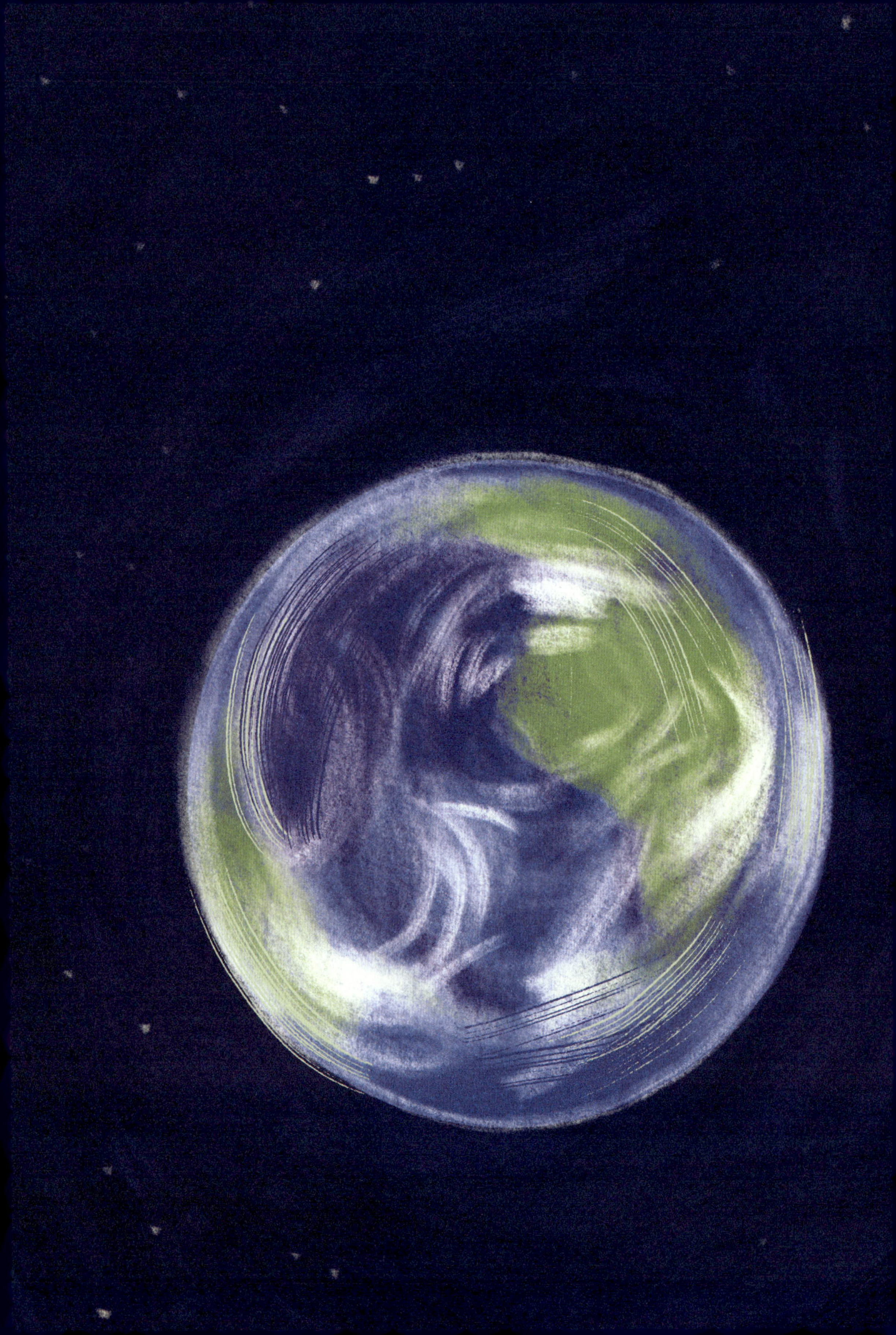

If you think the future seems
scary or feel like no one is
listening to you, know that
you're not alone.

All over the world there
are kids and adults working
to help us take better care
of our planet.

And there's always room
for more.

Are you with us?

Thank you to Natur og Ungdom
(Nature & Youth), especially the
activists in Førdefjorden Spring '22

Sources:

Climate Change Vulnerability Analysis for Oslo. Climate Report, Oslo, 2020. klimaoslo.no/wp-content/
uploads/sites/88/2021/03/Climate-Change-Vulnerability-Analysis-for-Oslo-short-version.pdf.

FN-Sambandet. "Klimaendringer." Updated March 21, 2023. fn.no/tema/klima-og-miljoe/klimaendringer.

Hessen, Dag O. The World at the Tipping Point. Oslo, Norway: Res Publica, 2020.

Thunberg, Greta. No One Is Too Small to Make a Difference. London: Penguin Random House, 2019.

First published in Norwegian by Aschehoug & Co. (W. Nygaard),
Norway, 2022, original title: La Skogen Leve!
aschehoug.no
Published in agreement with Oslo Literary Agency

Hippo Park
An imprint of Astra Books for Young Readers, a division of Astra Publishing House
astrapublishinghouse.com
Printed in China

Publisher's Cataloging-in-Publication Data
Names: Dåsnes, Nora, author. | Bryn, Lise Lærdal, translator.
Title: Save our forest! / Nora Dåsnes; translated by Lise Lærdal Bryn.
Series: Cross My Heart
Description: First published in Norwegian in 2022 by Aschehoug. Original title: La skogen leve! | New York,
NY: Hippo Park, 2024. | Summary: Bao faces a challenge unlike any she's faced before: the PTA wants to
raze down the students' beloved forest, removing the space where she and other students have always
played—integral to their lives and the environment they call home.
Identifiers: LCCN: 2023921508 | ISBN: 9781662640735 (hardcover) | 9781662640742 (paperback)
|9781662640728 (ebook)
Subjects: LCSH Climatic changes--Comic books, strips, etc. | Nature--Comic books, strips, etc. | School--Comic
books, strips, etc. | Friendship--Comic books, strips, etc. | Graphic novels. | BISAC JUVENILEFICTION / Comics;
Graphic Novels / General | JUVENILE FICTION / Social Themes / Activism; Social
Justice | JUVENILE FICTION / Science; Nature / Trees; Forests
Classification: LCC PZ7.7.D368 Sa 2024 | DDC 741.5--dc23

First American edition, 2024
10 9 8 7 6 5 4 3 2 1

Design by Nora Dåsnes and Mary Zadroga
The author created the art digitally in Procreate.
The titles are handwritten by Nora Dåsnes.
The text is set in INK-LoujainScript, and handwritten by Nora Dåsnes.

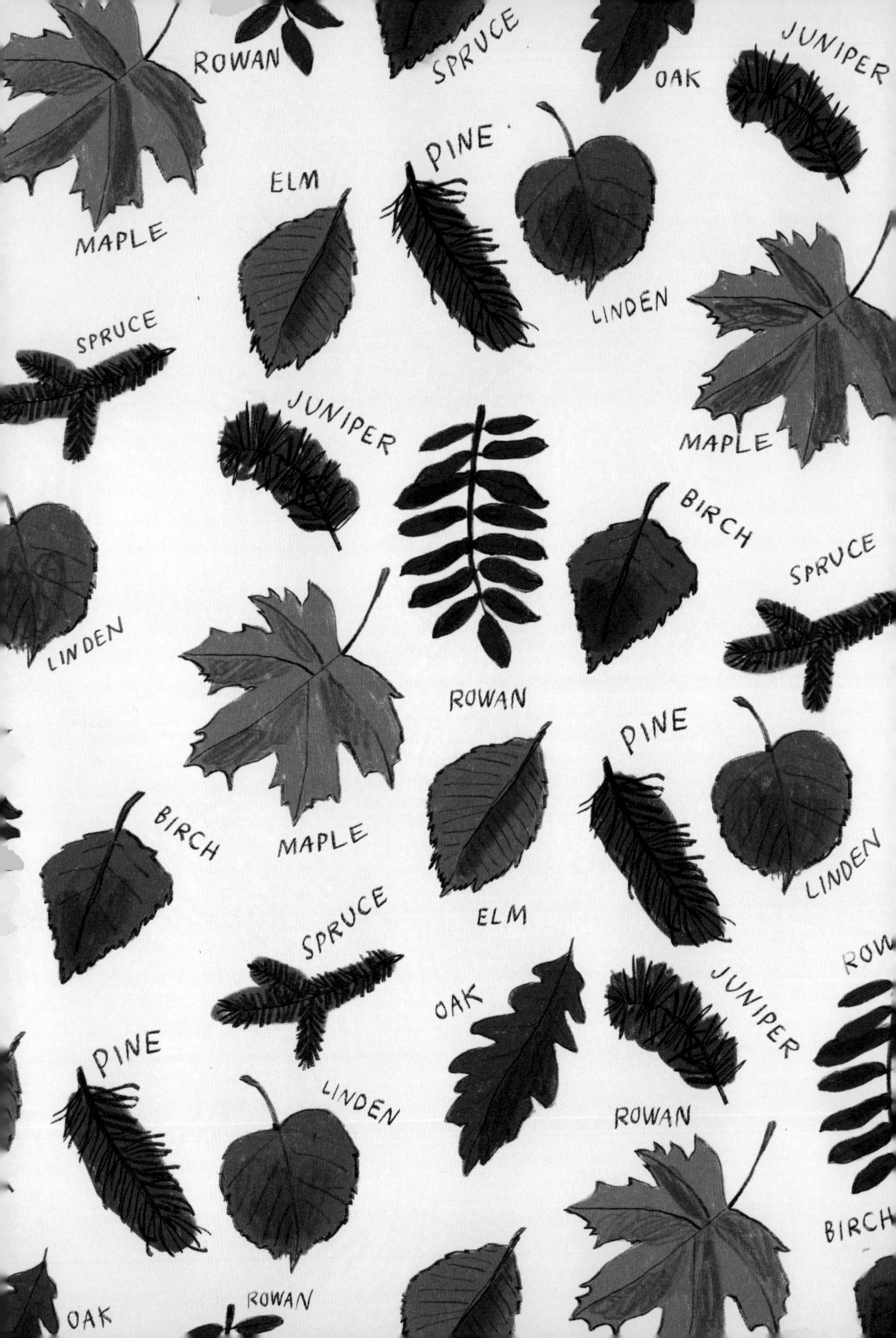
ROWAN
SPRUCE
OAK
JUNIPER
PINE
ELM
MAPLE
LINDEN
SPRUCE
JUNIPER
MAPLE
BIRCH
SPRUCE
LINDEN
ROWAN
PINE
BIRCH
MAPLE
LINDEN
ELM
SPRUCE
OAK
JUNIPER
PINE
LINDEN
ROWAN
BIRCH
ROWAN
OAK